Contents

Prologue
21/08/2675
15:29 Earth Standard Time
03:51 Local Time

Leyton Foresc

The air was still, cold and bitter. So cold that it would cause a person to cease breathing if they found themselves outside without the proper protection.

Even with his combat armour keeping the bulk of the cold at bay, Agent Leyton Foresc of the Office for Intelligence and Research Development could still feel the icy chill penetrate his lungs with each breath. Clouds of deep grey passed overhead, occasionally blocking the moonlight and shrouding him in momentary darkness. Snow fell gently against the eerie backdrop. Covering the leafless trees in a thin white blanket.

He walked down the barren wasteland of target zone Charlie on the ice planet out on the fringes of human expansion. He, like everyone else stationed on the planet, nicknamed it Chillzone to give it a more regular name. On all official and unofficial records, the planet did not exist. It bore no designation number or location reference in any United Planetary Nations database. If anyone ever asked for a stellar map of the sector – though he was assured that there were plenty of people already in place to make sure no one ever would ask – they would not see the planet there. Anyone with kit powerful enough to see it, who may search the night sky and stumble upon it, would immediately be persuaded by members of the Military Intelligence Division assigned to make sure their secrets remained secret to forget about their discovery. There were some things that only select people were ever meant to know; the public was only told what they needed. It was a fact he had accepted some time ago as being a necessity for society to continue. People could not handle the truth. Especially if it defied what they understood to be the truth. If they did learn the reality of the world, society would collapse. And if he knew it would happen, his superiors knew *how* it would happen.

Leyton shouldered his weapon and scanned across a plain of dead trees covered in ice and snow, illuminated by the moon. Boulders littered the landscape. Ice formed a protective sheet across bodies of water. Large rodent like organisms they called frost rats that fed on mosses, rushed out of the cover of one bush to that of another. Larger creatures that preyed upon them followed eagerly, hungry for their next meal. Somewhere out there, there was something far more dangerous than the lesser predators before him.

'Hey boss,' crackled the voice of his second in command, Agent Jerome Houghton. 'You got a minute?'

'You do realise that you broke radio silence, don't you?' Leyton hissed, conscious that he was not to raise his voice. Any unnecessary sound could jeopardise the entire mission.

'I wouldn't do it unless there was a very, *very* good reason,' Jerome retorted.

'Go ahead,' Leyton sighed, refusing to bite against the attitude he was being given.

His friend was an exceptionally good agent. His downfall was that he had a horrible tendency of thinking he knew better than everyone else, acting like he had a position of command even though it would never be his. Itching for a chance to prove Leyton wrong in front of an audience. He would correct his latest display in poor attitude when the mission was over. There were plenty of punishments and diminutive duties that could do that.

'Orb-sat has got movement. Lots of it. They're only going after you and Hatty.'

Leyton stopped in his tracks. He and several other agents were currently playing bait with their objective. The mission was simple: capture as many ice wolves, a strange and dangerous local organism designated as an alpha predator, as possible. They had been stationed out there for months, tracking the local packs and observing their movements and habits, collecting samples wherever they could. All for the scientist they were with them to then compile for the upper echelon at headquarters back on Earth. Then the order came through that they were to move on them and acquire the assets. No matter the cost. He tried to ask for a reason why there was the sudden hurry, but no one could or would tell him. If the base commander was telling the truth, she didn't even know either.

The ice wolves were dangerous creatures. The fact only he and Hatty were being pursued caused him a few problems. The ice wolves spread their resources wide and targeted multiple prey to ensure they always caught something. Why were they only after them?

'What's happened with the others?' he demanded. 'Have they gone and bugged out or something? What's their situation?'

'It's just you and Hatty left, boss,' Jerome admitted without hesitation. 'The others are dead. Can't say if the wolves got them or they slipped off the edge. Some of the routes you chose for them covered rough terrain. All I know is they're gone.'

His heart must have stopped for two or three seconds. Was Jerome exaggerating to try and secure a position for himself, or had he planned a route that forced them to run to their deaths? He had spent hours with the base commander planning the options, making sure everything went the way it was supposed to go.

Leyton looked up at the trees. The branches shifted direction, the wind now blowing toward him. It would carry his scent and the scent of everything in front of him, including his team. Like sharks to blood in an ocean the wolves would narrow in on them and pursue with everything they had. They may have been in combat armour, but their equipment still had the stink of flesh on it.

'How close are they?' Leyton asked.

'Too close,' Jerome answered. 'Orb-sat has them put at less than five klicks away. You do not want to know the numbers. Just keep running.'

'Great. When you can't see is when they can see you,' he whispered, quoting a childhood nursery rhyme. Though it was hardly a sweet lullaby; more like a fairy tale of old that told the story of children searching for something and stumbling into the den of evil monsters that would catch them when their guard was down. Leyton took a breath then spoke calmly. 'Hatty?'

'I know boss,' Agent Tallow replied with a hint of anger in her tone. 'I can hear the updates.'

'How are you holding up?' he asked her.

'I don't want to die,' she answered. 'Not like the others.'

'Just stay focused,' he said, ignoring her tone. She was experienced but had never been on an assignment like this. None of them had. He opened his tac-pad on his left gauntlet and pulled up a map of the area. He located their positions. 'I'm going to get you through this. Okay? Now, by my estimates I'm about a klick due West of you. Confirm?'

'Confirmed,' Agent Hatty Tallow answered.

'Right. That means if we bust our asses, we can regroup in time to lead the assets to a new site. Houghton, how quickly can we re-deploy your team and move them over to Echo site?'

They had smaller teams at six other sites. Should something go wrong with the original plan, which it could very easily do so, it was essential that they had fallback plans in place. Alternatives to ensure the mission was completed no matter what.

'Give me ten minutes,' Jerome answered smugly. 'All we need to do is get up and hustle.'

That was perfect. He had already predicted there being a shift in the plan. This was not a standard operation. They were dealing with animals, not people, and these were animals they did not know enough about. It did not help him in the slightest that his second in command had waited until the last possible moment to give him the bad news. How could he have not heard anything over the comms beforehand? The others should have screamed out. There must have been interference from the storm trying to take hold from the North or from the canyons.

However, it was not the time to consider the details and all the possible reasons for the lack of communication. There were more pressing matters at hand. He could address them once the mission was completed and they were all safely back at home.

'Don't forget we've only got one chance at this, so keep an eye on us with orb-sat and keep us on track,' Leyton said. 'Hatty, when we shift direction and head toward Echo site just run as fast as possible. Don't stop no matter how much it hurts. Jerome, move everyone over there ASAP and get them all up in the trees. I want minimal units on the ground when we arrive. I need the wolves focussed on me. We can't afford for there to be any distractions. I need you with the professor and Medic Suttle in the APC. You keep them safe until the wolves are snoring.'

'Understood.'

'Remember, the wolves can smell you. They will react one of two ways after the trap goes off. Hopefully, they charge and don't turn and run. Hatty, let's get a move on.'

Leyton picked up the pace. If he avoided slowing down, Leyton would regroup with Agent Tallow in ten minutes; nine if the terrain was kinder than anticipated. From there to Echo site would be another five or six minutes, provided his theory was right. They could make it. They had to make it.

Slipping and sliding on the ice made manoeuvring the rugged ground incredibly difficult. It was a perilous run. The slightest misjudgement would throw his balance and lose him valuable breathing space ahead of the wolves. The wind started to pick up. Whistling by and drowning out the sound of his steps. Each gust threatened to knock him off his feet. His unit updated him that they were in position though this announcement was only a murmur over the sound of the wind. They made it faster than anticipated.

Then he heard it. A shrill cry carried by the gusts of wind stole his moment of joy, piercing the air like nails being run down a chalk board flecked with glass cracking under pressure.

It was the sound that the wolves had almost caught up to them. They were closing in for the kill, howling with excitement and anticipation.

'Boss!' Hatty cried, exhausted.

The agent ran into view through a thicket of dense trees to his right, moonlight glistening off her black armour. Her legs threatened to give way with every step she landed.

'Tallow!' Leyton cried.

His voice was strained, like speaking had become a challenge, and his muscles ached. Being so focused on just reaching the rendezvous point was enough of a motivation to make the fatigue unnoticeable, until there was a reason to think about more than just putting one foot in front of the other.

'How close are we to the others?' she gasped.

'Close.'

The response was a guess at best. He wanted to avoid lying to her but had to say something for her own morale. He had no idea how far out they were and could not spare the time to check his tac-pad for confirmation. Leyton didn't want to even risk wasting breath asking for an update on their status from the team. Any energy spent not running was energy wasted and could be the difference between life and death.

'You're not far off,' Jerome confirmed in his ear. 'About another minute and you'll be running straight under us.'

Good news. He needed to risk it. 'Everyone in place?'

'Affirmative,' Jerome said. 'They're in position with a clear line of sight on the passage you'll be coming through. There will be a crevice in the rock face ahead. Take it. When you reach the end, jump through the opening. We have a trip wire set up. You really don't want to be caught in the narco cloud. The rest of the team will tranq any that gets past it.'

'Good.'

Leyton tried to shift the conversation back over to Hatty, to motivate her to keep going. Before he could begin, he was cut off as the ghastly cry of one of the ice wolves pierced the snowstorm. They were far closer than he had anticipated. A second and a third wolf joined the chorus. Soon it became a deadly symphony crying out for the taste of blood as the wolves realised how close they were to their prey.

'Faster!' Leyton cried. 'Move those fucking legs!'

'What do you think I'm doing?' Agent Tallow retaliated.

The pair ran through the dead forest and into the crevice. It was a tight fit, slowing their progress down, with sharp jagged ice cutting through their armour as they brushed past it. Out the other side, the snow-covered field led up to a dense forest of dead trees and barren shrubbery. Somewhere above them in the trees was the rest of the unit, and up ahead he could see the outline of the APC, its silhouette broken against the darkness of the forest. Behind that was a convoy of All-Terrain Vehicles with mounted guns. Should everything turn bad they still had options on handling the beasts.

Another piercing cry echoed through the fissure behind them. It sounded like the wolves would jump straight out at them. Leyton pictured their claws digging into the ground, itching to rip open his armour.

After making it this far, there was no way that all their efforts would be for nothing.

Leyton gave Hatty a pat on the arm to usher them to finish the last leg of their retreat. They rushed to the front of the APC and waited. Baiting the wolves. Most of the pack pushed through the crevice and charged into the opening, triggering the trap. After the detonation he couldn't see anything in the thick cloud. Where his sight failed him, his hearing picked up on the thuds as the unconscious bodies fell to the ground. Only when the gas dissipated could they see the pile of unconscious wolves. Of the pack, a dozen or so had been within range of the narcotic cloud to have been sedated. Another ten had been able to stop before they reached the gas. They walked out of the canyon and into the opening. Mouths were open wide. Hungry for the chance to strike at them.

The moonlight faded as dense clouds crossed its path, plunging them into near total darkness.

His eyes slowly adjusted to the world. Red eyes glistened in the dark. Two pairs of eyes per wolf. The wolves held their position momentarily before edging toward them. His unit stayed silent. Not out of bravery or commitment to the job. No, this was fear running through them. Even though they were safe in the trees they must have been worried that if they failed, they had to get down alive or be left for hours until help arrived. Leyton looked around the various eyes until he locked his gaze with one set. These eyes stood over the others belonging to a larger body. Leyton stared as the ruby eyes glared back at him. A dangerous game of who would drop their gaze first.

As the ice wolves approached them, Leyton could feel his heart pounding in his chest like a percussion player performing a solo act. Facing these creatures to complete their mission was as exciting as it was terrifying. That fear was not for his own safety. If things turned sour, his priority was to get Agent Tallow safely on the APC before he could help himself. The team had to come first. That was the way it had to be.

When the wolves were in full view, the agents rained down potent tranquiliser darts from their positions above. Each target took a couple darts to slow down. A couple more after that to hit the ground. The last one standing – the same one that had locked eyes with Leyton – proved to be much stronger than the others and took more to be put to sleep. It could only have been the pack leader.

When the shooting stopped, Leyton ignored Agent Tallow's objections and dared to edge over to the pack to see if any were still awake. Thankfully, none of them budged and every one of them was in a deep sleep. These dangerous creatures were a difficult sight to take in. Four bright red eyes were imbedded in their elongated skulls. Within the mouth were two rows of razor-sharp teeth and a serrated tongue. Each of their four limbs was powerfully lean with muscle covering every inch of the leg. A thick coat of matt black and silver hair covered their leathery skin.

When he was confident that they were all down for the count and no more were waiting to make a late appearance, Leyton gave the instruction to his team to come out of hiding.

Personnel dropped out from the trees on their zip lines. Each one took up a defensive position before proceeding with the mission. The APC opened, allowing the medic, scientist and Jerome joined him outside. The Medic Suttle took one look at him and dove straight for his leg.

'When did this happen?' the medic asked.

Dom Suttle worked on an injury to his thigh. Something had somehow punctured straight through his armour and gouged his leg without him realising. It could be that the adrenaline surging through his veins had numbed him to the pain.

'Not sure,' Leyton answered. 'Must have got caught when going through the boulder fields. Didn't think the rocks were that sharp?'

'Well, you were wrong,' the scientist said. 'I did try to tell you that when you were planning the mission.'

Professor Samuel Ainslot. He was as intelligent as they came. As a xeno-biologist, he knew more about alien species than any other human Leyton knew of. Even though that intelligence was incredibly useful for them when they needed to understand what was going on it came at the cost of including arrogance. But he was not a bad person. A bit eccentric when he got going, yet still good hearted.

'I thought you was a biologist, not a geologist,' Leyton replied.

'I am,' Samuel said. 'Doesn't mean I don't need to understand the environments around me. Everything's been eroded to a sharp point because of the ice. You really should have paid attention.'

Leyton resisted replying with a sarcastic comment. He turned back to Dom. 'Are you done with my leg yet?'

'Just about,' Suttle said. 'I've given you a stimulant shot, antibiotics and plugged you with bio-filler before wrapping it up. When we get back, I'll give you some more pain meds. All being well, I think you'll be back to full strength in a week or so. Just try to not overdo anything in the meantime and let the filler do its job. You're really lucky that there's oxygen on this planet and that you have the gel layer in your armour, or you'd have died by now.'

'Do you think I don't realise that?' Leyton retorted. 'Thanks.'

'It's my job boss,' the medic responded, looking out into the distance. 'What about the guys we lost out there? I wish there was something I could have done for them.'

'So do I,' Leyton added. 'But we can't think about that right now. It won't do us any good. Check on everyone else. Make sure they're okay and good to go. I want to know if anyone is showing any signs of trauma. If they are, get them booked in for checks when we get back. We don't need anyone losing their shit when we're in the arse end of nowhere.'

'On it,' Dom Suttle answered.

Suttle ambled over to the rest of the team. There were another four field agents and a team of a dozen security personnel assigned to them out in the field. Back at base there were another several dozen personnel including more scientists, medical staff and security, with only a handful of additional agents to oversee everything that went on.

Agents were a luxury supply. Too many infiltrations had occurred within the UPN over the years for it to be an easy enlistment process.

'Right, Professor go check on the acquisitions,' Leyton instructed. 'You know what command needs. Make note if any of them have been injured. Tag them when you're done, log them and prep them for stasis. I need a full report by the end of the day.'

'You got it,' Samuel said.

Leyton turned his attention to his second in command, 'Jerome, how's it looking?'

'We've got the area secured and have a count of twenty-two wolves sedated for transport,' Jerome explained as the scientist rushed off with his tac-pad at the ready to take measurements, pictures and make notes on every specimen before they were loaded. 'No misfires and, unless Suttle reports anything, I don't think we've had any incidents worth worrying about among the guys still standing. Are we going to collect the bodies?'

'Only if it's safe enough,' Leyton responded. He wanted to bring them home so families could mourn. That indulgence wasn't worth more bodies though. 'The commander won't risk any more losses for a pickup job. Have a drone do a recon of the area when we're at base. We might get lucky. The area might stay clear long enough for a pickup crew to be despatched.'

'Understood,' his adjutant sighed. 'Command should be happy we've got these.'

Leyton snorted. 'We got the entire pack. They were hoping for just three individuals, a male and two females. They better be fucking happy. We've given up too much for them to not be happy with the result.'

'What the hell do they want these things for anyway?' Jerome asked.

'Hell if I know,' he said. 'All I know is they're destined for OSTAD. That means they're going straight to MID's very own black ops. Could be anything. Anyway, I need you to oversee the stasis pod prep. It doesn't look like we have enough pods for one wolf each. The pack's much bigger than we thought. May need to give them bunk buddies.'

'Understood sir. Don't forget to call in to command.'

'Don't worry, I was just about to.'

Jerome rushed off to the back off the APC to start unloading the stasis pods from the trailer. Each one was built with anti-gravity skids that helped them move across the ground with ease. Instead of taking two people or a piece of machinery per unit, it just took one person with a steady hand and good footing to move a couple of them at once. Each unit had several hours of charge in them before they needed to be plugged in. Once in there, the ice wolves would sleep and wake up as if nothing had happened after the correct dosage of drugs brought them round in a controlled manner. The eerie blue glow from the pods was sinister in the dark but was strangely pretty.

Leyton activated his tac-pad. The red glow of its screen lit up his visor. He swiped through the menus on the holographic display and navigated the layers of information, tapped into sub-folders and opened a live connection with his superiors back at the base. It wasn't answered by a standard comms operative; instead, he was put straight through to the base commander. He gave her a quick update and was given his orders to return to base to receive a full debrief.

Leyton quickly joined the rest of his team to assist loading up the wolves into stasis pods and moving them onto the trailer hooked to the back of the APC. It would be a couple hours until they were back to base and could relax.

'This is amazing,' Professor Ainslot said eagerly as the final stasis pod was secured in the trailer. Leyton sensed a lecture brewing. 'I've been able to locate unique facial patterns on each of the specimens so that we can identify individuals. I didn't realise it until I looked over the recordings, but it looks like we emptied their den when you brought them out. Looking at this, I think it's safe to say they work on a matriarchal hierarchy. Males are typically larger than the females. Not here. Look at that – the matriarch is the largest one and a few of the other females are just a little smaller than her. Then you have the males, and after that, the smaller females.'

'Do you think she normally hunts with the pack?' Leyton asked.

'I think there's a good chance she might do,' Samuel said. 'Best way to make sure she gets the best bits of the kill. But I'd say she led the hunt because of you throwing a shock grenade in the den while they were sleeping and pissing her off. It'll take a bit of studying to fully understand why exactly she came out, but I'd put my money on that being the reason.'

Leyton shrugged. 'We couldn't exactly wait for them to wake up. Come on, load up. We need to get back to base.'

The pair loaded up in the APC and with a sudden jerk they were on their way back to base. It was a three-hour drive through rugged terrain, the perfect opportunity for Leyton to shut his eyes and catch up on some rest. Back at Ice Castle, he was more than relieved to have the cargo no longer under his supervision. He was not fond of them, happier not having much to do with the wolves.

Pulling into the base's loading bay wasn't without surprise. Commander Nes Julough was there, waiting for them. She stood proudly in her grey suit, her greying hair tied back in a bun and her chevrons showing her rank proudly on display on her shoulders. She was a good commander, and he respected her. She always did her best to lead by example. Age had now stopped a lot of the physical leading but what she couldn't do herself she made up for by listening to people.

'Welcome back,' she announced as he clambered out of the APC.

'Thanks,' Leyton replied. 'What's the occasion?'

'You had a successful mission,' Commander Julough said. 'A successful, high priority, mission. Are you ready for the debrief?'

'Something tells me that I'm getting something other than a debrief now. With all due respect.'

'It's a new assignment. After we've debriefed this task, I'll be running through everything in detail.'

Leyton rolled his eyes. Not five minutes had passed and already he had a new job. 'Give it to me now. What is it we'll be doing?'

'You're to assemble an eight-person team, including Professor Ainslot, to join you in escorting the wolves back to headquarters on Earth. I relayed your success back to command and they don't want to wait for a heavy transport unit to arrive. You'll have a few days to rest before you're on the move again.'

'Alright then, what're our orders?' he asked.

Commander Julough answered, 'You're to take LSAGs all the way back to Earth. You will need to make five transfers on the trip. You'll have immediate clearance to embark from each gate. No cargo inspections. Once back in Sol, you'll be contacted by command and advised where to go from there.'

LSAGs. Light Speed Amplification Gates. A work of wonder. For anyone who doesn't have the means to enter the jump with their ship, these were the best way to traverse the vastness of space. Two giant, circular gates linked to make a powerful wormhole, allowing for precise travel across the galaxy. What would normally take months, if not years, only took a couple of weeks. These monoliths of human creation relied on massive energy supplies to run so their locations were limited. As much as the UPN told everyone they were put where they were needed, truth was they were put where the money was. If it weren't for the gates, colonising the known galaxy would have been too costly for

11

humanity and they would have been stuck in the small pockets of existence that they could reach at lower costs in a single lifespan, not the generations it would cost to get to these far-flung planets.

'Doesn't sound too bad,' Leyton said. 'How long will it take? I don't remember how long it took to get here.'

'You'll be travelling for two or three months,' Commander Julough replied. 'The first few weeks or so you will just be getting to the first LSAG. After that, you will only stop off at gate stations for resupply before going back on your way to Earth. We have a transport currently being retrofitted for the voyage. We didn't expect to have so many full capsules but I'm sure it'll be able to handle them for the trip.'

Two months. He didn't think it took them that long to get there to start with. He could have spent that long out there on the edges of civilisation that he had simply forgotten the concept of reasonable lengths of time spent travelling.

'But there is one more thing I need to let you know before we go to debriefing,' she added.

'What's that?'

'The administrator will be overseeing your return,' she said. There was something behind her words. Was it menace? A warning? Whatever it was, the message was clear. This was not going to be casual contact made. 'He'll be communicating directly with you the entire way.'

'The administrator? As in, the boss of the OIRD?' Leyton questioned. 'OSTAD?'

'Higher. The head of the MID.'

For him to be involved could only mean one thing. This cargo being brought back to Earth was top priority and part of a project under his personal oversight. No one knew who the administrator was. At every presentation he was to attend, a secretary or spokesperson went in his place. For every promotion or award ceremony he was to host, his second, Director Ruis, took centre stage. No one among the ranks even knew his name. Leyton had given him the nickname Puppet Master. Terrifyingly, the man always knew what was happening before it happened.

'This is that big?' Leyton cussed.

'It is which means you don't fuck up,' Nes stated. 'Or it's both our careers. Even when you leave, what you do is a result of my leadership of you. And he will punish us both if you fail. Do you understand?'

'Yes, Commander.'

12

'Good, I'll see you in debrief in fifteen.'

Commander Julough left him where he stood. Leyton could hardly believe that the administrator was going to be in touch with him. He let out a heavy breath, before catching up with the rest of the unit for debrief. How was he going to explain what was happening when he didn't fully comprehend it himself? More importantly, who would the additional seven agents be that he took with him?

Chapter 1
12/09/2675
06:32 Earth Standard Time

Duke Horren

Morning. At least that is what it was supposed to be when the lights in his room gradually brightened. On a space station floating near a moon on the outer edge of a far-gone solar system in the outer colonies it was impossible to know if it was day or night without a clock that was set to Earth Standard Time. It was standard practice for any UPN facility, civilian or military, to follow Earth time of a standard twenty-four-hour day if there was no sunrise or sunset. When it came to being on a planet, you had to go by two times. Local Time and Earth Standard Time. It could be six in the morning there but be ten at night Earth time. There were some planets where, by the time the sun sets, you have seen three Earth days. He avoided understanding inter-planetary time zones and how the think tanks back on Earth made everything make sense. It was less of a headache that way, easier just to accept things as they were.

Sergeant Duke Horren slowly came to from a deep sleep. He had dreamed about his first assignment after joining the Stellar Protection Force. How, his task had been to save a group of colonists on their way to a recently acquired planet after their ship suffered a malfunction. If he and his team hadn't arrived when they did, there was no telling how long the civilians would have been drifting through space for. Duke had a long service career from the marines to special forces that had taken him across the galaxy. He had visited strange and exotic planets that most of humanity had never heard of. Duke had even fought in battles they couldn't ever hear about. After spending most of his life there, Duke decided he needed out of that institution. He did not like the thought of always being at risk or being a disposable asset that politics could deny affiliation with if he were ever captured by hostile forces. He transferred for a safer detail that was still on the front line to serve out the rest of his time with. The Stellar Protection Force was the first line of defence and a bridge between the military and civilian worlds. They patrolled UPN space looking out for any threat and aided anyone that needed the assistance. He had spent many years there. Doing decent work. Not spending every day in direct line of fire.

It was a nice memory, but one that could not keep being added to indefinitely. This was the beginning of the end.

Duke had been away from his home planet of Olleraa for far too long. At thirty-seven years old, he decided it was time to hand in his notice to leave the SPF and the military behind. It had been too long since he last spent good, quality time with his mother. Now was as good a time as any to take up a change in career. He had done his bit for society and wanted to start enjoying his own life.

He sat up and looked at his room for what would be one of the last times. It was a simple billet, with a bed barely big enough to fit him in pressed against the wall with just enough space to walk around beside it. Modest decorations of awards, team photos from back in the day and a few carefully selected books were placed around his room. A wardrobe and shelving were hidden behind the wall to the right of the foot of his bed. One thick pane of glass was all that stood between him and the vacuum of space outside. A simple room, but it was his.

Duke clambered out of his bed to look at himself in the mirror. Duke's light brown hair was only slightly messy. It helped having it cut short. His blue eyes stared back at him. Weary but still full of determination. He wasn't the largest man out there, but that had never stopped him from doing whatever was needed to be done.

He got dressed and left his quarters. A voice from behind him caught Duke off guard.

'Where you off to in such a rush?' It was his friend, Sergeant Peter O'Connur. 'I thought we were having breakfast?'

Peter was one of the few people stationed out there that Duke could trust and call a friend. They had met a couple times through his career before Duke joined the Stellars, when he was with the Tactical First Strikers, and had carried out several assignments together whilst in the SPF. His chestnut brown hair was groomed near to perfection as it always was. Peter always did like to be well presented, no matter the time of day. The burly man held two flasks of coffee and handed one to Duke.

'Change of plans. I'm handing in my notice,' Duke replied.

'Thought as much,' Peter said, not even surprised. 'Care to explain why?'

'Walk and talk?'

Sergeant O'Connur nodded politely. Duke led the way. The rounded corridors of the station, reaching round in an eternal circle, were a uniform cream colour. Each segment of the outside corridor that did not house rooms had a large, windowed seating area showing the endless void of space outside with the eerily dark celestial body of the local moon hovering nearby. The only light to prove it was there coming from the station. The windows on the inner curve revealed the central stalk, a long shaft that housed units to keep the facility running, office and living spaces for senior members of the crew stationed there and was topped by the command centre, where several other habitation and facility rings were held in place by long, intertwined, corridors layered above and below their own ring.

'I've done a lot,' Duke Horren explained. 'Since joining the marines, I've had a good life. A good career. But I've stuck it out long enough. I want to try have a life now. A life of my own. See places without worrying about my head being shot off. Think I've earned it.'

'Get married, settle down and all that bullshit?' Peter added with a smile. 'Why don't you just stick it out for another couple years? You'll get a better pension at least that way.'

'I could but... no, I'm not getting any younger and I can't keep putting it off.'

The pair stopped at the first link-pod port. It was like a traditional elevator, except it could go along vertical and horizontal tracks.

'You sure about that?' Peter asked. 'I mean, where are we going to find anyone like you?'

'I'm sure you'll eventually find someone. I'm going to catch the next pod over.'

'Okay man, give me a shout when you're done. I'm going to head to the gym for a few rounds,' Peter said. 'Good luck.'

Duke watched his friend depart then took the capsule that would transport him to the stem of the facility. It was only a short walk once there to his superior's office. This part of the station was much nicer than his sector, the colours were more cheerful and the hallways lavishly more spacious and decorated with real plants and artwork. Even the recycled air he breathed in this section seemed much more planet-like and natural.

The heavy metal door he stopped at looked like any other. The only thing to make it obvious who lived there was the black name plaque to the right. One knock, a sharp response to enter and Duke was standing before General Baalshuk. He was not an imposing person physically.

He was old, antiquated, and small in stature, with pale eyes standing out against his olive tanned skin and pure white hair. But his words carried the authority of someone half his age.

'Sergeant,' Baalshuk said. 'What a pleasant surprise. I wasn't expecting to see you. Is everything okay?'

'I know sir,' he replied cautiously. 'Can I take a seat?'

The general gave a courteous nod of permission then spoke once he had sat down. 'I apologise for the bluntness, but you don't typically come over for a talk. I must ask you, what exactly is this about?'

Duke hesitated. That did not happen much, not to him. 'Sir, as you know I'm not exactly young anymore.'

'Neither am I! I'm long past my sell-by date and growing closer to my expiry date every day,' Baalshuk retorted with a chuckle. 'What're you trying to say? After my job? I never realised that you secretly wanted a promotion.'

Duke sighed. There was no point delaying further, beating around the bush or otherwise. He plucked up the courage and spoke confidently. 'I want to hand in my notice, sir.'

'Leave? I really wasn't expecting that one. Are you sure?' Baalshuk asked, nearly choking on the words. The look of shock and disappointment could not be hidden and was painful to see. 'You do realise that you only needed to do a few more years and you get to retire with a full military pension for life with military benefits to remain on your citizen pass.'

'I know but I've thought this through… I am very sure about it,' he admitted.

'If you mean to retire from front line work, I can always have you transferred to a desk job. It would be nice, boring, and more importantly for you, away from the front lines. That would be the least I can do for you,' his superior said, trying his best to talk him out of it. He was doing well. The support system in the UPN was poor at best. Not everyone had access to half of what he could receive with a full service.

'Sorry sir. I need to give you my notice. There is too much I simply do not have. I don't have a family of my own. I don't have a life outside of the service. I don't have anywhere off station to call home. This rig has not let me have one for more than a weekend off for as long as I can remember and even that isn't exactly off site. Here in the ass-end of nowhere, my spare time is spent reading or in the gym or the bar because if I left the station, by the time I get to the nearest planet I'm already a week into my next patrol. I'm sorry but I've made up my mind. I need to do what's best for me and not what's best for someone else, sir.'

There was an awkward silence left in the wake of his statement. He had said what he needed to. That was what mattered. The expression on Baalshuk's face was difficult to look at but he held steady. The general left his desk slowly, as if rising from a funeral sermon. The man walked over to the cabinet at the side of the office, rummaged inside it momentarily with the clinking of metal rattling out from behind the scenes, then returned to the desk. A large bottle full of whisky, courtesy of Earth judging by the label, and two metal cups were placed in between them.

'And there's no trying to negotiate you out of this?' his superior finally managed to ask.

'There isn't, sir,' Duke answered apologetically, not feeling sorry at all.

'Then it calls for a drink,' Baalshuk said remorsefully. 'I need a moment to take this in.'

The general poured them both an extremely healthy portion of the liquid. Duke sipped at his pleasantly, enjoying the taste of something from Earth. It tasted distinctly different to whisky brewed off-planet. Not even the liquor produced from his home world tasted anything like it. This really was something that the people of Earth could do right.

'So, you're calling it,' Baalshuk muttered. 'Be one hell of a void without you here. You've built quite the history in the UPN Military, Horren. The Marines, then you joined the TFS and then moved on to be a part of SETS? All before coming here. And you even took the drop in rank to come here.'

After leaving the Special Execution of Tactics in Space division of the Marine Corps, Duke had had to drop from the rank of Lieutenant to Sergeant. There were no positions for someone of his rank in the Stellar Protection Force. No room to make one. That was fine by him. A drop in pay, but it was worth the reduced risks. He had been a lot happier. Bored, granted, but happy in himself that he wasn't in any real risk most of the time.

'That I did,' Duke admitted. 'I will miss it. It's been one hell of a time.'

He took another sip of his alcohol. He savoured the richness of the flavours.

'I'd be sad if you didn't miss it. What do you think you'll do with your freedom?' Baalshuk asked.

Duke shrugged. 'Not sure yet. I will need to do a bit of recon first, see what there is out there for me to do. Maybe find work after some time to adjust. Something low-key. Try and buy some land back home near where my mother lives and make a house for myself. Find out what women my age are like nowadays. You know, the usual.'

'You can take the man out of the military,' his superior laughed, enjoying his military-style attitude to life outside the military. Baalshuk's face then turned a little sterner. 'Look, I can't let you go that easily. I know that statutory notice is one-month Earth Standard. Can you give me more? Can you at least do one more patrol? Go out there and train your replacements with the basics just so they can take over from you. Please don't make me invoke Article Four of the State Services Act and order you to stay.' When Duke didn't answer straight away, Baalshuk pushed on, 'I'll tell you what, you do this for me, and you get your pension as if you did the minimum twenty-four years' service. I can't promise, but I'll try and get the military benefits for you as well. Call it a goodwill gesture if you will.'

It was going to be much longer than he wanted. He hoped for one month's notice. Not six. But six months for a full pension in return was a very tempting offer. And at least he would still be young enough to start up a life when he returned to the station and fund it no matter what happened.

'Alright then, you've got a deal,' Duke replied, finishing off his drink. 'I'll stay for one more tour. Then I'm done. Not a day later.'

'Thank you,' General Baalshuk said, with a proud and thankful smile. He topped up both cups. 'Thank you. I do appreciate this.'

'You better do,' Duke replied with a chuckle. 'When's the launch?'

'I'll schedule a launch in three days. Got to give the paperwork back to command to start everything for your retirement. Consider between now and then as free time. No active duties. I will send across the profiles of the NCOs I want you to train up later today. What patrol you take and how you train them is completely up to yourself. Make it as difficult or as easy as you want. But it's all in your hands and I want them to be up to standards by the time you're done. You can even take whichever crew you want to pilot the patrol ship. If they are even half as good as you when you come back it will still make them great assets.'

'Thank you, sir,' Duke said taking another drink.

'So, tell me, off the record, how long have you been thinking about this move for?' Baalshuk asked.

Duke flicked his eyes up to the ceiling, trying to count back the days to the weeks to the months. 'A while.'

'That long, eh?' General Baalshuk said thoughtfully.

'That long,' Duke replied with a smile. He took a sip of whisky. General Baalshuk had good taste in alcohol. 'But like I said, I'll miss this. It's all I've known.'

'I have to say, I do envy you having the gall to do what's right for you,' Baalshuk stated. 'Few people here have the stones to do anything like that. Fewer still can be so sincere about it directly to me. I appreciate your honesty. Whatever you do next, if you decide to work in some shithole or suit up and go corporate, I'll give you the best fucking reference you could dream of if you need it. And if you ever get stuck, you come to me. I owe you a hell of a lot. My door and this station will always be open to you if you need help. I promise you that.'

'Thank you, sir,' he said, feeling a little watery eyed at the sentiment.

'Call me Sanjeep,' Sanjeep Baalshuk said. 'I plan for us to part as friends, not colleagues.'

Duke smiled and finished his drink. He left the office after they talked some more and met up with Sergeant O'Connur at the bar in the top outer ring of the station. The place was for non-commissioned officers, though there were a few commissioned officers who were friendly with the ranks that joined them and outstanding recruits who showed promise were given permission to enter. Out of the large window covering most of the wall was a beautiful view of the system. He could see the moons and planet nearby on the backdrop of stars. To the inner side were a series of large booths. Each one had a large screen showing different sports, shows or news channels from across UPN space. An all-round good atmosphere.

They had both gone through two beers and a portion of fries at the bar before either of them said a word to each other.

'It isn't going to be the same without you,' Peter said.

'It's going to be weird for me too, y'know,' Duke replied with a forced laugh. 'But like we've always said. Got to look out for ourselves.'

Peter clinked his bottle of beer against his own. 'I hear that. What did he say in there to you in there then? Is he pissed?'

'Definitely by now. I had a few drinks that Sanjeep insisted on,' Duke joked.

O'Connur barked a laugh that shocked people nearby into glancing over. 'Really? Sanjeep? You two are on first names basis? Now you really do have to tell me what went down.'

Duke went through everything that went on in the conversation then paused as he finally came up to the part where General Sanjeep Baalshuk asked him for his help. Then spoke slowly. 'He asked me to give him one last tour, train up replacements. In return I'll get full pension early. Maybe benefits as well.'

'Wow, he must be desperate to offer that,' Peter O'Connur exclaimed.

'He did seem it.'

Duke took another swig of beer. His tac-pad went off on his wrist with a beep. He removed it from his gauntlet and activated the holo-screen. A message from the general. He opened it to read the message holding profiles of the three replacements that he was to take out. None of them were familiar names. He wondered what unit they served with or if they were new to the station. He spun the pad around to Peter.

'Take a look at this,' he said. 'Any idea who these guys are?'

Sergeant O'Connur let out a long whistle. 'Got your hands full with this lot my friend. Corporal Arche? She is a tough one that will have your nut-sack if you even think of saying something she doesn't like the sound of. I think she is assigned with Vanguard team. Corporal Udal'e? He's a book boff. How he passed physical is beyond me. Not surprised you don't know him, keeps to himself a lot. But Corporal Moasa? Now that is what you call a soldier. Not so good at playing nice with others though. Enjoys a good fight a bit too much if you ask me. But when you get into a fight you better take him with you. Always the last one standing from a sparring session.'

'Great,' Duke muttered under his breath. 'Any suggestions?'

'Don't show weakness,' Peter laughed. 'They'll have you before you know what's going on if you do.'

He scoffed at the obvious comment. 'Noted.'

'Where are you taking them? Any ideas?'

Duke shrugged, 'We've not got that far yet, but it's my choice. And my choice of training. I have a couple of days to think it through.'

'I'll help you with that,' his friend said with a cunning smile. 'I have a few unsettled issues with Arche so will think up a couple things to make life Hell for them. But for now, another round?'

'I'm not going to say no,' Duke said gleefully.

Jesa

Jesa woke in a pool of sweat, gasping for breath. The air was humid and damp. It was too hot in the ship when she had to sleep. During long distance jobs, multiple jumps through hyperspace were required. Between each jump, she would drift through space while the hyperspace drive cooled off ready for the next jump. In these moments of vulnerability, she needed to do everything she could to keep a low profile and achieved this by shutting down as many of the ship's functions as possible. That included the air con and air recyclers. It kept her safe from unwanted passers-by taking an interest in her ship. It was for the better that she had woken up – it saved her from her dreams.

She clambered out of bed. Her olive skin shined with a sweat that made her look sick. The healthiest part of her were her black eyes and black hair. After considering herself acceptable, Jesa made her way through the ship, passing by the artifacts, weapons, technology, and other contraband that she was under instructions to transport across the solar system. Had she not been the owner of the vessel, she would have never guessed that several of the floor and wall panels could be unfastened to reveal empty spaces that could be used in desperate situations to hide from boarders. Or they could be used to keep legitimate salvage secret for her own enjoyment later. Each compartment was lined with reflective properties so that only the most advanced equipment could see through, even with the small eyelets that allowed the occupant to look out. Of course, those were not features that came pre-built into the ship. It had been a wreck when she bought it. 'Buy a ship or be released,' was what her master had told her. 'Released' meant thrown out of an airlock. Part of the code was no one got out easy. If a smuggler could not contribute, pay their own way, or wanted out, then they were dealt with. So, she bought the best she could, which wasn't much. Thankfully, her master had helped with renovating it and bringing it up to speed at the time. It was a price she took a long time to pay back.

The ship, though, was hers. She gave it the name the *Saridia*. It was the local dialect from her home meaning The Hopeful. It drew in comments, judgement, and mockery. It didn't matter. They would never appreciate just how important the vessel was to her. How much of a symbol it was for her sanity that there would always be hope. The piece of junk became a functioning cargo ship. From there, it gave her reason to expect something good to happen to her in the future.

On the flight deck she sat back and sighed while looking out to the nothingness of space. Jesa quickly looked over the diagnostics. It was fortunate for her that her ship was small. It ideally needed at least two crew members to pilot but could be done by one. Everything was fine and no one had been anywhere near her. Not even in the same system. That was good. She listened to the clacks of gears and the rumble of the ship as the engine ticked over with minimal output. To her, her ship was welcoming her back to the bridge.

'Yah, yah, I managed to sleep a little, thanks,' she told her ship, speaking in her space station slang. 'It's the dreams that keep me up. D'ya know? I know I've got you. Only need you. You have my back, yah?' She looked to her right where a co-pilot would have been seated. The empty chair looked isolated. Vacant. Almost as lonely as she was. 'But company would be nice... yah? No, you're right. Too much risk. Safer to go it alone.'

A smuggler's life was a lonely one, if you did it right that is. To do it wrong meant you put your faith in people who would betray you in the end. When that happened, chances were that you died. That had almost happened to her, once. But only once. Never again. She remembered it like yesterday. Fresh into the hot seat of her first job, so fresh that the pain that the branding on her hand of that metallic circle with the flaming dagger, the mark of the syndicate, was still throbbing. Jesa had put together a small team of more experienced smugglers from the syndicate to show her the ropes on what to do. They delivered the cargo with no incidents. On the return flight though one of them, an older man with a taste for blood, turned on them. He demanded a greater share of the pay because, he said, he brought the most experience. He killed one of them and maimed another two before he was killed himself. So much blood among their own over a payday. Even though her cut increased by a fraction, it was still a clear message. People caused trouble. After that Jesa vowed to never be a part of a team again. It was much safer to run solo.

Since then, she had run dozens of shipments over the course of nine years. Now at twenty-seven, she had more experience than most people far older than her on how to survive in the galaxy. Mainly because more people were interested in a young woman than they were an older man. That meant being tough. She also knew the people to avoid and the people she could play if it meant making the job easier. Jesa knew the

23

best routes and shipping lanes to take to avoid traffic or to avoid high risk zones. This shipment though was the biggest and longest haul she had ever done. Most jobs were a few weeks at most, occasionally a month. This one was destined to take her months to complete. The payout was going to be huge. If she worked out everything correctly after her master took his large cut, she would almost have enough money to buy her freedom – or at least enough freedom to not feel like she could be pushed around so much. That was a good feeling. So good her heart raced a little.

A fraction of her cargo was the usual that she was assigned to transporting, consisting of weapons, ammunition, precious stones and lavish paintings. There were some technological items, navigations systems and communication logs ripped out from Outer warships lost in the numerous wars. These human items were purchased by buyers in the Sol system. One buyer was from Earth, and they must have had deep pockets with what they purchased. The bulk of her cargo consisted of alien artefacts that were all acquired by the same person.

Ostad was her contact at the shipyard when she eventually reached Earth. One part of the large payload was something quite scary yet intriguing. A skeleton. Not a human skeleton or that of an animal. It was a strange reptilian-human creature known as a Shauari. The thing was giant, at least nine foot tall. Each finger and toe were tipped with claws and a bony frill crowned its skull. Its tail was well over five feet long. A mouth full of jagged teeth grinned down at anyone who stood before it. It frightened her to consider the thought that it was once a real thing prowling the galaxy. But it wasn't the first she had known of it. Stories had flown around the outer colonies for as long as she could remember, but no one could ever prove anything. Jesa thought they were just feeding tall tales to make a name for themselves. Now though? It was possible that they were telling the truth. She tried to wonder what the use would be for the bones. Having something like that as a decoration was morbid. It wasn't going to any museum. Nothing she transported was for the public eye. The answer to her curiosity was not for her to know. She just needed to transport it to Ostad. Then it would be their nightmare.

Jesa looked out to the stars. There was nothing around her for light-years. She reflected on what her owner had told her before leaving.

''You're ready for this,' Barbaros Indalle had told her.

He was the leader of the Ayuindi Syndicate. A gang of thugs and mercenaries that, on top of their other activities, recruited smugglers against their will to do the riskier work of transporting goods for them. That way, if they were captured it wasn't their own hand selected crew that was lost. Barbaros' group was one of the most feared organisations in the outer colonies. He led his crew with an iron fist, anyone deviating from his plans swiftly dealt with. The fear of facing his wrath was what kept his ranks in order. His right cheek was burnt after an explosive went off near him during an assault by a rival gang. He had scars around the rest of his face from shrapnel in the same attack. Barbaros was a large man, muscular with a heavy build. This size was used deceptively. New players always presumed he couldn't hold his own against them. Barbaros quickly corrected them with his speed and strength. He had come into possession of Jesa after he and his people massacred her family. She did not want to work for him. Jesa wanted to have a life that was hers, and she struggled to stomach doing the bidding of the man responsible for the death of her parents. But his methods ensured she did what he told her to without question.

'Are you sure?' she had asked, wincing at the time expecting him to beat her for questioning him. Barbaros had just given her the biggest job she ever had, and Jesa was still in disbelief.

'I am. If you're not ready, you'll die. If that happens, I will have to arrange for someone to find your ship and finish the job for you. Don't want that, do I? Make sure it doesn't happen. How's the arm?'

Her left bicep had been bandaged up after his security guarantee had been implanted into it. An explosive. That way if her ship went off course without good reason, he could make sure the cargo wasn't sold without his knowing. More importantly it stopped her from running away. Running as far as she could go to the places in space that he would not find her.

'It itches,' she had answered. 'Why does it itch?'

'Because you know it's there. You know it shouldn't be there. But I need to put it there. Keeps you in your place that way. You know how shepherds use animals to control their flock? I'm the shepherd. You're my flock. That is my animal to control you and keep you where I need you to be. And I'll know if you're not. Don't you even think otherwise. Compre?'

Jesa did not realise that she had started to scratch at her arm until she felt blood start trickling down her bicep. It still itched, even after several weeks of travel. She wiped the tears from her eyes.

Jesa couldn't remain where she was. There were dangers that, amazingly, were more deadly than her master. All throughout the outer colonies amongst the several warring factions that shared control of the territories was something much worse. A species that made their wars that lasted for years, gang hits that destroyed buildings, families, and murders committed in the most horrific ways, look trivial. There were murderous aliens that swarmed and plagued the people that lived out there. Crevari. They patrolled in hoards and destroyed everything they could reach. These creatures were what nightmares were afraid of, and they were rife in the area. Always hunting. Always searching. Always hungry.

She fired up the engine on her ship for the next leg of the journey. The hyperspace drive charged up then on her command carried her vessel across the stars faster than the speed of light. Planets, stars and everything in between hurtled past her in a dazzling display of light and colour.

Safely in the jump of slip space, she activated a timer to drop out in exactly twelve hours. It would be enough time before she needed to recharge the drive and to still have reserve to make an emergency jump if she needed to. Jesa felt her stomach rumble, demanding a meal. She left the flight deck, walked back past the cargo over to the kitchen area. It was a small unit with a microwave, a single stove, and a sink offering drinkable water – recycled and foul tasting, but drinkable. A few cupboards were full to the brim with ration packages. For the journey she was expected to make, it was not going to be enough. Jesa had to alternate her meal consumption. For every four days travelling, she would have one day eating normally and the other three days she would have to cut her food intake to a third of her daily requirement if it were to last. To get more cargo loaded onto her ship, her food had to be reduced to fit it and to ensure weight did not affect the range of the *Saridia*.

Jesa tried to remember when she last ate a normal portion. She thought past the hunger. Two days ago. Jesa sighed. She would have to endure another reduced calorie intake day. That meant no food for another six hours.

To keep some form of normality and create some form of distraction from the daily torment she went through, Jesa had developed almost obsessive habits. She routinely spent an hour tidying everything up after herself and cleaning her bedroom at the start of every day. She then progressed onto doing a daily inventory check. Not that anything could go missing out in the middle of space when she was the only one there. This time it was the weapons and ammunition to count. All the standard issue weapons and the intriguing ones that Ostad had bought. Tomorrow it would be paintings. She had a checklist to confirm the item, its location and condition. That way, if Barbaros ever doubted her or a buyer tried to pull a fast one, she could prove she had checked its condition routinely.

Everything was there. Nothing was missing. It was as predictable and mundane as anything could be, but it helped. Jesa could look past how hungry she was for a spell. She slipped and knocked one of the assault rifles. Jesa immediately winced at the prospect of being attacked by Barbaros or his henchmen for costing him hundreds of credits. Like every other time, she quickly realised he wasn't there to hurt her. But the threat of him and his heavy hand looming over her was still painful. She wept as loudly as she wanted any time the terror he inflicted became too much to handle. No matter how much she was rewarded she was always punished more severely than she deserved when something did go wrong. It made no difference how hard she tried. It was a feeling she could not shake off.

She gasped for air and whined, 'I wish I was home.'

For far too long Jesa only had the company of the memories of her parents to keep her safe. After their murder, she had no one except her master. He was everything to her. Friend and felon, protector and attacker, hope and dismay. Jesa wept more. Even if she were home, there would be no gravestone. No burial. Her parents would have decomposed and returned to the planet years ago by now. There would be no sign of their existence except for her memory of them. She desperately wanted to see her family again. Feel their embrace. Hear their voices.

There was all the time in the world to carry on crying. But she had another hour and half until she could eat. It would be slop, but the ration portion she had planned on eating was supposed to taste like beef. Real beef. Not the herds of Briden Beef from the outer colony ranches that tasted sour. This one though was delicious. Jesa hoped to taste the real thing when she got to Sol. If Barbaros permitted it, of course.

Even her dreams were terrified of imagining simple luxuries.

She carried on with finishing her audit. Jesa needed to remain focussed.

Leyton Foresc

Leyton sat in the passenger seat on the flight deck of the Sphinx Class transporter. He watched while the world of slip-space cocooned their vessel. A lot of people lost themselves in it; they said it was beautiful, awe inspiring and enticing. It gave him a migraine. That, though, was better than staring at the blue luminescence of the stasis pods, seeing the eerie silhouettes of ice wolves, and listening to the professor going on and on about how amazing they were. After a few weeks of travel, he desperately needed to get off the ship. He needed to breathe fresh air and clear his head. Anything to have a break.

'How long until we reach the LSAG?' he asked the pilot.

'About an hour or so,' the pilot replied. 'It's going to be a quick-drop out of slip space then straight to the LSAG to go home. You'll want to get your team ready, especially the professor. I don't think he'll handle the exit well. You know those academic types - they don't have the stomach for it.'

A quick drop. Dangerous if a ship wasn't designed for it. More so for the occupants if they were susceptible to the rapid changes of reality. Any drop out of a jump was supposed to be steady to stop passengers' internal organs from failing and occupants passing out. Depending on the size of the ship, the drop could be anything from a half-minute to several minutes. For them, the drop would be over in a matter of seconds. It took weeks of training to become tolerant to those stresses, not necessarily immune. Even though the professor was a member of the agency he had never been subject to that sort of training before. If anyone were going to feel the symptoms it would be him.

'Understood.'

Leyton Foresc vacated the flight deck and clambered down into the troop bay, which doubled up as a cargo bay, where the rest of his team was sat. During the trip, aside from mealtimes this was the first time all of them had been in the same space. Jerome walked over to him before he could assess what everyone was doing.

'ETA sir?' he questioned, with a tone that demanded an immediate response.

Leyton hesitated, glared at him as a visual reminder that he didn't answer to him, then responded, 'Just over an hour. You might want to get comfortable.'

Leyton brushed past his second in command and clambered over to Agent Suttle. 'Dom, make sure everyone's ready for a quick-drop out of the jump. And give Samuel a sedative. Don't think he'll stomach the return to real space.'

'Got it,' Dom replied. 'I'll get him it now. Gives it time to take effect.'

'Thanks,' he said. 'Right. Everyone, listen up. One hour until we come out of slip through a quick drop. You all know what that means.'

'Buckle up?' Agent Kari Fellstrum answered.

'And wait until the professor here starts to scream like a little girl,' Specialist Ray Schottler added with a sinister chuckle.

'Enough of that,' Leyton snapped before any further taunts could be made. 'We're all on the same team here. I trust him more than any of you about those things were escorting. If anything goes wrong, he's the only one who'll tell us exactly what to do to fix it. Am I clear?'

'Sir,' both agents replied in tandem.

The rest of his team, Hatty Tallow, Jake Deulche and Onyx Perretti remained silent. None wanting to be on the receiving end of his wrath. Once the professor had been given sedatives to ease the passing into real space, Leyton carried out his rounds to ensure everyone and everything was securely in its place. Content all was in order, Leyton went to his seat to buckle in. He pulled down the overhead restraints and waited.

'Hey, Sammy,' Hatty called out while the sedatives were still taking effect. 'Remind us again, why were you posted to the Ice Castle?'

The scientist looked over to Leyton for permission to answer, and only spoke once he received the nod. 'I specialise in alien biology where the subjects show superior signs of intelligence to other organisms. That includes things such as pack animals or alpha-class organisms. I've dealt with things as small as a hamster and three times larger than an elephant. I also have experience in human level intelligence life forms and other, lesser, aliens of primitive intelligence. You know the aliens we're working to have trade agreements, peace treaties and so on with? I've studied their anatomy too. I could tell you all their strengths and weaknesses, how to kill them... how to save them...'

'Which means?' Onyx asked.

'He's the smartest person on this transport and is in the top twenty most prized intellects back at base,' Leyton answered. 'There are very few people in the galaxy smarter than him in the field, which is why the boss wants him protected at all costs. Just like those wolves. It's a lot easier to replace us than it is to replace either him or the assets. I suggest he's shown a little more respect.'

Leyton glanced over to Agents Fellstrum and Schottler. Both now wore soured expressions for having their lack of importance pointed out and either glared at Leyton or looked away. Better they were quiet than causing unrequired tensions among the team. That was one headache he did not need.

The announcement came that the quick drop was imminent. Leyton Foresc tensed up, as he always did. The sensations were not pleasant. When they dropped out there was a power surge throughout the ship that overloaded it in a magnificent display, like fireworks only for them. The lights went out. Wall control panels sparked up before setting ablaze, and the transport shuddered violently. This was not a standard fast drop from slip-space. Everyone panicked, screaming out to understand what was going on. This had never happened to any of them before. Leyton kept his mouth clenched tightly to hide how terrified he too was while he jumped out of his seat to tackle the electrical fires that erupted.

Then the commotion passed. The ship stopped shaking like it was caught in turbulence. They were in complete darkness. The stasis pods glow had dimmed.

'Sir, are you seeing this?' Jerome said as the red glow of emergency lighting clicked on.

'I am,' Leyton answered. 'Professor, please tell me that's a good thing.'

'It isn't,' Professor Ainslot whimpered, half cooked with the sedatives. 'It means they're... not connected to a power supply. Those pods... they're designed to have a few hours of charge before the wolves start to wake up... We need to put them on battery support... Now... Extend the charge supply... Buys us several more hours.'

'Fucking hell, how many pills did you give him?' Leyton asked Agent Suttle.

'I only gave him an extra one, just to be safe,' the medic said with a shrug. 'I didn't think he would be that much of a light weight. It'll wear off soon enough anyway. Was only meant to stop him hurling.'

'This is not my day... Break the battery packs out and hook them up. We need to make sure they stay under,' Leyton ordered.

Everyone unlatched themselves from their seats and rushed around the troop bay for the batteries. It was like clockwork. As soon as a battery was safely removed from its housing unit another agent took that power cell and connected it to a stasis pod. One by one the pods started to glow in their bright blue light once more. Each power unit took several minutes to attach and in the small space they could only have a couple agents wiring them up at any one time. Anyone not connecting power cells could only watch on helplessly.

Unable to be of any assistance in the troop bay, Leyton left the job to oversee the battery installation to Jerome. He clambered onto the flight deck and strapped into the passenger seat. Alarms were blaring, and warning lights flashed on every monitor. A thin layer of smoke began to gather in the air from the electrical fires. The smell of leaking coolant pierced his sense of smell.

'What happened?' he demanded. 'Are we under attack?'

'Attack? If only! It's those damn stasis pods back there. They take up so much juice!' the pilot said. 'We were only retrofitted to take a dozen of them. This many? Coming out of the jump was too much. It fried the circuits. We needed more power than was available to keep the shields up. Tried to re-route the auxiliary power but that wasn't enough.'

'What the hell were we doing trying to fit them all on here if we couldn't handle it?" Leyton asked.

'You tell me!' the pilot retorted. 'I tried to tell them the order was dangerous. That we should wait for a bigger ship. But the big boss wasn't going to wait.'

'They rushed it,' Leyton recalled. Too eager to have their assets returned to Earth. Greed was a dangerous thing. 'What do we need to do now?"

'Ideally? Land and get to work with the repairs. I've plotted a course for Gorucia. It's a planet right next to the LSAG we need to take. Once the repairs are done, it's up and out.'

'How long will that take?'

The pilot shrugged. 'Depends on the extent of the damage we've taken. Best-case scenario, it's going to be at least a day of repairs. If we're unlucky it'll take us a few days. That's if we have a safe landing too.'

'What do you mean by that?' Leyton asked.

'The damage done so far is bad. I can guarantee it won't be an easy landing.'

The battery packs did not have enough charge in them to last the eight hours, let alone a couple days. Leyton needed another way back to Earth, and he needed that option to be presented quickly.

'Okay, thanks.'

He left the flight deck in a hurry. Leyton found a quiet corner in the transport and opened a comm link with the administrator on his tac-pad. After leaving the Ice Castle, he was contacted by the head of the MID. From that moment on, the only person he was to talk to outside his field team was the administrator. No name was given. It was all very mysterious. He was used to secrecy, but this made Leyton uneasy.

When the comms was answered he wasted no time with greetings.

'Sir, we have an issue. Coming out of the jump, the stasis pods fried the circuits. You loaded too much onto the ship. We're heading planet side for repairs, and we've connected the pods to battery packs, but they won't last long enough for us to get the ship up and running again. More so, if our ship couldn't handle a jump then it won't handle the LSAG. Which means we can't bring back the assets. Please advise what we can do.'

There was no response for several extended seconds. He could feel his heart beating faster and faster, threatening to break free of his chest. He heard the frustrated sigh, then a deep breath.

'Confirm, are you going to be landing on Gorucia for your repairs?' Administrator asked. His British accent was strong, tired but powerful enough to keep Leyton's attention.

'Yes sir.'

'Okay, there is a docking facility on the coast of the Great Lake. I have a landing bay allocated for you; coordinates are being sent to the pilots as we speak. They will take you there. By the time you land I'll have paperwork for you to take a loading ship onto a civilian holiday cruiser currently in orbit around the planet, the inter-planetary liner *Galactic Passage*. It is part way through its voyage. Destination, Earth. Your cover story is that you are a security team for hire, and you are transporting high value goods. I'll ensure you have authorisation to acquire a storage room for whatever use you need. You just make sure no one knows about the wolves. No one.'

'Understood, sir. What exactly are we transporting in this scenario?'

'Good question,' the administrator said approvingly. 'With the cargo being classified, you don't know. All you know is that the containers are refrigerated and need to be powered at all times. If anyone asks, you're not paid to know. Ignorance buys time and is more believable than an elaborate story. By the time you reach anyone who asks for paperwork everything will be arranged for you to get past them.'

'Thank you, sir. Our mission parameters?'

'How you handle everything from here on out is up to you. I will only step in if you need me to. Get those assets back to Earth and make sure no one learns what you're bringing here.'

The administrator cut the comms. Leyton sighed deeply. Their mission was supposed to be simple. The equipment they had was too advanced for it to be believed they were a simple security team. Anyone with an ounce of training would spot that instantly. They would have to pack everything up into security cases if they wanted to keep their gear. Whatever they did, they needed to hide anything that showed who they really were.

'Time to earn your pay,' Leyton muttered to himself.

He ordered everyone back to their seats and to buckle in as they approached the landing bay and briefed the team on the change of plans. As expected, Jerome took it as an opportunity to show how good he was, immediately boasting ways they could get by the security personnel at the docks and completely ignoring the administrator's assistance so that force would not be required. Fellstrum and Deulche both wanted the strong-handed tactics to be used. Professor Ainslot had barely woken up. As a result, he was more than happy to go with whatever his orders were. The rest of the team was open to suggestions. When Leyton told them they were to use stealth and deception, Jerome made it known that he was not happy with the decision but was quickly silenced when advised the way on the ship was arranged by the administrator. They stowed their armour, automatic weapons and more ammunition than was necessary in scan-proof containers, leaving only their sidearms and one spare magazine of ammo each on display. Gorucia was not a high-risk place and had no high value facilities. Leyton didn't know of any security teams that required heavy armaments there.

The next thing on the agenda was for the pods to be blacked out so that no one could investigate them and see their cargo.

By the time they landed, the pods were secured together in four great oblong packages and all outside facing glass sides were painted over with black spray to hide their contents. They had their story straight and in conjunction with the paperwork Administrator had sent across to them in time for their landing. Leyton bid the pilots farewell and led his team off the ship. The early morning sea air hit him first. Salty, fresh, with a gentle breeze. Sea birds called out in the distance. The intoxicating combination was refreshing. It felt good. Much better than being at the Ice Castle. Leyton imagined that it would be even nicer if the sun were up. He showed the shift leader in charge of their landing bay the paperwork on his tac-pad allowing them to use the bay.

The busy streets outside their bay were a shock to his system after spending months out on the ice planet hunting wolves, looking over his shoulder every day expecting the shadows to hide threats. On Gorucia, it was completely different. So many people. An unknown potential number of hostiles. Every corner hiding unidentified threats. The very real possibility of collateral damage should anything go wrong, and their cargo stolen or worse still escape, hung thick in the air. Like an ever-present force that couldn't be seen, only felt. Adrenaline coursed through his veins ready for the first sign of danger. His hand was always held stiffly beside the grip of his pistol.

Finding the loading bay for the liner was not difficult. Giant holo-banners and signposts pointed them toward the loading docks. And way above them, in the atmosphere, was the liner itself. It was barely a small, shiny pill in the sky. But it hung there waiting for them to arrive. They boarded the first vacant transport shuttle and claimed it for themselves, deterring anyone else from joining them.

It took off gently, slowly gaining altitude, and when they were in the atmosphere, they unfastened themselves from their seats and looked out of the portholes to have their first up-close look at the vessel that would be their home for the next few months. The vessel was a brilliant silver with flowing waves of pale blues and greens streaking down the side. From bow to stern the liner had to be close to a kilometre long and had from what he could count at least fourteen decks. The front of the ship was shaped like two bows crossed at the riser that were pulled back, ready to release the arrow. The top limb was about a third of the height as the bottom. The horizontal section reached back and joined in a diamond shape with the main hull of the ship. The body of the ship itself looked like an arrow with a single fletching reaching down from the middle to rear like a giant rudder. A single maintenance corridor bridged the void between the fletching and the lower limb of the vertical structure. Somehow it all pieced together in some elegant grace. The bridge stood proudly on top of the hull, sitting on a stalk of four decks as if they were a pedestal for it.

'You see there, below the loading bay,' Leyton said, pointing to the lower decks at the rear of the liner. 'I want us to set up shop down there. Okay? I'll be on point with Schottler when we're on board. Everyone else, make a perimeter around the professor and the assets. No one gets close. Clear?'

'Understood,' his team announced.

'We don't say a thing to anyone that they don't need to know,' he added. 'Jerome, make sure the professor doesn't get too friendly with anyone. Loose lips and all that shit.'

Beatrice Lenoia

Dawn. It was four thirty-seven in the morning. She was as tired as anyone but, after spending the past several weeks without experiencing a natural sunrise, there was no way Captain Beatrice Lenoia was going to miss it. Not even the false light shows on the ship, designed to impersonate a sunrise or sunset, could replace the real thing.

She stood in her smartest uniform, her jet-white hair tied back and kept hidden under her naval cap, on the bridge of her ship, the *Galactic Passage*. A luxury liner that has sailed the seas of space for years with many more years of service to come. She served all classes of society. Dignitaries. Upper class. Middle class. On occasion, lower class when they could afford it. The one thing she was ashamed to admit was that they had never taken on alien life forms for a cruise. All their places of docking were human controlled, and not that appealing for the aliens. One day, she hoped that inter-species relations with the alien societies at peace with humanity would improve to the point where she could take humans to these truly alien worlds and bring aliens back to humanity's society. That would be a privilege to go down in history.

They were docked in atmosphere around a planet called Gorucia, directly above a metropolis called Horizon that spanned for miles on the coastline of the Great Lake. It was not really a lake. More like an inland sea. But the inhabitants thought it more endearing or romantic to name it a lake. The sunlight shimmered around the atmosphere at first, eclipsing the planet for a moment. The light gracefully shined on the ocean below them. Waves twinkled under the morning rays. When the light reached her, it warmed her dark skin. Beatrice groaned with satisfaction as the heat radiated through.

She absorbed a few more seconds of the rays before opening her eyes. People were already piling onto shuttles to be brought up to the liner. Those that were finishing their journey with her had disembarked yesterday. Her ship would be full of fresh faces soon enough, eager for excitement.

Beatrice was about a third of the way through her voyage. After leaving Earth, stopping off only at Mars and a couple lunar colonies on the moons of Jupiter, they had soared through space for several weeks in the jump. They dropped out into real space to admire the many spectacles space had to offer enroute before arriving here. Millions upon millions of light years away. They still had more to go and see with a few more planets to stop off at along the way.

Once her new guests were onboard and settled, she would depart for a quadrant so explosive with star births that it was a constant light show – a crowd pleaser. From there it would be onto a series of planetary reserves, planetary spectacles, gas giants with rings of ice, comets and a series of strange phenomena before heading back to Earth. Each leg of the trip came with little additions that the passengers were not expecting. They paid for the trip of their lives. They were going to get a journey that was once in a lifetime.

'Captain,' Franklin Hender said.

Her first mate and adjutant, he was a long serving member of her crew. A relic, with the grey hair and weary eyes to prove it. He had another ten years' service on top of her, and she was not exactly young herself after a long and fruitful career in the military before she turned to be a captain on a civilian ship. There was very little that he didn't know about running a ship and keeping a crew in order. A lifetime of experience and knowledge. Yet with that age he carried himself like a young man in his twenties, ready for whatever life had to throw at him. He was well respected amongst the crew, and passengers found him approachable. A truly good person.

'Yes Franklin?' she answered.

'I have crew on hand ready for the first delivery of passengers to embark. Things will run like clockwork.'

'Good.'

That was a given. She never really had to give him any instructions. Things were always in hand. All Beatrice needed to do was see the progress being made.

'Do you want any coffee?' he asked her.

'Of course,' she replied. 'Why wouldn't I?'

'Who knows, you might want another hour of shut eye now you've had your sunrise?' Franklin suggested with a smile.

It was a very tempting thought. Her eyes were heavy from lack of rest. The sudden relief that everything was coming together was helping to relax her eye lids. But there was no point. She was awake now. Sleep could wait until they had started their voyage. The needs of the passengers came before her own needs.

'I'll live,' Beatrice said. 'What about resupply? Is that underway?'

'We're at about forty percent complete,' her adjutant answered, handing her a cup of fresh coffee from the pot at the back of the bridge.

'We have several more containers of food and drink to be loaded up then it's all toiletries and cleaning supplies. We should be done in less than four hours.'

She took a sip of the coffee. It was good. Beatrice did pride herself on her taste of coffee. 'Very good.'

'But we have one thing that I think warrants a closer look from you on the manifest,' Hender stated, while analysing his comm-pad. 'A last minute change.'

'What is it?'

'We have several containers being loaded up. They'll be coming with us all the way to Earth,' he explained. 'They were not on the original manifest. Apparently, their safe transport is a high priority. Comes with their own security detail too to make sure it reaches Earth okay. It has all the required authorisation from the United Planetary Nations Military too.'

'Come again?'

Her ears pricked at the thought of there being cargo that was signed off by some suit back on Earth to come on board her ship. Why would the UPNM use her liner to transport goods? Why not use their own vessels to bring their goods back? Especially if it was marked as high priority. It didn't make sense.

'Classified cargo is being loaded with its own security detail. The signature on the documents reads OSTAD. No idea what that is. But it comes with the UPN seal stamped on. You ever heard of them before?'

Beatrice shook her head. She beckoned her first mate to send the paperwork to her comm-pad. It was UPN Military certified indeed. But worse, this was UPN MID level clearance. Secrecy. Something that Beatrice couldn't stand. Secrets were trouble waiting to be unleashed. Beatrice had encountered spooks throughout the UPN far too many times to not recognise the threat they posed to friendlies. She could not have such cargo on her ship. Not for the safety of her passengers and crew. Those people could look after themselves. Intelligence only ever brought dangers. Beatrice refused to have such things onboard.

'Have it rejected,' she ordered.

'Believe me I've tried,' her first mate answered. 'All my rejections have been rejected. They've requested Cargo Hold N-E to store their cargo in and I've had no choice but to let them.'

Rejected rejections? Her years in the military and meeting red tape first-hand taught her that this meant one thing. There was someone *really* important behind it. Just as significantly, the security team had taken a storage room in the furthest reaches on the lowest deck as far from people as possible. Keeping their secrets out of sight did nothing but encourage her suspicions. Beatrice relaxed her hands that she never realised had been clenched into tight fists. A nervous reaction whenever her anxieties were tried.

'Come on! What have we lost so some suit can have something brought back to Earth via us?'

'We've lost about two weeks' worth of dry food,' her adjutant said. 'Maybe more. I've already scheduled for a resupply at the next docking. It'll only need to be a top up to make up for what we've not been able to take on now. A hindrance but it'll give passengers an extra hour or two to enjoy themselves to keep them out of the way.'

'I guess that's better than it could have been,' Beatrice groaned, massaging her brow.

With one last look to the outside, she turned and walked across the bridge, leaving the viewing platform behind, toward her command chair. She had over a dozen key crew working around the clock on several stations positioned in two neat, split semi-circles in front of her chair. The only stations not there with them on the command deck were security and engineering. While security was on the other side of A-Deck outside the brig, engineering was down in the engine room. It gave her chief engineer oversight of the beating heart of the vessel. Each control station focussed on a different aspect of her ship from life support and communications to navigation and radar. Each piece of information was almost useless when working alone. But together, they provided her with a clear picture of how her ship was at any moment in time. Each member of the key crew worked furiously to keep things moving.

She had complete faith in their abilities to keep them in one piece and they had absolute trust in her ability to command in return. They followed her instructions to the letter. Even on the occasions when she tried to push them too much.

Beatrice took up her seat. She keyed a command into the control panel on the right arm of her chair and the lights in front of her dimmed. The windows turned opaque, hiding the planet below from view. A map of the galaxy glowed in a holographic projection over the holo-table in front of her chair. After a couple seconds, the map zoomed in on a sector showing many stars and even more planets. Then it drew closer in on a quadrant. A red line reached out from a planet half blue and half green, nearly at a halfway mark from start to finish on her voyage. Gorucia.

She eyed the space in between Gorucia and their next destination. It was a long way away. There had to be something that they could do in between as a surprise addition to the trip. Something to break it up. One planet caught her eye. Vesvi. It was a lovely planet full of natural hot springs that spanned for miles at a time, the likes of which did not exist anywhere else in the known galaxy. It would make for extra value for money. Plus, she could use a spa day herself. God knows she deserved it. That would be added to the agenda after they'd stopped to view a comet cluster gliding through space in what was nicknamed 'the Hailstorm'. That would be programmed into the navigation system once they departed the planet.

As the first passengers were settling on her ship, Beatrice felt fatigue catching up with her. She should have heeded Franklin's advice. She needed to move. There was only so much that she could do from her command chair. Beatrice walked around the bridge, getting a feel for the full crew, and stretched her legs. Butterflies started to erupt in her gut, as they always did in the moments leading up to a launch. It was easily the best part of any voyage she went on, reminding her what it felt like to be young and experiencing the galaxy for the first time all over again.

A notification came through over the comms from her crew overseeing arrivals – everyone was now on board. Cargo was fully loaded and secured into position. All hands were on deck ready for departure. She marched to the command chair and took her seat.

'Systems check?' she requested.

'All green, Captain,' replied Franklin Hender, standing over Mike Volk on the helm. 'We're ready to pressurise and push away from the docking station on your command.'

'Okay, close the loading doors, pressurise and pull the docking tubes back,' she ordered.

When she was told that it was complete, Beatrice instructed them to push away. Dozens of bursts of gas on the starboard side of the *Galactic Passage* worked in sequence to guide them gently away from the orbital station. Once clear of the platform, they glided through space leaving the planet behind.

'Status report?' Beatrice asked when it looked like they were clear of anything man-made.

'Clean departure,' Franklin answered. 'Pushed away nicely and we're still all green sitting at about fifteen kilometres from any structure, a safe space to enter the jump from. Won't interfere with the LSAG.'

It was unfortunate that they were not going to use the LSAG to speed up their journey, as the structure was a unique experience to go through. But their route took them in a completely different direction. That meant dropping out of the jump periodically for the passengers to recover and to see the sights.

'Understood.' Beatrice opened a communication link with engineering. 'Chief, you there?'

'Loud and clear Captain. What's up?'

Chief Engineer Allua Jons was a chipper person. For her to be anything less than happy was unusual. Even when angry, she sounded like she was on top of the world. She was a brilliant engineer. Even if it looked fine, she could spot a faulty shaft, worn-down washer or a circuit containing a blown fuse with only a few simple checks. On top of that sought-after ability, she had the foresight on what was going to need to be replaced before it started to go wrong. She was an asset.

'How's the jump drive?' she asked.

'Primed and ready,' Allua answered. 'I've had to do some patchwork to the cooling systems. That last jump put a bit too much stress on the tanks. Stayed in it a few days too long between charges.'

'Will they hold?'

'They will, but we really do need to get these replaced when we get back to Earth. I did try to warn you that the cooling system was on its way out at our last stop. You didn't listen.'

'I know you did,' Beatrice said slowly, remembering the engineer's last report. 'It will have to do until we get back to Earth. They'll have the equipment needed to replace the system. We jump in ten.' The officer turned to her adjutant with a weary grin. 'You good?'

'I am, Captain,' Franklin said with a smile. 'What's going through your mind?'

'Sleep. Once we enter the jump, I'm calling it for some rest,' Beatrice admitted.

'Smart choice,' Franklin Hender whispered softly.

They soon reached the jump point. By law, all vessels, unless under an emergency, had to be at a minimum safe distance from a planet before entering slip space. That way they ensured that planets and more importantly civilisations did not suffer from the sudden, instantaneous, forces expelled when a ship entered the jump. To go into a jump within atmosphere could easily demolish a town or severely damage a city, if not worse.

The automated warning rang out, advising that they would soon be leaving real space behind. Beatrice shifted in her chair as the portal opened ahead and they were absorbed into a realm outside reality. It was beautiful entering the weird world of slip space. A spiral of colours and lights entombed them. Somewhere in the distance was the event horizon, their end point looking like a pin prick of light. This was her view for the next week. There were worse things to look at.

Her world became distorted. Blurry. Now it was time to sleep. If she waited any longer, she wouldn't make it to her cabin. Beatrice conceded command to her adjutant and vacated the bridge. It was a certainty that she would sleep through lunch.

Chapter 2
19/09/2675
14:30 Earth Standard Time

Leyton Foresc

Leyton and his team had successfully acquired cargo hold twelve on Deck N, the one that he had every intention of occupying. It was the furthest storage space away from any other living being that they could have taken. Once everything had been positioned and set up to make a functional command station, they found a main conduit and spliced into the ship's power grid. Thankfully, the stasis pods were able to last on battery life long enough to be plugged into the mains. Leyton was assured by their specialist that on a ship that size there really was no risk of them short-circuiting anything important, which meant they could charge the battery packs so they were prepared should they be needed again.

Specialist Schottler was able to successfully hack into some of the ship's systems, granting them access to security footage from the numerous cameras, ship schematics, nav logs and comms links established. Everything. The only person who would see anything more was the captain herself.

Jerome had been able to acquire several tables from one of the nearby storage rooms to set up somewhere for them all to sit and eat or go through briefings together. There was no need to go out and potentially mix with curious eyes. They didn't need their cover story to be challenged.

The rest of the team had opened the weapon cases and prepped all their kit in anticipation of something, if anything, going wrong that needed to be sharply resolved. He wanted to avoid heavy handed tactics. The 'any means necessary' clause in the mission parameters unsettled him. Nothing was worth any methods to complete. Leyton was more concerned that most of the people on the cruise ship were civilians. Innocents didn't deserve to be put at risk. He dreaded to think how many times would he have to remind them of his orders to make sure the safety latch on those weapons stayed on?

The professor had requested each of the pods be lined up neatly so he could view and scan each specimen in turn. Samuel had rushed around from unit to unit like an excited child. Back in the Ice Castle, he barely had time to log the specimens and name them before he had to sit back and watch while they were in transit. Now he had the space to work with and a long time to carry out his research in with no risk of disruption. Of any of them, he was the only one that was genuinely excited about the voyage taking so long.

He on the other hand had done a lot of research on the ship's captain. Captain Beatrice Lenoia, a military officer turned civilian. From the moment he saw her name, he recognised it from somewhere. The more he delved into her personnel file, the more obvious it became why he recognised her. She had taken part in a long, drawn-out conflict that had cost many lives, and had taken part in defending a planetary siege, the Siege of Vulcair. The official reports stopped there. Not even his clearance levels gave him access to look behind the blemishes of censorship on her files. That left him with not that much more to do when it wasn't his turn to patrol.

For lack of anything better to do, Leyton joined with the professor to see where he was up to with his study. He was apprehensive of the responses he might receive. Biology wasn't a strength of his, nor did he find it that interesting.

'It's fascinating,' Professor Ainslot stated like he was asked a question. 'Just through appearance you can see that there are distinct social standings in the pack. Here's Spike, their matriarch. She is the only one with the large protrusions around her jaw, back of the head, shoulders and spine. I have three more females that are significantly larger than the other members of the pack, but not as large as Spike. I'm not sure what their purpose is to the pack yet though. I've designated them Ruby, Sapphire and Amber. Not as good as a diamond, but still worth something. They might be the next in the chain of command, potentially contenders to take control of the pack from her in a challenge for matriarch. Or second in command. But I'm hoping that we can find some answers with the scans.' He held up his tac-pad that showed a three-dimensional image of one of the wolves. 'I'm carrying out scans on each of them so that I can analyse them inside and out, straight down to their blood vessels. I'm not hoping for much in the way of understanding their behaviour. Bit difficult while they're asleep. What I can try to at least get to know is what makes them tick. See what their biological makeup is and what could potentially hurt or help them.'

'What else can you tell me?' Leyton asked. 'What about the males?'

'Well, the males are smaller than the three females I've just mentioned but are larger than all the other females,' Samuel explained.

'And there is a significant proportion more of them. Realistically I could do with another couple packs of them to see if there are any patterns in their structures and numbers. Without the comparisons, anything I learn here may be nothing more than an anomaly. But I think that it's highly suggestive that a significant proportion more males means that they are the ones to hunt most of the time.'

'Wow, talk about being under the thumb,' he scoffed.

'Tell me about it,' the professor replied. 'It's a good job you basically went knocking to bring them all out otherwise you'd have only got the boys by the looks of it. But it makes sense. If the female is the biggest and strongest of the pack, then it only stands to reason that the males hunt to prove themselves as worthy suitors when it comes to breeding season. Whenever that is for them.'

'I still find it weird how there's, what, three types of female and only one type of male,' Leyton said. 'How was it that you said Spike can tell the difference between them? And this might sound like a stupid question, but if we call Spike the alpha wouldn't she have an omega? A bigger male to get down and dirty with?'

Professor Ainslot shrugged. 'Come over here. See these two males? Look at their faces. It isn't obvious straight away because we aren't used to seeing them up close, but they have different facial markings. This one has the crisp white to the sides of the eyes while the other one has a beige colour on the forehead. Aside from that, it would have to be different scents and even pheromones that they give off to tell each other apart. Animals have a good sense of smell. If they're able to have a social hierarchy like this, then it's only logical they have a way to recognise each other. What you said though about her having an omega is a good observation. There's nothing obvious though to show it. Either they don't have a tell, the tell is a little more subtle or we left someone behind. I can only potentially comment on two of those.'

'Okay then, so we know that they can tell the difference between each other and that the main female is bigger than the rest,' Leyton recited. 'And you know what you want to look up. I have a question. Why would command want them?'

'Even if I knew what they wanted them for, you know that's classified,' Ainslot retorted. Of anyone there, he was the only one that had any idea what their use would be. 'I wish I could tell you. I don't even know the full reason myself. What they told me was that they are vital to the war effort and improvement to the UPN military. But I have a few speculations for what they mean.'

'Anything you can tell me?'

The professor sighed, looked around and leaned in close. His voice was hushed. 'I know that command wants to experiment on them and study them in a controlled environment. These things have incredible communication skills. What we hear as awful noises is meant to disrupt prey and give clear communication to other pack members at the same time. In low light they succeed with their red eyes. That is why they have thrived so well out on that ice planet, where it's dark most of the time. Think how successful a night mission would be if you sent a pack of these into an enemy base after an E.M.P. goes off before you rolled in with the dog whistle. Or how much more improved base defence or prison security would be against escapees if they had a pack or two of these. That's my educated guess. I will know more when we get back to base.'

Leyton Foresc stepped back a moment. Could that be a real possibility? Command wanting a living weapon to send in before the troops. A potential boost to security resources? The thought had occurred to him, but Leyton didn't really think that it was a possibility. As far as he was aware that sort of thing had been prohibited by the United Planetary Nations Council decades ago under some human-animal rights convention. Thinking about it, their potential use was not something he was comfortable with, regardless of the benefits. Animals were not meant to be used like that. He had committed a lot of questionable acts that were well outside legal conduct to complete the mission objectives. All those times however were different. It was always technology that was going to be used on UPN planets that needed to be retrieved, assassinations of hostile dictators and key personnel or the destruction of an enemy facility key to disrupting movements. Even sabotage and the apprehension of known terrorist groups. Yet, if he had been capable of all that then it stood to reason that he should be comfortable with transporting animals for tests, and with putting civilians at serious risk.

He wasn't comfortable with the notion of it.

'Keep me up to date on your progress,' he instructed, feeling his stomach tighten as he spoke. 'If something seems interesting or unusual, I want to know.'

'You got it,' Professor Ainslot said.

When he worked his way over to their social area, he slumped back into his chair and held his forehead in his hands. There was too much information for him to take in one go. First, learning a little about the

46

ice wolves. Second, realising that chances are they were to be weaponised. Third, and most worrying, he'd learnt that he was not the same person he had been. There were things that he drew the line at. Leyton Foresc groaned as his head began to ache.

'Want to talk about it?' Jerome asked, taking the chair beside him.

'Yeah,' he replied. What he didn't say was that he didn't want to talk about it with Jerome.

'Allowed to talk about it?' his adjutant questioned, knowing the difference between the two key words.

'Not in the slightest,' Leyton said. 'I wish I wasn't even thinking about it to be honest.'

'Is it about the cargo?'

He nodded, trying to find the right words to use.

Jerome exhaled heavily. 'I can't really help if you don't let me.'

'I know,' Leyton sighed. As annoying and as infuriating as his friend was, Jerome was still his friend. 'I know. I just sometimes wish I knew what the long-term game plan is with command. Like this. These things. We've never caught animals before. We're not poachers or in the animal trade. I want to know why we need them.'

'Do you remember what you once told me?' Jerome asked. 'Asking more questions than what you're paid to understand the answer for will force you to lose sight of what you've been paid to do.'

It was nice to see that his subordinate had taken in what he had said. There was something quite humbling when someone you had taught was able to shed reason on your situation with your own lesson.

'That was a long time ago, wasn't it?' he said.

'It was,' Jerome laughed. 'But you were right. I think you've got to take a step back.'

'I'll be fine. Still, this just doesn't sit well.'

'Doesn't have to,' Jerome said. 'The only thing I'm bothered about right now is that the power doesn't go out.'

'That wouldn't help us much either,' Leyton joked. 'Anyway, if I need another chat, I'll give you a shout.'

'You know where I am,' Jerome said, slapping him on the shoulder before leaving him.

'Same place as the rest of us,' Leyton grumbled under his breath.

Leyton Foresc just stared for a while at the stasis pods, torturing himself with the possibilities for their purpose if the professor was correct. Again and again the words went through his mind. Several times, the answers seemed so obvious to Leyton. Then the next moment they were guesses at best. He couldn't work it out.

Leyton eventually managed to pull his mind away from the wolves' potential uses and onto the more present threat that Jerome was right to hint toward. How well prepared were they to tackle an outbreak of a full pack? The odds were not in their favour should that happen. If he had people on patrol, as he should do to keep up appearances and keep the ship's crew at ease, his forces would be down to just a handful at a time in that room. They would not be able to sedate or eliminate them in case of a breakout. A failsafe was required.

Without a word to anyone, he left the room and found another cargo hold that was packed the rim with barrels of grains and rice just down the hall. He opened a one-way message for Administrator to receive. That was the difficulty of slip space travel. There was no way to generate an immediate comms link to anyone outside as he was moving position too quickly in the jump for a link to be established.

'Administrator,' he started. 'Please advise. A potential circumstance has been brought to my attention that I have suggestions for but need authorisation on how to handle. In the unlikely event that the wolves escape the stasis pods, can you please confirm how we should contain them? With limited ammunition, I can't guarantee we have enough narcotics to put them all back to sleep to re-contain them. I feel a complete lockdown of the room would be best suited to keep them contained in there. Me and my team would then hold the deck from anyone finding the wolves and relocate to a new position for command. Out.'

That led him to a worrying prospect. If they did wake up, they would need to be fed. It was not like they packed food for them. There would be no way to feed them safely. How could any of them be so foolish as to think things would go according to plan? There was no contingency if they woke and needed to be fed. He would bring that up with the administrator when he got back in touch.

'I need a fucking drink.'

Duke Horren

In the days leading up to their departure, Sergeant Duke Horren had worked closely with O'Connur to figure out the best way to handle his trainees. It had been difficult. Tedious. There were things about each of them that was going to be difficult to deal with.

Ronan needed to learn how to control his anger. His temper had put him in a serious amount of trouble repeatedly. However, his leadership skills were impressive. And more importantly he knew how to take orders and put up a fight. Abe was an intellect. A tactical person. He was able to formulate a plan as quickly as anyone could. But he was the opposite of Ronan. He was no fighter. He had the skill to fight but not the strength or the will to; a bookworm who found safety in theory over practice. Joane however was a fighter and a tactician. The best of both. With completely new issues that needed to be resolved if she were to find success in the military. She had a history that was distressing to read about, but it explained her extreme dislike to men. In her mind, women were capable of more than any man and she had to prove it any way possible. It didn't matter who she upset to make it known how good she was. Everyone had a point to make.

They boarded the *Griffin* class patrol ship from the hangar. The vessels were ugly, boxy things with retractable wings to make them capable of both in atmosphere and space travel. And they were huge. So massive that they would not fit into any of the hangar bays around the station and could only be accessed through docking tubes and loading skiffs. They had three decks with two separate purposes: living and working. In the living deck, the top deck, there was space for twenty passengers and the ship's crew with facilities to sleep in individual or twin cabins, eat, relax and look after personal hygiene. From there anyone could reach the flight deck. The first of the working decks consisted of the troop bay, a small cargo hold, briefing room, med bay and armoury. The troop bay was the only way on or off the patrol ship with two docking airlocks, one on the belly and one to the side both with extendable docking tubes, and a loading ramp at the back of the ship. Underneath the troop bay was the second working deck that held a workshop, the engine room and a refrigeration unit for any deceased. It was a known fact that during military operations, people would die. Bodies needed to be stored somewhere during transit to their final resting place. The fridge was installed solely for that purpose. When on-board, with a full supply of food and drink, a full crew could last over six months before needing to restock.

Shortly after detaching from the station and pushing to a safe distance the team entered the jump. Their helmsman, Ivan Zenkovich, had promised a smooth transition across space for a few hours. Zen was an experienced pilot and could navigate most environments with ease. They had worked together on previous missions and Duke trusted his skill.

Their first destination was an asteroid field out in the middle of nowhere. The band of giant rocks criss-crossed a massive expanse of space outside of human colonised territory. That would give him a chance to test their team working abilities.

The team had enough time to stow their kit and become acclimatised before Duke brought everyone down to the briefing room. It was small for a briefing room with twenty seats around a rectangular holo-table. Zenkovich sat with his feet propped up on the edge of the holo-table while his second, Petty Officer Valentina Rodriguez, had control of the ship in his absence. Arche took a place at the corner as far from everyone else as possible. Her bleached blonde hair was short, sharply styled and brushed to one side to keep her pale skin and brown eyes exposed. Moasa and Udal'e were sat with a seat between them. Ronan Moasa was an imposing force with his giant stature and sleeve of tattoos on his tanned skin. He towered over them with the physical presence of a giant warrior. Abe clearly looked uncomfortable. His nervous smile was easily seen on his brown skin. Duke sat at the edge of the table with the asteroid field delicately hanging over it in a holographic display.

His next words had to be carefully chosen. This was his first big announcement after introducing himself when they arrived on the patrol ship.

'As you know, the whole point of this patrol is to train you all into a team of leaders. To do this, I have several tasks, simulations and leadership lessons planned to put you through your paces and prepare you for taking on a command of your own. Our first session is going to be here in this asteroid cluster. We will be dropping the three of you off here.' He stood up to point at one of the rocky objects. 'You have to work together on this and make it over here.' Duke gestured toward another celestial body. 'You'll have twelve hours' worth of air in your tanks, twice as much as you realistically need to complete the task, and about half the required propellant to stabilise and direct with. In order compete the task, you must work together. Trying to do this alone *will* result in failure. Any questions?'

'What's the point of this?' Ronan asked. He spread his arms wide. 'I don't think we need to worry about rock hopping when we're patrolling a trading port or doing a random inspection of a hauler.'

'You're right, our job shouldn't ever need us to jump asteroids. That's something for someone else to do. This is an assessment to put you in high stress situation for me to get a baseline on you all. I need to know who needs what guidance, and what training is required, to give me a hope in hell of getting you up to standards. This will test for everything I need to decide what's best for you. Anything else? No? Okay then, how long until we land Zen?'

'We'll be there in... two hours thirty,' Zenkovich replied checking the time on his tac-pad. He held it much the way civilians would hold their comm-pads, casually and with no consideration to how expensive it was.

'Okay then, get geared up,' Duke instructed. 'I want you ready in two hours. Dismissed.'

He shut off the hologram and left the briefing room. Duke quickly changed into his combat armour. The armour was highly versatile, able to be used in atmosphere and out in the vacuum of space. Each armour plating sat on top of a ballistic gel that hardened with the increase of force striking it. In theory, it was supposed to be able to protect the wearer from a sniper round fired up close. It didn't quite work that way when put into practice on the battlefield.

Sergeant Duke Horren waited in the troop bay for everyone to eventually arrive. There was no need to wait in solitary. He could have been up on the command deck with the crew, but it was nice to have time alone. There wouldn't be much opportunity for it for the rest of the patrol if his fears came to culmination. There was no real hope of the trio of trainees to gel and work together on their first sortie – their personalities clashed far too much. He hoped they would start in good spirits, that they would hold long enough for there to be some success.

His hopes were already too high.

The arguments between them had started long before they even reached the troop bay. Arche had bombarded the other two with comments to degrade and emasculate them. Moasa had, as expected, retaliated with an equally vicious response that would have had him locked up on most worlds. Udal'e managed to distance himself completely from the others. He did his best to avoid being involved in the conversation, avoiding looking in their direction.

It was not a great start to working together.

Duke Horren had shut and sealed the troop bay from the rest of the ship by the time Zenkovich landed on the starter asteroid. Once he had vented the atmosphere out of the compartment, Duke opened the loading ramp to release the trio into the void. The troops bounced along the surface of the rock until they figured out how to activate the gravity pads on the base of the armoured boots so they could walk normally. Duke waited until they were a safe distance away from the patrol ship before signalling to detach from the rock. When they had safely pushed away from the asteroid, he closed the ramp, re-pressurised the compartment with breathable air and joined the helmsman and navigator Valentina Rodriguez on the flight deck. As if his mind was being read before he joined them, Duke found a calorie bar, a lump of compressed food with a full meal's worth of nutrition in a single wrapping, and a coffee waiting for him at what had become his seat.

'How's it sounding so far, Zen?' he asked.

'Noisy,' Zenkovich responded.

'Me and the girls don't even sound this bitchy on a night out after a few bottles of wine,' Rodriguez added for emphasis.

Duke shook his head and had a bite of the granular calorie-rich bar. 'What're they saying?'

Ivan scoffed the notion of repeating what they said, 'Have a listen.'

'I really think that we need to aim for that asteroid first,' Abe was insisting. He sounded scared. *'It's the closest and we'll only be off course slightly. From there it's really easy to get from point to point.'*

'Come on little man,' Ronan replied. His tone was not exactly harsh but was a little patronising. *'If we aim for that big one there, we can at least be a good part of the way in.'*

'Yes, but the risk of missing is too high,' Udal'e retaliated. *'By the time we get there-*

'Look,' Ronan Moasa said. *'We can do this.'*

'But-

'Trust me!' the giant of a man insisted.

Joane Arche laughed mockingly over the two of them. *'Look at you two. Don't even think to ask me what I think about this? Too afraid that you'll be wrong?'*

'Not afraid in the slightest,' Moasa said. *'Just don't think you'll give a good answer.'*

'Well, I don't need you two,' Joane retorted with a huff. 'You two will only slow me down. I can get this done without you. Just watch me.'

'Yeah, with a mouth like that I guess I'll hear you before you reach the finish line,' Ronan mocked. 'Come on Think Tank. Let's leave little miss can do it all to get through this on her own. We've got an asteroid to reach.'

Ivan Zenkovich turned off the speakers and turned around with a smirk on his face. 'I think they'll kill each other before the asteroids crush them.'

'You and me both,' Duke replied.

After only four hours of the twelve-hour exercise, Duke had to make the call to bring them all in. Ronan had gotten himself stuck in a weak section of an asteroid where it caved in under him. Abe near-enough refused to move out of fear of getting his calculations wrong. Joane, however, was floating out into space and entered a state of panic the likes of which Duke had not heard for a long time. The three of them were sat next to each other as instructed watching a replay of events on the holographic projection above the holo-table in the briefing room. From the moment they split into two teams then all went their separate ways. When the four-hour recording finished, everyone remained silent. No one said a thing.

He stared at them, waiting for someone to speak. When they remained silent, Duke turned off the hologram and spoke slowly. 'Anyone care to tell me what went wrong?'

'Obviously, those pig-heads thought they were better than me,' Arche started almost immediately as if waiting for the moment when she could say something. 'They just had it in for me from the start. You had it in for me as well. You have only one female out here on this training exercise. Why not two or more? You're just bullying. Got me here just so you can say you're including me.'

'Oh, that's what it always comes down to with you!' Ronan spat. It was clear she hit a sore spot with him. 'What? Because we have dicks, suddenly you're the one that's a victim? Half the shit out of your mouth is you just blaming everyone for the fact that you have something to prove. The rest of it I stopped listening to. Probably more bullshit. We'd have been fine if you just swallowed your pride and stuck with us.'

'Actually,' Abe interjected, 'I think—'

'And you, smart-ass,' Joane screamed, cutting Abe off in an instant. 'Not even got a pair to tell us where to go? I thought you were smart. Why didn't you guide us?'

'I did say,' Udal'e replied, quietly.

'What was that little bitch?' Arche asked. 'I didn't quite hear you.'

'Whoa, you're the only bitch here,' Ronan said. 'Leave little Petal alone.'

'Enough!' Duke bellowed. His face turned red as his fist slammed into the table. 'If anyone speaks unless I order them to, the speaker is going to taste the edge of this table. Am I clear? What went wrong is none of you are actual leaders yet. You're just trying to prove you're better than each other. Arche, I'll be a gentleman and say ladies first. My review of you is that you *are* a bitch. You can wipe the sour look off your face before I do it for you. You're in the military, not the girl scouts. The enemy doesn't give a shit that you're a female. You're just a target. So why should you be capable of any less than the person next to you? But on your personality, you need to be prepared to take exactly what you give. Understood? I get that you have history, I really do. But you need to realise we're all on the same side, fighting for the same flag, keeping the same people safe. Your attitude that men are out for your blood and are simply wrong isn't wanted. Not at all. You're out here because General Baalshuk thinks you have promise. And the fact that you're the only female shows you have more than all the others that aren't here. All that said and done, I am going to say this once and only once: You are the same as everyone else and you have the same goals as everyone else. Because I have my bits and you have yours doesn't mean there's an agenda. We all bleed red at the end of the day. You're a soldier. Act like it.'

'Yes sir,' Joane whimpered.

She looked like she'd been told her entire life was a lie, that nothing she had ever done had any meaning behind it. He kept his expression blank. She needed to be knocked down a few pegs before her perspective on life got her into some serious trouble. Or worse, pushed someone to a place that they didn't need to be and be what she said they were.

'Udal'e, you want to elaborate on your idea you weren't allowed to have a say in?' Duke asked, activating the hologram once more from the start of the task.

'Sergeant,' Abe replied. 'If we landed where I was initially suggesting, it would have taken us a little way off course. However, we could have gone to either of these three asteroids afterward then after two or three more little jumps land on this big one here. A bit of a hike across and we'd have had a clear run to the rendezvous point.'

'Good,' Duke said. 'So why the hell didn't you say anything?'

'Well, they didn't give me the chance,' he explained.

'And? You're supposed to be a soldier! If you can't tell your team to shut up, how can you make a civilian to follow your instructions so you can get control of a situation? You need a pair. Pure and simply. You'll always be pushed around, but when you know that you need to step up and tell someone they're wrong, do it. As long as you can prove why they're wrong. If you can't prove they're wrong, let *them* prove they're wrong for you by carrying out their plan. You will not get a recommendation if you can't be a leader. Being a leader is making people trust that you know what you're talking about.'

'Yes Sergeant,' Udal'e whispered.

He turned his gaze to Ronan who for some reason had developed a smug expression. 'And you, Ronan, you actually tried to start a team with Udal'e. The only one of you who attempted any cooperation. Granted, you could have tried to enforce it differently, but you tried. Where you let yourself down is you were so stubborn and set on proving you was the best you set an impossible task that was risky. Just like Arche you took yourself out of the mission. I have no doubt you can hold your own but you're just as likely to be your own worst enemy. You need to think about everyone else and work with what they can do. Not expect everyone to keep up with you.'

'If they can't keep up then that's their problem and the UPNs for recruiting them,' Ronan said with an air of arrogance in his tone.

'Or it's you that's a little more blessed. Look at you. Your ancestors went to mainly a water world with increased gravity. Your people grew bigger and stronger than most humans ever could naturally. You have one up on a lot of people with your strength. Don't let that be your downfall.' Duke paused and assessed the trio. 'Go get a wash, clean your armour and go get some food. After that you rest. Dismissed.'

He waited for everyone to leave before slumping into a chair. He had not realised it was going to be so difficult. It was fortunate that he had time on his side to get them into shape before giving them their own command. Once he was sure he had removed any expression of remorse or regret from his face, he left the briefing room and went to the flight deck. Another cup of coffee waited for him with an aspirin.

'How did you guess?' he asked Zen.

'I could hear you and you took your time coming up,' the helmsman answered. 'It doesn't take a genius to work out the shouting followed by eerie silence is not a good thing. Where're we going to next?'

Where to indeed. There were plenty of places they could go to from their position. Had the training or debrief gone a little better, there were several planets with different terrains to overcome to drill cooperation and respect into the team. This would take more than that. The trainees needed to understand what they were working for, and why they joined the UPN.

'Let's go to the Juntah,' Duke suggested. 'That'll give them a wakeup call to what their responsibilities are going to be.'

'Good shout,' Ivan said. 'Val, plot us in, will you?'

'Done,' Valentina replied. 'You take too long to tell me to do things.'

'On your go Sergeant,' Zen said.

Beatrice Lenoia

It was just a few days into the jump. Already Beatrice was feeling restless. She had spent her time either pacing around the bridge or down in the gym. Anything to keep her mind occupied. This, she knew, was not her normal behaviour. Typically, she would be walking the halls of her ship, meeting and greeting passengers to see what they were enjoying or not enjoying and hear what they were hoping to encounter, all so she could gauge how to plan the next encounter. She might have been on someone's payroll and not responsible for the programme, so bore none of the responsibility for satisfaction feedback, but this was still her ship. She oversaw making sure everyone on-board was comfortable and happy.

Not now. The unexpected arrivals on Gorucia weighed heavily on her mind. One of them was always stationed outside the door to the cargo hold they occupied, on guard. Two more patrolled the lower decks, moving between L Deck and N Deck. They paid close attention to anyone that was on shift nearby and did their best to steer them away from the lower deck. No more than two other personnel left the lower decks at any time, and they always returned with food from the restaurant for everyone else. One of those to venture out routinely was a tall, well-built man, in his mid to late thirties. He had short, dark hair and carried himself with calm confidence. She the posture – it was someone in power. But there was something else about his stance. This man knew what he was capable of. If anyone came up to him and he did not like them he could handle them with ease. That was a scary person to have on board.

The rest of the security team were a menacing site. One was more unnerving than the rest. A dark-skinned man, with a buzz cut with strange blocky patterns shaved into it, looked threatening even when smiling. His eyes were constantly looking around. Like a predator constantly in search of prey. This one seemed to be the second in command. Everything about him put her at unease.

Beatrice had his face seared into her memory for safe keeping. Whenever he next ventured out, she hoped to see him and question him. Hopefully then Beatrice could understand more about these people.

'Captain?' Franklin Hender asked. 'Are you okay?'

'Fine,' she whispered.

'Obsessing?'

'Not obsessing,' Beatrice replied. 'Assessing. Can you bring up the security footage of them and their cargo please? I need to see it from time of embarkation to reaching the cargo hold.'

Franklin bowed his head. 'Of course.'

The holographic projection of the security footage floated over the holo-table. It went through the motions of going back in time to the moment they boarded a few days ago then played from there. Led by the same man who had captivated her attention moments ago, they brought in cargo in three separate packages with their exteriors had been painted black. They did not want anyone to see what was inside, but a faint blue incandescence reached out of the seams where the containers met. Each package was about five-foot-high and floated another half-foot off the floor on what could only have been gravity suspension skids. It gave more credence and support to the paperwork that they belonged to the Military Intelligence Division. One person always had a handle on the packages. The others circled around them and constantly glanced around to keep people away. That was, all but one of their teams. There was one man that caught her eye. He had mousy hair that looked as skittish as a small dog in the middle of a busy street. Was he scared? The way someone always nudged him on and said something to keep him on track suggested it. Maybe he was new or was there against his will. There was no way to tell for certain.

She flicked through several camera feeds to follow them, trying to see what was inside those units, until they were inside their chosen location. In the hold there were too many blind spots. Which was expected. It was meant to be a food storage unit. Not much happened in food storage. She could barely see anything going on.

Beatrice might not know what was in those containers, but she had identified the one person who would tell her if she asked in the correct tone.

'Franklin, if this guy comes up to the upper decks,' she said, pointing at the man with the mousy hair, 'alert me straight away. If anyone is going to tell me anything about that cargo, it's going to be him.'

'But Captain, what about the privacy demand on the paperwork?' her adjutant responded. 'It was crystal clear that they were to have whatever they required to get their product back to Earth. And we can't breach privacy rules without just cause. Especially military privacy. I hate to say it, but we don't have just cause.'

'We do have reason for concern,' she corrected.

It was a distasteful method, to think up a particular reason for investigating someone. One that she had used several times in the past during her time in the military to root out infiltration cells of enemy forces within their ranks. That did not make the move any less necessary. Doing what was required gave results. Although she would need to alter the method to suit the civilian ways of handling dangerous circumstances. Besides if they had nothing to hide, they would not object. She just needed the questioning to be on her ground, on her terms, with her crew around.

'You do?' Franklin asked.

Beatrice stabbed her eyes in his direction. A cunning smile crossed her lips as a perfect plan formed. 'Of course. They get approved paperwork signed by the MID in order to board my vessel. Not only that but they come on-board with weapons. They have several containers that have who-knows-what inside. It might turn out to be nothing. But... say that those documents are forged... we've breached our duty by not following it up. These people are potentially terrorists that have great, no, perfect forgers on their side. Everything about them says they're dangerous with one man potentially working against his will for them. For the safety of my crew, passengers and that suspected hostage I have reasonable concern that whatever they're transporting is dangerous. That means I now have the grounds I need to question them further and in person. Ask Security Chief Henendez to increase security around the lower decks. I want to know all their moves while I draw up the required paperwork to do something about them. Understood?'

'Yes Captain,' Hender said.

Her glare returned to the security footage. She wished more than anything that she had access to facial recognition software scattered throughout the ship. That would have made life much easier for her. With the input of a simple request, the database would have been able to find out if they were friendly personnel or people they should be in fear of. She flicked the footage back to real-time feed of the storage space they occupied. After several minutes of staring at the projections she saw a sudden strobe of flashing light and shadows being projected across the floor of people and right-angled shapes. Something electrical had discharged. It was not a torch being lit – it was much too bright for that.

'What is that?' she whispered to herself.

Beatrice replayed the footage from the alternate angle. The same shapes flashed then faded away. With the only difference being she could see someone get up and rush toward something out of shot of the camera.

She pondered for a moment. Something like that had to be faulty equipment. How could it be something else?

Beatrice opened a comm link with her Chief Engineer, 'Jons, can you carry out a system check for any power surges that have just happened?'

A couple of minutes later Allua Jons replied, her breath heavy as if she just ran to her station. 'Aye Captain.' Then a minute later she reported in, 'There were several minor power surges just now. Most were compensated for. There was a small overload in the lower cargo holds. Nothing to worry about. Maybe they didn't quite get their kit set up right? Although it doesn't explain why we had an overload…'

'Understood,' she said. 'Try and see if you can find what caused it and keep me updated. I want to know if it was us or them for certain. Out.'

The lower decks were a realm that she barely had any input in with. The engineering team looked after themselves and the decks with precision can capability. If it were of concern, Allua Jons would have said something. Beatrice would catch up with Chief Engineer Jobs later to see what she found or did not find with her checks.

Without warning her stomach let out a terrible roar. A flicker of embarrassment washed over. Her cheeks heated up. There were a couple small chuckles amongst her crew. Even a delighted smile from Franklin. He walked over to her.

When Adjutant Hender spoke, there was amusement in his tone. 'When was the last time you actually ate something, Captain?'

She hesitated. When had she last eaten? A glance at the bridge clock over by the forward viewing window told them it was going on five-thirty in the afternoon EST. She last ate directly after working out that morning. And for her morning started at six.

'It doesn't matter,' she shrugged, avoiding eye contact with the man.

'Captain, I suggest you go and eat something,' Franklin said. 'I promise nothing is going to happen until you're back in that chair.'

Beatrice nodded, smiled then vacated the deck. A short trip down the elevator took her past crew quarters then onto D-Deck, and then on to the main corridor leading to the food hall. It was just above the forward observation deck, a luxurious and large glass-walled room, with a wide balcony level above that gave people a bird's eye view of everything going on and its own bar area. A chandelier dangled gracefully in the centre of the room. She walked over to the buffet table, helping herself to tastes of the outer colonies. Noodles with a type of meat not too dissimilar to pork infused with a wild wonder of spices and greenery. And for good measure she picked up a platter of mixed cooked meats. Beatrice took her place at the officer's table and ordered a glass of red wine to go with her meal. With a relieved sigh she started to feast.

Occasionally, she looked up to see everyone else there enjoying their own meals. Families having a wonderful time conversing, laughing, and talking about the sights that they had seen, or hoped to see soon. Couples taking a long romantic break, enjoying a quiet meal before returning to their cabins. Tour groups of elderly travellers enjoying their retirement to the fullest. The odd business class voyager taking a more luxurious route to their destination.

It was nice to have space to breathe. Beatrice was able to think only about herself and focus on what she wanted. Her body had been aching for a couple days now from the effects of minimal sleep, low food intake and constant stress taking its toll on her.

When she finished her meal almost an hour later and collected a dessert, a simple bowl of ice cream, she had eaten about half of it when she saw one of the recent arrivals dressed in black. A female. She was staying well out of everyone's way. Beatrice waited for the woman to collect some food before making her way across the food hall to speak to her. At the halfway mark, a large group of passengers – judging by their various ages, an entire family – rumbled by in front of her, blocking Beatrice's path. When the route ahead cleared, she had lost sight of the woman.

'Franklin,' she said into her comm-pad. 'I need your help.'

'What can I do, Captain?' he replied sharply.

'I saw one of the new arrivals in the food hall. She's just collected some food and I've lost visual on her. I need you to locate her.'

'On it.'

She walked out of the food hall before instinctively making her way down the hallways toward the rear of the ship. From there she could take an elevator down to the lower decks and hopefully get in front of the woman that had been able to disappear. She just needed to know where to go.

'Captain, we've lost sight of her,' Franklin informed her. 'I've gone back over the footage from the food hall. I can see her enter and leave through the main entrance then head down the corridor. After that though, it's like she just vanished out of thin air. She moves out of frame of one camera right into a crowd of people and doesn't appear in the next one.'

Beatrice stopped in her tracks and let out a forceful sigh. 'What are you trying to say?'

'I'm saying that I can't see her at all. You really need to come up here and take a look. Tell me what I'm not seeing.'

She clenched her teeth and held back the curses to nothing more than a faint whisper. 'I'm on my way… Dammit!'

Jesa

Another nightmare.

The last few nights Jesa had had the same vivid dream of when her parents tragically died. No. Not died. Murdered. To die suggested that it was natural. Peaceful, even. There was nothing natural or peaceful about how they went, and it haunted her all too often.

The dream was the same every time. She was twelve and in the back of their jeep to go with them to work in the fields for the day instead of studying for school. Normally a neighbour would look after her while they were out. But the woman that usually did so was sick, and so with no one else to look after her, her parents had no choice but to bring her. School was not free in the outer colonies. Not enough money was provided to fund it through the local government and the Colonial Investment Grants set up by the Central Colonies weren't given to the Outer Colonies. That was what her dad had told her. It was why he had to spend long hours out in the fields working, and why he spent most nights crying while her mother tried to calm him and reassure him it would all be alright. He spent a lot of time apologising to her for not being able to give her the life she deserved. He would also tell her that he was working on a way to correct that, to give her a chance at life that they never had. She believed him. He always worked so hard, was always up late trying to invent something to make the harvest quicker, easier, to bring in more crop and in turn make more money. Jesa never had many luxuries. But she had something that no amount of money could ever buy. True, undying, abundance of love.

It was hot outside as they drove under the giant orange sun at the centre of their solar system. So hot that her chest felt clammy on the inside. Not even the breeze from driving quickly could cool her. Jesa had resorted to using a piece of scrap paper as a fan to give some relief from the heat. They reached the plantation to bring in that days' harvest; hengdu crop. A chewy plant that had a lot of calories in. Enough to make sure an adult was well fed and could survive considering there weren't many other options in the way of food. It was an expensive crop that people were willing to pay high sums for because of the nutritional benefits it offered. And her parents were one of only a handful of farmers that not only had the crop to grow, but the right planting conditions and optimum weather all year round to generate a higher percentage of good crop. They gave a lot of people work on their plantation.

The store houses lined the dirt track where the harvested crop would naturally dry for a few weeks to improve the longevity of the crop. Fields as far as the eye could see ran down the plain between the mountains marking the perimeter of her parents' property. Each high standing stalk was topped with a huge, beautiful purple flower that looked more like a thistle and several giant leaves to soak up the sunlight with small branch-like vines lining the stalk holding onto the crop to be harvested. If she never left that life, she wouldn't have any complaints. It was beautiful, just like her parents.

Mid-day was when it all happened. The syndicate flew in with their gunships after hitting several other farmsteads in the region already. Jesa never learnt of those hits until she first set foot in their base. The rumbling of engines overhead was what they heard first; then they saw the vessels coated in obscene images and the syndicate logo of a flaming dagger nestled within a metallic circle. Fear set in. The farmhands didn't run straight away. They just watched, a sense of wonder and confusion gripping them, as if they were trying to figure out if this was even real. Panic did not take hold until the ships fired its first salvo of rockets down at the ground, sending clouds of black smoke and red flames into the sky. First it was the store houses that were destroyed and engulfed in flames. The plantation then started to take the hits as the attackers tried to force out anyone hoping to hide amongst the crops. Smoke thick with contaminants billowed into the sky in giant plumes of death and destruction.

Her father took hold of her, hoisting Jesa over his shoulder with unnatural ease, then gripped her mother's arm tightly with his free hand before they began to flee. He stayed calm, knowing what needed to be done and focusing only on that. They tried to make it back to their jeep. People were jumping out of the gunships and shooting their guns into the farmers that tried to put up a fight or flee. It didn't seem to matter to their attackers. Everyone was a target. An explosion erupted where a rocket landed just a little way to their right. The blast reached the jeep and it detonated. The forces from the explosion hit Jesa and her family and sent them flying. Her head hit the ground.

Jesa did not consciously remember much after that point. Regardless of if she was dreaming or awake, events normally were a blur by that point. The more she tried to see, the harder it was for clarity to come forth. It was also usually at that moment where she woke up in a pool of sweat. This time was different. Jesa could not wake from the torture. She wanted to wake up so desperately, but instead, the dream continued, vivid, dangerously accurate, horrifically real. Her subconscious had regurgitated the scenes in a dreadful film reel that she had to relive.

Jesa finally came to from hitting her head on the ground. She looked to her side. Her mother was not moving. The woman's eyes were wide open and red, her face sprayed with blood, mouth open, trying to gasp for breath that couldn't be taken. Jesa could not see her legs or one of her arms. There was no sign of her dad. The battle raged on all around them. People screamed in pain. Farmers tried to flee. Gang members hollered and howled in joy at the carnage they were bringing. Jesa started to cry in grief. She was going to die all alone. Worse still, she wasn't going to die straight away. Just because she was young didn't mean she hadn't been warned about men like their attackers and what they enjoyed doing to young girls who couldn't fight back.

A man stood over her. He was missing half of his lower jaw, replaced with metal moulded into the shape of a mouth. He looked at her as if he had just seen something delicious, eyes wide, almost drooling with anticipation. Her father rushed over out of nowhere and punched the man unconscious with a single strike. He took hold of Jesa and with tears streaming down his face ran with her toward the distance. She cried for her mother. Pleading for her father to turn around and rescue her. Even though she had no real concept of death, Jesa instinctually knew she would never hear the woman's voice again and her pleas were futile. Then her father cried in agony. She was dropped once more. Her dad was on his knees clasping his leg. The blood staining his trousers red. He barked for her to run. Told her to just keep running and to not look back. She stood up, legs sore, hesitated and made it a few feet then slipped on a branch. Her ankle had been twisted in the fall. Jesa rolled over to see a new man, a large man with a black mohawk and tanned skin, standing over her father. They exchanged words that the big man seemed to find funny. The man shot her dad once, twice, three times. Three merciless bullets. He fell to the floor and didn't move. She started to sob. Jesa couldn't remember the last time that she told her parents she loved them. How she wished that times could stay as they were.

The man walked over to her and smiled. It wasn't a hungry smile like the other one had. The man seemed genuine. He brought himself to her level, and looked her up and down casually, assessing her.

'I'll look after you,' he had said. *'My name is Barbaros. I'm here for you now.'*

'I want my parents,' she snapped back.

'They were never good enough for you,' Barbaros retorted. *'You deserve better than that. I'll look after you right.'*

Barbaros forcefully took her hand and brought her up to her feet. Jesa's injured ankle collapsed under her weight. Barbaros caught her, lifted her up and carried her back to his ship. They passed the bodies of her father then her mother. She belonged there. With them. That was where she needed to be. Where her heart desired to remain.

'Mother!' she screamed at the top of her lungs. Hoping that her voice would resurrect the woman she turned to when in need from the grave.

Jesa was back in her ship. Not out in the fields. She could breathe filtered air. Not the hazardous smoke that choked with each mouthful. Her mother was no longer around. Nor was her father. No one was. It was just her, alone travelling through Jesa brought up her knees, tucked them in tight against her chest and cried for a while. The day she lost her parents was the day she lost her freedom. A freedom they would have done anything to make sure she still had. Not only that, but she had control over her own destiny stripped away from her.

Jesa hated Barbaros. Her thoughts always teetered on giving in and doing whatever was necessary to free herself of that monster. Fear of him, however, outweighed her hatred. She had no idea what he would do to her if she failed him or if she tried to revolt against him. Stand her ground and be her own person. She had seen too many times the sorts of things he was willing to do to people that disappointed him. Even his friends.

Her arm started to itch. It always itched more when she thought of him. A reaction of how he was the reason for the thing in her arm.

Jesa clambered out of bed and went over to the flight deck. As to be expected she was right on course for the next destination. It was a gang-controlled outpost that was initially set up as a trade port called Juntah. It had its own law enforcement that was merely there to make sure fights did not get out of hand and to send reports to the UPN. They knew their place there. Because of the criminal element being in control of the station, it gave smugglers a safe place to refuel and resupply without risk of being reported to the Centies. More interestingly, unlike the Centie worlds, Juntah was a multi-species society. Humans and aliens lived there and worked closely hand-in-hand. Everyone was there for a reason. Wouldn't find that in any of the central systems – people there were too prejudiced toward aliens. They were lucky to even have trade agreements. Once she was back in the jump, she would be there in a few more days. Her timer said she had to wait another six hours before enough time passed to avoid jump-flu. Jesa had suffered with it once. She had been bed stricken and her bones ached for a week. All because she didn't take long enough breaks between jumps.

Jesa had breakfast and just sat there, looking out onto the goods she was transporting. The Shauari skeleton glared back at her. She tried to imagine the colour of its eyes. What colour its skin must have been. Did it have smooth skin or rough scales? Hair or feathers? How intelligent was it? It was of no importance to her if she knew any of that. She would still be smuggling goods back to Barbaros after she was done with this shipment if she was to learn any of that. It would have just been nice to know.

'What's up big guy?' she asked it as if expecting a response. 'Can't talk, yah? Probably for the best. Wouldn't understand a word you say, I reckon.'

The skeleton stared at her blankly, intimidating even in death. She wondered if the creature had once possessed a soul. Did aliens die and go to their own version of Heaven, or did they just cease to exist upon death?

'I can't believe I've resorted to talking to a fucking pile of bones,' she cursed out loud. It humiliated her to admit how alone she really was. A communication link request alarmed from the flight deck. It took a couple moments for it to sink in that this was an incoming transmission and not a figment of her imagination. 'Who the hell?'

She returned to the flight deck. The transmission coding said it was from Juntah. Who was getting in touch with her? Jesa flipped the switch to accept the comm link.

'Juntah Outpost to unidentified craft, you are in Outer Colony controlled space. Please confirm your vessel code and business here,' a gruff voice instructed her.

'This is *Saridia Two-Zero Dash Eight-Three-Hotel*,' she replied. 'Trajectory is for Junta Outpost, yah. It's a resupply and refuel stop. No more than twelve hours then I'll be out of the way.'

'*Saridia*?' the man asked to no one other than himself. '*Saridia*… Ah yes, we received word to expect your arrival, yah. You have more cargo to pick up, compre? We have a hangar bay assigned for you. I will send across your landing authorisation codes shortly.'

'More cargo? What do you mean?' Jesa asked.

'Well, it means more stuff is going onto your ship for you to take to the Centies, yah,' the flight controller answered bluntly. 'Nothing to worry about. It's only a small package. We also have instructions to top up your food. Plot your arrival and prepare for remote docking controls once you enter proximity. You will be met in the hangar, compre? Out.'

Just as she was getting used to speaking to someone that was not herself the conversation was over. A shame. In a few days at least, that would be different. She would be able to eat to her limits and speak to other people as long as they were not the police of Centies. If she did speak to cops, even in casual conversation, and word got back to Barbaros she would be best doing herself a favour and jumping out an airlock without a vac-suit. Chances were, he would find out too. Barbaros had eyes everywhere that he had any influence.

'Nice talking to you,' she muttered. 'Should do it again sometime, yah. Maybe grab a cold one? Doesn't have to mean anything.'

Jesa sighed. It was one of those times she tried to remember how her parents sounded just so that she could imagine them giving her words of advice. Saying things that would empower and encourage her to tackle her obstacles. Anything to get her by. Instead, all Jesa could picture was their faces. Lips moving but making no sound. Having heartfelt words that she was never allowed to know about. It hurt that she had to remind herself that they would never be there to guide her again. And that Barbaros was the one to blame for that.

Her arm itched again.

Jesa set the autopilot to launch automatically into the jump once enough time had gone by to ensure a safe journey. Confident that she had done everything she needed to, Jesa rotated in her seat and started to daydream. A few more days and she would be around people again. Real people. There would be no need to continue to talk to herself. And air. Recycled air that had to be topped up from time to time from gas hauliers, but air nevertheless that carried smells that weren't hers. Noise that wasn't the *Saridia* or herself. She could barely contain her excitement. And there was a food top up. They would fill her up as much as they could before the weight was too much. Jesa celebrated by eating a full meal. She satisfied the hunger that had been handicapping her for weeks. With each mouthful, she decided on what flavour pouch of food she would enjoy for each meal up until reaching the station.

An alarm cried out. Jesa pushed away from the helm, her seat following tracks in the floor, to the navigation station where it locked into place. A blip on the radar. She watched its moves intently. The blip came a little closer to her, then another showed up. Her heart raced a little faster. More blips representing ships continued to appear until there was at least a dozen of them. She could feel her heart beating violently, trying to escape from her chest. Jesa brought up a visual of the ship on her long-range sensors and gasped. She recognised the harsh design, wide structure and deadly weapons from all the survivor accounts.

Crevari. Aliens that hunted for fun and killed indiscriminately. She had never seen one in person, thankfully, or even a holograph of one. She wasn't sure that anyone able to snap a picture of one survived long enough to show it. But Jesa had been told too many terrors about them and what they were capable of. They were hive-minded, insectoid creatures with four legs and two arms. Their bug-like eyes gave them a two-hundred-degree line of sight, and they had a hunger that was never satisfied. The Crevari searched the galaxy looking for their next sport as a swarm, converging on their prey within an instant, using their superior numbers to their advantage. To her knowledge they didn't have a home planet anymore. The rumours said that they had ventured from another galaxy entirely and floated through the void of space until they reached the Milky-Way. The entire population lived on their ships and roamed between the stars living on the spoils of their last attack. Very few victims ever escaped once the Crevari had them in their sights. Even fewer survived once they were within their claws. The best way to escape was to stay far away and never get caught. That was the advice she had always been given.

Jesa shut down her engines, the life support and all non-essential systems until all she had was the navigation station. The aliens didn't have the same way of observing the local space as humans. Instead of radar pings and visuals, they looked for radiation trails and heat signatures. If she wasn't giving anything off, there was less for them to find her with.

She waited. Watched. Prepared herself for the upcoming slaughter. They started to edge closer to her, following the trail she must have left behind. Then something else came up on her sensors. Another ship. Not a Crev. Human. Jesa wanted to warn them, to tell them to turn around and get out of there. But she couldn't. To do so meant giving up her position, making herself a victim. Jesa felt sick as she watched the fleet react to the new arrival, turn on the spot and speed up for the kill. Their deaths meant she could live. Once the ships dropped off her sensors,

Jesa fired her engines and hurried away before they returned to the hunting ground. With the amount of fuel she would use to get out of the area as quickly as possible, it was a good job she was heading to Juntah. But Jesa was potentially leading them straight to it. She veered away from the station so that if the Crevari did turn and chase her they wouldn't be led straight to those millions of people. Families. Men, women and children. They didn't deserve to die. Let alone die at the hands of the Crevs.

Jesa got back on the comms, 'Juntah Outpost, this is cargo ship *Saridia*. I will be later than expected to berth. Be advised, Crevari are in the area.'

'Mayah! Crevari? You serious?' flight control replied.

'Very, yah,' she stated. 'They're not heading your way or following me. They got another target. I'm taking a detour to be safe.'

'Where are they going?' flight control questioned.

Jesa quickly tried to picture the territories in that direction. 'They're heading toward Salvage Pass.'

'Thanks for the heads-up, yah,' the man at flight control answered. 'We'll have evacuation teams on standby and will let all ships in the area know they're going to have trouble if they don't get out of there soon. Fly safe, yah. Out.'

Fly safe. Words that never applied when those things were out there. Jesa set her course and kept going. She would resume course after about a half days travel. Would be enough time to shake them and make sure they weren't following her. Or at the least send them in the wrong direction so they didn't reach Juntah.

The worrying thing was that they had never ventured into this sector before. Had everything dried up in their known hunting grounds? Or were their numbers growing that much they needed to widen their territories? Times were changing too quickly. It was one of the few times she wanted the Centies to come to the outer worlds. They would be strong enough to take them on. Why hadn't they done it already? Did they want the outer colonies to die off?

Chapter 3
27/09/2675
19:13 Earth Standard Time

Duke Horren

Juntah. A miserable place for the many and a treasure chest for the few willing to do whatever it took to survive. Somehow the local law enforcement just managed to keep it under control; and that was because the local gang leaders kept the calm in their own way. Police would only step in if they had no choice when someone who was not affiliated with a gang had been killed. Even then, the SPF was usually called in for assistance in case things got a little tricky or hard to handle. It was a huge spaceport for trading that had been built into the side of a monstrous lone asteroid orbiting the local space. More than fortunate that it was in a near empty solar system and ran no risk of ever colliding with anything. At fifty levels in height and over a few kilometres wide it was a moving metropolis outside of entire control of the UPN. It was a law unto itself.

Duke watched their approach for a few minutes while the team assembled in the briefing room. Once they had been approved for landing in one of the docking bays, he left the command deck and joined the others. They were all suited, as requested, in their combat armour. Ronan looked bored and the others appeared to be anxious.

'Okay, we're now on our final approach to Juntah,' he announced. 'What can anyone tell me about the place?'

Corporal Udal'e raised his hand and waited a second before speaking, 'It's a trade port, Sergeant. A stop off for goods being traded between the outer colonies.'

'Yes,' Duke said. 'Anything else?'

'It's controlled by gangs,' Corporal Moasa added. 'There's cartels, chapters and just local thugs that run things.'

'Well done.' He turned his look over to Corporal Arche. 'Have you got anything?'

She hesitated. A reaction that was out of character for her. This was a sore spot for Arche, and Duke knew it. Arche lost a relative a long time ago there, a female relative. What the police report stated explained her attitude to men. Intentionally making her give an answer was to force her to speak about the place. It was a lesson of putting even the most powerful of emotions aside to be professional.

'They have no effective police force here,' Joane Arche said through gritted teeth. Her voice struggled for a moment. 'Can you please tell me why we're here? Why're you're doing this to us?'

Arche received curious looks from her peers. Duke, however, felt a bit of pride that she spoke of the team and not just herself. Intentional or not, it was a good sign.

'This is so you can watch and learn how we do things from a leadership perspective,' he explained. 'We'll all be going in and doing a walk around. I'll be pointing out the signs to look for to see who's a victim and who's a criminal, who needs us to talk and who wants us to keep on walking by. How to read the language that isn't spoken.'

'Why are we learning that?' Abe asked. 'We're not going to be there long enough to get to know anyone. That's a job for the police, right? We're military.'

'We are military, that is true,' Duke agreed. 'But that doesn't make us any less a face for the UPN. Our duty in the UPN is to protect the citizens. Our role with the SPF is to bridge the military world with the civilian. Out here in the Outer Colonies, this is more important than you could possibly imagine. The people out here have no connection to the Central Colonies and barely anything for the Mid-Colonies. Doing this shows that we are still here for them. To help them. Not to oppress them. No one wants to follow a leader that they feels is controlling their every move. Most people that live in places like this think we're just out to rule them with an iron fist.'

Duke activated the holo-table and an image of the station appeared. A sequence of colours flashed; each one associated with different areas and purposes.

He looked at the trio for their attention and continued. 'As Udal'e said, it's a trade port. Goods come in, get traded and go out. They are for mainly the outer colonies but also a few things are sent to the central colonies. There is home-grown produce but it's minimal. They are heavily reliant on food being brought in. None of that food, or very minimal, comes from the central colonies. Near enough all the food imports here are from outer colonies only. That means as far as they're concerned the UPN doesn't care about them. They have no reason to think we do. No humanitarian aid comes in with food, clothes, education. Nothing. Grants from the UPN Central Fund are usually used up by the time they get to the Mid Colonies. That's where Ronan and Arche, your comments come with relevance. The law is minimal. Why? Because the police force represents the UPN and anything they do is the heavy hand of the UPN trying to impose tyranny, dictatorship and supreme rule over them and take away any independence they have left. So, police only do something if they have no other choice. They're left to play politics. Then to fill the void, gangs came into power and created their own law. We have a few known gangs out here.'

The holographic projection flashed on all the upper decks and covered most of the hangar bays. In each flash was the symbol of a dark angel wielding a sword and mace engulfed in flames.

'The Devil's Cavalry is probably the biggest shuttle-gang that's present,' he continued. 'The Juntah Chapter believes heavily in protecting the civilians here provided the civilians do as their told and don't speak to anyone that isn't one of their own. Anyone says anything and the entire family is punished. They're beaten and forced to pay them for years later. If we're to be cooperative with anyone, it's them. The second they think someone has ratted them out to us, they will go to war with everyone.'

'What about ones we're to not cooperate with?' Ronan asked. He wore the grin of someone hoping for a fight.

Duke sighed. 'Corporal Arche?'

'The O.C.C. The Outer-Colonies Cartel,' she answered shakily. 'They use this station as the main port of distribution for their drugs and weapons.'

'How do you know that?' Abe asked her.

'I…'

'She lost family out here. To the cartel,' Duke explained. It was incredibly dirty laundry to have out in the open but exposing it would help to tone her attitude down. That and he would spare her any indignities by saying it for her. 'It was a cousin of hers. She was stationed out here on one of her first details when she became a cop, believing she could make a difference. She arrested a member of the cartel who got drunk and was waving a pistol around in front of his friends. Just wanting to show off. Problem was that his friends were all high and the guy she arrested was the boss' grandson. They put the deck on lockdown then stormed the police station in retaliation and to free the kid. There were no reinforcements with most active units assigned to distractions elsewhere. Once identified, she was beaten, raped and forced to cut her body for their own pleasure. But it also acted as a warning – don't touch the cartel.'

'It didn't end there,' Joane Arche whispered. Tears rolled down her cheeks. 'When it was over... she...'

'She couldn't carry on,' Duke finished. 'She took her own life not long after that. These guys are the worst of the worst and don't care who gets in their way. Only reason the UPN didn't go sooner was because they took their sweet time telling anyone. By then it was too late.'

Corporal Arche hung her head in shame and mourning, the memory still fresh and just as painful. Duke walked over to her and placed a supportive hand on her shoulder. She squeezed his hand in return. Udal'e and Moasa both shared her grief and offered support. Showing more compassion than Duke realised they were capable of. She eventually smiled and wiped the tears from her eyes to continue.

'We stick together on this,' Duke explained. 'You start to wander away you tell the rest of us. Stay in my line of sight. This is still a training exercise but a live fire one at that. Go grab your gear from the armoury and wait in the troop bay.'

Duke Horren armed himself with the standard issue assault rifle and two pistols with ammunition to spare. Arche and Udal'e also took up assault rifles and pistols while Moasa armed himself with a shotgun and assault rifle. No sidearm. Unorthodox. Though it was not like they had many people to share the weaponry with and he was the right size to control both. Duke wasn't going to pull him on that. He would however mention something when it was over. Regulations were regulations after all.

'Zen,' Duke said over the comms. 'Remember to lock up when we jump off.'

'Don't worry, I will. If anyone comes knocking, we're only interested if it's food or alcohol.'

'Good to hear.'

Sergeant Duke Horren lowered the rear loading ramp to give them access to the hot, stuffy environment of Juntah Trading Outpost. The immediate smell of exotic spices, oil, fuel and sweat was overwhelming. The noise of the hustle and bustle of station life deafening. As their eyes focussed on the individuals walking by, Joane and Abe both gasped. Not Ronan. He was surprisingly calm about it.

Udal'e cleared his throat. 'Sergeant, are those...'

'Yeah. Aliens,' he answered as the odd bipedal and quadrupedal organisms passed them by. 'For a lot of the outer colonies, aliens are quite the regular thing. Facilities like this are usually the first places aliens come to within human controlled space. We don't see many back home in the central or even mid colonies, unless they're there for official reasons. There are no colony outposts that way for them to shelter in, and people there aren't so accepting of aliens. Hell, Earth struggled accepting people who lived on different continents for centuries because of their skin colour and we came from the same planet. Can't say you're surprised the central worlds are still touchy about them, can you? Out here, they're all on the same page. No one is better than the other. Everyone is just wanting to scrape an existence here. For the most part. There's some that think the aliens are only coming to take their homes, their livelihoods. Most know that's not the case. Let's get it moving.'

Swarms of humans and the odd alien moved around the hangar. Some were waiting to try and sell anything they could to any would-be punter. Others begged for money. The debate was what they were going to use that money for. Most of the passers-by were either working or on their way to work. All looked over when the four of them walked out and onto the station deck. Many people gave them a wide berth. Avoiding them like they had contracted some foul ailment.

This was the seventh time Duke had ever set foot inside this outpost. He was far from happy to be back because of the risks it presented. His previous experiences had been dangerous but went as expected. His first time resulted in a couple of broken bones. The most recent expedition out there only suffered several heated arguments with the locals, with nothing more dangerous than language being thrown around. Every time was a unique experience for him.

He led the squad through the hangar. They were on level thirty-one, near the mid-section and at the heart of Chapter territory. He kept his eyes open for hostiles, his finger never far from the safety catch on his rifle.

They did a sweep of the level. Dozens of stalls, tens of shops, row after row of storage bins and vacant units littered the deck. There were a few homes around the edges. Some built into the rock itself. And lots of eyes watching. Their reception was warm compared to what it could have been. No one greeted them, but no one started anything. The locals just wanted to be left alone. The team did as they wanted and kept their distance. Nodding to the occasional friendlier-looking person or alien. The squad double backed once they reached their limit and headed for the nearest elevator to go to the next level. A man screamed in the distance a few streets away. His roars of anger were tremendous. Duke automatically fell into a combat-ready state as he led them toward the outburst. An alien child burst through the crowd carrying a loaf of bread followed closely by a grown man with a large gut and long bushy beard. The little girl scuttled through the crowd and took cover behind him and his team.

While the man was pushing his way over to them and the human roadblock called Corporal Moasa, Arche knelt to eye level and removed her helmet to show a friendly face to the child. Joane smiled and the kid smiled back, her pale pink skin and large white patches around the eyes making her look even more innocent. She had a much smaller nose than humans and one digit less on the hands. A Yusian child. Physically she was thin, much more so than her species naturally was. They were from a quadrant much closer to the centre of the galaxy. The planets they colonised were much like Earth but with reduced oxygen levels and slightly less gravity. When the first members of the species came into environments suitable for humans, they were overpowered by the abundance of oxygen in the air and quickly became addicted to it. Their children however grew up with a tolerance and felt little to no such afflictions to breathing the air but also grew taller than they naturally would, giving rise to the skinnier stature.

'It's okay,' Corporal Arche said to her.

The girl continued to smile until the large man made himself known, trying to peer around Ronan. She cowered immediately to stay safe.

'The girl, hand her over to me,' the man demanded.

'Care to tell me what for?' Duke replied. His hands stayed on his rifle.

The man pointed at the loaf of bread. 'She stole that. Snuck round the back and took it. I don't care that she's a kid. She stole from me. I'm taking her to the Chapter. Let her parents suffer for it.'

Duke knew some of their rules and the punishment of children was something that they did not adhere to if kids were young.

'Bit extreme, don't you think?' Duke asked.

'What do you care? Aren't you about upholding the law?'

Duke laughed and stepped in front of Ronan so there was only a small space between him and the shop owner. 'I care because she's a kid. Yes, punishment should be given. But to hand the kid over to the Chapter? That's a bit overkill, isn't it?'

The man snarled. 'Then I'll report you too.'

'For what? For stopping you from beating a kid?' Ronan questioned. 'Please, only a little bitch beats on a kid.'

'Say that again!' the man retorted.

'Wait!' Corporal Arche yelled. 'How much?'

'What?' the shopkeeper questioned, glaring at her.

'How much is the bread?' Joane asked.

'Six credits,' he replied with a vicious cough and a greedy smile. 'Ten if you include cost of damages from taking me away from my shop.'

'How about five credits and we don't report you to the Chapter for intentionally wanting to handle a child?' Joane countered, holding out a handful of coins. 'I know they'll do worse to you for… man handling the girl.'

The shopkeeper took one look at them all, bared his teeth and took the money then left. The crowd looked at them with amazement. Some of them even cheered them for defending one of their own.

Corporal Arche smiled at the child again. Are you okay?'

She nodded and leapt at her into a deep cuddle. Joane reciprocated the hug and then gave her the remaining credits the shopkeeper never received from his demand.

'You take these as well,' she instructed. 'I'm Joane.'

'Tziene,' Tziene replied quietly.

'How far do you live?' Arche asked her.

The little girl shrugged then pointed down the main street. 'Way, way. Down and down and down and left.'

Duke had forgotten how so many aliens struggled with the English language, or any human language for that matter. But for Tziene to speak with an accent they could understand was a sign she was born and bred here. She probably had very few friends that were human to learn from. Tziene most likely would barely speak more English than a ten-year-old human when she grew up. But her offspring would learn more. Maybe a couple generations down the line and her family tree would be fully integrated with the humans.

'Show us where you live,' Duke requested. 'We'll make sure you get there safe.'

The four of them escorted the girl through the level and home. When they saw her parents greet her Arche waved her goodbye and they returned to the task at hand. Duke was impressed at Joane's quick thinking to settle the dispute in order to save a child's life, and that of her family, by the simple act of paying for the food herself. She couldn't afford to do that for everyone. This one-off though would surely win over hearts and minds even if only temporarily of the locals.

That was the sort of quick thinking he needed to instil into the troops if they were to pass.

They managed to quell a few more disturbances during their recon of Juntah. Arguments mainly. There were a few alcohol and drug fuelled brawls that they were able to separate. The police showed up at a couple of the events and were happy to have little to do in those instances. Word had travelled quickly of their light-handed method of handling events. People would look at them more favourably, even greeting them in the various languages that were spoken there, of which Duke only recognised a couple. He led them back to the elevator when a call for help from the Juntah Police Department came over the comms on a security channel accessible only by UPN personnel. The station was under attack from the cartel and by the sounds of it the gang was winning.

'What do we do?' Abe Udal'e asked.

Moasa scoffed the question. 'What do you think? We have ourselves a rescue mission.'

'Serious?' Abe said shakily. 'Sergeant?'

'We have a duty to help,' Duke replied. 'And we have the means with which to help.'

'Yes!' Ronan exclaimed with excitement.

'Arche?' Duke asked. 'Your thoughts?'

She did not answer straight away. He looked at her intense stare through her visor. The desire to have revenge. The need to bring someone to justice.

'Let's go kick some ass, Sergeant,' Arche answered.

Duke smiled. He radioed the police to let them know support was on its way. The four of them worked their way down a few levels and followed the directions given by the police. It was not long before they only had to follow the gun shots. When they reached the police station, the various buggies and carts in the streets, police and civilian, were either shot up or burnt out. Shooters dressed in khaki baggy trousers, bullet proof vests and balaclavas or stolen military grade helmets were pushing through the streets assaulting the station. The cartel. There were well over a dozen of them that they could see, and most definitely more that were out of sight.

Duke stopped them only so he could give his orders. He and Ronan swung left while Abe went with Joane and circled over to the right of the battle to flank the assailants. Duke and Corporal Moasa crouched low, weaving between the cars, until there was no chance of missing a shot. He fired first and took out three cartel members that were lagging behind the others with three controlled bursts from his rifle. When a fourth dove round the side of a police car to get the jump on him Ronan put the man down with a quick blast from his shotgun.

The pair fought through a few more cartel members that thought they could stop them until they were inside the lobby of the police station. It wasn't quite quiet. Muffled gun shots could be heard down the corridors as the battle continued. Doors were riddled with bullet holes. A couple bodies were callously left lying around where they fell. Blood, papers and wreckage carpeted the floor. Voices approached them from somewhere nearby. Out of the shadows, five gang members marched into view. Some were on the ground floor. The rest were on the balcony above looking down. Their weapons aimed at the two of them. They knew they had arrived.

'What do we do Sergeant?' Ronan asked.

He looked everyone over again, checked his ammunition counter on the side of his rifle, and breathed calmly. He had half a magazine remaining. They were probably fully loaded and had both the low and high ground. 'There's some cover over to your right. When I start to shoot, you make a break for it. Understood?'

'What will you do?'

'I have somewhere to hide,' Duke lied. He was going to just draw their fire and hope for the best. As long as Ronan was okay that was all that mattered. 'You just do your bit, okay?'

'Understood,' Ronan grunted, readying his shotgun.

'Ready?' Duke asked. 'Three... Two...'

Duke almost finished the countdown when a chorus of gunshots rang out from his right. All five of their opponents collapsed where they stood. He never fired a shot. Neither did Ronan, as much as he would have wanted to. A group of men and women dressed in black leather jackets, baggy trousers, and shin-length boots, with wild hair styles of various colours, stepped casually out from the side, howling and hooting in celebration. The shuttle-gang. It seemed the Juntah Chapter was in a hurry for a piece of the action too.

When they locked eyes with Duke and Corporal Moasa, the cheers ended almost immediately to make way for a stand-off between the two sides. Duke attempted to find out who they were and to calm the situation while trying to stay numb to their persistent taunts as they goaded for a fight now that they had the fresh taste of blood.

A single gunshot was fired, ending the commotion. Footsteps approached Duke from behind. Arche and Udal'e hurried over with another member of the gang following calmly. He was a skinny man but the way he carried himself couldn't hide the fact he was a dangerous person. Pasty white with grey eyes and a spiked mohawk that had been allowed to grow a little too long at the back. His jacket had a triple-patch on the back and something on the front. A logo.

'Don't shoot them,' Corporal Arche insisted. 'They're with us.'

'Care to tell me what's happening?' Duke requested. He kept his weapon at the ready, already having two targets picked out that could be eliminated with ease.

'It's like this, yah?' Mohawk said. 'Your girl here saved a kid. A kid on my turf. That goes a way-way. Long-o way-way. We repaying the debt, yah. Boys, circle. Eyes everywhere, yah? No cartel fucks come anywhere near, compre?'

'And you are?' Duke replied.

The man smirked, as if it were the most ridiculous question he had been asked. He casually walked up to him until they were glaring each other in the eye. If his visor weren't in the way, they would have been nose to nose.

'My people call me Deadman. I'm president of the chapter here,' he answered. 'Anyone I don't like, dead. Get me, yah? Not you guys, you guys we help today.'

Duke readied himself for a fight, taking the name as a threat. 'Why help us? What do you get out of it?'

Deadman shrugged. 'Point your gun somewhere else, yah? Then we talk some.'

The bikers did have the advantage of numbers. If there was any harm meant for them, they would have been killed by now. He sighed and lowered his weapon, holding his trigger hand away from the rifle for added trust.

'Yah, he get me,' the biker said then turned to his crew. 'He get me! No shooting friends, yah?' He turned back to Duke while laughing in joy. 'Now we talk some. I help because you help us. We do this and maybe you let us clear up a problem we all have, yah? And when we done, we get left alone to keep it quiet? No badges.'

'What's he talking about?' Abe asked.

It took Duke a moment to translate what Deadman was trying to ask. When he worked it out, he almost felt like he had insulted himself for not suspecting it sooner. It was obvious what the Chapter wanted. And one less enemy was always a good thing until they could deal with them.

'He's going to help us clear the cartel out of here,' Duke explained. 'But when it's done, he wants to be able to claim some territory off them.'

'Some?' Deadman barked, falling almost into hysterics. 'All. We want them gone, yah? Done. They be dead men, yah? No one want them here. They bring white and low-dow here. We not about drugs, compre? Drugs ruin us. Make us into animals. We're better, yah.'

'No,' Duke said. He thought carefully about how to keep the devil they knew in good favour. 'We need the status quo. I'll speak to the chief here when this is done. Smooth things over as best I can. I'm happy for you to take some territory and have the upper hand. But you help the police. You cooperate with them, and you tell them where there is trouble. You get too big, I'll be back. If I come back because the cops need me, you'll never ride again. Get me?'

'Oh, big man,' Deadman chuckled. 'I like you. We have same brain, yah? I agree. One small print.'

'What's that?'

The biker pointed to Duke's tac-pad. 'I need you; I call you. You help.'

'If I can,' he replied. 'No can do if I'm on the other side of the galaxy.'

'Yah, yah, I get you,' Deadman said. He held out his hand. 'Deal is bondage. Yah? My word good. Your word?'

'Yeah,' Duke said. 'My word is good.'

He took the biker's hand in a tight grip. A deal with the devil to hopefully keep the peace a bit longer. It was a sacrifice he was willing to make and support. He wasn't sure how the station's captain would react to the news, but Duke would find a way to make it okay. If Deadman tried anything, he would ensure that it was the last thing he did.

The group stayed together and began their efforts to reclaim the police station. With the extra fire power, it was going to be a lot easier.

Leyton Foresc

Leyton kept his eyes closed, though he had woken a half-hour earlier. Sleeping was so much easier when out of a jump. There was no reason to rush out of what had become their sleeping corner. Nothing was happening. No alarms, no raised voices. Not even a hint of a rumble from the engine. It was the good life to not have to worry for once. He just listened. Agents Fellstrum and Tallow were somewhere around the eating area talking about Earth and what it was like – Fellstrum had never been, Tallow had lived there for a few years growing up. Schottler was typing away on the equipment he had plugged into the ship's systems, most likely learning everything that he could about the ship after the earlier fiasco of the makeshift plug-in overloading. That was a sticky situation. While Schottler and Houghton worked on repairing the damage he had to go explain to security and engineers that it was nothing and everything was under control. Had they not bought it, his agents would not have hesitated in doing whatever was necessary. The professor meanwhile was busy away muttering to himself. Leyton had no idea what he was saying, but even if he could hear the professor, he highly doubted he would know what the words meant.

The others were either patrolling or guarding. It was good to know that they were carrying on with their duties as normal.

When Professor Ainslot started to go wild with excitement at something he had discovered, Leyton could not continue pretending to sleep. He forced himself out of the makeshift bed. Samuel was in a frantic state rushing between a couple of the stasis pods. When the professor glimpsed his approach, he nearly yanked Leyton's arm from the socket to show him something displayed on the tac-pad.

'Agent, you have to see this,' Ainslot insisted. 'I–I can't believe it.'

'Can't believe what?' Leyton asked.

'I didn't think it was that season yet!' the professor exclaimed as if he never heard the question.

'What season?'

Professor Ainslot continued with his excited gibberish, 'I mean, I would have like to have seen the demonstration to understand better how they carry out their rituals.'

'Professor,' Leyton said, trying to steer the conversation to something he could follow.

'It would have made for a great research paper to describe how it happens, why they do what they do and how long it lasts for but—'

'Professor!' Leyton bellowed, taking hold of the man by the shoulders. 'What the fuck are you talking about? I do not have the patience to ask questions you're not going to listen to so either answer me or stop fucking talking!'

Samuel looked like he was going to wet himself. Like a child that had never been told off before and got a taste of discipline for the first time. He started to quiver and breathed sharply, taking short breaths. Leyton closed his eyes for a moment and sighed. He had gone a little over the top with his reaction but in his defence, he had been needlessly disturbed from his rest.

'I'm sorry,' he said. He put extra effort into keeping his voice calm. 'But speak sense. I don't know what you're trying to tell me. Start from the beginning. Okay?'

The professor nodded rapidly and gasped as he initially spoke, 'Yes. Sorry. Just excited. Sorry.' Ainslot paused as Leyton released him from his grip then continued. 'As you know I've been carrying out scans on each of the specimens. Two of them are showing definite signs of being pregnant!'

Pregnant? Leyton looked over to the ice wolves. None of them exactly looked plump as if they were carrying a litter. They all looked quite slender except for the top four females. They were bulkier than the others anyway. But more to the point there were two wolves that were expecting a litter. This was so much more than what he was expected to provide. Having a bonus such as that was enough to give him leeway, in some shape or form, to move out of field work. Leyton needed that change.

'Are you sure?' he asked excitedly.

'Positive,' Samuel replied eagerly. 'I triple-checked the two of them to make sure I wasn't seeing things. I don't know why I couldn't tell the difference before. Maybe they don't show the signs. They must still need to hunt even when pregnant? Judging by how far they have developed according to the scans, I'd say they're not far from being born. I just hope that being in stasis doesn't affect them.'

'What do you need to do'

'I'm going to need to do tests and scans. Now that I know they've got pups on the way, I have something to monitor.'

'What do you mean?'

'Think of it like a patient in a hospital. If you only see the symptoms and not the cause, you're going to do generic tests. Now I know they're pregnant, I can fine tune my tests. I need to see if the pups are still developing and at what rate. A slowed rate of maturity would indicate either that stasis is slowing them down or they are naturally pregnant for a long time. A faster rate... Well, that shows that stasis does nothing and they're going to be born regardless of if the mothers are awake or asleep. Once I've been able to establish how it affects them, I can look to calibrate the sensors on the pods to also keep me updated on the pups. At this moment I have no idea if they're even alive or not. Just that they're there.'

'Okay, so let's say they come to term while the mothers are still under. What do we do when they come to giving birth?'

'I honestly don't know," Professor Ainslot answered. 'Personally, it's a risk I don't want to take. I'd be much happier reviving them and letting them give birth while awake. Don't want to find out the hard way if they could or couldn't give birth in stasis.'

'That means more work for us,' Leyton sighed.

'It does," Samuel concurred. 'But do you want to be the one to tell the boss that two wolves died in childbirth and lost their litters because we did something we weren't sure about?'

'I guess not. If they all do survive, how many pups can you expect?' Leyton asked.

Ainslot scoffed while shaking his head and picked up the tac-pad. 'It's too difficult to say right now. I'm more interested in the fact that they're there. A stab in the dark, I'd guess anywhere between four and nine is a realistic range per litter without further examination. In the wild I would expect at least half of the pups to die in the first year as food became scarce. So, they would need more pups to make sure some survive to adulthood. When we get back to base, that will be a one hundred percent success rate with births. We will be able to establish a breeding programme. The journals I could write!'

'And never publish,' Leyton added sharply. 'Don't forget this isn't a scientifically or even university sanctioned expedition. It's Intelligence Division classified. You don't publish anything about them. Not until you're allowed to.'

Professor Ainslot sighed, his head slumping and shoulders falling. 'Which will be never. I'll still write them for my own benefit to share with the rest of the division. Making these discoveries and not telling people about them, about what's out there, it just goes against what I became a xeno-biologist for. I wanted to study alien organisms for humanity to be able to understand them, appreciate them and preserve them in a way we failed to preserve animals back on Earth or even learn about any benefits they could give us. To make a discovery like this and not be able to tell anyone is… Well… Shit. I mean, we caused so many species to die out. I want to preserve anything I can.'

'I understand,' Leyton said. 'I really do. Don't you think I feel the same when I know months in advance that some fucker is dangerous? To know we must give a bad guy a target to attack and put people at risk to capture them? Innocent people. It isn't a good feeling. But we suck it up and deal with it. Think of the bigger picture. Our study of these will have a purpose. We just need to be patient and trust that the guys in charge know what the hell they're doing.'

'I guess so,' Samuel muttered.

'Okay,' Leyton said, patting the man on his shoulders. 'You keep at it. Let me know what your next discovery is. But next time, do me a favour and just tell me. Don't go off on one.'

'Will do,' the professor replied.

Leyton smiled at the man and left him alone. His tac-pad chimed with the receipt of a message. The name of the sender put him on alert. Administrator. The message instructed him to make immediate contact. They were out of a jump so he could do that. Leyton told Schottler that he was stepping out then left for the same cargo hold he used before and requested the communication link which was answered within a few moments. As it was last time there was only his own video being sent. He still had no idea what the administrator looked like.

'Leyton,' Administrator said.

'Sir,' Leyton replied.

'I didn't realise that you needed me to guide you through protocol,' the Englishman started. 'Would have thought you would know what to do.'

'I know procedure. I just wanted to confirm that was what was best, sir.'

'Fine, I'll entertain you,' administrator said. 'You are correct to use the cargo hold should they escape from stasis, and I approve of the requirement to have an alternate room for your team to occupy. I don't see what the problem is or what was difficult about it.'

'Thank you, sir,' he said. 'My concern is food. In the instance they wake up, how would we feed them? We didn't exactly bring any raw meat for them. That and I don't particularly want to worry about how we get the food in there without releasing them.'

'I'm sure that there are food stockpiles on the ship. Use them. If you're not in a position to have ready access to the food, then put yourself in a position to have access. If you're worried about how you'd feed the wolves, think about how you could make it safer and prepare for it. You have the knowledge to do this. I know that you have been in more difficult situations. Use your head. Understood?'

'Yes sir.'

'Good, now we have that cleared up is there anything worthwhile you need to report? Or do you plan to give me more reason to question your position as a Field Lead?'

Leyton cleared his throat before speaking, 'We have had... a development.'

'Explain,' Administrator insisted.

'Two of the females are pregnant. We are looking at between eight and eighteen pups in total.'

'That is a development,' Administrator said, pleasure noticeable in his voice. 'Do you know if the pups will survive in stasis? This is the first I've heard of for a long time. Don't think I've come across pregnancies in transit in my lifetime.'

It was a first for science that any of them knew of. The initial studies had rarely included pregnant organisms traveling in stasis. Those that did mainly used smaller organisms like mice and rats. There was too much red tape blocking them from venturing down that route, too many ethical questions. Too many protests disputing the female body and how it should be used or what it should be subjected to. In the end, it was accepted that, while tests on larger organisms were still being carried out, pregnant individuals would be advised against stasis travel.

'We don't know,' he explained. 'The professor is trying to figure that one out. We don't even know if they're alive or not. Which brings me to another problem.'

'What is it now?' the Englishman sighed angrily.

'According to the professor if they do need to give birth, we will most likely need to revive them. We don't know enough to not revive them. And that means putting them somewhere safe. Will the same instructions from before be applicable in this scenario?'

'That does not even deserve an answer,' Administrator snarled. He wasn't wrong. And it wasn't like he was absent of ideas on containment strategies. Leyton was more testing his responses to see what his limits would be. 'These organisms are some of the greatest acquisitions this division has ever come into possession of. They are essential for my research and our progression. They must make it here alive. You have a temporary holding pen, do you not? You work out what you think you're supposed to do for yourself. I can't hold your hand through everything. Just ensure the professor makes the pups a priority if they are born.'

'I will do,' Leyton said flatly.

'Good. Keep me updated. Out.'

When the comm link had cut out he cussed under his breath, 'Fucking asshole.'

There was no need to be as abrasive as that. No need to be so rude. But Leyton did get a hint of the thought pattern. The administrator wanted these wolves and their pups. He was going to get them. And Leyton would make sure they arrived.

Leyton left the room and instantly radioed for Jerome to come meet him. It didn't take his friend long to arrive. He had been on the upper decks scouting patrol patterns and positions of importance to the ship's crew. A move he insisted was essential to give them a tactical advantage.

'What's up boss?' Jerome asked.

'We have a thing,' he explained, starting out vaguely. 'Two of the female wolves we've captured are pregnant. We have no idea if they will give birth in stasis or if the pups will die. I told the boss, and he wants us to make sure we bring those pups back to Earth, alive. We might need to wake the girls up. If we have to do that…'

'We don't have the resources to put them all back to sleep for the rest of the trip,' Jerome said, finishing off the sentence for him.

'Exactly,' Leyton whispered. 'But we have the storage unit. I don't know if it'll do until we get back to Earth. They might outgrow it.'

The expression in his friend's face told a story. He was aware of what the consequences were. His eyes listed each of their potential options, growing wider with each choice as his concern increased. It was a nice change seeing him unsure of what to do and being out of his depth. Maybe it would teach him some respect. When he managed to gather the strength to overcome the speechless episode he spoke quietly.

'What are we to do if that happens?'

Leyton shook his head. 'Administrator pretty much said do whatever we need to do. But whatever we do, he wants those animals in one piece.'

'Okay,' Jerome said sharply. 'If that's what is required of us.'

In the briefest of moments Leyton saw a glimmer of something in his friend's eyes that he seldom saw. Yet had always known to be there. The hunger for power. For recognition. Lurking under his collected exterior until rearing itself on occasion. He had seen it enough to know he was prepared to do whatever he had to. This had now become his opportunity to show just how deserving he was. He had killed strangers in cold blood on assignment and dug metaphorical knives into the backs of his peers in the field to make a name for himself. It was why he was so good and now was why he was so dangerous. The look in his eyes this time could not hide something else. A change in his temperament.

Leyton would be the next one to fall victim to his will if he were not careful. It was a good thing that he recognised the look. Gave him some form of an edge.

'We do it on my say so,' he corrected.

'The administrator told you to do whatever it takes?' Jerome questioned.

'He did but I'm telling you we deal with it how *I* see fit. There are things I'm not prepared to do and while I'm in command we do it my way.'

'You might not be prepared to do exactly what the boss says. Well, guess what? I am,' Jerome retorted, with a tone of self-imposed superiority.

'You had best remember in that case who is in charge on this,' Leyton hissed, jabbing a finger into his friend's chest. 'So, until I say otherwise, we're doing it the way I intend to do it. Not yours, and not his. Let's go. And not a word of this to anyone. I'll tell them when the time is right.'

He guided his friend back to their holding bay. While he ate, Leyton could not take his mind away from the danger he was in, both physically and in terms of status. There had to be something that he could do to postpone future events. Steer the potential backstabbing away from him. Telling the rest of the team about what may be needed was an option. Make his opinion of it known from the word go. Trusting them would help them trust him. Or he could do away with Jerome, make him out to be the untrustworthy one. With no one to contend the idea after doing away with him, it was most likely the only path that would pay off with minimal backlash. That brought him onto the next problem. Who would support him should Jerome start to break relations down?

It was well known in the division that a lone agent rarely had success. Those that did have success were put on such a high pedestal that they were practically untouchable. Immortal. He was far from that. He needed allies. Leyton had to know who he could trust to support him and who he could depend on to turn against him.

He focussed on his friend as the agent returned to the others. Jerome spoke to the rest of the team casually. At least whilst he was in front of him, Leyton could tell their conversation was still private.

He caught Agent Suttle as the medic walked by to join the others. 'Hey, you got a minute?'

'Of course, boss, what's up?' Dom asked.

'I need you to carry out a psyche eval on everyone,' Leyton instructed quietly. 'Keep it hush-hush. I need to know everyone is still up to the job. Think you can do that for me?'

'Of course,' Agent Suttle answered. 'It won't be as good as a shrink session, but I'll be able to tell you who's a problem and who isn't.'

'Good, I need you to start with Jerome.'

'Any reason why?' the medic asked.

'There is… But I don't want you to get too involved in the whys. Not yet at least.'

Dom gave a firm nod, collected his food and left to join the others as intended. Jerome glanced over at Leyton when the medic joined them. Suspicion rife in his glare. His subordinate was right to be concerned. Leyton would find out what was going on in his mind and he would be ready to tackle anything that was thrown his way.

His own paranoia though had put him off his food and he barely touched it. Leyton grimaced as he forced himself to finish it. Every ounce of strength would be needed.

Beatrice Lenoia

They had an extra couple days following the comets through space, their tails of ice slowly melting away and leaving beautiful trails of blue and white in their wake. It was a truly marvellous spectacle. Each individual part of the cluster of hundreds of pieces of ice and rock was destined to carry on being thrown around the solar system for a millennium without any risk of being stopped in their tracks.

Beatrice stood on one of the several observation decks at the fore of the ship where the cross sections met amongst the passengers as they watched the spectacle unfold before them. Children gasped in amazement, asking more questions than their parents could answer. People started to find their philosophical purpose in life as they made entirely irrelevant statements that sounded wise and wonderful until the words were picked apart. Then they became idiots who wanted to sound smart. And others merely felt like they were getting more than their money's worth.

Gazing at the comets hurtle along their trajectory made Beatrice feel lonely. Even the rocks and ice in the comets had other rocks and ice to drift through space with. How she wished she were back home, with her family. Just a few more months and she would be. Equally though she wished they were all there with her. Her husband, Earnest, children and many grandchildren. They would have loved seeing this show. Then they would understand why the job was so important to her. Why civilian life offered more for her than the military. Sure, she had been able to see dozens, maybe even hundreds, of other planets. That though was always on deployment. Fight after fight. Never the chance to stop and just appreciate what it was she was fighting to defend. Now Beatrice could enjoy and savour the moment.

After another half hour of being lost in the tranquillity of natural beauty carved from before the time of humanity, she returned to the bridge. There were matters that still needed to be resolved. Her key crew had been able to learn that there had in fact been an electrical overload in the cargo bay that their new arrivals occupied. What caused the overload though was still unknown. It most likely had something to do with what the security team brought with them, even if there wasn't any proof, but she had to accept that there could simply be some faulty wiring that engineering had overseen. To add to the problems, when her engineers tried to get to it so that any damage could be assessed and repaired the occupants insisted that it had all been resolved doing whatever they could to make sure no one entered.

Franklin and Security Chief Henendez updated her on the most recent events that they caught on security. The pair explained that two of the security would always speak in private away from anyone else. The leader and someone they hadn't quite identified. They could not hear anything being said though. Which was odd. Her crew should have been able to hear them. Maintenance crews were still working on fixing the issue that confused them. What had been done to emit the sound in just that one room? Whenever their conversations ended, the one that seemed to be in charge looked uncomfortable around the other. Like something had been said or suspected. Was he really in charge? Or maybe a power struggle. At that point she was worried about cabin-fever setting in. Beatrice massaged the sides of her skull and sighed with frustration.

'Pain killer?' Adjutant Hender asked.

'No, thank you,' she groaned. 'I need a bullet at this rate.'

'No need for that,' Franklin insisted. 'Think of the mess you'll leave for us to clean up!'

Beatrice burst into a brief fit of quiet laughter. It helped alleviate the stress she was feeling for a moment. 'No, I guess that would be most unprofessional of me. Wouldn't it?'

'And selfish,' Franklin added.

'Yes,' she laughed. 'And selfish.'

'Go on, what's up?'

She took a deep breath and forced it out quickly. Humour still did nothing to completely ease the tension that was going through her.

'I just don't understand,' she said. 'I really need to know what cargo they're transporting could be so important that requires them to be armed and constantly around the goods. If it was that important, they really should have just arranged for a private transporter of their own to take them to Earth? Would make more sense.'

'You would have thought so,' Henendez agreed. 'Unless what they are transporting needed to be plugged in to a power source. I mean it would explain the power surge.'

Beatrice looked to the security officer, eagerly awaiting answers to his statement. 'What do you mean?'

'Well, for a team so small they shouldn't be using a major ship like this. Just something small,' the Security Chief said. 'It wouldn't need much power to run. This ship though, has power to spare. That's the only difference between the *Passage* and whatever they would contract out.'

'Makes sense,' Franklin concurred. 'If you can't use what you've got, you go and get something you can use.'

It was so incredibly obvious. In all her years of command on any ship, she had never had a power surge like that before in the cargo holds. There had rarely been an instance when something was connected to the ship's energy supply that didn't belong there. Beatrice pulled up a chart of energy consumption on the holo-table. She mitigated the power consumption accounted for by travel in slip space and compared the figures to standard levels at any other point in time. Before the security embarked with their cargo, usage was comfortably in the middle of standard levels. After their arrival though that average consumption had noticeably increased to just below higher than average levels. Beatrice wasn't an engineer but even she knew if that continued, they could start to see certain lesser systems start overloading. Her ship was not designed to be at that level of power usage consistently. No matter how nominal the fluctuation was to the size of her vessel. Everything eventually took its toll. Anything longer and the likelihood of something going wrong increased on a daily basis.

However, there was every chance it could have been coincidental, that the power surge was because of the number of repairs that had been needed. And that it had nothing to do with the security team. If she incorrectly accused them of wrongdoing, of being a threat to the passengers on her ship, it could all backfire on her. The last thing she wanted to do was go around upsetting members of the UPN's MID. What she needed was further evidence that it had something to do with their occupancy.

Beatrice changed the charts to a view of the ship. Most rooms displayed a vibrant green colour to show stable consumption levels. The engine room would periodically show amber, orange and red levels of usage. A periodic cycle as coolants kicked in to keep the engine from overheating. The cargo room, when empty, had shown as green. Once occupied it changed to amber and at the time of the power surge that colouring flared up to red for a split second before easing back down to amber. But it never went back to green.

There it was. The proof that she needed that these people were the ones responsible for the power surge. What had they done to the cargo hold? What did they have syphoning electricity from her ship? She needed to do something about this. The risks of not acting were too great. Civilians could not be left in the firing line.

'Henendez, You're with me. Assemble a four-man security team for me,' Beatrice announced. 'Tell them to meet us at elevator five on F Deck. We're going down to the cargo hold. I want answers before anyone else is put at risk. Franklin, you've got the con until I get back.'

'Do you want to tell me what's going on?' her adjutant questioned.

'She's doing something about a problem,' Henendez answered. 'Isn't it obvious?'

'But why now?' Franklin replied.

'You know how I've been waiting for the right opportunity to invoke threat of security of this ship against them? Here's my chance. Chief, with me.'

Before her adjutant could object, Beatrice got up and left the bridge with the security chief in close pursuit. The man watched her every move with the eye for detail she wasn't offering. Making sure she put no step out of place. She traversed the ship and marched through the hallways and never paid attention to anyone trying to speak to her. They could all wait until she had finished her mission. Their problems were most certainly going to be less than hers.

The team had gathered as requested. A mismatch of personnel. One man was quite mature, probably mid-forties, and carried himself the same way someone would if they had spent a life in the military. Another man was equally mature but clearly had been in a lethargic role with a well-formed and rounded gut. Her other members of the security detail were a young man and woman, fresh into security most likely. The girl seemed more bothered about looking pretty than taking a job seriously with the amount of makeup she had on. Completely unprofessional. The boy was a bundle of nerves. It was not the best team she could have taken, but they would have to do.

She barely led them down a few decks when she was presented with the man she had assumed was in charge. The tall white man was imposing, his black hair short and with piercing brown eyes that sparked a memory she couldn't quite recall. His smile was calm and collected. The name tag on his tactical vest said *Foresc*. An unusual name, probably Martian. He was flanked by two of his peers; one male and one female and both were incredibly intimidating with the cold, emotionless expressions they wore. It was a tactic she recognised – meet a threat with an equal show of strength.

'I'm assuming you're on your way down to see me?' Foresc said.

'As a matter of fact, I was,' Beatrice answered. She wasted no time in politeness. 'I need to view your cargo.'

'You do?' he asked, smirking. 'Why did it take you so long?'

'Because your paperwork had the right stamps on,' Beatrice said. 'And it took me a while to have justification. Classified or not.'

'Oh?' the man responded. 'And what's that?'

'I need to know that whatever you have brought with you is not going to cause anyone any harm,' she explained. 'Our ship has recently experienced a power surge, a power surge that we *know* originated because you tapped into the ship's power grid, without my consent, to power whatever it is that you brought with you. I refuse to accept that you have only brought refrigerated units. Standard fridges do not take that much power. I need to know what it is you have because if we keep having these power surges, there won't be a ship to travel on.'

Foresc shrugged, 'Is the entourage necessary?'

'For you? I hope not,' Beatrice said. 'Now, are you going to let me have a look?'

'No,' the man said sharply. 'I can't. What I can tell you is, yes, we have had to tap into your ship's circuitry. We probably should have told you before and I'm sorry we didn't. We could have avoided all this. But I cannot and will not give you access to the goods. What I will say is we are transporting products that need to be kept super-refrigerated. On ice if you will. They have to stay sub-zero temperatures, and that requires a lot of power. If we open the fridges now, before we have them in the proper facility, for you to have a look into, it'll risk damaging the product.'

'Okay, so why not use your own mode of transport?' Henendez questioned.

'The honest answer is we wanted to use our own. We'd be home in just over a week's time if we had our own mode of transport. The problem is that the fridges are state of the art, and it takes a lot to keep them going. They screwed our transport up, and nothing we had immediate access to would have kept them powered until alternate transport arrived. So, my superior was able to arrange for us to come aboard your ship. It will take us a lot longer to get home. Either way, we'll get back and we'll be back with the cargo intact.'

She scowled at Foresc. How much of what he said was true? Regardless of the number of untruths most likely just spoken, she was sure that he was honest about using their own transport if they could.

He had confirmed the suspicion Henendez voiced. They needed her ship for its power supply.

'I still need to see the cargo,' Beatrice said. 'I have a manifest for every piece of cargo we bring onto this ship, except for passenger's luggage. It is standard practice to know what comes into my cargo holds. For our own security reasons. So, if you will step to one side?'

The man blocked her path as she tried to sidestep him. She tried again, aiming for the other side, and he still moved to be a barrier that she could not get past. His arms were spread apologetically but still covered a wide enough area to still be an obstacle. Setting up a line she was to not pass. Yet his eyes were far from that.

'I'm sorry but you can't,' he told her. 'I'll tell you what, give me your comm-pad link and I'll send you the comm address so you can get in touch with my superior so he can put in writing if you have permission to view our cargo or not. I can safely tell you that the answer will be a *no* but if you get it in writing, you can stop trying.'

'Have it your way,' she hissed. Disappointed that she couldn't get any further.

'Look, we don't want to cause trouble. Your guys stay out of our way, we'll stay out of theirs. We just want to get home at the end of the day.'

The smile that he wore, though soft, was clearly showing strength that he tried to hide. As she supplied the link address to her comm-pad, Beatrice turned to leave then remembered something. There was a member of the team that could give her the insight she needed into their activities. Maybe there was a way to make the guy slip up and give her an idea on what she was dealing with.

'You have someone with you,' Beatrice started. 'A skinny guy. He seems really anxious on our security footage. What can you tell me about him?'

'He's our scientific advisor,' Foresc replied instantly. There was no sense of conversation in the tone. 'He's awful in public. Only time we've seen him calm and happy is when he's working.'

'And he's with you willingly?' Beatrice persisted.

Foresc barked a hysteric laugh. 'Willingly? Hardly! If he had the choice, he'd have been back at our site minding his own business. Can't expect anyone to willingly leave what they enjoy doing to go halfway across the galaxy, can you?'

'I guess not,' Beatrice conceded, relating immediately to the scientist's plight. She could hardly say she was happy being sent on some of her assignments in the military and did nothing to hide her feelings. 'You don't know him well, do you?'

Foresc shrugged. 'How well can you know someone you haven't worked with before? He's come with the cargo. When we get to Earth, he'll go his own way to wherever he's assigned to with the cargo. We'll go the other way with our pay ready for the next job. Are we done?'

'We're done,' Beatrice replied.

She left before she had a chance to see that smug look on his face again. That was something she could do without taking another look at. And his eyes. Something about them scared her. He had the look of someone that had killed before. Of that she was certain. Beatrice answered all the questions and concurred with the majority of the statements from Security Chief Henendez as they hurried back through the ship, the rest of her security escort in close proximity. They did not slow their pace until she was back on the bridge. She relayed the conversation to Franklin and that ended with everyone agreeing to wait and see what the security detail's supervisor said whilst keeping a close eye on their activities.

She was not keen on waiting around but that was all they could do. Hopefully, they would get something sooner rather than later.

Beatrice kept the *Galactic Passage* near the comet cluster for another few hours before announcing they would be departing for their next destination. That would be another week and half in the jump with three twelve hour breaks in between. That meant they could be waiting a long time until they received a response once the message was sent. She left the bridge under Franklin's capable control once more and retired to her cabin for a long-deserved attempt at rest. Most likely it would be restless as those eyes haunted her or that smile plagued her with its almost pervasive glimmer.

Jesa

The Crevari never came back for her. Their ships were well out of sight within an hour or two of fleeing the area. She wept for the people on the ship that had to take the hit for her to survive. Jesa had confessed to the Shauari skeleton just how much the Crevari had scared her and how to avoid their bloodthirsty needs she would have happily scuttled the ship or thrown herself out the airlock just so they didn't eat her alive. There were more dignified ways to go, but it didn't matter. Anything was better than being subjected to that alien race.

She reached Juntah Outpost without any further issues, just a little hungrier than she had intended to be. All those plans to eat disappeared, along with her appetite, out of fear. She guided her ship through the traffic flying in and out of the station. The various small, personal craft sped by carelessly as their pilots tried to show off their skill or displayed complete disregard for safety. All the larger haulage craft slowly meandered through to their loading hangars. Ready to unload their precious cargo to keep the citizens of Juntah fed and watered or to supply the businesses so that their owners could make a healthy profit. All were just targets at the end of the day for organisations like the syndicate to hit for a quick score. Her bay was quite open, enough space for a dozen ships. Cranes loomed over head to make unloading easier. Landing clamps lay in wait for the vessels too specialised or too large to come with landing gear. Drones soared all around, controlled by local reporters and drone enthusiasts hoping to catch the next big thing on camera.

Jesa clambered down the port loading ramp and into the docking bay she had been given and breathed in the smell of the bottom end of society. Scents of grease and fuel from the ships, street food and citizens with poor personal hygiene engulfed the air – the smell of what she now associated with home. People and aliens alike bustled by her. She could barely control her reflex to tense up around the aliens; every one of them was a potential threat. Humans were lesser beings to them, or prey. All they wanted to do was take over human controlled planets and depose them of their rightful place in the galaxy. Humanity was not worthy in their eyes – at least, that was what her parents had told her. What Barbaros had also convinced her was true. Things wouldn't be so difficult for humans if they stayed where they belonged on their own planets. Maybe that's why the Centies stayed put and didn't venture out. Wanting to protect their own first from the aliens. If any of them even looked at her funny she would not hesitate from retaliating.

Her instructions received on her final approach were simple. Once docked, Jesa was to go to a bar in one of the loading docks to await her cargo while dock crew re-stocked the *Saridia*. She took a deep breath and kept her head down as she walked through the hangar until she heard a voice, a familiar voice, calling her from the distance.

The distinct shape of an old friend could be seen heading her way through the crowd. It was hard to not see the robust figure who stood a shoulder width wider than most people and thick hair that was moulded into the most eccentric shape. A smile was uncontrollably plastered on her face as he approached. When she reached the man, they embraced momentarily in a tight hug.

'Jesa! Glad you made it okay,' he stated joyfully.

'Ghavvis,' she replied as she released him from the embrace. 'Mayah! What're you doing here? Last I knew you was out prospecting for the boss, yah?'

'Yah, I was,' Ghavvis said as he guided Jesa through the crowds. 'Found a few new places for big boss to set up outposts. Plenty of potentials to make it worthwhile for a long time. Some of them weren't quite what he expected. Wasn't too happy, compre?'

Potentials. Settlements, the small and upcoming ones without a recognised police force, or businesses that were small and isolated that would offer quick and easy plunder. Or the well-developed establishments that were questionable themselves so if they were involved in something, they wouldn't go crying to the UPN out of fear that they would be caught themselves. That meant the chances of retaliation were smaller. Plenty of gunfights occurred when prospecting because looks could be easily deceiving. Especially if it was a mining town just starting out. They were resources that businesses defended fiercely since the only products worth mining in the outer colonies were expensive, precious metals used primarily in the military. More death came about there. Most places prospected were a bust. The sites that were able to be a payoff either paid out less than was put in or paid the way for the boss to get fatter and drink into unconsciousness while everyone else managed to eat just enough to be content but not full.

'I see, so what're you doing here? Juntah isn't exactly on the table for prospecting. Neutral ground, yah? No need for you to be here. Waste of your time.'

'I've been sent over to make sure your new cargo is loaded up safely, compre?' he explained. 'It's a good job too. The cartel is growing real quick over here. Think their balls bigger than their egos.'

'Mayah, that isn't easy,' Jesa said.

'I can tell you what is easy, yah? Anything being bigger than their brains. Even their tic-tac dicks. They so ballsy, they attacked the police station here not too long ago. Trying take the precinct, even with SPF here, to take over the station. Didn't count on the SPF getting help from the chapter! The Centie puyas are still here after sorting it out.'

She stopped in her tracks. Puya, a horrible outer term for UPN military personnel. 'Mayah, why the hell did no one think to get a message to me? Don't think I need to know that they're here before I land? What if they clocked me?'

Ghavvis shrugged, 'They didn't clock you. Besides, would it have made a difference? You couldn't turn around. Got supplies to pick up and the cargo. Can't say no to the boss.' Her friend held her arm softly and felt her cheek. 'And get food to put in you. Dead smuggler not a good smuggler. Come on. We get food first then we go do business.'

Jesa hummed thoughtfully as they continued through the crowds. It was nice to be around her friend, the one person she was able to trust. The only one to show her how to do things the right way, the safe way, and not see her as an object for their sexual desires. He came into the fold much in the same way she did. Only his strength made him more useful on the frontline of business for Barbaros, which is why he didn't stay in smuggling for long before he was made an official member. To most, he had a lucky break. For Ghavvis, everyone else was lucky. They stopped for food at a food stall. Ghavvis insisted on paying and she wasn't about to stop him. Barbaros still had most of her credits, keeping them to ensure she didn't try to pay for her freedom. Those she did have, she needed to save for an emergency. Jesa got through at least two cartons of Noodle Brovznii before saying a word, enjoying the noodle dish with a thick, heavy soup base lathered in spices and herbs with a topping of meat. She wasn't sure exactly what the meat was, but it didn't matter. Food was food. On the third helping and her fourth cup of water, she looked up thoughtfully. Her eyes had started to swell with tears. Jesa wished the moment of feeling safe didn't have to end.

'Are you okay?' Ghavvis asked. 'Not seen anyone eat like that in a long time.'

Jesa weighed up the consequences of saying how hungry she had been, how her hunger was always there, even when she'd eaten. Why she was so hungry. This was her friend. Not an enemy. Better still, not another smuggler. There would be no risk of their conversation going back to Barbaros. 'Hungry. All the time. Boss loaded up the *Saridia* real good. Had to lose food space for the cargo to fit. Needed to make it last, yah.'

'Mayah! Jesa, loni, how you holding up?' her friend gasped.

She shrugged. 'Gotta do what the boss says, compre? He says jump, we don't ask how high. Just do it. He says I got to give up food to make the delivery, I give up food to make the delivery. If not, he won't need to feed me for much longer.'

She fought her tears back. Ghavvis wrapped an arm around her shoulder and gave her a gentle hug. 'He not here now. You're safe with me, yah? Come, you eat up. Get another in you. We can go after. Need to keep your strength up, yah?'

Ghavvis paid for another two pots of noodles that Jesa happily wolfed down before making a move. The pair of them dropped a few floors down to level twenty-nine. This level was the primary route for supplies in and out to keep the outpost fed and watered with enough resources arriving to run the station for three weeks within forty-eight hours. Most of the containers filled with supplies came from all reaches of the Outer Colonies. Some managed to work their way over from the Mid-Colonies. Probably bringing over real meat or better, maybe even protein-rich nutrition bars. All goods arrived in massive containers. Anything less than several tonnes was taken elsewhere. It was not worth the time if they could barely feed anyone.

They marched through the maze of containers waiting to be unloaded and distributed amongst the citizens, dodging the workers operating the mech-loaders and shopkeepers bartering for cheaper goods to sell on. They continued to talk and had steered the conversation to reflect on all the events that had gone on since they last saw each other. Ghavvis had lived an eventful life over the last couple years. He had been in several shoot outs, fell in love half a dozen times during his travels and had even been through a spell of having a bounty on his head as he climbed the ranks in the syndicate. Ghavvis swore blind that somewhere out there he had children that he would never see. Meanwhile, the most exciting thing to happen to Jesa was fighting off scrappers who thought her ship was an empty vessel drifting through space on a power down, and dodging military vessels that were carrying out routine patrols. When she mentioned about her brush with the

Crevari, her friend looked like he had seen a ghost. Jesa wondered if that was how she looked whenever the name was mentioned.

'Crevs? You saw fucking space-stalkers?'

Jesa hummed a confirmation. 'Was on a power down. They didn't come near me. Don't think they saw me. They were too busy with another ship to care about me.'

'Scared?'

'Very. Thought it would be the end of me, compre?'

'No kidding… Mayah…'

She nodded softly. 'Real scared when I put the burn on to get out of there. I thought they might have turned to come after me. Called it in with the station when in the clear. Hope they don't come here.'

'Me too,' Ghavvis said. 'Guess I know where I'm not staying. Come on, nearly there. Just over this way.'

Her friend led her through to a bar hidden behind a wall of containers. The sign above said it was called the *Forgotten Lodge*.It was a dark, badly lit place with no windows. The sort of location that would offer drinks with the potential of a stabbing on the side, if you were lucky. Jesa was guaranteed to be cleaner wiping her feet when she left. Shady looking buyers drank and made bets, some would be buying drugs, and others offering services both violent and non-violent. That was not for her to know. If she showed the slightest amount of curiosity in something that wasn't her business, she wouldn't be given the chance to listen in a second time. Jesa kept her eyes forward. Never making eye contact with anyone around her. Any opportunity to start something would be taken.

However, she couldn't help but smile. She was happy that it was a human-only bar, with no aliens allowed. Meant that the aliens weren't going to try to buy the bar any time soon, manipulate the drinks to make them more addictive, and force the patrons to keep coming back for more so they could take all their money. That and it meant she wasn't around their smell. Some aliens let off a putrid scent after they consumed alcohol. Others just simply stank because they had a different concept of being clean. Jesa could relax.

Ghavvis bought them both a beer and found a seat for them tucked away in a corner. The booth was simple with a dark metal table between two small metal benches. Screens set up behind both benches gave the booth some privacy.

'What's my cargo going to be?' she asked, kicking things off straight away. The sooner she was on the move again, the better.

'Just one case, yah,' Ghavvis said after he downed half of his beer. 'Won't weigh you down so shouldn't affect your food. Not a clue what it is. Sealed up. Under orders not to have a look.'

'Retinal key?' Jesa asked.

'No,' her friend answered. 'No retinal, no prints. Not even a lock and key. Just the boss' threat. It's all he needs, compre?'

'Mayah, the threat that big?'

'Yah. He even had it brought in by one of the captains from out in the Wild Sector. You know that shit's bad out there. Need all the bodies we can put there, yah? If they pull a captain, it's serious. Apparently, we have a buyer that's willing to pay a fortune for it in Sol. More than the boss thought they would pay.'

'Sol?' Jesa questioned. 'It isn't Ostad, is it? How much they paying?'

'Five mil. Story goes, Barbaros thought it was only worth a few hundred. So, he tells the buyers it's for sale at one mil. Ostad comes along and trumps all the bids. Slams down the big five, yah. Tells the boss he'll pay half now, half on delivery if they sell to him straight away. That's what the boss did. How did you know about Ostad?' Ghavvis replied, looking shocked that she knew already. 'Thought we weren't supposed to know about other jobs?'

Five million credits? Not even the skeleton was going for that, and that was her most valuable piece of cargo at two million. What exactly was it she was taking on that could cost that much? A weapon? If it was, then she didn't want anything to do with it. Something that cost that much, but was that small, was going to be deadly.

'Most of my cargo is for him,' she explained, keeping the conversation on topic without giving away any details. If anyone around the pair heard anything either of them said, they could quickly expect to be attacked and mugged. 'Wish I knew what it was all for.'

'Who knows how these Centies work?' Ghavvis joked. 'Think they rule the place, yah, the lot of them. Have all the money. Just buy what they want. If we say it's not for sale, they throw more money at it because they know we'll eventually say yes. Fuck, we'd say yes if they offered a years' worth of rations so that we didn't have to go hungry. Galaxy would be a better place without them.'

'Maybe, but when they have all the money, we need them to keep buying from us,' Jesa said. 'Keep the money coming out here for us.'

'Or we just take over their operations, yah? Have their jobs. Their money. Their planets. Just don't have them to ruin everything with laws and taxes that help them and do run us into the dirt.'

'And be like them in a few years' time?' she retorted. 'No thanks. I'm happy being an outer.'

'Good point,' her friend said, taking another healthy mouthful of beer. 'Anyway, got the package holed up in here. When we're done, I'll get it for you then you can get going before the puya start carrying out spot checks on everyone down here. They've not done one yet. Only a matter of time, compre?'

'I know, last thing I need is to be caught up in one of those. Hot goods don't sell, even if the buyer really wants them.'

'Amen to that. Like the code says,' Ghavvis said.

The code. Everyone had one, even the SPF. Their smuggling code was a simple one: Sell them cold, hide them hot. No one asked questions about yesterday's news. Everything she transported had been hot once but was now ice cold and no longer being talked about. That made it sellable. Meant they could put a price on it. It was a code Barbaros instilled in everyone. Her arm started to itch.

'What mood is the boss in?' she asked, shaking a little at the mention of him.

Her friend pulled the most perplexed expression at her. 'Why you asking?'

She scratched the unsatisfied itch on her arm. 'I need to know if he's being serious about this.'

'About what? The job? He always serious about the job. Never jokes.'

'No not the job… This,' Jesa replied, gesturing to her arm as she continued to scratch the itch.

'You mean he tagged you?' Ghavvis questioned, his eyes widening with shock. 'Mayah, what did you do?'

'Was given the job,' she whispered.

'You didn't piss him off?'

Jesa shook her head. 'No, just got the job and was tagged.'

Are you okay? How are you holding up?' he asked.

'Badly,' Jesa admitted. 'Not sleeping too well. I keep having nightmares, and it's so itchy, I just want to take it out. I don't deserve this. I never did anything wrong.'

Ghavvis took her hand, gently rubbing it with a thumb, and looked her dead centre in the eye. 'I know you. Boss man doesn't, but he thinks he does. He just sees a number taking his things and looking after his money. Expects everyone to betray him unless he gives them a reason not to. Give me ten percent of your cut when you get paid, and I can get that thing set to being unresponsive to remote detonations. I can't take it out and it will still go off if he's within a five-meter range with a clicker, but anything further than that and he can't do a thing to you. Should help you sleep easier at least.'

'Really?' Jesa asked hopefully. 'You can do that?'

'Damn straight I am,' he said with a smile. 'My ship's on this level. Can do it there, yah.'

'What will happen to you if he finds out?'

He smirked and finished his beer. 'Fuck all. I've got a couple tools registered to dead guys in my locker. No one knows I found them or took them. He won't know a thing unless he shows up mid-procedure. Let's get another round in or two then I'll get that switched off for you before we get the package.'

'Sounds good to me,' Jesa said. A genuine smile crept onto her face.

Ghavvis smiled, encouraged her to finish her beer and quickly returned from the bar with fresh drinks. After a couple more relaxed beers, no longer talking shop but reminiscing about happier times, they went to his ship which doubled up as a workstation with a larger than standard workshop. She strapped into a chair and let her friend do his work. It was a quick procedure, but it still stung to the point where she had to bite down on a piece of leather to make the pain tolerable. When it was over, her arm was bright red around the implant and the itch was still there. But Ghavvis reassured her that what he did was going to work and that she was safe. Jesa felt better knowing that she could not be killed any time soon by the boss. It felt good to feel a bit of freedom.

After a brief celebration, that resulted in yet another drink – this time strong moonshine, his own brew – the pair returned to the bar. Jesa was left alone at the counter while Ghavvis went through to the back to get the case. Jesa was lost in herself, feeling more than happy about her newfound easing of restrictions. Maybe it was the alcohol. Her head was a little fuzzy. She didn't care. It was nice to feel positive. Optimistic. Safer.

The door opened and shut to two new arrivals. The hushed murmur of secrets being discussed silenced. Someone was here that wasn't supposed to hear their discussions. She cautiously glanced toward the door. The arrivals wore the silver-grey armour of the Stellar Protection Force. Jesa immediately felt herself sober up as her heart rate increased.

They were there. They had to walk in just as her friend went to retrieve the package. Nothing would attract attention more than a case being brought out of the back area and handed over to her when no one was looking.

'Fucking puyas,' she cursed under her breath, turning away from them so they could not see her face. She had no idea if she was on any Centie database. The best she could do was make sure she didn't find out. 'Mayah. Fuck no, this can't be happening.'

Jesa quickly opened her comm-pad and signalled the alert to Ghavvis that they had visitors. His response was swift, advising that he would be out soon, and she was to follow his lead without question if they were to make it out. She did not respond. She just waited another minute or so. The footsteps of the SPF soldiers were slowly getting closer. Each thud meant she was almost surely going to be questioned and arrested. They were bound to know about her ship, that it was smuggler owned. How could they not. Jesa was almost able to guarantee they also knew about the contraband she was in possession of. Her heart raced. Ghavvis calmly rushed out from the back without giving off the amount of pressure they were under in his expression, a large silver case in hand, and took hold of her arm. He guided her around the bar area, putting obstacles between them and the soldiers, then led the pair out of the building and into the bustling streets outside.

On the streets, their pace sped up until they were nearly sprinting. The SPF cried out for them to stop. Their pursuers were soon catching up to them as their attempts to put as many bodies between them as possible failed to lose the soldiers. Ghavvis gave her a push and the instruction to run. Together they hurried through the crowds until they were back in the maze of containers. There, the pair split up. They could circumnavigate the storage boxes with ease and had their location to regroup. The SPF were out of sight. That could only mean they were having difficulty keeping up with them. Jesa pushed past everyone in her way, ducking under exo-drivers using the massive mechanical suits to carry smaller crates to their new destination, and clambered over a few containers to get a little further ahead. All while checking behind her for the SPF to make sure they were not tailing her.

She was winded as one of the soldiers tackled her from the side to the ground. Her ribs ached. They had gone around and somehow made it ahead of them.

'Stay down,' the woman, Arche by the name on her chest plate, told her. 'Want to explain why you was running from us like that?'

'Not to you,' Jesa replied.

She kicked the woman off with as much strength as she could muster and carried on running until she regrouped with Ghavvis. He was gasping for breath. She was curious how her friend could be so out of shape while living the life of a prospector. Jesa would ask him when they got out of the mess. He'd be safer coming with her now. At least she would have the company she wanted.

'Did you shake yours?' Jesa asked.

'For now,' Ghavvis replied.

'What're we going to do?'

'Here,' he wheezed, handing her the case. 'We're not going to outrun these guys. I swear the one tailing me just spoke to some friends. If they have a patrol ship, that means we're going to be dealing with another... what? Dozen or so of them? That'll be two dozen.'

'So, what do we do?' Jesa questioned. She already knew what the answer was going to be, but hoped, prayed, that it would be something else.

'I can buy you some time.'

'What? No!' she hissed. 'I got to get you out of here! Compre? You're coming! We're in this together. The boss will understand!'

'No, you don't have to do anything for me,' Ghavvis told her. 'All you have to do is get this to the buyer. If this came from a captain, then this is worth more than the price they put on it. That means it's more valuable than me and you combined, and you know it. Now you go. I'll hold them off. Just go. Get out of here.' When she tried to respond, he pushed her away. 'Go! I'll see you again soon. Don't you worry, yah?'

'But I can't leave you,' she whispered.

'You're not leaving me,' he said. 'You're just finishing the job.'

'I'll come back for you,' Jesa said.

'I know. Now go!'

Jesa nodded and ran through the crowds as fast as she could. She did not look back. Her ship would have been refuelled and restocked by now. Hopefully they had been unable to find out which ship was hers so that she could make a clean escape. All she needed to do was get in and take off then finish the job. When it was done, Jesa would be back to find her friend.

She would indeed see Ghavvis again and hoped that he would be well. If not, the puya SPF would pay for it. One way or another, there would be consequences if he had been hurt.

Jesa continued through the streets and only stopped when she was at the base of the boarding ramp to the *Saridia*. She looked back to the crowds of people and aliens, a tear rolling down her cheek. She boarded her ship without a final word and was given immediate permission to take off. The outers looked after their own.

Chapter 4
08/10/2675
04:52 Earth Standard Time
15:21 Local Time

Beatrice Lenoia

Hot springs were completely underrated. The rejuvenating properties of the heated waters enriched with natural minerals; steam rising gently to enshroud everyone in a gentle blanket of warm air; the sense of relaxation. It was intoxicating. There had to be a law to make attending them mandatory at least once a month.

Beatrice was still waiting on receiving word from Foresc's superior. The message was sent over two weeks ago and there had still been no response. Red tape and bureaucracy clearly still had its place and was being used to keep her from the truth. It made the jump feel like it had taken months to finish. That though gave her time to think. A benefit or a hindrance depending on perspective. Beatrice had a myriad of options on how to handle her guests, most of which could potentially be more problematic than result in supplying a solution. In the end she decided to leave it until the response was received. Who knew – it could be good news.

The *Galactic Passage* docked with the space elevator above the planet Maugavai. Most planets had them installed. They saved having the atmosphere full of space faring vessels and was much cheaper to run. The energy needed for a single warship being launched from a planet's surface to break atmosphere could be used to transport enough people to the top of a space elevator to fill thirty ships. Most of these elevator platforms were plain, simple metallic husks that were to hurry passengers onto their flights. This one however was beautifully designed with carpets, painted walls with paintings mounted, and decorative features. It even came with restaurants, hotels and other amenities for overnight stayers waiting to climatise to the rotational orbit of the planet. At peak capacity, Beatrice estimated that up to twenty ships could dock with the multi-level platform at any one time. One by one the passengers had disembarked and took the thirty-minute ride down one of the carts to the planet's surface. It had taken her a couple days to complete enough paperwork from the voyage before she could descend to the planet to taste some relaxation for herself. When she went down to the surface, a smile beamed across her face.

Once Beatrice had finished speaking to the passengers, hearing what they thought of their trip so far and teasing them with glimpses into what else they could expect over the rest of the journey, she had been able to find a quiet spot in an upper-level pool, perched herself right at the edge of the spring and fell asleep for a couple hours. She left her body floating in the hot spring water, the heat working its way through and easing all muscle tension. She was only disturbed by a waiter, a Trodensit male, offering a drink. They were big, strong creatures that loved hot environments. The males were either pale pink or brown in colour depending on maturity, while the females were orange, green and other vibrant colours. They had large eyes and a small tuft of hair on the top of their heads. By her understanding, this was a cultural style, not a natural one.

They were not the only species there. A quick count allowed her to estimate that there was at least another dozen alien species working or visiting. Bipedal organisms, quadrupeds and even those that slithered made their way around the springs. All aiming for one thing; to have a care-free day.

When she finally woke and accepted an alcohol-free mocktail, a strange concoction with bands of greens, blues, reds and silvers in the glass, Beatrice gazed over the springs. Steam created a permanent thin cloud that hung above the spring waters like a canopy. Huts for geothermic saunas and spas were dotted all along the waterfronts with a bar slotted in between every dozen or so huts. The main building for this resort was nestled at the base of the cluster of a couple dozen pools.

The planet was highly active with volcanicity. It was that activity that allowed for the natural springs to form over the land masses in the numbers that they existed in. There were three main bodies of land and five oceans. No sentient natives inhabited the planet, only basic fauna and flora. Any sentient organisms living on the planet had migrated there for the easy, laid-back life. The local fauna ranged from small amphibious and reptilian organisms to massive sea creatures of legendary proportions that lurked the depths of the oceans. She wondered what else could be lurking in the murky abyss. There were many excursions for people to take, if they could afford it, to see more than just the springs. That was what made the site such a good detour from their schedule.

She remained at the pool side for a further two or three hours, enjoying the drinks and food, before deciding that was enough relaxation until the next destination. She showered, dried off and re-dressed then made her way back to the space elevator, just an hour-long trip by an all-terrain vehicle with a very comfy cabin. The space elevator stood prominently in the skyline like a dagger being plunged into the planet. Strange reptilian-like birds flew in the sky, and unusual four-legged animals marched over the land. She was one of only five people to board the cart capable of carrying forty people at a time. The transition from in-atmosphere to space was a wonder of its own when there were no pressure changes through transit thanks to the gravity dampeners built into each capsule. When in the bulbous platform at the top of the stalk of the elevator, Beatrice almost lost her footing in shock of convenience. The skinny man that she had wanted to speak to, that she hoped to speak to, was looking around the space elevator platform. To her added pleasure he was venturing around without a babysitter. A perfect opportunity.

Beatrice approached him. 'Hello.'

The man seemed to jump a little but hid it well. He wore the expression of someone who was fascinated with the structure.

'Hello,' he replied pleasantly.

'Lovely view from up here, isn't it?' she asked.

'It really is,' the man said, smiling as he looked out the nearest window. 'A magnificent piece of machinery. You know that if these would have been made into a government funded project seventy years earlier, twenty years after they were proven to work, we could have avoided two financial crashes that ruined the UPN for a decade at a time each?'

'I did not know that,' Beatrice answered, intrigued by the fact and glad that he was making the steps to engage in conversation. It helped that she was in civilian clothing, so she was not immediately recognisable as the ship's captain. 'What brings you out here then?'

'Work,' he said with a nod. 'I get to see a lot of things with work. More than most people would ever dream of seeing.'

'Oh really? Are you an engineer or mechanical surveyor?' she asked, gesturing to the platform they were both in. She knew he was a scientist. Asking something as vague as that to a scientist would easily tease out arrogance. No one liked being labelled incorrectly.

'No, no, no, I'm no engineer,' he said, laughing and flashing his hands. 'These things can barely put up a flat pack. Never mind something like this. No, I'm a scientist. A xeno-biologist to be precise.'

Aliens. He studied alien organisms. The team currently occupying her cargo hold had fridges that held unknown cargo which required a xeno-biologist to oversee them. It could only suggest that there were aliens or alien-related products on board her ship. Why else would he be there with them and look as nervous as he had done on the security footage? What aliens were they? Were they even alive?

She needed to continue digging to find out just how much danger they were all in.

'Have you been down to the planet's surface yet?' Beatrice questioned.

'Not yet, no,' he said while shaking his head slowly. Remorsefully. 'Would like to have the time though. I've heard of the different types of animals out there. I mean, the last time we knew of reptiles flying was in the age of the dinosaurs. Here? We have the piliapa. Actual reptiles with wings – mini dragons if you will. And the tagasami that rules the oceans. Have you ever heard of a whale-like animal so big that it could swallow a small transport ship and still not know what they've just eaten? I mean... wow. The life here! Easy to see why sentient life couldn't have evolved though. Too much of a challenge for food. Nothing here could ever eat enough to fuel the development of intelligence.'

'Why don't you go? We're going to be here for a few more days.'

'I can't,' he said. 'I've got to stay here with our cargo. Just need to be on hand at all times with it.'

'Can't anyone else, you know, watch it?'

'They could,' the man admitted. 'But I don't want to trust them with it longer than necessary. It's... it's not something that just anyone can handle. I know what to do with it. I want to keep it that way.'

'So, what have you been working on then? To be all the way out here,' Beatrice asked, chancing her luck. 'Seems a bit far out.'

'Research,' the man answered sharply. She was pushing the wrong buttons and needed to be careful. 'I go wherever I'm told to go and study whatever I'm told to study.'

'And you've got whatever it is you're studying on here with you? Is that why you're here? Is it something you can tell me about?'

'No, I can't,' he said. His voice was shaky. He began to look around, as if expecting someone to be watching him. 'Look, I got to go.'

'You really don't need to,' Beatrice insisted. 'I didn't mean to pry. Just curious.'

'I really need to go. I shouldn't even be here.'

'Are you sure? Can't even spare a few more minutes?'

'No. I really need to get back. Sorry.'

The man rushed away back to the *Galactic Passage*, leaving her to think about the conversation. What was he researching? Had he brought some of that research with him onto the ship? Was it the contents of the fridges that required him to be there? She desperately needed answers for all those questions.

Beatrice clambered back onto to the ship herself and, after she had changed into her uniform, returned to the bridge. She wasted no time to check her comm-pad. No messages received yet. How much longer would she have to wait? Was the answer going to be no, she could not have any information about what cargo they were transporting through her ship? The suspense of waiting was nauseating. Like a child waiting to find out what is under the wrapping of their present and won't be given a hint what it is until it's unwrapped. The difference was now it was up to someone else to give her permission to unwrap someone else's gift.

'What's the look for?' Franklin asked.

'Just really frustrated,' Beatrice sighed. 'I really want to know what they're doing down there but I can't decide what to do until the guy's superior gets in touch and says something to me. It's just taking so long.'

Franklin shrugged. 'If it's political, you'll be waiting a while. Those guys only know one speed: slow. It gives them time to justify whatever they say.'

'True I guess,' she muttered.

'Maybe try this guy's patience and go back down? Take a few extra bodies with you. Showing up again might prompt him to hurry up and say something. I could go. Or Henendez could. See if the guy just doesn't like you?'

Beatrice smiled at her adjutant. 'Thank you, I'll give it a couple days first. Then we'll see if I've had any contact or not. If not, be my guest and go down.'

Franklin Hender courteously nodded. As he left her side, Beatrice took a moment to collect her thoughts and focus on what she did have control over. Their next destination was a couple weeks jump away to visit a nebulae cluster where new stars were being born. This though would mean no communications could be received, as there would be too much activity going on for any comms to make it through the clouds. Their schedule dictated they were to leave in a couple days. Beatrice decided that she would delay that and make it four days. Doing so not only gave the passengers more time to rest, but it also gave her a little extra time to receive a response from the man's superior.

Beatrice opened a radio link with the Chief Engineer, 'Jons?'

'Yes Captain?' Allua Jons replied cheerfully.

'I want a full system check and report. We've got a few more days out here before we go. I want to make sure that my ship is in full working order before we depart,' she instructed.

'Aye Captain, I'll have a report for you in forty-eight hours,' the Chief Engineer said. 'You want me to try and get access to the cargo hold?'

'If anyone can do it, it's you,' Beatrice said. 'Do whatever you have to do and get in there. You can take up to seventy-two hours. Get the report as detailed as possible.'

'Understood,' Allua replied. 'Out.'

Beatrice waited a few minutes in silence, trying to decide what to do now that there was quite literally nothing to do during that time other than the usual daily routines. It was quite a difficult task.

Jesa

Jesa had abandoned him. It was at his instruction, but that did nothing to make the fact that Jesa had left Ghavvis behind any easier. He had done so much for her when she was in need, and she had been powerless to help because of the risk of losing her new cargo to the puyas. Another person who had meant something to her that had now been taken. Not by illegal criminals like her. But by the legitimate criminals ordered around by the UPN. Terrorising the Outers like it was their right to just because they had established civilisations. Puyas thought they could come wherever they wanted and do as they please.

Everyone was trying to take something from her. And everyone managed to do just that. How long would it be before they started to take away her soul? She already had her dreams, something deeply personal and precious, taken away from her. They belonged to her nightmares that in turn were policed by Barbaros, the Crevari and the UPN.

She had made a couple random jumps since leaving Juntah Station over the course of about a week then put herself back on track to her destination of Sol. Anything to try and lose the UPN ship that had come after her. For the last week, Jesa had been sailing smoothly carrying out vital repairs to the *Saridia* to make it space-worthy again. Carrying out her evasion jumps had nearly ripped her ship apart with not stopping long enough to recharge the jump drive safely. If she had done another couple jumps like that, her ship would have exploded with the stresses. Jesa managed to patch up a couple of the rips in the inner hull, re-secure a few pipes that had been shaken loose and keep the engine from overloading too much. Everything external would have to wait for when she next made it to a dock to be repaired, and that would be months.

Jesa wished that she never had to make such drastic manoeuvres, but it had to be done. The SPF soldiers would not be able to trace her after those jumps. She could barely retrace her own steps. That was a good thing. At least where she needed to be didn't change.

Jesa spent a few extra minutes making sure she was still on the right route. After what she did, there was no room for error. She needed to make sure that she could reach Earth. Once she crossed the Prosper Line, an imaginary band that the UPN and its major allies put around the central and mid colonies to separate them from the outer colonies, there would be no allies. No one to turn to for help, and no one that she could trust, until she reached Earth. Even then, the people she was to deal with she couldn't trust to be honest. Once confident that there was nothing else to consider or plan for, she left her ship on autopilot to return to the cargo bay.

'I can't believe it,' she sobbed to the skeleton. 'What would you have done, Bones? Huh?'

That was a stupid question. Something of its size wouldn't have had any issue in fighting off the SPF puyas. After all the stories she had heard about the Shauari, there should have been no doubts of their capabilities. She thought of how the creature would have easily ripped the SPF personnel apart limb by limb and devoured their flesh with a ruthless hunger, crushing skulls with a single bite, immobilising its prey with a single lashing from its tail. A true challenge for anything inferior in size.

'You wouldn't have left your friend behind, would you?' Bones just looked at her with that empty glare from the eye sockets staring through her. Judging her and yet not even noticing her at the same time. 'I bet you'd have died fighting rather than live running away, yah? Wish I was as strong as you. Would have been able to help him. Would be able to help everyone in the outer colonies.'

Then it struck her. Maybe Bones didn't play well with others. Barbaros had only been able to acquire one skeleton. There was nothing to suggest there were others. It was possible that he lived a solitary life with no one else to rely on, worrying only about himself. Much like she did. It was safer that way. Simpler. Didn't have to rely on people. No connections or emotions to affect decisions. Just the need to survive.

'Guess we're not too different then, are we?' she asked Bones. 'I'll leave you alone. Bet you can't stand listening to me going on and on. Speak to you soon.'

She left the Shauari skeleton in peace to go to the source of her woe. The reason why her friend was stuck on Juntah, imprisoned by the SPF soldiers, with a Crevari fleet somewhere in the area. Her stomach tightened at the thought of losing him to them. Nestled in one of the few remaining spaces of the hold was the case she had fled with. She pulled the container out of its place and took it to her cabin where she sat on her bed staring at it for an age. What was in there? Why was it so important that it was worth Ghavvis sacrificing himself and cost so much to sell on? Where did its contents come from? Her hands quivered at the possibility of opening it and finding out. Jesa pulled her hands back and looked to the doorway. No one was there. Just her. It didn't stop her from checking the hallway outside. Had to be sure that

Barbaros wasn't there, or one of his many informants hadn't tagged along to spy on her. Jesa returned to her bed. Her hands reached out to the case and were softly placed on it. She gasped in fear and looked towards the doorway of her cabin as she unclasped the latch, fully expecting Barbaros to enter in a fit of rage at opening something that wasn't hers. When he did not show himself, Jesa flipped the case lid to reveal its contents. She needed to know what had been worth sacrificing Ghavvis for.

Crystals. Beautiful pale green crystals. Seventeen of them that were shaped like long, hexagonal tubes about eight inches in length and two wide with one end housing groves as if it was designed to be slotted into something. Most of the precious stones were shattered and broken into thick shards, positioned in the case as if they were about to be put back together. The few that were whole were kept together at the centre of the collection. Proudly where eyes were supposed to be attracted to. It was on those whole ones that it was easy to see tracking lines carved into the outside and imprinted on the inside of the crystals like what would be found on a micro-chip.

'What the hell are you?' she whispered to the objects.

She picked one of the complete crystals up. It was light and looked like it should have been brittle even though handling it proved it was far from that. The crystal was smooth. Even the defined edges were far from being sharp. She could not work out what it was. Maybe it was just like a computer processing chip. Why would it look like one if it were not one? Who had owned it previously? Or the crystals could simply be ornaments. Meant for a life as nothing more than decorations in a display case.

If it was for the same buyer as everything else, Ostad. Jesa could only believe that it came from the same place that the Shauari came from; a lot of her cargo already did. Her head started to hurt as she raced through all the possible connections everything had with one another. It became unbearable. That was why smugglers were never meant to think and just did the job like a mindless drone, she guessed. Barbaros always did say that people ended where they were meant to be under his leadership. That everyone had their own purpose and to try to reach something you wasn't meant to achieve was a waste of time and resources. It was upsetting to remember that. To make her feel like she would never break free of the shackles that imprisoned her, not because she didn't deserve to, but because she wasn't meant to.

Jesa put the crystal away, locked the case and returned it to its place. It was not going anywhere any time soon so if she wanted to go back to it, she knew where to find the case. There would be plenty more opportunities to have a look at them and ponder their purpose.

Her stomach rumbled furiously. It was not her time to feast that day and she had already eaten most of that day's rations already. There was not much left to eat, and her strength was starting to fail. The temptation was almost too much to handle yet Jesa couldn't have her food yet. It needed to be saved for later so that she had the strength to carry out the checks on her ship. She decided to retire back to her cabin and fell asleep once more. Sleep came very easily to her thanks to the hunger. Barely any strength remained to stay awake.

The darkness instantly consumed her, and her dreams came to life. She was back on the station, but it wasn't quite the same. It was dark. Even with the lights on there were dark shadows enveloping the building fronts. More so, Juntah was empty. No cargo containers filled with goods. No food stalls on the streets. Not even any people or aliens to work the machinery and eat the food. She searched for what must have been hours to try and find someone else. All the shops were closed. Crew offices that were meant to be staffed at all times had their shutters pulled down that remained shut after repeatedly slapping the metal to get someone's attention. Even the bar where they encountered the SPF was absent of its less than civilised clients and those places were never vacant. She turned the corner and couldn't believe her luck. She found someone. Ghavvis was still alive and stood in front of her facing off to the side. He held the case with the strange crystals in, keeping it close to his chest. Her heart jumped with joy. Jesa started to run over. He must have just not heard her when she was searching the station for someone. Then he turned to look at her. Where his eyes should have been there was just a black void, a perpetual darkness with no ending. He started to speak to her, but no words were spoken. There was silence while his lips moved. Somehow though, she knew what he was saying. The words permeated in her mind. He was telling her that she should not have left him behind. That she would suffer for it. Ghavvis begged her to tell him why she left him. Why she didn't ignore his instructions and come back for him. He told her of all the terrible things that the SPF had done to him to give up her location. Where she was going. How they had brought him to the edge of death just to find out. It struck her like a knife being plunged into her heart. Not that she wasn't already hurting inside and did not already feel like she carried a led weight in the pit of her stomach made of guilt for what she had to do.

Jesa tried to plead with him, try to make him understand that she did not want to leave him and that she only did as he instructed. Her words fell on deaf ears. Or maybe she was unable to speak. She couldn't tell which as Ghavvis carried on demanding answers from her. A hand was placed on her shoulder. Another human, one of the citizens of Juntah, was there. They too had the same endless darkness for eyes that Ghavvis had and spoke without saying anything through their silent lips. Another hand was placed on her shoulder. This time an alien. They kept appearing out of nowhere. Each time from where she wasn't looking. Each one of them asking her why she left Ghavvis. Demanding to know why she had abandoned him. Wanting to know why she didn't care about her kin. None of them wanted to listen to her. Or they didn't care.

When she was ready to give in attempting to explain, exhausted from trying, she closed her eyes to weep. As the first of her tears hit the floor, the voices stopped. Jesa looked up in shock to find that the station was empty once again. Barbaros walked up behind her. She could feel his presence, lingering, before she dared turn to face him. Unlike the others, he still had his eyes. He just stared at her. There was anger, disappointment and even sadness in his expression. The man stood there. She tried to tell him she was sorry, that she would never fail him again, begging for a second chance. Barbaros never uttered a single word to her. When she was gasping for breath after collapsing to the floor in tears, Jesa looked up at him. Barbaros smirked at her briefly before he pulled out his comm-pad and tapped a button on the screen. Time from that moment seemed to move in slow motion. First the device in her arm heated up, slowly becoming over searing hot. Then it whined in a single high-pitched tone. Finally, the flames erupted out of her bicep as it detonated, separating her arm from her body before the blast started to work on the rest of her body. The moment she felt the pain, felt the agony of being torn apart into hundreds of tiny pieces from her arm to the rest of her body, she woke from the dream. A warning siren rung out from the flight deck. How long had the alarm been crying out for? How long had she slept through it? According to the clock beside her bed, she'd been asleep for at least five hours. It felt like it had barely been a few minutes. The siren kept crying for her attention so she could deal with it.

She shook the weariness out of her system, caught her breath and rushed to the helm. Jesa took up the controls and checked everything over. She had an unknown ship within long distance sensor range. It seemed to be on an approach vector with her. Jesa decided to test the notion that it was pursuing her. Better to be safe than sorry. She changed direction, waited, and it altered its own trajectory to get in front of her. Coincidence maybe. Jesa repeated the process another couple times. Each time she repeated it, the new ship adjusted to get in front of her. It was clear that Jesa was being followed and worse still they were constantly altering to be ahead of her ship. Who was it though? Another smuggler that knew what cargo she had and wanted to take it for themselves? A team chancing their luck at an easy pay out. Worse still, she knew that marauders and Crevari patrolled this area. If the ship belonged to either of them, she was as good as done for unless she could get help. Regardless of who they were, she needed to get out of there.

Jesa altered her direction once more and increased thrust to maximum. It too sped up to a speed that would put the vessel ahead of the *Saridia* before she knew it. While Jesa had a little time to prepare until the ship that was following caught up to her, she scanned it. It was a Stellar Protection Force vessel, a Griffin class patrol ship. Was it the same one that brought the SPF soldiers to Juntah? Or was it a new one that had been alerted to her escape and was now after her?

Either way, her options were limited. The vessel was much faster than hers was, and she could not outrun them. Handing herself over was not on the table. There needed to be another way out of this mess, some way she could get away from them. Her only option was to get a head start and somehow achieve a speed that they wouldn't follow.

'Maybe...' she whispered as she thought up a potential.

Jesa stared at the console in front of her. Once she started the process there would be no turning back. She reached to the controls and started to charge the slip-space drive. The maximum safe speed was not enough to outrun them. She needed to go faster to be fast enough for her to escape. It had to be enough. Doing such a thing came with risks though. The maximum speed was there for a reason – so that the pilot didn't kill themselves exceeding limitations. If it went wrong, not only would she die but she would repeat the stories of the first ships to attempt to go into the jump. How they imploded and tore holes in reality itself.

The *Saridia* rumbled and vibrated as the jump drive charged up. Her teeth ground together in anticipation. Desperate times called for desperate measures. Her console flashed ready to enter the jump. She reached out and pushed the button. The wormhole opened before her. The incredible speed achieved was more than her dampeners could adjust for. She was being crushed in her seat, pushed back as if an anchor had been dropped at the event horizon of the wormhole and the chain was wrapped around her. Maybe she could hold on for a few hours like this. It would have to be enough. She needed to make it out of there.

Leyton Foresc

'You did what?' Leyton barked, towering over the professor in ill-placed outrage.

He had just learnt that the ship's captain had questioned Professor Ainslot. His anger had boiled over when he learned that the questioning did not take place on the *Galactic Passage* but on the station platform at the top of the space elevator. His orders had been simple and easy to follow: stay within the confines of the cargo hold at all times. It was for the professor's own safety. Not only did he leave the cargo hold and their deck, but the professor left the liner entirely. Not only that, but his dramatic exit would have only stoked the fire of curiosity the captain was already feeling. The only thing stopping Leyton from placing a single round in his skull for such a serious security risk and insubordination was that the academic had come straight to him and confessed what had happened. A man that willing to confess upon their return was someone worth giving a second chance. They rarely forgot the lessons learned.

'What were you doing leaving the ship anyway?' he demanded. 'I told you that you needed to stay.'

'I know. I couldn't help myself,' Samuel Ainslot admitted. 'I wanted to see the planet. I did want to try going down and study some of the animals. But it would have taken too long. I realised that if I were to go, I'd need one of you guys with me. I just looked at the planet from the platform. You have to believe me. I just wanted to study the wildlife there and see if any of the rumours were true.'

Scientists. In too much of a hurry to get their next fix of information. He relaxed at the notion that Samuel knew he had overstepped the boundaries with his curiosity.

'And how did she end up questioning you?' Leyton questioned. 'What were you doing to get her attention?'

'Nothing! She found me and must have recognised me from somewhere,' he explained with a shaky voice. 'I was just looking around the station after a quarter of an hour of staring at the elevator. Started to talk to me, acting all nice. In normal clothes, I didn't realise it was her straight away. When she started asking about why I was out here, about my work, I knew I had to get out of there. So, I left.'

Leyton paced around the cargo hold. The captain had a hunger to know what they were doing. She was not going to stop until she knew.

That sort of adversary was one to be watched closely – they would do whatever they could to get what they wanted. It was exciting to have a mental challenge like this after weeks of nothing. Yet, it was troublesome. Leyton was already dealing with a subordinate that was hungry to take power. Forcing him to look over his shoulder. He didn't need a second front to battle from.

'Alright,' he whispered. 'I'll figure out what we do about her. We can't have her going around questioning everything we do. While I do that, you are to stay here. Got it? No more venturing out like that. We have too much to lose if you lost your shit. And she knows you're the weakest link out of us all. She'll target you again and again until you cave. I need to avoid that.'

'I understand,' Samuel answered.

'Good. Anyway, where are we at with the wolves?'

The professor had learned that, even in suspended animation, the pups were going to continue to grow at a standard rate. Stasis could not slow their development. And by the physiological differences between the pregnant wolves and the other larger females, Samuel had concluded that they couldn't have been far from giving birth. That meant they needed to bring the wolves round so that they could give birth successfully. His team had been working tirelessly to erect and fit the containment unit they brought. The structure was a large, makeshift container that had been hooked up the electricity grid to electrify the walls and power the door lock they installed. It looked like it shouldn't be able to hold anything. Jerome insisted that it would be fit for purpose. How long it would last though, was a bridge Leyton hoped he didn't have to cross.

'As you can see, the cage is ready,' the professor answered, gesturing to it casually. 'Got it plugged in to the ship's power grid so that we can keep the door locked. We just need to take them out of stasis and get them inside it.'

'And the cameras?' Leyton asked, gesturing toward the cameras in the ceiling. 'Can't the guys up on the bridge see everything that's going on?'

Jerome stepped up from the other side of the room. He'd been listening in on their conversation, something he had done a lot of lately. Trying to look like he wasn't paying attention but clearly taking note of everything that was being said. It had been going on since Medic Suttle carried out his evaluation – an enlightening read once completed. Dom Suttle had figured out that while everyone, including Leyton himself, displayed increased occurrences of anxiety-related stresses because of the situation, most of the team was perfectly fine. Emotionally most were still well balanced. Hatty Tallow was lonely. She missed the people back at base and was just looking forward to getting home. Kari Fellstrum and Jake Deulche were both bored, itching for something to happen. They had too much energy and no way to burn it off to bring down their stress levels. Onyx Perretti was cool and collected still. Longed for a fight though. He always had violent tendencies and the lack of conflict wasn't sitting well with him. The medic didn't seem to care about that as much as he was concerned with the looming onset of galactic fever. Like cabin fever it was an alteration to personality, but a person didn't need to be isolated to suffer. Just needed to be confined within a spaceship for extended periods with no way to escape. Onyx was starting to feel lost, trapped, believing no one else felt like him. Yet, it was Jerome that was the biggest concern. Medic Suttle had learnt that he had become more secretive. Defensive. Even the most basic question was an attack against him. A suggestion became an accusation. The agent was hiding something and struggled to keep his emotions locked away. He also had a lot to say about Leyton and how poor his leadership was. Never though able to quantify with evidence how Leyton wasn't fit to lead.

'Schottler's been able to hook up the camera onto a sort of loop,' Jerome explained. 'As far as they know, it's an empty space that we will all continue to avoid.'

'Good,' Leyton said. 'Let's get them moved in there now. How long will it take for them to come round?'

Professor Ainslot answered swiftly. 'After I've injected them with the drugs to wake them, it'll take approximately two hours until they're back on their feet. Five until they're fully awake and aware. But we may need to leave the pods in there with them, I don't think we'll be able to get them safely back out. I hope command has more of these because they smell of us. The wolves will most likely break them to eradicate anything to do with us.'

'I'm sure command has replacement fridges,' Leyton said. 'Move them into the cage and start the preparations. Jerome, oversee the move and make sure everything is still secure before waking them up.'

'You got it,' Jerome replied. 'What are you going to do?'

'I've got to make a call,' he explained. 'I'd rather not but I have to do it.'

Leyton left the professor and his friend to move the ice wolves. He quickly paced through the corridors to his cargo-comms room. He opened a comms link with the administrator of the MID. There would be questions on his progress. He still had to secure a fall-back base of operations if things did turn sour. That he would arrange once the wolves were awake. Most likely would be best off using that room. One thing at a time. It took several connection request attempts before his call was taken by an assistant, a young man by the voice, then transferred through to the administrator.

He thought over what he needed to say about the result of the professor's tests. He would need to have confirmation on how they were to exactly keep up with the food demands and what their limitations were, even though the head of the division had already made it clear that there would be no restrictions. Leyton needed to hear him say the words one more time. He couldn't proceed in good conscience without that talk, and even then, it would still be with great reluctance.

Finally, the call was answered.

'Do you have any idea what time it is?' Administrator questioned, his tone saying he had just been woken up. 'This had better be worth it.'

'I have an update for you,' Leyton said.

'Could it not wait?'

'I don't not believe so, sir, no,' Leyton replied. 'We have to wake the pregnant females. The pups have continued to grow in stasis. If they are to be born in stasis, they will either kill the mother or die without the booster shot to help them survive the freezing process.'

'Understood. Do not forget my instructions. They must be brought back healthy and intact.'

He let out a sigh. 'I understand. Sir, how do you want me to feed them?'

'Did I not make myself clear before?' Administrator snapped. 'Raid the ship's storerooms. You're in the cargo area, right? Don't need much imagination to know that you'll have easy access to food. If that fails, there is a lot of fresh meat on that ship. You can either take the food to them or make the food walk right in there for them. This is more important than you realise. Am I clear?'

'Perfectly, sir,' Leyton said. 'I will keep you posted on any further developments.'

The comms link closed. Leyton sighed. It was clear what his superior was hinting at. He could not do the latter. These were the people he swore to protect against hostile forces, that he had devoted his life to keeping safe. All on board were loyal to the UPN or at the least friendly. They followed the same flag that he did. Why would his boss give such orders for reasons not known? Secrets or no secrets there was no current war with the UPN that could justify the order. Collateral damage was not needed. There were always ways around killing your own. Leyton was determined to make sure of it.

He closed the pad on his gauntlet and returned to the cargo hold. The creatures had been successfully moved into the cage. Professor Ainslot stood on top of one of the capsules, analysing the animal inside with his tac-pad as if there would be some advantage to looking down on the wolf. Samuel looked over to him with a smile of approval.

'We're on schedule,' he announced proudly. 'I'll be initiating the revival process shortly. Got to make sure the pups are still stable first. If I rush it, we could lose them.'

'Don't let me keep you,' Leyton said. 'Take as long as you need. We can't disappoint the administrator.'

'Understood,' Samuel Ainslot replied.

He nodded and turned to Jerome, 'Organise a food raid. We need raw meat and lots of it. Go onto the station platform for it. Take as much as much as you can.'

'Why there?' Jerome questioned. 'We've got food here.'

'Because if we take food here, we'll only slow our return down when they realise there's not enough food to feed the passengers,' Leyton Foresc explained. 'If we take food from the station, they'll just have to call a resupply and hopefully think that someone fucked up an inventory check.' When Jerome grumbled acceptance of the order, Leyton turned to Samuel. 'Hey, professor, I know what you said before, but do you think we can try to pull one of those stasis pods out before they start trying to chew us?'

'Why?'

'Because we need somewhere to store their food until we next reach a space port to top up. And those fridges are the best thing we have to store it in.'

'Maybe then, if we're quick enough after the ejection stage,' Professor Ainslot said. He did not look convinced by his own words. 'But you will have to be quick. I can't guarantee how quickly they'll be ready to hunt once the drugs take effect. Their hormones might wake them up a little sooner.'

'You gave us hours earlier?' Leyton replied.

'That's a best-case scenario,' Samuel explained. 'In reality, it could be a lot less. I don't know everything yet. We've got a lot of firsts to contend with: the first births ever documented for the wolves; the first defrost cycle from stasis. I can't tell you anything more specific than what I'm telling you now. All I can do is theorise, document and amend theories as I learn more.'

'Fucking scientists… Okay, this is what we'll do,' Leyton said. 'As soon as those pods have cycled the defrost process and we can get one out, give us the nod and say so. We'll be in and out in less than a minute before they have a chance to realise what the hell is going on. Jerome, take Fellstrum and Deulche with you onto the platform. Get all the meat you can carry. The fewer times we need to go for supplies, the better.'

'Understood,' Jerome and Professor Ainslot said together.

The following couple hours were tense to say the least. The computer consoles on each of the stasis pods buzzed as they completed the sequential processes of reviving the wolves. Bit by bit, chemicals to wake them were introduced as gasses into their pods, reversing the process of putting them under and cleansing their systems of the stabilising components required to survive the deep freeze. Once the first pod ejected open, sliding the body out like a corpse being brought out of a fridge in the morgue, they moved quickly. Leyton worked with Agent Schottler and Tallow to ease the ice wolf out of her container. The matriarch, Spike. She looked at them with weary eyes that did nothing to ease the feeling she was already wanting to tear them all limb from limb. They eased the female creature onto the floor. She twitched, fighting with all her strength to fully wake up so she could get to her feet and feast on them. They rushed the stasis pod out of the cage, shut the door and waited with their weapons at the ready as it locked. An electric hum signified that they were safe.

Even though his heart was still racing, Leyton felt relief that they were safe and made it out with the stasis unit intact. Leyton sighed. He wanted to cheer. To celebrate. But this was not the time. They now had to contend with wolves that were awake and going to multiply.

Over the next few hours, Leyton watched as the wolves came round. Once awake they tried to break out of the cage in a desperate bid to attack their captors. The wolves gnawed at the metal bars, pushed at the gate to force it open and even tried to dig under and through the metal floor. After those attempts failed, they cried out for the rest of their pack to come to their aid. When that failed, they fell silent and paced.

126

Spike very rarely took her eyes away from Leyton whenever she wasn't attempting to break free of her prison. They watched each other intently, rival leaders trying to calculate the upper hand. The other wolf, designated as Crest because of her spines on her head looking like a sloping crest behind the skull, rarely stopped pacing. She was constantly assessing every aspect of her surroundings.

The professor was terrified, enlightened and excited all at the same time. He carried out more studies now that they were up and about, analysing their movements, capturing their vocalisations and biometrics with a constant smile on his face.

Several hours later, and several more cups of coffee in their system, something changed that caught his attention. The wolves stopped what they were doing. Their red eyes were a constant glare, not particularly looking at anything, just staring into an infinite abyss. Then their stance changed. They shook. Something wasn't right. Leyton had stayed awake to make sure they didn't attempt another breakout – this wasn't that. Professor Ainslot was asleep. He would surely know what was happening.

Leyton rushed to the professor. 'Hey, wake up!' When Samuel did not stir, he gave him a gentle kick to wake up. He wondered how the guy could sleep so easily. 'Get up and don't forget your pad.'

The professor rubbed his side, grabbed his comm-pad and joined Leyton at the cage. The wolves still stared into nothing as they shook in pain, squealing and hissing. Spike was the first to do something different, a fermenting gurgling sound emerging from the pit of her stomach, much like the sound of sludge being forced out of a small pipe. Crest soon followed suit with the sickening sound.

'What's going on?' Leyton asked.

'Your guess is as good as mine,' the professor responded. 'But I'm recording.'

That was not the response Leyton needed. 'Fuck recording! We need answers! Are they dying?'

'I don't know,' Samuel replied. 'I wish I could tell you. I'm learning as you are. But we can't do anything about it. Just watch.'

The gurgling continued a little longer before a peculiar substance started to eject from their mouths in large clumps. It was a strange murky gloop that looked like mucus, the colour of muddy clay. They created a base layer under their feet then both animals then paused from the secretions and shook violently, quivering as if they had been caught in a blizzard with no protective layers. The gurgles became diluted with shrill shrieks of pain.

'Oh god, don't tell me they're dying!' Leyton pleaded. Was it something to do with being brought back to consciousness? Were they having a reaction?

'I don't understand what's going on,' Samuel said, tapping instructions into his tac-pad. 'Their vitals look acceptable. Heart rates are quite high but not dangerous. It doesn't make sense.'

'What do we do?' Leyton demanded.

'I don't think there is anything we can do except wait for them to stop,' the professor answered softly. Panic struck him to the core.

All Leyton could think about were the consequences of failing. What would happen if he did not bring back the pups, even though they were not a part of the original plan. The administrator wanted them. Needed them, even. If he didn't get them then Leyton would lose more than his command. Possibly he could be found guilty of something worthy of disgraceful dismissal and removed from the agency... or worse.

The shrieking diminished into heavy breathing and gipping. Both animals began vomiting the strange murky secretion by the gallon. They only stopped to breathe and drink water. First, they covered the entire floor with enough of the sticky, gloopy substance that it overflowed from the cage and towards their occupied space. The secretion quickly lost its liquid characteristics and solidified. Hot steam rose from the floor, creating a putrid mist from the heat of the substance. Spike and Crest moved to vomit all over the cage walls, creating a think enough layer of the unusual stuff to cover two thirds of the way up with very few breaks in the sticky layers. They stopped, gasped for breath then could be heard collapsing in heaps breathing deeply. Leyton could feel his heart start to race, threatening to break out of his chest. Was that the moment they died?

He looked to the professor and the rest of his team. They all wore the same concerned expression. Should they go in? Leyton needed to know what was happening. He couldn't leave their survival to chance. The risks of being wrong couldn't outweigh keeping the administrator happy, could it?

'Professor, please tell me they're still alive,' Leyton pleaded.

'They are,' Samuel answered, analysing the data on his tac-pad. 'They're weak but their vitals are stable. They've exhausted themselves doing that.'

His heart was saved from sinking, but equally chilled as the reassuring sound of cooing called out from behind the wall of residue. The high pitched, quiet whine was eerie. A hushed noise that sounded like crunching snow carried by the wind through a forest. Completely alien to anything he had come across before, yet familiar. He didn't know which was more unnerving.

'Okay,' Leyton whispered the repeated himself with more confidence. 'What the hell is this?'

'It's their den, I'm guessing,' Samuel said. 'Feel the heat? They're keeping conditions at the right temperature. Ready for birth. Probably gives the pups more chance of survival. And the whole thing makes it private for them.'

'But they didn't do anything for ages after they woke up?' Hatty Tallow questioned. 'Why now? Why not earlier?'

'They might have woken up, but their bodies will have just been taking some time to catch up,' the professor answered excitedly. 'This is them getting caught up and realising what their bodies needed them to do. Or at least that's my theory – I'll know for certain if they start to give birth soon.'

The man was as excited as a child in a games shop. Any more excitement and he might burst like an overinflated balloon. The wolves would without doubt keep him occupied for a while.

Leyton let out a heavy sigh. With one less thing to worry about and one more success for the team, he could focus more attention on the pressing issues he had on his hands. Such as the captain of the ship and her insistence on finding out about their mission. She needed to be dealt with. Somehow. First thing was to know exactly who he was dealing with. She wasn't just some civilian captain. No, her personality had military origins.

Leyton let out a yawn. It wasn't the time to play detective. Too much time had slipped by since he last slept. He retired for some well-earned rest. This would be a task that needed a rested mind to focus on, not one that was exhausted. He hummed the tune of the lullaby he always turned to in challenging situations as he drifted off.

Duke Horren

After reporting the altercation to the station that he had called home for so long, Duke and his team remained at Juntah for another few days. They needed to wait for the commotion of the attack on the police station to calm down and for the local forces to establish a tense yet essential truce with the Juntah Chapter so that they could work together against the cartel and help maintain the peace for things to go smoothly. It was going to be a difficult transition for the local police. The police commander was as hostile to the notion of working alongside criminals as was to be expected. Like a carnivore being told it had to befriend its favoured prey. However, it didn't make the decision any less necessary for them. Hopefully, the alliance would pay off in the long run. Duke did feel bad for leaving so soon. If he had the choice, he would have stayed there for a couple more weeks. Help set the boundaries and required structure of command. Staying though would not have given his soldiers the training they needed, and he didn't have that sort of time to spare.

The following week, he pushed his team harder through their theoretical and physical training. They had proven to him on Juntah that they could work together, use initiative and, above all else, handle themselves in a tight spot faced with unknown threats. Now he wanted to see just how much it took to break them. When they weren't being pushed with strategies and moral dilemmas, he had vented atmosphere to the absolute minimum while they were resting, then timed their response speeds in complete darkness without gravity. That was just the start of the training he had in mind. There are many other ways he could break them to find out just who they really were.

Coffee in hand, Duke clambered up to the flight deck while the soldiers were sleeping. No mid-sleep surprises this time. They had earned a break. Ivan was asleep at his post, feet up on the control panel. Valentina however was wide awake. Her eyes glanced over the various streams of data that were flooding through her station. The ship's system diagnostics, radar sensors and comms channels. By the expression on her face, Petty Officer Rodriguez was looking at a ship running fine.

'Want some company?' he asked her.

'Sure thing,' she replied without turning away from her station. Val didn't even flinch. Must have heard him coming up.

He took up his usual seat and sipped at his coffee a while. They were on the slowdown from dropping out of the jump. The space they occupied was quiet for the moment, with not much activity by the way of planets or comets, but the location did have a nice view of the Milky-Way. That beauty hid a dark secret. The sector was renowned for being a deadly zone for pirates and opportunists. Duke noted that the weapon's systems were primed.

'How's the hunt going?' he asked.

Ever since leaving Juntah, they had focussed on a secondary mission he had started to locate the female that had outrun Arche and Udal'e. As soon as he was aware of what had happened, Duke instructed Ivan Zenkovich to place a trace on any ships that departed Juntah at a hurry. A place that size, and with its political status to the UPN, there was not much more they could do. To their benefit there was only one departure, and it was a known smuggler ship on their databanks. One that had been elusive for years. Something about her rush to be as far from them as possible was intriguing and he needed to know what she was hiding. With the tracer in place, they were able to track her, for the first week, and see where she was going until her ship was too far out of range for them to follow after she performed a series of random jumps. From then, there was little more Duke could do. While he was training the troops, Zenkovich and Rodriguez were scoping nearby systems as frivolously as possible, hoping to catch a glimpse of her ship.

'So far, no joy,' she answered. 'We know she's somewhere… out… wait a minute.'

A red light abruptly started to flash on her control panel. She typed furiously into the console for a couple seconds, analysed a hologram of the system and zoomed in on a single blip at the edge of the system, then turned around to smile at him.

'We have her!' Valentina exclaimed. 'Ivan! Wake up!' When he did not stir straight away, she repeated her instruction while giving him a sharp slap to the head. 'Wake up!'

'What?' Ivan replied. 'I'm awake.'

'Well get off your ass and look at the scanners, we got sight of her at last,' Valentina instructed.

'On it,' he said.

Duke sat back and watched as Ivan Zenkovich did his thing at the helm. He made a sharp change of direction and sped up to close the distance between them and the vessel on radar. They were gaining ground. When they had covered most of the space separating the two vessels the smuggler ship quickly changed direction. Ivan was just as reactive to adjust their own trajectory. Their target held steady for a moment, then evaded them another few times before they altered direction one final time to speed up beyond what it should have been capable of. Ivan grunted, complaining that what they were doing wasn't safe, then pushed his own ship to sub-light speeds to catch up to their target.

'Hey, Ivan,' Rodriguez stammered. 'You're seeing this, right?'

'Fuck, yeah I am,' Ivan Zenkovich replied thoughtfully as he flipped switches and pushed at buttons. 'They're readying for a jump entry. Val, prime weapons. I want to disable their engine.'

Duke could see the vessel, a pinprick at first, slowly growing in size as they approached. When it started to fill the forward viewing window, he could see evidence to support the helmsman's announcement. The event horizon glistening around the wormhole being produced by the slip space drive stood in front of the backdrop of space. It was beautiful to see, and it was massive.

'Hey, is that supposed to be that big?' Duke asked.

'Not at all,' Ivan said.

'They're pushing their drive beyond max; the thing's a pressure bomb,' Valentina added. 'One wrong move and that ship explodes.'

That was not good. In a matter of seconds, the vessel was going into slip space and could end up anywhere faster than they could have anticipated. It was too risky to fire a missile at them.

There was one other choice. It was dangerous, but it needed to be done. He was done guessing where she was going and wanted an end to the chase.

'Don't shoot. Follow her,' Duke ordered.

'But they're going into the jump?' Valentina said.

'I know,' Duke said. 'We're going into their jump with them.'

'Um Sarge I don't think that's the best idea you've had,' Ivan said.

'I never said it was a smart idea,' he retorted reluctantly. 'Just do it, we can figure the next bit when we're beside her. The thing is big enough to hold the two of us.'

Ivan Zenkovich sighed heavily. 'On it.'

The patrol ship sped up drastically. They closed the distance in a matter of seconds, just as the wormhole had fully formed and opened to engulf the smuggler ship. They were both in the jump and moving dozens of times faster than light. Their target was a little bit ahead of them, but their ship was much faster. They would catch up in a half hour or so. At that point they needed to act fast and with precision. If they left it too long the smuggler could randomly drop from the jump and leave them behind, losing them for good. Drastic measures had to be taken if this was to remain under his control.

'Team brief in three,' Duke announced. 'Need you both in the briefing room too for this one. I'm waking up the others.'

He flipped the emergency alert switch at the back of the flight deck. The entire ship went from being well lit to being plunged into a flashing deep red of danger. Any rooms that had their light turned off would now be strobing in the warning colour. Duke hurried through to the lower deck and took a seat in the briefing room. The pilots were the first to join him. By the time the others arrived the flashing lights had automatically returned to the standard lighting.

'What the hell's going on?' Moasa grunted, rubbing the sleep out of his eyes.

'Is this another training session?' Arche asked. 'Just drifted off.'

'No, we've got a live mission,' Duke explained. 'But I need you guys to agree to it because it's dangerous.'

'Dangerous how?' Abe questioned. 'What're we doing?'

'We're going to do a mid-jump, ship-to-ship dock. If Ivan can't line this up straight or she drops out of the jump, we're all dead,' Duke answered honestly. He waited a moment, looking over everyone's concerned expressions, and resumed speaking. 'It's risky and only a handful of documented attempts have resulted in success. But I trust his skills and we either do it or run the risk of losing the ship we've been tailing the last couple weeks. It's the girl that gave you guys the slip. I want to know why she's running from us. If even one of you doesn't want to do it, then we don't do it. It's that serious. Does anyone have any objections to doing this?' When no one made any comments or responses he carried on. Thankful didn't come close to describing his emotions. 'Okay, thank you. Ivan, Valentina, do whatever you have to. Get us docked. We'll prepare for boarding.'

The ship crew vacated the briefing room and returned to the flight deck. Their heavy footsteps pounded on the metal as they rushed up to the ship. Duke pulled up an image of the vessel on the holographic table. Its picture rotated slowly on its axis for all to see.

'This is a Nymph class hauler,' he explained. 'It's popular with smugglers because it's old. That means most of their systems run on outdated software and equipment. While we've moved on and hoped that this stuff is junked, they're holding onto the past because that's where we've left them. That, and parts are cheaper for repairs. Much cheaper. When Ivan has docked up here on the upper airlock, we'll be entering just ahead of the living quarters and in the engine room. Unless it's been modified, everything between there and the flight deck is just cargo space. We're most likely going to have hidden compartments to contend with as well. Just to keep things interesting.'

'Objectives?' Arche asked.

'We take the ship and make sure we have the female, and anyone else on the ship, in custody. Moasa, you've got defence on this one,' Duke said. 'So, you stay around the living compartments and don't let anyone past if you don't recognise them. Arche, I want you to search engineering. When you're done there and have given the all-clear, you're with me and Udal'e. We'll search the cargo hold together and make our way up to the flight deck.'

'Sergeant, what if she opens fire on us?' Udal'e asked.

'Do we know if she's armed?' he questioned back.

Abe shook his head. 'Not a clue. But I wouldn't think a smuggler would go anywhere without some form of defence?'

'In that case, if she opens fire on you, then you return it,' Duke answered. 'Your lives come first but do your best to make it a disarming shot. I want to be able to question her. If you do have to take the kill shot, then take it. Any more questions?'

'Yeah, why the hell am I running defence?' Ronan complained. 'Why can't chickenshit do that?'

'All part of your training,' Duke explained. 'He needs to learn to be a man and you need to learn how to let others do the heavy lifting. If no one has anything else to say, get geared up and ready in ten. We're dropping through the lower airlock.'

Once assembled and in the troop bay, Duke and the team waited as Ivan Zenkovich lined them up behind the smuggler vessel then sped up to be right on top of it. Over the next few tense minutes, they could only wait and hold onto the handrails above them while listening to Ivan's cuss under his breath at the difficulty of the task. Their ship latched onto the docking port with a heavy, metallic thud. Gears and cogs whirred as the connection was made airtight. A high-pitched squeal screamed out as atmosphere was created in the airlock and docking tube. Once the green light showed everything was okay, Duke flung open the airlock hatch and stepped back for Ronan to drop through the tube, open the smuggler ship's airlock door and secure the area below.

When the all clear was announced Duke followed through and was closely followed by the remaining two members of the team.

'Okay guys,' Duke said. 'You know the plan. Ronan, keep your eyes open. Joane, secure the engine room and everything in-between here and there. Report in after every room. We need to know where you are at all times. No risk taking. When you're done, haul ass and regroup with us.'

'Understood, Sergeant,' Corporal Arche replied.

The team split up. Duke led Abe into the cargo hold. Moving slowly. Each step carefully placed. They started looking behind every carry case and piece of contraband, knocking on all the wall panels they could reach and stomping on every floor plate that wasn't covered by goods. Joane Arche cleared out the eating area, sleeping quarters, washroom and engine room with ease. When she caught up with them, Joane reported that there seemed to only be one occupant in the ship and judging by the clothing, the person was indeed female. Duke led Udal'e and Arche through the rest of the ship to find the smuggler.

They walked past a wall of trinkets and the cargo hold opened up. All three soldiers stopped in their tracks as they took in just how much of the ship was made of cargo hold. They realised how full the ship was.

'Sergeant?' Udal'e asked. 'What the hell?'

Easily two-thirds of the vessel was designed to hold goods. Containers lined both sides of the cargo hold with a central reservation made of a mixture of shelving that reached the ceiling and tables, creating two walkways that led a person past all the rare and wonderful trinkets from the black market. Every surface was piled as high as physically possible with the expensive goods, ranging from gems, jewels and paints through to weapons, ornate pieces of armour and carry cases. Not a spot was empty. A lot of wealth locked into place on one ship with one person to protect it all. A ship that had no weapons to defend with. His heart went out to the smuggler. She would never stand a chance if things went wrong. She probably knew it.

'A standard smuggler ship,' he explained. 'Once they have them, smugglers gut the insides to create maximum space, fill them up and send them on. Poor girl has to go to wherever she's been told to go with all this and no protection.'

'My God,' Corporal Arche gasped. 'How could anyone want to do that for a living?'

'False promises, trickery, money problems or imprisonment,' Duke answered. 'Take your pick. It isn't a pretty lifestyle like you see in the movies. It's dangerous. Tough.'

Too many people had died just for being in that line of work, doing everything they could to protect the goods their controllers instructed them to transport. He had seen to it many times that individuals stopped smuggling permanently. Not once had Duke considered that they were more afraid of their handlers than they were of him and the SPF.

'Is she even a hostile?' Abe asked. 'Are we sure she's not just another victim?'

Duke shrugged. 'That's what we're going to find out when we get her. Come on, let's keep going.'

They continued through the cargo hold. Duke looked in a few of the cases out of curiosity. Amongst everything else he had already seen, there were unexpected finds like fossils, strange black rocks and bullion. There were even hundreds of thousands of credits. Duke wondered what they were for. What he found more unusual were the lack of porthole windows in the hull of the vessel. Clearly someone wanted to make sure no-one could see what was inside.

'Sergeant, can you come over here?' Abe called out from up ahead.

'What's up Corporal?'

When he replied, Udal'e spoke hesitantly with a tremble in his voice. 'I need you to tell me what this is.'

He rushed over to find the soldier looking up at a terrifying skeleton that towered over them. It was so tall that it couldn't be stood upright. They had to make it lean forward to fit into the hold. It was an imposing humanoid creature with strong reptilian features.

'What the hell is this?' Duke asked, repeating the question.

'I was hoping you could tell me,' Abe replied. 'This thing is freaking me out.'

'Save it for later. Keep your head in the game; we can worry about it after we apprehend the smuggler,' Duke instructed. 'Securing her is our priority. But this is a good find. Someone back at base will have a fun time studying this before it gets locked up as evidence.'

Duke left the skeleton behind, admiring the length of the tail trailing it as he walked by, with one thing in mind: search for the hidden compartments he knew were there. It was an old trick. Hide in plain sight then either run or attack when the intruder's guard was down. Duke tapped on many of the walls in the vessel hoping to find the hollow spaces hidden behind them. Most of the checks were false. A couple proved to reveal hidden rooms that were empty. Abe had equal success, or lack of with no smuggler hidden away. Joane soon reached the flight deck and reported in that there was no one. She immediately started screaming in pain moments before a loud thud led to her crying out in obscenity. Duke called for Corporal Udal'e to join him at the flight deck. Corporal Arche stood pounding on the door in a fit of anger.

'What happened?' Duke demanded.

'She must have had one of those compartments in there,' Joane growled. 'Bitch stunned me on my way out, pushed me then locked it up behind me. No idea where she came from.'

'Abe, have a look at the controls,' Duke instructed. 'See if you can force an override.'

'Probably not,' Udal'e said. 'But I'll try.' Abe looked through the door controls for a couple minutes. 'Like I thought, can't force it open. Be a bit stupid if boarders could easily force their way onto the flight deck when you've holed up there for safety.'

'Alright no need for the lesson in being an asshole,' Duke snarled. 'Is there any way around it?'

'Maybe, let me see,' Private Udal'e muttered slowly, carrying on working on the controls. 'I can mess with the atmosphere controls. That might force her out if she wants to breathe?'

'Do it,' Duke said. 'Arche, when she's out, apprehend her straight away before she gets her breath back. No cheeky punches. Understood? We need her to be in the best mood possible, so she cooperates.'

'Fine,' she replied reluctantly. 'I'll do my best.'

Duke stood back as the soldier worked around the controls. The hiss of atmosphere being vented took over the silence. A dial showing the dropping oxygen levels appeared on the control panel. The level dropped slowly from safe amounts of oxygen into levels of concern then into the lower section of dangerously low concentrations of breathable air. If she had any respiratory equipment in there, they would be waiting for hours. Judging by the condition of her ship and its patchwork to stay afloat, that was highly unlikely. With that being the prevailing theory, his only fear was if she was stubborn and stayed in there, they would need to hope the welding kit in their workshop would cut through the door to retrieve her body. Hopefully, she was not that stubborn.

As the air became unbreathable, they could hear her gasps for air become louder. Her fists pounded against the floor violently in panic and desperation to stand her ground. She fought it for as long as she could, screaming obscenities at them all demanding for them to leave her alone, until it was unbearable for her. The door slid open. The woman fell to the floor gasping for breath. Duke quickly pinned her to the floor with Joane until Abe applied the restraints.

She was very skinny, just as Arche and Udal'e had reported after Juntah, with long brown hair, dark brown eyes that were nearly black and golden-olive skin. She trembled as she tried to stand still, swaying from side to side. She wasn't high or on drugs. She had no strength left in her, her face gaunt and her skin was tight from weight loss. Her eyes were constantly searching for a way out or looking longingly at their weapons. There was something else in her eyes. Fear. Pure, animalistic fear. Not of them though. Of something else out there. A fear he rarely ever saw this close.

'Who are you?' Duke asked her.

'Won't tell you Centie puyas anything, yah,' she snapped.

A local to the outer colonies. Most likely, she was going to be an enemy until he could prove she was anything else. Especially with the cheap jibe of calling him a Centie puya. A puya was a disgusting term for someone that worked for the UPN military. Centie, a derogatory term for someone from the central systems. Put them both together and it was a standard insult used by the Outers.

'I thought you wouldn't,' Duke replied, ignoring the comment. 'But fact is that you're now under arrest and we're in control of your ship. At some point, if you want a chance of walking out of this, you will talk to us. Take her on board. Put her in the troop bay for now. We'll clear out one of the spare cabins to house her in.'

He wished they had a brig to use. Griffin class patrol ships were never meant to take on prisoners. That responsibility fell to the larger ships. This was the best alternative he had to keep her secure.

'Understood,' Corporal Arche replied.

'I wouldn't do this if I was you,' the smuggler insisted.

He stabbed his eyes at her. 'Do what?'

'Take me prisoner,' she explained.

'Why's that?' Duke asked.

'Sergeant, I don't think it's wise to entertain her like that,' Udal'e said.

He waved off the comment his solider had made. Duke glared at the woman for a response and when she did not reply he repeated himself. She returned his stare, pursed her lips and sighed.

'If only you knew, yah,' she said cautiously. 'You wouldn't be so smug if you did.'

'Then why don't you tell me, so I do know?'

'Because if I tell you or not, I don't think it'll help either of us,' the woman said.

'And what if I think I can help?' Duke asked.

'I wouldn't believe you,' the girl hissed. 'Why should I believe you? You're a Centie, yah. You do nothing but hurt us. Hate us. For who we are. You all take and don't give anything back but pain.'

Again, with the insults aimed at anyone born in the central systems. He had that insult thrown at him so many times it no longer phased him. The outer colonies had a significant dislike to the central planets, seeing them as the ones who had everything and who gave nothing away. To an extent, that was true, but only because the outer colonies refused to accept any help extended toward them in their drive to achieve total independence or collaborate into federations, alliances or unions that fundamentally were against the UPN. That was a truth they also refused to accept. It was easier to live in a reality where they were hated and were free to hate in return, rather than one where they were the cause of their own problems.

'I can't tell you why you should believe me,' Duke admitted with a sigh. 'I don't think there's anything I can tell you or do to prove to you why you should believe me and that is because I don't think you really want to believe me.'

'Damn right I don't want to believe you,' she spat. 'You'll just lock me away and do whatever you want with me.'

Duke shook his head. 'That's not true and I think you know it. I'll let you calm down before we talk.'

He stopped Arche and Udal'e before they took her away to analyse her one last time. Her skinny structure was not natural. She had not been eating properly for a long time. Weeks or even months. Duke Horren quickly inspected the kitchen supplies. She had food but depending on where she was going it may not have been enough. They had more than enough food to spare.

'When you've got her secured, give her a full meal and some water before clearing out a room for her. Okay?' Duke instructed before turning back to Jesa. 'You're one skipped meal away from collapsing and being really unwell. Won't be having that while you're under my care.'

Chapter 5
19/10/2675
16:09 Earth Standard Time

Duke Horren

Duke had instructed Helmsman Zenkovich to drop out of the jump shortly after they had secured the prisoner in her new room. They were not going to be travelling into an unknown and potentially hostile territory if he could help it. The only problem was that they dropped into an unregistered area. He had no idea where they had wound up. Petty Officer Rodriguez looked over the charts to see where they were. So far, she had a good idea that they were in a location known as raid space, an area that housed thieves, murderers and villains. There was never a time when someone wasn't on the scanners to make sure they were alone.

Whilst she was doing that, Duke had to rethink his strategy. He still needed to keep training his soldiers but at the same point he needed to break the prisoner down so that she would speak to him more freely. While they trained, running zero-G exercises, tactical theory and weapon checks, he kept her in as much isolation as possible – a torture method, admittedly. However, the time spent alone should make her more susceptible to his questioning. When they gave her food, it was quick entry into the cabin, placing the food then leaving. Not a word was to be spoken to her. Duke Horren could have reduced her food, but the girl was malnourished as it was. Feeding her less would have been counterproductive, and he couldn't see someone physically suffer like that. It brought back too many memories.

That treatment had been going on routinely for the past week. It was long enough – now was the time to get some answers from her.

Duke ordered everyone out of the troop bay and for Corporal Moasa to bring the prisoner through. He had Ronan sit with her for a while to intimidate her, staring at her while cleaning his rifle, sharpening his combat knife and polishing his armour.

When the soldier left, Duke waited before making a move. He pulled up a weapon container and sat down in front of the woman. They stared at each other in silence for several minutes. The cold, blank expression on her face was forced. Her eyes could not hide the fear. Was it fear of him? Or was it as he suspected, a fear of something else? Time to find out.

'Tell me, what was a girl like you doing out on Juntah before bugging out faster than a rat jumping a sinking ship?' he asked.

'Trading,' the woman replied. 'Taking in the views. Then realised what time it was and that I needed to get home before it went past curfew, compre?'

Duke rolled his eyes. 'Right. Because there is so much to see out here obviously apart from stars, more stars and a whole heap of nothing.'

'It takes a certain person to really appreciate it all, y'know?'

'I know what you're saying,' he chuckled. 'What were you out there buying?'

'Souvenirs, spices, the works,' she answered sarcastically.

'You don't say?' Duke replied. 'You know, I saw that skeleton on your ship. How does someone get one of those? Don't think I've ever heard of alien skeletons that look like that being sold on the market there. Or anywhere in the outers.'

He was no interrogator, but he knew interrogators from his time in the Special Forces and had spoken to those that had been interrogated. They all made similar remarks. It was the ones who befriended you that made you slip up. The ones that were aggressive of course had success. In those instances, whatever information was acquired could not be as well trusted because the victim could so easily just start babbling and saying things that they thought the interrogator wanted to hear to make them stop. The friendly ones developed trust. He was not much of a friend, but he could be friendly and ask a question that did not directly implicate her in anything but when answered could offer what he needed to know.

'Find a trader,' the woman said with a forced smile. 'Someone that deals in bones preferably.'

'And if I don't know anyone or can't find someone that does?'

'Dig up a Shauari grave,' she suggested. 'It seems that one works too.'

'Shauari?' he asked.

'Yes.'

'What exactly are they? I've never heard of them.'

The woman shrugged. 'Not a clue. I've heard stories about them and from what they say, yah, I think they're reptiles. I mean, look at that thing. You cannot tell me that looks like an avioid or mammoid?'

He knew of a lot of alien species that had come to be known over the last couple of centuries. There were so many in fact that they could not even categorise them by solar systems. They had to go through categorisation by traits or resemblance to known creatures from Sol. As far as Duke was aware, there were only a handful of species that fell into the reptilian category. Of those none of them looked like that. This thing was unique by its own standards.

'What can you tell me about them then?' Duke asked, taking advantage of her talkative attitude on the subject.

'Not much. I'm no scientist or anything. I just hear the stories, yah? They're supposed to be savage things that occupy the space beyond the outer colonies. Don't know much else about them.'

'Have you ever seen one?'

'Alive? No. This is the first time I've ever seen one of them, and I don't ever want to see one in the flesh. Not after seeing that thing.'

The woman fell silent. Glaring at him. He was not going to get much further on that subject. The fingers on her hand started to twitch. Her arm soon followed. Something was aggravating her. Had he been wrong? Was she on drugs and needed the next fix? Maybe she had a trap waiting to be sprung.

'What else you got on there?' Duke questioned.

'Lots of stuff.'

'What sort of stuff?'

'Have a look.'

'What don't you just tell me?'

'I can't tell you.'

'Why is that?'

Her eyes went cold. Her hand reached up and scratched her bicep violently. She'd been resisting an itch. 'He will kill me if I tell you. Then kill you for finding out.'

'Who is *he*?' Duke asked.

'I–I can't tell you,' she whispered. 'He is too dangerous. He will kill us all.'

'Tell me who he is,' he demanded. 'I'm more capable than you realise.'

The woman shook her head. 'I can't. He will kill us.'

'I don't die easy,' Duke replied.

'He will kill you,' the woman whimpered.

'Try me.'

'No!' She screamed. Her shrill voice cut through the troop bay, echoing through the rest of the ship. She scratched at her arm again. 'I can't! I won't. No.'

Whoever this person was that she answered to, he be terrifying. What did he do to her to force her to react by scratching her arm? The fear in her eyes. The trembling of her jaw, the short and rapid breaths, shuddering as she breathed. Duke now knew that it wasn't him she was afraid of. It was the man who owned her. It hurt him to see her suffer that way. How many of the people that he had been despatched to detain, that fought back and had to be killed, were like her? How many should have had the chance to live? More depressing, how many more were out there waiting to be rescued from such a life? A life that he had taken with the squeeze of a trigger.

He took a deep breath then exhaled sharply. For Duke to have any success, he needed to prove why he could help her; why he could be trusted.

'From where I'm sitting, you can either talk or stay silent. Either way we have enough to detain you with what you have in your cargo hold, regardless of if you admit to what you're doing with it or not. You have a ship full of contraband that will land you in an orbital prison for an awfully long time. It doesn't end there. You evaded us back on Juntah and have managed to attack a member of my team when we boarded. That all says you're doing something illegal which not even the best defence can protect you from.'

'Why don't you just take me to prison then?' she asked.

'Because I honestly want to help you' he answered. 'I could send you to prison but your boss will just recruit someone else, and the cycle begins again with someone else losing their future. Someone else being imprisoned in this life, doing these smuggling runs, taking the flak so that someone else can gain power and stay free. I need to know who you work for and what you're doing with your cargo. From there not only can we apprehend your boss, but we can get rid of the buyer at the same time. Stop both ends of the cycle. The supply and the demand. You tell me that and you have my word that I will help you. I'll be able to vouch for you, reduce your sentence, or even help you avoid going to prison altogether.'

'Screw you,' she spat. 'I know what you damn Centies are like. If I tell you anything you find useful, you'll just fuck me over.'

Duke sighed. 'I want to help you. I really do. If I must, I will bargain. But be nice.'

'You won't bargain. You'll just lie.'

'You have my word,' Duke said, holding his hand up in an oath style gesture.

'What are you going to do then to prove that I can trust you, puya?' she snarled.

The woman was listening and clearly open to the idea of bargaining information. That was as good a start as any he could have hoped for. He had to be selective with his words now he had a chance. And find the right place to strike a bargain with.

'Without knowing much else for certain, the best I can promise is that you will not be alone,' he explained. 'I will be there, by your side, to see the fairest and best result from your trial when this is all over and offer you protection until then.'

'You need to do better than that,' the woman insisted.

Duke sighed. What could he offer her that she really wanted? Something that would earn her trust. Who was she? She scratched her arm again. There was a tattoo on her right hand – a metallic circle with a flaming dagger through it. A long-lasting branding to show that she was property, that the person she was scared of also owned her. The tattoo was small, probably smaller than it should have been. She must have been taken at a young age. Failed by the United Planetary Nations as a child. What would someone like that want? What would give someone abandoned, imprisoned and probably abused faith in him? She continued to scratch her arm. It was not a natural itch. Something was causing that reaction. What was under her sleeve? She was a smuggler under ownership, travelling alone with all that contraband. Goods that carried a hefty value on the illegal market. She'd been tagged.

He smacked his lips as he thought carefully. 'To fix everything that's already happened to you, there is absolutely nothing I can offer you. Nothing. As much as I'd like to take any pain back I can't. I can offer you though a chance to get out. That and I will be able to have that thing taken out of your arm you keep scratching at.'

For an eternity she did not move. Not a flinch. Not even a blink. She sat there staring at him.

'How… How do you know?' she soon asked.

'I've seen a lot of people like you; one person I know who's been through it is on this ship,' he said. 'There are a lot of people out there that do what you do, and worse still, some of those do it voluntarily. Those that are like you… I've seen die. They've either been blown to pieces, or I've had to kill them. Before they could be given a chance to survive. I was never fast enough to notice the signs, to make the connections and save them. Let me save you when I get you back to base.'

The woman breathed sharply through her teeth. 'If you're lying to me, I will ruin you before my master gets the chance to. I promise I will sell you out. Ask your questions.'

'Understood,' he said with a smile. 'Thank you. I guess I'll start with the easy one. What's your name? I don't like talking to someone without a name. I'm Duke. You can call me Duke.'

'Jesa,' she answered. 'The name's Jesa.'

'Jesa what?' he asked.

'I don't remember,' Jesa replied. 'It's just been Jesa for as long as I can remember.'

She *was* taken as a child. There were no limits to some people out in the galaxy. What else had she lost to those people? It never failed to chill Duke to the core to think about the potential answers.

'Okay, Jesa, what can you tell me about your owner?'

'He's dangerous, he owns an army... he has an armada of smuggler ships, gunships and probably has something bigger somewhere.'

'A name?' Duke requested.

'Barbaros Indalle,' Jesa said. 'He is the man in charge of the Ayuindi Syndicate. They pretty much run the outer systems.'

'What do they run? Apart from smuggling illegal cargo, weapons and that sort of thing?'

Jesa took a deep breath, readying herself for a list, then spoke slowly, 'They do weapons trade, some people trade, hustling, gambling... extortion. Hit settlers, money heists...'

'All the dirty jobs,' Duke surmised. 'Sounds like a really good guy.'

'Far from it,' Jesa whimpered, her voice shaking. 'He... has a way to make the people he owns do things for him and when they get caught, they're too scared to rat him out.'

'Like using the tag?'

She nodded. Her eyes watered as she fought back tears while glancing around rapidly, trying to find an apparition of her owner.

'He's going to kill me,' Jesa sobbed.

Duke placed his head into the palm of his hand as he tried to process the fear the man, Barbaros, inflicted on her. It hurt him to see her like that. To be so vulnerable, even though she was safe. How could anyone live like that? That though meant he was the sort of person to always know where his possessions were. At all times. 'Jesa, he won't touch

145

you again. Okay? What about keeping tabs on the things he owns? He has the way to keep you in line so that you're afraid of him. But how the hell does he know where you are? For all he knows, you could be pissing off to sell the loot and keep the money for yourself.'

Her face flushed red with embarrassment. She started looking around, unable to look him in the eye.

'Jesa?' he said. 'I need to know because if he has a way to track you, then he knows where me and my crew are too, and I will not risk their lives unless I have to. Please help me keep them, and you, safe.'

'He has tracking systems in every single ship, shuttle and truck he owns,' she whispered cautiously. 'But the pilots never see them installed. The people that install them... We rarely ever hear about. Don't know if he kills them when they're done or if they never leave the base and just do that all day.'

'You can't tell me where to find it? Just that it's there?'

'I'm sorry,' she answered quietly. 'It's the way he does things, yah?'

'What else can you tell me?' Duke asked.

'No more. Not today. I can't. I still don't know that I can trust you.'

'Last words?' he asked her.

'For now,' she said. 'Find that tracker. Let me know I'm safe then I'll think about sharing more with you.'

'Okay, I'll arrange for you to be returned to your room,' Duke said. 'Thank you.'

He left Jesa in peace. His soldiers had all been listening in from the briefing room. They looked at him patiently waiting for Duke to speak first as he entered.

'What are her portions at?' he asked them.

'We're feeding her approximately eight hundred cals a meal,' Arche answered. 'Why?'

'Up it to a thousand,' he instructed. 'She's cooperated this far. Get her back to a normal weight. Okay?'

Joane Arche nodded curtly, 'Understood.'

'What are we doing about the intel she gave?' Abe asked. 'Should we flag it to command?'

Duke hummed thoughtfully in response. What were they to do with the intel? Where should they even start? She had supplied a few things to go on, most of which would have to wait until they got back to base where they had access to the right equipment before they could act on it.

146

'We're not going to report it until we have some certainty that what she's said is true. As much as I want to believe her, she might be telling us what we want to hear. No. First things first,' he said. 'Corporal Moasa, I need you to… Corporal? Are you okay?'

Ronan shook his head as he realised where he was after staring thoughtfully into empty space. 'What'd you say?'

'What's up?' Duke asked.

'That name she gave… It sounds familiar,' Ronan Moasa explained. 'I don't know why.'

'Have a think on it, okay?' Duke asked. 'If you know anything about them, I want to know. In the meantime, I need you to search that ship of hers. Find that beacon and disable it. I don't care how much you rip out. Just get it found.'

'Consider it done,' his soldier replied.

Ronan jumped out of his seat and left the briefing room. Duke expected nothing less, given the gravity of the potential situation if the tracker was not located. Even though Corporal Moasa would love the fight, he knew that there would be no fight if gunships showed up and blasted them out of space.

'As for you two, I want to know everything there is to know about her owner,' Duke instructed. 'I need to know everything he's wanted for, who he's wanted by and anything that gives an idea of how dangerous he is.'

'What are you going to do?' Joane Arche asked, her tone suggestive of him not getting involved.

'I'm going to bring coffee through,' he answered with a smirk. 'Then I'm going to see what I can do to help.'

He activated the holo-table, input his permission authorisation codes to give them all the access to files as needed, then left to bring back three cups of coffee. Each of them, with coffee in hand, worked through the wealth of information that was readily available about Barbaros and his syndicate in the databanks. Yet for all the files that referenced either topic, they barely found anything to start with. Just news reports of crimes and deaths that the syndicate was suspected of committing and collections of eyewitness statements that gave barely any information. Nothing substantial enough to confidently state Barbaros was responsible could be found. It took them almost an hour before they managed to start uncovering the dark secrets Duke needed to know, none of which he was quite prepared to take in. He fought the temptation to turn away and stop reading.

Barbaros appeared to have gotten into the world of crime at a very young age. He was still just a teenager when he was first arrested for theft and assault; he nearly killed a guy who wasn't exactly a pushover. Over the next few years, before he was even an adult, he was arrested a further eight times for increasingly violent crimes. Barbaros then disappeared for six years, locked up in a medium-security prison for severely beating several people in a fit of drunken rage single handed. Then after his release, the man became a notorious super-villain, seeming to roam just outside the reach of the law for an exceptionally long time. He started with a small crew who then took over several other gangs across his home system in the space of two years. Once he either removed all immediate threats or reduced their capabilities to being nothing more than petty street thugs he set his sights on controlling huge swathes of space covering a couple dozen solar systems. With such a huge space to work from for his expansive enterprise, his influence was suddenly felt in the central colonies, his dominance even reaching all the way to Earth herself.

A tingle ran down Duke's spine.

Barbaros' presence did not end there.

On the UPN Inter-Planetary Police Commission's most wanted, he and his syndicate were ranked number nine. The only gang to make the list in its entirety since the inception of the chart. The man was hunted by military police, militia's, bounty hunters and the IPPC's top division, the Investigation of Serious Criminal Activities unit. None of whom had any success apprehending him. Barbaros' syndicate had killed thousands of people over the years, a substantial number of which he took personal claim to. Men, women, children. It didn't matter. All were targets. They had taken hundreds of thousands, potentially millions, of hostages to receive rapid sums of money quickly. Jesa wasn't the only one that had been branded to show them as property. There were thousands of smugglers, drug runners and hit men that had been forced to work for him through tags being implanted into them. Extortion, theft, smuggling, drugs and various other activities increased his reputation amongst the authorities. In the outer colonies, the UPN was not too welcome. They were not able to put their forces there without facing repercussions. Even if it was for the benefit of all. So, Earth had placed a reward for his capture. An even greater reward for his head. As disgusting as his crimes were, his mugshots showed someone with an even more disturbing glare in his eyes. The bloodlust of being wronged lingered in eyes set in a large face, topped with a short mohawk.

The shiver chilling his spine grew in intensity. A series of images flashed in the back of his mind from his time in SETS. All the worst, most malicious military regimes, terrorist groups and militias had nothing compared to this man.

Then Duke read statements made by defectors. Traitors to the syndicate. They were fearful to the point of paranoia, in a constant state of looking over their shoulders. Many were hunted for days and weeks on end through the planets, tortured with ferocity and murdered with methodical precision not long after their statements were made. Those that survived quickly retracted their comments, claiming they had taken too many drugs prior to make their words worthless. Or they would announce that they had made a terrible mistake.

A man that was, through provable reputation, to be feared. Duke's heart really did reach out for the victims of this man's dangerous drive. Jesa was, for all her reluctance to help, a victim too. She did not want to help Barbaros but was in a position where she had no choice but to do so. She could not be held complicit in a man's crimes that she did not want to be involved with. That would help his case to defend her when they got back to base.

The hours went by. Coffee had to be resupplied on numerous occasions. They had even forgotten about their appetites. They only stopped their research when Ronan walked into the briefing room and dumped a small box with a crystal blue centre, torn wires and all, onto the holo-table.

'I need a fucking drink after that,' Corporal Moasa announced.

'Well done,' Duke said with a smile. 'Guess it wasn't easy?'

'Easy?' he scoffed. 'I've had to lift so many panels and flooring covers... Fucking thing is a death trap. It's a few jumps away from falling apart. All that jumping around she did could've killed her. But this was tucked away under a pile of wires and pipes. Missed it like ten times. They did a good job hiding it. I can safely say that we ain't being tracked any more though. How's your book club going?'

Duke laughed. 'I wish I didn't read most of this. Let's just accept that it's a good job this guy isn't tracking us anymore.'

'That bad?' Ronan asked.

'That horrible,' Duke corrected.

'Nothing I can't handle,' Corporal Moasa stated. Itching for the fight.

Duke Horren shook his head. 'I wouldn't be so sure.'

He trailed off. Only the four of them for the next few months would be even remotely aware of Barbaros Indialle's crimes. And what hope did Jesa have after his retirement? Any promises General Baalshuk made upon his return would not be guaranteed to last. Was now the time to retire? Duke couldn't just leave like that and expect her to fend for herself.

'You okay Sergeant?' Abe questioned.

'Fine, I'm fine,' Duke answered lightly while scratching his head. 'Let's call it a day. We'll carry on with more theory tomorrow. Take Jesa back to her room. After that, it's your time.'

He turned off the holographic table and ushered his soldiers out of the briefing room. When they left, he slouched back into his chair. The thoughts rushing round his mind were overwhelming. It did not take much effort to work out that now the tracker was removed, Barbaros would have people at every port looking out for Jesa and her ship. If that failed, the thug would most likely have all the information from the numerous sources in his possession around the galaxy to know that the SPF had her. That put every soldier with the UPN in the line of fire if she was special to him. The numerous star systems he was known to have a presence in. The countless more that he could operate within. Anyone operating in the outer sectors was at risk.

Duke's head started to throb with pain as he tried to grasp the concept of just how vast this man's reach was. Duke finally left the briefing room and took his place up on the flight deck with Ivan. Valentina was asleep in her cabin she shared with Joane until her next shift. This time there was no coffee waiting for him. Instead, a cup of vodka was handed over.

'Figured you needed that more than that brown muck,' Zenkovich said pleasantly.

He took a sip, breathed in sharply at the strong bite of the alcohol, then replied, 'I do. More than you can believe. Thanks, Zen.'

Ivan laughed, drank his own vodka, and leaned back in his chair. He sighed, muttered something in an odd Russo-Sino combination, then spoke, 'What are we doing then? Are we calling it? Am I plotting course home yet?'

'No, not yet.'

The helmsman made a strange throaty sound. 'Oh? Why not?'

'I need to find out what's happened to her,' Duke answered.

Ivan turned around; his eyes fixated on him. 'What's this about? Thought you were retiring?'

'I was, I am,' he said hesitantly before releasing the weight of the universe through a heavy sigh. 'Fuck. I don't know now is the honest answer.'

'Talk to me.'

Though he had not spoken to the pilot much, Duke quickly realised that the man was far wiser than he should have been. He quickly looked around to make sure there was no one behind them. He did not need anyone else to hear him.

'I used to be in the Tactical First Strikers,' he explained.

'Shit, for real? You were a Slayer?'

Slayers. The nickname given by all in the military, regardless of branch, for the Space Marines Special Forces. They went into places before the main marine forces arrived to take the glory. As such, they would eliminate more enemy forces in the first few hours than any other unit. And take the heaviest losses.

'Yeah, I was in the TFS,' Duke said. 'But when I was there, I'd put away a lot of people like the guy that owns her. I killed a lot more that were fighting for their cause. How many of them though were like her? Now that we have her in our custody, I feel like I need to do something about it. You remember that event, a few years back? The Portik Tragedy?'

'I remember,' Ivan nodded.

'I led that mission,' Duke admitted reluctantly. 'Slaughtered so many that day. I didn't even think about it until the shooting stopped. When it did stop, that's when I learnt how many of them weren't adults... how many of them were kids. Then the tags went off. I don't know how many got left behind to die. My first thought was to get my team out of there. I've had that hanging over me since.'

Ivan Zenkovich chuckled then stared at him with a smile. 'Salvation.'

'What?'

'Salvation. She's your salvation to correct your past.'

'Didn't take you to be the religious sort.'

'Didn't take you to be the sentimental sort. Either way, if you feel this strong about it, I say stay and see it through. You will only hate yourself if you don't.'

Duke hummed thoughtfully. He finished his cup of vodka and held it out for a top up. He needed to continue to talk things through. Make sense of it all.

Beatrice Lenoia

It would be just another few hours until they left the jump. They were almost at their next destination but needed to drop into real space for a final time to give people a chance to rest and enjoy the view before the final leg of this part of the voyage.

Beatrice leaned back into her chair. The last few days in the jump had been torturous. She had finally received word from the security personnel's superior before entering slip space, and it was not what she wanted to hear. Beatrice, and her crew, was not allowed to know what was being transported. The message advised she was only allowed to know that it was imperative that the goods reached Earth in perfect condition and that they were to supply whatever was required by the team upon their request. Other than that, she was to have no interaction with them. Adding to her frustration, Allua Jons failed to work out what was going on in the cargo hold controlled by the security team. They had every possible entry point covered and were prompt to respond to every attempt to get close.

To take her mind off the negative she had slightly adjusted their route. There was a pulsar star – a spectacle that few people would ever see. It was extremely fortunate that they were within range of it to make the deviation worthwhile. Had she not instructed the *Galactic Passage* into the jump when she did, they would never have had this opportunity. Because of the nature of the star, she had run the system diagnostics several times to make sure their shielding could withstand the effects of the radiation. They would be able to survive a short stay there before the drain on the shields proved to be too much.

She groaned and glanced at the digital clock projected onto the wall. EST was three-thirteen in the afternoon. Beatrice needed a break. The repeated fourteen-hour shifts, along with the endless additional hours spent overthinking, had finally caught up to her. She had earned a break. Franklin Hender would be able to handle the ship for a few hours without her.

Beatrice made the handover, left the bridge in his capable hands, and strolled down to the entertainment hall on deck D-a for the afternoon entertainment. Deck D was a large deck in itself, twice the height of a standard deck. As such, there was a second level within it, housing arcades, fun houses, family events, movie theatres and an entertainment hall. It was the entertainment hall she intended to go to. There was a show on with a specific performance that she liked, a type of comedy-musical duo, performed by a couple. The husband a singer, the wife a comedian. They were a regular occurrence on her voyages and a must have that she personally requested be a part of the trip before they departed. This was their first performance that she was able to get away from the constant stream of work to see.

Beatrice steered away from her usual, healthy, option and ordered a burger and fries with a beer. While she was off duty, she was going to enjoy herself for those few hours. Most likely she would head back to her cabin halfway through the afternoon to rest but for now, she would have fun. The food and drink would nicely kickstart her time to relax.

When the opening act started, she hardly paid attention. It was a group of performers interacting with the audience. They carried out games and little competitions handing out prizes from small gifts to trips up to the bridge to see how the ship is run. The first half of experience went well, and the crowd was enthralled with the entertainment. After eating, she tried to relax. Beatrice watched the show but couldn't enjoy it. Something niggled in the back of her mind. There was only so much she could take of only half enjoying the performance before she gave in.

She set up her comm-pad and started to work through the numerous reports that had been submitted, analysing the stock checks, power consumption and the vast swathes of documents and messages received prior to entering the jump. She signed off everything that she was happy with, returned everything else she was not happy allowing to happen and then responded to several messages. Her replies would send out once they dropped out of the jump. Until then, they would sit waiting to send. The power consumption though was of significant concern. The room that the security team occupied was absorbing three times more power than her bridge took when operating at maximum capacity then it jumped up to five times capacity several days ago. She desperately needed to know what was going on in there.

Yet, the information she read was always the same. Never changing. No way to see any new details that would prove something was going on. And, until the occupants were doing something illegal, there wasn't anything else she could do to ease her suspicions. She reached out to some old colleagues back in the navy. Specifically, the Naval Intelligence Division, and gave them the name Foresc. Sure enough, they had replied.

The man was an enigma, almost a ghost. There was plenty about his life before the military and during the academy. But from day one after his graduation, everything had been redacted. She could see years, mission names and sentences that, when read out of context, were either ambiguous or made no sense at all. But they all said the same thing to her – to stay on her guard with him. He was dangerous. Assuring her that low-level operatives, even mid-level, had more available to see on their files than he did. But he was still UPN. She wanted him off her ship, but they were on the same side.

Beatrice had no idea what to do.

Her head started to ache from overthinking, and her eyes stung with the strain of looking at a screen in dim lights. If she carried on like this, she would burn herself out. Beatrice tore herself away from the work and looked around the room.

Large swathes of people entered the hall and equal numbers left. Families. Couples. All different ages. Everyone after a good time, most only arriving for the main act, which was a showstopper. The jokes were nothing short of genius, and the music equally captivating. Their laughter was infectious, and she lost herself in how relatable it all was. Tears came to her eyes when she wished her dearest Earnest were with her to watch them. His humour was dry, callous, and highly inappropriate but he would have enjoyed this display.

A break in the performance was brought to her attention as the lights dimmed a fraction before shining bright again. Bright enough to light the way to the bar. Beatrice looked down at her beer bottle then to her comm-pad and back to her empty bottle. They still had more than an hour until they dropped out of the jump. She could spare the time for another drink. She had earned it after all.

The officer pushed herself away from the table then paused before she stood up. The hairs on the back of her neck started to prick up. An uneasy feeling loomed around her. It was the same feeling she got back in the field when a hostile had locked eyes on her from a hidden position. She instinctively moved her hand to her side where a pistol would have once been. Her heart raced, her eyes constantly shifting without moving her body trying to find the source of the uncomfortable sensation. She was exposed. Tensed up for the impending attack which never came. The feeling passed. Whatever had triggered the sensation was no longer there.

She rotated in her seat. Amongst the commotion of people making their way to either the bar or the rest rooms, there was no way Beatrice could spot whoever had her back up. She decided it was best to end her personal time so she could report back to the bridge where she would be able to relax and feel safe. That second drink would have to wait.

Beatrice was out of breath by the time she reached the bridge. Beer, junk food and a fast-walking pace were not the best combination. Her crew all looked at her, surprised. It was a fair enough reaction – she was meant to be having a good time for another hour or two.

She sat down at her command chair and pulled up the security footage from the entertainment hall, trawling through it until she could see herself eating. Hender tried to see what she was doing, and when she did not respond he wisely opted to leave her alone. She watched the footage several times from numerous camera angels and hit pause when she found him. Foresc! He had been so close, barely three feet behind her, looking right over her shoulder. His right hand reached to his waist for what looked like a pistol. Maybe a knife. It was difficult to tell what the metallic object he reached for was. Maybe it was a moment of weakness. Possibly it was the alcohol. No one would be so mindless to make a move like that in plain sight of spectators, yet she couldn't see the logic. Her heart pounded with fear.

'Captain?' Hender said calmly, insisting she told him what was wrong without saying a thing.

'He was going to kill me,' she whispered. 'He was right there. Right there! And I had no idea he was that close. I could tell he was there but… but… He could have done it.'

'Let me have a look here,' Franklin said, leaning into the projection. 'That wasn't a weapon he went for. See here. No, he was reaching for… I don't know what that is. A comm-pad?'

How could she have been so quick to panic? Foresc wasn't reaching for a weapon to do her harm with. It was a comm-pad. No, it was a tac-pad. How would members of the MID escorting the packages to Earth have that sort of equipment? It was just another question that she would never have an answer to.

'I'm sorry,' she whispered. 'But he could have been reaching for a weapon!'

Her adjutant gripped her arm firmly silently reminding her that he was there, and that she was not alone. 'I can see. He didn't though. Did he? And he didn't attempt to hurt you. You're still here.'

'I know.'

'And you're back here now. You're safe. We're all here for you.'

She looked up and smiled at him. 'Thank you.'

'It's okay,' Hender said. 'I'll arrange for double shifts on security. Make sure people get checked at all main venues and before they move up the elevators. I'll even add extra security for the bridge. We won't risk anything happening. Now, let's try and figure out what this guy saw that made him reach for his pad. Then we can work out what to do next.'

It was a good plan. She racked her mind for what she had looked at, fighting through the worry, anxiety and concern that came with having been in such danger, and the only work she had open that would be of interest was the power consumption being astronomically high for a standard cargo hold and the information she had received from her old colleagues in the navy. Considering most of the man's files were redacted, that meant it had to be something to do with the power levels. Beatrice couldn't see the importance of that. How did the high-power consumption and the fridges force the man to reach for his tac-pad? What Beatrice knew was that the sustained abnormal usage would ultimately result in something bad happening to her ship. What that would be wasn't something she could explain. She needed someone who knew how machines worked better than she did.

'Get me Allua Jons,' she instructed. 'I need her here as quickly as possible.'

Hender nodded and after making the call Jons arrived in rapid time, still covered in grease from whatever she had been working on. The expression on her face said that she had not quite finished the job and needed to go back to complete it.

'You called for me, Captain?' she said, controlling the annoyance in her tone.

'I need you to advise me on this,' Beatrice explained, pointing at the hologram. 'I need to know what could drain that much power and what the consequences will be on the ship.'

'Do you know what they have in the room?' Allua asked after a few minutes' analysis.

'These,' she answered, pulling up on a separate projection the footage of the security team boarding her ship with the massive crates that had thin beams of blue light trying to escape at the seams. 'I've no idea what these are though. They say they are fridges to keep a product cold. I don't know if I can believe that.'

Allua Jons took a closer inspection of the objects, analysing every angle of them. Much akin to a shark circling potential prey trying to work out if it is food or not. The engineer cocked her head to one side.

'There's not much that size that needs to take in that much electricity,' she explained. 'A standard fridge? I'm calling bullshit on that. A collection of stasis pods would probably need this much electricity. What I'm looking at doesn't tie up.'

'What do you mean?' Beatrice questioned.

Beatrice had used stasis pods before on deployments. The navy pods were much bigger and bulkier than the objects brought onto the ship. She never understood the power required to run them; it was never a requirement to know. All that mattered was that they worked. But these didn't look like stasis pods.

'Stasis pods use a lot of power. A hell of a lot. And they're big. Bigger than these. See how many pods there are? They should need a hell of a lot more juju than what we're seeing being used here. I'll have to think about what else they could be. But fridges? Beggin' your pardon captain but that is grade-A bullshit. They are not standard fridges and they're not stasis pods; at least no pods that I've ever seen. Whatever they are isn't public knowledge.'

'Understood,' she muttered under her breath.

Beatrice remembered the consequences. How catastrophic it would be if the persistent power drain were allowed to continue.

'I've also been running the numbers. I have a concern,' Allua Jons said.

Beatrice looked up. 'What is it?'

'As it stands, life support is being tested,' Allua explained. 'This power drain from those *fridges* is really taking a toll on it. If that goes, I don't think I need to explain the knock-on effect.'

That she didn't. If life support went, it wiped out almost everything that was needed to keep her, her crew and her passengers alive. There would be no temperature control so things would either heat up or drop to lows that couldn't be survived. Artificial gravity would go. In itself, weightlessness didn't sound like a bad thing, but when people panicked accidents happened. That and when the artificial gravity returned, how many people would be low enough to survive impact? Or hovering away from objects to avoid being impaled? Then there was the all-important airflow. There would be no fresh, recycled oxygen to breathe. People would start to suffocate not long after the systems shut off. They couldn't lose it.

'Can you, or your best engineer, go check life support?' she requested. 'I want to make sure that it's not being overloaded. Do whatever you can to make sure it stays functional.'

158

'I'll go,' the engineer said. 'If there's anything we need to be worried about I'll find it. I will report in once I've completed the checks.'

'Thank you.'

When Allua Jons left the bridge, Beatrice resumed inspecting the systems and reports until the *Galactic Passage* dropped out of the jump to return to real space. Ahead of them was the pulsar star. She gave the announcement for the passengers to gather at the viewing decks to see the celestial object. At first it was nothing more than a dim blip in the distance. Over the following hours the spec grew until the orb was in full view. Initially, it did not seem too exciting, just another celestial object. But when she polarised the windows and changed the spectrum settings, the dull star suddenly switched into a wild and vivid star in constant activity. The wide range of colours showing the various types of radiation being emitted created a beautiful entity.

After about a half hour of enjoying the scene, a warning flashed in front of her conveying an overly concerning message. Radiation was hitting them. And lots of it. Enough to cause some concern for their safety if they stayed there too long. She instructed Laurenne Vellai to keep an eye on it while she opened a communication with the chief engineer.

'How are the checks going?' she asked.

'Slowly,' Jons advised. 'But so far, I've found a few things I need to get swapped out as soon as possible that have already been fried, preferably when we're out of the radiation zone of the pulsar. Can't believe things haven't gone bad already with how messed up things are. Give me another two or three hours and I'll have the full report for you.'

'You haven't got that long, sorry,' Lucy Mills stated abruptly from the life support station. Her face flushed red with embarrassment knowing she had just spoken out of turn.

'Report,' Beatrice Lenoia instructed sharply.

'Shielding is already at sixty percent efficiency and dropping fast, Captain,' the life support officer explained. 'Whatever's taking the power down in the cargo hold is diverting power directly away from the rear shields to maintain nearby systems. Power is being re-routed from the forward shields to boost them up a bit.'

'How long have we got?' Beatrice questioned.

Mills turned to face her terminal and checked the numbers, then double checked them, before answering, 'We have two hours tops until the shields fail entirely, Captain. If we want to make a jump, we have less than an hour to decide. After that we had best hope we're on our way out so we can charge up the drive.'

'Chief, are you hearing that?' Beatrice asked over the comms.

'Unfortunately, I am!' the engineer called back. 'I say get us out of here and do it quick. I'll make whatever repairs I can make while we're in the jump then finish them off when in real space. If that security team has compromised us, we need to get un-compromised.'

'Agreed,' Beatrice said. 'Franklin, get us out of here. Sound the alarm. Departure in thirty minutes. Should be enough notice for people to get ready.'

'Where to, Captain?' her adjutant asked.

'It doesn't matter where,' she stated. 'Plot random coordinates. Emergency protocol. Save any more questions for later. Just get us to safety.'

'Aye, Captain,' Hender replied.

Her adjutant went to work coordinating with the bridge crew and security team. Together they ensured that all the passengers were safely secured in their cabins in preparation for the jump. All she could do in that time was wait and hope for the best. Everyone else had the situation under control. Or at least she thought they did. The panicked commotion of updates from key crew repeating information spouted not long ago was poor stress management –all signs of civilian training. Military training was more stringent. It taught people how to accept they were afraid and to see past it so they could make rational decisions. Then again, there was never a reason for civilian crew to have that level of training.

In the fleeting moment that her eyes shut to blink, she was back on her old ship. They were part of an armada despatched to quell an uprising out on the edger of the Mid-Colonies that threatened to disrupt UPN control in that sector. Apart from structured updates, she could only hear people breathing and typing instructions into their terminals on the bridge or relaying messages to the shipmates throughout the vessel and making those instructions once. Anything that was outside their primary duties was not of their concern. Not even the battle going on around them outside could distract them from their duties. Her heart seized up for a moment. It was such an age ago and that mentality still existed within her. Her heart started to beat again as she opened her eyes and demanded silence on the bridge. The order she gave was clear. Only speak when it was essential.

They entered the jump.

The sudden rush of power from a short charged jump overloaded several circuits. Fortunately, most of the systems held up. Those that didn't hold popped and sent showers of sparks raining down on everyone around. Occasionally discharging sudden bolts of electricity. Bridge crew rushed to tackle the electrical fires that started to rage, dousing the areas to subdue the blazes. There were reports of similar incidents throughout the ship but somehow no-one was injured. Only shaken up. They would live.

Outside was a mess. Instead of the beautiful swirl of distant stars and space being warped as they traversed the jump there was a fiery thunderstorm that shrouded the ship. Like a portal leading straight to the bottom of a flaming pit. Terrifying did not begin to explain it. She'd never seen anything like it. Nor did she ever want to see one again.

'What destination have you plotted?' Beatrice asked.

'Random. Unknown. As you instructed.' Adjutant Franklin Hender answered. 'But we will be exiting from the jump in approximately five minutes.'

'Understood,' she said. Beatrice re-opened the comms link with Allua. 'Chief, be ready with the damage report for me. I don't think this is going to end well.'

'Don't worry, I'm ready for it,' the engineer answered. 'We just put out the fires down here.'

'I don't think you are,' Beatrice whispered after she ended the comms.

All they had to do was survive the exit. That was it. Beatrice kept trying to focus herself on that to take her mind off the chances that if their systems could not handle entering slip space, chances were that they would fail on the exit.

She crossed her fingers and waited. Hoped. Prayed even.

'Please…' she muttered under her breath.

Leyton Foresc

The rough exit from the jump was far from enjoyable. Leyton already felt like he could have thrown up because of the smell coming from the wolves' den. Extreme forces pushing down on him threatened to make that feeling a reality had he not snapped a peppermint sniff, supplied to help suppress feelings of nausea. The shock of the exit even hushed the constant cooing from the wolves for a short while.

Once stability had returned to the ship, he and his remaining agents present in the cargo hold sprang into action. The lights had dimmed, sparks flying out in massive arcs from the electrical connections and electrical discharges flashed as the ship's circuitry overloaded from re-entry. While patching up the damage and putting out fires, he kept an eye firmly on the light on the door controls to the cage to make sure they still showed it was locked. If that cut out the two protective mothers would rush out to keep their litters safe. His team remained as calm as they could, though there was panic in their actions, each one expecting the worst to happen. None more so than the professor who, once he had finished throwing up all his meals for the last twelve hours, screamed in desperation for the wolves over his own life. It took them several attempts at following Schottler's instructions to make the room safe once more. Leyton checked the door controls again. The light was still on, confirming the cage remained locked. At least that was a success.

'What the hell happened?' Jerome asked.

'We've dropped into real space,' Leyton answered, assessing the minor burns their equipment had sustained. 'The shields must have been pretty depleted to do this.'

'How would the shields get this depleted?' Schottler asked.

He looked around the room and hung his head with shame for having not thought of it before. 'Us. We must have drained too much from their systems to power all of this. Fuck. If they were already suspicious of us before, then this is not going to end well. Jerome, find out where the hell we've ended up.'

'On it,' his second in command said. 'I'll triangulate with any nearby sites.'

'Okay. Schottler, get hold of everyone that's on patrol,' Leyton instructed. 'Bring them back.'

'Yes boss,' Agent Schottler said.

With the two agents carrying out his instructions, Leyton checked the surveillance feed Schottler had set up for them to oversee the pups that had been born several days earlier. They had grown a lot in that time, already twice as big as they had been at birth. Their features were already more defined, more ice-wolf-like. Professor Ainslot couldn't understand how. The academic thought that they should have taken weeks, if not months, to get to that stage. Not days. As expected, Professor Ainslot worked tirelessly to understand their development process.

The matriarch had given birth to seven pups. The second female, Crest, had produced five. Another twelve wolves. From a security point of view, this was going to be a nightmare. Fourteen organisms awake for the rest of their journey. Already it was proving difficult to keep their food and water supply going and to clear their den from excrement meant using valuable tranquillisers to ensure the process was safe.

The pups were all suckling or fighting for somewhere to suckle. Their mothers continued to coo and lick them as they did at birth. A delicate touch. This side of them was not the lethal creatures capable of killing a man with ease that he had encountered on their home planet. They were almost peaceful. There had been plenty of times when he had encountered something that looked peaceful. A woman with a young child. A villager. A family pet. Almost just as many times they turned out to be more dangerous than their looks suggested. Only once was he caught out by something that appeared innocent. His first op when he was a rookie to the world of the MID. It was a simple assignment to retrieve an informant from a hostile base. A man pretending to be disabled led him to believe he didn't need to restrain him. Leyton was very wrong that day. Lucky for him, his field lead was not so easily fooled and saved him. Leyton's vow to not drop his guard was extended around the wolves.

'Professor, how're the new-borns?' Leyton Foresc asked, unable to tear his eyes from the monitor.

'They're well,' Professor Ainslot replied weakly, injured from the drop out of slip space. He analysed some data on his comm-pad. Leyton could not understand any of it. 'Thankfully that exit didn't disrupt the power to the pods or the cage, it Just gave me a headache. Aside from that, they're developing quite rapidly. I think in a matter of weeks they'll be large enough to start eating solid foods. Once they can do that, they'll be useful to the pack and could potentially go on hunts with them not long after that even if just to learn how. Makes sense that they would. They only need the strongest to be able to survive.'

'Survival of the fittest,' Leyton whispered.

'Exactly!' Samuel made no effort to hide his excitement. 'But if you look at the females. You can already see that they know which ones are most likely to survive in the wild. Their attention is mainly on the larger members of their litter. The ones taking the attention of their mothers. They're the ones most likely to be fed. The runts are almost entirely overlooked.'

'What does that mean for us?'

Professor Ainslot sighed. 'It means we can see how underdeveloped they are, I guess. We can sort of assess the minimum amount of food required for a pup to develop into a healthy adult. I'll need to keep an eye on them though. In the wild the runts would die naturally as food became scarce. I don't know how much that would change things. The ones that should die the parents might even kill off and eat them to thin out the weak. Oh, and that's not all of it!'

'More news?' Leyton asked.

'The other two senior females?' the scientist started, pausing for theatrics like it was required. 'They're also pregnant. They're not that far behind in their gestation. They must have mated a couple weeks after Spike and Crest. Scans suggest we could see another fourteen pups, roughly. With this equipment I can't give anything more specific yet, but we'll have a minimum of another ten, eleven pups.'

The excitement to see the birthing process all over again, with more opportunity for success, was clear in his tone. Leyton could feel the anticipation for further research hanging thick in the atmosphere. The professor rushed his speech with the urgency of someone unable to contain their excitement and was not holding still for longer than a few seconds.

'How long until we have to thaw them out?' Leyton asked the scientist.

'Don't want to leave them in longer than another few weeks. I'll prep the sedation kits closer to the time so we can safely put them in the crate.'

'Good. Keep it up and you know the drill. Let me know if anything else changes,' Leyton instructed. 'If you need a break to get your energy, take it. You've earned it.'

'I will.'

Leyton turned on the spot, taking his time to take in everything he had learnt, before heading over to Jerome. A quick count said that they had another six dozen tranq darts available to use. What should have lasted easily in excess of the time taken to get to Earth would now have to be halved. Did they even have the resources to get back with all the wolves in one piece? Leyton needed to change his methods and even changing the layout of the den so that they didn't need to waste darts needlessly to keep the wolves alive.

'Is the team on the way back?' he asked Jerome.

His second in command was with Schottler at their command station. They were looking at the monitors with intent. Some showed security footage. Others, a map of the local space.

'They shouldn't be too long,' Jerome replied. 'And I got our location, pinged it off a few of our bases. We're about seven sectors away from the nearest outpost., in an unchartered zone. All our facilities are in the same direction.'

'Good work, send the coordinates to my pad. I'm going to try update the boss,' Leyton said.

'Do you want me to come with you on this one?' Jerome asked. 'I heard the professor talk about a couple of the others being pregnant too. With everything going on, it might be worthwhile having a second voice in case you miss something. You don't want to leave out any details for the boss.'

The hairs on the back of Leyton's neck pricked up. It was not normal for his subordinate to even suggest something like that. At least not so overtly. There was something going on that Jerome Houghton hoped to keep quiet. Most probably was trying to weigh in and prove he was more capable to the administrator.

'Over here,' Leyton snapped. He took his friend to one side and made sure Jerome was backed up against the wall. When Leyton spoke, his words were short, controlled yet still reverberated with anger. 'What the hell is up with you?'

'Nothing,' Jerome replied sharply.

His friend tried to hedge out of the way. Leyton refused to let him, an outstretched arm preventing that. A wrathful glare locked his eyes in place.

'Bullshit. Talk.'

Jerome hesitated then returned the glare back at him. 'I don't think you're cut out for the job anymore.'

'Come again? I don't think I heard you right.'

'You heard me just fine,' the agent insisted, trying to be more than he was. 'Your judgement isn't the same anymore. You said it yourself. You won't do what the boss says. The boss! He's the guy that the Supreme Speaker of the House of Representatives listens to. This is the guy you would shoot first, ask questions later for. And now you, what, think you can go against his orders because you don't feel like it?'

'I'm *prepared* to go against his orders if I need to,' Leyton corrected. 'I am not prepared to do whatever is necessary like he expects. This ship has civilians on board. Civilians. You know what that translates to? People that can't defend themselves. Whatever's necessary does not include them in my books. I signed up to protect them. Not kill them. If you think you can do a better job than me, then put it in writing when we get back. Until then, shift that chip off your shoulder and get back into line before I decide you're not cut out for this. Do I make myself clear?'

'Crystal,' Jerome scowled. 'Are we done?'

Leyton did not speak. He simply nodded and with a firm slap to the shoulder left his second in command alone. He returned to his communication room and initiated contact with the administrator.

'Agent,' the Englishman hissed softly. 'Good news I trust?'

'It is,' he answered. 'We have twelve pups. All in good condition and developing quickly.'

'That is good news,' the administrator replied. 'Very good indeed.'

'There's more, sir,' Leyton said. 'Professor Ainslot has advised me that the other two high ranking females are showing signs of pregnancy too and aren't that far from giving birth.'

'Another dozen pups,' his superior whispered with a strange hunger. 'That is certainly better news than I could have ever anticipated.'

'Yes, sir. However, I do have to make you aware of some bad news.'

Puppet Master did not answer straight away. He took his time. When he did speak, he did so with a cold absence of emotion. 'Speak.'

'I think the ship's captain is onto us,' he advised. 'She carried out an emergency jump that nearly ripped the thing apart because of the shield levels already being low. I think it's the stasis pods and cage that have drained too much power. Before the jump though, I did some recon and spied on her. She's obsessed with the energy consumption and has tried to find out anything about me. That's going to be her justification when escalating things.'

'Understood.' There was a moment of silence before the man spoke again. His words were slow. 'I don't care how you do it, but you must take control of that ship. I have done my research on the officer in charge.'

'So have I sir,' Leyton said. 'Her name is familiar.'

'She used to be a captain in the UPN Navy and led the attack to break the Siege of Vulcair. I can guarantee that she will not stop until she has you all off her ship. Take the initiative and take control.'

'There are civilians on the ship, sir,' Leyton stated. 'I can't put them at risk.'

'You will do as I say!' Administrator barked.

Before he could give any rebuttal and stand his ground, Jerome burst through the door and into the conversation. Jerome rushed over to Leyton. Judging by the expression on his subordinate's face, it was a charade. There was no hint of urgency in his eyes. No suggestion that he had even been earnestly in a rush. Leyton fought every urge to say something he'd regret.

'Jerome, what's the meaning of this?' Leyton demanded, trying to keep his anger under control.

'Boss,' Jerome said sharply. 'We have a situation. A group of engineers and ship security are on their way here. I think they're going to do their best to have a look in the cargo hold. I don't think they're in the mood for fun and games anymore.'

'Where is everyone?' he asked.

Puppet Master was demanded to know what was going on. Clearly upset that his instructions were being ignored. Leyton ignored him. His priority now was knowing about the situation at hand. Not listening to an overpaid Brit that sat on top of some self-made pedestal dictating who had the right to live or die as if he was some god.

'We got Tallow, Perretti and Suttle in the cargo hold,' Jerome answered. 'Fellstrum and Deulche are still somewhere on the upper decks making their way back to us.'

That could work in their favour, provided that everyone followed their instructions to the letter. He quickly formulated a plan then turned to his tac-pad and advised Administrator in brief before disconnecting the comms link. He pulled up a schematic of the ship for a quick glance over to confirm his thoughts. Jerome Houghton stared at him. A rage flickered in his eyes.

'Let's get back to control,' Leyton ordered. He anticipated Jerome to not be prepared to move without any answers to the questions clearly bothering him.

'Really? Just as easy as that?' Jerome laughed in disbelief. 'After what I've just heard? Not a chance. You'll want us to just use harsh words on their security. No. I'm taking charge on this before you start hugging the enemy and get us all killed.'

'Enemy? Who the fuck do you think you are to call them the enemy? We're not at war with the crew. It's their taxes that are paying your fucking salary. Paid for the research that went into that combat armour you're wearing. Put bullets in your weapon you're carrying. These are the people you lace up your boots to protect. They're not our enemy, whatever you think.'

'Tell them that when the shooting starts.'

Leyton hung his head and shook it slowly, holding his breath to keep in the brewing frustration. He then growled like a wild animal, 'I have no idea what's going on in that head of yours or where this attitude has come from. But here's some reality for you: you know every time we go out on deployment? Every time we put our necks on the line. It's to protect them! They don't have any idea what we're doing here and are taking it as hostile. I'd do the same if I were them.'

'That means we need to be more hostile to keep them in their place so we can complete our job,' Jerome countered. 'We're field agents. Not fucking pussies. We do all the missions the public is to never even know were happening, go places they've never heard of and fight enemy they don't know exist. I'm not letting them push me around. And while I'm at it, what the fuck was with the medical assessment? All those questions and the psyche eval? I don't know what you're getting at but I'm not having any of it.'

'No, you don't. We do this my way. Understand? As for the assessment, your health and wellbeing are my priority. So that evaluation is for me to have a better understanding of how this mission is affecting you. You've had it. It's been assessed and I will update the boss when we get back. Accept that it's what I wanted. Now stow your shit. I don't want another comment. I'll deal with you when we're done.' Leyton Foresc opened a comms link with the rest of the unit. 'Team, suit up. Combat armour. We've got company on the way. We're doing a meet and greet.'

He closed the comms and barged past his second-in-command, then led the way back to the cargo hold. Ray was at the control station, his mouth moving rapidly, most likely in conversation with his two field agents still deployed. Aside from Ainslot, his team had armed themselves for a firefight; all except Agent Suttle. The medic looked sheepish, like he did not want to be there. It wasn't like him to not want to get involved in a mission like that. He was a sort of moral compass for them.

'What's up?' Leyton asked him, keeping his voice low so no one else could hear. 'Why aren't you getting your gear together?'

'You know I'm on your side here but... these are civilians we're dealing with,' Agent Suttle said. 'I can't do it. I'm on this team as a medic.'

'And you're still a field agent,' Leyton stated.

Medic Suttle scoffed. 'I'm a medic first and foremost. I have the oath keep people alive. I'll fight and defend myself. I'll put down fucking monsters that threaten my safety if I must. But I won't kill civilians, I just won't. You can't tell me to.'

Leyton sighed. The sentiment was not only with him then. Dom also understood the fact that they were civilians. Not an enemy force.

'Suit up and follow my lead, okay?' he muttered. 'We'll be fine.'

'We won't,' the medic whispered. His eyes were fidgeting from left to right.

'What do you mean?'

Dom hesitated, took a shaky breath and spoke quietly. 'The psyche evals. I've been going over the results and something about them just doesn't add up. I feel like I'm missing something.'

'Okay, keep it to yourself for now and I'll catch up with you later. We can go over it together. Try and not think too much about it until then, got it? Only we are going to know about these results,' Leyton then turned his attention to the entire unit. 'Guys, as you already know, the ship's security team is on their way here with their engineers. We need to go scare them off. Schottler, you'll stay here with the professor. You're our eyes and ears. Everyone else is with me. We will only use non-lethal force unless it's necessary that we fight back. Keep it clean. We keep their attention on us while we're there so we can buy some time for Fellstrum and Deulche to get back. Are you all clear on that? Good. Let's go. Ray, tell us where we're headed.'

Following the instruction given by Agent Schottler, Leyton led his team through the corridors and up a few decks to meet the force of a dozen personnel head on. A man in security armour stood at the front of the group with a large shield the same size as himself attached to his left forearm and a stun baton wielded in his right hand. To his side was a woman with black hair and oiled up overalls wielding a hefty wrench and a tool bag.

'Have we got a problem here?' Leyton asked, holding his sub-machine gun to his side in a less hostile pose but keeping it on display to show that he was prepared to use it. With a twitch he could bring it to bear in and eliminate all immediate threats.

'You tell us,' the man stated. 'What's with the firepower?'

'Call it insurance,' Leyton answered. 'What's with the posse?'

The security guard smirked. 'Consider us bailiffs. We're in the middle a problem with the ship and the only place that is causing us issues is the cargo hold you guys have been living in. We need to get in there, now, to fix the problem to make sure we all get home safely.'

'Problem?' Leyton asked casually. He hoped his face looked as calm as his voice. 'We haven't had a problem. Think you must have a faulty wire or something somewhere telling you it's us.'

'Funny, smart-ass,' the man said. 'Unfortunately for you we've already checked that. No faulty wires apart from in your room. Now we're not asking. We're here to tell you. You are going to let us in, and we are going to fix whatever you've damaged then send you the bill. And depending on what we find, we couldn't care less what permissions you have with you to justify being here, or what paperwork you've got to keep us away. We're dropping you off somewhere with your cargo so no one else is put in danger.'

'Sorry, that's a no-go,' Leyton said. 'Your captain has already been told that only us are allowed inside and that we're here until we get to Earth.'

'Just keep talking,' the guard chuckled. His face though was far from amused. 'You know what? If you're not going to step aside, I'll have you move aside.'

The man took a few steps forward. Onyx Perretti stepped up to keep him back, but the guard heaved the agent to one side using his shield with ease. Leyton shrugged, squared up to the guard and raised his weapon with menace. The two glared at each other in silence waiting for either one of them to back down. When it was clear neither would, Leyton took a deep breath, sighed, then clipped the man round the jaw with the butt of his weapon. It was an option he'd have preferred to avoid. It would go one of two ways. For their sakes, he seriously hoped it would be the more peaceful option.

'Last warning,' he snarled, pointing his weapon at the guard. 'Back off. Now.'

'Wrong choice,' the guard said, a slight smile lifting the corner of his mouth.

Briefly, the pair fought furiously, ending only when Leyton's team stepped up with their weapons targeting each member of the security personnel opposite them. Leyton wiped a small trickle of blood from his lip where the guard had caught him with a lucky jab and stretched out his shoulder to loosen it after taking a few hits from the stun baton. It was a good job he had worn his armour otherwise he wouldn't have stood a chance.

'Either you can go, now, or we start to shoot,' Leyton advised. 'It's your choice but I don't want to waste bullets on you. We're on the same side, after all.'

The guard started to speak, giving a little speech on why they were not going to back off, but Leyton couldn't focus on the words. In the background of the hallway, a pair of shadows moved through the darkness with swift precision. Fellstrum and Deulche revealed themselves from their positions to join the standoff. Kari struck first, digging a knife into the throat of one of the engineers. Jake Deulche incapacitated a security guard with a hefty clubbing blow to the back of the head. The female engineer turned around and with an impressive swing of her arm hit Agent Deulche in the chest and she immediately let loose with another few strikes, pummelling the agent to the ground without mercy. Jerome let off a few rounds at a guard who attempted to fire off a couple shots at Agent Fellstrum. None of it was going according to plan.

'Non-lethal!' Leyton barked, grasping at Jerome's collar and dragging him back trying to reinstate control. 'I said non-lethal!'

'I told you, tell that to them,' his second in command hissed. 'This is my operation now.'

'The hell it is.'

Leyton harshly threw the man out of his grasp and turned back to the battle. Onyx Perretti was in a fist fight with one of the guards. Agent Tallow and Medic Suttle were working together to wrangle with a larger engineer who was quite easily out powering the two of them. The engineer carrying the wrench and two other engineers had hold of Agent Deulche and were being covered by the lead guard and his shield as they retreated through the corridor.

'Radio the captain,' the guard ordered loudly, though his voice was barely audible over the commotion. I need you to tell her we need to put out a mayday. Immediate assistance required, and we're coming in hot with a prisoner. Get a cell ready.'

Two engineers tried to take hold of Kari to claim another one of his team but quickly left her alone when she fought back. Leyton fired a few warning shots their way to deter them further. The ship's crew hurried out of sight down the corridor with their prize. His soldier. Agent Deulche was now in their control. They were battered and bruised and in no state to aid his comrade just yet. Leyton Foresc ran over to Kari's side and guided her back to the safety of the unit.

He opened a comm link with Agent Schottler. 'Ray, get on the comms network. Expect an emergency beacon to be sent out. I want that shit cut off before it goes. No one hears a thing. Understood?'

'On it, boss,' Schottler replied sharply. 'Will radio in when it's done.'

The comms cut and Leyton turned his attention back to Kari. 'Are you okay?'

'Fine now, thanks for the save,' she replied.

'What's the next move?' Jerome asked. His finger was still wrapped around the trigger of his weapon, eager to continue the fight. 'Are we going to run with our tails between our legs? Maybe walk up to them unarmed and ask for a quick death? Or even hand over our weapons, let them end us with our own kit!'

'We get back to the cargo hold,' Leyton said sharply. 'We regroup and rest then plan the next move. Until then we don't do anything. We do something now and it'll only end badly. They're not exactly going to be in a hurry either.'

'What about Deulche?' Kari asked, scowling at him with a look of hatred on her face. 'We can't leave him behind like that!'

It did pain him to make the decision so quickly. No one should be left behind. The choice was made easy, regardless of what he told his team because he was in the knowledge that the ship's crew were not killers. They were civilian engineers. Basic security, not trained for a war. He would be safe with them. They, on the other hand, needed to get their heads straight.

'We have to leave him for now,' Leyton said slowly. 'We go back, regroup, catch our breath then plan the next move. It's the smart play.'

'You're going to kill him!' Agent Fellstrum spat.

He could feel his blood start to boil. 'We're going to save him. Don't you dare doubt that. We will get him back. Right now, this is not the time. They've got the upper hand. We're hurt, worked up and ready for war. None of us are ready. We strike them when *we* have the upper hand, and we hit them on our terms. Not theirs. That is the end of it. Okay? Let's move.'

'Boss, I've cut all comms out of the ship entirely,' Schottler said over the comms. 'Couldn't single out the emergency beacon. I think they got a couple bursts out before I cut it off though. Sorry.'

'Dammit, it has to be fine,' he cussed. 'At least you caught it. Please tell me they can't get anything else out?'

'Not a thing,' Ray replied. 'They're not speaking to anyone unless we let them, or whoever comes to save them gets close enough to read S.O.S.'

'Good,' Leyton said. He glanced over his shoulder to see Jerome and Kari talking between themselves. 'I'll catch up with you when we're back. Out.'

Jesa

The Centies were not the demons and scum Jesa had been brought up to see them as. Her first contact with them had proven that they were far from it. Jesa was being fed a healthy portion of food, three times a day. Was not put through a daily torture routine. They even spoke to her like she was one of them. There were no beatings, no foul words and no threats of endangerment. There had been a gradual easing of the restrictions that were imposed upon her. The more honest her words were when she spoke about her owner, the more she started to trust them. From there, the freedom she was entitled to increased. She was free to wander their ship, provided she was escorted or constantly under a watchful eye. There were rooms that were off limits to her, as to be expected. But she could eat with them, learning more about them as she listened to them speak. At times, she felt like a part of them. When the soldiers had a training session, she had to vacate back to her cabin so they could keep their training sessions private. She was still a prisoner after all, and she had accepted that. If she was in their position, Jesa wouldn't have done half of what they were doing for her.

There was a feeling she had that mattered. A feeling of safety. They were not going to harm her, and she had the impression that the SPF soldiers wouldn't let anything harm her either. It was nice to feel safe. Her sleep had not improved much during that time. Nightmares of her master still plagued her slumber, but when she woke, she knew that under the watchful eye of the SPF she was away from him. Comfortably out of harm's reach. It eased the pain from the dreams. She was able to drift off back to sleep when she calmed down after each terror.

She had woken up early that morning in a sweat. Morning, according to the clock in her cabin. It was unusual and difficult to get used to, as she had never worked to Earth Standard Time before. It felt wrong working to the Centie's time zones. Barbaros had appeared in her dreams again. In it, Jesa had woken up alone; only, it was quiet, the hum of the ship was absent like they were drifting through space. There was no commotion of laughter, conversation or training. When she left her cabin to investigate the silence, there was no one around. Not a sign of the soldiers or pilots. Their armour was all that was left behind in the troop bay, galley and the flight deck. Coffee was left unattended. Weapons were scattered around half assembled. Possessions cast aside

174

like garbage fresh to be disposed of. She searched every room as thoroughly as she could. Jesa even scoured through her own ship. Nothing. When she returned to the troop bay, the doorway she was not allowed to go through that led to the armoury was open.

'You weren't open before,' she muttered.

Jesa walked toward the door. The other side was shrouded in darkness. She took a deep breath, held it, then walked through. The room on the other side was lit up. Jesa turned around to find that the door she walked through was gone. Instead, there was a stone wall behind her. She placed a hand on the solid material, disbelieving what she was seeing, and felt the cold touch of stone. Jesa walked down the hallway and gasped in shock at what she saw. This was not an armoury and certainly did not belong to a patrol ship. It was as if Jesa had been transported into the crypt of a cult. She stood in a massive square room built from giant stone blocks and lined with cages that housed a central, monstrous looking metal pedestal on a raised platform. At the head of the room was a raised metal chair. Skeletons occupied several of the cells lining the space. In a few others dotted around was the crew of the patrol ship. Resting upon the pedestal was a large, heavy looking book. Sat on the chair, a giant person shrouded in shadows could be felt glaring at her.

An unseen force pulled her, encouraging her to step down the small passageway toward the book like an invisible rope tied around her was being reeled in. The crew screamed at her from their confinements. Some were in terrible pain. Others tried to warn her, telling her to turn around and run as fast as she could. To get away. Jesa wanted to comply with their requests. She could not. The force that pulled on her had Jesa by the hand. Guiding her against her will, Jesa walked up to the pedestal. The black, battered leather-bound book seemed to fall open before her on its own. There were no words written down. Not even any pictures were drawn in. Instead, the pages were decorated in pastel shades of colour that seemed to trigger unusual sensations in her brain. The colours seemed to alter before her very eyes in a fluid motion. She flipped a page, looked at the next colour-filled pieces of paper, and winced as a searing injection of pain throbbed from behind her eyes as images flashed in her mind.

With each new page turned she saw every opportunity she ever had to go against her master but did not. The chances she had to get away from him and chose not to because of the fear. There were even flashes of every time she had been rewarded, every time she had been praised and every instance where she was made to feel just like a daughter. Jesa then saw something that had not happened, that she hoped was just a nightmare. Barbaros was tearing her flesh apart with jagged, four bladed knives while she was strapped down to a metal table, still conscious. When the pain was too much and she was close to passing out, he would ease back only to return moments later after she caught her breath to carry on attacking her. It was the results of when it was discovered that she disobeyed her master. Jesa never heard him tell her that in those flashing moments. The intense hatred and fury that he was radiating during the torture told her what the punishment was for.

She had to wonder. Was it so bad working for him? Obeying him? When he did reward her, she was rewarded. And he did not hurt her for no reason. Yet he did still hurt her, and he still showed no trust. That tag was in her arm because of him. If she really mattered to him, if those times of being rewarded were so special, he would not have done that to her.

'It isn't so bad after all, is it?' the shadow figure said, its voice eerily familiar, as it repeated what was on her mind.

'It is when you tag me, Barbaros,' she snapped.

Barbaros leaned forward in his seat, pulled back the hood that had hidden his face and stared at her with dead eyes. 'You are my property at the end of the day, yah. I have every right to… put insurance in place. Compre?'

'It doesn't make it right,' Jesa retaliated. 'You stole my life!'

'I saved you!' Bloodlust, anger and venom resonated in his words. 'You had nothing on that planet, yah. Nothing! Just dust with no hope of escape. A pitiful life.'

'I had a family,' she muttered.

'What?' Barbaros questioned.

'My family!' Jesa screamed. 'I had my family. My family that you stole from me!'

'Parents that couldn't give you a future,' Barbaros scoffed. 'If I hadn't come when I did, you would still be on that planet, barely having a life. Probably would have been sold off to some farmstead to marry their eldest just to be a mother so your parents could still have a living, yah? I saved you from that place. I gave you somewhere to belong. I gave you purpose. You are who you are now because of me!'

She could not reply. How could she? He was right. That was the life for almost every woman on that planet in the end. It was a simple life for a reason. Even though her father wanted more for her, he probably wouldn't have been able to provide it. Would he?

'Now,' Barbaros continued, bringing her focus back onto him, 'come back to me. Come back to where you belong.'

Jesa shook her head. 'No.'

There was a sudden flash of pastel colours in her mind. The pain returned to her once more.

'Let's try that again, shall we? Come back to me.'

'No,' she said more firmly.

Barbaros sighed heavily, his eyes weary with disappointment. He clicked his fingers and as she blinked: Sergeant Duke Horren was on his knees in front of her shackled to the floor in thick, heavy chains. The Centie was exhausted, battered and weakened. Bruises marked his face, and blood stained his uniform. Her master took out a large pistol and pointed it at the soldier's head. Duke mouthed for her to say no. His eyes pleaded she stayed strong.

'Now?' Barbaros said.

She hesitated. Her answer was not quick enough. The trigger was squeezed, and the muzzle flash woke her from her dream. In a daze she looked all around her cabin, trying to find the body of the sergeant that she knew was not there. To make sure that he had not been hurt. Her arm itched with a fiery rage that took several minutes to appease.

Once she returned to full lucidity and her heart rate had calmed down to a normal rate, Jesa clambered out of bed, got dressed then quietly walked through the emptied passageways of the patrol ship. One of the men was snoring in their bunk. Someone else was rolling around, their bed groaning under each turn. The galley was empty. That was perfect for her. Jesa sat down with a cup of coffee and shivered in the cold room. The realism of her dream was still at the forefront of her mind, haunting her every thought. She never noticed someone enter the galley and sit down to her left until after they had wrapped a thick, itchy blanket around her shoulders. Valentina Rodriguez. The woman was exhausted but still had the energy to smile.

'What're you doing up?' she asked. 'Aren't you tired?'

'Bad dreams,' Jesa answered. She scratched her arm.

'Want to talk about it?'

She shook her head. The truth was she did want to speak about it, to know if what she was feeling was normal. But Jesa couldn't say a word to the woman. The notion of talking about a dream had been beaten out of her. It was weakness. More than that, dreams were readable. A

177

person could learn a lot by someone's dreams and secrets could be given away without even realising it just by paying attention to the details they gave of their time asleep. There were no secrets to keep from people who were being so kind to her, that seemed genuine, but the habit to avoid conversation was too strong. After all, she was an Outer and they were Centies. It was too soon for her to be able to trust them. For the next few minutes, they sat in silence drinking their coffee.

Rodriquez stood up and gestured for her to follow. They joined the helmsman, Ivan, on the flight deck. He had his feet up on the controls and was relaxed with his seat set back. The man didn't move. His chest so still it was like he wasn't breathing. He had to be pretending to be asleep. People were never that still in sleep.

'We giving guided tours now?' he asked slowly.

'Easy up there, she's got her demons,' Valentina retorted. 'Think she could do with the company right now.'

'What's up, kid?' Ivan questioned. He still did not stir from his stony stance.

'I don't want to talk about it,' Jesa replied. Her arm started to itch, and she tried to resist it but failed.

Ivan twitched, sighed and turned around to look at her. Those black eyes were so empty yet so full of emotion. She couldn't work it out. 'The sergeant told us about that thing in your arm. Sorry to hear that your owner did that to you.' He turned momentarily to look in a small bag tucked away to his side and pulled out a small vial of thick, syrup-like red liquid. 'This will help. Rub it on your arm once every twelve hours. When we get it out of you, it'll be once a week.'

'What is it?' Jesa asked.

'My own creation,' Helmsman Zenkovich answered with a grin. 'Soothes the nerves. Makes it go tingly for a little bit then you feel nothing until it wears off. Don't get it anywhere you don't need it. Trust me, you won't thank me if you do. Oh, and don't ask me what's in it or I can promise you'll stop using most of the things in the washroom.'

'How do I know it'll work?' Jesa questioned suspiciously, eying up the strange substance.

Ivan took a deep breath and lifted his left sleeve to reveal dozens of scars. 'Toward the end of the Federation War, my ship was immobilised mid-battle. It was one of the last ones still operational. Everyone else was bugging out. No one was left to help us. We were boarded. The marines did their best, but the Feds were too much. They overran the ship and killed everyone they came across like it was open season. Then when they got to the bridge, they stopped killing. I was taken prisoner by the Feds with the rest of the bridge crew before we could scuttle it or put up a fight. We were taken to a penal colony. Not a PoW camp like we thought we would be. Turns out they needed the extra labour mining resources to keep up the war with the UPN.'

'Mayah!' Jesa exclaimed. It wasn't just the outer colonies that had it rough. The central colonies were also subjected to the same sort of conditions. 'That's awful! What did you do?'

'I tried to escape a few times while I was there. Like hell I was going to stick it out. Trust me, it wasn't easy. Damn near killed me a couple times. One time, I nearly made it to safety. After that, they had enough of it and started putting tags in me.'

The Federation War was a conflict between the Federation of Hulsari States and the United Planetary Nations; unsurprisingly, the Hulsari states were part of the Outer Colonies. The collection of planets wanted not only their independence but to force out all signs of Earth from their territory and outlaw the UPN. But they didn't want to wait for policies and legalities to be formalised to allow it. They opted to act by force and declared war by taking out the small UPN fleet posted in the area at the time. Little did they realise that for four years after that attack the United Planetary Nations would fight with a fury that few had seen for an age. It was no wonder why the Feds took prisoners when the UPN was knocking down every wall. It was the only way to keep them at bay and buy vital time for their war effort. Jesa never realised that they also took to tagging people that tried to escape. The last she knew; it was inter-stellar law that prisoners of war weren't to be tagged.

'Tags? Multiple?'

Ivan Zenkovich nodded. 'At first, it was one at a time. Each time they put one in, I gnawed at my arm to pull it out. I refused to be made to feel like cattle and the dumb fucks didn't realise that they never set the tamper trigger. Then they finally put several in that were all interlinked. Tamper triggers switched on. If I touched one, they all went off and that wouldn't just be the end of my arm but the end of me. After the war, the UPN eventually found me and everyone else they had at the lunar prison. They had me unconscious for nearly seven hours to get them all out of me without setting any of them off. In the end, the tags were all taken out at the same time. It was the only way to do it. Part of the wait with being unconscious was waiting for the robot to come that could take them out at the same time. Humans would make too many mistakes. But the thing I remember the most about the tags? More than the nightmares? The itch. That fucking itch. It never ended. Most nights I wished I could cut my arm off. Would have done if they let me. See that scar there? Tried it once. Knife was still in my arm when they stopped me. Can't look at a cage without feeling the urge to scratch my arm anymore. Thank fuck for the other POWs or I would have gone insane. What's your trigger?'

She warmed to him and his sincerity. To think about what he had been through was tough. It was heart-breaking, putting her experience into perspective: worse things could happen. Yet the news was reassuring all at the same time. He had come back from that terror. There were scars to prove it, that he could survive, and he was sat before her. But more than that, he *knew*. He knew the horrible sensation that the tags caused. That need to get it out at any cost as a body rejected the foreign object. He knew that there were triggers. No one could lie like that and have the physical scars to go with the statements. Not unless they were severely messed up in the head. Ivan wouldn't be in control of the patrol ship if he was that unstable.

'My owner,' she admitted. 'Every time I think of him… It itches.'

'Here,' Ivan said. He took the liquid out of her hand, applied a couple drops to his thumb and rubbed it into her scar. Like clockwork it went tingly as if a static charge was pricking at her skin. Then it went numb, and it was gone. There was no itch. Only constant calm. A much welcome relief. She sighed and stared endlessly at her arm. Expecting the itch to return with a fury.

'Thank you,' Jesa whispered when she was able to accept it worked.

'It's okay,' the pilot replied, handing her the vial of liquid back. 'On this ship if you're not a threat then you're one of us as far as I'm concerned. We look after each other. You haven't tried anything which says to me you're not all bad. Maybe a little misguided and defensive but not a bad person. And the big man likes you. So that helps.'

She smiled at the crew. They smiled back. It helped put her at ease knowing for certain that they would look after her.

'You know, between the three of us,' Ivan Zenkovich started. He looked over his shoulder toward the rest of the ship. 'I think you're going to stop the sergeant from retiring.'

'Retiring?'

'Yeah, this is supposed to be his last job,' Rodriguez confirmed. 'But the way he talks about you, I think he's pretty set on making sure you stay safe.'

Her stomach felt light and fluttered, like she had just found out she was the favourite child. He was going to sacrifice his own future for her. Someone that he barely knew. Someone that he was meant to imprison for being a smuggler. Almost like how Ghavvis had sacrificed his own wellbeing for her to escape.

Ghavvis. What had happened to him? Where was he now? Was he still on Juntah Station? Had the Crevari turned around and attacked the station in their absence? Jesa wished she knew where he was and that he was safe.

It had been a couple days since she last gave any new intel on her owner. Maybe it was their interrogation method. She could easily be succumbing to fatigue through being made to feel so at ease when she should be on edge. Or possibly her heart had simply been won over by the sacrifice and effort the crew and squad were making for her. Regardless of what the reason was, Jesa felt almost compelled to help more.

'Can I speak to him?' she asked.

'Excuse me?' Zenkovich questioned.

'The sergeant, I need to speak to him,' Jesa explained.

'Why?' Ivan replied.

'I want to talk. I want to tell him whatever he needs to know.'

'Are you sure?' Valentina Rodriguez asked her, placing a hand on her shoulder reassuringly. 'We don't expect you to.'

Jesa nodded. 'Yes, right now I am.'

'Go get him,' Ivan instructed the co-pilot and when she bolted off the flight deck, he turned to her and smiled. 'Thank you. He will really appreciate this.'

'I will have my price,' she whispered. She would need to know about Ghavvis. If he had been harmed, she would certainly not want to help. They would be the people that Barbaros and her parents warned her they were. 'There's something I need in return.'

'Everyone does,' Ivan Zenkovich said, not even remotely surprised by her statement.

Chapter 6
28/10/2675
09:51 Earth Standard Time

Duke Horren

The intel that Jesa supplied a few days prior was more than Duke could have asked for. She had given up coordinates of key positions, base sizes and even the names of high-priority individuals that were vital in Barbaros' operations. Every shred of information was immediately passed onto High Command. The very night after he had been woken to the news of this change of heart from the prisoner, Duke slept like he had never slept before. He did not stir. The next day the training sessions continued as normal, although a little more light-hearted. For several days they were to survive on zero-G and lose as little muscle mass as possible, ideally staying within five percent loss. The only safe places were the flight deck and Jesa's room. In space, things went wrong. Ship's systems could be disabled. Lighting fail. Anything. When bad luck did strike, gravity was usually one of the first things to go as it was not an essential for living. This training was designed to ensure the team could operate seamlessly should the artificial gravity fail. It came with its difficulties to overcome. One over-push and they would end up slamming into a wall faster than they could control. A misplaced arm and they would be spinning uncontrollably. Using the facilities was a messy operation for the inexperienced, but it had been a pleasure to watch everyone meander through the weightless void. A work of art watching them eat in zero gravity. There was one benefit to it all which deserved merit: there was no need to adjust to get comfy when sleeping. All that they had to do was tie themselves to harnesses near their beds to remain close to the vents providing a constant airflow.

Every morning he woke, Duke was refreshed. Some people needed to have an extravagant holiday to rejuvenate themselves, but a night in weightless bliss was all he needed. A few days of it and he felt like he was a new man. Once ready he immediately began a strict twenty-minute exercise routine using a workout machine built into the ceiling of the troop bay to push his entire body. The first of three through the day required to ensure there was no deterioration. Such a machine ensured that he pushed as much of his body as he could while taking up the least space.

Afterward, his mandatory medical assessment. As a leader he needed to set the example and prove that his standards were not only achievable but realistic. He hoped the soldiers would learn the importance of making sure the tasks at hand could be achieved. Duke passed the medical with ease, if anything his body had improved because of the extra rest and more intensive workouts he went through.

When his soldiers eventually woke from their slumber, they went through a similar procedure before breakfast. Each of their test results flashed on his tac-pad in quick succession. Abe was his only concern. While the other two were able to maintain their muscle mass, his had fallen by well over four percent. One more bad day and he would surely fail. Something was holding him back from reaching his potential. When the others were putting everything into keeping up their physical strength, Corporal Udal'e read one of his books. Whatever the reason for it, the soldier needed to be reminded on what his priorities needed to be. Books were good when on down time with nothing else to do. They would never complete the training exercise for him.

'Come with me, now,' he told Abe as he finished his meal.

Duke led him from the galley to the briefing where no one could hear them. Thankfully Jesa had learnt enough of his mannerisms to not ask what was going on when they climbed past in the zero-G. She looked very much at ease in the float, not needing to hold onto anything. He couldn't do that anymore. For a short while, Duke and Abe just floated in the briefing room. He stared at the soldier. Abe wore a smug look on his face as if it was all a joke. When he'd left him to wait a while in suspense, he cleared his throat.

'Why are you here?'

'Excuse me?' Abe replied.

'Answer the question.'

Abe smirked as if it was a stupid one to be asked. He then gave a poor excuse. 'I'm here to learn the skills I need to learn to take over after you retire. Sergeant.'

'No, why are you in the military?' Duke asked. 'Because it certainly isn't to fight.' He paused. He realised the error in his retort. Abe had been drafted after his family forced him to enlist. He changed his tactics. 'I saw your medical results. I've seen your attitude. I've learnt your personality. You read a book and think you know how to do things. Not once have I heard you try to practice speaking confidently. I don't see you strip your weapon and put it back together like the others do. Don't see you take apart your armour just to know how it all fits to then put it back together. No extra workouts just to push yourself a little more.'

'So what? You want me to be like Ronan?' Abe scoffed.

'No, I want you to be a successful soldier. Unless you start acting like one, I'll recommend you get shipped planet-side to sit at a desk for the rest of your career.'

'What?' the soldier questioned. Abe's expression changed as he started to see the reality of his decisions. "You can't do that."

'You heard me and yes I can,' Duke growled. 'You can be more than this. Carry on like you are and you'll do worse than get yourself killed in the field. You'll get everyone around you killed. Do you want that on your conscience?'

Abe shook his head. 'What do I need to do?'

'Do what I say,' he answered. 'More than that, prove you want to be here. Right now? I don't believe you do want to be here. Okay?'

'Okay,' Abe whispered. 'Sergeant?'

'Yes?'

'Do you think I can do this?'

'I don't know,' Duke replied. 'For all I know, Ronan could fail while you could pass with Arche. It depends on what you choose to do next. I suggest you buddy up with Ronan and train with him. You are to learn everything that you can from him. Understand how he does things. Why he does things. And more importantly find out the consequences if you don't do things correctly.'

'Yes, Sergeant,' Abe whispered.

'There is no shame in admitting things aren't as easy as you thought they would be,' Duke said. 'Are you still wanting to do this?'

'I am,' Abe answered.

'I suggest you go and prove it to me,' Duke replied. 'Because I don't want to have this conversation again.'

'Understood,' Abe said. 'I won't let you down.'

'You'd better not.'

They parted in silence with Abe leaving the briefing room first. Duke followed shortly after. His heart weighed him down with doubt and worry like a lead weight being dropped into a bottomless pit. He hoped that the soldier would heed his words and do what was required. That Corporal Udal'e wouldn't disappoint him. Duke desperately wanted to be able to give the message that they all had passed.

Duke swung himself through the doorway to the troop bay, heading for the galley for a coffee. He barely made it into the compartment when he saw Jesa hanging in free float above him. Her brown hair floated as if she was submerged under water. She had put on weight and looked healthier now. He was confident that if he left her overnight and came back to her in the morning, she would still be alive and would not have died of starvation. He was happy that she would survive.

'What was that about?' she asked, gesturing behind toward the rest of the team.

'Needed to give him a pep talk,' he explained, making sure it was clear that he wasn't going to say anything further about it.

Jesa nodded thoughtfully. Her lips were pressed, ready to speak, but she just looked away from him. That wasn't what she wanted to say. Jesa needed an excuse to get the conversation going. She wasn't going to find that on her own.

'What's up?' Duke asked. 'Something bothering you?'

'What's going to happen to me when we get back?' she blurted out, after taking precious time to consider the correct words to use. 'You said you'd try to help me.'

Her eyes swelled with tears, like a reservoir filling to the brim in a storm but not quite enough to breach its constraints. When the liquid did prove too much, her tears would not be able to roll down her cheeks. They would float aimlessly until gravity was restored. Duke couldn't leave Jesa wondering exactly what her fate held for her.

'Sadly, that depends on my negotiation skills,' Duke admitted. 'After doing everything I can for you, I can't promise anything other than you'll be safe at all times.'

'What could happen? Please. Tell me.'

Duke spoke slowly and with care. 'Best case scenario is you will be reprimanded under supervision by the time I'm done. I'll play the defector card for you and that you need to remain under protection. Or you only want my protection. That way you'll stay free. Either way, I'll be pleading for you to be out of secure holding. How supervised you are will depend on the results of the intel you've given and what a mandatory psyche evaluation when we get back the station states. Need to make sure you're not a sleeper unit. The more positive hits we get, the better for you. Worst case? You're tried for crimes against the UPN but get favourable terms due to your cooperation. You'll be put in protective custody at a penal station, medium security. Max will be eight years. It won't be the best, but you'll be comfy. You won't go without, and good behaviour works wonders on the length of a sentence.'

Sadness still resonated in her eyes. It was to be expected. Yet, Duke could also see a form of comfort in knowing what the extent of control will be.

'Hey, don't think about that just yet. Okay?' Duke insisted.

'Bit hard to,' Jesa murmured.

'I know,' he said. 'But it hasn't happened yet. I don't know what the brass back on Earth will say. All I can tell you is that you will not be alone when we get there.'

'Thank you.'

She smiled a sombre grin. Duke placed a reassuring arm on her shoulder and smiled back. There was not much more he could do, and he believed she was aware of that. He only hoped it would be enough for Jesa to hold onto. He needed her to be strong.

A klaxon chimed three times, stopping any further concerns from being voiced. He looked around toward the flight deck, ultimately hearing the call from Rodriguez for him to join her and Ivan.

'Shout me if you need me, okay?' he told her. 'I'm only up the decks.'

Jesa nodded and pulled herself aside for him to go by. Duke floated through the troop bay and up to the next deck. He hoisted his way past the soldiers in the galley, clambered up to the flight deck and let his feet gravitate toward the floor. Duke smiled as his feet hit clung to the floor once the effects of artificial gravity on the deck took hold. It felt good experiencing the gravity once again. His bones ached a little as they got used to feeling weight once more. Duke clung onto the backs of the crews' seats.

'What's going on?' Duke asked.

'We have a distress beacon,' Ivan Zenkovich replied. 'Sent on a broad spectrum for United Planets frequencies.'

'What're they saying?' Duke questioned.

'Have a listen,' Ivan said.

The flip of a switch and the panicked voice of a man spoke out. 'To all nearby UPN forces, this is Franklin Hender of the interstellar cruise ship *Galactic Passage* captained by Beatrice. We are currently under assault from armed stowaways. I say again, armed stowaways. We have dead and injured personnel and have had to make an emergency jump that has severely hindered out functionality. We are in need of immediate assistance. Please hurry. I have included—'

186

Ivan killed the transmission, swivelled round in his chair and shrugged. 'Transmission is cut short there. Don't know what happened. Systems might have cut out or, if what they're saying is true, they could have been forced offline. Think this would be an interesting live one for the trainees if you think they're up for it.'

'It does sound like a good one for them, doesn't it?' Duke said. Granted, civilians dead or injured was far from ideal. He couldn't help but see the potential benefit to his soldiers to have this sort of experience. 'A really good one. Do we have coordinates? What else do you know?'

'We sure do,' Ivan said. 'Thankfully they were embedded in the message otherwise… we'd have had to triangulate their position.'

'And that would have taken forever,' Valentina added.

'I got you,' Duke whispered. 'Have you checked them?'

'First thing I did before I called for you,' the helmsman answered. 'It's not good. Comes from an uncharted sector. Heading close to Crevari hunting routes. We're the closest ship by at least two and a half parsecs. No other UPN ship can be there quicker. Can't say for anyone else though. It'll take us just over a week to get to them. I can cut it down to five days at a push if we only stop once for a really quick breather… I'd get everyone ready to chuck up at some point or pop pills if we do that.'

'And the ship?' Duke questioned.

'It's a luxury liner,' Valentina explained. 'She's quite famous. Always has the best food. Has some of the best reviews. Costs a fortune to go on. I'd never be able to afford a trip.'

'You could if we buddied up for a single bed,' Ivan said, chuckling slightly at his own joking flirtation.

'Oh please, you wish,' Valentina laughed.

'Believe me, I do,' Zen sighed while laughing.

'So, we've got rich people on a ship with stowaways,' Duke said. Hostage scenario was the most likely one. No one took a ship with rich people unless they wanted ransom money. If they didn't get what they wanted, more would surely die.

'Have I got the green then for go?' Ivan Zenkovich requested.

'Fucking Crevari. Why do they have to be round here? You have the green light,' he replied. 'We're going to be there and done before the Crevs get wind of them. Get us to them in a week. Try to avoid any delays. Report it to Command. Let them know what's going on. I'll go brief the team.'

'And her?' Rodriguez asked, gesturing toward the troop bay. 'What're we doing about the girl?'

'She's coming with us for the ride.'

Both crew members turned to face him. Then Zenkovich spoke, slowly. 'Are you sure that's wise? What if she tries to break out? Or worse.'

'We don't really have a choice,' Duke shrugged. 'We haven't got the time to drop her off somewhere then come back and I don't want to risk that boat being raided by the Crevari in the meantime. Do either of you want to risk that? It's what we've got to deal with. Besides, I don't think we have anything to worry about. And I'm sure you don't either. Get gravity back online please.'

He left the flight deck to find the three soldiers waiting for him in the galley. None of them looked overly happy at the returning gravity without any warning. Some food had splatted on the table and all their cups of coffee was now pooled on the floor.

'Thanks for the heads up,' Corporal Moasa groaned.

'You're welcome,' he grunted in return.

'What's going on?' Corporal Arche questioned, equal displeasure in her voice. 'Why'd you flip on the gravity?'

'We've got a job,' Duke explained. 'An emergency beacon has been picked up.'

The trio laughed and looked at him with amusement while Duke stood there trying to work out what was so funny about what he just said. Either disrespect or doubt.

'Are you sure that it isn't just another test?' Abe Udal'e joked. 'Maybe a little setup? I think we've earned a break about now, right? You have just had us go through weightless training.'

Doubt. They were right to be judgemental. All he had them do, with one exception, was run the trio through tests, drills and practice scenarios. Each one started out serious, much like the real thing, only to be revealed to be a test. They had never been in any real danger even though they thought they were at the time. He would be just as doubtful if it were the other way round.

'This time it's not a test,' Duke said. 'I wish it were. Armed stowaways are on a luxury liner and have attacked the crew. People have been killed and hurt. They need our help.'

'Killed, Sergeant?' Joane Arche asked.

'Yes, killed. It means we're going in combat ready with live ammunition.'

'Do we know their numbers? Don't they have their own security to stop something like this happening?' Abe questioned.

Duke sighed. 'We don't know a thing about them or why the security failed. The transmission was quick and not a lot of detail was given. All we know is that they are armed and willing to use lethal force. We have no idea how well trained they are, who they are or what they want, though we can assume with the people on board that they're after ransom money. Either way, we're going. We're the closest help they've got and we're going ready for a fight.'

Corporal Moasa grinned with joy and spared a glance at his peers, his eyes lingering on Udal'e. 'Are you sure we're *all* ready for this?'

'I know that individually we're not,' Duke answered honestly, firmly. 'But we need to be ready,' he paused as the transport lurched into a jump, 'because we'll be there in less than a week. We're going into an extended jump. If you start to feel sick, say something. We'll get the meds ready.'

'Where are we jumping to?' Arche asked.

'I didn't ask the location,' Duke replied. 'But it's roughly a few parsecs away.'

'A few parsecs?' Abe muttered, opening the mapping on his tac-pad. 'Sergeant, does that put us where I think that puts us?'

'Forget that. We're doing that sort of distance in a few days?' Moasa spat, the sound of concern ringing in his voice. 'Are we even going to stop?'

'We'll be stopping once,' Duke explained. 'About halfway through. We'll stop for half a cycle. Give you all chance to chuck your guts up then come round before the second leg of it.'

Abe wanted to say something. It was clear from his posture, his quivering lip, his frequent glances at his peers. Duke chose to look past the body language. Abe was already onto the delicate predicament they were in while Duke needed it secured. Ronan paced like a prowling beast itching to make its strike. He couldn't be there fast enough. Corporal Arche simply looked annoyed, probably assuming this was all some decision made against her.

Then a voice that Duke had forgotten about called out. One that did not have a say, but whose opinion mattered just as much, nonetheless.

'What about me?' Jesa asked. 'Aren't you going to, like, send me to one of your bases first for processing before you go out?'

'Yeah, what about her?' Corporal Moasa concurred. 'We can't keep her with us, she's a damn liability. No offense, kid.'

'We can't take her back. There isn't enough time to do that and get back on track to the liner. Even at full speed, non-stop, we would wind up being far behind the nearest fleet instead of being ahead. She'll remain on the ship the entire time, watched by Zen and Rodriguez,' Duke explained. 'She won't be getting in the way. Not that she would try anyway.'

'What is so important that we can't just leave it for the main force?' Arche asked. 'I don't want to sound like Abe on this but we're just four soldiers and two ship crew. What use are we going to actually be? On top of that, if it is a hostage situation, they won't kill the hostages straight away. They need them for the money. They'd only start killing when negotiations go wrong, in order to prove a point. It won't make a difference if we go back. We're best just leaving it for the main response force to deal with.'

'Briefing room. Now,' Duke instructed. 'Jesa, please stay here.'

He guided his soldiers away from the galley, through the troop bay. Jesa was not to hear this conversation. He had no doubt the Crevari were something she was very much aware of, and afraid of, from her time smuggling. She didn't need to know about the risk they would be posing on this venture. Enough was going through her mind as it was.

'Do you want to tell us what's going on that we need to get there so quick that we can't leave it to the main force?' Joane questioned. 'It's not like command have never done it before.'

Duke looked them all dead in the eye as he spoke. 'The liner that's been boarded that we're on our way to? It's in Crevari space.'

'Crevs?' Ronan questioned, noticeably displaying fear in his tone. 'What the hell are they doing in Shit-face County?'

'That's what I'd like to find out too,' Duke said. 'But that's also why we can't leave it to someone else to fix. If we waste any time, those murdering fucks will get them if the stowaways don't do it first. If we let that happen there's no point anyone even going out there to help.'

'And why can't we let Jesa know?' Abe asked. 'If she's coming with us, shouldn't she know? I'd sure as hell would like to know.'

'She's got enough to worry about as it is,' Duke answered. 'I don't want her knowing unless we have no other choice. If we tell her what we're doing, we run the risk that she won't trust us anymore. We'll be just as bad as her master. I can't have that. This is to protect her. Understood?'

His troops muttered in unison as they understood what was at stake. Duke was thankful for their compassion.

'What's the plan when we get there?' Ronan questioned. 'We can't exactly fuck this up.'

'We get there, find out what the stowaways want, secure the ship, apprehend the attackers then get them on their way,' he explained. 'Either way, we need to be quick. I'll refine the details on the way. But remember, not a word to Jesa about the Crevari. Leave them out of any conversation.'

Duke hoped for her sake they did leave that detail out of it. The poor girl needed a break. A chance to feel safe. Secure. Free. The ship needed to be that for her, and he'd make sure of it.

Leyton Foresc

The air in the cargo hold had become almost unbearable. The mucus-based substance the wolves had lined their nest with was putrid. Adding the additional two females to the cage had only made the smell worse. It was so bad now that most of the team refused to take their helmets off unless it was absolutely necessary, letting their respirator filters clean most of the foul smells before inhaling or using their air tanks periodically for the taste of fresh, clean air. Leyton, on the other hand, merely wrapped fabric around his mouth and nose to filter some particulates out. He had gotten used to the smell and could tolerate it. On a positive note, it was not difficult to get volunteers to take up patrols or to stand guard. Even with the prospect of an attack looming from the ship's security, everyone wanted anything that didn't involve enduring the stench any longer.

The rift between Leyton and Jerome, like the miasma around them, had intensified. Jerome had at first formed himself a tightknit unit with Agent Fellstrum and Agent Perretti. The three of them were united with their distrust in him for allowing the ship's crew to take Deulche. Every time the two of them spoke, Jerome would find as much as he could in the words Leyton spoke to question. Taking any opportunity that he was presented with to prove that Leyton was no longer a worthy leader. Little did his second in command realise that he was in charge for a reason, yet the subordinate continued to try. Each attempt made the cohesion Houghton had with his group solidify a little more. All the aspects that Medic Suttle had pointed out in his psyche-evaluations were more prominent. Each of them had issues that under standard field conditions were controllable. Out in the middle of nowhere in unusual circumstances, they had no restraint. Those issues were now taking dominance over their mindset. Pushing their stability to the edges of human limit. Where Jerome was pushed to find a reason to show he was the true leader, prove that he was the man he boasted he was, Fellstrum latched onto the ideals that would bring her the results she wanted for herself and Perretti followed whoever would satisfy his bloodlust that had been teased with the skirmish against the ship's crew.

Suttle and Tallow were not as much a threat as they were a concern. Dom was not a fighter by nature. He could fight, there was no doubting that, and he was a very efficient agent. But Leyton knew the man from previous missions. He chose his fights carefully, putting faith in the better man to avoid conflict. If what the tension in the air foretold came to reality, he trusted the medic would choose correctly. Kari had reverted into herself. She knew what was right. What should or shouldn't be done. But she didn't want to see the team fracture. She was a stark contrast to the person she was on the ice planet.

The only person that he had no concern about was the professor. He was so deep into his work, and oblivious to the emotional tension permeating the air, that he didn't pick up on the divisions or care to choose sides. The man simply wanted to do his work. A man worthwhile trusting to choose with his head over his heart.

Professor Ainslot had been keen to keep Leyton up to date on the status of the wolves and their pups, ignoring Jerome's insistence that he be kept in the loop too. The two new mothers-to-be were settled and cooing for their pups to be born, as if being around other pups triggered the natural need to communicate with their offspring. The first batch of pups were growing rapidly and exceeded the professor's expectations. They were almost at the stage of solely requiring solid food. The pups were noisy and boisterous, stretching their vocal cords for the first time, trialling their lung capacity as they played with each other. They ran around their mothers and fought each other over who was top dog in the litter with their playfighting sessions. Leyton was not sure who was more vocally full of energy – the professor or the pups.

His tac-pad chimed: a call incoming from Puppet Master. He reluctantly left Jerome in command and vacated the room to walk down the hallway to his makeshift meeting room. Every step of the way, Leyton predicted a call over the comms announcing a mutiny. He returned the call. The administrator wasted no time in answering.

'Update,' he demanded sharply. 'Now.'

'The crew of the ship is aware of us, sir' Leyton explained. 'There was an altercation with the ship security and one of my team has been captured.'

'Captured?' the administrator replied slowly, almost patronisingly as if he was aware of it. 'Why didn't you alert me sooner?'

'I have it under control,' Leyton stated. 'We'll get him freed.'

'Make sure you do. We don't need any loose ends. And the cargo?' the administrator asked, showing almost no concern at all for his team member. If anything, the man seemed almost bored by it. As if he had already listened to the report a few times over. 'How are the pups?'

'The cargo is secure,' he answered. His words were spoken through gritted teeth. How could his agent's life be so insignificant to Leyton's superior? 'The pups that have already been born are developing and the professor has got a lot of research to go over. The other two females that are pregnant have settled. All other pods are still operating at full capacity.'

'Good,' Administrator said.

Leyton cleared his throat, 'But I do have a concern, sir.'

'What concerns you this time?' his superior questioned in disgust.

'Space, sir,' he answered. 'It was a tight fit with just the two litters. Now there's another two litters to be added.'

'What do you think you need to do to solve this then?' Administrator asked patronisingly.

'Make space.'

'Yes,' Puppet Master said. 'And you can achieve that by?'

Leyton paused before speaking. He needed to choose his next words wisely as the Englishman continued to antagonise him. 'By giving them a bigger enclosure.'

'Exactly. Release them,' Puppet Master said bluntly.

'Excuse me, sir?' Leyton said. 'Did you say release them?'

'You heard me right. Have you got a problem with that?'

'I do,' Leyton snarled. 'I haven't got anywhere to move my team to. We are outnumbered by security staff who have eyes on us.'

'I suggest you find somewhere to relocate to that you can keep under your control then, out of reach of the wolves if you want to keep your unit alive,' Administrator said. 'But when I tell you to do something, you will do it. Am I clear?'

'Sir,' Leyton hissed.

'Good.'

Leyton could not fully comply with the order that he was given. There were things that his conscience would not allow him to do. Even if he wanted to, there were obstacles that needed to be overcome. Once the wolves were released from their pen to roam the storage room freely, there would be no way to ensure they would be controllable when it came to extraction. That room would become their home – and animals defend their home against intruders.

'Sir, how will you remove the cargo when we arrive back at Earth with it?' Leyton asked.

'All things depend on your success. But I have a team briefed and on standby to secure the assets once you arrive with them.'

That first sentence held his attention. What was there about him that could be needed more than just making it back? He already had an immeasurable task at hand that was made more difficult as events developed.

'What do you mean it depends on my success, sir?'

'I need you to get the ship back to the Sol system and have it under your control,' Administrator said as if that was an easy thing to do.

'With all due respect sir, none of my team knows how to pilot a ship,' Leyton said. 'I can guarantee we can have this ship under our control but that's about as far as I can go with that.'

'I know,' Administrator retorted. 'Don't forget I already know everything about you and your team. I'm the one who made you who you are now. I've deployed a specialist team from another division I'm in command of to meet you at your current coordinates. They will be bringing a pilot capable of piloting large vessels. When they liaise with you and help you bring the ship back to Sol, you will rendezvous with my research and development station, the *Vestibule*. It's in orbit around Pluto.'

'I've never heard of the *Vestibule* before,' Leyton said. 'Why?'

'The same reason why the public doesn't know about you and your work,' Administrator said. 'Secrets keep people safe. You should know that.'

'Sir. And can I ask, why Pluto? I thought we were supposed to be reporting back to Earth?'

'That was the plan before you advised of the four litters, when they were going to be easy to transport. Now I need more space and fewer eyes. I also have units there that can very quickly be converted to suit the requirements.'

Fewer eyes. The statement itself was obvious with its meaning. The civilians were to not be involved in the transfer of the wolves. That could not be avoided easily and meant that the administrator's definition of by any means necessary got wider. Possibly, just possibly, he was reading too much into the words.

'Sir, the civilians?'

'What about them?' Puppet Master asked.

'What are we doing with them?'

'They're just victims of another interstellar accident,' Administrator declared bluntly, confirming his first belief. 'That's what's going to happen to them. There will be no witnesses that are not on my payroll that survive. But I do have to warn you, you have company on the way.'

'Company?' Leyton replied. 'What do you mean?'

Administrator let out a frustrated sigh. 'I have bad news for you. I have been advised that the emergency beacon that was sent out before you shut it down got picked up by a Stellar Protection Force patrol ship. At this present moment, I don't know how many people are on the patrol ship. What I do know is that the vessel is headed for your position and if it's at max capacity... you could be looking at a lot of firepower. Too much firepower to contend with. You need to take the ship as soon as possible and deny them access to the *Galactic Passage* until my team is with you. Only then will you have the required firepower to fend them off.'

SPF. They may not be special forces, but they were tough soldiers. They had to be. The low life scum that the local law enforcement refused to fight put up too much resistance for basic grunts. That was the sort of opponent who the SPF were deployed to fight. They even stood as a first line of defence against the many nations that were currently at war with the United Planetary Nations. For a man who knew everything though, Leyton expected the administrator to know the numbers on the patrol vessel.

'How come you don't know the numbers, sir?'

'Excuse me?' Administrator spat.

'You run the agency,' Leyton explained, cautious. 'We are the ones who give the military their intelligence and tell them where they are going to be deployed. One of the things we learn in training is to know more about our friends than our enemies. How do you not know what's on a patrol ship under UPN control?'

Administrator grunted and muttered something inaudible, a curse. 'You will mind how you speak to me, understand? Now, I do not know because this was not a sanctioned mission. Off the books. What I do know is that the ship is assigned to a training voyage being led by a sergeant close to retirement. I will keep you updated as more information comes through.'

A retiring sergeant. Someone that most likely carried more years of front-line service than most senior officers combined. This was going to be a tough guy to fight against but not impossible. Leyton's mind drifted over to the other part of his superior's statement. The training element. This meant that he was most likely going to be up against raw recruits. Given the morals of his team, there was a fifty-fifty chance that they would want to kill them regardless or take pity on them and let them live.

'Do you have a name or any intel on the sergeant?' Leyton questioned. 'And how do you suggest we hold them off?'

'His name is Duke. He isn't a pushover. Once you have control of the ship, all that you have to do is jump. That or seal all air locks and blast doors. This isn't the first time you've taken a ship. Don't make me remind you how to do the job you've perfected. Am I clear?'

'Yes, sir,' Leyton grumbled.

All those times he secured a ship controlled by hostiles were nothing in comparison to this. These were innocent people and fellow soldiers. One group he could shoot on sight. The other he was meant to keep his rifle steered away from. There was nothing similar in what had to be done.

'To make myself clear,' Administrator growled, 'you are to relocate your team to a new position. Once secured and my team has liaised with you, take control of the ship. Release the assets so that they do not starve. Bring the vessel to the *Vestibule*. Forget this ever happened. Then proceed to the next mission. Am I clear?'

Leyton clenched his teeth together and spoke quietly. 'Crystal, sir.'

'Good,' Puppet Master said.

The comms cut and he was left in silence. A rock, a hard place and a mouth full of teeth. This was not a hand that should be dealt to anyone.

His fist slammed into one of the crates. There was no way he could let the passengers die. Equally, there was no way he could fail knowing that the administrator would ensure he never saw the light of day again if he did. He could live with the deaths of the civilians on his conscience. That was an art he had reluctantly mastered after several missions where he was unable to rescue those in need. Leyton could not, however, live with a bullet between his eyes. It was a sick, tortuous choice.

The art of self-preservation was not a tricky one to understand, nor difficult to make. That was how Puppet Master made it into being in command. The administrator clearly knew a person's choice before he even gave them the options by setting them up to make whatever decision he wanted them to make regardless of their personal opinions and feelings. That gave him everything he needed to maintain a position of power. Everything was just politics, keeping everyone precisely where he needed them and making them do what he needed.

'Wish I was on my way to fucking Veralaa,' he hissed, thinking of the planet paradise that everyone dreamed of going to where the sand was a deep red, oceans a perfect blue and the drinks never stopped being poured. He had only ever been once. On official business of course. Leyton could never afford somewhere like that on his salary.

He shut down his tac-pad and returned to the rest of his team. No one reacted to his entry. Each one of them stared fearfully toward the pen where a strange chattering sound emanated quietly. The door had buckled around the lock where the wolves appeared to have tried to escape. Even the cage walls had been damaged in a desperate bid for freedom. His agents had their weapons were at the ready. Even Professor Ainslot was hesitantly carrying out his research, flinching at every sound the creatures made.

One more attempt at breaking free and there was a good chance the assets would manage to bust out of their confinement. Once that happened, the slaughter would be immeasurable. His team would barely last. Hopefully their suffering would only be brief.

'What's going on? When did this happen?' Leyton whispered, as though he was being stalked by a predator keyed in on noise.

'About a minute or two after you left,' Jerome answered. 'It's weird. They all started to panic like something was going on. Was close to giving the order to get everyone out or put them down. Then they just stopped and started making that noise. Haven't stopped.'

He scowled at the explanation. 'That doesn't make any sense. What have you done to them?'

'Not a thing boss, not a thing,' Jerome said. 'It's like something spooked them. They tried to get away and when they realised that they couldn't... they just froze. Waiting for it. Whatever *it* is.'

'I don't like it,' Leyton said. 'What do you think scared them then?'

'Not a clue,' Jerome answered.

'It wasn't anything we did,' Hatty added. 'We've just been doing our thing. Nothing new.'

'Professor, your thoughts?' Leyton asked.

'Something's bugging them, for sure,' the professor concurred.

'What could scare an apex predator like this?' Leyton questioned, trying to get a better understanding of their situation.

Professor Ainslot locked eyes with him, sighed and scratched his head. 'Normally? Natural disasters can cause an apex predator to get this scared. Or a superior species. One designed to hunt the apex. But out here on this ship? I haven't got a clue what could be doing this. I have a few working theories that could potentially explain it but nothing worthwhile yet.'

'Give me your best theory,' Leyton ordered.

'Well,' Professor Ainslot said, extending the syllable. 'My best ones are either there's something wrong with the ship that they can sense or there's something out there like a black hole that they know is nearby. Whatever it is, if they're scared then I think it's safe to say we should be scared too.'

'I can tell you it's nothing to do with the ship,' Schottler announced from his station. 'Ship's perfectly fine.'

'Okay, so where does that leave us now?' Jerome asked. 'Apart from thinking a black hole is going to fuck us over.'

'Back to where we were a few minutes ago,' Suttle announced then, while pointing at the pen, asked the question that he was dreading being asked. 'What do we do when they get so scared, they decide they're getting out and don't stop until they do? We have more than just them to worry about.'

Leyton felt something twang in his chest and a rapid sinking feeling in his gut. He was unsure of what to do now. Tell the truth? Some of the truth? Or none of it? He had to consider the variables. All those variables relied on Jerome and how he would react. He chose to give some of the truth but not all and only what he considered safe to supply the team. It went against how he felt but it would give the best outcome.

'I just had a briefing with the administrator,' Leyton announced abruptly. 'We have to prepare to vacate this room and find somewhere else to fortify. I'm under instructions to allow the wolves out of the pen if they become too cramped, which they already are. There are some difficulties that we'll have to overcome but they're nothing compared to the preparations that we now need to do.'

'And what's that for?' Jerome asked suspiciously. His tone was that of someone who knew more than he admitted, something Leyton would have to keep an eye on.

'That distress beacon we cut out?' he started with a sharpness in his voice. 'We didn't get to it fast enough. Now, we have a UPN patrol ship on its way to investigate and provide the crew with some assistance. That means we need to take control of the ship and get out of here as soon as possible to avoid them.'

'Why do we need to do that?' Onyx questioned. 'What's so bad about fighting back?'

'Because if we do that, then they'll put out their own distress call that we won't be able to cut off,' Leyton explained. 'If that happens, this ship will be marked by the UPN Navy. We won't get anywhere near Earth without being stopped.'

'That happens and we're out of the job,' Hatty added.

'Fuck that shit, I like having a job,' Kari said.

'What are we waiting for then?' Jerome said. He brandished his weapon eagerly, chomping at the bit to prove why he was better than him. 'Let's go for it.'

'Yeah!' cried Fellstrum. There was a mixture of hope and rage in her eyes. 'We're coming for you Jake!'

'I've got the first kill,' Onyx Perretti yelled.

The more trigger-happy members of the team spurred into action with the octane energy of fresh recruits oblivious to the risks of the universe. Fellstrum and Perretti had their weapons loaded for action. They even rushed to the ammo cases to take extra. Both had their eyes on the door when prepared, ready to leave the room at a moments' notice. Suttle and Hatty were not so eager to march on in a bloodthirsty rage. They hung back waiting for their orders. Professor Ainslot and Agent Schottler stood watching. For the briefest moment it felt like they were on a school yard. Where he led the typical school kids, Jerome led the bullies, and the professor filled the role of school geek with Ray Schottler. He could have laughed had the tension not been so high.

'Take a breath!' Leyton barked. 'We are not killing anyone else. You hear me?'

'You can't be serious?' Jerome hissed. 'They have Deulche. We're going to get him back then we need to take the ship. It's a no-brainer. People are going to die. I don't know about you, but I say it should be them instead of us that die. Don't you think command would want it that way?'

'Care to ask that again?' he asked. It was more of a challenge than a threat. When Jerome backed down, he turned to face the team. 'We'll make a move for the command deck in a few hours. When we enter the passenger decks, we will go through the crowds, not around them. While there are civilians in the way, we will not be engaged by the ship's crew. They won't want to risk any collateral damage, and while we're armed the civilians won't come near us and try to play hero. It'll buy us some time to prepare and some much-needed cover. I'll lead the mission. Houghton, you stay here with Schottler and Ainslot. Keep them safe in case anyone comes poking their noses around here while we're away. Everyone else will be with me. For now, go check your gear and get some rest. I'll plan the route then we make our move.'

His team acknowledged their orders and went about their preparations. Combat armour was checked to ensure it was fully working. Tac-pads synced up with armour systems to make sure vitals were communicated. Bullets loaded up into magazines. While they were busy, Leyton took a seat in the corner of the room and brought up a glowing map of the liner on his tac-pad. After selecting the destination of the bridge, routes were automatically devised, each directing away from guaranteed areas of large congregations of people. He needed cover, but not so much that the civilians might go against his hopes of staying compliant. Of the eight different options presented to him, Leyton disregarded five of them instantly. They would either take too long or led them into areas where an ambush was almost guaranteed. The remaining three were good options, taking them through passenger quarters and away from facilities that would certainly be staffed by the crew. It was just a matter of choosing the right one.

Jerome pulled up a chair in front of him. Their eyes locked. The air between them was charged with anticipation. Leyton prepared himself for a fight. The enraged look of hunger for power was raw in his agent's eyes was unnerving. His subordinate wanted to say something. Or do something. The latter unlikely. He had had every opportunity previously to do something and never did. When the intimidation act failed to have any effect, Leyton took the lead and spoke first.

'I've told you before already to be careful with how you're speaking to me,' he said flatly.

'That was before you started to take things into your own hands, to defy orders given by the boss,' Jerome replied sharply. 'What gives you the right? You're not the administrator. You're just a lead field agent.'

'Then what gives *you* the right to decide who lives and dies if I'm a lead field agent and you're my subordinate?' Leyton countered. 'This is my team. This is my mission. I have done this job long enough to know when people don't need to be killed. This is one of those times.'

'Oh, so you're above Administrator?' Jerome asked. 'You can pick and choose which orders to follow while I have no choice but to follow yours?'

Leyton shut down the holographic projection above his gauntlet. He focussed on his second in command like a bull preparing to charge down a matador. 'Right now, yes. You're blinded from your own conscience by the mission. By the payoff when it's over. Your own progression. Can't you see that? These are civilian families. Security teams trained in how to say *no* with authority. A civilian ship's crew. Not soldiers waging war. We're better trained than most soldiers ever will be. There is no logic in using force against them. I refuse to follow orders without a good reason. If these people were all mad psychos, terrorists and murderers then yes, I would follow the mission parameters to the letter. Not now, no. This is simply wrong. It doesn't sit with me.'

'For you, maybe,' Jerome hissed. 'Not for me.'

'And what do you mean by that?' Leyton demanded.

'I know what the orders are. I heard them. Remember? So, we will do things the way the boss says they're to be done.'

Leyton scoffed at the attempt to take control from him. There was no chance of that happening any time soon. Leyton scratched his chin, looked away for a moment then took hold of Jerome by the scruff of the neck and pulled him down to press his head against the table between them. He pushed the man's face into the metal surface, feeling him squirm beneath his armoured palm.

'You listen to me,' he growled. 'Because this is the last time that I'm going to have this conversation with you. I am not going to kill civilians. None of the team are going to kill civilians. Not on this mission or any other afterward. You will follow my orders and if we must go down this road again, I'll space your ass before you even realise what just happened to you. Now you go, get some chow down you and learn your place. Get out of my sight and wait for the order.'

'That's why you're benching me,' Jerome said. 'You don't want me to prove I'm right about this. That you're not fighting for the cause anymore.'

'I'm benching you because I don't trust you. Simple as. You don't follow orders. And I'm afraid that you'll do something that'll get us all killed. Focus on your job. Keep the professor and Schottler safe, and I'll consider filing a positive report when we get back. Put you up for recommendation to have your own team. Anything that gets you away from me quickly.'

'Understood, sir,' Jerome said as he walked away.

Leyton returned to his plans quickly, seeing the routes and considering the potential consequences and threats awaiting them at every turn, on every deck and through the entire mission. After he would research the sergeant leading the patrol ship enroute to them. He needed to know whatever he could about this incoming obstacle. Yet he could not shake the need to constantly check on Jerome. What was he saying? Who was he saying those things to? Was he being listened to? Some of the things his subordinate said did not quite fit, like an ill-fitting jigsaw piece, with his conscience. Something else had to be going on. Every time he tried to focus on his task at hand, his mind drifted. Jerome's voice and his words whispered at the back of his mind. He glanced over to his second in command. That false smile that all was under control couldn't hide the rage the man permeated.

For his own safety Leyton decided that he would be best to stay in his combat armour as much as possible. That and making sure he kept his weapon loaded, with the safety off, at all times. If Jerome turned on him, he would start with anyone loyal to him and sway them to his own agenda. He needed to be ready for that eventuality.

His head throbbed. The mental anguish he was being inflicted pierced his mind like a super-heated steel blade. He wondered if Administrator ever felt like this. All he'd need is a painkiller and that would be enough to see him through the last of the planning until he could get some rest. Leyton hoped when he did rest, his team would have his back.

Jesa

Emptiness. Darkness. Eternal abyss. Those were the things that had filled her slumber over the last few days. There were no dreams, no images, not even any voices. Just dark silence. It wasn't pleasant, but it was better than dreaming of Barbaros, and providing her with a much-needed break. More than that, she was able to realise something: his hold of terror on her had faltered. If she felt safe enough to sleep without seeing him in her dreams, then it could only mean one thing. Jesa awoke with a smile as she realised it. She was free of him. Really free. The man could no longer hurt her, and she believed it as the truth.

She left her cabin and made her way to the galley to have some breakfast. A sludgy bowl of oats flavoured with syrup and cinnamon. It was simple, but better than what she endured on the *Saridia*. She was joined by Ronan. He too had a large bowl of oats with what looked and smelled like bacon Actual bacon. She'd heard of this but never tried it. Pigs had never been introduced to the outer colonies. She wondered how it tasted. Judging by his protective stance over the meal, Ronan wasn't in a hurry to share.

Arche and Udal'e soon joined them for breakfast, each taking a seat around the table with their servings of sludge brightened with a variety of toppings or spices. Immediately the conversation shifted to what they were going to do that day for training. Ronan joked that it didn't matter because he would outdo them all, while Joane challenged that with friendly competitive rivalry. Abe tried to reassure that intelligence outperformed strength and skill. It was funny. When she had first met them, it was easy to see how distant they were from each other. Now? They were comrades. A family unit. The way they looked at each other had changed. The trio no longer took every opportunity to cut their peers down with sharp words but spoke warmly. Affectionately. Kindly. How could people so different in personality have been brought together with a joint desire to serve and protect the UPN and its people? For that matter, how could she, a woman who despised the UPN for so much of her life, now be breaking bread with them.

The sergeant. It was all down to him. Had to be. He was the only common feature of their lives. He was a person that inspired unity.

What wasn't clear to her was why they all came into the military. What was it that put each of these Corporals on the path to be on that ship with her.

'What got you guys into the military?' Jesa asked. 'Why do you want to do this? Put your lives on the line.'

'You go first,' Corporal Moasa said to Joane Arche.

'There are a few reasons. Mainly, I needed to prove myself,' she admitted reluctantly. The honesty was painful for her. That much was easy to tell. 'I was always intended to be a boy. My parents prepared themselves to have a boy. Everything they bought was for a boy. The sports gear, action figures and how they furnished the baby room. Then I came along... and my dad was disappointed in me for how I was born. Ever since then, I've had to do everything I can to be better than a boy. What's the best way to prove my dad's wrong for being disappointed than by joining the military? Be better than a man in a man's world and all.'

'Shit, we didn't know that part,' Ronan said. 'You kept that quiet!'

'I know,' Arche muttered.

'I'm sorry to hear that,' Abe added.

'So am I,' Jesa whispered, feeling instantly guilty for even asking.

Joane wiped away a tear. 'It's okay. I made it this far, didn't I? It's not something that I really intend people to find out about. That and what happened with Hearra...'

Corporal Arche had a look in her eyes that she recognised from her own expression. She had lost someone dear to her. Someone so important that without them they were less of a person. Jesa didn't know who this Hearra was. It was clear though that something had happened to her that pushed Joane into joining the military.

Corporal Moasa caught her gaze then politely gave a vague explanation of who Hearra was and what had happened. It cut Jesa up knowing that Outers had done that to Arche's relative. And she had been persuaded to hate the Centies for the crimes they committed when her own people were performing horrors that were just as disgusting.

Jesa wanted to take the conversation away from Joane. It wasn't fair to keep attention on her. 'What about you Ronan?'

The giant of a man smiled. 'It's a sort of rite of passage that I have to go through. My home planet isn't a part of the United Planetary Nations government, but it's strongly allied with them with an agreement that the UPN Military can use their planet to host a base of operations in the sector if its people can be recruited for ten years minimum in the military. If we want to do longer, we can do. So, we join the military and for the most part serve our ten years. It teaches discipline and how to fight in a war so we can protect our families and our people should we need to. The more senior we are when we come back, the more respected we are in the tribe.'

'That's actually quite nice,' Joane said softly. Her voice hushed. 'I didn't think you were the sort of person to be that... poetic?'

'I'm not, but my planet is, so y'know. Don't have a choice. Besides, if I didn't do this then I would never have left the planet.' Corporal Moasa leaned back in his chair and finished the last of his breakfast. 'What about you Abe? How'd you get into this?'

'My family,' Udal'e answered sternly. Almost as if he was ashamed. 'My entire family is a family of military veterans in some form or other. All my brothers are war heroes. I'm the youngest of five and I needed to break out of their shadows. I wasn't ever the strongest or the most disciplined. I wanted to be a businessman.' He laughed at the thought of how different a career that would have been. 'I mean, it would have been easy. Nine to five. Safe work. No weekend work. Time off. I could have made a success of myself safely. But no. Before I could even decide anything for myself, I'd been signed up by my family.'

'I don't understand?' Jesa said. 'I thought it had to be you to sign up? Others can't sign up for you, can they?'

'Certain people can with the Authorisation Against Defection or Avoidance Act,' Joane explained.

'What's that?' Jesa asked.

'It gives parents or legal guardians the right to sign up a person under the age of twenty-five but older than sixteen to the military without their permission if they feel the person in question is doing everything that they can to avoid the military without good reason,' Abe answered. 'To be exempt, you need to be employed in a core service industry, medical, law enforcement, professional, that sort of thing, already well established in a successful career or medically not cleared. I wasn't any of those, even though I was planning to run a successful business.'

This was disgusting for Jesa to hear. As much as a parent may love their child, to make such an important life decision as that for them without their consent was horrible. No one should have their life chosen for them like that. She knew that better than most. Her life had been chosen for her illegally through murder. But this was a law that allowed parents to do it. How could someone be legally allowed to do such a thing?

'Why is that a law?' she demanded. 'I can't believe you Centies would allow that sort of thing.'

206

Ronan shook his head. 'It was a needed evil. Before our time, probably when the sarge was still a kid, there was a huge movement where people refused to fight in a war that threatened Earth. There was an uprising in Sol. Mars tried to break away from the UPN and took control of all Martian based ships. Most of Earth's fleets were out on campaigns on the edges of UPN territory. With a heavily reduced fleet and help weeks away, Earth was losing, badly. And fake propaganda spreading lies was putting people off joining the military to help save their home. They desperately needed troops and they didn't want to use conscription. The government was afraid of the backlash. So, the law was made to let parents and guardians put family members in the military and boost the numbers. That way, it was the families to blame. Not the government. After the uprising, the law remained and was kept quiet. It's mainly officers that use it now to keep the military in the family, and because they know about it, they do it in a way that no one finds out about it.'

'My grandpa is an officer in the Army,' Abe added. 'He knows all this stuff and he's the one that pushed to have me signed me up. Can't really go against him. To speak out I'd be disowned by the family. Kicked out. Stripped of everything they have ever given or would give me. Worse still, I'd be doing him the greatest of dishonours by going against his wishes. I couldn't live a life knowing I've dishonoured and disappointed him. So even though I have the right to leave, I can't.'

A fate worse than being in prison. At least criminals were put in prison for a reason and for the most part had the chance of getting out early. There were things about this supposedly civilised quadrant from humanity's birthplace that Jesa really was glad did not happen in the Outer Colonies and stopped with the Central Colonies.

'What about the sarge? Any idea why he—'

A warning siren blasted for a moment then ceased, cutting her off mid-question. Everyone stopped what they were doing and waited. Ronan Moasa chuckled at her confusion.

'What was that?' Jesa asked.

'Warning klaxon –– it means that we're dropping out of the jump for our halfway breather soon,' he explained.

'But we don't need a warning, do we?' she questioned. 'It's not like we've never been in a jump before or it's a bumpy ride to drop out of the jump?'

'Normally, you'd be right,' Corporal Arche laughed. 'We're coming out of a long jump in a patrol ship after moving faster than standard. What's the longest you've been in slip space for?'

She shrugged, 'About two days. Maybe three. Didn't feel too great afterward though.'

'How fast were you going?' Abe questioned.

'Normal, maybe point-seven of max jump speed?' Jesa replied.

'We've been going longer and faster,' Joane explained.

'I take it that's not good?' Jesa asked.

Ronan shook his head, walked over to the counter, rummaged in the drawers and cupboards, then returned with a sick bag. 'Keep this close. Let's just say you'll need it.'

Jesa took the bag and waited in silence. A few minutes later, the usual sensation of dropping out of the jump washed over her. It was nothing exceptional, something she had done many times before. It took Jesa a couple of minutes before she felt her body slowly react to the change from prolonged time spent in the jump to real space that the soldiers had hinted toward. Her skin turned pale, and her palms clammy. Cold sweat poured from her skin. Her mouth filled profusely with warm saliva before the inevitable retching as she vomited into the sick bag. The longer the vomiting continued the more she felt like she wanted to die, and by the time the sickness passed, she felt like she was not that far away from death. Jesa's limbs were heavy and weak. She struggled for breath. The taste of acid and breakfast lingered a little too long in her mouth to be comfortable.

Ronan smiled kindly at her and took the sick bag away from her. He returned with a fizzy liquid and gestured her to drink. It had a strange citrus taste, or what she believed to be citrus flavour, and almost instantly she could feel her stomach easing its wrath on her. The disgusting flavour in her mouth was washed away. Her head buzzed with a strange numbness as exhaustion set in. The soldiers spoke around her, but she couldn't make out their words. Ronan Moasa took the empty cup away for her then helped her out of the galley and to the flight deck with the crew and Duke. They took one look at her and nodded, as if they expected her to be brought up to them. She was so occupied with watching Ronan leave that Jesa never realised the sergeant approach with an emergency blanket to wrap her in. The warmth from the rough material helped calm and relax her. She hummed delightfully as she felt herself sinking comfortably into the chair.

Duke gave her a warm smile, a pat on the shoulder and returned to the conversation with Ivan and Valentina. She closed her eyes and listened as best she could. The words she could make out were mainly jargon that she had no intentions of ever understanding. Some of the information she could understand, coordinates, speeds and simple words saying they were near hostiles. But she remained quiet. Grateful that she was not alone and that they clearly cared for her well-being. The presence of a man looking at her could be felt on the other side of her eyelids.

'How're you feeling?' Duke asked.

'Like shit,' she replied weakly.

Jesa could sense Duke smiling at her. 'Have you popped any pills yet?' She could not think of an answer and when she did not reply he rustled with a container and continued. 'Here, have a couple of mine. They'll take the edge off. Might send you to sleep. Better to be sleeping than feeling rough, wouldn't you say?'

A soft smile crossed her lips at the caring gesture. She opened her eyes long enough to take the tablets. Jesa was disappointed when they did not do their magic straight away.

'Where are we?'

'We're in sector three of the Miksmal Straight,' Duke explained. 'There's not much out here in the way of scenery except for a few rogue planets and asteroids. No friendly fleets for weeks. Perfect smuggler route. Also, a dangerous route.'

'Dangerous how?' she questioned. Something about the location name stirred thought in her mind. It was familiar.

'There are pirate stations out here,' Duke explained. 'The worst of the worst from humans and aliens alike make up their numbers.'

'It's not just that that we've got to worry about,' Valentina said.

'What else is there?' Jesa asked.

'We're about half a week away from reaching the ship to answer the distress beacon,' Ivan explained. 'That puts us a few weeks out from where we're actually meant to be. I hope this isn't a trick or I'm going to be pissed. But if anything goes wrong, we're nowhere near anyone that can actually help us.'

Jesa didn't reply. Her mind was going around the location name, remembering why it was familiar. The Miksmal Straight was one of the main trade routes in the area, running straight through several provincial territories and was considered a neutral zone. Cargo ships were allowed to have an escort of gunships to protect them from attack but were never allowed to be the aggressor without facing heavy repercussions. It didn't stop pirate raids though. She knew that the pilot would have his finger on the trigger of the ship's weapons, keeping an eye out for anyone showing too much interest in them. And there was something else about that strip of space. It had another danger. A threat that she spent a long time staying one step ahead of. One that would be the end of them all one day when it grew strong enough.

'This is Crevari hunting grounds,' she murmured.

Duke sighed. 'It is.'

'And you didn't tell me. Why?'

'I didn't want to worry you,' he said. 'You've got enough on your mind as it is.'

'Are there any nearby?' she asked.

'Not a thing,' Ivan answered. 'Got the scopes set to max range and primed to pick up Crev frequencies. They're not getting anywhere near us without me knowing about it.'

'Or us doing something about it either,' Valentina added. Jesa knew she meant shooting them down at the first chance they had.

'We wouldn't let anything happen to you,' Duke said.

'Then why did we stop here?' Jesa questioned, her voice trailing as the medication started to take effect.

'It didn't matter where we stopped,' Duke replied. 'It would have been Crev space regardless. The cruise ship is slap bang in the middle of it all. Of all the places to stop, it stopped there. And I must tell you... we're not leaving until we've finished at the cruise ship. We won't be out here any longer than we need to be though. Don't fancy staying in this sector and I don't want to leave them out here either.'

'Because they'll kill us all if they find us,' Jesa said.

'Exactly,' the sergeant said.

'Crevs don't discriminate,' Valentina added. 'They kill us all the same. Central, mid or outer. All we are to them is food.'

'And we're almost there?' Jesa asked. She opened her eyes slowly. Everything was blurry until she blinked a few times.

'That's right,' the sergeant answered.

'How long do you think we'll be there for?'

The sergeant shook his head. 'I don't know. Hopefully no more than a few days.'

'Sarge, we're going to get some food. You want anything?' Ivan asked while heading out of the flight deck with Rodriguez.

'We're okay,' Duke replied. 'Thanks.'

The sergeant stood there watching over her, protective. She felt safe. No matter what happened to her now, whatever the threat may be, she knew that the man and his team would do everything in their power to save her. That was easy to see. Though at first a bitter pill to swallow, she was glad to have succumbed to their better nature and forsake her former life. That didn't mean she wouldn't yearn to be behind the controls of her ship and carry on working to keep herself safe. That part of her life was almost second nature.

What had she done to deserve that sort of kindness? Surely none of the information Jesa had handed over could give enough reason for it. Somehow it had been enough. For some reason, the soldier was showing her not pity but pure good intentions.

'Thank you,' she whispered.

'What for?'

'Being so kind.' Her eyes closed again. The vibrations of the ship lulled her to rest. Or was it the medication's effect strengthening on her? 'I didn't think you Centies would be so kind. That you could be so kind.'

'There's a lot the outer colonies don't think or believe about those of us from the central colonies,' Duke answered. His voice seemed distant. Thoughtful. 'There's too much propaganda floating around, too many half-truths and half-lies. Too many coincidental events that justify thoughts. We aren't as bad as people say. Not saying we're saints but we're not bad.'

'Why do you think the Outers hate you so much?'

Duke hummed thoughtfully. He was probably smiling at her. 'I think some of it is lack of education. Probably a lot of it is lack of education or the facts being kept hidden from you. You guys think we hoard the resources we produce and share only the best with the central colonies, the okay resources with the Midi's and give the Outers the scraps. What no one that thinks those things realises though is that even in freezers fresh stock degrades in quality. It takes weeks or even months for goods to get to the outer colonies. The fresher stuff will be inedible by then. The best needs to be consumed quicker and that's by the central colonies where it's freshest. Then from there people sadly get what they are given. Then we have money that causes problems. Doesn't need to be an outer verses central argument. Taxes are a constant rate for everyone but because the outer colonies have higher cost of goods thanks to import charges, the financial burden is felt more there than in the central colonies who have more disposable income. Add to that the

211

fact that crime in the outer colonies is rife, murder higher than the central average and corruption amongst the separatist factions putting central funds to bad use, and this makes us in the central planets seem privileged or that we don't care. All of it just divides us.'

'And the wars?'

'They don't help. But when one cell of terrorists is protected by every man, woman and child? It isn't safe for us. We can't pick and choose the enemy in that situation. Too many risks. Every time we deployed soldiers out there, everyone we saw was the enemy. Had to be treated like they were the enemy to keep our forces safe. That in turn made people who were not exactly friendly but not exactly enemies become fully fledged enemies. Things turned bad too quickly all too often. And there was never any winning for either side.'

The wars in the outer colonies were the things that people like Barbaros preyed on. Gave meaning behind their words which without them events carried no meaning at all. When they said the central colonies were on their way to them to wage war and murder the people there, their kin, the UPN was there to make those fantasies become reality. She had been brought up to be at first wary, untrusting, of anyone under the UPN flag. Then under her former master's control she learnt to truly hate them as his lies were proven to be truth. Like the Burning of Hela, where the UPN Navy bombarded the city of Hela into radioactive slag. They were told it was an attack to slaughter civilians in a bid to further their control over the outer colonies. She knew that there were several dozen militia factions in the city and that they had carried out several coordinated attacks in the weeks beforehand. Killing hundreds, if not thousands, of innocent people in UPN-controlled territories. What the people in the outer colonies weren't told though was that Hela had been mainly evacuated by covert UPN forces. Yet, even knowing that, at the time Jesa had been ignorant to the atrocities the outer colony factions had committed themselves in the name of their causes. She only saw the murderers in charge of the UPN fleet raining warheads down on the city.

She remembered the carnage of the aftermath of one of the UPN assaults. Barbaros showed her the images to strengthen her will to his cause. The anger she felt. The sick, relentless feeling in her gut of loss consumed her and pushed her to aligning more with him. But how was she rewarded for the loyalty that she had shown? She was tagged. He would have disposed of her at the push of a button.

Jesa opened her eyes once more. Duke sat staring at her with the warm smile a father would wear when looking proudly at a daughter.

'Do you have family?' she asked.

'I have my mum back home. A few cousins and other relatives.'

'But do you have a family of your own?'

He shook his head softly. 'Never had the time. The UPN always came first. It's why I want to retire. I want to have a life that's mine, and to try to have a family while I have the energy to keep up.'

It was always a good reason to get out of anything. She felt sorry for him to have given up his life to protect people that he would never meet. Civilisations who would never know the sacrifice he made. More people that did not deserve his selfless act than those that did. Maybe she didn't even deserve it. She was a stranger after all. And he was prepared to give it all up for her.

'Anyway, get yourself to bed and rest,' Duke instructed. 'We go back into the jump in a few hours. It won't be as bad next time we come out of the jump. But you need to get some sleep.'

Jesa nodded her head and staggered weakly out of the flight deck to her cabin. Arche aided her through the sleeping quarters from just outside the galley until she was in her room. When Jesa felt her head hit the pillow she drifted away back into a deep sleep. While she faded away, returning to the world of slumber, she hummed a melody her mother used to sing to her as a young child. When she was still alive to sing it. A lullaby that had been passed down through the generations. Then her father would join them with the song, and they'd sing it together. The words flooded back to her as if they had only just been sung to her, even though she had not sung it for so many years. It was a song of family. Of love. Of being together.

She felt a little embarrassed when she realised that Arche was still in the cabin with her, but it did not deter her. Jesa carried on humming until she drifted away.

The people who would keep her safe deserved to hear it. Her adoptive family deserved to know the song. Everyone deserved to have a family. Even those who never had the time for one before. Especially the ones who should have a family.

She lost herself in the sweet melody and could hear her mother there singing with her. She could feel her holding her. Gently brushing her hair until she fell asleep. Her father would join in with his deep, husky voice that was powerful yet soft, superior to all their but somehow still equal. A tear fell as she could see them smiling at her. She was happy that she had found a new family, one to love and protect her as much as they did. That would make sure she was the best she could be. Even if they were Centies.

Beatrice Lenoia

The uneasiness her crew felt had continued to permeate since the assault started. They received very little chance to catch their breath from the continuous onslaught, and it was grinding down on them. It had been a few days since the security team showed their true colours and launched their attack. They seemed intent on making their way to her bridge. In response, while her more experienced security crew held them off, her engineers locked down as many of the bulkhead doors, pressure doors and blast doors as they could to keep the attackers secured in the engineering deck. They had even gone as far as to rig the maintenance tubes connecting the luxury quarters at the bow of the ship to the engineering decks at the stern to blow as a last line of defence. Just in case their assailants tried to use them to get around the lockdown imposed on them. It would be troublesome for her crew but at least everyone would be safe. All the while she insisted that Communications Chief Rhys Dolga was wrong when he told her that the comms was completely jammed. That something was stopping them from communicating with the outside. Hoping that some of the distress calls they put out would be heard by someone was all she had left. Their mental strength was being tested beyond anything they had ever trained to handle. Each member of the crew was ready to collapse at an instant. Beatrice wasn't prepared to give up the only thing they had left to hang onto.

The pressures though were heavier for Beatrice. She could not show any weakness. She needed to be stronger than the strongest of her crew, to remain a pillar of support for those that needed it. Her fatigue had to stay hidden, kept close like a dear secret that could never be uttered. She pushed to be always present. Be the leader that they were all looking for. Beatrice only left the bridge when she absolutely had to for rest or to inspect the passengers and crew. She went as far as insisting food was brought to her, so she never had to leave her post unnecessarily. Everyone seemed to follow that example.

Then there was the burden of staying on the float through space. Going against the requests of the crew to leave. As much as she wanted to return home too, to bring everyone on-board to safety, she knew they needed to stay put and wait it out. Help was on its way. It had to be. Their beacon she was sure was sent out had been travelling for days before Dolga said the messages weren't getting through. Surely the UPN or at least a UPN-sympathetic fleet, station or patrol had to be

215

within that range. But she had not heard anything back yet. No one answered. Or maybe they had, and it was taking time for help or responses to reach them? Then again, if their outbound transmissions couldn't send that only meant that inbound communications couldn't be received as well.

To add to her worries there was the matter of the passengers. She had made the decision that they would not know a thing about what was going on. No announcements. No slip of the tongue. Total silence about anything to do with their predicament. The only thing she allowed the passengers to know was that they were experiencing a technical issue that needed to be repaired and that they were to stay above F Deck under penalty of being fined for breach of security. By now she was sure they knew that something else was going on, that things weren't as she portrayed them to be.

The first couple of days were amicable. People accepted the excuse that something had happened and that they needed to stop for repairs. When the time spent stationary persisted, people started to make their feelings known and rumours that weren't really rumours began to spread like wildfire of occasional gunfire being heard from the lower decks. Seeing blood stains on the floor that weren't there before after the crew rushed through did nothing to dissolve the suspicions. There was only so many times the crew could tell them that it was a fault with the piping they were hearing or that someone got hurt fixing something before they stopped believing it.

Beatrice tried to take her mind off it all and looked over the energy consumption statistics for the fourth time since her shift started. There was a second cargo hold, a little smaller than the first, with unusual amounts of power being consumed now. Thankfully, the amount under consumption was reduced in comparison to the first. It was clear what was happening. The stowaways had spread out. But why? What was making them spread out from that initial room and need more space? How many more of them were there? Beatrice tried to access the security feeds for both rooms and everything in between. Each camera came back with no input. They had all been taken out. Or she had been cut out from them. Whatever their assailants were doing there, they were making sure it stayed private.

'Hey.'

Beatrice nearly jumped out of her skin. Adjutant Hender stood beside her. His eyes rest upon giant bags that took up most of his cheeks.

'How's the lockdown going?' she asked him, quickly yawning after with exhaustion.

'It's tough shutting them in while they're attacking us at the same time,' Franklin answered. 'We've been able to get most of the doors secured. The pressure doors are sealed from our side so there's nothing they can do to open them. The bulkhead doors however they keep going back to. It's like a game of cat and mouse. While we're sealing one door, they're either trying a new one or going back to one that we've already sealed to try and bypass it. There's just not enough of us to keep one step ahead and stay safe at the same time. It doesn't help that we have a couple more injured.'

'How are the injured?'

Adjutant Hender sharply inhaled. The hollow look in his eyes told of the loss before he spoke. Her hopes sank in an instant.

'We've lost another two,' Franklin Hender answered quietly. 'Our first aid stations are not hospitals. The longer we're out here, the more of our injured are going to die. I'm sorry, but I must recommend strongly that you reconsider your decision and get us into the jump for the nearest outpost. I don't care where. An Outer occupied station, a Midi planet. Anywhere. Just somewhere with a hospital and a security team. Please. We can claim mayday when we get there.'

'We can't,' she replied, the lump in her throat making it difficult to speak. 'You know we can't. We need to stay, at least for a few more days. For all we know help is on the way right now. They might even be about to come out of the jump.'

'Yes, but help might *not* be on the way as well,' Adjutant Hender countered pessimistically. 'We might be waiting to die a slow death.'

'I know,' she sighed. 'Give me a little longer. A few more days. Please. I know we'll be safe until then.'

'Okay Captain, I can do that for you,' Franklin said grimly. 'But I need you to listen to me when I think it's too much. We have passengers to think about. We can't put them at risk on the hopes of help arriving.'

Beatrice smiled and mouthed *thank you* to her adjutant. 'How's the prisoner?' she asked as a change of topic. 'Has he said anything yet?'

She had not been to see the prisoner since they captured him. That was something she wanted to avoid at all costs. He had been a part of the group responsible for the deaths of some of her crew. If she went in there earlier, there would be no telling how she would have reacted. It was safer for him that way. But it had been a while since her last update. Beatrice needed to know what was going on.

'Still complaining and making threats. Nothing new there.'

Beatrice placed her head into her hand. 'He hasn't said anything that's useful to us?'

'Not a thing,' Franklin admitted reluctantly. 'He just makes threats that his friends will come save him, kill us and then scupper the ship as payback.'

'Charming,' Beatrice muttered.

'Oh, he was a lot more charming with his wordings,' Adjutant Hender said. 'That was the polite version. What are your orders, Captain?'

That was the million-credit question. What were her orders? There were so many things she wanted to do, that needed to be done. So many things she was trained to do. But all of that was a past life when she was younger, fitter and more, importantly allowed, to carry those actions out.

There was once a time when if her ship were boarded, as ships under her command had been on a few occasions when she served, she would have broken protocol, abandoned her post on the bridge to join the ship's compliment of marines in combat. If there were survivors from the hostile ranks, she was one of the officers present for the interrogations. She was as ruthless in a gunfight as she was inflicting the right amount of pain to get the answers she needed. It was all an age ago now. The memory was nostalgic, empowering and woefully sad that her prime had been left in the past. A fact that her heart clung onto with steel claws carved from warfare.

And what was she doing now? Looking over information she knew like the back of her hand. She could almost predict what the ship diagnostics would read. What someone was going to say or announce. Progress to provide anything new was slow. She was older but she was not retired yet. There was more she could be doing. She could be more useful.

'To hell with it,' Beatrice cussed, pushing herself out of her command chair. 'I'm going to the brig.'

'Ma'am?' Franklin said. His expression was as confused as it was startled.

'I want to see if I can't get anything out of our prisoner myself,' Beatrice said. 'It's not like I'm much use right now.'

Franklin looked at her with concern. Understandable, really. Her frustration couldn't convince anyone that her thoughts and actions were logical or planned sanely. She considered the possibility of her attitude being illogical, an impulse decision to make herself feel better.

'Is that wise?' he asked her.

'Probably not,' she shrugged. 'But I need to see what I can do.'

'At least don't go alone,' Franklin asked.

'I'll take the on-duty guard with me,' Beatrice said. 'Don't worry I won't be alone. You have the bridge.'

Beatrice left her post, walking past the two men guarding outside and made her way to the brig at the back end of A-Deck.

A single guard stood outside. Nathaniel Knoxx, the deputy security officer. He leaned up against the wall, bored with his duties most likely. He was not remotely bothered by the commotion made by the prisoner inside the cell. His dark, battle-hardened face presented scars that could only have been earned through conflict. His left forearm had something non-regulation strapped around it, a sort of metal sleeve with a raised box. She would ask about that later.

'Ma'am,' he said politely while he bowed his head in respect.

'How's he been?' she asked.

'He's nothing short of a little shit that needs to be taught a lesson in respect, pardon my language,' he replied.

She waved down the apology with a smile. 'Speak freely. It's not exactly a standard situation we're in.'

Knoxx went ahead to tell Beatrice how their situation was less appealing than when he was stationed at Mars during the Uprising – a bloody campaign by a terrorist group known as Red Dust Rising to take Mars from the control of the UPN. She had never taken part in the United Planetary Nations' campaign to retake the planet. But she had heard the stories. The stress that it inflicted upon people was unbearable to consider. The guard told her all the details. How they were constantly at risk. The threats. The losses. She never appreciated just how many lives had been lost in the struggles.

That conflict was preferable to the guard because everyone knew where everyone stood and what they would do. How every member of the RDR would kill any UPN personnel without a second thought. On the *Passage*, there was no telling what the stowaways would do. They had the means to lay waste to everyone. Take control. And they didn't do it. It was a dark thought that Beatrice had considered but was reluctant to admit to.

Their talk moved to being more personal. Knoxx admitted how he suffered from an injury that he couldn't afford to have treated but the Veterans Assistance Committee refused to give him the financial assistance required. To make matters worse for the man, he struggled to find work afterward. No one wanted a broken soldier that could easily be containing countless mental traumas. That was until he got a job working security on the liners.

It was heart-wrenching to listen to. To know someone who gave so much to the UPN had struggled to get anything in return was enough to make her realise just how privileged she really was. He deserved more than this. But she was prepared to take the chance that he would happily live that life again.

'You want a change of duty? Prove some people wrong?'

'What're you thinking, Captain?' His eyes widened at the potential answer she could give.

'I want to know what he's doing here and who he is,' she explained, pointing into the brig. 'And I'm willing to do whatever it takes to make him talk. But I could use a hand.'

A cunning smile crossed Nathaniel Knoxx's lips. 'I'm in.'

The deputy security officer opened the door to the brig and led her through to the six cells. Each cell in the whitewashed and well-lit room had thick bars, designed to hold three prisoners. Thankfully, there was only the one prisoner occupying the cells. There were no witnesses for what was about to happen. He sat at the back of his cell and glared at them until he recognised her rank. The prisoner swaggered over with a confidence that prisoners would typically show when they were exactly where they wanted to be. She would happily wipe the smirk off his bruised and beaten face.

'See they've brought out the big guns,' he said. His jaw barely moved as he spoke. Probably due to the swelling from injuries sustained during his capture. 'What are you going to do Granny? Give me a telling off? Spit at me when your teeth get stuck in taffy?'

She waited for him to come to a stop at the cell and rest his hands on the bars. A glance and a nod to Knoxx was all the veteran needed. His lightning reactions had hold on one of the prisoner's hands. The fingers were bent back in an uncomfortable angle. He tried to keep his scream stifled but it would not be held back for long. She had no doubt that Knoxx would make him sing for her if she asked.

'My name is Beatrice,' Beatrice said calmly, once he stopped screaming. 'Not Granny. Care to tell me yours?'

'You can get fucked,' he spat back.

'Wrong answer.' In response to her saying that, Knoxx pulled back on the fingers a little more and splayed them then she asked over the sounds of his screams, 'Care to try that again?'

'It's Agent Jake Deulche,' the man snarled. 'You happy now?'

'Agent?' Beatrice asked. 'You a spy?'

'If I need to be,' Deulche said. 'Depends on the job we're doing. I'm a field agent.'

How worn out was he to talk like that? Or was Nathaniel that aggressive that there was no build up? Either way it gave results she was happy with so far.

'Who do you work for then?' Nathaniel Knoxx replied. 'Which government sent you out here?'

'Same people you pay your taxes to pal, the UPN,' the agent laughed.

'You're lying!' Beatrice cried.

Knoxx pulled back on the agent's fingers again. There was no way he could be working for the same government. How could that government, the UPN Government, sanction these people to shoot at her and her crew, putting the civilians on-board at risk? There was no justifiable reason she could conceive of that would justify it. The man had to be lying.

'If you can, I say you scan my identity chip, then you'll know I'm not lying,' Deulche insisted through gritted teeth.

'Do it,' she instructed.

'Yes, Captain,' Knoxx said.

Every member of the UPN service was implanted with an identity chip designed to show their clearance levels, the branch they worked in, and their rank or position. That way, they would be easily found by drones and at check points within UPN sectors. Or a body identifiable if the identifying markers were beyond recognition. Fortunately, even though the brig's terminal couldn't carry out facial recognition, it did have a scanner to carry out checks on prisoners to see if they were known criminals who also were implanted with chips. The system would work exactly the same. The guard went to the control panel at the end of the room and returned a few moments later after carrying out the scan from sensors built into the security cameras. Agent Deulche had retracted his arm and retreated to the other side of his cell where he could not be assaulted again.

'He is UPN, but it's classified,' Knoxx said. 'No idea about anything apart from his name and that he is a part of the UPN within the OIRD.'

That was of no comfort to Beatrice. Even if he was a member of the UPN, he had killed her crew. She could not in any good conscience be okay with that. Being on the same team was not going to help the prisoner. He would face justice when she was finished with him.

'So, what exactly are you doing on my ship?' she demanded.

'We're not meant to be here,' he admitted. 'Would rather not be here. Our ship got busted. We needed a new ride and yours was the nearest one that could do what we needed. The big boss got us a way on-board. The field commander didn't want us to kill anyone. But you lot wouldn't just leave us alone. Took things into our own hands and then you got me.'

'Those containers you came on with,' Beatrice said. 'We know you were taking them back to Earth.'

'Clever girl,' Deulche mocked. Confident now he was out of Knoxx's grip. 'Glad to see you can read the papers we provided.'

'What are you transporting in those fridges?' she asked. 'I need to know.'

'Fat chance I'll tell you that one,' the prisoner retorted. 'What I will tell you though, is that we're under orders to get the goods to Earth no matter what. So good luck if you think you can stop us because we don't fail a mission.'

Beatrice wanted to go in and slap him round the face, just to make herself feel better, before doing whatever it took to get him talking again. But he had at least given her some information to explain what was happening.

Whatever they were transporting was high enough in value that they were prepared to kill to make sure it reached its destination in secret. Had she not been so persistent in finding out what that cargo was, systems may have still failed, but would they have even come under attack? Would her crew still be alive? If so, then why were the rest of the prisoner's team so insistent on assaulting them now? What about their objective had changed? It could have been to release the prisoner. More realistically, they had realised the ship was not moving. If they were not going anywhere, it meant their cargo was not any closer to being brought to its destination. The only way they would get back on track to Earth is if they were in command of the vessel.

'We're done here,' Beatrice stated and started to leave the prisoner.

'What's happening?' Knoxx asked.

Beatrice waited until they were outside the brig and the door had slid shut before answering, 'They're going to keep attacking until they take the bridge. We need to formulate a plan to hold them off until help arrives.'

'And a failsafe? Need to have a backup plan if things don't work out,' the security guard said.

'Yes, we'll also think of a failsafe,' she agreed. 'Come on.'

Chapter 7
04/11/2675
16:23 Earth Standard Time

Beatrice Lenoia

The strength that Beatrice had discovered through the plight that they found themselves facing ran strong in her veins. Her eight hours of sleep turned into five, and that was more than enough. While she lay in bed waiting for the last few hours to tick by, she still had energy to spare. It was as if the strength she owned an age ago had never left her during all those years out of the military. Just lying dormant within her subconscious waiting for the perfect time to come back. More importantly, it felt good. It felt right. She was the woman that she should have stayed as once again.

Over the past couple days, she had further success in subsequent interrogations. At first Agent Deulche showed resilience. He refused to concede any further information. Then he started to give up a little intel after much persistence.

Beatrice had a team of nine field agents in total to contend with, one of whom was a professor. The other eight remained in the depths of her ship. Seven of them were fully trained to kill. They were armed with military-grade weaponry that they had been able to bring on-board in sealed containers. Now that they were known, there was no reason for them to remain within the shadows to act covertly or with restraint, and nothing to stop them from doing whatever was necessary to complete their mission. It made for a formidable enemy to contend with.

Beatrice could not take laying around in bed any longer. She marched over to the bridge once dressed and ready to resume command of the *Galactic Passage*. Her crew was weary. Anyone would be hard pressed to find a station without a pile of coffee cups to help the crew power through their extended shifts. She was proud that they had persisted through everything and could only hope it was the example that she led by that encouraged them. Adjutant Hender sat at the command chair. He stared at security feeds and ship diagnostics.

'How's it been?' She asked as she approached from behind.

'Not bad,' Hender yawned. He stood up to give her seat back. 'Thankfully, they've been pretty quiet down below decks. Just been tense. No one can relax.'

'Understandable,' Beatrice muttered. 'Have we had any updates on the injured? Have there been any more fatalities?'

'No one else has died,' Franklin answered. 'As glad as I am about that, there is a downside which is the injured aren't getting any better any time soon. It's taking its toll on the morale of the crew, having seen their friends die. Don't know how much longer they can hold up for.'

'And you?'

Her second in command looked down at her. His eyes were wet with tears at the thought of putting how he felt into words. There was no need for him to answer her. She felt the same. No loss was a good loss and the prolonged time without assistance made everything feel worse. Made everything they did seem futile in the grand scheme of things.

As Beatrice pulled up a more detailed tactical view of her ship's vitals, dancing in its mesmerising display of holographic light, an alarm cried out. A warning light flashed repeatedly plunging the bridge in and out of a shade of deep red. When both warnings were turned off and calmed down her heart started to pound. That was not an announcement from an internal system error. It was something external their long-ranged sensors picked up on that triggered the alarm.

'What was that?' she demanded quietly. When no one answered, she spoke louder and with more authority. 'Someone tell me what that was!'

Shortly after the commotion of people seeking answers began, Eric Schaps on Sensors and Scopes screamed out with their discovery.

'A stellar-storm!' he cried. 'It's about thirty minutes away.'

If it wasn't a group of armed stowaways raining havoc down on them, it was an act of God being thrown their way. Stellar storms were a rare phenomenon, for a long time thought to be a myth. Stories told by smugglers and long-distance haulers to scare visitors to their bar. Then they were discovered by a military vessel on a peacekeeping mission that barely made it back in one piece. Roaming clouds of electrically charged dust that generated enough electricity to short out most ships glided through space for as long as anyone knew with no telling how long they could last for. If they ever did die out. Not much was known about them due to how rare they were and how unpredictable they could be. They were known to range from a few hundred meters to tens or even hundreds of kilometres in size. Their speeds varied from being nothing more than a crawl to being as fast as a vessel moving in sub-light speeds. Smaller vessels rarely stood a chance if caught in them. Many were destroyed within an instant. Thanks to its size, her ship stood a chance.

'How big?' Beatrice requested.

'Assessing… It's a Class-Four. We're looking at about fifty-seven-K wide and roughly twenty-two high. It's heading straight for us and we're going to hit it dead centre in less than half an hour. Sending the telemetry to your display now Captain.'

The radar image showing the storm cloud hung in front of her, replacing the schematics display that had been there moments prior. It was to their starboard side, and it was giant. A Class-Four Storm was two grades off the largest known storms that had been seen. She had to pull the magnification back to the point where her ship was dwarfed by the electrically charged cloud to grasp the full scale of this monster approaching. Something as monstrous as that could not possibly be a natural occurrence. There had to be another explanation for it.

There was no way they could outrun it on sub-light engines alone. No matter which way they went. Either it would get to them before they were out of its reach, or they would avoid the body of the storm but the electrical discharge around it would still hit them and potentially short them out. The only chance they had was to make another emergency jump. But with help hopefully on its way and a power drain affecting their systems, the latter was not an option she was prepared to take.

That meant only one thing.

'Sound the general alarm,' Beatrice announced. 'All passengers are to either return to their cabins or gather in the galley. I want crew waiting on standby to provide aid where required. They need to strap in tight. I want as many of our security personnel as we can spare guiding the passengers to safety. We're going to ride this one out.'

'Aye Captain,' came the unanimous response from her crew.

As the warning bellowed out through the ship, her adjutant cleared his throat. 'Captain, are you sure you don't want to reconsider leaving? We really should get out of here while we can.'

'Negative,' she stated. 'I'm sorry but we just can't. I know what you said before. And I know what I agreed to. But we can't. Help is on the way. It has to be. We just need to survive this. Am I clear?'

'Clear. What will happen when the storm hits us? Suggesting that we actually survive that part of it.'

'*When*,' she stressed, 'we survive, our shields will be done. Most likely our entire ship will enter a full shut down and go through an emergency reboot. It'll be cold for several minutes. Really cold.

There'll be no gravity. No lighting. Air filters will be off, and we'll be relying on whatever oxygen there is remaining in the air. So that means we'll have about twelve hours of air, which is enough. When the backups kick in while the main line comes back online, we'll have about three hours of minimal systems. That'll include emergency lighting, oxygen, some heat and other key life support measures. No gravity still and no engines. Then we'll be back up a few hours after that and running but chances are most of our internal systems will be incapable of handling the power surge of coming back online after being forced to shut down from the storm. We will no doubt have plenty that needs to be repaired to get back on the move.'

'And that's the better option?' Franklin sneered. That personality didn't suit him, but it could be forgiven. 'Tell me, what do we do if help arrives and we're not receptive because everything is shut down? What if someone tries to hail us and, because we can't reply to tell them where we are, can't find us? How about this one, what if our guests decide to take advantage of the outage and come in all guns blazing? Because last I checked we haven't got control over most of those doors shut on the lower decks. They're just electronically locked. No electricity, no locks. All they have to do is flip the panels and manually open everything we've shut, if they think that far ahead.'

When in a state of panic and stress, he did ask the right questions. Even if they were in the most inappropriate tone. In a less-threatening situation, she would have found the time to be proud of his capability when times were bad.

'We act as required,' she answered. 'If they attack, we respond and hold them off as long as possible. For now, try send out a message. Broad channel. I want anyone with a tugboat and a comm-pad to be able to pick it up. Tell them we're going to lose power due to a storm but are holding ground. Request assistance as soon as possible.'

'Captain,' Franklin Hender muttered. 'We don't have comms yet. We're still cut off.'

Beatrice screamed out of frustration. 'Dammit! What is there that we can do to tell people what's going on?'

'Not a lot. Carrier pigeon, maybe.'

'Don't give me the fucking lip!' she hissed and immediately regretted reacting on impulse. 'Sorry.'

'It's fine,' Hender spat.

Beatrice removed all eye contact with her subordinate. She felt bad for her outburst. It wasn't necessary. She was just as scared as he was about their situation, if not more because she had responsibility for everyone on her ship. Beatrice would make up for it in time, when it was appropriate. Franklin left to oversee the bridge crew as they worked on things that were still in their control. She pulled up the ship's integrity levels and started to analyse it all to confirm her own mental calculations of the fallout from the storm were correct. Repetitive and monotonous but it ensured nothing was overlooked.

The main areas that would experience damage were sections of her ship with high power consumption, shielding, life support and her bridge. The power behind the storm would overload them. When they went, that meant the engine room, entertainment venues, security system and the cargo rooms occupied by the agents would start to falter. In order to save as much of her ship as possible from the storm she needed to reduce the liabilities by disconnecting as many key systems as was safe to from the grid. If it wasn't on or in use, the chances of it being damaged were cut.

'Hender!' Beatrice barked. 'We need to shut down every console, station and system not necessary to running the ship.'

'Aye Captain,' her adjutant replied. He was not in the mood for her after the onslaught she had just put him through

One by one, the lights started to go out. Everyone shut down their consoles once the systems they oversaw had been safely deactivated. All that they had left operational consisted of life support, shields, artificial gravity and minimal security systems.

She closed her eyes as the last light went out in the bridge, opening to a world of darkness with only a few glowing screens providing light. The air became tainted with a bitter chill. Not too cold, but cold enough to see the mist of warm air in the glow. Beatrice pushed away from her command chair to look out the viewing window. Without any artificial lighting from her ship, the stars, galaxies and other stellar objects seemed to shine much brighter than normal. Each super-sized ball of fiery gas, the many clusters of worlds and every extraordinarily large flash of a supernova was beautiful. Gems on a black sheet waiting to be plucked out of the nothingness. If there had not been a threat hurtling toward them, she could have happily stayed like, staring into the eternal depths of space.

Over to the right was the mass of substance that threatened them. Every second, several brief explosions of electricity cracked silently in the void of space, each one the size of a town. Yet with all its danger, it too had a strangely elegant place in the cosmos. Like a forest fire being seen from a distance, it was just as dangerous and equally beautiful.

'Captain!' one of her crew blurted out over the comms from the security station next to the brig, so quickly it sounded like he forgot to breathe.

Lenoia dashed across the deck to her chair and took the comm. 'Report.'

'We're going to have company,' the guard stated. 'Four of the agents are heading mid ship and two heading stern. All armed. I think they're making a break for the upper decks.'

Not now. Not when she had an adjutant that had warned her about such things happening, telling her to get them out of there. When there was a storm on its way to destroy them. He was going to be smug about this if they survived. She shook that thought out of her mind. It had to be *when* they survived.

'Where are they now?' she asked.

'They're on L Deck.'

'Leave it with me,' she ordered. Lenoia cut the comms with the guard and opened a link with Security Chief Henendez and Allua Jons. 'Henendez, I need you to gather as many personnel as you can spare. We've got a few of our prisoner's friends heading out of the lower decks. They're almost on deck K. Take the chief and a few engineers with welding kits. I want you to make sure they don't get far. Seal them in and be as quick as you can.'

'On it,' Carlos Henendez replied.

'Do I get to have a gun?' Allua requested after a moment of hesitation.

'No,' Beatrice replied. 'That's what the security team is for. You and your engineers get your job done. They'll make sure you don't get hurt.'

'Understood.'

'Jons, we'll meet you on deck G,' the security chief said. 'Don't go any further without us.'

'I will do,' the engineer replied.

'Okay, act fast,' Beatrice instructed. 'Keep me updated. Out.'

She closed the comm link.

An intense, sudden headache started pounding her brow. That look on Adjutant Hender's face didn't help either. After the pain subsided and she regained her composure, she returned to monitoring their situation. She had the security footage side by side with the system diagnostics and countdown timer for impact.

It would take another seventeen minutes for the storm to reach them after getting everyone on task.

'This is going to be fun,' she hissed.

Leyton Foresc

Leyton hid round the corner from the corridor on their next available way out of the depths. He had spent half of the current magazine in his SMG firing at what might as well have been shadows. Leyton, Agents Tallow and Perretti, and Medic Suttle were once again trying to breach the upper decks from mid-section. While they were there, he reluctantly sent Jerome and Fellstrum to the rear of the ship to try and push up past the engine room.

For some time now, they had been unable to make it to the passenger decks. Let alone the crew decks and the bridge. Every attempt they made to reach the bridge and take control of the ship was thwarted by the ship's crew sealing every door between them and that objective. Each time they made an advance, they ended up fighting for control of a hallway, passage or maintenance shaft, and each time they were not fast enough. Admittedly he was happy to take his time with the task. Anything was better if it meant they didn't have to kill anyone. Every time they were pushed back, he took it as an opportunity to either double back or call it for a few hours. His stall tactics were not going unnoticed. Leyton had several arguments with Houghton in the process.

That was until they heard the klaxon, warning of imminent danger. He had no idea what it was for but as soon as it blasted out the team felt the urgency to break free. And they had had enough of his time wasting.

To his relief, this time there was only one person at the bulkhead waiting for reinforcements to arrive to hold them off. This would be easy, but they needed to be quick this time. If there was any delay, there would be no telling how it would go down with Jerome should they all fail.

He signalled a countdown with his left hand. When he reached zero, his team provided cover fire while Leyton stepped out from their protection with a calm swagger in his step. The defender cowered in safety, making Leyton's approach all the easier. His agents held their fire once he was in position. In the space of the second it took the lone ship security to peer back, Leyton shot three rounds that incapacitated the victim into a whimpering wreck.

'See you're still letting them live,' Perretti muttered.

'Course he is, they're civilians!' Medic Suttle replied.

'Who the fuck cares?' Onyx questioned. 'They're in our way. We need to deal with them however we need to.'

'We care,' Tallow snapped. 'We're not murderers like you.'

'Shut it and move, we're running out of doors!' Leyton ordered, steering them back onto their goal and not to each other's throats.

The four of them took off at a sprint, with he and Hatty alternating to provide cover for the team as they pushed forward. The next bulkhead was ahead of them. All they had to do was make it past there. The stairwell to the next deck up wasn't far after that if the schematics held true. His foot was close to crossing the threshold. He had to be first. He needed to take control before Jerome. He feared what would happen to the crew if his second in command made it before him.

He felt the hard, cold touch of steel slamming into his helmet and cracking the visor. Or his face slamming into the metal. It was impossible to tell which during the moment. Regardless, it still hurt as his head reverberated on the inside of the helmet. Leyton fell backwards letting off several rounds in response until he hit the floor. He managed to glance the business end of a large wrench between the cracks of his visor receding out of sight. His comrades let off several rounds of their own in response before pulling him back and hiding behind a support beam. The ringing in his ears started to ease and focus began to return to him.

'What the fuck was that?' he asked as Suttle immediately took the helmet off him to start checking his face over.

'A wrench,' Hatty answered, a slight hint of pleasure in her voice. 'Surprised you didn't break it when it hit you.'

'Oh ha-ha. My neck fucking hurts.'

'Boss, keep still,' Medic Suttle insisted. 'It's a bit of whiplash you've got. Nothing serious. But I need to make sure nothing's broken.'

'If it is, I'll break their face more,' he said.

'Foresc, we have more contacts,' Perretti said. 'If you want to do this, we need to make a move now and you need to be ready to put them down.'

'Negative,' Leyton spat. He grunted as Suttle pulled his face back forward. 'We're not killing anyone. There are always other ways.'

'Should have fucking gone with Jerome and Fellstrum,' Onyx Perretti grunted. 'They'd have fought back and done whatever was necessary.'

'Save it!' Leyton commanded. 'When we're done here, I'll deal with you and straighten you out like I did Houghton. Hurry it up, Dom. We don't have all day.'

Dom's checks were painful, but he was given the all-clear, needing only a quick stimulant shot and some pain killers. Leyton got back to his feet and led his team back to the bulkhead. Aside from the gun shots being exchanged, the only thing that stopped them in their tracks was a simple announcement over the terminal system.

'Sixty seconds to impact. Shutting down all non-essential systems. Brace. Brace. Brace.'

There were no alarms. No sirens. The lights dimmed before shutting down completely being replaced by dim emergency lighting. Amber warning lights engaged, strobing the corridor in a circular motion. The air was colder. Even the gentle hum of air recyclers that were a background noise that could be ignored had been turned off.

'Impact from what?' Hatty asked.

'Not a clue,' Leyton answered. 'But I don't like it.'

He found himself breaking into his usual tune as the uneasiness of not knowing what was going on set in. It made him feel vulnerable and exposed. This was not the environment he was trained to fight in. As a lead field agent, he was expected to have as much understanding of the situation and environment as possible. He needed to think fast if he were to save his unit.

The ship's crew was talking loudly. They were insisting on the door between them being shut and welded together. It had been their mantra over the last few days, but this seemed more urgent.

'Thirty seconds to impact,' the terminal system announced.

Whatever this impact was going to be, Leyton wanted to be on the other side of the door before it hit. His need to be on the other side of the doorway was primal. He couldn't say why he needed to be there; he just knew in his gut that it was needed.

'Move!' he barked. 'Get to the other side of that door!'

The two sides exchanged shots with, to his relief, poor accuracy. Their last-ditch attempt to charge them was thankfully stalling the ship's crew from being able to close the door. It bought him enough time to force his weapon through as a show of force with his finger safely away from the trigger.

Before he could push his way through, he felt it. At first it was static cracking in the air. His hair stood on end. Something told him there was imminent danger. That something was going to happen that threatened his very life. His heart raced as adrenaline flooded through him. Then the lighting flickered into darkness. A thunderous sound of a million thunderstorms unleashing all at once roared outside the ship and within it at the same time. The *Galactic Passage* groaned under the strain it was being put through. The terrible commotion travelled down the corridors with deafening ferocity. The ship started to violently shudder and shake as the full force of the impact struck. Leyton was flung into the ceiling, walls and floor like a rag doll, only coming to a stop when he found a piece of piping to latch onto that threatened to come loose under the brutal vibrations.

When it finally stopped and everything came to rest, there was silence. The very air around them was still. Everything that could make a sound was peaceful. Even he and his fellow humans were silent. As if they had forgotten how to breathe. In the darkness there was no telling who was alive if anyone. Was he alive? Was this what it felt like to be dead?

Leyton felt a twisted relief when people started to moan in agony as they caught their breath. It was a good sign that he was still alive. The commotion of people trying to get to those that were injured sounded unusual. The way the clothes rubbed was like that of swimming without water. Why would they be swimming? Leyton tried to stamp his feet on the floor but hit nothing. His leg jolted to a stop when it couldn't reach out any further. He reached up with his hand knowing that the piping was running horizontal to the wall and felt the solid surface. But this was vertical. He was at an angle. A ship in space couldn't list like a ship in the ocean on a planet. The artificial gravity had gone.

They were all floating.

'Everyone, report,' he instructed, pushing away from his pipe to free float.

The feeling was nauseating. In the dark he had no idea which way was up or down, with no concept of his bearings. Already he'd forgotten where he'd just pushed away from, and vertigo started to set in. He slowed his breathing and focussed.

'I'm breathing,' Agent Tallow gasped. 'Think I've had the wind knocked out of me.'

'Think I've broken my nose,' Perretti stated. 'Pretty certain I've got a few new bruises too.'

'Dom?' Leyton called out when the medic did not reply straight away.

'Not good boss,' Agent Suttle responded painfully.

'What's up?' Leyton asked, feeling lost with not being able to see his medic to help him.

'Feels like a broken rib,' Agent Suttle replied. 'Don't think I've punctured anything though, so that's a good sign.'

'Hang in there. Hatty, crack some sticks, will you?' he instructed.

A trio of cracks echoed down the hallway and the eerie glow of yellow from three glow sticks lit up the area. It didn't faze him that they were all illuminated to the ship's security. He had an injured agent that needed tending to, and by the sounds of it they had their own to deal with too. That gave him confidence that they were not going to waste their time attacking them.

Agent Tallow tossed one of the glow-sticks over to him. After righting himself, once he could tell he had somehow turned the ceiling into the floor, Leyton glided through the air to Medic Suttle. The agent floated in mid-air clinging to his chest and had his eyes closed in pain.

'Hey man, you got to talk me through this,' he said. 'I'm no medic.'

Agent Suttle grinned, took off his helmet and spat out a bit of blood. Hopefully, that was not a sign of internal bleeding. 'If only it was that easy. I'll need to get this armour off before we know just how bad it is. Right now, that isn't going to happen.'

'Tell me about it,' Leyton muttered. 'Okay, what else do you need?'

'Gravity,' Dom said. 'I need gravity. If it's bad enough for me to spit up blood, then you can't do anything until we're rooted on the floor.'

'Hey, I can see them!' someone screamed from the bulkhead door.

'Stand down!' Leyton yelled back. 'We've got injured here. I'm sure you've got your own to deal with, right?' He turned his attention back to Dominic. 'What do we do then?'

'Back pouch, I've got something that'll help,' the medic said painfully. 'Should be a blue plunger. Stick it in my neck. Will take the edge off until we get to base.'

'Hatty, you take over,' he instructed. 'Perretti, keep an eye on them lot in case they do anything we don't need right now.'

'What're you doing?' Agent Perretti questioned.

'Trying the comms, need to find out how the others are.' He opened a comm-link with Jerome. The static feedback was horrendous. 'Jerome, you there? Jerome? Report.'

'Here,' his subordinate replied. The response was filled with static and broken, making understanding the response difficult at best. But at least they had a response. 'I can barely hear you. Too much interference. The fuck happened?'

'We don't know,' he answered. 'How're you guys holding up?'

'We're a little banged up. Had to pull Fellstrum down from the rafters. But we're safe. No crew around here. You?'

'We're okay, Dom's bust up. Just hoping that no one wants to shoot at us while we're sorting shit out,' Leyton said. 'We need to regroup. Give me a minute to work out what we do next.'

'Boss,' Agent Schottler said, taking over his conversation.

'I'm here, what's going on? How're you two doing down there?' Leyton asked.

'We're okay, for now, but the power's gone,' Ray said, his voice quivering fearfully.

'Tell me something I don't know.'

'No, Forese, the electric powering the pen is gone.' There was a heavy thud in the background with an aggressive bark of a wolf intent on freedom. Ray cursed in surprise while the professor yelped in terror. 'And I think they know it.'

The assets. Without the power to keep them under lock and key they were going to break free unless Agent Schottler had backup to help contain them. Leyton needed Schottler to remain in control.

'Keep talking Ray, you keep talking to me and keep calm. Got it? Can you get out?'

'Let me try the door,' Schottler said. He grunted and the door could be heard creaking as Ray tried to force it open. 'Okay, I think we can manually open it. It won't be easy. But we can do it.'

'Right, get the professor and open that door together then get the hell out of there. Understood?' Leyton ordered. 'Just get out and run. We'll meet you enroute and figure out the next bit together.'

'On it,' Schottler answered.

Leyton closed his tac-pad and turned to his team. 'Right, you heard me. We're going to extract those two. Dom, how're you doing?'

'Not any better than a minute ago,' the medic replied. 'Aching like hell. Don't think I can come with you on this one.'

'What're we going to do?' Agent Tallow asked. 'We can't bring him if he's not able to fight.'

'And we can't leave him here,' Perretti added gesturing over to the ship crew.

Leyton thought carefully for a moment on their situation. He weighed up their options and there was only one situation that favoured them. 'Fuck it.'

'What is it?' Dom asked.

'We need help. A lot of help if we're to even have a chance at having a handle on this,' he explained. 'Wait here.'

'And what about our orders?' Agent Perretti hissed as he floated down the corridor. 'You said it yourself. These people aren't meant to survive. Our orders are to kill them. I say we do it!'

'Fuck the administrator. Our primary is and always has been to safely transport the cargo that is now trying to break free. There's no point fighting them if we're going to die. If we're to survive, we need help.'

He took hold of Dominic's tactical harness and, to everyone's protest and curiosity, pushed through the hallway toward the bulkhead held by the ship crew. Leyton cried out for the crew on the other side to hold their fire, that he was coming through with injured.

'What the hell are you doing?' a man asked from behind the door.

'Trying to save your lives,' he answered. 'I need you to look after my medic and I need to borrow some of your security if we're to have a chance at that.'

'What're you talking about?' another person asked from the shadows.

Leyton sighed. He had to give them something. They could not be given any details that would compromise the mission, but they needed to know the severity of their predicament if they were going to help. 'We brought some cargo with us that is going to break free any minute now. I have personnel down there who if we don't save, right now, will die. My medic can't come because of his injuries. I need you to look after him. I have no time for debate. If you're going to help, I need you to come now. If you're not going to come with me and my guys now, then please just be good people and keep him safe.'

Leyton pushed Dom gently through the doorway and kicked his way back down the corridor. Agent Tallow readily joined him, appearing to be happy that they were no longer fighting other people, while Perretti gave him a disgusted look before silently falling into line. Upset that he had so easily handed over one of their own to people who in his mind were the enemy. Three of the ship's crew joined them. It was not much but it would do. They only needed to rescue his team and seal the wolves in the lower decks.

He radioed in with Jerome and liaised to meet a couple decks down before they were anywhere near their command station.

One of the ship's crew that joined them carried a large metal wrench in her hand and wore the uniform of an engineer. At least he could put a face to the person who was behind the aching jaw. She was the pretty

237

one he had seen on his recon missions. Someone that didn't quite suit an engineer's uniform. She had a strong arm.

'What exactly are we dealing with here?' the engineer asked as they traversed down a deck. 'Electrical discharge like the rest of the ship? Got a toy that's been fried?'

'No… it's something worse.'

'Boss, we got out of there,' Ray Schottler said over his helmet comms. 'But…'

A loud thud boomed in the background of the comms. A couple of the creatures bellowed and roared in victory. Their icy shrill cry ran painfully through him.

'What is it? Ray?' he replied, bringing the group to a stop so he could focus.

'They're loose,' Agent Schottler gasped. 'Shit boss, they're loose.'

The blood drained from his face and his palms turned sweaty. His agents were in trouble, and he wasn't anywhere near to save them. 'Go, move it! Protect Professor Ainslot at all costs. You hear me? Get out of there.'

'Understood sir!' screamed Ray Schottler. 'Come on professor, we're getting you out of here.'

'Let's hustle,' Leyton said. 'They won't have long.'

They charged down the corridors listening to the commentary. The two agents frantically rushed through the air to reach them. The piercing cries of the wolves blasted through the comms. They were gaining on them. His team was closing in too. He hoped they would reach them first. Agent Schottler cried out in panic. Shots were fired erratically as the agent instructed the professor to keep moving. The gun shots intensified, and the screaming shifted from terror to screams of pain. The wolves had reached his agent. He couldn't listen but there was no comm link with the professor to switch to. Leyton heard everything as the wolves tore Agent Schottler apart. The joyful sounds they made as they feasted on his agent drowned out Ray's cries of help and his pleas for someone to save him.

Then it ended. Ray was dead, the only solace was that his suffering was over. A strange purring that sounded like glass cracking under extreme weight was the last thing he heard before Leyton disconnected the comm link.

A single tear fell down his cheek, his teeth clenched tight in anger. How could he have left them with such minimal assistance? He should have left more bodies in the command station in case something went wrong.

The following several seconds were a blur as the rage fermented into a physical outlet. By the time he came round, his throat felt like he had just eaten sandpaper one sheet at a time, and his fists were sore, most likely bruised under the armour. Everyone stared in shock and concern.

'Sorry,' he said hoarsely. Leyton floated in suspense. He wasn't sure what to do or think until he heard the familiar voice of Samuel Ainslot down the corridor. It was faint but distinct. He remembered what he was doing and sprung back into action. 'Professor!'

He led the team toward the commotion of scampering hands and feet on metal. Trying to move in weightlessness and failing. The professor dragged himself round the corner, throwing his awkward body into the wall across the hall. He forgot how uncomfortable the man was due to no training in zero G's. Leyton flung himself forward and caught the intellect to bring his freefall under control. Down the corridor the ice wolves screeched and scampered as they fought through the lack of gravity to catch up to their prey.

Are you okay?' he asked him.

'Schottler!' Professor Ainslot yelped. 'He-he's dead. They got him. I couldn't do anything about it. I'm sorry!'

'I know, I know. It's not your fault,' Leyton ushered for calm. 'You stay here with the others. I'm going to go on ahead.'

Leyton flung himself through the weightless void and down the corridor, going back down the same route the professor had taken. Once round the corner he stopped propelling himself in great leaps. Against animals that had more grip behind their manoeuvrability he would be at a disadvantage in mid-flight. Taking shorter jumps, he would have more control and presented himself with more opportunities to perch himself against the walls to take any shots required. Without even realising it, he was halfway into his tune. How he wished he were in the woods. That sort of environment was a lot safer to be in, with more places to hide and more ways to survive than in a metal tube.

Someone reached out and grabbed his shoulder, bringing him to a complete stop just at the base of the stairwell. It was one of the ship's security.

'What the hell is going on down here that's got your friend killed?' the man demanded. 'Something we need to know about?'

He replied sharply. 'It is something you should know about. But now is not the time to talk about it. And yes, it's what got my agent killed.'

'If it killed someone then I need to know,' the security guard stated. 'And I need to know now.'

'You see my friend back there with the busted face? He's dangerous,' Leyton said. 'What we've got out here makes him look like a pacifist. Right now, it isn't the time for storytelling. Okay? I just need to see where they are and secure them.'

'Well then you can wait here. I'll find out for myself,' the guard instructed. 'I need to make sure you're not pulling a fast one.'

'You really don't want to do that,' Leyton insisted. 'You don't know what's out there. It won't end well.'

'Then tell me.'

'I can't,' Leyton said. 'Not yet. I just need you to trust me on this. I need to go on ahead and secure the area. Then I can tell you.'

The guard gave no reply, not acknowledging the warning. Leyton attempted to stop the man from going. Restrain him as best he could. There wasn't anything he could do to prevent the guard from pushing onward. He drifted on into the darkness until he was out of sight. Leyton hung back. As much as he wanted to help him, Leyton wanted to live. Wanted to help the rest of his team survive. He couldn't do any of that if he was dead.

He heard nothing at first. Just the strike of armour and thick leather against metal as the guard propelled himself through the corridors. The sound faded away to nothing more than a whisper when it was replaced with the shrill cry of fear before the blood curdling screams of agony and the roars of the wolves as the guard found their cargo. His stomach churned as the creatures could be heard feeding on their fresh kill.

The rest of the group had rushed over with Jerome and Kari now regrouped. They were visibly not happy at the new joint venture. Thankfully, they had the decency to keep it to themselves and not make a scene.

'What do we do?' Hatty asked under the eerie glow of their glow stick.

'What do we do...' he muttered under his breath, thinking about their next course of action. 'We move back up a level. Seal them down here. It's all we can do for now. It should hold them long enough to give us a chance to formulate a plan.'

The engineer shushed him whilst he was finishing speaking. 'Do you hear that?'

He wasn't sure what she was telling them to listen for. The security guard was dead. Leyton could only hear the crunch of bone and split of armour as the wolves fed, the disgusting sound of the creatures slurping up every last piece of flesh.

Underneath that noise, though, was a background noise. A low hum gently reverberated through the floor.

'Backup power,' the engineer said smugly.

The low whir rumbled through the ship as life was restored to key systems. Lights began to return, the occasional one popping under the sudden surge of power returning. Section by section the corridor before them lit up. Protected by the shadow of a couple bust bulbs, the silhouettes of five wolves gathered around what had once been the guard. The light around them glistened on their red eyes like rubies hanging in the dark. Globules of blood and pieces of clothing floated throughout the air.

'My god, what are they?' the engineer questioned.

No one answered. Fortunately, she was in that much shock at what she could see that she didn't follow up and persist for an answer. That though was the least of her concerns. The last time he checked there were only four adult wolves awake and none of the pups could have developed fast enough to become adult sized already.

'Professor,' Leyton whispered. 'Did you release any more of the assets while we were gone?'

'None,' Professor Ainslot replied.

'Fuck, they're breaking out of their pods,' Leyton cursed.

'How?' Hatty Tallow asked.

'I thought they were supposed to be on magnetic locks?' Jerome added. 'And how come the last lot took hours to come round?'

'They're supposed to be,' the professor explained. 'But they only work if there's power and we're not there to fit the battery packs, are we? Without us to administer the drugs to gradually wake them up, they're waking up quickly, panicking and breaking out of their pods. The drugs force the hibernation state to persist, making handling them safer.'

'Alright then, so what do we do now there's more than before?' the remaining security guard asked.

'Exactly what I just said. We lock them down here. Stay together. It's our only chance,' Leyton explained. 'We do that, and we might stay alive.'

'Who put you in charge?' the engineer questioned.

'For now, I did. We can discuss it later when we're out of here.'

241

When no one, not even Jerome, challenged his command, he focused back on the wolves that his eyes had never left. They were still feasting. This was their chance to get away.

'On my command, we make a move,' Leyton said. 'I'll take the rear and cover you. Make our way back the way we came. Get ready. Now!'

They kicked their way back up the corridor to the nearest flight of stairs. They barely reached the first corner when the wolves caught their scent. They let out a terrible roar and began to chase them in the hunt for fresh meat. As the team glided through the metal hallway ribbed with bulkheads, blast doors and compartment locks, the harsh scratch of claws gripping into the walls and floors followed, edging closer toward them. The first flight of stairs was a godsend. They pulled their way up but by the time they reached the top their pursuers were already at the base.

'Move it!' Leyton called out as he fired off several rounds at the wolves before following.

Agent Hatty Tallow started to fall behind. The gap between her and the rest of the team was growing by the second. With a strong push Leyton propelled himself through the air, took hold of Hatty and flung her to the others while he hurtled back toward the wolves that pursued them. Leyton quickly regained control by holding onto a railing and immediately opened fire on one of the creatures as it attempted to clamp its jaw down on him. While it was stunned by its injuries, he took his opportunity to escape. Safely at the top of the stairwell, the engineer reached out and pulled him through a doorway to temporary safety.

'Get going,' he barked.

He slowed his pace as he pulled himself down the corridor, always keeping his aim on the stairwell, making sure he was holding onto something to maintain stability. Each time a wolf dared to round the corner, he let off a burst of bullets to keep them at bay. After several solo attempts, the entire pack rushed round and charged for him.

The door wasn't that far. Couldn't have been more than a couple dozen feet away yet felt like it was the furthest distance he had ever needed to cover. Almost everyone else was on the other side waiting by the door. The security guard remained at the halfway point, letting off shot after shot to cover his escape. He took cover behind the guard to reload.

'Go, I'll meet you on the other side,' Leyton said. 'I'll hold them off.'

'You won't make it,' the guard replied firing more shots. 'You go, you're more use to them than me.'

Before he could even begin to object to the guard's statement, Leyton was sent flying through the air by a forceful shove. He bounced off the floor and through the doorway. The pressure door was manually shut on the guard's instruction as the man started to fight the wolves on his own. Leyton quickly regained full control and propelled himself back to the door in time to watch the guard through the porthole as he fought valiantly against the creatures only to be another victim. He cursed and struck the door in remorse. He could have saved the man and still made it out. He just knew it. Leyton shouldn't have let him have the final say.

The sombre moment was brought to an abrupt stop when Leyton was forced to turn on the spot to then be struck round the jaw with a vicious right hand. The engineer glared at him with eyes almost as wild as the wolves. Hatty and Jerome pushed their way over to him to help. Leyton held a hand up to waive them away. The engineer deserved that one.

'You had better start explaining what the hell those things are,' she hissed with watery eyes. 'That's two more people that have died now because of you.'

Gravity returned as the systems resumed normal function on backup power. The group dropped to the floor. It felt good having feet on the ground even if the gravity felt a little weaker. While most landed perfectly fine, Professor Ainslot was far from graceful with his landing, stumbling as he regained his footing. The engineer was ready to swing another punch at him if he didn't answer or gave an ill-advised response. There was no way he could avoid telling them about their cargo now. Not after what they had all seen, and now that they were released from their confinements.

'I need to speak to your captain,' Leyton said.

Jesa

By the time they had returned to the jump, Jesa had slept for over ten hours without as much as stirring. From then on, she had been allowed to spend more time around the soldiers. The restrictions that had governed her were noticeably lifted. There were fewer limitations to where she could go – the only room understandably off-limits was the armoury. Even if they trusted her, she was an outsider, but everyone seemed to speak to her fairer than before. Jesa could even be a part of the training sessions they were having. It was interesting, learning how they approached scenarios. The more she was around them, the more she could see how Barbaros had been so wrong. More than that, she could see how Duke Horren had been so right.

After a long training session, Jesa sat in the troop bay. She stared at the lower airlock where her ship was attached. She had told the sergeant and his troops about every one of the goods she was transporting except for one. The crystals. She did not know what they were. To her, there had been no point saying anything about something she didn't know about. It would have been pointless. Maybe she had been wrong for thinking like that. But now she had a reason to come clean about this last little piece of her former master.

Jesa climbed down the docking tube and into her ship. It had been the first time since being boarded by the SPF that she had returned to the *Saridia*. Jesa clasped at her mouth in horror as she gazed upon the innards of her ship.

'Mayah! What have they done to you?' she asked her ship.

Ronan had made a mess of the place in his search for the tracking beacon. Panels had been ripped from the walls and floor and piled in messy heaps. Holes littered the floor where he had dug deeper. The loot she was transporting had been scattered and strewn around carelessly. At least her ship could be repaired, and the clutter cleared up. That would be a job for later. Jesa would try to recruit Ronan to help her. He was very mechanically minded and seemed to have a talent for anything that had a mechanical purpose. If not, she would ask Duke if she could get some help.

Jesa cautiously walked past the disarray to where she had stowed the crystals. The case didn't appear to be damaged. A good sign that they should still be as they were before. She took the case to the kitchen area, set it on the table and lifted the latches. To her relief, the crystals were all in the same condition they had been left in. She sighed softly and smiled at her luck.

'What are you hiding down here for? Not trying to make a getaway, are you?'

Duke's voice came out of nowhere. She had no idea he had even followed her through to her ship. Jesa nearly pushed the crystals off the counter in fright. When she composed herself, Jesa felt more at ease with his gentle smile.

'Oh yah, of course. Don't think I'd want to leave you, compre?'

Duke continued to smile. 'So, what're you down here for?'

'I didn't tell you about everything that's in my cargo,' she explained. 'I didn't mention these.'

'Why not?' Duke asked.

Jesa shrugged. 'I didn't think they were important enough to mention.'

'What are they?'

'I know just about as much as you,' she said. 'All I know is they were bought by the same guy that bought that skeleton. And most of the cargo.'

Jesa turned the case around and waited. The sergeant stepped up and analysed each of the crystals. So far, he always knew what to do. Maybe he would know what they were and what they needed to do with them. Duke returned the crystal he was holding to the case. He let out a thoughtful hum and closed the case.

'Mind if I take them for one of my squad to have a guess at?' he requested.

'Go for it,' she said. 'It's not like I need them anymore, compre?'

'Thanks, because in all honesty I haven't got a clue what they could be for. But you said that these and most of the stuff here is for the same buyer?'

Jesa nodded sharply. 'Same seller and for the same buyer on Earth. Some guy called Ostad, yah. Doesn't look like they'll just be ornaments. Must be something useful?'

'Maybe. Safe to assume that they're probably from the same source then I think if they're in the same shipment, hm?' the sergeant surmised. 'If anyone's going to know what to do with these, it'll be Abe. He's too book-smart to not have an idea.'

Duke lifted the case to take it away. Before he could go anywhere, he paused. His eyes closed and his body swayed. He stumbled forward and had Jesa not nudged him awake he could have easily carried on falling forward until he hit the floor. She'd have been lying to herself if she said there wasn't a small part of her old self that would have liked to see that.

'Are you okay?' she asked.

'Just a bit tired,' Duke Horren admitted. 'Not slept too much.'

'You haven't? Why not?'

'I've just got things on my mind that I can't seem to shake.'

'What is it?'

Duke shrugged. 'The guys. This assignment. I'm just hoping that they're ready for this. I can't help but worry that they're not so I'm doing everything I can to make sure they're as prepared as they can be. But for me to do that, I'm spending more time working than resting.'

'Why are you pushing yourself so much for them?'

'Because it's my job,' he explained. 'They're my soldiers. They need me to guide them so they can be effective leaders. So that they can all come home in one piece after every mission. I don't want their deaths later in life on my conscience.'

'Don't you ever, you know, get tired of trying so hard for them?' she questioned.

'Honestly? I did think a few times at the start of the patrol about giving up on them, turning around taking them all back. For the first couple weeks I couldn't see them ever gelling together and working like a team. They were always at each other's throats. Didn't want to know each other. But look at them now. They're making progress and I can trust them to cooperate. They might not like each other, but as long as they can work together that's the main thing. It means that all my hard work, patience and tolerance has paid off. There isn't a better feeling than knowing you've done something to improve someone.'

'It's nice to see that you don't give up,' Jesa said.

'Like I'm not prepared to give up on you,' Duke Horren replied. 'Look, I know I'm not an Outer. I know there's still things that you can't let go of about us. But when we get back, I'll do whatever I can to keep you out of a cell and under my supervision.'

No matter how many times she repeated those words to herself they still didn't sound quite real, like it was all a charade meant to deceive her. But it didn't make the words he spoke any less meaningful. The fact he wanted her under his supervision meant that she had a better chance of having more freedom. Jesa smiled softly at him with eyes watering ever so slightly. She wanted to believe everything he said, and she knew he would prove that his words could be trusted.

'Thank you.'

'Come on, let's see what Abe has to say about these things,'

The pair of them left her ship and returned to the patrol ship. Duke shouted over the control panel in the troop bay for Corporal Udal'e to join them in the briefing room. The soldier joined them a couple minutes later, disturbed mid-work out, and stood waiting for his orders.

Duke opened the case show him the crystals. 'I need your help working out what these are. Think you can do it?'

'I can try,' Abe Udal'e said as he delicately took one of the precious stones out from the case. He analysed the cylindrical piece carefully.

'What do you think it is?' Duke asked.

'I don't know. Never seen anything like this for real. I mean... look at these lines. They're almost like processors.'

'Seriously?' Jesa blurted out, feeling proud that he had come to the same conclusion she did. 'I thought I was completely wrong with that idea.'

'Well, yeah,' Abe said. 'Crystals can store so much data. We're only just using them the right way now in the labs. They're trying to store artificial intelligence and anything else that takes a lot of processing power on them. If they can manage that, we'll be able to advance ourselves and not worry about slowing down. This thing? If it is a processor, I want to know how much data it can store. And I want to know what it plugs into.'

'If it can store data, then that means there's information on it to read. Right?' Duke asked.

'Exactly. And who knows what information there's stored on here. It could be anything,' Abe Udal'e replied.

Information. Jesa could only imagine the sort of information the crystals held. Ship schematics. Building plans. Educational material. Maybe even a history of the crystal's creators. Would it advance humanity altogether or give the holder of the crystals the upper hand in the political battleground of human existence? What would happen afterward? Would the ones in power with the information stored on the crystals be benevolent and forgiving, aiding all humanity to reach their full potential? Even those in the Outer Colonies? Or would they be ruthless and aim to take over colonised space? Rule over the human race with an iron fist. The possibilities were both exciting and terrifying. Jesa wasn't sure if she liked knowing that possibility or not. Being in possession of them was a responsibility she would have been happier not having.

Jesa thought of her parents and how she missed them. Their warm smiles that brought comfort whenever she was in need. The ability they possessed to hear something long and complex and pick out only the things that mattered to them. Life was so simple then. There were fewer evils out there, back when the most complicated piece of equipment was a harvest collector. Now she had something that held who knew what secrets before her that was just a bit shorter than her forearm. And no one actually knew what it was.

'Is this something you think we can work with to try and read?' Duke asked.

'With what we have on the ship? Not a chance,' Abe answered. 'We'd need a science lab and people a lot smarter than all of us combined to work out what the crystals have stored on them. But I'd really like to be there when they crack it. I'll have a think and come up with the best people to go to with them.'

Duke Horren smiled. 'Thank you. Go on, get back to the others. Have some rest.'

'Yes Sergeant,' Abe Udal'e said as he left them.

They didn't take the crystals back to her ship after repacking them but instead the pair remained in the briefing room. Duke put the case in a cupboard under the holo-table and locked it with a key code combination then slumped down in a chair with a heavy sigh. She joined him in taking a seat around the table. They sat there in silence. Jesa didn't know if the sergeant wanted to be alone or not but the expression he wore said that she shouldn't leave him alone. He was tired, probably frustrated, and now he had another problem to solve.

'You know you don't have to do everything alone,' she said softly.

'I know,' Duke said. A smile subtly spread across his face. 'But there are some things I can't ask others to take responsibility for.'

'Doesn't mean we wouldn't help if you needed it, yah,' Jesa replied. 'What are we going to do with the crystals? Should we put them back on my ship?'

'No. We'll keep them here. If that's okay. When we get back to the station, I'll hand it over to the general back at station and hopefully we can find out what's on them.'

'That sounds like a plan,' she said.

Jesa felt a strange sense of affection for the sergeant, as if he really were that father figure who had been absent from her life for so long. He seemed to know what to do in every situation they faced, was forgiving and yet forceful when required. Someone that she could respect without question and without request. Must have been why he was in command on the mission. It was easy to see that if it had been anyone else to come across her ship, she would not have been so fortunate.

They didn't say anything. There was no need to. She was simply happy to be there in his company. That was enough.

She stared at him. He sat there with his uniform on. It fit perfectly. The sergeant's stripes on his arm didn't fit. He was confident. Skilful. Intelligent. A natural leader. Yet his rank didn't fit the picture.

'Can I ask you something?' she said softly.

'Sure thing,' Duke replied. 'What's up?'

'You're only a sergeant,' Jesa started. She weighed up the best way to word her question. 'How come you never got promoted? Were you not good enough?'

The sergeant laughed gently. Like it was an inside joke that only the two of them had. He smacked his lips as he leaned back. 'I didn't want it. Simply put. I got into the military because of the old man. He was the best during his time in spec ops. He moved up through the ranks. Quickly too. Was a captain the last I knew. Every time he came home, there was always a story to tell that I wasn't allowed to know. If anyone asked, he'd deny everything I ever said. Then one day he didn't come home.'

'What happened?'

'I don't know. Tried to find out but because it was while on assignment. I was told it's classified and hasn't been permitted to be disclosed yet. Which means for all we know; he could still be on assignment or dead. Broke my mother's heart. She still waits for him. On the plot of land we have, there's a dirt landing pad. She goes there a few times a day to speak to him. Hopes that one of these days she'll go there and find him standing there with a ship behind him. That the classification of being dead was incorrect.'

'I'm sorry,' she whispered, understanding the pain better than most but still being completely oblivious to the scars that were close to his heart. 'How come that stopped you from wanting a promotion?'

'While I was young, I made the connection that he didn't come home because of his rank,' Duke explained. His voice was barely there in the room. His eyes were clearly back in time. A few tears rolled silently down his cheeks. He continued without expecting any sympathy. 'The lower the rank, the fewer high-risk missions he went on. He was home more often than not. It was when he was a Lieutenant that he started getting the shit that put him further from home for longer with fewer reinforcements. Then he kept getting promoted and with each promotion he was gone for longer. After he didn't come back, I promised myself that day that I wouldn't be that man. I wouldn't be away from my family for anything. Not even my duty. Just need a family to fulfil that for now.'

There were no words that could do anything to comfort him or respond with. He truly had given up everything for the United Planetary Nations. If there was ever a poster boy for getting out of the UPN it was him. He deserved more than what they gave him. More than what they offered him. She would be his family. She would give him the reason to come back. They shared the silence together. Mulling over the words that had been spoken and even the words that remained unspoken.

'Thank you,' Duke said out of nowhere. She cocked her head at him. Why was he thanking her? When she didn't reply he continued. 'I appreciate you telling me about these. Is there anything else you want to say while we're here?'

Her mind immediately drifted to thoughts of her friend. Ghavvis. He was equally kind-hearted, in his own outlaw-ish ways. Had made sacrifices as well. The last she knew he had been apprehended. She never thought to ask about him before when she gave up the information. For good reason. Jesa had been a prisoner for some time. Now she was free she could speak just as freely. However, she did make it clear that she had her price. Now was the time to cash in on it.

'Not as much say as ask,' Jesa said.

Duke leaned back in his chair as he spoke, 'Go on.'

'My friend back on Juntah, Ghavvis, helped me escape,' she explained. 'Your soldiers got him when he held them off for me to get away. I want to know he's okay … I need to know. I want him to be safe.'

'I can't promise an answer any time soon. We're a bit too far right now for an instant response and the guys back on Juntah have a mess to clean up first. But when I can ask, I will do I and I'll let you know as soon as I have an answer, okay? We left him there with the local police. I've got someone I think I can trust to make sure he's okay. As long as he isn't attached to the cartel there, he should be safe.'

'What happened with the cartel?' Jesa asked.

'They tried their luck and got their asses handed to them,' Duke said proudly. 'Made a couple temporary allies while we were at it.'

'And there's no way we can release him? Or speak to him?'

Duke shook his head. 'I'm sorry. We can't. Not while we're out here with a job to focus on. Afterward though, we will do. I promise.'

'Okay.'

It was disappointing. An unanswered question was frustrating at the best of times. This, though, was hurtful. It was her friend she was asking about. It wasn't much and it wasn't unreasonable. If Jesa was asking for them to let her go, she would understand. But she wasn't. She didn't want to have to wait for an answer about his life. Those were not good thoughts to go to sleep with. The only thought that could help Jesa rest easier until she got word was knowing that if it were bad news, the sergeant would most likely have known by now.

'Sorry it couldn't be better news just yet,' Duke said. 'But there's still time.'

'It's okay,' Jesa sighed even though it wasn't. She still needed to know. 'Just wish he hadn't been there and someone else made the drop. That it wasn't him getting locked up, compre?'

'I know what you mean.' Duke crossed his arms and looked up thoughtfully. 'If I don't hear anything after I call when we're done, I'll have us go back to Juntah first thing. We'll inspect it and see what the score is. Sound like a deal?'

Jesa nodded. At least one way or another she would know what happened to her friend.

She left the sergeant and returned to her cabin. Her arm had been itching for a while. It started with the thought of her family. Even though it wasn't about *him*, Barbaros had been the one to take their kindness away from her. It had been some time since it last itched. Jesa applied the ointment that Ivan had provided and almost instantly felt the relief. The control panel beside the door blared into life with the announcement by Rodriguez that they were coming out of the jump in the next couple hours. Jesa decided to try and get some sleep before they got there. It would at least pass some time and she would be out of the way of the soldiers while they made their final preparations before arriving at the cruise ship.

One more obstacle to overcome before they could go back for Ghavvis.

'I won't leave you behind,' she muttered under her breath as if everyone were listening in. 'I promise you.'

251

Duke Horren

As Duke gazed upon the *Passage,* his first impression was that it looked exactly as he imagined a luxury liner to look. Pristinely built, with smooth curving stretches of metal reached back gracefully. The thick glass of the viewing platform at the front glistened under the glimmer of their spotlights. Scorch marks littered the hull like it had been caught up in a fire storm. Some sections of ship's exterior had been breached by whatever struck them. Faint lights could be seen shining from the inside. Most presumably emergency lighting. From the bridge Duke could make out the faint silhouettes of people walking around with flashlights.

'Looks like we've found our ship,' Zenkovich stated.

'The hell happened here?' Valentina gasped.

'Good question,' Duke said. 'Any ideas? It doesn't look like an attack.'

'Nah, not attacked. Most of that is superficial. Couple breaches probably from something overloading. Best thing I can think of is they flew straight through a star,' Ivan answered. 'Either that or someone flew around with a flamethrower. But it should still be space worthy if they've sealed the blast doors around the breaches. Why they're not moving though I couldn't tell you.'

'Have you tried to hail them?' Duke asked.

'I've been trying,' the pilot stated. 'The signal's not getting through. It's like something's jamming them but... wait a minute. You see that?' Ivan pointed toward the rear of the ship as they flew down the length of the vessel. 'That's electrical scorching. No, it can't be.'

'Can't be what?' Duke replied.

'A stellar storm,' Ivan Zenkovich said gravely. 'Never seen one but you'll be hard pressed to find a pilot that hasn't heard of them. Explains why we can't hail them. All their circuits will be fucked.'

'Okay. Find us somewhere to dock,' Duke said. 'I'll get the team ready.'

'Will do boss,' Ivan replied.

He quickly slid down the ladders and marched into the sleeping quarters to wake the team up. Within fifteen minutes they were up, kitted out with a standard assault rifle and pistol with a pair of flash-stun grenades and were waiting in the troop bay. Duke checked the team vitals on his tac-pad. Not only could he see everything from their heart rates, blood pressure and amour registered injuries, but Duke could also have a read on external factors such as chemicals detected in the atmosphere and radiation levels. If he ever was without a weapon, that was the next best thing to save his and his team's lives.

Jesa sat in one of the chairs watching their every move as they prepared and went over the plan. She was to stay on their ship and help the crew with anything they instructed her to do, which she was more than happy with. It was music to his ears.

The plan was simple. Make the immediate area safe, then proceed up to the bridge and liaise with the ship's captain. From there he could ascertain the full extent of the damage then focus on the boarders that had threatened the crew. He silently prayed none of the hostiles were waiting for them, and that they had not killed anyone else.

Their patrol ship docked with the liner on its starboard side, emitting a heavy thud as the docking tube latched with one of the vessel's several air locks. For Zenkovich to successfully latch onto the liner while the smuggler ship was still in tow was nothing short of impressive. When the docking tube pressurised Duke opened their airlock hatch. A quick countdown and Ronan tool the lead to open the secondary hatch granting them access to the *Galactic Passage*. They sealed themselves into the airlock and manually cycled through the pressurisation process before being allowed access into the liner.

It was dim and even though the ship was larger than most apartment complexes with its floor space, it felt claustrophobic in the dark. Glass lined the floor where bulbs had been blown and mirrors had smashed. Sparks and flashes flew out in an epileptic light show from damaged wires and circuits. All it needed was bodies and this could be the scene of a mass murder from a horror film.

Yet not a soul was in sight. It was eerie how empty it was.

To his delight there was working artificial gravity and according to the read outs on his HUD there was also breathable air. At least he knew it was airtight and secure.

'Where the hell is everyone?' Corporal Arche asked.

'I don't know,' Duke replied. 'Udal'e, shut the airlock. Zen, you read me?'

'Loud and clear boss,' the pilot replied over the comms. There was a slight bit of static in the transmission. 'How's it looking in there?'

'It looks like they got hit hard by the storm. No-one has shown up yet but I'm not taking any chances. I'm locking the airlock behind us. Don't want anyone to sneak on the ship for a quick ride out of here.'

'Understood. We'll keep you updated if anything comes over this way knocking.'

'Good. Catch up in sixty. Out.' Duke looked up and down the corridors, trying to decide which way to go. He then gestured for them to go left. 'This way. Keep your eyes open for any signs or maps. This place is too big to keep guessing our way around. Remember, we need to find the bridge.'

The soldiers gave their acknowledgements and went ahead to navigate the hallway. After a few twists and turns, encountering no-one, the corridor opened into a large foyer area. They'd reached the dead centre of the vessel. Had everything been in perfect condition it would have been a wonderfully lavish entrance. Now it was a dank place void of joy. To their relief they even found a map of the ship outside several elevators. They were on D-Deck, just a few levels below the bridge. The elevators appeared to be the only direct route up to the bridge from there. Their problem though was the ship seemed to be running on emergency power, meaning they were unable to use non-essential systems, including the elevators. They needed to find another way up to the command deck.

'So, what do we do?' Abe asked cautiously, panning his assault rifle back down the corridor they traversed through.

Duke fell silent, thinking of the right answer to give, when a faint sound pricked his ears; amplified by the audio receptors built into the helmet. There were people talking somewhere on that deck. Lots of people. But the noises were faint, almost muffled as if there were closed doors between them.

'You guys hear that?' Duke whispered.

'Oh yeah,' Ronan replied. 'I can hear it.'

'Any ideas what that sounds like?' Duke asked the team.

'Sounds to me like a trap,' Corporal Moasa answered.

Corporal Arche nodded her head. 'I agree. Can't be that easy to find them.'

Duke shouldered his rifle. 'Moasa, take point. Udal'e, you cover our rear. Arche, you're behind me. Ronan, get us on the move. I want to be wherever that noise is coming from. See if we can't spring the trap. Might get lucky and find someone that knows what's happening.'

'You got it,' Ronan said.

The unit moved carefully through the hallways, clearing each room they crossed as they went along. They passed cheaper cabins, storerooms for cleaning supplies and amusement facilities. Still, not a person was to be found. Duke was fearful that they were walking into a trap. It was a predatory tactic that animals and humans alike had adopted – gather the weak in a single place to attract the strong on the predator's terms. Right now, he and his team were the prey.

When they came close to the source of the sound, the team automatically split up to circle around what turned out to be the galley. Inside it seemed that most of the passengers and crew on board the ship, if not all of them, huddled together. They shivered in fear. Every one of them glanced around as if they were expecting something to go horribly wrong at any moment or for someone to tell them everything was okay. Duke looked around for any signs of hostile presence. People were scared enough for there to be a threat present. But the civilians were looking to the exits. If there were enemy embedded, they wouldn't be waiting outside. They'd be clinging to the shadows or out of direct line of sight.

He determined that it was safe enough to step out. When he made himself known to them, there were screams of terror that only ended when Duke lowered his weapon to usher in the calm. He announced who he was, what he was doing there and that he needed to speak to a member of the crew. A member of the ship's security eventually stepped forward when they determined it wasn't a trap. Duke quickly re-iterated who they were and what they were doing there before they were led away from the galley. The guard explained that they were indeed hit by a stellar storm and that since then they had been running on backup power while the engineers worked on bringing the engine back online. They clambered up one of the nearby emergency stairwells to A-Deck, passing the crew quarters on the way up. On the bridge, a collection of weary, exhausted eyes fell upon them, most wearing the obvious uniforms of naval crew and a few in black attire carrying weapons.

The armed stowaways. They had taken the bridge. Even if anyone could have replied to their comms requests, they wouldn't have if they were there.

Duke didn't spare a moment to consider why the guard had not told him about their presence. He simply reacted, bringing his rifle to bear. His team followed suit. When the people in black armour responded and created a standoff, a woman wearing the uniform of the captain shot out from the command chair to stand between them.

'All of you, hold your fire!' she cried.

'Aren't these the guys that you wanted our help getting rid of?' Duke questioned. His finger delicately danced with the trigger, teasing it to be squeezed in an instant.

'We are, but we're the only ones here who know what the hell is going on and are best positioned to deal with it,' a tall, well built, man said.

'Oh really? From here you look like the people who are holding the passengers and crew to ransom,' Duke retorted.

'Sergeant, what do we do?' Abe asked.

'Can I put a bullet in them yet?' Ronan added, clearly itching to do something other than stand still. 'I can get most of them before they get us.'

'Ease off,' Duke instructed before turning back to the man in black. 'Tell me what's going on then.'

'Put your weapons down first,' the man replied. 'Then I'll talk.'

Duke snorted. 'How about I meet you halfway? You tell us what's going on then I'll lower my weapon if I think you're not full of bullshit.'

'How about you do as *I* say on *my* ship?' the captain snapped trying to take control of the situation. 'You will all lower your weapons. Now. This is not a war ship. Put out any of the windows and we'll all be dead which means all this testosterone bollocks will be pointless. Okay?'

She had a point. Civilian ships were not made for internal conflicts. They weren't even up to standards for ship-to-ship conflict. Unlike a military ship, all it would take was one badly placed shot and they would be sucked into the vacuum of space before the blast shields could contain the bridge. On a military ship, the glass was minimal and significantly reinforced. Designed to take hefty strikes from point defence cannons, missiles or torpedoes before giving way.

'I'll be the better person and lead by example,' the man in black said with a smirk as he conceded.

In a single swift motion, he and his team lowered their weapons.

'Alright then,' Duke sighed, lowering his weapon. 'Now can we talk?'

'Sure thing,' the man in black replied.

Duke and the SPF personnel were invited to the command chair where they were introduced to the ship captain along with her key crew and the personnel in black armour. It was nice for him to be able to put a name to their faces, albeit a cause for concern to learn that one of the members of the armoured stowaways had been a prisoner on the ship.

The one they called Deulche had been tortured and bore the bruising of harsh treatment. He made a mental note to keep an eye on him. Revenge would be quickly sought after at the first opportunity by someone subjected to that sort of cruelty. Regardless of if they were on the same side or not.

'What's going on then?' Duke asked.

At first no one said anything. The people in black looked at each other, daring someone to step up and kick start the briefing. The leader of the team, Leyton Foresc, finally came forward and explained the course of events that had brought them onto the *Galactic Passage*. It was for all factual purposes a good story. One of the sorts of tales that soldiers would tell and reminisce over a beer about. Yet it was terrifying to learn about the wolves. Beatrice would interject at intervals with her interpretation of events which would cause a brief verbal disagreement that at times nearly boiled over back into conflict. Emotions were still raw and clearly still painful.

The professor came forward when order had been restored to give them details about the wolves. He identified them as apex pack predators that were a very real threat. Professor Ainslot had even named them all, apart from the pups, and could differentiate between them on sight alone.

By the time Duke and his team were brought up to speed they were left with more questions than they had answers for. The more important of them though couldn't be left unanswered.

'What exactly was the purpose of catching them?' Duke asked, noting that no one had given out that piece of information during the briefing. 'It's not like they're going to make good pets. More importantly, where the hell are you taking the wolves, and who for?'

The dark-skinned man with eccentric patterns in his buzz cut hair, Jerome Houghton, gave Leyton Foresc the death glare. Silently imploring him to not say a thing. Or was he judging him on what he did say? Either way it was a good thing. Whichever way Jerome reacted was going to determine if what Leyton said was the truth or a lie.

'We have some ideas,' the leader of the team answered. 'But none of us have been told what their purpose is. Above our paygrade. Just that we're supposed to bring them back to Sol.'

'Sol?' Arche screamed. 'That's where Earth is! Do you realise how fucked up things would be if they got out?'

'That's why we have a secure facility away from Earth,' the professor insisted.

'How far from Earth?' Beatrice asked, sharing the same suspicions as Duke.

'Far enough that we have everything in hand,' Houghton snapped.

'You do realise how fucking funny it is saying that you have everything in hand, but your cargo is loose on the ship?' Ronan asked.

'Keep talking about things you don't know anything about and see how much I fuck you up,' Jerome Houghton snarled.

'Keep running you mouth like that, and I'll introduce it to my fist,' Corporal Moasa retorted.

'You do that, then you can tell me what metal tastes like,' Jerome countered.

'Easy,' Leyton Foresc said calmly. 'We're not out to start a fight.'

'Say that for yourself,' Jerome spat.

'Wouldn't even be a fight," Ronan stated.

'Back to topic!' Duke bellowed out. 'Who is it you work for?'

'Same people as you,' Leyton answered.

All three members of Duke's squad shouted their disbelief at the statement as an all-out uproar. None of them wanted to believe it. For Duke, it seemed possible. It gave credence to how they were able to so easily get last minute access to the liner. That and the equipment they were packing. It was all standard issue Spec-Ops gear for the UPN. And the insignia of a metallic raven with its wings' spread wide was that of the United Planetary Nation's MID.

Which unit within the MID did they work for? Who was that desperate to have the upper hand over all other governments in the known space that they would work in the shadows and use unofficial methods to transport dangerous organisms across the galaxy to Earth? What would their use be? They were the first examples of this organism. Whoever was to receive them would need to study them. Research. That was it. Research and development would be the area they had to work for. Only they would want something that no one else knew about for themselves.

Yet, the guy was a spook. An agent. He was a trained spy and operative. How much could he believe and how much should have been ignored as a lie?

'Got anything to prove you are who you say you are?' Duke requested.

'Not a thing except for these,' Leyton replied.

Jerome Houghton shot a stabbing glance at Leyton as the leader of the team took out a combat knife. Duke took the blade and looked it over. At a glance, there was nothing obvious. A deeper inspection revealed the faint insignia etched at the base of the knife. They were only ever issued to people who successfully became field operatives.

'Agents.'

'Field agents,' Leyton admitted, confirming his thoughts. 'My unit gets sent just about everywhere. I suggest you leave it at that.'

'Why is that?' Duke questioned.

'Because you aren't cleared to know anything else,' Leyton stated. 'That and you don't want to know more than you should. It's too dangerous.'

'Is that a threat?' Duke replied. 'Because I suggest you check the legality of all those people you've killed on this ship before threatening me.'

'Stand down,' Beatrice screamed before their disagreement could escalate. 'Sergeant, yes, I asked for your help to apprehend them. But that was before we found out there were fucking wolves on ice in the lower levels that are now awake. Right now, this isn't helping. I have dead and injured crew. He's lost someone too and is offering to help contain them so that no one else has to die. Considering his team has the most knowledge about them, I suggest we use that information. Right now, my only thought is I need my crew and passengers to be safe. I need your help to do that.'

'Have it your way then,' Duke said. 'I have a couple questions for you. How do we contain them and where are they now?'

'We have them in the lower decks,' Leyton answered. 'We're not sure how far up they've moved but the captain here has people patrolling and there's been no breaches that we're aware of.'

'The wolves will most likely be establishing a new territory,' Professor Ainslot added. 'They won't venture out unless they have to for a couple days.'

'Can you pull up the schematics of the ship on a hologram?' Duke requested. He walked over to the holographic projection as it appeared above the holo-table. 'As far as you're aware, where are they sealed? I'm worried that they're trapped but not contained.'

'We last had them locked in around here,' Leyton said, hovering a finger over the mid-section of a corridor a couple levels from the belly of the ship. 'We were set up down here at the lowest cargo hold. The litters will still be down there with the females while the males are moving upward on the hunt.'

'What're their numbers?' Duke asked.

'Thirteen adults and two litters of pups that have been born,' Leyton said. 'Another two females were gestating the last we knew. Possible that the new pups are born by now.'

'How much does it take to put one of these down?' Ronan asked. It really didn't matter if it was a human or an animal. All that mattered to the giant of a man was the fight.

Professor Ainslot cleared his throat, 'We're not sure. What we do know is that they're tough. They can take out prey three times their size without taking as much as a scratch.'

'They can take at least a half mag of an RFSM-thirty to the face from mid-range,' Leyton added, showing off his sub-machine gun as an example.

'They were still standing after that?'

'Still trying to kill me after that,' Leyton replied, laughing off what was clearly a troubling incident he had been through.

If one of them could survive that, it would take something of higher calibre to put them down. Something like his RFAR-Ninety-Two assault rifle or a shotgun would potentially work. That though he was reluctant to find out for himself.

'They're down here, and you last shut the doors here?' Duke pointed at the locations on the hologram of the ship they indicated the incidents had taken place, returning them back to the task at hand. 'How about we shut everything off two decks up. Gives us a chance to do it before they realise what's going on. Can you highlight every door and deck hatch along this stretch of the ship?'

Beatrice brought up the various thresholds in a bright yellow. Along the intended deck were three main corridors running with a couple maintenance shafts between them. There were about two dozen ways down to the deck below, scattered along the three corridors all the way to the engine room at the back of the ship.

'We got one problem,' one of the agents, Medic Suttle, said while gesturing to the engine room. He had suffered a broken rib during the electrical storm but thanks to supplies on the ship he had been able to get patched up enough to be back in the fight. 'Look at all the doors here. There are way too many to shut. Can guarantee that by the time we even get half of them shut the pack would be onto us by then.'

'Most likely, their sense of smell and hearing is too good to let that go unnoticed for too long,' Professor Ainslot added.

'But if you see here, below the engine room, the doorways down there sort of converge to just a few passages?' Beatrice pointed out. 'We seal these off then we're saving ourselves some work.'

'At that point though we'll be going into what's now their territory,' Ainslot explained.

'I say we move in twelve teams,' Duke announced, summarising everything everyone was saying with the environment and the task at hand. 'Start in the middle and work outward in both directions. Makes twelve fronts for the wolves to deal with. All we need to do is get into position before they can react. From there we have the advantage.'

'That might not be as easy,' Hender said, joining in with the conversation.

'What do you mean?' Leyton asked.

The ship's adjutant joined them at the holo-table. 'Jons would be a lot smarter than me at this, but we don't have much power which means most of the doors aren't operating. The ones that are dead, we have to manually shut.'

'Like you were trying to do to us?' Leyton questioned.

'Exactly,' Lenoia said. 'Which means you need to remove the panel to access the manual controls.'

'And that's a hit and miss on which doors are manual or not,' Duke muttered. 'If we keep a good pace, we might be able to pull this off.'

'We'll arrange for the chief engineer to show you the fastest way of taking the panels off,' Franklin Hender said.

'Thanks,' Duke said.

That would slow things down for them. They needed the pace, but they needed to get it right. At least the wolves couldn't open doors. Once they were shut, that was it. Containment completed.

'How confident are you that this will work?' Beatrice asked him.

'He should be quite confident,' Leyton answered with an impressed smile before Duke could reply. 'It's a good plan. We have numbers on our side so this should be successful.'

'Okay then,' the officer said. 'Can you help arrange a guard to help keep an eye on the corridors for a couple hours before we make a move? I want my crew to help you, but they're exhausted and need to rest. I can't have anyone falling behind.'

'Will do,' Duke said. 'Agent, can we trust you and your team to help?'

261

'As long as you don't try anything then we're on the same team,' Leyton answered. 'Try something, anything, then you find out for yourself what happens.'

Duke smiled, retaining a calm composure. 'Keep threatening me like that and you'll find out how well you stack up against me.'

He felt the presence of Ronan stepping up behind him. Duke was strong thanks to his past and training. Moasa was so much stronger than he was. Duke was confident that if he were to lose the fight, Ronan would more than certainly finish it.

Leyton took one look at the larger man and stood down. He stepped back a little but somehow still held himself with the confidence of being in control.

'We'll be ready and back in one hour,' Leyton Foresc said. 'Where are we staying?'

'You can stay in one of the amusement rooms,' Beatrice said. 'I'll arrange for someone to show you there.'

'Thanks,' Leyton said. He sang a tune as the agents walked away. It was familiar. A lullaby, maybe.

Duke Horren waited for the agents to be off the bridge then sighed and looked to the captain. They both knew that the truce would be a difficult one. The look in her eyes told him that. They also told him something else.

'How long has it been since you served?' he asked.

'Excuse me?' she replied.

'How long?' he repeated. 'It's all over your face that you served. The way you look at things.'

'Did twenty-five years,' she answered. 'Left about ten years ago.'

'Least you can give a straight answer,' Duke joked. 'Let's get to work then.'

Chapter 8
08/11/2675
02:41 Earth Standard Time

Beatrice Lenoia

Beatrice was exhausted. The shift watching the corridors had gone smoothly according to Duke's report – if 'smoothly' was a word that could be used to describe the repeated arguments and high tensions that nearly led to a two-man war. Leyton insisted on joining Duke on guard duty once his team had set up in their new quarters. The agent made things tense enough with his transparent yet secretive attitude. The repeated half-truths when answering the sergeant's questions were too much. Intentionally or not, they got to Duke and resulted in an argument that only ended when Beatrice's crew stepped in to have them separated for the rest of their watch. Somehow, they managed to make it through the rest of the watch without attracting the wolves either. Much to the relief of Beatrice.

After the two-hour guard duty, she had the agents, SPF personnel, her own crew report to the bridge for the briefing. As expected, her people were far from okay with being in the line of fire. They voiced their concerns, and those concerns were heard but her decision was final that they were helping. There was no debate to be had. Duke divided them quite evenly. One agent or SPF soldier per crew member with the rest of her crew pairing off with each other. They were assigned their corridors and directions before they were dismissed to their duty.

She watched the last of them leave and, as the bridge was eased into silence, felt helpless being confined to her command chair. Beatrice knew that she had to be there. She needed to have control over the situation. Her crew was scared. The Stellar Protection Force personnel were limited in their numbers. It was impossible to tell if the agents were truly on their side or not. The only certainty was that all were now under her direct command. That, and the curse of time, meant that she wouldn't be able to run from one end of the ship to the other anywhere near as quickly as she once could do. If at all. There was a time when Beatrice would go for a run through the corridors of a battleship or a carrier twice a day, every day, without a second thought. Nostalgic thoughts now.

'Captain,' Hender called out from comms. 'We've got word from Truss that their agent has fallen behind.'

Engineer Truss. He was assigned with Leyton. What was the man doing to fall behind? Was he secretly concocting a plan with his unit to go against her and her crew and the SPF? Maybe he was sabotaging the ship. She needed answers.

Beatrice opened a comms link with the agent. 'Leyton, this is Beatrice. What's wrong? Your assigned partner is in position without you. Report.' He didn't answer and she turned to the professor who remained on the bridge. 'What is he playing at?'

'I don't know,' he answered.

'Stop lying!'

'I'm not!' Samuel Ainslot cried. 'I haven't got a clue what he's doing. If I did know I'd tell you.'

'Why should I believe you?'

'Because I'm not one of them! I'm just a scientist!'

'You're a part of the agency!' Lenoia screamed.

'You're a part of the military, doesn't mean you're the same as the army,' Samuel retorted. 'But I don't know a thing. I'm telling the truth.'

She muttered something under her breath then returned to the comm link with Leyton. 'Agent, report. What the hell is going on?'

'Sorry Captain, had to check my kit. Something was loose and I needed to secure it,' he answered. That was a blatant lie. She knew every one of them was ready before setting out. 'I'm on my way to position.'

'Understood,' she said. 'Out.'

Beatrice would take up the matter with him when the task at hand was complete and everyone was back, safe and well. He was lying to her. It ate away at her. She desperately wanted to know what he was doing. Was he placing a booby trap? Maybe sending out a comms burst. Either way she would find out.

'All teams have checked in. We're waiting on the signal Captain,' Duke said over the comms a few minutes later. His voice boomed over the intercom for the entire bridge to hear – this was information that everyone needed to know.

'Understood,' Beatrice replied weakly.

It took her a moment to prepare herself. If events over the next several minutes went wrong, even if only by a minor detail, then they were all almost certainly in perilous danger. Someone could easily not seal a door correctly. In the rush they may even skip a door by mistake. A bulkhead door may be stiff and poorly maintained and take too much effort to close. Or the teams may not be as fast as the wolves and are beaten to an opening. From there it was an easy route to the civilians who still huddled for safety in the galley. The inevitable slaughter that would surely follow wasn't worth thinking about. She shuddered at the possibility of it.

Her hands clenched onto the arm rests of her chair. Knowing the consequences unsettled her.

'You are a go in ten,' Beatrice told him.

A countdown flashed up in her mind's eye. Each second ticked by. The milliseconds took an age to go down. The seconds lasted for as long as a millennium. When she got to five, Beatrice started to count aloud for everyone to hear. Once her count hit zero Duke cried out for everyone to move, his voice frantic yet hiding the pressure he was under.

They were all in his hands now.

The voices of everyone commentating as they ran along their routes was overwhelming. So many people speaking at once to announce that they sealed their door and were moving onto the next one. One by one they shut every opening they came across. Within several minutes, they had reached the halfway point. However, their biggest obstacle was still to come – the engine room.

'So far so good,' Franklin Hender commented with early relief in his voice.

Beatrice immediately hated her second in command for saying that phrase. When someone said that something always went wrong.

The wolves could be heard over the comms. Their cries were faint at first but were gradually getting closer. Some cried that they were starting to see silhouettes heading for them as they sealed the hatches and doors. Her heart rapidly pounded in her chest. The suspense was almost too much to handle as updates informing them that the wolves were getting closer came over the comms with increasing frequency. The heart rushing anxiety was too much to handle when they heard the almighty cry of agony over the intercom, the effort behind the heavy thud of a door being closed and the laboured breathing of survival.

'What's happening down there?' she demanded. Her heart rate had rocketed with every worst-case scenario passing through her mind and thinking up a plan of action for each one to keep as many people alive as possible. 'Is everything alright? Someone report.'

'Captain, I've sealed the door.' It was one of the agents, Jerome if she recalled rightly, that spoke. He sounded in pain.

'What happened?'

'One of the wolves. It beat me to position. The engineer that was with me, he didn't make it. I tried to warn him. But he didn't listen. I'm sorry. I tried.'

'I'm sure you tried your best,' she said hoping that the words were true, resenting the fact it was another one of her crew to have perished. 'Are you able to continue?'

'Negative,' he groaned, letting out a slight groan of pain. 'They got my arm pretty good. I need to head back and get it fixed up.'

'Understood,' Beatrice replied. 'I'll have your medic ready for you on Deck C and I'll let the others know.' She turned to her adjutant. 'Inform Medic Suttle of the incident. Assume blood loss and large open wounds. Tell him to wait on Deck C.'

'I'm on it,' Hender said.

'What's going on?' Duke gasped over the comms. 'Talk to me Captain.'

'We have casualties,' she explained, fighting back emotions she didn't want to explain. 'My engineer's down and one of the agents, Jerome, is injured. He's having to come back. I need someone to finish his sector.'

'Understood,' Duke said. 'I'm on it.'

'Fuck's sake!' cried Leyton through the comms. 'What's he done?'

'One of the wolves got him,' Beatrice reported. 'Focus on securing the lower decks.'

'Don't worry lady, we'll get it done,' the agent replied.

The chatter cut dead and she made a point to not reply to Leyton. Anything she did say could potentially distract him from the task at hand, jeopardising the others.

When the joint force finally reached the engine room at the stern of the ship, the bridge itself seemed to hold its breath eagerly. They were at a crucial point. She waited. No one dared breathe. The team was in the danger zone, with the wolves closing in. Then it all went silent. Not a sound was made. Beatrice Lenoia was worried that it had all gone wrong, that any minute now there would be the screams of civilians under attack from the ice wolves. The knot in her stomach tightened as the seconds went by. When the message finally came through that all doors and hatches had been sealed off, the bridge erupted into a medley of celebrations and euphoria. Even the joyful cries of her crew, SPF soldiers and agents over the comms was deafening. She could have sailed the ship on her own with ninety percent of the engines failing and successfully berthed at port and even that feat of skill would have been nothing in comparison with what they had just achieved.

'Captain,' Franklin muttered at her side. His face was long. Sad, even.

'What is it?' she whispered softly, placing a hand delicately on his.

'I'm sorry for ever questioning you,' he said. His eyes filled with tears at his sense of disappointment in himself.

She shook her head and smiled. 'You had the best intentions of everyone on this ship at heart. That's what matters okay? Go. Celebrate.'

Her second in command smiled back, wiped away the tears and joined the crew to congratulate them all on their parts. She didn't move. Her heart was still weighed down with the weight of events to come. Disaster had been averted but they weren't in the clear yet. Beatrice now needed to focus her attention back on the agents. Even with the wolves secured and the SPF on-board, there was nothing holding them back from finishing their mission of taking control to transport their cargo to Earth. Even if Agent Foresc was on their side. She forced those thoughts to the back of her mind for the time being so that she didn't take the moment away from her crew. They needed the win.

Without realising it until she was in the thick of it, the bridge crew had turned the focus of their celebrations onto her. Like she had been in the lower decks shutting the doors and the bulkheads with everyone else. She calmly waved away the applause only to embrace her crew individually for their efforts, recognising who they were and that what they did was above and beyond anything anyone could have asked for.

When the Stellar Protection Force and agents returned to the bridge, her bridge crew welcomed them with a hero's welcome. Each one slapped on the back in acknowledgment. As soon as her engineers joined them with Allua Jons at the forefront, her head lulled to face the floor. The mood instantly turned sombre. No one knew what to say. There was nothing that could be said.

'We did it,' Allua Jons said quietly.

'You did,' Beatrice replied with a delicate smile.

'Your engineer did well,' the sergeant said, placing a hand on the chief's shoulder. 'He did more than was asked of.'

'Thank you,' the engineer responded, smiling at him.

'It's okay, and you did well too,' Duke added.

Allua Jons blushed and shied away. Beatrice had never seen the engineer turn that shade before. Jons turned to her and spoke, 'What do we do now?'

'We need to get the ship up and running again,' Beatrice answered. 'How long do you think it'll be before you get the ship ready for sub-light and light speed travel?'

'I can't say without looking over everything again,' the chief said. 'I'll look over the numbers and the ship read outs then update you.'

'Take your time before you make a start, let's just be happy we've shut the doors for now,' Beatrice whispered softly, squeezing her engineer's hand for comfort. 'Enjoy yourself then go over everything after some rest.'

'Okay,' Jons replied and left to join her engineers in mourning and rejoice.

'Captain, we'll stay with you until you're able to move and make it to UPN controlled space,' Duke said after it was certain they were alone. There was something he wasn't saying. Something troubled him. 'If you need it to speed things up, you can have help with the repairs. Ronan's not much of an engineer but he knows how to fix things. Anything to get moving from here sooner.'

'What is it?' she asked. 'What's the hurry?'

'We're in Crev space,' he said flatly.

'Oh God,' Beatrice gasped.

It had been years since that word had ever been uttered around her. She had lost too many ships to that hoard of roaming murderers. If anything was to send her back into the military, it would be the chance to eradicate every last one of the alien race and make sure humanity never had to be subjected to that kind of threat again.

'I want to get out of here as soon as we can,' Duke said. 'We might have sorted the wolves out but if a patrol fleet of Crevari finds us, there's nothing we can do but fill my ship with as many people as I can and go.'

'Agreed,' Beatrice said. It was a bitter pill to swallow, accepting that there was no way they could save everyone if the Crevari found them. It was either some survive, or none survive.

'When we're in friendly space we'll stay in close support until allied forces come to evacuate everyone on board,' Duke said. 'Then the wolves will be under their jurisdiction to deal with. If they even make it that far.'

'What do you mean?' the academic asked.

'He means,' Beatrice started, 'that they must be destroyed.'

'I'm sorry, but no,' Professor Ainslot blurted out as he rushed over to them. 'You can't destroy them. I need them for my research. We keep them alive. Don't transfer them just anyone. They can't be. We need specialist equipment and the right level of security to control.'

Duke massaged his brow. 'Those things are too dangerous. We can't risk them getting out into the public. All it takes is this sort of thing to be repeated on a planet. They could decimate entire populations before anyone had a chance to stop them. I won't risk civilians for a science project.'

'It's not like we don't have the kit to keep them contained,' Samuel Ainslot insisted. 'We have more than you think back at base. They won't get out. I can make sure of it.'

'Much like you did here?' Duke retorted. 'Because you did a good job of that, didn't you?'

'That wasn't my error,' Professor Ainslot snapped. There was a fire in his voice. 'I did everything right. I can't prepare for a myth hitting us the way that storm did. It won't happen again. I'll make sure of it. Don't destroy my research needlessly. Please.'

The man was a true scientist. Research above sense and completely lost in his work. She needed to make him see sense and reality, not lofty dreams of future success.

Beatrice sighed and gave her thoughts, 'Yeah, and those things are not from Earth. Are they, Professor? They're not even from our solar system or any human colonised planet under the UPN or any other flag. Professor, I'm sure you'll agree that they don't belong with us just as much as we don't belong with them. Let it go, okay?'

'Don't argue with them,' Agent Leyton Foresc instructed his scientist. 'We just lost someone else to the wolves. This isn't what we signed up for. This isn't what *I* signed up for.'

'But my research,' the man whined. 'I need to understand so much about them! I won't get this chance again.'

'Just stow it for now, okay,' Leyton ordered. 'Make predictions based on the research you've already been able to do. It's not like you can do much now anyway. I'm sure that if we can get one contained, we'll be permitted. Until then, work with what you've got.'

'Yes boss.'

269

Professor Ainslot left them, reluctantly taken under the wing of Jerome. Beatrice couldn't help but notice that both the professor and Leyton were not overly keen on that member of their team. It was something that needed to be understood better. Any rifts in their team, any sign of the dangers, she had to be made aware for everyone's safety.

'What's the deal with you and your guy there?' Beatrice asked. 'Don't seem to be getting on too well right now.' When he didn't react straight away, she persisted. 'It's easy to see so don't even try and pretend that nothing's happening.'

'Okay,' Leyton said in a hushed voice leaning forward. 'Okay. We're having a disagreement. He wants to follow orders to the letter. I don't. This is for me to sort out. But not a word of this to anyone. I don't think he's being entirely honest with me. If he gets wind of anything I'm thinking, I can guarantee I'll never find out and things will get worse.'

'I understand,' Beatrice whispered. 'Can you tell me what it is?'

Leyton Foresc shook his head and looked away, silently saying that part of the conversation was now over. She respected his position and wasn't going to advance any further with that for the time being. There were more important things than a shake up in the ranks.

'Agent,' she said. 'What actually happened when you fell behind earlier?'

Leyton scoffed. 'Told you, needed to check my equipment.'

'Please, I've known people just like you for being on it with their kit,' Duke countered. 'You're the sort to never not be ready. So go on, what was you doing?'

'I just fell behind,' the agent repeated. 'Like I said, I had to sort my kit. Something wasn't secured right. Look, I still got the job done.'

'You still got the job done, yes, but we need to know what happened,' Duke Horren said. 'How do we know you didn't plan on the guy being killed?'

'I'm trying to save you! And you accuse me of that? You know what? You're really full of shit if you think you can accuse me of that and expect me to cooperate. Think again.'

'Look, we needed to know, it was suspicious,' Duke explained.

'Piss off!' Leyton Foresc snapped. 'You're accusing me of intentionally killing your guy. I'm trying to help you lot. Why would I have told you anything if I didn't want to help? If I wanted to kill any of you, I could have ordered my team to open fire on the bridge before you got here then wait outside the airlock when you arrived. But I didn't.'

'How about you take it easy and see where we're coming from?' Duke requested. 'You have to admit it's dodgy. You're a field agent. You guys are never not prepared.'

Leyton scowled at the sergeant. 'Well, I was this time. It's not exactly an everyday situation, is it?'

'We're sorry for accusing you,' Beatrice said, hoping to calm him down. 'Look, take cabin thirty-seven on B-Deck. It's available. Freshen up and rest. Have some time to yourself. We'll talk about this later when we've all cooled off.'

'Thanks,' Leyton muttered before leaving the bridge. 'Be back later.'

'What was that about?' Duke Horren asked after the agent left. 'Why are we giving him the pamper treatment?'

'If he's not an enemy, I'd rather it stays that way and keep him on our side,' Beatrice said. 'You do what you can to keep people like that in your favour. I still think he is hiding something. We'll come back to him in a while and see if we can find out what he's not telling us then.'

'Okay, I'll speak to him later,' Duke said. 'Try and patch things up.'

The signs of a good man. Someone who was prepared to make the steps to forget the past. She had a lot of respect for a person like that.

'A word of advice, be upfront with him,' she suggested. 'Accept the fact you pushed him and let him know you're sorry. And another word of advice?'

Duke tilted his head in curiosity. 'What's that?'

'I saw how my engineer looked at you,' she said with a grin. 'Break her heart, I can guarantee she'll break your face.'

271

Leyton Foresc

The sergeant had been everything that the reports on him said and more. He was, quite literally, a walking legend with a string of military successes and military heritage of exceeding calibre. And humble. Leyton had been impressed by the accolades alone. Then he saw him in action The man had formed a team out of strangers and managed to get everyone working together. Even though they lost another person, the ship was secure. The passengers were safe. It felt like his soul was a little cleaner. And best of all, he didn't feel any remorse for going against his superior's instructions. Leyton Foresc had done what was morally right, what a decent human being would do, and it felt good. Even if the sergeant was right to have made those accusations, he was still in a good mood.

He retired to his designated cabin. He showered, then slept for a few hours, leaving him feeling refreshed and rejuvenated. Once awake and dressed, he let out an almighty sigh. The tac-pad on his gauntlet pulsated with a light. He had received a message while he slept. Administrator. Leyton sent a comm link request to his superior. While waiting for the connection to be made, he quickly checked that there was no one out in the corridor and kept the door shut. This was one conversation that he wanted no one to listen in on.

A chime signalled that the link had been made.

Leyton spoke calmly, 'Administrator.'

'Agent,' Puppet Master said. 'You ignored my comms link.'

'Yes sir,' he replied. 'I was resting.'

'At a time like this?'

Leyton shrugged, for no one to see, 'It's early morning. I needed to sleep. We have the situation under control, so I had the time.'

'Under control?'

'Cargo is contained in the lower levels. We're one down. The ship's engineers are currently working on getting repairs completed so that we can get the liner moving again.'

'And the SPF soldiers? Have you dealt with them?' The question sounded almost rhetorical as if he didn't need an answer. Why was that?

'We have a temporary truce,' Leyton said sternly. 'It was the only way we could secure the objective successfully.'

There was an eerie pause before Administrator spoke, 'I gave you an order. That ship was to be yours and the soldiers kept off it. You told me that you would take care of it.'

Before they had begun the process of locking the wolves away in the depths of the ship, Leyton had fallen behind to send a quick message to Administrator. He had briefly explained to his superior that they were trying to contain the wolves in the lower levels which would in turn allow them to take control of the ship more successfully. Leyton had avoided making any mention of the SPF and their arrival at the time.

He knew then that he would have to face the music for his decision when it came to light. Now he was facing it and now was the time to make it known without uncertainty what his stance was on the mission parameters. That there were things he simply would not do.

'Yeah. You did and I took care of it my way,' Leyton said. 'I found a way to contain them without anyone else dying. I'm happy with the results.'

'I see. What gave you the authority to go against my instructions? You know what the result is going to ultimately be. Be the good man now, it doesn't matter.'

'I understand sir. With all due respect, I wasn't about to slaughter civilians for you so you could keep your hands clean. I'm not going to do something like that. There's no reason for it.'

'No reason?' Puppet Master questioned. 'No reason? Really? You are not the head of the division. Not even the head of a facility of your own. You're a lead agent for a field unit. You are not at liberty to understand the reason behind anything I tell you to do. All you need to know is that when I say I want something done, it gets done because I say so.'

'I at least have the right to know what's going on,' Leyton told him. 'Especially now that you want me to kill innocent people for it to stay secret.'

'No, you don't,' Administrator replied. 'All you need to know is that if my intelligence is correct, these specimens are going to be desperately needed for humanity to survive the coming years.'

'What the hell is that supposed to mean?' Leyton demanded.

'Chess.'

'What?'

'I play a game of chess every… single… day. My day doesn't end when I take my name badge off. I must be two, three, four… as many steps ahead of all our competition as is needed. Prepare for everything.

Threats everyone knows. Threats some people know about. Threats that haven't even been recognised yet. If I tell you even an ounce of what I knew, considering you're out in the field, you wouldn't be allowed out of my sight for risk of the information falling into the wrong hands. That's if you were to even stay alive. You know there is a chain of command for a reason. I'll take your morals as a result of exhaustion just this once. But you will listen to me and accept that this is not something you need to know any more about. Understood? This isn't a game. You're not a child that gets to throw a strop when you don't get your own way. You're a soldier. An agent. Start behaving like one.'

What was there that could require the ice wolves to help humanity survive? What could be that dangerous that it wasn't to be well known yet? He realised that there was no point pursuing the subject further at the moment. Maybe when he got to Earth, he would try to clarify it. 'Yes sir.'

'Now, your reinforcements are less than a week out,' Puppet Master explained. 'Because of your insubordination I will be assigning the squad commander of the unit to relieve you from your duty. Is that clear?'

'It is,' Leyton growled.

'Good,' Administrator said. 'I am aware that you have also revealed to the crew of the ship and SPF personnel details of the mission?'

How would he have known that? That was not disclosed on any comms with the administrator at the time nor with any of his team over comms. That meant either the administrator had his comms bugged or there was someone else in his ranks in conversation with him. Both of which were more than likely to have happened. He had to manipulate the conversation in his favour to find out whatever he could from someone proud to boast they knew everything about this internal espionage.

'Excuse me sir?'

'How much have you told the crew?' Administrator questioned.

'Only what they needed to know so that I could get the assistance I needed to secure the cargo,' he said, partially telling the truth.

'Anything else?'

'What makes you think I would have told them more than that?' Leyton questioned.

'I have eyes and ears everywhere,' the administrator answered. 'Even around the people I would like to trust.'

'You're spying on me,' Leyton snarled. 'Why? Who with?'

Administrator scoffed. 'I spy on everyone. Friend and foe. Especially my friends. You don't get far in our business trusting friends.'

He had a traitor in his midst. The question was, who? With four definite possibilities he could not say for certain who it could be between them. They each bore the potential to be the one with a knife primed for his back. Equally, was it the ones he least suspected? A helpless professor would definitely be one to go unnoticed in acts of espionage. Or a friendly medic that valued life over all else would get by without catching a second glance. A willing agent who was always there for him to rely on.

This was always a risk with working in intelligence. People turned on each other eventually. It was only a matter of when.

Even if he did not approve of it, Leyton was proud and scared of the skill it took to lie to him in order to keep a secret like this from him.

When Leyton started out in the agency he would have lied to his mother, sold his childhood best friend's arm and stolen a credit from an old woman trying to get a shuttle bus home if it meant impressing his superiors. Anything if it meant progressing through the ranks. Someone showing that sort of voracious appetite for progression was a dangerous opponent. That was not the person he was anymore. His loyalties to the agency were not as strong as they were before this assignment. After what was expected of him, how could he be loyal to the agency when the targets were civilians?

Duke, however, was a person he could be loyal to. They may have their differences, but he was a good man. A trustworthy man. Someone who valued life. Leyton couldn't betray someone that may genuinely want to save his agents from certain doom should it be needed.

Maybe it was time to tell them what was going on. Time to come clean. There would almost certainly once again be repercussions for the actions that had been taken. But if anyone were to be able to help him it would be that man.

'What are my orders then while we are waiting?' Leyton asked.

'Hold position and keep an airlock clear for them,' Administrator said. 'When they arrive at the *Passage*, direct the team to the bridge. They'll take it from there.'

'The SPF is still here,' Leyton reminded him. 'They will put up a fight when the reinforcements arrive.'

'And?' Administrator pressed. 'Your point?'

'Give me comms with them,' Leyton requested. He prepared himself for the lie. 'If they can let me know when they're here I can be better prepared to give them access to the ship so they can come onboard safely. Without detection.'

'How much preparation time will you need?'

'About six hours before,' he said. 'Will be enough time to get everyone into position without any suspicion. If I leave it too late, they'll suspect something.'

'Okay. I will forward them your link. They will be in touch. Be careful though. Do you remember the soldier I told you about, Duke? I've done more research on him. He's seen almost as much action as you and survived worse. If he gets wind of any of this, you're a dead man. Make sure you get him first.'

'Understood.'

'Out.'

The communication link cut. Silence set in. A powerful sensor of relief overwhelmed Leyton in such a rush he could have easily lost all stability. He had just successfully lied to the most well paid, professional deceiver in the galaxy. Not only that, but he had an ally that was more capable than the rest of his team. Things wouldn't be so difficult after all. They had a chance.

Leyton turned to walk out of the room and find the sergeant but when the door opened, he was greeted by the angered face of the very man he wanted to find. He must have heard the parts of the conversation that were not meant to be taken out of context.

'Sergeant, how's it going?' Leyton asked casually.

'So and so,' Duke said. 'You?'

'I'd say the same. What're you doing here? I didn't ask for a booty call.'

'I came by earlier, but you were asleep. Was just going to ask if you wanted a drink, try and find out exactly what's going on with you and try to see if you're on my side or not. Make things easier for us. You know?'

'I see,' Leyton replied. 'Guess you've made up your mind before speaking to me?'

'Guess you could say that,' Duke Horren said.

'How much did you hear?'

'Enough.'

'We really need to talk about it before you throw a punch,' Leyton said. 'I promise you that you haven't heard everything.'

276

'Don't really think there's anything to talk about.'

Leyton took a deep breath, grit his teeth in anticipation then spoke, 'Trust me, it isn't what you think it is.'

'I bet,' Duke scoffed, clenching his fists tightly. 'Not the first time someone's told me that to get on my good side before they backstab me.'

'We really going to do this?' Leyton sighed, accepting that this wasn't going to go his way.

'Oh yeah,' Duke said with a snarl. 'We are.'

'Do me one favour then?'

'What's that?'

'Make sure the first one really hurts because you won't get a second,' Leyton instructed.

Duke gave a cunning smile. 'Where's the fun in that?'

The SPF sergeant landed the first punch. To his credit, it was a good punch that rattled Leyton's jaw. A really good punch. Had it been a little closer to his chin and a few teeth may have been chipped or knocked out.

As the fight got underway, there was no telling what was a punch or a kick and what was a chair, a desk or a wall that he was thrown into. The only clear answer was that it hurt. At first, he didn't retaliate. Instinct and training told him to feel out his opponents at first, let them give their best shot. It allowed him to quickly assess their fighting methods, strengths and weaknesses while his foe wouldn't learn anything about him and waste valuable energy. When he started to notice the coppery taste of blood in his mouth after a sharp hook around the jaw Leyton stepped up to the fight, rivalling the SPF non-com step for step. He was indeed as tough as the administrator indicated he would be. Not bad for an out of practice Slayer.

The fight awkwardly progressed out of the cabin and into the hallway. Members of the key crew avoided them, unable to decide what they should do. They stood around, gasping in shock at the chaos. The sergeant held his own with surprising ease. But he wasn't Leyton's enemy, and he was starting to hold back. He needed to stop the fight so he could explain what was going on. When the opportunity presented itself, Leyton got behind the sergeant and held him in a headlock until his struggling eased.

'Sergeant, you need to stop this. Please,' Leyton insisted. 'You need to listen to me.'

'I need to stop you!' Duke snapped.

'You don't understand! I need you to hear me out.'

He pushed the pair apart and held out his hands in a hold off gesture. They glared at one another with the bloodlust of primitive man out to get their next meal or fend off a potential rival.

'What is there to understand?' The SPF soldier asked. 'You're under instructions to kill me.'

'No. I'm not. Well, yes. I am. But I don't plan to. I'm not your enemy. I don't want to do that.'

A look of confusion washed over the sergeant's face. 'The hell does that mean?'

'I have information you need,' Leyton stated. 'Information you clearly missed out on that would put what you did hear into the correct context.'

'What like? How to put me down for good?'

'Like the fact that my boss is sending reinforcements under the impression that I'll have secured this ship and got you lined up to be easy prey for them,' Leyton explained. Once again, there were no bad feelings about committing what amounted to treason. It was all worth it. 'But trust me, I'm on your side.'

'Come again? There are more of you on their way here?'

He shook his head sharply. 'No, not agents... A specialist unit. Don't know anything about them.'

Leyton took a moment to compose himself, to take in just exactly what he was doing. To make sure he was okay doing this. Leyton opened his mouth, but no words came out. He glanced around the hallway. There were eyes everywhere, ears all around. Too many people had seen and heard his statement for him to be comfortable carrying on in public.

'Sergeant, we need to take this conversation away from here,' Leyton said. 'I can't risk any of my team finding out about this.'

'What? Why not?'

Leyton Foresc walked up close to Duke Horren and spoke quietly. 'Because I don't like what I've been instructed to do. This is why I want to help. But I just found out I have a mole in my team. I have no idea who it is, or when they started feeding information to the administrator – but he point-blank told me he had someone keeping tabs on me. Right now, I can't trust them, not any of them. None of them must know we're having this conversation until I know who it is otherwise it'll fuck everything up.'

'How can I trust you?'

'Because I have no reason to lie.'

'Anyone can say the same thing,' Duke said. 'Give me a better reason.'

Leyton sighed and spoke quietly. 'The fact that we're having this conversation means that I'm not going to have much of a life if we fail. If that's not good enough, look in my eyes and tell me that I'm not fucking shitting myself.'

He was right. The fear in the agent's eyes was genuine. Leyton was tense. It wasn't enough to earn his trust entirely. But it was enough to let him have the chance to prove himself.

'Alright then. But we'll do this my way. We're going to get all this out in the open with people that can listen. Now,' Duke said. He opened a comm link to his team and the bridge crew. 'Guys, keep your mouths shut and head to the bridge. Get there as fast as you can. Don't bring any of the agents or ship crew with you. Captain, secure the bridge. Only key personnel you trust to be there.' He turned his attention back to Leyton. 'You, you come with me and don't leave my sight.'

'I guess I earned that.'

'You did. But I want you to earn my trust back. This is your chance.'

Leyton smirked. 'Do I at least get an ice pack? My jaw hurts.'

The pair laughed. It hurt like hell. He had some severe bruising. Maybe a slight fracture on a rib or two. An easy fix by the medic. Nothing really to worry about but enough to make him think twice about laughing again. Or stepping up for another round with the soldier. He was a good fighter and didn't even break a sweat.

They didn't say much as they walked to the bridge. Duke walked with an ever-so-slight limp, clearly hiding a knee injury. He wasn't about to pretend to be so brave. Maybe if Leyton showed how much he was hurting would earn him a couple of sympathy votes. The smile on Duke's face was gentle. Playful, even. It told him everything he needed to know. They knew how each other felt. It was strange how their brief skirmish had built such an unusual connection.

By the time they reached the bridge armed guards were already stationed outside – clearly the captain making sure that they were not interrupted. To the captain's credit, her crew had been reduced to just a handful. Beatrice Lenoia was present with her adjutant and a few key crew members. The three other members of the SPF stood in a group at the edge of the holo-table.

No one spoke to them. Only stared.

'What's this about?' Beatrice asked.

'The agent has something he needs to tell you all,' Duke said, slapping Leyton on the back. 'Go on. Get it over with.'

'I never told you my mission parameters that my boss gave when I initially told you what I was doing on your ship,' he started. 'Originally it was to go unnoticed. When two of the females gave birth and another two were expected to give birth, we realised we didn't have the resources to keep them contained and alive, which I informed my superior about. I was told to relocate my team and release the wolves so they could feast on the passengers and crew. I refused to do that. I've been keeping my boss updated with some false and some incomplete information throughout it all. And I just learnt that I have someone conspiring against me. There are certain things that I have kept out of my updates with him. He brought up something that I haven't told him. He could only have learnt it from one of my team that I've been telling you about the wolves and our mission here.'

'You have a spy in your midst,' Beatrice stated.

'Ironic, isn't it?' Leyton Foresc whispered. 'Which is why I didn't want my team here.'

'Why don't we just deal with them then?' Ronan Moasa asked. 'It won't be that hard if we have the upper hand.'

'It's not that simple. It's not just them we have to worry about.' Leyton walked to the centre of the bridge and stood before the captain in her chair. To some comfort, Duke joined him. 'Well, my boss has deemed me to be incompetent because of my insubordination and not wanting to kill everyone here. In response he has a second team on the way to relieve me of my command and take the ship to transport you all back to Pluto. When there, you're all as good as dead. I can almost guarantee that I won't be around much longer when we get back to Earth after all this.'

Beatrice sank into her chair and placed a hand to her face. 'Do you have any idea what their numbers are?'

'I don't,' he admitted. 'But what I do know is that they should contact me six hours before they arrive here so I can prepare. I had to tell him I needed the heads up to be able to get you all into position to make taking the ship easier.'

'It gives us something to work with,' Duke said. 'I can easily make a plan if we have that heads up.'

'And do you know who you can trust from your team?' Beatrice questioned. Her voice was on the verge of giving up hope.

280

Leyton shook his head softly. 'I haven't got a clue. I only just learnt someone was feeding information to my boss behind my back. No idea if they've just started it or been doing it for a while. At the moment I can't trust anyone.'

'Is there any way you can find out?' the officer requested.

'There is, but it'll take some time and when I start the process, we need to be ready for shit to hit the fan once it's complete,' Leyton explained.

'Understood. We'll wait until closer to the time. The less time they have to react gives us the advantage when your reinforcements arrive,' Beatrice said. 'How long is that going to be?'

'Less than a week. Administrator didn't give any specifics. Guess he doesn't trust me.'

The captain was stopped from replying when her adjutant called from the comms station. 'Captain, we have a breach. The wolves have found a way out of the lower decks using a maintenance shaft!'

'Fuck, how did we miss that one?' Ronan Moasa shouted.

'How many wolves?' Beatrice cried.

'Three, at least,' her second in command answered. 'They're not far from engineering.'

Leyton and Duke shared a glance before Leyton spoke, 'Civilian? Crew? Anyone in the area?'

'We have a half dozen crew members in the vicinity,' Adjutant Hender explained. 'We're already pulling them out of the area. No civilians are... there...Oh shit, we got kids down there!'

'Kids?' Beatrice screamed. 'What the hell are they doing there? How many?'

'Must have snuck down when we eased the restrictions for people to return to the cabins,' her second replied, shrugging his shoulders. 'Little shits must think they're being clever. There's four or five of them.'

'Sergeant,' Beatrice said. 'Can you and your team extract the kids and keep my engineers safe to seal the wolves again?'

'You bet we can,' Duke said. 'Send the details to my tac-pad.'

'I'm helping,' Leyton declared.

'No, you're not,' Beatrice countered. 'I need you to tell me everything you can about your team, so we all know what we're up against. The sergeant can handle this. Can't you?'

'I can,' Duke answered. 'If I get stuck, I'll shout for help. Come on guys.'

Leyton watched as the non-com left the bridge with his team. Ready for the fight that no one could prepare for. He sighed and turned back to the officer with his arms widespread in submission. 'What do you need to know?'

'Everything.' She glared at him with steely eyes that offered no disguise for the anger swelling inside.

'Sure thing. Well…'

Leyton went through the members of his team and the psyche evaluations that Medic Suttle provided. With each piece of information provided he could feel himself becoming more disassociated with the agency, his team and his former self. Everything went against the grain, and it felt right. Leyton only hoped it would buy him the trust he needed to put things right. Maybe when it was done, he wouldn't need to look over his shoulder. At least not straight away.

Duke Horren

Duke charged through the hallways to the rear of the *Galactic Passage*. He had been assigned the chief engineer, Allua Jons, to help lock away the wolves. She and his team kept up with him; he could feel their tense anticipation of combat. Out of his troops, Udal'e was the most ill-prepared mentally for the fight. Arche surprisingly wasn't far behind him. He expected her to be a little more confident. Moasa, however, was more than ready for it, almost lusting after the threat of imminent death. Allua on the other hand was an enigma. If she was afraid, she didn't show it. And with a heavy welding pack and bulky tech-pad strapped around her shoulder was showing his team that a civilian could match them. The map on his tac-pad led them down several decks.

He slowed the pace down. He wanted to save the kids but not at the expense of his team. It hurt of him to think of it in such simplistic ways, but children were a risk. There was no way around it. Duke would do his best to save them but saving them was pointless if he lost his team during the effort. His team could fight. The kids couldn't. He checked the map of the deck.

'Jons, tell me where we go from here,' he requested.

The engineer came in close and hovered her finger around the hologram. 'From what the captain said, the wolves have come up back here. Realistically, I want to shut them back on the other side of the door. It's going to be the easiest way to have them secured again.'

'But getting them back there is going to be tricky,' Duke replied.

'How did we miss this?' Abe asked.

'We rushed it,' Chief Jons sighed. 'Overlooked that any of the shafts on the lower decks that might still have been open down below. This must have been the first door that opened for them to crawl out of. Those shafts are meant to take you from the bottom straight up to the top.'

'So, if we lock them on the other side of the door here, how do we stop them from moving up to the next open door above us?' Ronan questioned. 'Didn't think that through, did you?'

Allua Jons threw him a wicked smirk. 'Actually, I did. Every two decks there is a blast door cutting the shaft off. These are supposed to be automated, but there's a hand lever to either shut or open them. If we can get them through the door, they shouldn't expect a drop on the other side. While they're falling, I can weld the blast door above the

283

entry shut before coming back through and then shut the door. Provided that there aren't any others that are open. But we can cross that when we've contained them here.'

Sergeant Duke Horren looked it over. It was a sound plan. He didn't like the fact that someone, by the sounds of it, would have to play bait or at least trick them into going back into the shaft. But it was all they had, second to a shootout that wasn't guaranteed to go their way.

'Come on then, let's move.'

Duke and his squad raced along the deck. They needed to find the children first before the wolves did. He couldn't handle the thought of not making it there first. There was something uncomfortable and soul destroying about a child dying. He always hoped that he would never have to see another child needlessly die again.

'Sergeant,' Ivan said over the comms in his ear.

'Zen, what's up?' he replied. He held his breath as he checked a corner.

'I've been given access to the security footage,' the pilot explained. 'Figure that Lenoia lady wanted someone who knew what they were doing overseeing you.'

'Then why don't you move aside for Valentina?' Duke joked.

'Funny,' Ivan jested. 'Seriously though, with that and your helmet cams, I'll be your eyes and ears. There we go, I've got sight of you. You need to keep going forward and at the third intersection take a right. The kids were around there playing a game or something just now.'

'And the wolves?' Duke asked.

'I don't have sight on them just yet. But we're looking. I'll keep you posted.'

'Thanks, out,' Duke said. 'Come on guys, we're not that far.'

'Sergeant, what do we do about the agent?' Abe asked. 'We can't trust him, can we?'

'He's ready to rat out his own team just to keep the passengers safe,' he replied. 'Not sure how much I believe him but if he's telling the truth I'd like to think we can trust him.'

'I know what I'll do if he's trying to lead us into a trap,' Corporal Moasa growled. He couldn't tell if the growl was out of savage hope or out of anger.

'Steady on,' Duke said. 'We wait and see what happens.'

'Sergeant, hold up!' Ivan hissed over the comms.

The squad stopped advancing and clung to the walls, expecting hostiles to burst out from nowhere. Nothing happened. Was this Helmsman Zenkovich overreacting?

'What is it?' Duke asked. His breath was light and soft to attract as little attention as possible.

'I can see the wolves. They're not far from the kids. I don't think it's a smart thing to go there,' Ivan insisted.

'We're going to at least try,' Duke said.

They covered the corridors in a swift, sweeping motion. Glass crunched under their boots with each step. His heart raced in his ear.

A laugh. Not a laugh, a giggle. The sound of a child having fun. It was muffled by a door or a wall. Duke signalled for the team to start searching the rooms when a door opened round the corner and another young voice could be heard crying out that she found someone before huffing in defeat as she found no one.

'Arche, get her. Keep her quiet,' Duke instructed.

'On it,' Corporal Arche replied.

Ronan found the child they initially heard giggling. A young boy, barely seven, with mousy hair and teeth too big for his face. He'd grow out into them eventually.

'What's your name?'

'R-Ruben,' the boy stammered.

'How many of you are there down here?' Duke asked. 'You know you're not supposed to be here, right?'

'Are we in trouble?' the boy whimpered. His eyes swelled with tears of fear.

'Sergeant, the wolves are getting close,' Ivan hissed in his ear. 'You don't have long before you need to make a move.'

'Not if you can tell me who else is here and where they are,' Duke insisted calmly, de-polarising his visor so the child could see his face.

'There's six of us,' Ruben said. 'There's me, Jo-jo, Guntburgh, Mai and Loden and Ali.'

'Okay, thank you. Where are they?'

Abe announced that he had one child, shortly followed by Joane with another two. Four down, two to go.

'I don't know,' the boy answered. 'We were playing hide and seek. Can't play it if you know where everyone is.'

He had a point, the little smart aleck. Joane returned with the three children they had found. A fifth came running round the corner with Ronan. By the exclamations they had all made, that meant the last one to find was Mai. The kids huddled together. Each one terrified of what might happen to them.

'Abe, where you at?' Duke asked.

'Just a couple corridors away,' Udal'e replied. 'I can see the last one now. Hey kid! Get over here, it's not safe!'

'Shit! Duke, he shouldn't have done that,' Ivan Zenkovich cried out. 'The wolves are heading for-

The shrill cry of glass breaking in a vicious wind roared down the corridors. Duke felt his heart stop. The kids wailed in terror, crying for Mai to be brought back to them. The wolves were going to get Abe and Mai unless they helped.

'Joane, get the kids out of here,' he instructed.

'Sergeant, I can help you!' she insisted, not wanting to be put on baby-sitting duty.

'Help me by helping them,' Duke replied. 'No offense, but Ronan is better in a fight than you. He has a better aim and is stronger than either of us. It's not up for debate. Go!'

'Yes Sergeant,' Arche said reluctantly. 'Come on kids, we're going.'

'Let's get a move on Ronan,' Duke said. 'Somebody talk to me, what's going on?'

'I've got the kid,' Abe answered. He was panting heavily. 'The wolves are right behind me.'

Ivan quickly chipped in over the comms, 'Behind? They're practically on him. Take your next right Sergeant and they'll be right in front of you.'

'How many?'

'Four of them,' Ivan Zenkovich answered.

'Got it.' He held his hand on Jons' shoulder. 'Wait here until we tell you it's safe to move.'

'Sure thing, boss,' Chief replied, hanging back as he moved forward with Ronan.

Abe was sprinting down the corridor toward them with the child in his arms. The four adult ice wolves were closing in on them.

'Abe, drop and slide!' Duke barked.

His soldier complied almost instantly. Once Udal'e was below eye level, Duke and Ronan opened fire on the wolves. Instinctively they aimed for head shots but when those failed to put them down, they switched their aim for the legs. If the creatures weren't going to be killed easily, the next best thing would be to handicap them so that they could buy themselves some time.

286

Udal'e joined them in the defence against the wolves after he put Mai down behind them. The child screamed. Terrified and deafened by the automatic fire. Jons rushed over to take the child to one side for her safety.

'We can't hold them off forever!' Ronan announced.

'I know, I know!' Duke replied.

'What do we do now?' Abe Udal'e asked.

Duke felt his stomach knot. He didn't know. Abe persisted for a response when he didn't answer straight away.

'Give me a minute,' he demanded.

'You don't have a minute at this rate,' Ivan advised in his ear. 'You need to think fast, and I don't think you have many options.'

'I know we don't,' Duke replied. 'Jons, how many ways out are there from here?'

'Too many for us to handle,' she answered. 'Can you buy me a minute to think?'

'We'll give you thirty seconds,' he said.

The wolves were gradually getting closer to them. One dropped to the floor, not dead but severely injured. They were getting there. They just needed more ammunition. If they had that, they could have finished the job there and then. Duke Horren was sure of it. He turned to face Jons when his mental timer had passed the stated time for an update to find she wasn't there. She was gone. The child remained and looked at him oblivious to what had happened with the engineer.

'Shit, where is she?' he asked. 'Ivan, can you see her?'

Before the pilot could answer he heard tapping and rattling that wasn't coming from his team or the wolves. It was behind the beasts. Then she appeared out of a corridor waving and screaming for them to follow her. The beasts wasted no time in obliging, smart enough to know an easy meal when it was in front of them.

'I don't believe this,' Ivan coughed. 'She's leading them back to the maintenance shaft.'

'Without us? Fuck me, come on let's give her backup. Abe, give me your ammo then get the kid out of here.'

Fresh ammo in hand, the raced after the engineer and the wolves while Abe departed with the final child back to safety. First it was the engineer that was out of sight. Then the wolves dropped out of visual as they darted after her round a corner. He hoped that when they caught up to them, they beat the wolves to her.

Zenkovich kept him posted on her position then fell silent as the maintenance shaft was ahead of Jons. Even at their distance, they could hear the panicked scream of the woman and the vile outcry of the wolves as they neared their victim. The heavy thud of something colliding with metal at speed silenced the beasts momentarily before their own terrified roars faded out of hearing range.

'Ivan, what's happening?' Duke demanded as they rushed for the shaft.

'I don't know,' Ivan said. 'I saw her go through the door then the wolves went through after. I haven't got any visual in there.'

'Fuck! Come on Ronan.'

She needed to be alive. Duke had already lost one civilian on his watch. He couldn't accept another death.

He almost dove through the shaft as he looked down. The wolves were already climbing up again, though one of them remained at the base of the shaft, hopefully killed by the fall and their defence against them. But no sign of the engineer.

'No,' he whispered, immediately dreading the worst.

Sparks started to rain down on him from above. Jons secured herself in the shaft with her feet as she used both hands to handle the welding kit and fuse the blast door together at the seams, preventing anything from moving further up the shaft.

'Hey, it can't be that bad that I'm still alive, can it?' she asked mockingly, glancing down with a seductive grin. 'I mean how many chances do you have to get a view like this and get away with it?'

Flustered by the sudden change of circumstances and the innuendo proposed by the engineer, he aimed his rifle back down the shaft. 'Good point. How long do you need?'

'Another fifteen seconds to secure it, why?'

'It's going to get loud,' he warned. 'And you might need to move faster.'

Several bursts were fired from his rifle by the time the engineer was ready to come down. Somewhere between the rush of him pulling out of the shaft and Allua clambering down, the chief engineer lost her footing. Taking her hand to stop her fall nearly ripped his arm from its socket. The weight of the engineer and the welding pack was not an easy load to pull through the hatch even with his combat armour taking most of the strain. Once they were safely through, and shared a relieved smile with each other, Ronan closed the door and locked it. Chief Jons jumped back to her feet and welded the metal slab shut.

They did it. They managed to trap the wolves back in the lower decks without losing anyone. And best of all, they saved the kids. It was an incredibly good day. The relief and grins on each of their faces was enough to make the risks worth it. Duke rubbed his shaking hands together as the adrenaline continued to race through him.

'What about the other shafts?' Ronan asked.

Allua Jons smiled at the giant, 'Already on it. Got my best engineers there while we had this group here. Animals aren't as tactical as us.'

'She's not wrong,' Duke concurred. 'But good work with that.'

'Thanks. Good job there, muscles,' Allua said, backhanding Ronan's arm. 'And you didn't too bad either,' she added as she walked past Duke, winking and looking him up and down. 'Come on, first round is on me.'

'Sarge?' Ronan said, watching as the engineer carried on walking back down the hallway.

'Yeah?'

'Is it wrong that I'm a little scared by her being calmer than me right now?' Corporal Moasa asked.

He shook his head. 'Nope.'

'How about that I quite like it?'

'Nope,' Duke repeated.

'It's not?'

'If it is, then I'm just as disgusting as you,' Duke said with a smile. 'Come on, she said drinks on her.'

'Maybe she means literally,' Ronan muttered hopefully.

'Hey, now that's just filth,' he laughed.

At the bar on the ship, it felt odd to be able to relax and have a drink while danger was still lurking. But it was a relief, and the beer on board was delicious. Fresh and hoppy, brewed at a Mid-Colony brewery. Duke was with Allua, his squad and a few of her engineers. Even Leyton and a couple of his agents joined them. For what felt like hours they laughed, drank, and felt at ease. All the while, Duke felt his gaze always drift toward Allua. She was extremely attractive, with flowing hair and twinkling eyes. She was one of the first women that he was able to speak freely in front of, spend time with, and enjoy being around. Every time either he or Allua spoke, their eyes locked. They took in every word each of them uttered. She'd blatantly flirt with him, and he'd be incapable of hiding the redness in his cheeks. At times, people would make outright jokes at their clear flirtation. Others were subtle. Yet, Duke was surprisingly unshaken by their comments and jokes. If anything, he couldn't hear them for most of their conversation.

As their company started to filter away back to their cabins or duties, they remained in each other's company. Unable to stop talking, refusing to bring their time in each other's presence to an end.

'Thank you for this,' Duke said, gesturing to the empty bottles on the table before them. 'I've had a really great time.'

'Oh no, that's never a good thing,' Allua replied, taking a sip of her beer and rolling her eyes.

'What do you mean?' Duke asked.

'This is the part where you tell me you like me, but you've got a girl back home,' the engineer explained. 'That as much as you want to give me the time of my life you don't want to break my heart.'

Duke burst into momentary laughter. 'No! Nothing like that. I don't have anyone in my life. Or a home to go back to, to be honest.'

'Fuck off!' Allua Jons exclaimed. 'How do you not? Have you seen yourself?'

Duke shrugged. 'I've just never had the time to meet someone. Even if I did, I'd be gone for too long too much of the time. Guessing you're single?'

'What gave it away?'

'Well, you're not exactly shy with your flirting,' he explained.

Allua shrugged gently with a smirk. 'No point hiding how I feel.'

She gently brushed the hair out of her face. Even such a simple move was seductively carried out. Their eyes locked. Duke fought every tipsy urge to look at her lips then back to her eyes. He wanted to. That way she would have the visual suggestion of what he wanted.

'I like that,' Duke said, finishing his drink.

'Should hope you do.' Allua was about to say something else when her comm pad went off. She sighed in frustration, looked at the message she received and smiled softly. 'Duty calls. Don't go thinking that this right here's over. I'll be back to finish this talk.'

'You better do,' Duke replied.

Allua smiled, winked and left. He couldn't help but watch her as she left. Her hair swaying with every step. The contours of her body moving. When he realised that he was staring, Duke shook his head softly.

'Easy boy,' he told himself.

If she was returning to her work, it was only right that he too returned to his squad. But not before he had a strong coffee back on the patrol ship.

Jesa

Jesa struggled with her emotions. She had been beside herself with worry. Duke had risked his life and she had been there to watch the whole thing, unable to assist in any way. She had watched as he fought to keep the children safe from harm before ultimately saving the engineer and sealing off the lower decks to keep the passengers safe. Once the ordeal was over, she found herself in floods of tears that this man, this father she never had until now, had almost died right before her eyes and somehow survived. Zenkovich eventually managed to ease her emotions and took her from the flight deck to the galley.

He brewed her a coffee and sat in front of her with warm eyes.

'Care to tell me what that was about?' he asked her, smiling softly.

'It's nothing,' she said sharply. There were some things she wasn't ready to admit to the Centies. Having a heart that cared for them was one of those subjects. 'Just forget it.'

'No, tell me. What got to you then?'

She felt her cheeks flush. Jesa shied her face away from direct view with her hair. 'You'll laugh.'

'I won't,' Ivan said. 'I promise.'

Jesa hesitated then almost blurted out her emotions within a single breath. 'He's been just like a father to me. Stupid, yah? But he cares. He's nice. He's not like other people. He wants the best for me, and he's made me feel safe.'

'And you were afraid you were going to lose him?'

She nodded. 'I lost one father. Don't want to lose another. Can't lose another.'

'Why was that so hard to say?' Ivan Zenkovich asked her. When she shrugged, he answered the question for her. 'It's easier to not say your feelings than to admit them. Isn't it? In your heart, you still don't trust us. Maybe not hate us. But definitely don't trust. Don't think you really want to trust us just yet. To tell me you're scared to lose a Centie would be admitting to yourself that you can trust us. That you want to trust us. And it's a bitter pill to swallow.'

'You speak like you know how it feels, yah?' she replied.

'Better than you can imagine,' Zenkovich whispered. 'Growing up, I didn't know my dad that well. He was always working. One day, he got a call from his best friend. His friend worked the business with him and had a gambling addiction. His friend owed a lot of money he couldn't

292

afford to pay. So, he gambled the business, and lost. He killed himself not long after, out of shame. My dad had to accept that his friend had an addiction he had failed to fully appreciate. He still lives with that guilt, refuses to accept it and carry on. You on the other hand, you have time to accept that we are not as bad as you were brought up to believe and do something about that mentality.'

'I'm sorry to hear that,' Jesa said softly. 'I really am.'

Ivan shrugged. 'It's okay. Life is what it is. I've been through a lot. Learnt a lot because of it. Know how to best look after myself thanks to it. When you get to my age, you stop getting too overwhelmed because you've been able to learn how to deal with things.'

Almost a necessary evil to be spoken to like that. It did put things in perspective for her though. She had lived so much of her life believing what people told her without seeing it first-hand. At no point had any of the Centies told her that they were amazing, wonderful or perfect. They all had flaws that they wore on their sleeves not out of pride but out of recognition that they were human and did nothing to try to hide that from anyone. How had Jesa been so blind for so long to this? Then she answered it for herself in a single word: Barbaros. He had drilled a lot of reason and rationale out of her as a child. Being away from him revealed all the lies for what they were and held a candle close enough to the truth that she wanted to keep looking for. It was beautiful.

Yet she was scared. With the newfound truth that had been discovered came the threat of everything she learnt not being what she hoped for. Changing the world around her from what she had known to being worse than it was before. Much like a child on the day they learn that the fictional character they had grown to love is no longer real. Only this time she had the option to choose what she did. Should she remain in ignorant bliss to the reality of the universe or take the risk and discover the truth for what it truly was?

Jesa decided that it was all worth it. To learn about the cosmos and accept the Centies into her life, for better or for worse, meant staying around these people that had taken her in. They no longer looked at her as a prisoner but as one of their own, giving her freedoms within known limitations. Not forced like Barbaros had done.

'Thank you,' she said.

'It's no problem,' Ivan replied. 'Just remember, while you're on here you're one of us. We care for each other in our own ways.'

Jesa finished her coffee and followed Ivan Zenkovich back up to the flight deck. Valentina was in full control, watching the team return to the bridge and, after that, the bar for drinks. Jesa wondered how good the alcohol was from the central systems. She doubted it could match anything that was Outer made.

'How long have you all known the sergeant for?' Jesa asked randomly. She couldn't answer why she needed to know but if they were as much a family as they said they were, then, surely, they had known each other long enough to be considered a family.

'I've known the sarge for a couple years. But I've known Zen here for eight,' Valentina said.

'Ivan?' Jesa asked.

'Near enough since he joined us at the station so... About five years?' Ivan Zenkovich answered. 'Val only became my co-pilot a couple years ago. We've ferried Duke for most of his assignments in that time. Why'd you ask?'

'Just wanted to make sure you weren't just telling me things to make me feel good, I suppose,' Jesa explained. 'Couldn't be too safe.'

'I hear you,' Rodriguez said. 'But you're in good hands with us. I wouldn't agree to be assigned to anyone here if I didn't like them.'

'Exactly, can't trust someone you don't like,' Ivan said. Apart from trust that they might backstab you at some point.'

Jesa smiled softly. 'So, what do we do now?'

'Now? We wait,' Ivan said. 'We keep an eye on the scopes, keep up with what's going on and make sure that we're secure at all times.'

'Doesn't that get boring?' Jesa asked.

She couldn't bear the thought of just sitting around any longer; not after spending an age waiting to reach the next drop off with nothing else to do. Jesa fidgeted in her seat with anticipation.

'Usually, no,' Valentina said.

'We usually have enough to worry about, like hostiles arriving at any moment,' Ivan Zenkovich added. 'Things aren't as boring when you've got enemy ships threatening to strike at any time. But this time round, it is a little boring. We're not expecting anyone any time soon.' When she fell silent and he could feel her looking around for something to do, Ivan turned around in his seat to look at her, 'We could play cards, you know?'

'What are you thinking?' Jesa teased, feeling the same giddiness she had when gambling in some bar or back street tavern.

'How about Unervo?'

'What're we playing for?' she asked, eagerly awaiting the stakes. This was a game that she had played with many punters and won repeatedly. Helped fund a few little luxuries she enjoyed.

Ivan and Valentina grinned and seemed to silently agree on the terms.

'How about loser buys the others a drink?' Ivan suggested.

Jesa smirked. 'You're on.'

The game was underway. It was fun. During the first round she got lucky, with the perfect hand. She played and almost immediately got the win. The next two rounds went to Valentina. The fourth back to her. Ivan was getting frustrated but still in high spirits. He was about to play his hand that he claimed was going to get him on the board when a warning alarm went off.

'The fuck?' Ivan exclaimed.

The pilot left the galley and ran to the flight deck. Within an instant he was screaming in anger and frustration. He returned with a worried look on his face.

'What is it?' Valentina asked.

'We've got company,' Ivan Zenkovich hissed. 'Come on, arm up. You too, kid. All hands-on deck for this one.'

'What?' Jesa questioned as she was pulled out of her seat and down to the troop bay.

'We've got a few agents nearby. Looks like they're trying to find us. Doesn't seem like they know exactly which airlock we're strapped to yet. We might have a truce right now but I'm not taking any chances.'

Ivan opened the one door that she was not permitted to go through leading to the armoury and gestured her in. Weapons lined all sides. Assault rifles, shotguns, pistols, explosive grenades and non-lethal grenades. Spare sets of combat armour were stacked ready to be donned by the wearer. Bulletproof vests were stored on shelving. Zenkovich quickly picked up a smaller vest and forced it on her and secured it before she knew what was happening.

'Here, take this,' Ivan said, handing over an assault rifle already loaded. 'Follow my orders and we'll be fine. Val, you get one too. Come on, now!'

'But I haven't fired one before,' Jesa stated. Her hands trembled as she held it.

'Well, you're going to learn quick,' Ivan explained. 'Safety's off. Point, pull the trigger, let go on my order. Okay? You've got this.'

Ivan Zenkovich led them back into the troop bay. He gestured for Jesa and Valentina to go to the right side of the troop bay while he took the right. All had their weapons aimed at the airlock door.

'Steady,' Ivan snarled.

All Jesa could hear was their heavy, panicked breathing and her heart pounding. She was terrified. The weapon felt heavy in her hands. If she had to, would she really be able to pull the trigger? Would she be able to actually take another human's life? Would she be able to save a fellow human if it came to it? When the enemy never came knocking, Ivan was the first to relax. He gasped a sigh of relief and lowered his weapon. Jesa instantly lowered hers and removed her finger from the trigger.

'Val, go check the cameras,' Ivan Zenkovich ordered.

The co-pilot ran up to the flight deck. Moments later she gave them the all-clear, the threat had moved on. Their laughter was infectious. The feeling of dodging death was an amazing rush. She could see why some people joined the military, a militia, or a criminal organisation – not for the hopes of pride, glory or riches but for the thrill of facing death and surviving.

'Okay then,' Zen said. 'Unervo?'

Chapter 9
13/11/2675
09:17 Earth Standard Time

Leyton Foresc

Leyton had taken several calls with the administrator. Each one he made sure Duke was around to listen in on. There had to be complete transparency if they were to believe him when he said he wanted to help. It didn't faze him. Every piece of information taken was recorded and saved onto the sergeant's tac-pad. After each briefing, he earned more trust.

He gave up so many secrets and spent that much time with the SPF, however, that the divisions between him and his own unit grew by the second. Jerome had clearly rallied those on his side to him. Hatty, Dom and Samuel remained loyal to Leyton. Yet he still couldn't trust any of them. How did he know that those he was close to were not the ones feeding intelligence back to Administrator behind his back or when he was not around? He didn't. It made trying to believe in them difficult and for them to believe in him equally challenging.

Leyton and Duke breathed a sigh of relief after the most recent update. They had just listened to Administrator recommend that the second team wasn't far out now, just a couple days, and that everything was in place for them to arrive at the *Vestibule*. He also endured further reaffirmations of the change in leadership once the reinforcements docked with the *Galactic Passage*. Still no numbers on how many members to the team there was. All he knew was that they weren't agents which meant there was no way to predict tactics when they arrived.

They had set up shop in the brig for the briefings. The most secure place in the entire ship that either of them could think of. Away from the bridge, away from the crew quarters and more importantly away from the rest of the agents in his unit. Leyton sipped on his coffee while Duke had yet another refill. Neither of them could muster the energy to speak straight away.

'Another bust, then?' Duke muttered.

'Sorry,' Leyton said, massaging his brow. 'He's the head of the agency. Like he's told me before; you don't get there by trusting

297

people. He'll keep his secrets close to him and only reveals things when it benefits him or when he has nothing to lose.'

'Let me get this straight because I think I'm starting to get it; we need to get him in a position to tell us something he doesn't want us to know because he thinks it'll benefit him by telling us it?' Duke said. 'Easy.'

'You can say that again,' Leyton laughed. 'But at least you're getting the picture. This guy is dangerous by every standard.'

'I can tell... How close are you to figuring out who the leak is in your team?' Duke asked.

'Nowhere close,' he admitted. 'It's difficult. Like I said, once I start it'll take some time and when I'm done, we need to move because once I know, the mole will know I know.'

'And at that point things will start to get fun.' Duke took his cup off him and refilled the coffee before carrying on. 'Okay then, we'll have to make a move soon. We don't have long before your backup arrives, and I'd like to have the leak dealt with before they get here. Sorry to be so shit about it, but it had to be said.'

'It's okay, I get it,' Leyton replied. 'Just been a tough one to come to terms with.'

'You think it's your old friend, Jerome, right?' Duke Horren asked.

'He's my first guess, yeah,' Leyton answered.

During one of the briefings, Leyton has listed to Duke and Beatrice who he thought was the mole within his ranks and who he thought couldn't be the mole. Jerome Houghton came up at the top, followed by Fellstrum and Perretti, while Deulche was close to the bottom of the list because of the time he spent out of play. The likelihood of him being the source of the espionage was very minimal. Leyton had also explained why Jerome was at the top, which left Duke with no doubt that it was most likely his second in command.

'Why don't we rough him up then and find out?' Duke suggested. 'If it's not him, then the person who it is will be rattled. Not only would we have dealt with your most significant threat, but we've let them know quite publicly that we're onto them. If you panic, you make mistakes. They might give an update and we'll be able to catch them in the act or find evidence of it at the very least.'

'It's a good plan, but it wouldn't work. Sorry,' Leyton advised. 'I'd love to say I know how to persuade the information out of him, but he's good. Incredibly good. He'll either feed you misinformation or will not answer a single thing. Then the divide will worsen because everyone will think I'm against them all. No… we need to stick to the plan and do this my way.'

'Just not sure how to do it?'

'That's right,' Leyton said.

'Let's make it on our terms then,' Duke said. 'How long will it take once you start the process for you to find out who it is?'

'It'll take between three and five hours to finish the process. From there it'll be a case of getting the mole on their own before they lose their shit.'

Duke contemplated what Leyton had just said, then spoke slowly and carefully. 'So, we need to have your agents out of the way. Far enough away from the civilians that there'll be no collateral when the mole finds out we're onto them.'

'Hate to say it, but the furthest we can go is the deck where we cut off the wolves,' Leyton stated. 'That's the only place where there won't be any civilians caught in the crossfire.'

'You reckon you can get your team down there without arousing suspicion?'

Agent Tallow and Medic Suttle would be easy to get down to the lower decks. Onyx Perretti most likely would comply with his orders. The others would be reluctant, at best. Professor Ainslot however needed to stay out of it. This wasn't his fight, but to keep him separated for his safety wouldn't go unnoticed.

'Not really. Once I tell them to go down to the lower decks and tell the professor to stay topside, they'll start to ask questions and will be on edge.'

'Dammit, we'll have to chance it then. Come on, let's alert the captain,' Duke said. 'We need the upper hand before the others get here.'

Leyton stopped the sergeant from leading the way. There was something else that he wanted to clear up and speak about first. Something that wasn't to do with the wolves, his agents and the reinforcements on their way. Something that he really needed to find out about.

'You going to tell me, or do I need to ask?'

Duke cocked his head to the side and stared blankly at him. Oblivious to the meaning behind the question.

'You know, the engineer,' Leyton added with a cunning smile. 'How's things going with her?'

Duke grinned widely, like a teenager with a crush. After they secured the maintenance shaft, the two of them joined the engineer for drinks with the rest of the sergeant's soldiers and some of his agents. Duke and Allua seemed to hit it off almost straight away. It was clear that she was into him almost as much as he was into her. After that the sergeant and the engineer had met a few times. Leyton persisted to satisfy his curiosity until the sergeant started to explain what had been going on.

It appeared that the two were really getting along. They would grab a bite together and have a drink. Or even patrol the corridors together. They seemed to handle a conversation flawlessly. More pleasantly he was enjoying her company. When he pressed for a little more information, the sergeant told him that before they left the *Galactic Passage* he had every intention of keeping in touch with her and, all things permitting, seeing her again. That in itself was a win for the man and was worth celebrating when the time was right.

Duke quickly gestured for the two of them to press on, red in the face with embarrassed containment of youthful excitement. The pair left the brig to take the short walk across the deck to the bridge. The delay was more than worth making to have that talk, to have the interaction that told him the sergeant was able to trust him. They interrupted a debriefing Beatrice was giving to her key crew and quickly ushered everyone away so that they could have privacy with the officer. Only when they were left alone did Leyton say it was okay to talk.

'What's going on? Care to tell me what all this is about?' Beatrice demanded. Her eyes were wide with concern.

'We're going to draw out the mole in my ranks,' Leyton answered. 'And when we do, it's not going to go well.'

'What do you need me to do?' she asked.

'Clear the lower decks, now,' Duke explained. 'No one is to go down there.'

The captain's eyes searched for something, anything, to explain what was going on. 'Why now? What's happening?'

'It's not going to be long until the second team gets here,' Leyton said. 'If we don't act now, we'll be outnumbered and outgunned for sure. And I'd like to have the advantage when they get here.'

'And what're the chances of success?' she persisted; her eyebrows raised with curiosity. 'Will you be able to contain them once you know who the mole is?'

'In all honesty, not good,' Leyton sighed. His eyes drifted toward the floor, workstations, ceiling, anywhere she wasn't. When his gaze returned to her, she was not impressed at the attempt of avoidance. 'If we take a full security team, everyone will be against me. Which means a fight from two fronts. If I go alone, it could go one of three ways. I either walk out with allies or walk out with enemies. Or I could be dragged out in a body bag. But one thing is for certain, I'll know who the mole is. I'll know who I can trust and who I can't trust.'

'We need you walking out of there knowing who we can or can't trust,' Beatrice said, slumping deep into her seat. 'I can't accept anything less than a win. I've already given the passengers a brief about what's going on. Had no choice in the matter. But I've also told them that we're safe if they obey the rules. They need to be able to go about the passenger decks freely to stay controllable. I can't lock them down in their cabins or the galley again. Not so soon.'

'If you need to lock them down to keep them safe, then you need to lock them down,' Leyton said. 'I'm sorry but their safety is more important than being at risk of pissing them off.'

She was being too defensive for his liking. There were many things to fret about. Upsetting someone when there was a risk of them dying to keep them alive was far from one of those things to be concerned with. For a former military officer who had seen war and risked lives for a living, she was a lot more considerate than anticipated. Was this really the same person he had read up on?

This was the person who had led several major naval victories and had led the UPN liberation of several hostile planets. These were technically invasions, but the human propaganda machine from Earth worded them nicely to show how the United Planetary Nations saved the people of these distant worlds from their oppressors. Like what she did at the Siege of Vulcair.

'Fine,' Beatrice Lenoia conceded. 'How do you intend to lead them away?'

That was a question. How would he? Leyton needed it to be natural and in no way give away the true intentions.

'I'll have a change of heart,' Leyton said. 'I'll tell them that it's come to my attention that you're going to backstab me or something and you'll have me arrested when we get back regardless. I'll have time to think up a good enough reason when I get the process started.'

'Okay, then I think you should get started,' Duke said.

301

Leyton looked to the captain. When she gave a nod of approval, he took a seat to start the programme that allowed him to see everyone's communications. The privilege he had for his position would let him view everything that had been transmitted from a tac-pad owned by a member of his unit. He could see messages, hear voicemails, and see a full list of comm links established complete with recipient name. The problem was that everyone would know, when it was completed, that he had viewed their communication history. It was an age-old requirement for all scrutiny to be visible. Being transparent helped build trust in an institution where trust could be ill-afforded. Regardless, his actions would be seen as an immediate threat without justification because Leyton was supposed to be on their side. Not with the SPF.

Over the next few hours, the information slowly started to stream in front of him. Suttle and Tallow had shared several private messages discussing how Leyton had been behaving, asking if the other had any insight into what he was doing. To Leyton's relief, the medics kept their discussions about the mental health of the team completely confidential.

The professor was an odd one. He had made a number of voice monologues, saved onto his tac-pad. The wealth of information on his personal console was immense, as if he had documented everything that had ever happened in his life, using the tac-pad as a high-tech diary. But more importantly there was no attempt made by him, Tallow or Suttle to establish a comm link with someone outside the ship. That was a weight off Leyton's shoulders. The people he hoped were trustworthy were just that.

His interest spiked when he started looking into the messages from the others in his unit. They were all conspiring against him, each of them with an agenda. All apart from Perretti. But he was easily swayed by the arguments presented by Jerome that Leyton was no longer fit for duty, that his allegiance was no longer with them, and that he would be the end of their team because of his insistence on going against the administrator. They had even formulated a plan on how to overthrow him then deal with the SPF personnel. Quite elaborate really. Even the private calls made while on patrols were an interesting glimpse into their mentalities.

Then he found it. The one that was communicating with someone outside the ship.

'Got him,' Leyton announced quietly.

'You ready to make the call?' Duke asked.

'As I'll ever be,' he said.

'You do that, I'll get Ronan,' Duke replied. 'You're not going in alone and we need all the muscle we can get. I won't take no for an answer.'

Leyton didn't reply. A firm nod and to leave the sergeant to it was all that was required. He took a deep breath, sighed and opened a comm link with his agents. In the few moments it took for the call to be answered, he felt his heart race for what felt like a lifetime. He frantically thought up the best way to lure his team away from any collateral.

Jerome answered. His tone was anxious, angry and offended. 'Boss?'

Game time.

Duke Horren

Duke made sure he and Corporal Moasa stayed true to his word with Leyton. From the moment the three of them reached the lower decks, the pair had stayed at least twenty feet behind Leyton, keeping at least one junction away. The worst-case scenario was that they were caught following and were presumed to be stalking Leyton, not colluding with him. Their chatter had been minimal, and even their breathing was forced into silence. Leyton wouldn't even tell him who he had learnt the mole was, only that he knew who had been conspiring against him.

As a precaution, Duke had advised the rest of his team split up. Abe was to return to their vessel after intercepting Professor Ainslot to take the intellect with him while Joane remained on the bridge as extra protection. If everything went sideways, those were the two main targets that needed defending afterward and he intended there to be personnel that knew how to fight and defend themselves at both locations. The patrol ship was his main priority to protect.

To think that before he and Leyton had fought, Duke had been on the patrol ship just waiting for the right moment to go speak to the agent. It was when the smuggler asked him why he was pacing that he decided to make the move. She insisted that he give him another chance. Jesa was a good kid who had just been the result of an unfortunate series of circumstances of which she had no control over. He recognised that. If she was deserving of another chance, then why wasn't Leyton worthy? He too had been the product of his life and had been put in a predicament that he didn't want any part of. That too deserved an opportunity of redemption.

They reached the deck where the meeting was to take place. Duke slowed his pace down, dropping the pair further back to keep their distance. He kept to the shadows, racing between the dark patches and slipping past the light. There were voices up ahead. His steps turned lighter than air on water; a pin being dropped would have made more noise. Leyton turned the corner and his voice rose – the signal that Duke and Ronan were to stay back. Duke hugged the corner. Ronan Moasa stayed close behind.

'What's up boss?' Jerome asked. 'We got a green light to smoke those bastards or what?'

There was impatience in the adjutant's voice and something that sounded patronising.

'Easy Jerome,' Leyton said. 'We'll get them. Hatty, you got my gear?'

'Here you go boss,' the female agent said.

Whatever they thought they were about to do, they evidently believed they were going to do it there and then. Duke's grip on his assault rifle tightened, his index finger tensing. Ronan too was ready to round the corner when required. They kept listening.

'Thanks Hat,' Leyton said. 'The plan then. I have access straight up to the A Deck and I have been able to convince the captain that she doesn't need armed guards outside her door because we just want to get home now. Doesn't grant me instant access to the bridge though. The crew doesn't trust me that much. Means I need to ask for permission to come onto the command deck. When we get there, we won't have long to take control and need to be ready for a fight. The SPF are stationed on their ship right now. They'll come running to help once they're made aware of what's going on. Once we have control of the bridge, we seal it off then blow the docking connection with their ship with the override. Gets rid of their patrol ship in one move. We shouldn't have any problems after that. If we move now, we have a better chance of succeeding.'

'And the civilians?' Jerome asked.

'What about them?'

'What're we doing with them? Hit them as we see them or what? You've only told us what to do about the crew and SPF,' Jerome questioned.

'Just the ones who put up a fight,' Leyton instructed.

'Not our instructions,' Jerome replied. There was tension as he spoke. Anger even. Like a child reminding a disobedient sibling of their parents' rules. 'You know that.'

'No, they're *my* instructions. To hell with killing people that don't need to die. If the administrator wants to kill them, I'll give him my gun. I'm not doing it for him. Not anymore.'

Was that the mole as he had suspected? The second in command? It made perfect sense the more he thought about it. Seconds usually would do anything to take command, even if it meant going behind their superior's back. And he had a track record of showing what Duke would class as insubordination to take command. The added problem was that an adjutant in that mind-set would train harder to better develop their skills in order to reach the top. Another hurdle was they were also more likely to make friends and surround themselves with allies. Leaders were always to be respected, not liked. A second was the bridge between the two levels. The ones that were friendly and smoothed things over with the brass. When made to choose, people were more likely to go with their emotions. Duke tensed up.

'I don't think the boss would want to hear about this. You feel me?' Jerome asked.

Someone else spoke, Agent Deulche, 'What the fuck are you talking about, Jerome?'

'Oh, I feel you,' Leyton snarled. 'I guess you know then?'

'Know what?' Medic Suttle asked.

'You bet I know,' Jerome said.

'What the hell are you two talking about? Has this something to do with our pads being checked?' Agent Fellstrum questioned. 'Because that wasn't cool boss.'

'Our fearless field lead here found out something he didn't need to know,' Jerome explained. 'And he's here now to punish us all by fucking up the administrator's plans.'

'Now you know that's bullshit,' Leyton stated. 'I've defended all of you when you didn't deserve it. I'm just not standing for being backstabbed. I needed to know what was going on.'

'And now you know way too much,' Jerome snarled.

'What the fuck are you two doing!' screamed Hatty Tallow.

'Stand down!' Leyton barked.

'You first,' his adjutant snapped.

That could only mean one thing – weapons had been raised. Duke couldn't do anything yet, though. He needed to know where the battle line was and who was on which side. He would then know which ones were friends and who was a foe before making a move. Stepping out too soon meant everyone had a common enemy to focus on. All he could do was sit and wait while they bickered like children. It was almost embarrassing to listen to.

'Jerome, the fuck are you doing?' Agent Fellstrum asked.

'Well, our by-the-book leader here is going against our orders given by the administrator,' Jerome stated. 'I've been talking to the boss. Turns out he's had every chance to follow orders and he hasn't. When our reinforcements get here, they're taking over this mission and relieving him of his duties.'

'You're damn right I'm not following them,' Leyton replied. 'I know there's a better way about it that doesn't involve killing everyone.'

'And your way is in direct violation of our orders,' Jerome added.

'I'm not going to argue with you,' Leyton said. 'But what I am going to say is I won't let you do it his way. I'm sorry but if you get in my way, I'll have to deal with you.'

'Then you'd best deal with me now because I'm taking command.'

There it was – the battle line he needed. Duke took a deep breath and stepped out from round the corner, Corporal Moasa following close behind. Fortunately for them, Leyton was on their side of the corridor. Everyone stared at the pair with their weapons at the ready as they came up to stand beside the agent.

'It's his way or ours,' Duke said. He kept his rifle trailed on Jerome.

'Are you shitting me?' Jerome spat. His eyes were wild with rage. 'You jumped into bed with them? With the SPF? They don't know what the greater good is like we do. They look only at today, not to tomorrow. What we're doing now will make a better tomorrow. He'll destroy it.'

'He didn't jump into bed with anyone, he simply grew a conscience which turns out to be the same way of thinking as us,' Duke said. 'This is the score. I know you've got buddies on the way. I know none of you want to die as well. But if you choose the wrong side to be on the only thing that I can promise you is that you will not make it out alive. If I didn't trust this guy was doing the right thing, I wouldn't be standing next to him. Choose the right side. And choose it now.'

'Boss?' Hatty Tallow whispered.

'You choose what you think is right,' Leyton instructed. 'I won't choose for you.'

'You better be with me Tallow,' Jerome growled.

Agent Hatty Tallow wasted no time, stepping forward to stand beside Leyton. That was one on their side. The medic, Dominic, also joined them without hesitation. Based on the history of the one who had been captured and tortured, Agent Deulche, it wasn't surprising that he chose to stay on the opposite side. The second female, Kari, was a surprise to see joining Jerome and Deulche. After the report of Leyton saving her from the ship's crew Duke thought there would have been a little more loyalty to the lead field agent. The last agent, Onyx Perretti, also joined Jerome. Not a shock given how much of an itchy trigger finger he had.

Once each of them chose their side, weapons were raised. Fingers were placed on triggers with every expectation they would need to defend themselves. One wrong move and everyone would start firing.

'So, looks like I know who we're trusting and who we're not,' Duke stated.

'Shut up!' Jerome shrieked. 'You just shut your mouth! How could you all betray me?'

Leyton started to speak, but it wasn't his place to. He needed to be the dignified leader, the man that wouldn't lower himself to the levels of others. Duke reached out and pat him on his shoulder to take the lead. 'They betrayed *you*? You're the one speaking to your squad leader through your back end like it's going out of business while you talk to the administrator when he's not looking. Not even got the balls to tell him what you're doing. You're the one who's ready to kill the people you are supposed to protect. Would you do the same if your parents were here? Your family? No. You wouldn't. But you'd happily do it to get yourself promoted. You're the one betraying everyone. Especially yourself. And now you've convinced these agents, the ones standing there with you, that your way is the right way. Your way will only be the right way if you somehow survive which I promise you will not.'

'Don't listen to him!' Jerome yelled. 'He's trying to con you all.'

Duke chuckled. 'I don't need to con anyone. I'm the only one who's on the straight and narrow here. I can promise that anyone on my side of this standoff will have a better chance of getting out of this without consequence when it's all over.'

'What are you talking about?' Jerome demanded.

'You're bringing dangerous and unknown creatures to Sol, you're using a civilian transport, prepared to wilfully kill civilians who you currently have imprisoned under your hostile threat and to top it all you've successfully killed some of the ship's crew already,' Duke explained with an air of sarcasm. 'Are you seriously telling me that you'll get out of this without a scratch? Or that by the time I'm through with you, that you won't see the other side of a cell? Not even your precious administrator can save you.'

'Only if you win,' the man snarled, backing up a step, keeping his comrades in front of him as a human wall.

'You know what, Jerome?' Leyton asked, spotting his subordinate walking away. 'You're a spineless piece of shit. You could never own a fight you started.'

Jerome fired the first shot, making sure he could take cover before letting off the round. It was the opening for a brief fire fight, everyone scattering for cover in any room that was open and any crevice that offered protection. One person fell. To Duke's relief, it was Deulche.

Not one of the guys on his side. Though the medic did take a couple shots to the arm and shoulder. The guy was having bad luck on the ship with his string of injuries.

'Medic, you good?' Duke called.

'Fucking brilliant,' Dom wheezed. 'Never better. One of these days, I'll not get shot.'

'And one of these days I'll be a queen,' Hatty retorted joyfully.

Duke was happy they could be light-hearted, even if it was forced in the moment. He glanced at his ammo count on the side of his rifle. The sergeant had barely let off six rounds. The enemy agents would need to reload soon.

'You got a clear LOS on the guy?' Leyton breathed lightly over the comms. He spoke so quietly it was like a gust of wind.

'Care to give a distraction?' he replied. 'I don't want to have my head blown off.'

Leyton laughed so calmly it was eerie. When the shots started firing across the corridor, Duke briefly glanced around. In the split second his face left the safety of cover he clearly saw the three remaining hostile agents down the corridor. They were in his line of sight but the second he could take out one, the others would either have a meat shield or a clear shot at him. It was too risky to do it. The best they could do was fall back and regroup now that the two sides were clear. He pulled his head back round into safety.

'You see them?' Leyton asked.

'Oh, you bet I could see them. But I can't make the shot. Too risky.'

'So, what's the plan?' Ronan asked.

Duke slung his rifle, un-pinned both of his flash-stun grenades from his tactical vest and primed them before sending them part way down the corridor.

'Let's move,' he hissed over the comms as they went off. 'Leyton, you and Hatty get the medic. Me and Ronan will provide cover fire.'

The five of them evacuated the area as quickly as they could, bullet spray flying by them as they fled, each shot threatening to be the one to end them. Duke closed and secured every door they went through to slow down their pursuers until they were deep in friendly territory. Even then they only stopped to tend to the medic's wounds, which he found crudely ironic yet funny that of all of them to take a hit it was the one most qualified to fix such an injury. It took them a full can of bio-filler to plug the injuries and a couple shots of rapid bone regrowth serum to speed up the repair of any skeletal damage suffered. A couple more scars to his collection.

While the medical supplies started their healing process on Medic Suttle, Duke reflected on what had just happened. Standing in the corridor as if he was in a daze. Oblivious to all that was going on around him. It could have gone better for them. Duke knew that. He could have converted more if he had the time. But what he managed to achieve was more than enough. Duke had saved two lives. That was two people who could go home when it was done. He smiled only to be thrust back into the panicked predicament as he listened to the commotion around him.

'What just happened?' Hatty asked, panic starting to swell in her voice from the outset. 'My God, what did we do? What did *I* just do?'

Leyton and Ronan were too preoccupied with the medic to be of any use calming her down. Duke knelt in front of her and got her attention, forcing her to look straight into his eyes without touching her chin or even saying a word as if he'd hypnotised her. He waited until she was focussed on him and not just looking at him until he spoke.

'You did what you had to do in the moment,' he told her bluntly. 'You made a choice. I can't tell you if it's the right choice or the wrong choice for you but what I can tell you is you made the smart choice. The fact they could return fire on you, one of their own, shows to me that they couldn't give a damn about you. You tell me, what just happened?'

'I did what I could to survive. I had to pick a side. I chose the boss because... because he was doing the right thing,' she answered rapidly, taking deep breaths. Hatty slowly composed herself now she was able to think, and he needed to act fast to keep her mind in the right place.

'You did what was necessary,' he said. 'You protected those that showed they thought just like you, the ones that you could trust. You didn't side with a guy able to make idle threats and act on them. You sided with the guy who knew where to draw the line between the job and morality. It's more than a lot of people would have done in your situation.'

'You think?'

'I know. I've seen it when people had the chance to do what was right and didn't. It's easier to choose the easy option than the right one. Have your moment to do whatever. Cry, scream, whatever you need to. If you need to talk, shout out and any one of us will be there for you. But get your head back in the game. It isn't over until it's done.'

'Okay,' Hatty whispered.

'You'll be okay,' he said softly.

He patted her on the shoulder and joined the others as they helped the medic get his combat armour back on, now that his injuries were plugged and bandaged.

'You guys ready for the fight?' he asked the trio.

'You know I'm good to go,' Ronan said smugly. 'Can't I go back?'

'You think that's wise?' Leyton questioned.

'For them? Not a chance.' Ronan flexed his arms and cracked his knuckles. 'If they knew what was good for them, they'd turn and run next time they see me.'

Leyton looked to Duke, 'Is he always like that?'

'Near enough,' Duke answered. 'Dom, you good?'

'Give me an hour,' the medic replied. 'But make sure I get to treat you after the next fight, not the other way around.'

Leyton chuckled, like nothing serious had happened. 'Only if you stop getting in the way of enemy bullets. So, Sergeant, what's the plan?'

The plan. Duke needed to formulate it and get it right. An unknown number of hostiles were on their way with not enough time to spare, and three agents were loose in the lower decks, probably ready to carry out guerrilla warfare and hit them where it hurt with everything they had. No doubt they would be liaising with the administrator to tell him what was going on. Realistically the agents under Jerome's leadership should lay low until backup arrived now that they were now outnumbered at a ratio of almost three to one. For them to make an attack would be suicide. Which offered them valuable time.

First, Duke needed to find somewhere safe for him and his team. Somewhere they could hold up, formulate a plan and act on it, but still run if needed. That wasn't the bridge – they'd be cornered if the fight came to them and there were too many civilians to get in the way or be used as bargaining chips if things went wrong. There were no other locations on the ship that could act as a war room.

But there was one place that would be perfect. Home turf, for him at least, giving them the option to fall back well out of harm's way if the fighting became too intense to then come back onto the ship from a different angle.

Duke looked to Leyton and smiled. Leyton looked as bewildered as expected.

'Looks like I'm taking you lot home with me,' Duke said.

Jesa

Jesa had no idea what to make of everything. They had gone from being enemies with the agents, to being friends with them; to there now being a schism within their ranks, creating a separatist group that remained pure to their original mission, and a second group that were going against those original orders. It was like a bad episode of a comedy-drama show. Now, they had the three agents with a change of heart on their ship – no, the SPF ship. It wasn't her ship, though felt like it was, and she couldn't shake that. Her personal space was on that ship. Yes, she wanted the sergeant to patch things up with Leyton. Give the man a chance. This though was a bit much. Them being onboard was an invasion of her personal space that kept Jesa on edge.

Everyone was sat around the holo-table in the briefing room. Even the captain of the ship had joined them. The woman didn't seem to want to acknowledge Jesa's existence, looking right through her like Jesa was not worth her attention. Everything about her read over-privileged officer that thought she was better than everyone else. Jesa immediately didn't like her, even if in the end that didn't matter. Jesa was simply glad to be involved in the debate. It felt like her opinion counted, that she was important in the decisions being made. Duke had given everyone the briefing of what was happening, what was on the way, and what they needed to do to prepare for it.

The smuggler would have been lying if she said she wasn't afraid. The situation they found themselves in was terrifying. Known enemy were already on the ship, human and alien; an enemy force was on their way to them as they sat there in space with no means of escape; and somewhere out in the vastness of space was a Crevari fleet searching for their next meal. Jesa mustered all her will power and strength to try and stay positive. Her eyes went around the people present to scan their emotions. There was fear, just like she had, reservation, anger. Even eagerness. Then she faced the sergeant, and he was calm. The way he spoke about the matter was already expecting to see her way through it successfully. To see the hope that Duke seemed to be able to find with ease. To stay focussed on what mattered. She called on what she had learnt from his lessons to the soldiers that she had sat in on. All the theory, emotions and ways to calm the feelings. Taking deep breaths, focussing in on what she has control over and trying not let what hasn't happened have any impact on her.

312

'A couple days doesn't seem like long enough to get things together,' Beatrice said. 'My ship is not a warship or even a military vessel. It's a civilian luxury liner. My crew are not trained for this sort of thing.'

'No, but this is,' Ivan Zenkovich replied, patting his ship proudly. 'She can put up a fight, can't you girl?'

'And we're all ready for the fight,' Ronan added, flexing his arms with pride.

'Too right we are,' cheered Arche.

'Settle down! Skip the fact that we only have one combat worthy ship for a one on one, none of this helps us with the ship boarding situation we'll be facing,' Duke said. 'They'll probably have combat armour and would disembark their ship if we engaged then move through space to the *Passage*. Humans are harder to hit in space than a ship. Smaller targets. Meaning they'll board and can board anywhere they please.'

'Or take into account the fact that you guys have a second ship attached to yours which will affect manoeuvrability,' Leyton added. 'You can't forget that bit.'

'You saw that?' Ivan asked.

'You're damn right we saw that,' the agent said. 'All you have to do is look outside.'

'Okay,' Duke groaned. 'So, we have that contend with too if we engage. Well, where do we begin?'

Jesa listened for hours as they debated and argued on what to do. No one could agree on what was the most important issue to fix first or what their contingency plans should be. From ship systems to security, the group covered just about everything. They even debated who should have overall command until they were in full control of the *Passage*. What no one realised was that they were falling straight into the stereotype of Centie that Jesa had grown up believing. It was a sad sight considering how she knew they could be better than that.

In the end, they all agreed that they needed to focus primarily on fixing the *Galactic Passage's* engines so that they would be able to move again. According to the ship's chief engineer, the work required would take at least two days to complete if they worked round the clock. Once they were operational, then it would be up to the SPF soldiers and the agent turncoats to handle the defence of the ship to keep the hostile agents at bay, maintain observation of the ice wolves and handle the new arrivals when they showed up. All whilst other essential systems were brought operational, so they could make a jump to the nearest UPN position for assistance. They seemed to have it well planned out, with most of the details covered. Then the captain brought up the point of weapons. Her crew didn't have much in the way of weapons so were defenceless. Jesa didn't quite agree with Ronan surmising that it would be fun. The arguments on how to best execute the plan persisted. All three of the leaders put their best plan forward and reasoned their case ferociously. That was to be expected – Centies always liked to argue. If not for their own lives, then to control the lives of Outers while the Middies just put up their feet and waited for it all to blow over. No, she couldn't think like that. Not anymore. They were just trying to do what was right to protect the hundreds of people on that ship and the billions of lives out there in the galaxy.

Jesa cast her mind on herself as everyone continued speaking. So far, she had not made any contribution to the discussions. Nothing to make her presence worthwhile. There had to be something she could offer them. Something she could do to help. Her skill set wasn't for fighting, she spent most of her time running away from trouble. Even holding the assault rifle before was barely any help. Jesa was certain that had it come to it, she wouldn't have pulled the trigger. The only skills that could be of any assistance was her ability to evade humans and animals alike. The number of gang leaders that had deadly animals as pets and the equipment owned to find fleeing targets was terrifying. And Jesa had a knack for finding places to hide when on the run. That only gave limited use to the team, but one thing she did have though was a cargo hold full of contraband that had cost a lot of money to buy. There had to be something amongst it all that could be used. If her mental inventory was right, there were a few things that looked like they would do the job and do it more effectively than standard weapons.

She tuned back into the discussions to hear the closing statements as the briefing ended. It seemed to be that the sergeant had the final say in the plan, much to the captain's dislike. The anger in her face was prominent. Beatrice left the patrol ship swiftly when it was apparent that she didn't need to remain any longer. Jesa was content with her leaving. The woman didn't need to be involved with what Jesa had to offer to the team.

Jesa rushed for the sergeant and lead agent and took them to one side. 'I think I might have something that can help you.'

'What is it?' Duke asked.

'Well, I'm not sure,' she admitted. 'But part of my cargo is weapons, yah? Most are human. Some are alien weapons. They look like they might be useful.'

'Weapons?' Leyton questioned. 'Who are you, by the way? A little petite to be SPF, aren't you?'

'This is Jesa, she's a smuggler we picked up on the way,' Duke explained. 'That's her ship connected to us. Don't worry, she's a good kid. Was a little lost on the way.'

'A bit like me then,' Leyton replied.

'I guess so,' Duke chuckled. He turned back to Jesa, 'Show me the weapons you think can help. We'll take whatever we can use and distribute it. At this point, any help is better than no help.'

'Amen to that,' Leyton said.

Jesa led them into her craft. She had made some effort with the repairs. Things were a little more organised, but still out of place for the most part. She sifted through the mess until she found the weapons cases. She brought out all the containers she could manage. Jesa directed the soldier and agent to the cases that were massive and too big for her to handle. Amongst the vast arsenal of human weapons, pistols, sub-machine guns, assault rifles, rocket launchers, were the cases that held the unusual armaments belonging to an alien race. Strange things that looked like nothing humanity had ever produced. They were aged, rusted and beaten as if used extensively in a previous life. Each one was barbarically crude in a mottled brown and dark green colour with jagged edges, no scopes and strange green crystals embedded in the metal or spherical crystal orbs void of colour as if it had been sapped out of them slotted into the back of the weapons. The triggers, or what they presumed to be triggers, were for hands twice the size of their own.

The two military veterans examined the weapons with keen eyes. Trying to hold them was a challenge. The sergeant swayed as he tried to remain balanced while holding the largest of the weapons.

'Sorry to say it Jesa, but we can't use these things,' Duke sighed eventually as he put the weapon down and back in its case.

'I agree,' Leyton added. 'Shame. They look like they would have been fun to have a play with.'

'What? How come?' Jesa questioned, disheartened by the update.

'Whatever they are, they don't respond to us,' Leyton explained, holding one of the smaller alien weapons. 'See these pads around the grips? They're like our DNA scans on some rifles. By the looks of it, they're made to register a complete hand. I haven't got a clue what species they're for though if this is where a palm should be. And these crystals? They're on every single one. They're not decorative. Nothing this brutal would be made to look pretty.'

'Which means they have a use,' Duke added. 'Probably a power source.'

'Or ammo that's run dry, maybe,' Leyton said. 'The bottom line is, we can't use them this time. It was a good try though.'

'I'm sorry,' Jesa whispered solemnly. 'I didn't know.'

'Hey, it's okay!' Duke cried. He rushed over and placed his palms gently on her shoulders and waited until she was looking at him. 'You tried. I know this isn't your world right now. You've only been learning it for a couple weeks now. You'll get there. Okay? This sort of thing takes time. And the fact you're trying tells me you'll get there eventually. Keep your chin up.'

'I guess,' she muttered.

Jesa felt embarrassed. She could feel her face going red. Like a kid at school that tried too hard to be liked and couldn't live up to the hype they created about themselves. But the two men didn't laugh at her as expected. They didn't get mad at her. They would not even raise their voice in frustration. If anything, they looked at her proudly. Appreciating the fact that she wanted to help. Leyton then turned to the cases of human weapons that were in her possession.

'These though we can use,' the agent announced. 'The ship's crew have fuck all. This puts them in the fight. Not as well prepared as us but they can at least we can give them a chance.'

'Yah?' she replied hopefully.

'Yeah,' Leyton said. 'This is a big help, kid.'

That brought her back from the darkness of feeling like a failure. The two men helped her pack the alien tech away, moved the human gear into place, and returned to the patrol ship. Jesa tucked away to one side in the galley while everyone else was helping on the liner.

What was she doing? Why was she trying so hard? These were people with military training. Centies. People that served under the UPN. They might be nice to her, helping her, even making promises to free her permanently from her former master. She didn't know that they would do any of that for certain. For all she knew it was all a ruse to get her to trust them before they betrayed her. This was all way out of her depths. She wasn't anything like any of them. Jesa knew that she should still have remained in her cabin under arrest. At least she could do that right.

Leyton and the medic in his team both climbed into the galley and walked up to her, taking a seat opposite. They both smiled gently. The warmness was easing, but she couldn't relinquish the feeling of guilt in her gut. She had no idea who she was betraying. No idea what was right or wrong. Her entire universe had been turned on its head. Was she rushing to be a part of a world that wasn't meant for her? Or maybe she was trying find a reason to not be where she belonged. Trying to get back to what she had always known. If she couldn't trust herself, how could she trust anyone else?

'What's on your mind, kid?' Leyton asked.

'You know,' Jesa shrugged. 'I'm on a military patrol ship, attached to a ship with agents that want us dead inside and more people on their way to finish the job. We got Crevari out here. I'm just a smuggler. You are all soldiers. I don't belong here. This isn't what I was born into, not even what I've trained for. There's nothing I can do to help you. At least I could do what I was told to by my master and smuggle. Compre?'

'You're right,' the agent said flatly without emotion. 'There isn't anything you can do right now. And what you did before? Forget about it. That doesn't have to define who you are now. Doesn't mean there won't be anything for you to do later or other ways you can prove yourself. You've helped in a big way already with that cargo, and you never know what else you'll be able to do to help. But there is something I can do for you.'

'What do you mean?' Jesa questioned.

'The sergeant has told me about your situation,' Agent Leyton Foresc stated, pointing to her arm. 'We can get that tag out of you. Now.'

'You can?' Jesa asked hopefully. 'Mayah! Please don't be yanking.'

'Don't worry, I'm not. Well, I can't get it out of you,' Leyton said. 'But he can. And he can fix you up afterward too.'

'You'll barely have a scar,' Medic Suttle added.

'Really?' Jesa questioned.

'You better believe it,' Leyton said.

'It's not the first time I've had to do a tag removal,' Dom Suttle stated.

Jesa tilted her head and blinked. 'It isn't?'

'No,' the medic laughed. 'I've taken plenty out of PoWs when we've busted them out of prison camps or HVTs.'

'HVTs?' she asked.

317

'High value targets,' Leyton explained. 'Politicians, officials, that sort of thing. The sorts of folk that governments don't want to share.'

Until the agent's smile widened, and he leaned back confidently in his chair, Jesa couldn't believe what she was hearing. She felt overwhelmed that the sergeant had been honest and truthful with her. If she could trust him with such a huge part of her life, then Jesa knew she could trust him with her entire life. Her ties with that monster of a man were going to be severed. He wasn't going to be able to control her life for much longer. Jesa never realised she was crying until the medic passed her a tissue.

'Thank you,' she whispered. 'Thank you, so much.'

'That's alright,' the lead agent said.

'When can you do it?' Jesa asked, wiping away another tear, eager to get the procedure over with.

'Give me a few hours to prep,' Medic Suttle replied. 'If it's just the one, it'll be over within about ten, fifteen minutes. No biggie.'

'I can't wait!' Jesa gasped.

Her jaw ached from the beaming smile across her face. She was happier than she could have thought possible. Freedom. Even a life with known restrictions was more enjoyable than a life spent making a legacy for someone else to enjoy while having that same life threatened every second of every day. Jesa counted down the seconds until she could enjoy this freedom and see the tag that kept her tied in with Barbaros removed.

Jesa hurried out of the galley and into the troop bay. Duke was there as she hoped talking to the other agent, Tallow, and the rest of his team. When they locked eyes, he smiled and nodded. This was not the standard polite way of saying hello without breaking away from the current conversation. The look in his eyes told her it was his way of saying he kept his word, and that he would continue to do so. She smiled back. The same way a child would to a father that couldn't make it to their sports day then managed to show up out of nowhere simply to surprise them.

'Thank you,' Jesa whispered to him.

Jesa returned up to her cabin and waited with glee. Just a few hours and she'd have a life that could be hers. Not one that was forced upon her with an explosive or the threat of death. What would she do first? Why she even asked herself that was foolish. She would return the help and kindness she had been shown by the SPF. She would do whatever she could to help them. And the first thing she'd do, was try and help

318

with getting the luxury liner up and running. She had fought tooth and nail to keep the *Saridia* afloat through space. Learnt everything that made her tick. Had managed to educate herself on how to listen to a language that only a mechanic would understand. The flutter in the hum of a shield generator meaning a power flux. The shudder of the hull as a high-speed manoeuvre took its toll on the vessel to reveal weak spots that needed repairing or strengthening. Even how to take an engine apart to swap out components and put it back together. All transferable skills that could be used there since the more impressive parts of her cargo was of no use to them.

Hopefully, Duke would give her permission to help, to repay the debt she owed him. Maybe not him but most Centies thought of Outies as primitive, backwater inbreds that cared only for themselves but that was far from the truth in every way. They took debts owed seriously. Fulfilling a debt matters more than fulfilling family requirements or arrangements with friends.

She would prove her worth.

Only a couple more hours.

When the time came, she felt excited, nervous and in awe at the same time. It was just like a dream. Jesa couldn't believe it was happening as she walked into the med bay. She sat in the medical chair with Medic Suttle to her side. He had equipment on hand to carry out the procedure. Scalpels, anaesthetic syringes, towels and various other tools.

'You ready?' he asked her.

'Yah,' Jesa replied. 'Get it out of me.'

'Okay, you'll feel a scratch in a couple seconds,' Medic Suttle said slowly. She felt the sensation of the needle going into her arm. The medic carried out a couple checks to make sure she couldn't feel a thing and when confident that she would not be in any pain, he began. She looked away as he cut open her skin, pulled the flesh back and started the delicate process of disarming and removing the explosive device from her arm. Both were silent. Jesa didn't dare breathe for fear of shuddering and making the medic slip. Sometimes Dom would grunt and mumble as it proved to be a little more difficult than he had originally anticipated to remove. Probably inserted into her awkwardly on purpose to prevent it being removed. He persisted until she heard the satisfying sound of metal clanking in a metal bowl. A few moments later, Dom had her patched up and plugged with bio-filler then wrapped her arm comfortably in a bandage. Jesa turned to inspect the device that

319

had been removed. It was a small thing with a red and a green light embedded into it to show if the device was safe or if it was armed.

'How do you feel?' Dom Suttle asked.

'Never better,' Jesa said softly. 'I feel free. Thank you.'

'Don't need to thank me,' the medic replied. 'I'd have done it anyway. Thank the sergeant for telling me about it.'

'I will do.'

Dom pointed at her arm. 'Just take it easy for a few hours. Don't want to risk where I cut opening up again any time soon. I've plugged it with filler and applied a patch so once it's settled you can start using it again. If it does open, just shout for me. And take these when the numbness wears off. It's going to hurt like hell when you can feel it.'

'I will,' Jesa said, taking the pain meds off him. 'Thank you.'

She jumped off the bed. With a new lease on life the first thing she needed to do above all else was find the sergeant. He needed to know how grateful she was and that she was ready to help in anyway needed.

When Jesa united with Duke, he shared her joy. her happiness and relief. But it wasn't over. Fact was that the explosive still existed. It was still there with them. While it remained, Jesa was guaranteed to be haunted by Barbaros because the device would still be on the ship. Duke gave the explosive to Ronan who in turn configured it and sent the detonation controls to the flight deck. They launched the bomb out through the waste jettison chute. From the flight deck, they watched on a zoomed in video feed as it drifted further away from them. Jesa didn't smile as she detonated it. She scowled. Angry that it could have been inside her. Waiting to go off. As the explosion bloomed and died down, the scowl turned to tears. Tears that she had been so close to death. Tears that she no longer needed to worry. Behind the tears she cried, there was a smile. The smile only grew as those around her quickly embraced her. Holding Jesa closely as they felt her relief, her pain and her grief all at once.

Jesa could say confidently she was more at peace.

Beatrice Lenoia

On the bridge, within the safety of the company of her own crew, Captain Beatrice Lenoia took in the rapid change recent events had brought. She now had reduced threats to deal with in the short term. The engine was still down for repairs and as a result, wasn't generating anywhere near as much power as it should have been. Power that was running low by the drain that life support was having on the ship. Everyone looked to her for direction, for leadership. It was something that she struggled to offer them since the only thing she brought to the playing field was a winged ship. Beatrice needed to be back in control.

'Dolga, get me Security Chief Henendez and Chief Jons,' she instructed. 'I need them either here or on their comms in five. Hender, how're the passengers?'

'They're panicked,' Hender answered. 'They could hear the gun shots earlier when the agents had their domestic. Most of them obviously want to go home. Others are getting ready to riot. We have them contained to either their cabins or the galley.'

'Understood,' Beatrice sighed.

If the agents struck, the civilians would be the easiest targets for them to go after, and they were spread too far apart to give her crew a fighting chance of keeping them all safe. There needed to be a change in living arrangements. She could potentially bring them up into the galley and once that space was filled, start to filter them through into the first-class living quarters and the venues. At least that way there would be hope of defence against the loyalist agents should they strike any time soon, keeping potential casualties to a minimum. But depending on where their reinforcements docked that could potentially work against them.

'What're we going to do?' Franklin asked, seeing the concern on her expression.

Beatrice sighed. 'Honestly? Not a clue. I've never had to deal with anything like this before. It's all completely new to me.'

'It's been... interesting,' her second in command added, smiling gently. 'Why do you need security here? Thought the SPF were handling that?'

'Because as much as I trust them to do their job to keep us safe, I'd feel much safer knowing my crew, that I know and trust, are giving me information on what's going on within my ship,' she explained. 'And

I'd be happier having regular updates so I can make snap decisions without waiting for the SPF to guide me on what's happening.'

'It does make things easier when we are in control,' Franklin agreed. 'You going to tell me what was decided on down there?'

She waited until the security lead had come through from the security station, and Chief Engineer Allua Jons was on the comms from her station in the engine room, before going through the final decision made by her, Duke and Leyton. She recommended that they were to wait until the enemy attacked before doing anything. Even though they had the superior numbers, the agents had nothing to lose with taking out as many of them as possible before their help arrived. Spread themselves too thin and the enemy would surely take advantage. Once the engines were up and running, they would see where they were at then make a move from their current position to try make boarding her ship as difficult as possible. Her key crew protested some of the decisions, saying they had better ideas, but she waved them off.

'We will comply with their instructions,' Beatrice stated. 'That is final. But we are not going to be stopped from doing our own thing to make sure this ship stays safe and within our control.'

'What do you mean?' Henendez asked.

'Jons, do you think you can speed up repairs to the sub-light engines?'

'Possibly,' the engineer answered. 'I've got a few patches to make on the circuit board and a couple bits that need welding back together or replacing. Nothing too serious for the moment, just fiddly to get to. But when they're operational, I highly recommend that we don't use them at full capacity. We've taken too much damage from that storm. If we open her up past forty percent right now, I can almost guarantee we'll either fall apart or explode. Thirty is our safest bet.'

'Can you tell me what the fastest is you can get us to be able to use more than fifty percent thrust?' Beatrice asked.

Allua Jons thought for a moment. Beatrice could see the sums being calculated in her eyes. 'To be generous, if I have everyone working on it that I can get my hands on, we can get it done in a few hours. Being not so generous, we'd be looking at until tomorrow. But don't even think of asking about the jump drive. That's going to be at least another few weeks before it's remotely close to usable. We ideally need a replacement core bringing to us for fitting. Casing's fine, a few cracks that we can patch up to last until we're back at a space dock. But the core has been damaged. Only thing keeping it contained from having a complete melt down is the casing. Whatever we do, we have to do it fast because it won't hold forever.'

'Okay, try to get it done in a few hours so we're not running on minimal power any longer. When you're done, I need to know,' Beatrice said. 'I'll also need you to secure the engine room as soon as possible because once we can move, I want us to keep moving. That engine will be what keeps us alive long enough to get out of this mess. After it's been secured, send all controls and overrides for engineering to my chair. If we lose that room, I want to still be in full control of the engines. Leave no room for anyone to get around it. Understood?'

'You got it, Captain,' Allua Jons replied.

'Henendez, I want you to focus on the security cameras,' she ordered. 'Keep me posted at all times on the positions of the loyalists and the wolves.'

'But we don't know where they are,' he explained, as if she was asking an impossible task of him. 'This ship is huge, and they've already knocked out most of the cameras.'

'Don't you think I know that?' Beatrice hissed. 'What we can do is narrow where we're looking.' She pulled up a holographic schematic of her ship and a few areas flashed a bright white. 'These are the places we know for certain that the agents are not present. They're not with the civilians otherwise we'd have heard of more deaths by now and they're not with the wolves because they would have been torn to pieces themselves. They're most certainly not in our crew quarters or in the engine room.'

The light switched on in her security officer's eyes. 'I see where you're going. If I were them, I'd want to be private. No one to know what's going on.'

'Exactly,' she said. 'So, if we can tick off where they're not and where they're not going to be then the only places they can be is everywhere else.'

'And if we know where those blind spots are, we know where to avoid,' the security officer added. 'I'm on it.'

'Send Knoxx here too please when you go,' Beatrice requested. 'I want him to be assigned to me as personal security.'

'I will do, ma'am,' Security Chief Henendez said.

She smiled as he left her. 'Jons, you still there?'

'Yes, Captain,' the engineer replied. 'What do you need?'

'Are you able to take this conversation privately?' Beatrice asked. Her voice was hushed.

'I can do, why? What's happening?'

'I was hoping you'd tell me.'

There was a small pause before Allua Jons replied. 'I don't quite follow, ma'am.'

'The sergeant,' she said. 'I know you've been spending some of your down time with him. Are you distracted from finishing the job?'

Beatrice hated to admit it, but she had noticed the love interest between the two develop over the past few days. She did not approve of it. There was a time and a place for them to develop feelings for each other and this was not it. They were facing a life-or-death situation. No deviations from their survival could be accepted for anything.

'I don't see how that matters, ma'am,' Jons snapped. 'What I do when I'm needing to unwind for an hour isn't up to you.'

'It is when we need to be out of here,' Beatrice retorted viciously. 'Now answer the question. Are you behind schedule?'

'No,' Allua said in a short, harsh syllable. 'Me and my team are going to be done when I say we'll be done. Is there anything else?'

'There won't be,' Beatrice replied.

'Okay then, I'm going to get back to the engine,' Allua Jons stated. 'I'll report in when I'm done or if anything comes up. Out.'

As soon as the comms cut off, the officer felt her humanity ebbing away. That was not the way to do things. In desperate times, as much as they wanted to be free of the agents and the ever-looming threat growing closer by the minute, they all needed something to hold onto. For Allua Jons, it appeared that was now the sergeant. She shouldn't have made her choose their survival over her desire for some relief from the constant danger they were under. The engineer already knew what she needed to do. Allua would make sure the engine was operational, she knew that. Beatrice should have been calm enough to have remembered how capable the engineer was. Now, she was weighed down into her seat by a heavy lump resting in her chest where a soul should have sat.

How was it so much easier to manage this sort of a scenario when she was in the navy? Why was it difficult this time round? Was it her age catching up to her? Possibly. Age did change a person physically as well as mentally. Her tools too had changed since then. She was a worker. Her crew were her tools. In the military everyone was able to do multiple jobs, still being at the peak of their performance, no matter how tired. Now, people were good at what they did and that was that.

324

They weren't as sharp because the daily tasks asked of them didn't call for it on a regular basis.

She looked around and for the briefest of flashing memories she was once again back on the bridge of her last command as their naval battle ensued outside. Flashes of missile detonations erupted outside. Rounds from PDCs streamed by. Six armed marines constantly stood on guard on her deck. The crew worked quietly in perfectly silent synchronism with each other. Reacting to the slightest change in harmony. Her XO was always on hand to not question a single order unless it put someone needlessly in harm's way. Always there as a consul to affirm any beliefs or cast away any doubts. Beatrice had been so much younger then. Her glare more focused than it was now. Her body was far stronger with the help of youth.

Those were her proudest days. This wasn't her command anymore. The sergeant and agent were now in control of the situation. She was useless, merely there to make their requests happen. Beatrice was their second in command.

'What're you thinking about, Captain?' Adjutant Hender asked.

'It's nothing,' she said, holding back tears. 'Can you get me a drink, please?'

'Captain, talk to me,' Franklin insisted, bringing himself to her level so they could look effortlessly at each other in the eye. 'You don't have to go through whatever it is you have on your mind alone.'

'I'm not the person I once was,' Beatrice whispered. 'I used to be stronger. Calmer. I led fleets. And now look at me. It's just getting to me, now I'm realising it. That's all.'

'You're not, but you are who you are,' he told her. 'And I'm happy to be under your command. I'll be back with your coffee then we'll be able to look through the security feed with Henendez. More eyes will get through the monitors quicker. And it'll keep you distracted.'

'Sounds good,' Beatrice said.

'We're going to get home,' Franklin said. His eyes were filled with loving care and sincerity. 'You'll be back with your family. You'll see. Trust me.'

'I hope so.'

Her family. She loved them so much and missed them just as much. The love and respect they gave her was immeasurable, and the strength they possessed when united was unsurmountable. It was a family unit that she had built, that she had nurtured. She ached to be back with them, the weight in her chest growing heavy. Beatrice had the unnerving sensation she may not be able to tell them just how much she loves them again.

Chapter 10
16/11/2075
07:24 Earth Standard Time

Duke Horren

During the lockdown of the lower decks, Duke had faced off with the creatures that the agents had been transporting. He couldn't get their images out of his mind. Their jaws carried an overwhelming number of teeth, their four eyes ruby-red and filled with rage. The dark skin and fur with strips of white and pale blue covering their bodies blended them in with the darkened corridors of blown lighting. Their faces continued to haunt him after that fateful first encounter. In his sleep, the torment wouldn't let up. It intensified. Hundreds of them chased him through the abandoned corridors of the liner, an endless sea of death on the hunt. They had burst out of the lower decks as he patrolled the area. No one else was there to help – it was just Duke against the wolves. There were no blast doors, bulkhead doors or air locks to close for a moment's relief. Not even his patrol ship could be found. Duke's team had left him behind at some point. Most likely on his own orders. The myriad of ice wolves was almost upon him, their teeth inches away, each mouth vying to be the one that got to him first.

When he woke from his terror in a pool of sweat. Jesa and Ivan Zenkovich were holding him in place on his bed. Both showed relief that he finally woke. How long had they tried to stir him?

When he calmed down and his heart rate started to ease, they released their grip. Jesa helped him sit upright. He caught his breath and wiped the sweat from his face.

'Are you okay?' Jesa asked.

'Fine, I'm fine,' Duke replied. His voice was rushed, weary. They didn't believe him. 'Why?'

'You were having a bad dream,' the smuggler answered.

Ivan scoffed at the comment. 'Bad dream? That's polite. Sergeant, you were screaming and speaking in tongues. Not even a backwater Martian whose cousin, mother and sister are the same gal would understand you. Trust me, I know a few! You weren't in a good place wherever it was you were in your mind.'

'So, what was the dream about?' Jesa asked, looking up at him like a daughter would do to her father wearing a stiff upper lip when times were hard.

His stomach tightened. 'It was nothing.'

'It was something. You were screaming,' she countered.

With a reluctant sigh, he began to explain his dream, providing every detail, and quickly moved the conversation on from the subject, which his companions thankfully went along with for his sake. The less time spent dwelling on it the better for him. Duke didn't need to be reminded of the things that scared him.

'How long was I out for?' Duke asked them.

'About five hours solid,' Ivan answered. 'Before you ask, nothing's happened. There's been no attack, no sign of the hostile agents and no updates from the captain, nothing. It's been quiet. We thought we'd let you sleep. You kind of needed it.'

'Alright then,' Duke said. That had been a few days since the schism between the agents. During that time, there had been no sign of trouble. He didn't like it when things were silent for such a long period. It usually meant something was brewing. 'Where's everyone at?'

'Well, if we shout loud enough Leyton will hear you,' Zen said. 'He's been close by since we told him you were still sleeping.'

'Eavesdropping?' Duke questioned.

'Not a chance, he's too far away,' Ivan said. 'Think he's actually making sure you don't get disturbed. Anyway, the medic's making himself useful and fixing up a few people on the ship that have been injured. Abe's up on the bridge as our eyes and ears there. Everyone else is either patrolling the hallways or helping to fix things up.'

'Speaking of fixing up the ship, I'd like it if I can go back to helping out,' Jesa said.

'I'll arrange for someone to escort you to wherever you're needed,' Duke said. 'How's the arm?'

'It's healing nicely,' Jesa answered, checking the bandage on her bicep proudly. 'Thank you. A little tender still. The pain meds help.'

She had been a different person since having the tag removed and deactivated. A woman with a new lease on life. Jesa was rushing to offer her services to help wherever she could. She had been able to repair several key systems to help make sure the *Galactic Passage* didn't overload once the engines were fired up again. He was proud of her. This was all the sort of personality improvements he needed in order to argue the case for her to remain out of imprisonment, and preferably within his care.

'That's good,' Duke said. 'Glad you're getting there. Ivan, I need you and Val to hold the fort.'

'Where are you going?' the pilot asked.

'Up to the bridge.' He forced his way off his bed and gathered his equipment. 'I want to know if there are any updates that we haven't been told yet.'

'Okay, let me know if you need anything,' Zenkovich said.

In the troop bay, Duke was suddenly stopped by the professor shouting for him from the briefing room. The man approached him in the awkward manner a shy student would when stepping up to a tutor with an obvious question.

'Sergeant? You know that skeleton you have below in the other ship?' he started. Leyton evidently hadn't kept it to himself because the last thing he knew, the professor had not been on the smuggler ship. 'Is it possible I can look at it? My research with the wolves has, for all intents and purposes... well... has come to an end for the time being, and I'd really like to research that specimen while I'm not studying them. There's extraordinarily little that has ever been logged for this species. So little is known. This specimen that the boss told me about is completely different to anything that is known.'

'You mean you know about that thing?' Duke replied.

'I know a few things,' Samuel Ainslot explained. 'Not much though. No one knows much. Like I said, we barely have anything on record about it. But it's flagged as critical in our database. I really want to study it. Please. There's not much more I can do for you. Let me try and gather some data to add to the information banks.'

'Fine, but you can't be alone,' Duke replied after taking some time to think about what was being proposed. He opened a comm with Jesa. 'Jesa. Hey, I am sorry about this, but we have a slight change of plans. I need you to stay with the professor and let him research that skeleton you've got in your cargo hold.'

'Sure thing,' she sighed. Duke completely understood her reluctance. He needed someone there to make sure the professor didn't do anything wrong. He could trust that Jesa would keep him in check. 'If things change, can I help with the repairs?'

'I'll be the first to let you know you can help. Okay?'

'Okay,' Jesa muttered.

'Chin up,' Duke said. 'There's always something else to fix.'

Duke left the patrol ship before any new requests could be made and returned to the liner where he found Leyton patrolling nearby. Like a guardian, the agent had eyes on all the main corridors leading to their vessel. No one was getting close without his knowledge.

'Sleep well?' Leyton asked without turning his head.

'I think so. Will sleep better when I'm dead.'

Leyton chuckled at the remark. 'I hear that. Where you heading to?'

'Up to the bridge. Care to join?' Duke asked.

'Sure, not got much better to do now you're up. What's going on?'

'Just want to see what's happening,' Duke said. 'You might think up something to ask that I don't.'

As they traversed the ship, it was still unusual to see the ship bustling with almost normal day to day activities as the passengers walked around freely. Each one putting on a brave face to pretend that nothing was going on. Most though still called the galley home with others that had been moved to the first-class decks venturing back to what they knew. Duke would do the same with the officer's mess back at base. People knew where they belonged.

Children resumed playing in the corridors. They were a lot more cautious than children normally would have been, still managing to return to enjoying themselves to keep from boredom. The adults were in heated debate, trying to work out what was going on. When was it going to end? Were they going home? If only he could give them those answers. Their faces were long and drawn, weary. He wondered how many of them had ever felt like this before. If they knew how many people in the favelas, shanty towns and pop-up tent cities lived every day with this fear, would they still feel the same way?

Duke and Leyton were a couple decks below the bridge when Ivan contacted him and instructed them to pick up the pace to the command deck. When Duke tried to find out what it was about, Helmsman Zenkovich simply rushed a reply that it was bad news, and he was needed on the bridge.

'What do you think that's about?' Leyton asked.

'Was hoping you could tell me,' Duke replied. 'Any news on your friends?'

Leyton shook his head. 'Not a thing. No, they've been quiet for a while now.'

'Come on then,' Duke said. 'Let's go.'

The bridge was a different place now. No longer was it drained of life, vacant of purpose and run down with overuse. It was alive, an electricity buzzing through the air that had not been there since he first set foot on the *Galactic Passage*. The eyes of the key crew flicked between the multiple screens at their stations while their hands typed commands into the ship's system rapidly and their mouths remained perfectly sealed refusing to be the first to let out an exhausted yawn. It was impressive. He didn't believe the civilians had it in them to be so efficient.

The captain was hunched over the holo-table looking at a display of the local space with her second in command, a man that had become her personal guard and the head of security, Security Chief Henendez. It was a zoomed-out hologram of the liner, with the vessel being as small as a fist sat at the centre of the image. A red blip entered the space at the far left of the projection with an unknown transponder signal and unrecognised vessel registration codes underneath. Another ship, small but marginally larger than the patrol ship he had arrived in. This was the vessel that Leyton had warned them about.

Beatrice slapped the table in a fit of frustration before walking away with her hands behind her neck. Upon seeing the pair of them she let her hands fall to her side and waved them over to her.

'What's up Captain?' Duke asked her rhetorically.

'That,' she snapped, pointing at the table. 'It seems help got here a little early.'

'A little?' Leyton replied. 'They shouldn't be here for another day.'

'Oh well done, don't you think I know that?' Beatrice screamed. 'Weren't you supposed to get a heads up from them?'

'I was supposed to,' Leyton Foresc answered. 'Guess there was a change of plans when they found out I was onto Jerome and no longer on their side. Thought that would be obvious? How far out are they?'

'They'll be here in four hours,' Beatrice answered. 'I haven't got a clue what to do. The engines are barely functioning. We haven't run the tests yet to see if they'll even hold when they power up to anything that gives us a chance. We don't have the jump drive. Then there's the passengers. My fucking God, the passengers! What am I going to do with them?'

'How long until you're able to use the lifeboats?' Duke asked.

'In theory, we can use them now. Realistically I'd want a couple more hours to run diagnostics and simulations to make sure nothing goes wrong first. I don't want any of them jamming, short circuiting the system or self-destructing on launch.'

'We'll be able to think up an alternative plan if we can't use the lifeboats,' Duke said.

'Thinking?' Leyton replied. 'I've already got one.'

'You have? Go on,' Duke ushered.

Leyton stepped up to the hologram, pointing at the new ship. 'That isn't just any old ship. That's a frigate, Hades class. Stealth enabled. That means it has minimal weapons for a warship. Your patrol ship could be a match for it. It will be a tight one, but if your pilot is any good you can take it on. If they haven't brought a full complement of troops, then we should try to take that vessel. That will be our way of getting more people off this ship safely. It should have more than enough space for anyone we can't fit in the lifeboats.'

'What if it does have a full complement of troops?' Duke replied. 'There's only a few of us.'

Leyton shrugged his shoulders. 'We've still got to give it a go. It's our best chance.'

'How do you propose we do that?' Beatrice asked. 'It's not like we don't have to worry about a couple of your former buddies trying to hunt us down at the same time or that my crew aren't trained military personnel.'

'She has a point,' Duke said. 'We're far from in the best position to attempt anything like that.'

'You're right but we have to work with what we've got,' Leyton said. 'Our best chance is to lure them in. Make them come to us when they board the ship. Keep them moving in the directions we want them to move in. Then strike on our terms. Hit them hard and don't let up. They'll either stand and fight or turn and run.'

There was a fire in Leyton's eyes that Duke hadn't seen before. It was as if concocting a strategy was what he thrived on. It was effortless. Maybe he had been planning for this eventuality since he joined their side of the fight. Either way he was happy to have the man on his side.

'What do you propose when they get here then?' Henendez requested.

Leyton looked at the security chief. His eyes were steely, void of emotion. 'We use the civvies. They are just like chum. Those fucks on their way over? They're the sharks that are after that chum. We make things as easy as possible to lead them to the civilians and get them while they're on their way. Force them into kill zones. It's out best bet.'

'What the hell are you suggesting?' Duke demanded.

'Hear me out,' Leyton said, holding up a finger. 'We give them a clear line towards the galley, towards the civvies you've got in there. We position what resources we have in kill zones along that route. That way, they move where we need them to and hit them randomly in a territory they don't know. Keeping them at the disadvantage is going to be the only way we can get through this.'

'And if they fight through our defences?' Beatrice asked. 'What then? What's going to stop them slaughtering everyone on this ship starting with them after we've just led them straight there?'

Leyton grinned, as if he'd been hoping she would ask that question. 'I still have a few grenades that I brought. Didn't expect to need them but if they start to get the upper hand on us, we shut all doors leading to the civvies or the rest of the ship and we each pull the pin. Do what we need to do to make sure no one gets through and take out as many as we can while we're at it. Don't worry, we'll be too far in the ship to risk damaging the hull's integrity.'

Duke shook his head in disbelief. This was the guy that, not so long ago, was using the ship to transport the ice wolves they had imprisoned in the lower decks. It was too quick of a change of personality. 'I'm sorry but come on. Are you really going to put your life on the line like that? Because I don't think you will.'

'I've gone against the administrator of the OIRD. I've chosen this side of the fight now. For better or for worse, I might as well see it through to the end. I'm either dead here or dead planet-side when I get back to Earth or wherever. So yeah. No point half-assing it now that I've started. If I'm going to die, I'm taking some of them out with me while I'm at it and on my terms.'

'Dead? I wouldn't go that far,' Duke said.

'I would,' Leyton hissed. 'No one will even know I was alive when the administrator is finished with me now that I've gone against him. He makes people disappear for a living. Human, alien, it doesn't matter. He has that sort of power. People who can do that to you, can do anything they want to you. Should we lose this fight, I really recommend that you don't get captured because your lives will not be worth living when he's done. If you're not prepared to pull the pin say so and I'll have yours.'

'I'll do whatever I have to,' Sergeant Duke Horren replied.

'Wait,' Beatrice blurted, catching both their attention. 'Are you seriously considering this?'

Duke looked to the officer. Her concern was understandable, but misplaced. 'It's the best we've got apart from lying back and letting them get on with it. And I'm not prepared to wait for them to do whatever they want with me.'

'This isn't why you're here!' Franklin Hender stated.

'I can't believe it,' the officer gasped. 'You're supposed to be protecting my passengers and my crew. Not using them as bait.'

'Why not?' Leyton asked. 'I've read your file. You've done this before, and it turned out alright for you then. A little messy, but you made it out.'

Before Duke could process what Leyton had just said, the officer turned red with rage. She didn't say anything. She didn't need to. The look on her face was one of someone having a dirty secret uncovered that they had done all they could to keep hidden.

'Don't you dare,' she eventually whispered.

'What are you talking about?' Duke asked. 'What're you guys not telling me?'

'Our captain here—'

'Keep your mouth shut,' Beatrice hissed, cutting the agent off mid-speech.

'Our captain-' Leyton repeated but was cut off once again.

'I'm warning you!' she screamed.

'Oh, please quit it and get over it, we've all done shit we wish we could forget,' Leyton retaliated. 'She did a similar thing years ago. It worked out in the end. A lot of people died under her command as a result of it, but they got the job done.'

The officer fell silent. She cowered into her command chair surrounded with shame.

'What do you mean?' Duke asked, needing to know what she had done that she was so ashamed of she was prepared to make empty threats to someone that could have killed her with ease.

'You remember the Siege of Vulcair?' Leyton asked.

Duke nodded. It had been an exceedingly long time ago, a couple of decades. He was just a young man barely starting out in basic training. The siege had been to relieve a planet from the control of the Planetary Separatist Coalition, a collection of planets that believed in a free government away from the UPN. He wasn't opposed to alternative governments. The contrary, Duke promoted them. All of humanity under one rule would have been nothing short of totalitarian or even a dictatorship. But when it was forced on someone, and their decision based on if the trigger at the other side of a barrel would be pulled or not, that was rightly challenged. Which is exactly what the PSC did. Planets within their reach refusing to side with them were forced to join under penalty of death. Once the UPN got wind of this, they sprang into action. A war raged for years against this forceful tyranny to relieve people from the hardship. The campaign had been a drawn out one that cost both sides a lot of lives, trillions of credits in damages and took years to recover from. Vulcair was the first planet to be liberated from their control and had been heavily reinforced by the PSC in anticipation of UPN military forces arriving.

'I remember it.'

'Well, our captain here led the campaign that broke the siege,' Leyton explained. 'Instead of making the capitol ship of the fleet a ghost ship, she instructed it to go out into the open with a full crew and the rest of the ships in her fleet around the nearby moons. As expected, the enemy fleet couldn't resist such an easy target. Her fleet moved in on an intercept course when the flagship started taking a beating. Her ship took too much damage by the end of it. It was scrapped afterward. But more importantly they had to change tactics on several occasions, as Separatist ships went for the stronger targets to break out of the trap. Out of their fleet they lost over a half dozen ships and thousands of lives. So how she can say no to this is beyond me. It's the same thing with fewer lives at risk.'

'Probably because the crew on each of those ships knew the risks when they enlisted,' the officer retorted. 'They were doing their job. What was expected of them. The situation here is different because the people on this ship are civilians. This isn't what they signed up for.'

'Still surprised you aren't prepared to use them the same way you used your ship and the crew in the fleet,' Leyton muttered under his breath. 'But it doesn't matter what they signed up for anymore. Fact is we have no choice. It's all we've got.'

'There needs to be another way!' Lenoia screamed.

'Right!' Duke cried out. 'I'll make the call. We do it the agent's way. It's the only real option that we have until we have the *Passage* fully operational so that we can get out of here or we can start to pile the civilians into the lifeboats. Captain, have your engineers make sure everything is up and running for the lifeboats. I have no intentions of using them. However, I'd feel better knowing they're working if we need to use them. Let us know when the ship gets here and which airlock it's docking at. I'll direct the defences from there.'

'Fine,' Beatrice said, conceding defeat.

'Are we able to move?' Duke asked.

'We can, why?' Franklin Hender replied.

'Get us moving at the safest speed you can,' he ordered. 'Doesn't have to be much. Just buys us a little more time to get ready.'

'Captain?' the adjutant said, seeking permission.

'Do it,' Beatrice said. She turned back to Duke. 'But I'm coming with you when they do get here. I'm not sitting this one out.'

It was as if someone had just breached the forward viewing windows and the atmosphere had vented out into the void of space. It wasn't unusual for the ship's captain to chip in when needed, but to put herself in the firing line was unusual. Every commanding officer of every ship knew that they needed to remain safe so they could continue to lead and, when the time came, scuttle the ship if we need to. They only joined in the fight only when there was no other option because it was right outside their door. There were still plenty of options before that was required by her.

The look on her face told Duke that it was a fight he didn't want to partake in. He could argue until he was blue in the face that she shouldn't go, and she would still win. He sighed.

'Have it your way then,' he said.

Jesa

For well over an hour, Jesa sat in the background of her cargo hold and watched as the professor carried out scans of the Shauari skeleton, then processing those scans into readable information and interpreting the data. He would mutter every now and again to himself as he made new assumptions about how the creature came to be, what use certain features of its form were for, and where it could have come from in the galaxy. The constant monologue was amusing to listen to, like he was narrating for an audience that wasn't present at a lecture.

All the while, Jesa yearned to be on the *Galactic Passage* helping the people there and helping wherever her assistance was needed, doing something more meaningful. Babysitting was something she had never anticipated. A task that bore responsibility. That, surely, was a job for one of the crew? Although this would prove that Jesa could be trusted. Duke might give her more freedoms after they left the liner because she'd be proven to be trustworthy when not under their supervision. Maybe that's why he had assigned the task to her. A form of test.

Bored of sitting around, of watching his activity from afar, she jumped off the cargo crate she had been sat on, walked up to Professor Ainslot and peered over his shoulder. On the display of his tac-pad, two skeletons rotated in perfect synchrony. One was clearly an image of the specimen that she brought with her. The other skeleton looked a little like hers. It was noticeably smaller, a good couple foot smaller. The snout was flatter to the face to make it more human-like and there was no tail or head frill like her skeleton possessed. Curious that it could be so alike yet so different.

'What is that?' she asked. 'It looks like mine.'

'It's sort of like yours,' Samuel Ainslot replied. 'But not quite.'

'How do you know?'

'It's essentially a best guess right now. We have lots of bones that don't come from the same sample in our records. Because of that, we've taken the samples that we do have and generated this reconstruction based on the averages. But even though they're so different I think they're the same race of organism.' He was more excited talking about this than she would have thought was normal. Maybe that was what scientists were like. She'd never really known any that well before. All the scientists she had briefly met were recruited to make new ways of killing people for Barbaros. They were kept hidden

337

for days on end. 'Why this one's so big though, I would love to know. I want to say it's unusual, but we don't know enough about them to say what's normal and what isn't.'

'Annoying?'

'It's science.' Professor Ainslot waved his hand passively. 'Comes with the nature of the work. It's a lot of guesses and assumptions, disproving what we thought to be true and re-evaluating what we once believed was real so that we can hope to find the truth.'

Jesa looked back to the skeletons. She thought hard about why they were the same but different. The first thing that came to mind was gender. For most organisms, with several exceptions, the male was typically the larger of the species. They would typically also have display features to attract a mate. It could be that the tail, snout length and head frill was symbolic of strength or longevity? Or she could be clutching at straws to make connections that weren't there. Her head started to hurt.

'Is it possible your reconstruction is a female, compre?'

'That was my thought,' Professor Ainslot replied quickly. 'But look here. You see the abdomen and pelvic area? Proportionately, they're a remarkably similar size and shape. If they were different genders, then like other reptiles they would be significantly different. Granted this isn't like any reptile we know of and I'm just drawing the comparison on its skeletal structure with something closely related. But if my hunch is right, and they follow the same traits, a female of this species would have a different pelvic structure for reproduction. So, that means they're both males as far as I can see. This makes things interesting.'

'How?' Jesa questioned.

Professor Ainslot lowered his tac-pad and looked at her. He smiled and looked up at her with soft eyes, happy that she was showing an interest in his work.

'It means that either they are completely different species and we're looking at two unique discoveries at the same time, they originate from different regions of the same planet that requires different skillsets to survive so evolved a little differently to survive those environments, or the smaller one is a sub-class of the same species and would be subservient to the larger, superior class,' Professor Ainslot said. His voice was calm and soothing. Jesa had to repeat his words to understand what he was saying. 'However, without live specimens to examine, and the time to do it, I'm going to have a hard time getting the answers I need until I get back to a base to check the samples.'

The academic started to talk about DNA and genomes and various other biological terms that went over her head. Samuel Ainslot managed to see where he was going too fast for her, even if she was a little embarrassed to admit it. He was then able to explain the terminology that confused her in such ways that she understood and even gave nice examples that were easy to follow to help. Jesa could only wonder how much a man could talk about these things before he got bored or until their audience was bored enough to walk away. She hoped he would be the one to get bored eventually by his own voice because it wasn't something she was particularly interested in learning about. It was just another link to Barbaros that she would happily be rid of, and she had to be there to keep an eye on him.

'How did you get a complete skeleton? If you don't mind me asking.' Professor Ainslot asked. 'This is so rare. Unheard of even. I mean, my colleagues working in the field barely got an entire limb in one piece from their digs. To have a whole specimen this pristine... it's almost as if they found a live one and stripped the flesh away.'

'It was part of the job,' she explained with a shrug. 'I never asked where they got it from. Knowing too much got us punished. Or worse. Even if I could have known, I wouldn't have wanted to know anything about these things after the stories I've heard.'

'Stories?'

Jesa nodded. 'We have rumours about them in the outer colonies. The stories have been around for years. Longer than I've been alive, compre?'

'What sort of rumours?' Ainslot asked. He shuffled closer to her. Paid attention to everything she did or said like an eager schoolchild.

'People say that the Shauari are still alive, and that they occupy planets just outside the outer colony territories. Which sector depends on who's telling the stories. Some say that they live near the Pahs region, others as far as Yol and even Nexastile. People say they patrol overlapping boundaries, sometimes coming deep into human controlled territory. They say that the Shauari come and slaughter the people, stealing whatever they can. The stories say that when supply runs are made, the pilots find the towns, landing zones, everything just destroyed. Burning. People missing. Compre? Sometimes, they find survivors that managed to hide. They're crazy. Lost their minds. Say that the saw the Shauari. The pilots rescue the survivors and tell the stories. Never any alien bodies. Just plasma burns. Footprints. Sometimes blood. Dark green blood. But we don't have anything to test

339

it with and the Centies don't help. No evidence to prove the stories. Say that it's something other than Outers killing Outers. But I believe the stories.'

'No evidence?' Ainslot asked. 'How is that possible? When we attack somewhere, there is always something to say who was there. A recording, something dropped by accident. Blood. It doesn't make sense.'

'I don't know,' Jesa said. 'I've never seen them, nor seen an attack. I can't tell you. All I can say is what I hear in the rumours. Compre? That's not the scary part of the rumours, though.'

Professor Ainslot put his tac-pad down and stared at her. His eyes were soft and Sincere, like he was genuinely interested in, and cared about, what she had to say. 'What is?'

She tried to find the words and with a trembling voice, said, 'Apparently, the survivors say that when the Shauari are done raiding colonies, they take the bodies of the people they've killed and kidnap the ones that they let live. Not just anyone though. Mainly women and really young kids. Mostly babies. Every now and again they'll take the strongest man from the settlement.

'Kidnap? I wonder what for...'

'I don't want to know,' she answered quickly, cutting him off while glaring at the skeleton. 'I can't wait to see the back of that thing. Scares me.'

The professor sighed. 'I can get that. Me? I'd love the chance to see them. Study them. Understand how they behave, think and live.'

'Why?'

It was such an odd thing for her to hear. After learning about the rumours that tell of the notoriety about them and the threat that they posed to humans, why would someone willingly want to study it? It made no sense to her. Maybe she was just unable to see what he could. Or was he braver than she for following curiosity regardless of how dangerous the road could be.

Professor Ainslot smiled at Jesa. 'How arrogant would I be if I didn't want to? I'd be as bad as those people who believe that God created all life in the universe and put it solely on Earth and that anything else is the work of the Devil or false god. The galaxy is full of life that needs to be studied. Understood. Appreciated. We are all here for a reason. Those of us with sentience don't know what that reason is yet; we might simply be a part of the food chain. Or we might be destined to be the guardians of life that cannot choose its own fate. If I pick and choose what I want to study to suit what I'm comfortable with, I might as well pick and choose what I believe to be fact and fiction. At that point, I might as well stop all my research because you don't go into my line of work to choose what you study but more choose how you study everything.'

'Is that why you joined the agency? To discover life?' Jesa asked, finding herself curious to learn more about the man that didn't fit in with the rest of the unit.

Samuel laughed. 'No, I was actually recruited as a field agent to assist on a scientist on assignment that was looking into alien ecosystems that provided safe havens for known hostiles. Needing us to say if the ecosystems would beat the enemy before we were deployed. They knew I was smart when they took me away from the university I was lecturing at. But they didn't fully take into consideration that I had several degrees in xeno-biology until the higher-ups noticed I was smarter than the guy in charge of me.'

'Several?' Jesa interrupted. 'But... you're not that old?'

'No, I'm not,' Samuel Ainslot said with a smile. 'Only twenty-nine.'

'Mayah!' she exclaimed. He was not much older than her and smarter than most people. It was impressive to say the least. 'How did you manage that?'

'Just came naturally to me,' Samuel said confidently. 'Was able to take a few at a time. Anyway, after they found out how smart I was in the field, they transferred me out of the dangerous stuff to then go view, study and learn about the different organisms out there. It was mainly to discover things that were going to either be useful or dangerous to humanity. That way we could learn what would help us and what would harm us. I've learnt so much more than I thought I would in my time with the agency. We've discovered so many different chemicals that have medical use, variations of animals to further prove the theory of evolution and... well... aspects that have a more militaristic use.'

A true scientist. Discovery comes first. Violence a subject rather ignored. A good person, if not a little naive. Jesa wondered how he could have even been considered to be the mole. He wasn't a killer; he was barely even a soldier. Not even a liar. He was so open and honest with his thoughts and so obsessed with his work. The man barely gave himself a break from the research. It was impossible to think he could have been the one talking to the administrator. She was glad that he wasn't.

341

'What about you? How'd you wind up in all of this?' Professor Ainslot questioned. 'Forgive me but you're a smuggler running with the SPF. It's quite the remarkable turn of events that doesn't happen every day. Usually for a smuggler to do that they have to be an inside person for the UPN.'

'The usual way people do,' she said softly, hoping to not be taken notice of. 'I was kidnapped as a child. Watched my family die. Forced to go into smuggling to pay my debts for not being killed. Nothing good happened after that except for the Centies here finding my ship and taking me into their custody. They've near enough given me my freedom since I've been with them. I like being around them. It feels like home to me now. I don't want to leave them.'

'I'm glad they did that for you,' the scientist said. 'Freedom isn't something anyone should take for granted. And having a place to call home. Both of those are a luxury too few people have.'

Professor Ainslot gave her one last smile after his wise words before returning to his scans of the skeleton. Checking in detail the composites of each bone, the density of them, and trying to determine the age of the creature when it died. According to his commentary, he would be waiting a few hours before they were able to have the results required to make an educated assumption without more accurate equipment. He got excited when he saw the marks in the bones suggesting rapid growth at a young age. That sent him on a wild fury of questioning out loud what that would represent and why. Jesa smiled. He was like she used to be as a child before her family were murdered. Excitable. Inquisitive. Innocent.

Jesa wondered if he had a dark side. No one could be consistently nice like that. Or if he truly were that kind and naïve, how would he react when that innocence was taken away? It was always interesting for her to consider people's nature when they were upset or angry. It told her exactly the sort of person that they were when self-restrain was no longer an option. Samuel Ainslot wasn't so easy to read; maybe she would never know what it is that makes him tick. Or possibly she didn't want to find out. He smiled at her when he saw that she was watching him intently. Jesa blushed for a moment then looked away, trying to not distract him from his work. If she knew anything about his kind, it was that scientists were not the friendliest when distracted from their work.

The professor exclaimed a few more times as more revelations were made then immediately whined as new questions arose that couldn't be explained away. But he never stopped looking for answers. If anything, he searched harder for them whenever an obstacle was presented, just another challenge for him to overcome. She could never have that level of persistence. It took a commitment that she did not possess. Jesa quite admired it. There would be plenty he could teach her, if he was willing to. That would depend on if they survived the next few hours. Her heart groaned with the anxious anticipation of the soldiers coming for them.

She hoped they would make it out of there alive. To find out a bit more about this man before her. Understand why he wasn't like anyone she had ever met. He wasn't strong. He wasn't malicious. He didn't even appear to be remotely perverted. Jesa fidgeted for a moment.

'You are… unusual,' Jesa told him.

'I always told myself I was passionate,' he joked. 'My work gives me the satisfaction I need to be content with myself.'

'Why is that?'

Samuel Ainslot cleared his throat and explained. 'There are millions of species of animals and plants alone on Earth that haven't been fully researched. Humanity has colonised more planets with their own ecosystems than I can count; we haven't even scratched the surface of those. Let alone the sentient species out there and their individual evolutionary ladders we've encountered or have yet to discover. It's all worth getting excited about. It's the golden age of interstellar discovery. In time, I plan to have plenty of theses published categorising all these new species. And this gives me the chance to fulfil what I need to complete.'

'You are passionate,' Jesa replied with a smile. 'How much more have you got to do with this guy?'

Samuel laughed heartily. 'How much? I've barely got started! We're in for the long haul here.'

'Guess I'll make myself comfy,' she said.

'I would if I was you,' Professor Ainslot chuckled. 'You might even want to get yourself a drink while you're at it.'

'Don't you want one?' Jesa replied.

Samuel Ainslot shook his head and smiled softly, speaking with humour in his tone, 'No thank you. I need to keep focussed. Drinks are just a distraction from my work. I'm a man. We don't multitask too well. If I'm drinking, I'm not working.'

'Am I a distraction?'

'Hardly – it's nice to have someone to talk to that will listen to me. Even if you don't quite understand what I'm saying at times. Don't worry, I don't take it personally. I enjoy a difficult field for others to appreciate.'

'How do you know where to start with your research?' Jesa asked.

'Short answer, I don't know,' Professor Ainslot laughed. 'Most of the time, the really interesting questions I want to solve I can't work on until I know the basics. So, I've got a sort of chart of things that I work my way through each time I'm trying to understand something new and complex. Once I understand the basics, I can understand the more difficult things. Sometimes, I have to get creative with how I find the answers to the basic questions because things are missing or there is just not enough to go on. It keeps my work interesting; I can tell you that much! Anyway, go get yourself a drink. I'm not going anywhere. Not for a while.'

Jesa nodded and made her way to the galley of the patrol ship. She had to admit she did need the coffee and their coffee was surprisingly good. On her way out, she glanced at the professor with his back to her while he worked and smiled. It felt wrong to admire a Centie. Unnatural, even. But he wasn't like any other Centie she'd met, and nor was he anything like what Barbaros said they were. She was pleasantly surprised and was keen to get her drink quickly so that she could continue her own research to learn more about this man she had to keep an eye on. See what else there was about him that could turn the world she knew to be false upside down.

Beatrice Lenoia

The hostile ship slowed its trajectory to a casual approach, moving much slower than she would have expected. Like a shark coming in on its first inspection of potential prey. Testing the waters. Most likely waiting to see if the SPF patrol ship detached from the *Galactic Passage* to attack them or retreat. It put Beatrice on edge. There was no telling what the enemy force would do. In her mind, every delay meant they were one step closer to launching a salvo of missiles their way.

When the patrol ship did nothing, the frigate approached for docking on E deck. Duke quickly directed the teams into position. They sealed every pressure door and blast door that offered an alternate route to the galley just in time, disabling the controls at each door so they couldn't be overridden, and damaging the manual controls as they went to prevent them from being opened again. Beatrice left the safety of the bridge with her sub-machine gun issued from the SPF patrol ship and joined the personnel in the second to last defence position of the four lines of defence that had been established. Beatrice was determined to not be at the back of the defensive lines and reluctantly accepted that she couldn't possibly be anywhere near the front. So, she settled for this position.

She stood at her post with one of her own security team and a soldier from the sergeant's squad, Corporal Moasa. The giant of a man towered over them, his very presence making things seem safer. She received constant updates over her comm-pad from the bridge on the position of the approaching frigate until it had locked into place and breached the airlock. The attacking force secured the immediate area then went ahead to push through the already emptied corridors, following the route that had been pre-determined for them. It was going to plan. They wouldn't even attempt to change route. If anything, it seemed to be going too well for them. She expected the enemy soldiers to at least try to stray from the pre-planned route, but they didn't. Either they were that badly trained or they had no concept of caution.

Then the enemy reached the first line of defence; Duke, Agent Tallow and another member of her security team. For a few moments there were questions being asked. Agent Tallow almost instantly advised that the hostiles were not fellow agents. Even if the administrator said they were. That their armour was different, their equipment wasn't standard issue and even the tactics weren't the same. Everything about them was unfamiliar to her. Even the words of Leyton couldn't calm her down. It wasn't the first gun shot that sent fear down her spine. As the gun shot echoed over the comms, Beatrice was almost absent from it. A part of her mind worked wildly to tell her why it wasn't real and that she didn't hear a thing. It was the second shot that made her jolt with shock. The third, fourth and fifth shots solidified the reality that the time for waiting was over. The fight was now upon them. Blood was going to be spilled and there was nothing that they could do about it.

With only her imagination to interpret the commands, cusses and cries, she could only picture a worst-case scenario of the enemy pushing on through the first obstacle, and everyone falling under their show of strength where they stood. That was what it sounded like over the comms. It had to be chaos up ahead.

'Sergeant, sitrep?' Beatrice asked over the comms. When she didn't receive a quick response, with her heart in her throat, she repeated herself. 'Sergeant, sitrep? What's going on? Over.'

'We're a little busy here,' the SPF sergeant growled over the flurry of gun shots. 'Fuck me someone lay down some covering fire! I can't get a clear shot. Shit! Tallow, keep your head down!'

'He'll talk when he gets the chance,' Corporal Moasa explained as the fighting intensified. He didn't look at all bothered by the commotion. If anything, he looked like he was in his comfort zone.

'I know,' she muttered. 'I've just forgotten what it's like to be in a fight.'

Moasa shrugged a smile. 'It happens. We all get a little rusty. But—'

An explosion boomed down the corridor, cutting off the corporal. The sudden cry from Duke over the comms cut over the noise. 'What the hell was that thing?'

'Not a clue,' Agent Tallow replied. Her voice was pained and drowned by gun shots ringing over the comms. 'I've never seen it before. Take cover!'

Another detonation rang out down the corridor. At some point in the commotion, Duke rushed the hostile forces. He could briefly be heard fighting up close before being sent back, wheezing and gasping for breath. By the sounds of it he had been sent several feet by a single strike. Beatrice looked over to Corporal Moasa. Seeing the same expression of worry on his face did nothing to ease her concern.

'Fuck me they're strong. They're not even wearing power armour. That's it, we need extra firepower,' Duke yelled when he caught his breath. 'Fall back! Move it! I'll cover you. Team two, we're coming in hot. You ready?'

'As we'll ever be,' Leyton answered. 'Just don't stand in front of me when I pull the trigger.'

'Why would I do you the favour?'

Beatrice cocked her head and looked at Ronan. 'He doesn't have time to answer me, but he has time for that?'

'What can I say? You're wanting an update. He can't brief you as quickly as he can tell the agent better luck next time for an easy kill. We don't answer to command when in the heat of it.'

She never did understand that sort of banter between soldiers. Maybe it was because she had grown up in a different world and had had too many privileges to be privy to it. Or maybe he just didn't have the respect for her that she thought she deserved. Either way it wasn't important. Beatrice quashed those thoughts for another time. The fighting had escalated, and within a minute or two of the conflict reaching the second point, there were confirmed kills. To her dismay, one of them was a member of her security team. Another one. It pained her that the best she could promise her crew now was an empty coffin on Earth when it was over. When the female agent took a hit, the second line of defence dropped back to the third point. The enemy had momentum, superior numbers and greater tactics on their side which proved too much as that line too quickly became overwhelmed by the assault upon them.

Which led straight to her team.

Bullets peppered the wall at the end of the corridor, each shot threatening to ricochet toward them. People screamed in fits of rage, outbursts of pain and profound curses. She brought up her weapon and peered through the iron-sights, staring down the hallway with an itchy trigger finger. Her team didn't need to be told what to do. They followed her lead and readied themselves. The first person to round the corner was Leyton, immediately turning on the heel to provide cover fire as a member of her security team rushed into view holding a leg wound. He reached out and violently yanked another member of her crew into safety. She smiled at that gesture. Beatrice may not forgive him for killing members of her crew previously, but she could move on a little easier in knowing that he saved others. Duke soon joined them, firing his rifle wildly back in the direction that he came from. The female agent and another member of her security rounded the corner before they all hurried toward her. Beatrice Lenoia didn't want to believe the truth that those who were missing were dead. But it was something that she had to accept.

Duke and Agent Tallow were barely halfway across the distance toward them when the first hostile came round the corner after them, carrying what looked like a light machine-gun with a chain of bullets wrapped around their shoulders. The armour looked nothing like that of the agents. Instead, it was remarkably like the armour Duke wore, with minor cosmetic differences. There were decorative ridges running up the gauntlets and legs. The faceplate visor was narrower and more menacing, probably only revealing the eyes. An emblem was painted on the left of the chest piece, an emblem she couldn't quite make out at her distance.

The hostile readied their weapon and took aim at the two stragglers.

'Sergeant, down!' Beatrice barked.

Duke reacted instantly, dragging the injured agent down with him. With a clear line of sight everyone on either side of Beatrice pulled the trigger on their weapons. It took several dozen rounds to breach the armour the hostile wore. When the enemy soldier was finally felled, it was still too late to stop the loss of more life. Another member of her crew was killed and Corporal Moasa took a hit to his flank.

'You wanted a sitrep?' Duke asked as he and Agent Tallow joined them. There was a dent on his armour, the size of a fist, where he had been struck earlier. He let off several rounds back down the corridor as a pair of hostiles rounded the corner. 'Here it is. It's fucked. We've got at least another twenty guys back there still standing and out for blood. We've lost four with another couple injured. No idea how many of them we took out. The only confirmed kill is that guy you lot just took out. I don't know how much longer we can keep this up, because these guys are here for war and give zero shits about putting themselves in harm's way to win. To top it off, I haven't seen half the kit they're using before.'

'You and me both,' Leyton added. 'These guys ain't reinforcements. This is a fucking death squad. Whatever they are, I bet no one outside the agency has a clue either.'

'What can we do about them?' Beatrice asked.

As more hostile soldiers came into view and fired at them, she felt her control of the situation slipping away. They moved too quickly, far quicker than anticipated. This was supposed to be a fight on their terms. Not the enemy's terms which it was rapidly turning into. Her security team was losing the strength to continue. They were firing fewer and fewer shots and spent more time looking to the exits. Searching for the escape that she couldn't provide.

She had failed them.

Another member of her crew was killed. Their body slumped to the floor. Beatrice's lips quivered. These were more than just people that followed her orders. Everyone under her command was family. Every one of them a loved one that was near and dear. She looked up – the enemy was pushing forward. Each volley of shots fired toward their defensive line bringing the enemy closer to their position.

Corporal Moasa stirred back to his feet with a pained groan after the shot to the flank. 'I'll tell you what we're going to do. You're going to fall back and make an actual defensive line.'

'What do you mean?' Beatrice replied as Duke cussed under his breath.

The large man reloaded his rifle, took out his pistol, and charged forward into the approaching battle line firing both weapons in unison. In an impressive display of strength and speed, he mowed down the first two soldiers he encountered. The giant then fell into a brutal fight with several hostile soldiers. Seemingly taking the advantage. Beatrice ordered her crew back with the wounded until there was only her, the sergeant and Leyton aiding Corporal Moasa as he returned to them. The man had taken a severe beating and panted heavily in pain.

'Why'd you do that?' she questioned.

'Because I was the only one who could,' the soldier answered confidently, holding his sides as he composed himself.

A comm crackled into life across the hallway, barely audible over the incoming gun fire.

'Boss, you there?'

'Jerome?' Leyton answered.

'Hey boss,' the man's former teammate said. 'How's it going?'

'Well, considering there's a whole bunch of people out here to kill me I guess I'm doing okay.'

'It's what you get for being a turncoat,' Jerome stated smugly. His relaxed attitude was scary. How could anyone be so complacent?

'That's a matter of opinion,' Leyton replied. 'From my point of view, you betrayed me. You're the one who was talking to the boss behind my back.'

'If you did as we were told, it wouldn't have happened this way. Gather you've met the reinforcements? Are you finding them a little tough?'

'How'd you guess?' Leyton asked.

'They're not your standard grunts,' Jerome stated. 'I guess you'll never fully appreciate Project Terracotta. If you'd stayed on our side, you would have found out about it.'

The gun shots raged on, and the agent was having a casual conversation with his former second in command. It was as if he wasn't involved in the fight anymore. As if he was shielded from the slugs of metal that would kill anyone else. Beatrice reacted as a bullet bounced off the corner of her cover. She reached round and let off several shots down the corridor. The enemy moved out of the line of fire temporarily now that they too had suffered losses.

If that agent was not up on the same deck as them, where was he? And where were the others that defected away from Leyton? She needed to know. Someone as arrogant as Jerome would surely boast something that could give up information they could follow.

When she looked back at the agent, she made eye contact so that she had his attention.

'See where he is!' Beatrice hissed at him. When Leyton looked at her with confusion, she repeated herself. 'Where is he? Is he down below?'

Leyton waited for a break in the gunfire before speaking to his friend. 'So, where you at then?'

'I'm glad you asked me, actually,' Jerome said. 'You know when we were locking the creatures in? Where I was when one of the engineers died? You can find me there. Come alone.'

'You actually going to be there?' Leyton asked.

'You'll have to wait and see. Out.'

'Trap?' Duke asked.

'Trap,' Leyton confirmed, letting off a few shots now his conversation was over.

'Do you want backup?' Beatrice asked.

'I do, but I won't take it,' the agent answered. 'This is my fight.'

'Are you going to finish it?' Beatrice added, keen to know what he wanted to do.

'Only one of us walks away from this,' Leyton Foresc said. 'I plan to be the one to finish it.'

'Go,' she instructed.

'Shout if you need help,' Duke said.

'I will,' Leyton answered. 'Cover me.'

Beatrice, Duke, and Corporal Moasa leaned out when Leyton scrambled away from the battle. Beatrice watched him rush down the corridor until he was out of sight. The three of them pulled out of the firing line to reload, dodging the enemy's own salvo of rounds.

'How much ammo do you have left?' Duke Horren asked her.

She reached round her tactical vest, grimaced then replied, 'Not enough.'

Duke scowled, 'We'll draw those fuckers out, hit them hard then fall back to the last line. I don't know how much longer we can keep this up for.'

'We need to hold our ground there,' she stated. It was the obvious but saying it helped reinforce it in her mind. 'We can't let them reach the passengers. We need to get them off the ship.' The passengers. Beatrice opened a comm-link with Franklin. 'Franklin, how are the escape pods?'

'As ready as they can be,' her adjutant said. '

'Okay, we need to risk it. Start putting the passengers on them. Get them out of here.'

'I'm on it,' Hender said.

Beatrice took a deep breath, held it in, then slowly exhaled, trying to calm her nerves. It wasn't just the lives of the civilians she was worried about. It was all their lives. And selfishly, she hoped to be one of the lucky ones to make it off the ship too. She had her family to return to.

The footsteps carried on coming toward them. Duke announced his instructions, took one of his grenades and primed it, holding it for a few seconds before launching it down the corridor. After the explosion they took their chance to fall back. They couldn't fail. Too much was at risk.

Leyton Foresc

Leyton hadn't stopped sprinting since leaving the others to defend the ship without him. His legs ached, his body trembling in agony. Still, the physical pain was nothing compared to the emotional anguish he had to face. He would soon be challenging his friend. For Jerome to turn on him, to not trust in him and his reasoning, was an act that had to be answered for. The betrayal by someone he loved had happened many times before. A lover. A family member. A brother. But never from a friend.

Possibly he had made the wrong decision. Maybe his judgement had been clouded and he wrongly felt emotions over things he should have seen the logic of. A little bit of neural reprogramming would have corrected that and made him as obedient as a puppy without even realising that his thoughts weren't entirely his own. He would have been able to remain within the ranks of the agency and none the wiser to what had happened. Leyton quickly realised that those thoughts were wrong. He had made the right decision.

When he finally slowed his pace just ahead of the agreed meeting spot, footsteps thudded around in the dark. A hum echoed. A relatively jolly tune that inspired calm.

'Hey boss,' Jerome said, his voice carrying smoothly over to him. 'You alone?'

Leyton's former second in command and friend casually walked in a long circle around the hallway. Jerome's eyes were permanently locked on him. The few lights that still worked cast ugly shadows all around, some flickering wildly as their source struggled to emit enough light. Jerome's smile was sinister, cold and clearly hiding something. A hatch nearby was wide open. He had opened it.

Leyton approached slowly. He held his weapon in a non-threatening position primed to be brought to bear if needed. There was no way that he would be caught off guard.

'Jerome. You might be surprised at this, but I am. I don't backstab people like you do.'

Jerome jabbed a finger toward him, 'That's a cheap shot.'

'Doesn't make it any less true,' he retorted.

'I never backstabbed you. You turned your back on us.'

Leyton shook his head. The agent was still twisting the truth to make him the bad guy for having a moral compass. 'What's going on then? Where are the others?'

'Oh, they're not here. I've sent them to liaise with the soldiers and wait for me there with them. As for what's going on... You know, I've been thinking about this whole situation. About you having to die and all that.'

'Yeah? What about it?' he asked, silently taking the safety off his weapon.

'After all these years together, we've dodged death more times than I can count,' Jerome recounted. He seemed almost happy looking back in nostalgia. 'I've saved your life, you've saved mine. We're like family. You remember that time when we knocked out that comms array at the outpost on Trefalon?'

'Yeah, I remember,' Leyton answered. It had been a standard operation that, up until the last leg, had gone according to plan. They were never meant to destroy the comms array. Their mission was to disrupt separatist military activity and tag containers ear-marked for distribution, to see where they ended up and track how far the separatist movement spread. However, the enemy had been quick enough to abandon the outpost upon discovering their presence and, in their bid for freedom, attempted to call for help. The destruction of the array was a necessary mission update to ensure the outcome remained the same. In doing so, they couldn't be picked up and had to flee to a secondary pick-up location. 'What about it?'

'How long were we out in the wilderness for before we got saved? About two weeks?'

'Something like that.'

'And when we had to fight that big fucking thing—'

'—the hulshearn?' Leyton suggested, filling in the pause. It was a horrible creature that had hunted them through the jungles. It was almost the death of them, until they got lucky.

'Yeah, that thing. It wanted to chow down like there was no tomorrow when I fell into its pit. Even with your arm busted up you kept it away until I came to.'

'What exactly are you getting at? Stalling for something?'

'I am stalling – I want to give you a chance to come back to us!' Jerome exclaimed. 'I want you back on our side.'

'You know that isn't going to happen,' Leyton said flatly. 'I can't go back now. Not when you want to kill the people that I want to keep safe. Now, quit this bullshit and tell me what the hell you're trying to say.'

'I guess I can't be the one to kill you,' Jerome admitted.

'Oh?'

'Even with all this going on, we are friends after all,' Jerome said. 'I mean, how many times did you save me? Going against the code back then or not, you stopped me from dying. What sort of a friend would I be if I killed you? Even now. I know what my orders are and what you've done but the more I think about it, the more I can't be the one to do it.'

'So does that mean you're going to see common sense?' Leyton asked hopefully.

'I already do,' Jerome answered. 'I want you to change your mind. Come on, open your eyes! This is where you belong! You're just confused with everything that's going on. That's all. It'll all be clear when you come back. Please do what you know is right. Don't make me do this. I will have to if you don't come back to us.'

'You know I'm already on the right side of this fight. It's you that's not.'

'That's it though, you're wrong! You're not on the right side at all!' Jerome insisted. 'You're giving up the future of humanity for a few civilians. Please. I won't ask again. Take this chance. I'll make things right again with the administrator. I can't offer it again.'

Between his own thoughts and the desperate plea of his friend, Leyton felt a deep knot of regret form in his gut. Could Leyton really be offered repentance and return into the fold of the agency? Come back and do the work for the greater good of humanity without question. But was that what he wanted?

It wasn't. He'd come to the final decision that there had been too much death when it wasn't needed. A lot of the people he killed in his past had deserved it. Dictators, terrorists, and militia. There were some that never needed to die but did. Civilians though didn't need to suffer the consequences of their government's actions. He couldn't deviate from that. Knowing how people would side with him without having to be asked or coerced into siding with him was a powerful motivation and gave him strength when he needed it.

'Sorry man, I think being on this side suits me better.'

'That's a shame, you know?' Jerome said walking near the door that was wide open. 'God, I wish you were someone fucking else. It would have been a lot easier. Quick. Painless. No second thoughts.'

That triggered something in the back of Leyton's mind, like something gnawing at his head threatening to breach his skull. The door that led to the lower levels. There were no signs that it had even been hit from the other side. Glistening on the door was the dried crust of blood. The spatter was not what he'd expect from an animal mauling its prey. More like what he'd see if a blade had slashed through an unarmoured opponent.

'Hey, you know that engineer you were buddied up with to shut that door? What happened to him again?'

'He died,' Jerome stated as a matter of fact.

'I know that, but how? I don't think he died the way you told us he did.'

Jerome didn't answer for what felt like eternity. He fidgeted and paced. Avoided all eye contact until he settled in the middle of the corridor staring at the floor. It wasn't a nervous disposition. Jerome wasn't that sort of a person. He was more calculated than that. Calm. Always two steps ahead and never afraid to admit when he did something. His friend smiled. The grin evolved into a psychotic laugh that lasted only a few moments. He was losing his mind. What happened to him over the course of being stationed out in the middle of nowhere to coming on the *Galactic Passage*?

'What can I say? I needed to do it,' Jerome answered.

'Do what?'

'Kill him. You didn't really think it was one of those wolves, did you? They weren't anywhere near us. It was so easy too. I mean, come on, we're supposed to be killing these fuckers anyway. Not working with them. You really can't expect me to go behind our orders and hold their hands like we haven't got a job to do, can you? You can fuck off if you did. And you know what? It felt so good killing him. I'd sure as hell let one of those wolves take the blame to keep me in the clear but like hell I was going to let them take my fun away.'

'And your injury? If it wasn't because of the wolves.'

'All part of the act.' Jerome smirked, pulling back the bandages on his arm to reveal three claw marks running down the length of his forearm. 'I can't get away with it if I didn't suffer an injury. Needed to at least try and help the engineer. Oh, how I tried to help him. But the thing got me, and I lost my grip. There was no helping him. The best I could do was shut the door.'

'You didn't?'

Jerome grinned as he slid his knife out of its cover and admired it glistening in the dull light. Self-inflicted. The amount of pain making one of the cuts would have caused would have been enough to stop anyone from carrying out a second, let alone a third. To be that disturbed, he had to be close to psychotic if not outright insane. After so long together, Leyton was ashamed that he'd never picked it up before. More so, how was Jerome able to hide the full extent of his mental deterioration from Suttle through the psyche evaluation?

There were very few people he had ever met like that. All of whom had been serial killers, cult leaders or well-trained special forces gone bad. Each one Leyton was able to tell within moments that they were dangerous but this time he had failed to accept the signals. Had he let complacency and trust cloud his judgement on who Jerome really was? It did explain why the man was so efficient with his killing abilities and why he could manage to achieve one of the highest body counts and not need to speak to anyone about it.

Leyton had trusted this man without even considering that he could turn out this way. He really had been played like a fool.

'So where does this leave us then?' Leyton questioned begrudgingly. Closing the chapter of his friendship.

'Well, I can't kill you. I won't kill you. But it doesn't mean I won't let something else kill you,' Jerome answered.

Jerome glanced to his side. Leyton followed his eyes to the doorway. Leyton was closer to it than Jerome. He didn't wait to be the one that was reacting. Leyton charged forward and before his former friend could stop him, he reached the manual controls to seal the door. Jerome tackled him to the ground. The door was still closed. Their brawl was heavily stacked against Leyton. With the injuries he had already sustained and exhaustion setting in, Leyton took several strikes before being able to put up a fight and get back onto his feet. He quickly struck Jerome, before just as quickly disarming him of his knife. That did nothing to stop Jerome from regaining some control of the skirmish. The beating Leyton took was a good one, so much so that amidst the scuffling Leyton never realised Jerome had reclaimed his blade. When Jerome lunged at him, Leyton froze and could only watch as the blade came down, cut through the softer section of his armour where the shoulder padding met the chest plate and plunged into his flesh. It was far from the worst injury he'd ever suffered but it was still painful. His scream echoed through the empty hallways for no one else to hear.

The look in his former friend's eyes couldn't be quantified as anything but inhuman. Animalistic, even. His smile as he pulled the knife back out of his shoulder was sickening.

Leyton stumbled back, clutching at his wound until he slid down the wall he came to rest on. He wasn't dying. Just badly hurt and worn out. Leyton had been injured enough times with worse to know that much for sure. It didn't make it feel any less like he was dying though. Jerome paced from side to side in front of him, never taking his eyes away from his while putting the blade away. Leyton couldn't give up. Too much was on the line. Leyton lifted his good arm, pointing what should have been a weapon at his opponent, only to find his hand holding onto air. He must have lost it in the fight. His eyes immediately looked all around, feigning confusion to avoid arousing suspicion. It was a good distance down the hallway. Too far for a mad dash. He wasn't going to get to pull the trigger any time soon. Jerome stood in front of the bulkhead opposite him.

'You're not making this easy, you know that right?' Jerome said. A smile on his bloodied lips showed just how glad he was about it. 'God, I really wish you would have just come back to us.'

'Why does it matter?'

'You know why it matters,' Jerome hissed.

Leyton shook his head. 'It doesn't matter though, does it? I come back, I'm dead no matter what you say. The administrator will make sure of it. You're not exactly going to kill me. Seems this is my best option. At least I'm going on my terms.'

'You think? I wanted you to at least go with some dignity.'

Leyton spread his arms as wide as he could, which wasn't far and still hurt. It felt like he was ripping the flesh inside his shoulder. 'Tell me how this is letting me go with dignity.'

Jerome ignored the comment and walked over to the bulkhead lever opposite him. The mechanisms inside whined as he opened the door, leaving Leyton to look into the ever-consuming darkness on the other side of the doorway. Somewhere in there was the wolf pack, eager to feast.

There was no remorse in Jerome's expression when he managed to pull his eyes away from the opposing corridor. Only glee.

'It's lunch time!' Jerome cried down the hall. 'Come and get it! Get it while it's still hot! Here now. Over here!'

His voice carried down the dark corridor, echoing to no-one but themselves. After several minutes of silence, the response was returned.

A gust of freezing air from back on that icy planet rushed down Leyton's spine. The shrill cry of broken glass in the wind returned to haunt him.

'Nice one,' Leyton Foresc said sarcastically.

'Been a pleasure, boss,' Jerome replied, ignorant to the sarcasm.

'Do me a favour, will you?' Leyton asked.

'What's that?'

'Keep a chair warm for me in Hell.'

Jerome barked a laugh, 'Me keep you a seat warm? If you say so. See you there.'

'Yes, you will.'

Leyton watched his friend leave, his body disappearing into the shadows down the hallway while the echoes of his footsteps lingered. There was no emptiness within like he expected to feel. The emotional connection that had been there between friends wasn't there anymore. How long had Jerome not been a friend to him? It didn't really matter if he only just realised it.

The howls from the creatures carried on booming down the corridor, closer than before. He only had a few minutes before the wolves were upon him. He wanted to make sure he was as far from there as possible before they arrived.

'Agent, you there?' Beatrice asked over the comms.

'I am,' he groaned, trying to push himself up to his feet. His legs struggled to lift him.

The wound in his shoulder ached. He needed to plug it with bio-filler to stop the bleeding and start the healing process. But he was too exhausted to carry on pushing himself from the ground, and Leyton slid back down to the floor as his legs gave way. He gasped for breath. The pain of everything he had been through was finally hitting him.

'What's the situation?' the woman questioned.

'Jerome's on the run now. He's got me pretty good. I'm going to need medical if... when I get back. How're-' The cry of the wolves roared out once again, but they were closer. Much closer. How long had he been sat around for? 'Sorry, got to go.'

The sound of paws hitting the ground was rapidly approaching. He could hear their claws scratching on the floor. Some were great bounding leaps. Others were patters of smaller feet moving at twice the pace to keep up. The young pups with the adults. Probably being taken on their first proper hunt now that they had prey to go after. Or maybe they were just eager to explore with the adults.

Then they stopped. Leyton shivered in the silence. In the back of his mind, he expected there to be wolves on either side of him already.

The door was so close but seemed to be so far away. It needed to be shut to imprison the ice wolves once again. There was no way he could face off against them and win alone. He had no other choice. Leyton pushed himself back up the wall and made it to his feet with an agonising moan as he used all his strength to make it happen. He took a moment to regain composure. His head span as his body adjusted to being back on his feet.

He took a delicate step forward, only to immediately ground to a halt. Eyes as red as sparkling rubies stared at him from the bleak abyss. At least six sets of them. One of the ice wolves growled, it's cracking glass-like sound stealing his breath. Leyton edged forward a little more. If they didn't react, he could get to the hatch in less than four paces and possibly shut the door enough that only the less dangerous pups could squeeze through. They would be easier to deal with in a fight. If the wolves did react though, he wouldn't even make it halfway to the manual controls by the time they breached the threshold and escaped into the corridor. It was a risk that had to be taken. If they even looked at him wrong, he'd turn and run.

Leyton took a step forward. Nothing. They snarled at him, but they didn't budge. He took a deep breath. Another step. Still no movement. If he could get one more, that would be enough. As he took his final step, they snapped and hurtled toward him. The barks, howls and cries were a monstrous symphony vocalising their urge to hunt. Unable to stomach charging the last couple steps Leyton turned and sprinted away with the remnants of his strength, sliding briefly to pick up his sub-machine gun before rushing for the nearest exit sparing only the quickest of glances over his shoulder. There were seven of them. Three adults, or at least what he assumed were adults by their larger stature and more pronounced facial features, and four pups. Only weeks old and they were already as large as most medium sized dogs but with an attitude like the adults.

'Guys give me some good news because I've got some bad news!' Leyton pleaded over the comms.

'What sort of bad news?' Duke asked.

'They're out. The fucker got me and released them. I couldn't shut the door.'

Leyton had no idea who spoke and who didn't. The overwhelming outcry and cursing over the comms merely reflected how he would feel if he had the time to safely comprehend what had gone on.

'Where are you?' Beatrice questioned. 'How close are the wolves to you?'

'Up shit creek and about to feel what it's like to lose a leg,' he replied. Leyton turned and fired a burst of rounds at the closest of the creatures. The pups were far behind the adults now but still in sight. 'Let me worry about the wolves. Give me the good news.'

Leyton wheeled round the corner, down the hallway and up a flight of stairs. Every doorway he went through remained open; he didn't even have the seconds needed to secure them in place. The most he could do was slap the door controls and pray that some of them were still powered. Those that were still functioning slowly slid shut. Some never closed. Others only part closed.

'We're still holding at the last line,' Duke explained. 'We're five people down. They'll have lost just as many if not more. But they're not getting any closer. Looks like their numbers are thinning. Think they're regrouping.'

'Well, that's something,' he gasped.

'And the captain took a bullet. She's back on the bridge,' the sergeant added.

'You okay, Cap?' Leyton gasped.

'You focus on you right now, okay?' she replied. 'You're the one with those things after you. What's your position?'

He had no idea. He looked around, scanning every wall and every door for a sign. He passed one and immediately relayed the location to the officer. With a deep breath, Beatrice guided him down the corridors to safety. The wolves came closer, catching up to him with ease on the straights. The scratching on the floor was as haunting as a shadow. Always there and never wavering. Upon the final instruction, Leyton took a sharp right turn, tumbling as he shifted trajectory in a single whiplash inducing motion. The beasts were only set back by a few fleeting seconds. It was all he needed. There was a maintenance hatch further ahead. If Leyton could make it with time to spare, there was a chance he would survive.

Leyton fired off one last extended burst, forcing the creatures back just long enough to make his final move. He unlocked the hatch, pulled it open and barely closed it by the time the snapping jaws of death inadvertently barricaded him inside his sanctum. He sealed the hatch and paused as the banging continued against the bulkhead. His breath was shaky. He could feel his sweat inside the armour. Adrenaline was streaming through his veins a million gallons per second. His head was light with blood loss.

But he had survived. He managed to outrun the wolves and get to safety. Joyful celebrations though were not permitted. He had bundled his way out of the corridor to his new position only to seal the one entranceway out of the dozens he passed. The wolves now had a free range of the ship.

'I'm safe guys,' he quietly stated everyone over the comms. 'Thanks for the save.'

'That's okay,' Beatrice said. 'But we have a problem.'

'What is it?' Leyton asked, wheezing between words. 'Not that we don't have one already down here.'

The commotion of the beasts trying to gnaw their way through thick, space-worthy metal was admirable, futile and still concerning. He climbed up the rungs of the ladder in the maintenance shaft to the next deck.

'Things have really died down here,' Duke explained. 'The new guys have just disappeared. We don't get it. Why have everyone fall back when you've got the advantage? You'd at least leave a few people behind to keep an eye on things.'

'I bet the fucker Jerome has told them what he's done,' Leyton suggested. 'They'll be regrouping to decide if they finish us off or make it easy for the wolves.'

'Or they've found an alternate route around the defences,' Beatrice added. 'Either way the evacuation process is fully underway. We've already filled and launched two lifeboats from first class with another four nearly ready to follow.'

A muffled roar from the creatures below echoed up the shaft, reverberating in Leyton's ears, before dying off. They had given up for now, or so Leyton hoped. He hoisted himself out of the maintenance shaft. With those things on the loose, the further he could get from them the better chance he had of survival.

'Where do you need me?' he asked them. 'Right now, I'm just hanging around, you know, not doing anything.'

'Get up to the bridge,' Beatrice instructed. 'I want to try to formulate a counterattack against the soldiers or at least have a worthwhile defence and I need your help. You know how Jerome was trained. I might not be able to predict the wolves and their movements, but you have a chance of being able to predict what the agents will do next. That should give us one less thing to think about. And if the agents and these new soldiers are working together, it'll make things a bit easier for us.'

'Got it. Have some filler ready for me, will you? What about you Sergeant? What's your plan?'

'I'm holding the line. I've just spread what resources we have left as far as I dare,' he replied. 'Not all of us get to have a breather. So much for an easy job before retirement.'

Leyton sighed and let his head rest against a wall. That was exactly why he betrayed his former employer. People like Duke deserved a chance to live, to see another sunrise in atmosphere, taste the sweet flavours of liquor and to feel the touch of a lover, one night a week while a wallet lasted or every night for the promise of an eternity. This was his chance to put it right. He would get those civilians out of there. As many as physically possible. They were never to be a part of this. Then he would make sure Duke and his crew, and his own people, got off that ship too. Even if that meant Leyton needed to stay behind to ensure it. That way he would at least be able to know his conscience was a little cleaner before death.

'Pay your debts to Death,' Leyton instructed Duke.

'And Death will watch you until the time is right,' Duke finished.

It was an old saying, one that rarely spoken any more under the United Planetary Nations, but its meaning was simple and highly respected by those that knew it. If he who faced death accepted it and knew no fear, they would only die when they were supposed to. Not a moment too early. Not a moment later. And the fact that Duke finished the saying showed the respect for him was mutual in return.

Leyton finished the comm link and made his way up the shaft to the next deck to return to the bridge. He could hear the screams of civilians in panic somewhere in the distance as they struggled to come to terms with the evacuation process. It was going to be a long day before he could rest.

Chapter 11
16/11/2675
13:11 Earth Standard Time

Beatrice Lenoia

Red lights flashed ominously every thirty seconds, followed by the sharp automated announcement that an evacuation was in progress. So many drills had been run while berthed for such an event with her well-trained crew. Each session had been nothing short of textbook, as would be expected at the time in perfect conditions. Everyone behaved in those moments exactly as the manuals said they should do so that the evacuations were smooth.

This, however, was not a routine drill, and everyone was exhausted. They were demoralised and grieving. This was as far from a textbook situation as they could be. Most were not even trying to keep order or control amongst the passengers. Others were in floods of tears, begging their supervisors for a place on the next lifeboat. Some took the position of authority they held one step too far, being heavy handed with their methods of containing the civilians. It was a small insight to how fragile human society was when things stopped going to plan.

Looking at the security cameras that still functioned, people were clambering over anyone and anything that stood in the way of their bid for freedom. The limited crew they had available was overstretched, unable to control the flow of people. She tried her best. Ultimately though Beatrice was fighting a losing battle. After the first few successful launches, people started to barge and shove their way onto a lifeboat before it departed. It was chaos. No one listened to the instructions being given. After the first few overcrowded lifeboats were filled well beyond safe maximum capacity, she changed tactic. Beatrice took control. Since they couldn't be trusted on their own, she had all the passengers moved to the galley with the security team where they would have greater control over the flow of people with the number of crew she had at hand. That way they would then be able to choose how many left and made the journey to a lifeboat with an escort at a time. It made sure the lifeboats weren't crowded, offering the best chances of survival.

Within three hours she had sent another nine boats successfully loaded with civilians. It should have been more; it needed to be more. There were another twenty-nine boats on the liner for the passengers and crew to use. About sixteen of those though were in areas no longer under her control or too far from the galley to be a possible option. She needed to accept the worst-case scenario that there would be a sizeable number of passengers and crew who were not making it off the *Galactic Passage*.

The good news stopped there. In that time, there had been another two extended attacks against them. One by the agent separatists. The other by the new arrivals that boarded them. In both attacks, they had not reacted fast enough. Dozens of civilians were slaughtered. Men, women and children. No exceptions were made. She had reassigned Leyton to join Duke and their teams. They fought valiantly against the enemy to save as many of the civilians as they could. It lessened the blow, but the damage was done. The first passenger deaths took an immediate toll on her. They were completely innocent and didn't deserve to die.

'How many passengers have we saved?' she asked remorsefully.

'Hard to tell after that first scramble,' Franklin Hender answered over the comms. He was down in the galley maintaining command at the front for her with Security Chief Henendez. 'But at a guess, I'd say we've saved about one-fifty so far. Give or take.'

Approximately one hundred and fifty. That left hundreds more to be evacuated. After all the deaths, that number was impossible to assume. Beatrice didn't like the odds. She fought to remind herself that any quantity of evacuees was better than none.

'Next load?'

'Out in five,' he answered.

Beatrice pursed her lips ready to respond when her command table dimmed a deep red and security footage took priority over everything else. A group of eight ice wolves, five adults and three large pups, were prowling through the corridors toward their habited space. They must have been attracted by the commotion of panicked families. The wolves were heading straight for the galley. She barely had a half-dozen people in there. None of them wore anything more than a bullet proof vest, and none had training to handle the weapons they carried. Everyone else with military experience was engaged with the wolves elsewhere or were facing off against the hostile forces. To make matters worse, there were several doors wide open that couldn't be closed in time. With help too far away, they would all be slaughtered before they even had a chance to try escape.

'Oh God,' she whispered, immediately clutching at her mouth wishing she'd held her words.

'What is it?' Hender questioned. His eyes flitted up at the nearest camera.

Beatrice couldn't lie – could she? On one hand, she could tell the man what was going on and be completely honest with him, so he had a chance to prepare his team for what was round the corner. Alternatively, if she lied, they might not suffer until the last possible second. She could save them the mental torture of knowing the end was coming, knowing that they may not survive, until the last possible second. Would she like that? Would she appreciate the information being withheld from her? She knew how betrayed she'd feel to know that the powers above knew her death was imminent. If no one was kind enough to warn her.

'Captain?' Adjutant Hender's voice was stern and filled with fraught.

'You've got eight wolves on their way,' she weakly admitted. 'They're coming down the aft corridor straight for you.'

His response wasn't one of fear, or even one of anger. Regret and sorrow filled his tone as he replied to her, 'That's not good. What are we doing about the passengers?'

'We can't leave them in the galley waiting to die,' she sobbed. There was nothing she could do or say to make the situation better. It was her adjutant's life that was at stake, not hers. She couldn't decide how he died. She had no right. 'You and Henendez have my permission to do whatever you deem necessary from here.'

Franklin sighed. 'Understood. Evac crew, get ready. You'll have a fuck-load of shit scared passengers hitting you any time soon. The galley's been compromised.'

'What will you do?' Beatrice asked her second in command, her voice taking priority over any other replies he was receiving.

'The same thing you'd do. Whatever I can to buy these poor bastards some time.'

She listened and watched woefully as Hender and Henendez both directed traffic. They carefully positioned half the team around the aft entrance, while the rest scattered themselves around the rest of the hall. No one suspected a thing. To the civilians, they were simply rearranging themselves. Each one had a position to cause some distraction that would draw the wolves away from the civilians, even if only for a couple of seconds. In the end, seconds decided if someone drew another breath.

Franklin Hender glanced up at the nearest security camera. The smile on his face was a mask to hide a man not ready to die but trying his absolute best to come to terms with it. The signs of a man who could have had a command of his own. He would have made an amazing captain.

'ETA?' he asked.

'If they don't speed up, they'll be with you in a couple minutes.'

'Right. Well Captain, it's been a pleasure and an honour to be under your command.'

'The pleasure is all mine,' she replied. Beatrice was glad that he couldn't see the tears that ran down her cheeks. If she had listened to him from the start, would the wolves have been released? Would they have been under attack like this? Would Franklin still be about to die? 'I couldn't have asked for anyone better by my side.'

He gave her a nod through the security feeds. It was like watching events in slow motion. The pack methodically progressed through the corridors, each one sniffing at the air for the faintest scent and reacting to every sound. When they were just a breath away, animal instinct must have taken over. The pack held off just outside the galley for just a few moments, long enough for her to warn her crew of their position before they charged through the open doors. It was almost too quick to comprehend. The guards managed to let off dozens of shots, but it wasn't enough. Three of them were slaughtered where they stood. The wolves were killing indiscriminately. If it moved, breathed or locked eyes with them, they went for it. Hender managed to fall back far enough to give the order to open the doors separating them from the lifeboats and let the civilians flee. Not a breath later, a wolf took his life as he put himself between it and a child that had been the intended target.

Beatrice looked away and closed her eyes tightly. She couldn't watch the bloodshed. There were some things she had to observe as a leader, but that was not one of them. Her heart was already broken, and to resume watching the carnage would shatter what was left of it.

A new red light appeared above the command table. Beatrice looked to the new alert and immediately regretted her actions. The creatures had formulated a plan of their own. They had a small detachment go unnoticed through the corridors until they were in the direct path of everyone fleeing the galley. Somehow, they had managed to set up a pincer movement. Beatrice was powerless to do or say anything that would save them or stop them from running toward the threat. As the beasts ploughed through the panicked civilians, taking lives with devilish ease, the survivors scattered to find somewhere safe to hide in the ship or try make it to the lifeboats.

'Oh God no,' she whispered.

'What's happening?' Leyton asked, returning to the command deck.

She had almost completely forgotten that the agent was to come back to the bridge. After helping with the counterattacks to the strikes carried out by the hostile soldiers, he was instructed to return so he could offer tactical oversight to best predict the next move the loyalist agents and the companions would make. The problem was that they had now disappeared. They would have been in a blind spot where the ship's security cameras had been taken out. By the time they knew where the enemy forces were, it would be too late to react.

'Take a look,' Beatrice choked, struggling to get the words out.

'Shit,' Leyton hissed, taking over controls at the chair and turning away from the feed. 'I'm sorry about that. Are you holding up okay?'

'I've just watched my friend die,' she snapped. 'What do you think?'

'Sorry I asked,' the agent said.

'No,' she said with a heavy breath, regretting how she spoke to him. 'I'm sorry. Been a long time since I've seen anyone get killed. But... I've never seen anyone just... mauled to death before.'

'I hadn't either until I had this assignment,' Leyton confided.

The comms cracked into life. Allua Jons spoke. Her voice rushed and filled with panic. 'Captain, I have the engine stabilised. But I need help.' A gunshot cracked out, Allua Jons screamed, and then more gunshots followed. 'Shit! Captain, they're here. I need someone here. Now! Please! We won't last long.'

Beatrice pulled back control of the security feed and went straight to the engine room. The hostiles had surrounded the crew in there; some were already dead. Their bodies limp where they fell trying to flee from the danger. Everyone else was taking cover and hiding.

'I'm on it, find somewhere safe and take cover. Okay? We're going to get you out of there.'

'Please, hurry!' Engineer Jons pleaded. 'Please.'

'We will, just take cover,' Beatrice insisted. She turned to the agent. 'How soon can you get there?'

'I'll be there in no time,' Leyton Foresc replied. 'I'll liaise with Duke along the way.'

'Thank you. Go,' she ordered.

As the agent turned and sprinted from the bridge, she hung her head solemnly. Her engineer, a woman she respected as being more than a colleague, a subordinate, but as a friend, was now in danger. She couldn't lose someone else. Then it hit home that they were all in danger. That none of them were exempt. Death was indiscriminate with who it chose.

She turned to her crew. Each of them looked to her. Each wore similar expressions. They were sheep, and she the shepherd. They needed herding.

'What about us? What do we do now?' Laurenne Vellai eventually asked, realising that the next ones to need help would be them.

'Someone bring me up a map of where we are exactly in the system,' Beatrice explained.

The next instant, the local space shone over her from the holographic display. Empty. The area was devoid of anything except for their ships. The map zoomed out a couple dozen million kilometres. Two planets in close geosynchronous orbit with each other. A deadly dance, doomed to one day end in destructive collision to smash the planets apart. Any life left on them would cease to exist. Then, something else caught her eye. A dark and light side to each planet. It was faint but it was there. She had the map pulled back by another several dozen million kilometres. A star. A dying star at that, but still a cosmic vessel more powerful than anything humankind had ever created.

'What are you looking for Captain?' Laurenne asked.

'A way to make sure no one finds this ship and those things ever again if we can't win here,' she explained. 'If we don't, and they win, then those agents will just bring the wolves back to Earth. The cycle will start again, and others will have to die. That star will destroy every molecule of this ship and everything on it. Stops them in their tracks there and then.'

Someone let out a whimper. 'Does that mean...'

'Yes,' Beatrice answered sharply, sorrowfully. She refused to let that question be finished. 'It would mean those of us still on board will not see home again. I hope that we do not need to do this, that the sergeant and agent are able to find a way to kill those things and can take out as many of them as possible. But if they can't. If we lose too many people. If the other agents and those soldiers can take control of the situation.

Then they will win. We can't let that happen. Our duty demands it. I understand that this is not what any of you ever thought would be asked of you. For those of you who do not want to be here, if any of you want the chance to get off the ship, please make it known now. I will arrange for you to be escorted to the nearest lifeboat. I will not judge you because what I'm asking is not easy. Before you decide, remember that this is a last resort. I hope that we don't need it but if we do, we need to be prepared to take it. If you don't leave now, there is no turning back.'

Most of the crew made themselves heard. It stung that they wanted to leave, when they were needed most, but it was understandable. Self-preservation was the most basic of instincts and could easily prevail in desperate times. She arranged for a member of the security team to lead them away. With the bridge now down to just a handful of the key crew remaining the officer felt the threat of failure hanging over her.

To stop any more being tempted to join their comrades, she needed to say something. Beatrice racked her mind a million times over in a nano-second trying to figure out what she needed to say. She looked to all the famous leaders of history from the early modern era to the ancient world and to those from within her own lifetime. Of the myriad of things to tell them, none of the potential speeches quite sufficed.

She silently parted her lips, a tear rolled down her cheek and then words just flowed out without any input from her mind. It all came from her heart. 'Thank you for staying. All of you. I know it isn't the easiest decision you have had to make, and I know it's a terrifying one that no one wants to make. But I promise to exhaust all resources at my disposal to take any other option than to go headfirst into that star.' She pointed at the hologram that still hung in the middle of the bridge as an eerie reminder. 'I don't want to do that. I have just as much to lose as you do. I have a family waiting for me too. There will surely be people on here that won't choose to remain and are still here because they haven't had a chance to speak or get out. And there are many more that have already lost everything. Who will only leave an empty coffin for their families back home. This has got to be our contingency plan should all else fail. We have to stay strong that the sergeant and agent will find another way.'

'Glad to see you've thought one up. Contingencies are always good. Be a bit stupid to put all your bets on one horse.'

Knoxx had disappeared from her presence for several minutes. His words before parting were that he had something that he needed to grab. She took it as a secret message that he was jumping ship, and she held

369

no hope of his return. Beatrice was happy to see him come back. The guard wore military grade armour, most likely retained after his service on Mars and smuggled onboard with his personal items. More strikingly, he looked as calm as Duke did. Knoxx stood proudly in the doorway.

'Guard,' she said. 'Welcome back. Thought you wasn't going to come back for a moment there.'

He chuckled as he walked over. 'I can see how that came across. No honour abandoning my post. I didn't do it before. Wouldn't do it now. Especially while I've got the kit I need to do something useful.'

'Thank you,' Beatrice replied.

'No problem,' Knoxx said. 'So, we'll get a great suntan if everything goes wrong?'

'I guess so,' she replied remorsefully.

'Like you said though, hopefully it doesn't come to that. What do you need me to do?'

Beatrice smiled. With both the agent and sergeant out saving her crew in the engine room, she suddenly felt safer and less exposed to have someone with a background in combat, in defending a location effectively, back by her side.

'I need as many eyes as possible to monitor the situation. As you can see,' she said gesturing to the now all but emptied bridge, 'I'm picking up a few more jobs than I've had to for a long time. My hands are going to be a bit full.'

'Understood. Are the cameras diverted here?'

'They are,' Beatrice nodded.

'Good, I'll keep my eyes on them. If I see anything you need to know about, I'll shout out. If you don't hear from me, it's because it isn't a problem. Yet. You just focus on everything else.'

'Thank you,' she replied.

'Does the sergeant know about this?' Knoxx asked. 'Your idea?'

'He doesn't. Provided everything goes to plan, he'll never need to know about it,' Beatrice answered. 'Is that all?'

'Yes, Captain.'

It had to be all. She couldn't keep her cool to answer any more questions like that while trying to take on the duties of the missing key crew. There was too much to do. She glided from station to station, hoping to find some good news. Something good had to be out there.

Leyton Foresc

Leyton had quickly linked up with an understandably concerned Duke. He had to wonder what was going on the soldier's mind. Had Leyton had partners before? Yes, he had a couple ex-wives. They weren't exes because of foul play or infidelity. Those relationships ended because he couldn't be trusted. His partners had known about the nature of his work. Being so secret with his life left his exes wondering what else was being kept secret. They had been unable to trust him even when he was speaking honestly. But they had never been in danger before. Part of the reason why he didn't want a relationship any more was to avoid repeating the cycle of distrust in his loyalty to the relationship. Duke however had found a love interest that he had never had time for in his career. There was a fire raging within him. Duke never said a word. His eyes were focused on reaching the engine room. Not even the cries from others around the *Galactic Passage* could stop him from reaching his objective.

The battle was fully underway in the engine room by the time they reached it. Gun shots were being let off non-stop. There were screams of pain and fear. Leyton wondered how many had been lost while they were running the length of the ship.

'What's the plan?' Leyton asked the sergeant.

'I'll take the high ground,' Duke answered sharply. 'You take the low ground. Take your shots, move and take your shots again. Make them think that there are more of us than there are. If you get a chance to pull anyone out of there, do it. Don't waste time trying to round them up. Any survivors are better than no survivors.'

'Got it,' Leyton replied, and he carried on forward as the sergeant broke away.

He clung to the walls as he came closer to the engine room and peered inside. The battlefield that had once been a key room to the functioning of the ship was one that he didn't expect to encounter. A wrong move and everyone died. The assailants would achieve nothing. There were engineers and security alike laying where they fell. As expected, not a single body from the attackers. These guys were too good for the crew to be an issue. The squad of the hostile soldiers was easily located from his angle. Five were on the lower levels, six above on the gangways that ran across from one side of the engine room to the other with an aerial. In the distance, under the eerie glow of the light-drive core, was a small two-man security team and a few engineers cowering behind a workstation and several equipment lockers.

'Sergeant, you in position?'

'Just about,' Duke replied. 'You want to kick start this or do you want me to?'

'I've got it,' Leyton said.

Leyton took aim, and within a second fired off enough rounds to drop one of the attackers to a knee then finished them off with a second volley into the back of the skull. The four remaining soldiers on ground level immediately turned on their heels and took aim, as Leyton pushed forward to take cover behind what looked like a control board. Bullets ricocheted off the console as the enemy soldiers tried to stop him. Each bullet was shot with the intention of keeping him pinned down while someone pushed around to have a better position to take him out from. As the rounds kept slamming into his position, the secondary attack unleashed on the gangways above him. His assailants stopped in their tracks momentarily as they realised there was a second front to battle against.

That was his chance. With them distracted, Leyton quickly shifted position, moving behind the pipework to the port side of the engine room. Circumnavigating the forest of metal pipes as the enemy pursued him was not a simple task. What looked like an opening only led to a thicket of thinner pipes. The only sounds made by his pursuers was their footsteps. No voices, maybe keeping their comms private or not speaking at all. Leyton crouched behind some piping and waited. One set of steps approaching was too close for comfort. He came out of cover and took out another one of the soldiers in a short, controlled burst of fire that went through their visor. There were only two hostiles in pursuit of him now. The fifth on his level had to still be occupied with the guards and engineers he was trying to rescue. To make matters worse he couldn't actually see where the crew was any more nor did he know what the best route to take to them would be.

'Shit, I'm cut off from them,' Leyton said over the comms. 'Duke, how're you coping up there?'

'One down,' Duke answered. 'I'm pretty sure I've taken out another but couldn't tell you for certain.'

With no hope of any assistance, he had to figure this one out on his own. Leyton glanced around his cover. Still no sign of the third attacker. Without any time to waste, Leyton sprinted out of cover, dashed over and around the pipework to avoid the oncoming bullets and over to where he remembered the survivor's position to be. He located them and pushed the soldier he never had visual on back. A quick reload and he too took cover with the crew.

Only one guard remained and three of the engineers were still alive, all covered in blood that wasn't their own. He could only imagine how they had to be coping with what was going on around them. Everyone had their limits and the crew had been going through a lot for too long. It would soon be over at least.

'Jons?' he said to the engineer.

'Yes?' she replied.

'Good,' he risked a comm link with the sergeant. 'Duke, I got to the survivors. She's with them.'

'Thank fuck. Great news. Get ready to make a move. I'll make my way down to you in a moment. Just got something to sort out first.'

'What's going on?'

'I don't think they were here for the crew. It looks like they've got their own plans and that the crew stationed down here were just in the way,' Duke stated.

That didn't sound good. 'What the hell does that mean?'

'They're setting up a bomb,' Duke explained. 'Think they're trying to not leave any evidence.'

Leyton looked to the upper balcony. The remaining hostiles had Duke pinned down. One was over the other side of the engine room by the jump drive setting up the explosive. It wasn't complete yet. There was no way that the sergeant could fight through them, disarm the bomb, and get out of there to regroup with them. He couldn't wait for him. Chances were that the sergeant wasn't going to make it. Leyton needed to come up with a plan B.

'I'll try and hold the fort, just don't get yourself killed,' Leyton replied. He turned his attention back to the survivors. 'Listen up guys, me and the sergeant are here to get you out of here. The big guy up top's going to make his way to us, but I don't want to hang around waiting. I need you lot to stay down while I think up an exit plan. You,' Leyton glanced at the name tag on the security guard's uniform, 'Martins, how much ammo you got?'

'Last clip,' the guard answered.

'Okay, you stay behind the engineers and... Get down!' Leyton barked.

One of the enemy soldiers attacked them and was immediately pushed back. They had taken advantage while Leyton was discussing the situation with Duke. The guard opened fire behind him at another soldier that tried to flank them. Leyton reacted in time to watch Allua Jons slam a wrench through the hostile's visor. No wonder it hurt him so much when she struck him, if she could do that to the reinforced glass. Had the angle been a little more precise at the time, it could have been his face kissing metal. Leyton finished them off with a blast to the face.

'Nice arm,' he said.

'A girl's got to look after herself out here, y'know?' she said with a shrug.

'You can say that again,' Leyton chuckled.

It was easy to see why the sergeant liked her. But that was a lucky strike; there were still two more enemies to deal with on his level, and by the sounds of it, the guard had less than half a clip of ammunition remaining after that assault. When the next attack happened, someone would be dead. Leyton was determined to make sure it didn't come to that. The agent scanned the scene for their exit and spotted the way out. It was an almost clear run, with a few obstacles in the way, but if they kept a good pace, they could make it. All he had to do was keep his head on a swivel for the soldiers. The ship's crew wouldn't be thinking about that.

Above them, the sergeant pushed along the gangway toward the jump drive. The enemy soldiers were still huddled around the explosive and positioned at various points between Duke and the engine. He wasn't even close to reaching it and without any help probably wouldn't. Leyton reloaded and fired an entire magazine into the enemy soldiers from below. The distraction was enough to push a couple of them out of hiding for the sergeant to handle. Leyton swapped out magazines and turned to the survivors.

'Right, let's make a move for that exit over there,' Leyton said. 'We're not sticking around for the sergeant. Duke, we're getting out of here. We can't hold this position against another attack.'

'Got it,' Duke said. 'I'll be with you soon, nearly there now. Thanks for the assist.'

The fighting overhead intensified as Duke pushed forward. He cried out when he successfully took the priming mechanism from the enemy, ensuring the explosive couldn't be detonated. Duke then started to make his way down to their deck. Screams of confusion and anger roared out as the enemy soldiers realised what was going on and tried to stop him. Duke might have had a chance at getting down to them, but Leyton couldn't take the risk and hang around though. Four lives couldn't be put in harm's way for something that might not even happen.

'Let's go,' Leyton instructed.

Leyton leapt from cover and immediately caught sight of one of the soldiers. He opened fire, buying the survivors valuable time to break for the exit. The hostile fell back, their arms splayed, and visor annihilated by the repeated impact of bullets. A shrill cry erupted. The remaining soldier on the lower level made another assault on them now that they were on the move. The guard let off several rounds in self-defence until his weapon clicked empty. He fell to the ground clinging to his arm. Injured, not dead. The engineers took him to safety.

Leyton looked up in time to see the sergeant battling it out with the enemy force. Their fire and counterfire methods were amusing. All the enemy soldiers needed to do was attack all at once when Duke tried to counter them. Leyton let off a few precision bursts of fire to take attention away from the sergeant.

With an opportunity to escape, Duke bounded down from the balcony by sliding down one of the pipes to their level, leaving the remainder of the enemy soldiers behind. Together, the paid of them fought off the attackers for as long as possible. Eventually their combined efforts managed to take down a few more enemy soldiers. By now though they were running out of ammunition and couldn't keep up the fight for much longer.

'Get her out of here,' Leyton instructed. 'I'll cover you.'

'Got it,' Duke said. 'Don't take too long.'

'I won't.'

Duke ran over to the survivors, helping guide them to the exit. Leyton fell into line after them after finishing his magazine and reloading, drawing the hostile fire toward him. The remaining three hostiles carried on firing, hoping for a lucky kill to make up for their own losses. There was a pained scream and a desperate outcry from the sergeant. Leyton tried to ignore it. He couldn't allow it to distract him. Leyton fired several more rounds into the enemy before turning to join the others outside the engine room.

Upon Leyton's return to them, the group pushed deeper into the corridors before coming to a halt to tend to injuries when the noise of gunshots faded into nothing. They did it. The numbers weren't what Leyton had hoped for, but together they had been able to save four of them. It was better than none.

Allua Jons had taken a shot to the gut and was applying pressure to it to stop the bleeding. It was nasty to look at, but she was okay. They just needed to bandage the injury and keep the pressure until Suttle could address it. The guard with an injured shoulder had already strapped the wound. The others managed to make it out without much more than a couple bad grazes. Duke just stood there with a smile that seemed to glisten behind his helmet visor as it reflected the light above them.

'How'd you get on with the bomb?' Leyton asked.

The smile on the sergeant's face sharply turned into a grin as he held up a black and yellow cylindrical object. 'They're not doing anything without this. Tell you what though, they're tough sons of bitches.'

'You're not kidding, I've never seen anything like it before,' Leyton said. 'Don't think they've had much training though. Couldn't hit shit when they had the advantage. Clearly not done much time on the range. That didn't stop them though. Anyway, you have something important to do before we head back to the bridge.'

'What do you mean?'

Leyton rolled his eyes and simply gestured away and over to Allua Jons. Duke understood the meaning instantly, nodded and walked over to her. Leyton left them to it. There was no way to know what they would be talking about for the next few seconds. Probably not much, considering they had just survived a deadly fight. For them to spend some time together before they had to leave, while emotions were high, would be good for them. He couldn't explain why, just that it was right for them to have that time.

Leyton had a moment of being lost in himself where he reflected on everything that had happened since leaving the ice planet, and the journey he had taken. He did not regret a single decision. Everything led to where he was now. All the lives that were being saved were because he discovered who he needed to be at the right time, not who he was expected to be. A feeling of pride filled him. He was happy with his choices and the path he was now on.

Movement caught his eye, tearing his attention away from his thoughts. It looked like a shadow, dashing across the hallway back where they came from. His grip tightened around his weapon. His muscles tensed. Leyton was sure that he wasn't seeing things. The glint of a muzzle poking round from cover and he knew that there was no trick being played on the mind. The enemy had gone completely against what training would have suggested they would do and pressed the attack instead of retreating to regroup after significantly diminished numbers. The first of the remaining soldiers stepped out from behind a corner. Then the others came forward into view.

'Everyone down!' Leyton cried.

There was no way for him to see during the chaos of the surprise attack what unfolded behind him as he took out one of their attackers and injured a second. Duke turned to join him only to be tackled to the ground by Allua Jons as the third attacker turned their attention on him. Allua, in her desperately valiant act, took several deadly rounds to the torso. The guard avoided further injury but in an equally courageous act used his own body as a shield to protect the closest of the other engineers. Leyton charged after the surviving soldiers until they were out of visual, making sure that this time they really were gone. He returned to a sight of mourning.

Duke held Allua Jons in his arms. Without immediate help she was done for, and she knew it. He could see it in her face. She looked up at Duke. Too weak to talk. Injuries too much for her to hold onto life for much longer with. Allua reached up with a bloody hand, wanting to touch the sergeant's cheek but getting stopped by his visor. She placed the hand on his chest while Duke held her other hand tightly. They shared a silent moment together. Quite possibly sharing an intimate eternity that only the two of them would understand. Telling each other all the things it would take a lifetime to do. And then it was over. Her body fell limp and lifeless. Her head rolled back in a single jerk. After a second or two the sergeant's shoulders began to heave as he fought back silent tears.

'Duke,' he whispered. 'I'm so sorry.'

The sergeant held up a finger, menace behind every inflection telling him to remain quiet. He refused to let her out of his arms.

'Hey,' Leyton said, batting the finger aside. 'We've got to go. It isn't safe.'

'Not a word,' Duke hissed. His breath rattled with anger. 'Just give me this.'

'I can't. Not yet,' Leyton replied remorsefully. 'I'm sorry. We have to get out of here. You know that.'

'You can get out of here,' the sergeant snarled. 'I've got something I need to do first.'

Without a second word the sergeant delicately placed the engineer on the floor, briefly rest a hand carefully on her cheek as a sign of remorse after closing her eyelids then darted off down the corridor after the enemy that fled.

'Fuck. Captain, we've got a situation,' Leyton sighed over the comms. 'We've secured the engine room but... We've got casualties... Jons is one of them. We only have three left.'

'Oh god, please tell me it was painless?' Beatrice pleaded. The pain in her voice reminiscent of what Leyton heard in Duke's.

'I can't,' he said softly. 'But I've got worse news. Duke's on the war path now.'

'Is there anything you can do to stop him?'

The image of Duke storming off replayed itself in his mind's eye. The look of determination. The need to exact revenge. Leyton shook his head. 'Not a chance. All I can do is make sure he doesn't get himself killed and stay with him until he calms down.'

'Do it,' Beatrice ordered. 'Have the survivors go to the nearest escape pod. I've got eyes on you now.' Her voice stammered as she must have seen the body of Allua Jons and the carnage from within the engine room. 'I'll re-route assistance to your position.'

'By assistance, do you mean ...?'

'You'll get the big guy,' she answered, affirming his thoughts and hopes. 'I trust that'll be all you need?'

'That'll do just nicely. Out.'

Duke Horren

How could they do that? How could they kill her? And why did Allua have to sacrifice herself like that to save him? Their connection was deeper than he had realised, something forged in the flames of emotion that burned hotter than anything he knew of. Sure, they didn't know each other that well, and hadn't done more than talk and share deep conversation with each other. But that was the point. There was so much more that they had to do, that they needed to experience. Now he would never have the chance to go experience the things people should be able to enjoy after getting to know each other. He'd have to go on wondering what the highs would be, guessing how he'd handle the lows and the joys of everything in-between.

She was still there with him. Haunting him with her gentle touch. Her grit to hold on until the last moment. Allua's voice was soft. Weak. But she spoke to him, telling him that he was the best thing to happen to her since she came on board the *Passage*. Duke had set the HUD on his visor to pick up her vitals. He watched them failing and watched her die in his arms.

They would pay for it. He would make sure of it. As many of their lives as he could take couldn't possibly be enough to compensate for her life. It would be a good start though. They would start to understand what he was feeling by the time he was done, when he had their bodies stacked to the next deck. None of them would survive.

Duke stalked his prey through the corridors of the *Galactic Passage*. Where once caution would have told him to stop and check all corners and doors, anger and fury told him it was going to be okay if he walked by. That nothing would be waiting for him. It was like the severe intoxication of alcohol, the rage that filled him taking away all his inhibitions. all self-control and common sense. The proverbial red mist was fully in control of his actions. Shamefully, he was glad that it was. That way morality wouldn't stop him from doing exactly what needed to be done or allow him to show mercy where none was deserved.

Footsteps continued to rush ahead of him. Eager to get somewhere like phantom boots pounding the metal floor with no visible owner repeating the noise for the rest of eternity. But they were slowing down. Intentionally. They were where they needed to be. Where was that though? Was this where they had docked with the *Galactic Passage*? He had lost track of where he was on the ship now and there was no signage nearby for him to gain his bearings. Wherever the enemy soldiers were was exactly where Duke needed to be.

Duke slowed his pace down in turn to avoid being heard. He needed to retain the element of surprise if he were to take out a large enough number of them. Duke peered around the corner and could see a large collection of hostile soldiers gathered down the corridor. The administrator must have sent an entire platoon after them judging by the numbers that had been encountered before. There were about a dozen of them in the open. Some were clearly posted there standing guard. Others were loosely gathered as if they just arrived. One though stood out. This individual was much taller than the others, standing at least a head over them. They didn't wear the universal matt-black armour that the others had. This one wore grey armour with gold trim around the helmet, with a visor that gave a demonic aura to the person's presence. He must have been the commander of the unit. Not exactly covert with hiding leadership but with their fighting methods it may not have been much of a concern.

The two survivors from the attack in the engine room were talking to their commander. Most likely debriefing on the events in the engine room. He knew they told their leader they failed with setting the bomb when they were struck down with sharp strikes to the gut. One even took a knee from the pain inflicted. The pair staggered back to their feet, standing to attention once more as if nothing happened. Either their commander wasn't as strong as they were, or they could fight through the pain a little too easily.

This was it. The soldiers were distracted. Now was the time to strike; there was no better opportunity. He took the grenade he borrowed from Beatrice back when the assault first had started, before she had to retreat, primed it and rolled it along the corridor. One of the soldiers cried out at it and leapt onto the explosive, absorbing most of the detonation. Their body was ripped apart. Pieces fell around like a horrifying confetti shower. One death was not enough. Duke opened fire while the others were stunned. One went down with a burst of rifle rounds through the visor. Another took several gut shots and collapsed, down but not out. The others returned fire and pushed on down the corridor toward him. A quick reload and he let loose once more. Duke took out another two soldiers. Still, they didn't slow down.

Then the mist that had enveloped around him settled. Clarity returned and he could see clearly what he was doing. If he stayed there, he was going to die and Allua's sacrifice was going to have been in vain. That couldn't be her memory. Her legacy. To protect him only so he could go and get himself killed in her name. It did her no justice.

The enemy was still pushing forward while the commander casually walked behind the rest of his unit, overly confident by the strut in his step. Duke barely managed against one of these soldiers. There was no chance of standing up to them all. To do so would be suicide.

'Shit,' he cussed.

Duke fell back to the previous junction to make a fresh stand. There, as if provided by some unseen miracle, Leyton could be seen rushing toward him. He had a chance after all.

'Have you gone completely insane?' Leyton demanded, joining the fray with suppressing fire to hold the enemy at bay.

'Not anymore,' Duke said, firing back at the soldiers. 'Sorry about that. Don't know what came over me.'

'Forget about it,' the agent replied. 'We all do shit we're not proud of when things go wrong. You clearly had a moment. Let's just finish what you've started, yeah?'

'You got it.'

The pair held the attackers off until the leader started to act strangely, nearly panicking. The commander persisted in trying to see behind them, looking behind their own position, then spoke out.

'Squad three, fall back to the ship!' he ordered. His voice boomed out. Powerful. Deep. Calm. 'Protect it at all costs! If it's just them here, then the others are going back to the ship. They need it. Make sure none of them get anywhere near it. First squad on me. We'll finish them here and regroup back at the ship.'

Of the remaining eight soldiers that were in pursuit of them, five turned and tactically returned down the hallway. Tricked into thinking there was an assault on the frigate they arrived on because of the two of them holding the position. An unintentional benefit of the agent catching up to him. The remaining three intensified their assault, firing briefer bursts of rifle fire with less breathing space between each series of bullets, and rushed for the pair. Leyton and Duke took out one of the soldiers before the remainder were on them. Their gunfight turned into a fist fight that they were not going to win. Duke knew that from the first blow he received from the enemy commander – the leader was unnaturally strong. The pair exchanged blows with the precision of combat experience. Leyton fought with the same aggression, but they were both severely outmatched with their opponents in the hand-to-hand combat. Duke landed a lucky strike with the butt of his weapon, cracking the commander's visor to obscure their vision. He took the advantage to some success until the commander landed a breath-taking strike to his chest. A few punches and a sharp kick later, Duke was on the floor staring up at the enemy leader, dazed.

The man took off his helmet. His face was chiselled to perfection, with a defined jawline and white hair greased to one side with a perfect parting. Piercing grey eyes glared down at him. The skin was marked with a criss-cross of gridded scars like a chess board had been imprinted onto him. Duke wondered what could cause that. Duke even considered the possibility he wasn't human. It would explain the strength for sure.

'This ends now,' the enemy commander stated. His words were sharp, to the point and clear with no loss of meaning. The accent was unusual, nothing like what Duke had encountered before.

'Best get it done then,' Duke wheezed, still catching his breath. 'Because if I get back up, you've had it.'

The hostile smirked. 'I like the confidence. Shame it won't help.'

'Worth a try,' Duke Horren gasped.

'When I'm done, I'll take the component. Don't think I don't know about that. Then I will complete the mission.'

The commander took out their sidearm and aimed it at him. An execution. His finger wrapped around the trigger but didn't pull it. There wasn't the time. In the blink of an eye Ronan had tackled the commander into a wall and was overpowering the man. Corporal Moasa showed him what real, natural strength was. Within a few seconds the grey-eyed man had a bust lip, blood flowing from a severely broken nose that would take some modification to correct and the redness around the left eye that symbolised the brewing of a significant bruise.

Duke clambered back up to his feet. While Ronan had the leader under control, he helped Leyton with his opponent. The pair of them were more than enough to handle the one soldier. When one took a punch the other stepped up on the offensive. Sharing the role of defence and offence flexibly like a well-choreographed performance. The hostile had no chance to put up any form of defence.

As soon as it became clear the trio had the upper hand, the fight was over. White Hair ordered an immediate fall back, using the last of his energy to force Ronan onto the floor and to barrel into Duke and Leyton, before dragging his remaining soldier back in the direction of their ship. Another victory, with no casualties this time. To add to the success, he was still in possession of the component to the explosive device they set up in the engine room. Duke rolled his shoulder and clasped it immediately as something was too tender to move right away.

'Thanks for the save,' Duke gasped.

'No problem,' Ronan replied. He didn't sound remotely out of breath. 'What the hell is that guy anyway? He's like half my size and was almost as strong as me. Is he a cyborg or an android or something? And what the hell was up with his face? Didn't look like any dude I've seen.'

'Or punch like a normal person,' Leyton added, equally sore from the fight.

Of course. It made perfect sense why they weren't natural. A machine would have that sort of strength, speed and stamina. Though that theory had its own flaws. Being an android would explain the commander's precision, both options didn't explain the other soldiers and their lack of accuracy or skill. Something that only time would fix in a mortal. They were possibly cyborgs. Humans freshly fitted with machine parts with their flesh grafted back on. In a machine though, they would be defects. Hardly believable that defects would be allowed to go on unnoticed.

Either way, they were dangerous. A definite force to be reckoned with. Duke Horren was reluctant to see how dangerous a non-defective android would be. It was all theory and speculation.

'I haven't got a clue,' Duke said. 'But we've got to move. If they regroup now, we're boned.'

'Yeah, but before we do that, what the fuck are you doing down here taking them on?' Ronan asked. 'You have any idea how fucked I thought you was when the captain put the call out?'

Duke Horren sighed. 'I know. I lost it for a second there. They got her.'

'Who?' Corporal Moasa questioned.

'Jons.'

'What happened?'

Duke said weakly after he let out a heavy sigh. 'They killed her.'

'Shit man,' Ronan said. 'I'm sorry.'

'It's okay,' Duke whispered. It wasn't. It was far from okay. He needed to try to stay strong.

'Come on,' Leyton said, patting him on the arm. 'We need to get back to your ship. Keep the advantage on our side.'

'On your go, Sergeant,' Ronan said.

'I've got point,' Duke replied.

There would be time to grieve. He knew that. It was just easier to see now that everything had calmed down around him. Duke would remember her. Just like the gentle spring sun or winter snow that would always come back around so there was no need to worry about never seeing it again, he would always hold her sacrifice close to his heart for a future they would never know. She wouldn't die while in his heart and memories.

He reloaded his weapon and took the lead.

Jesa

When Duke returned to the ship with the others, Jesa immediately feared for his health. She worried that the man was hiding something serious behind his stance. His armour was battered and stained with blood. He would clench his arm periodically and persistently attempted to ease the pain he was in by adjusting his posture. The relief she felt when she found out he wasn't badly hurt was like hearing the news of someone surviving a tragic car crash with only minor injuries. When he took his helmet off and revealed the red puffiness around his bloodshot eyes, she knew that something else had happened. Something that had torn him up inside more than any bullet ever could. To see a man of his strength, of his hardiness, reveal how hard he had been crying was a difficult thing to see.

Jesa watched as he dropped his helmet and his rifle to the floor. His gaze was distant and vacant, his breath short and sharp. Duke staggered forward, slowly making his way toward the briefing room much like an exhausted drunk trying to get home after a night out. He barely made it twenty shuffling paces before he dropped to his knees and let out a terrible cry of anguish and sorrow that had been contained for far too long. Then he wept uncontrollably. His shoulders heaved like weights were being dropped on them then lifted repeatedly. Her heart shattered into a million pieces like it was made of glass and then repeatedly struck by a sledgehammer until it was dust to be blown away with the wind as she watched him suffer.

Jesa rushed over and wrapped her arms around him in a tight embrace. The sort she would receive as a child from her mother when times were difficult. She hoped to bring him comfort. Give him even the slightest bit of support that he had shown her. Leyton peeled her gently away from the sergeant. She didn't want to leave his side. Not when he was so clearly in need. She tried to fight him off to return to Duke. Leyton resisted and took her to one side, leaving the poor man to suffer in solitude.

'What happened to him?' she demanded. 'Why won't you let me be there for him?'

'Because he needs some space right now.'

'Why? Am I not good enough? Outer sympathy not as good as Centie sympathy?' she accused.

'It's not that at all,' Leyton answered, shaking his head. 'You should know that by now.'

'Then tell me!'

'You know that girl he was into? She just died in his arms,' Leyton explained. 'Took a bullet for him right after he saved her.'

'Mayah!'

Jesa couldn't believe it. The mental torture he had to be in. Having something start only for it to be stolen away prematurely. Her heart broke a little more. She needed to be there for him – he needed to know that he wasn't alone. Jesa knew exactly how it felt. They had both lost their loved ones, seeing them die right in front of their eyes.

'Tell me about it,' Leyton said. 'He just lost his shit and tried to take on all the enemy soldiers on his own before he regained some sense. Didn't think I was going to be able to get him back.'

'Mayah, is he okay now?' Jesa asked as the sergeant wailed again, tearing at her heart like a blade had been plunged into her chest.

She didn't mean emotionally. His condition was obvious. But his mental state was in question. Would he be able to keep his head straight to stay in the fight? Protect her when she needed him to.

'Well, he's not going to go on a warpath again any time soon,' the agent answered. 'Keep an eye on him for me, will you? I'm going up to the bridge to see what's going on. See what they need doing to stop this shit getting worse. I'll be back in a couple hours. If he tries to do anything that I'd do, call for me. Make sure he doesn't get off this boat.'

'I will do,' Jesa said.

Leyton released her from his grip, and she rushed back over to Duke. Her arms immediately locked around him before she eased him up onto his feet. Jesa guided the sergeant away from the briefing room and up to the galley while the agent left the ship with Ronan. There the pair sat in silence with a cup of strong coffee each. She knew better than to try and say anything. Nothing she could say would ever make the pain go away. Nothing she could offer would ease it. The silence would do him good to gather his thoughts and he would speak when he was ready. The main thing was that he wasn't alone and for him to see a caring face.

When he was finally ready to speak, his voice was distant, like he didn't really want to be heard or was speaking to someone else. His eyes were glassed over with a thin layer of tears.

'You know, I've had lots of people die in my arms before,' he said softly. 'More than I can remember. More than I can count. Gunshot wounds, explosives dismembering, impalements. The works. Doubt there's many ways I haven't seen a person die. In all that time, I've never felt like this.'

'How *do* you feel?' she asked.

'I feel... well... empty. It's like I can't feel anything. Any other time I would be able to shake the feeling, get on with the job and carry on. This time's different, though. It's my fault. Fuck. I should have been able to save her. I had all the right training, the right gear. She was right there. All I had to do was stand in front and I could have taken the bullet. I'd have had a better chance to survive it. I held her. She tried to speak to me. She was just so weak. I had her in my arms, and I couldn't help her. There was nothing I could do. And I've left her back there.'

'You couldn't have stayed there, compre?' Jesa said. She reached out and placed a hand delicately on his arm. 'It'd have only made you worse. Probably got you killed. And at least you've let out your anger, compre? You can think clear now too. But this, this is normal. You need to just think about here and now. Think about getting everyone that's still alive out of here, yah. We need you to help us. The crew. Your squad. Me. You can't help us if you're busy fighting yourself, blaming yourself for something that isn't your fault. And I need you. I need you more than you realise, yah?'

The sergeant smiled at her; his eyes full of appreciation for what she had said. She smiled back. Her intentions were to never give any profound, deep and spiritual explanations to things. All she aimed to do was tell him that everything he was feeling was understandable and that he couldn't have done anything more then but could do something now.

'Thank you,' he said. 'Just doesn't feel good.'

'It won't,' Jesa said. 'How... um... How long has it been?'

Duke looked at her and hummed with confusion.

She cleared her throat, a little flushed to be asking it, then clarified her meaning. 'Since you were last with someone.'

Duke chuckled softly. 'Yeah, I'm not going to go down that road. Don't think I could even give you an answer if I tried.'

That long. So not days, weeks or months. She was surprised. He was a good-looking man. He really must not have had the time to do anything but work. It had to have been a lonely life to go through what he had without sharing a moment with anyone. Even now, while she was there and the crew was around, he seemed absent. Lost. Maybe he didn't want to be found.

Jesa needed to steer the conversation away from that subject. The awkward tension was too much for her to carry on tolerating.

'What do we do now?' she asked.

'Now? We need to get as many people out of here as possible and we need to do it as quickly as possible,' Duke answered. 'No delays. Don't care how but we get people off this ship. Then, when we're done, we get out of here too.'

'Can I help?'

'You just stay here and keep safe,' the sergeant told her. 'I told you I wanted to save you. I can't do that if you're dead. On here, I know you're safe and I have a chance of getting you out of here.'

Jesa forced back the argument she wanted to make, 'Okay.'

'Besides, the professor is still down there. Isn't he? I still want you to make sure that he's not doing anything he shouldn't be doing.'

He was still there on her ship. The professor had been studying the skeleton nearly non-stop, ignorant to almost every attempt to make conversation with him. Even the non-stop commentary of the battles going on over the intercom failed to entice his attention. Nothing seemed to distract him. Except for her. While he made several theories that gained momentum every time the sequencing scans revealed credence behind his thoughts, Samuel would stop to look and smile at her. He had been able to surmise that the organism was indeed reptilian in nature and that it had the cranial size for a far superior brain than that of humans. All in the same breath as making sure Jesa was okay. During one of his distracted moments, he confessed that the one he was studying indeed had signs of rapid growth in its early and adolescent years before slowing down as it reached maturity. He believed that it had died at around a hundred years of age, though he admitted it would take additional tests to prove this for certain. Even then, he didn't see any significant deterioration in the bones to suggest that it was at the end of its lifespan. Which did lead the professor to suspect that its death was not quite so natural. Professor Ainslot had confided in her that he had no hope of ever finding out what the real cause of death was. Not without further tests.

And throughout it all, he had been sincere. Kind. And genuine. Not once did Samuel try to make a move on her or do anything that made her feel uncomfortable. A real gentleman. Few people ever spoke to her with the degree of respect that he, or Duke for that, did. As annoying as he was going on about how amazing his discoveries were or how many questions came from one new discovery, Jesa did enjoy his company. It was easy to be around someone that didn't have to hide who they were. Maybe he was a bit awkward and a bit blunt at times but that was his personality.

Duke smiled at her. 'Go. Get down there and be with him. Help him with his research. But don't let your guard down. Not for anything.' The sergeant placed something on the table between them. A cylindrical object. 'And keep this safe.'

'What is it?' she asked.

'You don't need to know,' he said. Clearly, she should have known what it was. He just didn't want her to panic. 'All you do need to know is that this needs to be kept safe no matter what. Those soldiers, if they come here, must not find it.'

'But what—'

'Keep it safe. Keep it away from them. Please.'

The look in his eyes. He was concerned. No, it was more than that. Duke was scared. He feared what would happen if this were back in their possession. If he needed it keeping safe, Jesa knew where she could put it. There were places on the *Saridia* that not even her former master knew about for things like this.

'I've got somewhere for it,' Jesa said.

'Thank you.' Duke finished his coffee and wiped the tears from his eyes before putting his helmet back on.

'What's going on? Is everything okay?'

'Everything's fine,' he replied. The smile on his face behind that visor was forced. 'I'm getting back into the fight. Still plenty of people out there that need me.'

'But Leyton told me to keep you here!' Jesa pushed her way out of her seat and stood beside him to stop him from getting up. 'You need to stay here.'

'I'm not needed here,' Duke stated. 'I'm needed out there.'

'You're grieving,' Jesa sobbed. He was doing something dangerous. 'You're not okay to go.'

Duke stood up, forcing her back, and placed his hands on her shoulders. 'Yes, I am grieving. I'll be grieving for a while. That doesn't matter to the enemy soldiers. I could be dying right now. It wouldn't stop them. They'll come for us regardless and we need all the soldiers we have out there. Helping. Doing something. Not here on the bench.'

'Don't rush,' Jesa insisted. 'You're no good out there if your head isn't in it, compre?'

'I know, I wouldn't go if I wasn't ready,' Duke said. He made his way toward the ladders that led down to the troop bay. 'I'll be in touch. You get down there and keep an eye on him.'

She followed him down to the troop bay and watched Duke leave. He couldn't have been ready straight away, surely. Either he was lying to her, which she thought was probably what was happening, or he was hiding a darker side to him that he kept hidden from all that allowed him to carry on when times were bad. When he was off the ship and the airlock had cycled and sealed behind him, Jesa clambered down the docking tube into her ship. Professor Ainslot was still working away. He had rolled up his sleeves and helped himself to a cup of coffee.

She looked at the strange object Duke left under her supervision. It looked like something she'd seen in Barbaros' arsenal. What was it? It wasn't a weapon like a pistol or a rifle, and certainly wasn't a club to beat people with.

All those times Jesa walked into the weapons locker, and she couldn't remember seeing anything like it. What she didn't understand was why this thing made her think of that room. Seeing rows upon rows of rifles, shotguns, rocket launchers. Cases of grenades, mines and CEDs. That was it. Concentrated Explosive Devices. They needed a trigger. She analysed the cylinder in more detail. There – the control circuit. All the user needed to do was input the detonation sequence key, insert it into the housing unit and get away before the countdown timer hit zero. Were the enemy soldiers trying to blow up the *Passage*? Did they have more of these stowed away? They had to. But the sergeant insisted she keep the trigger safe. Maybe they didn't have more triggers for their explosive. Either way, she had the perfect place to hide it for Duke.

Inside Jesa's cabin was a compartment built into the wall. A chute. Anything of significant value, illegally acquired contraband or incriminating evidence on a storage unit, was to be always left in there so if she were boarded it could be jettisoned before being discovered. It kept Barbaros safe that way. It also kept the contraband she wanted for herself away from her former master. Jesa placed the trigger in the storage space and synced it up to her tac-pad, courtesy of Duke, so that she could dispose of it at the swipe of a finger. No one would even know it had ever been there except for her.

Confident that it would be safe, she returned to oversee Samuel. He asked what had happened. She avoided the details; it wasn't her place to tell him about how Duke was feeling but he seemed to know, or at least have a gut feeling, without her being specific. He politely avoided asking anything else about the matter and returned to his work. Professor Ainslot would occasionally ask for help. Even when it appeared he didn't need it. Sometimes sparking conversation. Talking or not, she did find peace being around him and he was keeping her occupied.

Chapter 12
16/11/2675
16:52 Earth Standard Time

Duke Horren

Duke had endured the onslaught of Leyton criticising his return to the field. That in turn triggered Beatrice to say her piece. He managed to keep his emotions contained for a while, until he lost it and put them all in their place with why he was a better judge of his capabilities than they were. Once the atmosphere had settled, they were finally able to return to the important task at hand and search for the remaining survivors. He and Leyton paired up to take the rear of the ship to find survivors that had been spotted on the security cameras. This was where the cheaper cabins were. And where the remaining civilians would be in immediate danger. Within a couple of hours, the pair had successfully found and rescued at least a couple dozen passengers. The elderly, young and shocked. People that just couldn't keep up with everyone else. If not for their efforts, they would have easily been left behind.

As their search continued for the next batch of civilians Leyton was glancing over to him repeatedly. He could feel it. The air was heavy. Full of anticipation. He wanted to say something but could not find the words to use. He could only tolerate that for so long.

'What is it?' Duke asked.

'I'm just curious,' the agent said. 'What are you going to do when we're done here? When we get out of this.'

'When?' The entire situation seemed doomed to Duke. People were dead. Hostile forces were still present. The ice wolves were still a lingering threat. It seemed more of a case of *if* and not *when*.

'Well, if I didn't think that we're getting out of here then what is there to stop us from just scuttling the ship and being done with it? Nothing. It would have been so much easier if we let the soldiers plant the bomb then trigger it ourselves. Guaranteed to make sure no one makes it out. So, go on. What's going to happen when we get out of here?'

'First things first is to hail a rescue party, tell them to open up on the thrust and get them here as soon as possible to pick up the survivors,' Duke explained. 'There has to be UPN ships or at least UPN friendly forces on the way by now. The distress beacon has travelled for long enough. Then I plan to stick around until they're all picked up. I just hope they have enough oxygen on the lifeboats to last them until they get rescued or make it to the nearest colonised planet.'

'And me?' Leyton questioned.

'What?' Duke replied, bringing the pair to a complete stop. It was an all too familiar scene as he had with Jesa. He wondered why everyone treated him with the respect of an almighty being that controlled a person's fate. 'What do you mean?'

'What are you going to do about me?' the agent sighed. 'Since if I'm to get out of here, I need you.'

Duke hung his head. Thought carefully. There were protocols in place for people who committed crimes, regardless of if those crimes were under orders or not. The steps taken by an individual to make amends for their actions were also taken into consideration. Plenty of people had been executed for similar crimes. Many more in long term incarceration or work camps. What happened after his protocol requirements was entirely out of his control.

'I know what I should do. You need to be turned over to the UPN to be prosecuted for your crimes, given pardons for what you've done, and the guys making you do this brought to justice too. But we both know that because of your job, it won't happen like that. This is a different game to what I'm used to. So, in all honesty, I don't know. I haven't got a clue what to do next. But I'll think up something by the time we're done here.' When Leyton didn't respond straight away, instead just starring into the distance, he pushed for more. 'What are you thinking?'

'If you turn me in, I'm not going to prison,' the agent stated. It wasn't a threat. It was more a matter of fact. 'They won't let me make it that far. You know that.'

'What makes you say that? You'll be with me and my troops. We'd protect you and your team.'

'Doesn't matter. They wouldn't care if I'm in your custody or not. I'd be located and transferred to one of their most out of the way prisons. As soon as we return to Earth, my people will arrest me and probably have you guys arrested too for aiding and abetting. There'll be no court. No trial. Just a six-by-eight cell with two half-portion meals a day, four glasses of water and five hours sleep if you're left alone. No one will know we ever existed or still do. You know what our crime will be? Surviving when we're not supposed to. And that's if they take it easy on us. If they don't, we'll be dead not long after we return to UPN space. We wouldn't even be able to run. It'll be a well-timed hit. If they know we're alive and somewhere out there, they will hunt us down because we know something that the public isn't allowed to know about, and they need to make sure it stays quiet. Keeping secrets is their primary mission.'

Duke wanted to know why the agent was so sure they would be captured. They would be on his patrol ship on no course but their own to friendly territories. But then again, they were up against a threat that knew who they were. If there was any sign that they were alive, the administrator would surely learn of it. Duke realised that the agent's fears were quite rightly placed. And if they would be hunted down, their own personnel, then that meant the civilians were in no fairer position. Only difference is they didn't have the means to defend themselves.

The first snarl to break his attention from his thoughts was nothing more than a murmur. Rumbling behind them like wind carrying broken glass through a meadow. Duke shared a look of disbelief with Leyton, refusing to accept what the sound was. When the second growl reached their ears, they turned to its source in sync. Five of the creatures, one adult and four pups, stood at the end of the corridor behind them. The pups were taller than a large dog but small for their species. They had still developed enough to be able to make a kill once they got hold of their prey. The kill wouldn't be clean. It was a skill the pups were too young and inexperienced to have learnt. There was no telling how long they had been stalked for, like wild grazing livestock on a prairie.

'What do we do?' Duke asked.

'Try to not get eaten,' Leyton said flatly.

'Well, that's a given,' Duke scoffed while readying his weapon. 'You ready for this?'

'As ready as I'll ever be. Follow my lead.'

Leyton opened fire at the closest of the wolves. Duke joined instantly with the chorus of gunshots. The pup perished. A quick reload, and they started on the second while edging back, putting themselves one step away for every three bounds the wolves took. When the next pup slumped to the ground, they turned and ran as fast as they possibly could. Only after every several paces did they fire a controlled burst behind them to hold the beasts off.

They reached the end of the corridor, screaming at each other to keep moving. The wolves were soon out of sight round the corner but not so far away for the pair to feel safe. A door opened ahead of them, the occupants hearing their gun shots and the cry of the wolves. A hand reached out, beckoning them in. Fearful eyes looked out from the darkness. Duke and Leyton wasted no time, rushing into the darkened room and forcing the door shut, pressing their body weight against it. The scampering of feet outside ground to a halt. The remaining pups and adult sniffed around, picking up their scent but not able to work out where they were. A faint screeching howl from the below decks drew the wolves away in a mad panic. Something had happened that was more important than bringing down their next meal. It suited Duke fine. Neither he nor Leyton budged from their position until they were confident that the creatures were safely out of their vicinity.

A heavy sigh broke the dull background noise of the groaning ship, followed by the rapid breaths of people thankful to be alive. A cohort of survivors stood around the perimeter of the cabin. A man with a young child clutching his arm were closest to them, both wide eyed and clearly worried. A woman wearing a torn and filthy suit stood at the edge of the bed, frustrated at a situation that wasn't going her way. Two crew members cowered on the other side. They were shaken up. The expressions on their face were an all-too-familiar sign. Whoever they saw die was going to haunt them for the rest of their lives, no matter how much they drank to try to forget it.

'Are you here to save us then?' the woman in a suit snapped. 'About time, after we got cut off from the nearest fucking lifeboat. Thank you for abandoning us by the way. I will fucking take you all to court for everything you have for this.'

'Wow. Is that a thank you? You really have an attitude problem, don't you?' Leyton responded sharply.

'I what?' the woman demanded, taking a couple steps forward as if she meant to try intimidating them with her stature. There was a better chance of them being offput by the expression she wore.

'Well…' Duke started. There was a way to handle people like that, who expected everything and blamed everyone else when things went wrong. The way he preferred to handle such people wasn't exactly permitted so he needed to be careful. 'There aren't a lot of us. And you've all been spread throughout the ship by things out of our control. If you have any chance of surviving, it's with us now. I suggest you wind your neck in and shut it so that we can figure something out. Otherwise, people like you will get the rest of us killed with how much you like to bitch. Agent, plot us a route to the nearest lifeboat.'

'On it,' Leyton said.

While Leyton found them the route, Duke's comm crackled into life in his ear as Helmsman Zenkovich started to speak. But not to him.

Duke was given permission to listen in on a conversation. 'Take it easy comrades. We don't want any trouble.'

'If you don't want trouble then you will drop your weapon right now,' came the response. It was faint but clear with a tone that sounded far too calm. The speaker didn't want to be misunderstood. 'I will not repeat myself.'

'What if I don't feel safe to lower it?' the captain questioned.

'It makes no difference to us,' the male said. 'Comply or not, you will not be leaving this boat alive.'

'Why not?' Zen replied, stalling the boarders.

'None of you are to survive.'

Zen laughed. 'Isn't that giving away your evil plan?'

'There's no need to hide that from you anymore. We're going to end this regardless. We would have taken cooperation into consideration and shown lenience by making it quick for you. Where is the rest of your crew? And where is the trigger? We know your sergeant stole it.'

When Zenkovich wouldn't tell them what they wanted to hear, the boarders pushed on to search the rest of the ship to Zen's disapproval. As soon as they indicated going down the lower docking tube, the helmsman put up a fight only to gasp for breath after a brief skirmish.

'Stay out of there!' Ivan screamed weakly.

'Keep him here, I'm going to find out what he's hiding down there,' the man stated.

The next thing Duke heard was the terrified commotion of Jesa and Samuel being dragged from the smuggler ship into the troop bay. Their handlers were not gentle. His blood boiled – they were in trouble, and he wasn't there to help them. But there was nothing he could do. He was fixed to the spot, paralysed, only able to listen.

'Hey! Get away from them!' Zen barked, trying to do something to protect the pair.

Jesa cried out for help. Someone laughed at her fighting back. Professor Ainslot yelled, almost pleaded, for them to back away from her. It sounded like he was trying desperately to get to Jesa, and he must have had some success because it sounded like there was a brief scuffle that resulted in Jesa asking Samuel if he was okay, how badly his face hurt – most likely, he took a slap, and the helmsman wheezing for breath once more. Duke heard the distinctive voice of Valentina calling down at the boarders. The enemy spoke calmly but she didn't change her tone.

'Rodriguez, no!' Ivan Zenkovich screamed.

The crack of rifles being fired deafened Duke, Jesa's scream now barely a faint squeal in his ears. Someone screamed to look over to the docking tube leading back to the *Passage*. The gunshots unleashed once again. The line went dead after a desperate howl roared out. Not even the crackle of static haunted him.

He and Leyton both shared the same ghastly expression.

'You go, I'll get these guys to the nearest lifeboat… somehow,' the agent said.

'Don't get yourself killed,' Duke replied.

'What's that you tell me? Oh yeah. Wouldn't do you the favour,' Leyton laughed. 'Go. I'll get help to join you.'

Duke was out of earshot within several leaping bounds after leaving the cabin, regardless of the potential threats outside. The last thing he heard was the civilians asking what was going on and why he was leaving them behind while Leyton tried to reassure them that they would be fine. By the end of the corridor, Duke had almost stopped caring about the task at hand and the civilians that were still on the *Galactic Passage*. What mattered now was getting back to his ship. He needed to save whoever was still on board, or at the very least make sure his way off the liner wasn't in hostile hands intent on completing their mission to bring back the wolves.

He wheeled into view of the airlock, slowing to a crawling pace as he approached the docking airlock. His weapon was held steady at the ready for anything that dared step into his line of sight. The airlock door was wide open. Claw marks were dug deep into the frame. His heart stopped with the anticipation. He had been hoping that his ears were simply playing tricks on him during the open comms conversation, that he didn't hear what he thought he heard. An ice wolf was in the area. Duke edged closer, only to lose all restraint and rush on into the patrol ship the moment the pool of blood came into view. To his relief it didn't belong to one of his crew. The corpse was from one of the enemy soldiers, their back torn apart, the armour ripped open like it was paper. Two more bodies of enemy soldiers were left in the troop bay of his ship, and at the base of ladders leading to the galley was one of his own. Rodriguez, still with a rifle in her hand. She was crumpled in a heap. Probably fell from the gangway. Duke assumed she tried to get the jump on them from above while the enemy soldiers had the rest of the team in their sights.

'Fuck no,' he cussed.

Duke rushed over. She had been shot dead centre of her chest. In just a flight suit, with no armour, she had had no chance of surviving. As much as he wished she were still alive, he also wished the one responsible for killing her had managed to make it out okay so he could personally make them suffer.

There was no sign of anyone else. No blood trails, no bodies, not even the sound of frantic breathing or searching. That had to mean they had made it out, but there was nothing to indicate where they went. It was as if they vanished. Still, there was enough ship for someone to hide in.

'Ivan? Jesa? Anyone?' he called out, throwing caution to the wind. 'Professor!'

Duke searched the patrol ship for any sign of the crew. The flight deck was clear. Galley, cabins, briefing room and armoury were empty. Even the engine room was void of any life. Had prisoners been taken? It was unlikely after listening to the conversation, but it was possible. The best way to guarantee a trap would work was by having the right bait.

'Guys!' Duke cried, trying to keep his voice controlled as panic and concern surged through him.

Either his voice carried further than anticipated or the wolf's hearing was greater than anticipated. His calls were answered by one of the creatures somewhere out in the corridor of the *Passage*. Duke hurried over to the airlock and peeked around the corner. One of the adults was stalking him. This one looked larger than the others – much larger. A female, bearing extended head protrusions. He recognised which one this was from the briefing with Professor Ainslot. The matriarch of the pack, the one he called Spike, was heading right for him.

With no haven on his ship to hide in, he scrambled down into the captured smuggler ship. Cautiously he stepped backward through the wreckage, bumping into what seemed to be every surface and piece of contraband possible as he put as much space between him and the ice wolf as he could. His back was soon pressed against a wall leaving him nowhere else to go. This would be it. Duke was about to make his final stand without a hope of surviving.

A hand reached out from the dark behind him and took him by his hand, scaring him enough to instinctively raise his weapon ready for a fight. Jesa started at him, wide-eyed and afraid. Duke immediately lowered his rifle. Before he could speak, Jesa put a finger over her lips to signal for quiet and pulled him to the side of the ship and bundling him through a narrow opening. Helmsman Zenkovich and Professor Ainslot were cooped up in the tight space already. Zen seemed unscathed, though the anger resonating from him was palpable. Samuel was only just coping with the shock. The relief to see they were still alive was euphoric. Jesa followed him in, closing the panel behind her so they were entirely entombed in one of her several secret compartments for contraband she really didn't want to be found. Or herself.

'What the hell happened?' he questioned in a whisper.

'There were five of them,' Ivan explained. 'They were able to override the controls and forced their way onboard. The rest of us were down in the troop bay, Rodriguez was still up on the bridge. Val tried to get the jump on them. They either saw her attempt of a counterattack coming or anticipated that there would be more of us in hiding. But they got her before she could get them then—'

Jesa hushed the pilot, cutting him off mid-sentence. A low rumbled echoed down from the ship above them. The group was no longer alone.

They waited, staring through the thinnest of eyelets to see the contents of the ship. The ice wolf growled loudly as it scampered around above them. Her claws scratching along the floor as she searched for live prey. Spike sniffed the air with forceful determination to be sure she was on their scent before dropping into the smuggler's ship with a stumbling thud. The matriarch of the pack knocked over everything that couldn't be stepped over or around in her search for them.

Duke tried to estimate how far she was from him. Just a matter of meters, ten at the most. The wolf was bound to be able to hear everyone's breathing. Spike surveyed the ship, casting her eyes from one side to the other trying to pinpoint them, before prowling in their direction.

Six meters away. Spike stalked them through the cargo, sniffing wildly, furiously following their scent. Heading straight for them. Duke gripped his rifle, ready to use it even though at best he would only be able give the others a chance to escape while he held her off until his inevitable demise. Four meters away. Her four red eyes glared right at him like there was nothing blocking her view. Spike's face was covered in scars from what must have been contests for leadership or fights with rival packs. Several of the protrusions on her chin looked almost like tusks. She flashed her teeth, hissing with eager anticipation, drool raining down as she anticipated the taste of their flesh. Jesa gripped his arm. Ivan Zenkovich shuddered with a fear Duke didn't think he could feel. The professor quivered with dread. He was never meant to be on this side of his assignment.

Two meters away.

'Zenkovich? Sergeant!' Corporal Udal'e called out. 'You here? Anyone!'

Duke felt his blood turn cold. He never thought to warn the team about the situation. It was too late now if he was to save the people he was with. As soon as Abe found the body of Valentina his own mortified cry was muffled out by the shrill wail of the beast with fresh meat now within her reach. Nothing stopped Spike from rushing out for her next victim. She climbed up the hatch at speed. Barely a dozen rounds were let off before the distressed scream of pain took over.

Then there was silence.

He wanted to kill the ice wolves before. To make sure that they couldn't reach Earth. Now he wanted that one. That one had taken the life from one of his own soldiers. It might have been his own doing, but she would reap the consequences. Spike was going to die even if it cost him his own life in the process. First, he needed something that could hurt her. Duke knew that his assault rifle could kill a pup at the expense of a full magazine, and he also knew he wouldn't have the same success against an adult. He needed something stronger to take her out with. There would be something in the armoury for that.

Duke eventually dared to venture out from safety, much to the silent protests of his companions. Duke carefully ensured not a single footstep made a sound. He could still hear Spike feasting on her fresh kill, each bite crunching through armour and bone with spine shivering cracks. When he reached the final rung up to the lower airlock of his patrol ship Duke hesitated. He had the image of the beast waiting above him. Mouth open to allow him to move his head directly into it for an easy kill. He waited to build up the courage, fate daring him to take that fateful step.

A clatter back in the liner distracted the wolf. It paused from its meal. Another crash further in the ship tempted the ice wolf away. When Spike had hurried away to investigate the commotion, someone entered the ship. The airlock door was sealed. Footsteps casually strolled over to him until someone, not something, was stood overhead.

'Need a hand?'

'Ronan?'

'Still in one piece.' A hand reached down and pulled him into the transport. 'I got the message from Leyton to get here.'

'Thanks. What'd you do to get rid of it?' he asked.

'Threw some scrap metal down the corridor,' Ronan shrugged. 'Waited until she went on a wild goose chase before coming in. Poor fucker.' Ronan nodded toward Abe. 'I actually started to like him.'

'I know,' Duke replied, struggling to even look at the body. Ashamed that the death could have been avoided had he told the rest of his squad about the wolf.

'How'd she go?' Ronan gestured over to the body of the Rodriguez.

Duke shook his head. 'The soldiers came on board. She tried to stop them to save everyone else.'

'I'll get them for this,' Corporal Moasa snarled. 'Every last one of them.'

'Get in line,' Duke said. 'I'm first.'

'Sergeant?' Zenkovich called out carefully.

'Come on up,' Duke replied. 'It's safe.'

Ivan brought Jesa and Samuel up to join them in the transport. They were relieved to see a friendly face, but equally distraught at the sight of yet another member of their team felled. Udal'e had been ripped apart at the torso, cracked open like an egg. His innards were cast aside. His eyes were still wide-open peering through the smashed visor on his helmet. The final look of desperation on his expression. Not the way his soldier should have gone.

'What's the plan?' Ivan Zenkovich asked.

'You guys are going to hold the fort,' Duke instructed, handing the man his rifle and ammunition. 'Ronan, you're with me.'

With the pilot and their companions standing guard, Duke and Ronan took to the armoury. If an assault rifle was only able to hurt the creatures, then they needed to go heavier. They loaded up with shotguns, stocked up on extra shells and Duke took as many explosives as he could clip onto his tactical belt. He made sure to pack extra ammunition in a bag and a spare shotgun for Corporal Arche, wherever she was. If he could link up with her, she needed the extra firepower too so she could help with the fight.

Duke led Corporal Moasa back to the troop bay. 'Right, here's the plan. You guys are detaching from the ship. I've lost one pilot and one soldier – that's two too many personnel. I'm not losing anyone else so you're getting away from the fight. No arguments. You stay in orbit around the cruise ship. If that frigate starts to fire up, hit its engines with everything you've got to keep them here. If they get the upper hand, bug out. Come back for us when you've got reinforcements to help with the rescue. Understood? Just make sure you survive.'

'Understood,' Ivan replied. He put a hand gently onto Jesa's shoulder, silently urging her to either not say a thing or to not argue. She chose to remain silent. He glanced over to the professor and made sure he stayed quiet. 'What are you two going to do?'

'Regrouping with the others,' Duke started. 'I'll get Leyton and Arche to work with Medic Suttle and Agent Tallow to help with the evacuation so there's no one left on the ship. I've got business to settle with that fucker that did all this, and I don't think Ronan will say no to helping me out?'

'You bet I won't,' Corporal Moasa said.

That was it. Everyone followed their orders. Duke and Ronan waited on the *Galactic Passage* outside the airlock, watching as Helmsman Zenkovich took the patrol ship away from the fight. When they were safely away, and he was sure that they weren't under immediate threat, Duke turned to Ronan and nodded. They pushed through the ship with one task in mind. It was a strange throwback to the primal years of humanity where they were both the hunter and the hunted. Where every corner held a threat that wanted to kill them and prey begging for them to carry out the laws of nature. Yet it was exciting at the same time. A thrill that he used to lavish when he was younger and still under the belief that he was invincible.

No one else was going to die. Not if he could help it.

Leyton Foresc

Leyton had managed to get the civilians to safety with almost no issues, though a couple of them made ludicrous complaints. He managed to avoid berating the woman in a suit with a verbal barrage to stop her complaining. Others however, the child especially, struggled to keep up silently. They were tired and scared. Exhaustion affected the untrained and young mind differently. For them it was much easier to give in. Let whatever they were trying to escape from have its way with them. Anything to make the pain stop. He had long ago learned how to keep those thoughts quiet. Thankfully now they were on a lifeboat and out of harm's reach, at least for the time being.

After they had safely departed, Leyton had located his agents and was even able to regroup Corporal Arche of the SPF. She had been holding her position with a couple members of the ship's security against the enemy soldiers before they arrived, and she had done well. Together they had been able to take out a few hostiles and a few wandering pups that had broken away from the pack. They didn't suffer a single loss. Only injuries. He was even more surprised to hear from Duke. Leyton was quickly briefed about the events on their patrol ship and that Duke and Corporal Moasa were now heading into the depths of the liner hunting the wolves with Spike being their target.

The ship shuddered. His innards shifted in his torso, like taking a sharp corner a lot quicker than you realistically should. They were gaining speed. By the creaking and groaning of the already weakened hull it was a rapid and sudden increase in speed.

'Captain?' Leyton Foresc said over the comms with the bridge.

'Yes, Agent?' Beatrice replied.

'Are we moving?'

'We are,' she said calmly.

'We are? I think me and Duke missed that memo, sorry but… Why are we moving?' Leyton asked. 'And when did we agree on whatever it is you're doing?'

'I have to look at the situation we're in now for what it is. It's a no-win scenario. We have evacuated as many of the passengers and crew as we safely can. The ship is just about empty. At present, there are more hostiles than there is crew on-board. Our odds are not good. So, I need to make us a guarantee that this goes our way no matter what.'

When she didn't answer his second question, he repeated himself. 'Okay, so when did we get a say in this?'

'This is my ship, Leyton,' Beatrice hissed. 'I still hold the, albeit retired, rank of Navy Captain. My duty is to both save my passengers, which I have to the best of my abilities, and protect the integrity of the United Planetary Nations from all threats by any means necessary which I am doing now, and I am taking full responsibility for my actions.'

Her words were stern and forceful, but not without reluctance. There was no point trying to persuade her otherwise. He could see that. If he was to change her mind, he would need to do so by force. A sigh parted his lips. Leyton swallowed his pride and accepted that this had stopped being his show to run some time ago. It wasn't even the sergeant's mission now. They were just permitted to do what they needed, as long as it didn't interfere with her agenda.

'So where are you taking us?' he asked.

Beatrice let out a heavy breath. 'We're heading for the local star of this system. It's the only way to guarantee that we win, and they lose.'

A suicide run. She was going to send them all to their deaths. Not that she wasn't used to that kind of thing. Leyton kind of hoped that she had outgrown her old ways after how she reacted when he tried to bring it up before. Although he couldn't say anything about the reason for doing it or its efficiency.

'Okay, how long do we have?'

'On our current trajectory we'll be there in twelve to fourteen hours. But I intend to make it there before then. The sooner this is over with the better.'

There was enough time either way for something to go wrong or right. Any decrease in that time both improved their chances of success and took away their hopes for escape. An increase gave the enemy the time they needed to change the course of their fate. He really did hate how time worked like that.

'Understood. Will you be evacuating at all, Captain?'

'That is the intention but if I can't, I won't,' she answered, her voice still and stern. 'Is that all?'

'I guess so. I'm going to link up with the sergeant.'

'Have you heard anything from him?' Beatrice asked. 'I've been trying to get in touch with him but he's not getting back to me. I don't know why he can't radio in. I can get hold of the patrol ship but he's not with them. It wouldn't take much to tell me what's happening.'

'He's regrouped with one of his soldiers,' Leyton recalled, refraining from pointing out how she expected what she was not prepared to do herself. 'They've lost crew. He's hunting the wolf that killed them with Ronan.'

The officer's voice was slow and remorseful. Regretting immediately how she had spoken about the soldier only moments earlier. 'I… I am sorry to hear that.'

'I'm going to try get in touch with him to see where he is. I'll let you know when I've caught up to him and how he is. Out.'

He cut the comm link with the officer, pausing in the empty passageway of the liner. The signs of a frantic escape littered the floor like the plains of North America after a tornado ploughed through on its course of unintended destruction. Too much death had taken place. Every spark from blown electrics, drip of water from damaged piping and thud as objects fell from their resting position kept him on edge. Any sound could be an ice wolf coming round the corner. Each phantom of his mind was after him. In all his time during the Special Forces then working for the Agency he had never known of such a mess for no other reason than to transport cargo in the name of human existence.

He knew the mission was going to be difficult but not this taxing on his spirit. It was too much to take in without at least knowing what the bigger picture was. Even more reason for him to do whatever he physically could to make sure that anything that risked humanity, domestic or foreign, was dealt with to the best of his abilities. At least now they could divert their attention away from trying to do too many tasks to focussing only on the enemy present and ensuring they all went down with the ship.

All in a day's work.

'Duke?' Leyton said over the comms. 'You there?' When the soldier didn't respond straight away, he tried again. 'Sergeant! Come on you fuck. Duke, come in.'

'I'm here,' the sergeant grunted. 'What's up?'

'Not much. Just that if we don't get off his rig in the next twelve hours we're done for. The captain's running us straight into the local star. We'll be vaporised within the next fourteen hours. But wants to get there sooner.'

'Did you try to stop her?'

'Not a chance of it. She's retaken full control of the ship now that, as far as she's concerned, we've saved everyone that we can. There's no changing it now.'

The SPF soldier eventually replied with heavy reluctance. 'Understood.'

'However, there is still enough time for anyone still breathing to get any remaining lifeboats,' Leyton assured. 'But they won't be able to do it without us.'

'What are you thinking?' the sergeant queried.

'We split our forces. The rest of my agents and your soldiers will take on the boarders. If they attack their frigate, it'll cause an alarm and bring every one of them back to it defend it. Like what happened before. If they're all back at their ship, they won't be patrolling the liner or trying to capture any wolves. Gives everyone else a chance to get through the corridors safely.'

'So, they're distracting the enemy and taking a few bullets?' Duke didn't sound convinced by that option. 'Really? That might as well be sending them out for the slaughter!'

'Well, you know what they say, can't spell slaughter without laughter,' Leyton replied with a chuckle. 'But it'll work. They all know what they're doing. I understand the odds but when things get bad, they simply need to fall back to a safe place and make sure the soldiers can't follow them. By now they'll realise that this ship is star-bound anyway so they shouldn't venture too far back into the ship unless they want to die.'

'Guess you do have a point. What about us? You didn't mention us in your plan. Or the wolves.'

'I help you,' Leyton revealed.

'Come again?'

'I link up with you and we take out the matriarch which will bring all the others back to the lower decks if they're not already there. That way, all hostiles are preoccupied.'

Leyton wondered if something had gone wrong when the sergeant didn't respond. There wasn't even static interference or idle chit chat in the background. Just silence. As if their communications had been cut short.

'Okay then. Give it to me. How does us attacking the matriarch do that?'

'So, I was thinking this through,' Leyton stated. 'Spike is their main wolf. She's the one that they want to protect. If we want to distract all the other wolves and bring them away from everywhere else on the ship, concentrate them into one spot, then we need to get her.'

'Are you sure about that?' Duke questioned. 'It doesn't sound like a good plan.'

'It's the only plan worth pursuing,' Leyton said, doing his best to remember all the details Professor Ainslot gave him of the ice wolves. 'When we find her and force her into a corner, she'll hopefully panic and call for help. At that point all the wolves are going to come running to her aid. They don't want a dead leader. Soon as she's dead they'll just go into a bloodlust and come for us. That means if they're coming after us, they're not everywhere else.'

'What do we do after we've killed her, and the pack is after us?' Duke asked. A hint of aggressive scepticism in his voice. 'Because that's a big part of the plan you've left out.'

'If we want to live… we run,' Leyton said as a matter of fact. 'We run and don't stop until we're back on your patrol ship and off this thing. If we want to make sure everyone else has a better chance to live, we stand and fight for as long as we can and keep a door open to retreat through. If we want to die, we stand and fight and don't run. It's completely up to you.'

'How about we do the middle one?'

'Agreed,' Leyton said. 'What's your location? We'll make our way to you.'

With the sergeant's location received, Leyton led his team a few decks below. Once they had regrouped, they separated and put their plan into action with Leyton and Duke taking off for the lower decks instantly. Ronan was tasked to lead the joint team in a combined effort against the enemy soldiers to disable their frigate, attempt to take it if the opportunity presented itself or just hold their ground and keep the enemy occupied. Even though he was not the most experienced leader, Corporal Moasa was the best for the job out of the team. Their attack would give Leyton and Duke the time needed to reach the depths of the *Galactic Passage*. It was a long shot of a guess but an educated guess that Spike would have returned to the den by now. Leyton hoped he was right. There was no time for them to start the search from scratch.

When the gunfire erupted over the comms as the battle started, the pair picked up the pace. They hurtled through the passageways, past the numerous blast and pressure doors and down to the lower decks like they were both young men once again. It was difficult to stay focussed and ignore the ongoing narration from the combined forces and their assault. It sounded like every time they thought they were getting the upper hand they were only being fed a false sense of security for the inevitable counterattack that pushed them back. The troops needed additional help that wasn't there and couldn't be provided. They had to do their best with what they had. He and Duke both knew they would give all there was to give to succeed with the mission.

When he looked to Duke, he was expecting to see a man that was ready to give in with how bad the situation sounded adding to the grief he was already in. Indeed, the man looked rough. Tired. Battle worn. Emotionally drained. There was, however, a glimmer of the same rage he had heard over the radio still lingering in his eyes. But the soldier did need to stop. Lack of rest was catching up on him. They had time to spare for a breather.

'Are you hanging in there?' Leyton asked as they ground to a halt.

'Only just,' the soldier wheezed. 'Didn't realise how easy I've had it the past few years. Or how tired I am.'

'Happens to the best of us,' he replied. 'You need a boost? Got a couple stim shots.'

Duke waved away the offer. 'No thanks, don't need that stuff. We getting close yet? Need to know that if any more of my guys die it isn't for nothing.'

'I think so,' Leyton said as he gave himself a stim shot. The drug cocktail immediately alleviated the weariness his body was feeling. It'd last a few hours then would hit him hard once it wore off. 'Looks different with bad lighting now, you know?'

'Couldn't tell you,' Duke joked. 'This is all I've seen of it.'

Leyton laughed. 'You ready to go again?'

'I am, are you?'

'As I'll ever be' Leyton Foresc said. He reached out and grasped the soldier by the shoulder. 'Your guys will be fine. They're well trained and they've got each other. You've done everything you can for them. Try to not think too much about them. Let's get going.'

The pair quickly resumed the charge, rushing to the lowest deck as the shots continued to boom through the comms. Leyton brought them both to a halt once again. They were just a couple of decks above where the creatures most likely would have nested. He gestured for them to move slowly and carefully. The air started to get heavy. Power was fine, albeit a little sluggish. It wasn't the air scrubbers failing. They were working harder than normal but were still operational. There was something lingering within the atmosphere making it difficult to breathe. A thick, putrid smell. A familiar smell.

The wolves and the secretions used to make their den.

Leyton glanced over his shoulder and looked past the sergeant. He had the uneasy feeling that something was behind them. But no shadows, no sounds. It must have been his imagination. Nothing more than fear receptors in the brain making shapes and sounds he recognised appear when they were never there. Or putting something where he expected it to be, even when it wasn't there.

'What is it?' Duke asked.

'Nothing,' he said turning back to face ahead. 'At least I think it's nothing.'

'What did you see?'

'Not a damn thing.'

Duke rotated on his heels. His shotgun was raised and at the ready. 'I don't think it'll be nothing. Someone like you doesn't react like that unless there's something there.'

He was right, in the least-smug sense possible. His training had forced most of that out of him, to look for sources rather than react to tricks played on the eye. It helped that the sergeant didn't believe he was losing his mind. He was still scared though. He knew what they were facing, and this was now their territory. Not his and the ship didn't belong to the crew anymore.

They were just a deck away from the belly of the ship. The odour had intensified. It made breathing difficult. A light, putrid mist hovered over the floor. The heat radiating from below was immense, like entering the tropics after being in an air-conditioned capsule for hours. Only this was nauseating. The viscous, sloppy substance they secreted from their mouths was everywhere. As if they were extending the reach of their den as far out as possible.

'The hell is that smell?' Duke questioned as he lifted his boot off the floor, examining the gloop sticking to his foot. 'And what's this crap?'

Leyton shuddered. 'The nest. The other two females will have had their litters by now. If that is the case, that's another two sets of babies for them to protect. After all the pups we've killed so far, they're going to fight harder to protect the ones they have left once we get there. And this stuff? It's what they cough up to make themselves comfy. Try to not slip or get stuck. You got anything I can use or are you keeping all that?'

Duke scoffed with a smile. He unslung the spare shotgun, relinquished a couple barrels of ammunition and handed the lot over to Leyton. 'I want that back at the end of this, okay?'

'If we make it out of this, you can have it back and I'll even get you replacement ammo.'

'Thanks, which way from here?'

'This way,' Leyton said, shrugging forward and taking the lead. 'Just need to follow your nose.'

Beatrice Lenoia

There were things in life that were a given as going to happen, much like a prophecy. The sun would always rise. What went up would always come back down, within a gravity well. The events over the last several weeks had been far from predictable. There was no foreseeing what transpired. The occurrence shouldn't have even happened. Was there anything she could have done differently? Could there have been a way to prevent the lives from being taken away from those under her command on the voyage? Beatrice reluctantly accepted that the chances were that this was going to happen at some point. If not to her ship, then to someone else's. At least with it being under her command they had been able to do something about it. Any one of the other civilian captains, though highly skilled, would never have been able to keep themselves composed long enough to formulate a reactive plan like she had. It was a military operation that required a military response.

How many had she been able to save? Her last count indicated that twenty-five lifeboats had been launched, carrying over three-hundred passengers. Some of those boats were crammed. Others, barely full. An equally large number of passengers and crew were never able to set foot on a lifeboat. They weren't given the opportunity, their lives cut tragically short. The image of Allua Jons haunted Beatrice, her body left to rest unceremoniously back in the hallway leading to the engine room. Playing back the security footage of that tragic event was painful to watch. Yet, in an unusual way, Beatrice was able to find some peace. Allua sacrificed herself to protect Duke, and he was there for her while her grip on life faded. He kept her company. Made sure that she was not alone. She could only pray that he eased the passing enough that Allua wasn't afraid.

Lenoia found the strength take some solace in the number of lives saved. The collective efforts of everyone under her guidance meant people survived.

The *Galactic Passage* was hurtling through space on the sub-light engines. Her speed still increasing by the second. The distant glimmer of light that still looked dull enough to be one of the many stars in the backdrop was their destination. They were right on target.

Beatrice looked across the command deck. There was only a handful of key crew left. Half of them no longer had a role to serve, their tasks completed. She found little point in keeping them longer than required.

She cleared her throat to gain their attention, 'Listen up. We have our trajectory in place. All engine controls are at my hand. Vellai, Singh, Volk, Dolga, Schaps, you are all dismissed. Please make your way to the nearest lifeboat. I will follow you shortly with Knoxx, once we're confident that there will be no risk of being chased once we depart.'

There was a sigh of relief from all but one of the key crew given permission to leave. Laurenne Vellai politely objected to the order and stepped forward.

'We can't, Captain,' she said. 'We're going too fast.'

'What do you mean?' Beatrice asked. It may have been a lack of sleep, stress, or a combination of both, but she couldn't see what the young woman was getting at.

'If we get in those lifeboats now, at these speeds, we'll fall apart the second we jettison from the *Passage*,' Laurenne explained. 'The shields are too weak to give us a safety buffer and the lifeboats aren't designed for a rough exit. We're not going anywhere.'

The uproar was heart-breaking. How could she have overlooked that in her eagerness to get everyone else off the ship? To make sure their failsafe was in motion. Of course they were going too fast for the shielding to protect the lifeboats. Without shielding, the liner needed to be moving a lot slower. Because of that they were equipped with only the most basic shielding and dampeners to keep the occupants safe from more mild circumstances. At most the ship shouldn't have been going faster than twenty-five percent sub-light power for a safe break away. They were hitting at least fifty-five, maybe even sixty percent, with a damaged ship and minimal shielding. It wouldn't be long until the ship was falling apart with the stresses of high speed and the ever-increasing gravity from the local star pulling at them. If the *passage* was going to succumb to it all then obviously the lifeboats would too.

Beatrice could not for the life of her keep herself from falling victim to her emotions. She had failed this last faithful group that stood by her to the very end. She had waited too long before setting them free. There was nothing that she could do. Tears fell down her cheeks in raging torrents. The crew abandoned their posts to tend and comfort her, reassuring her that she had done everything that she could for them.

'Thank you,' she sobbed, forcing a smile through her trembling lips. 'I am so sorry.'

'You don't need to be sorry for me,' Knoxx said. His calm voice reassuring. 'I've survived more than most. If this is my time, I'm ready to go.'

'And you don't need to be sorry for us,' Singh added. 'We all knew we might not be going home if we stayed. You warned us. It's not like you lied. We accepted the risk.'

They were right, and that strangely made it so much worse because she couldn't be angry. If they had been wrong, she could have had somewhere to indirectly point the blame. Somewhere to take out her frustration, anger and disappointment at the same time to make herself feel better. Now she didn't even have that. But she did have them.

Something wasn't right. Beatrice had been too quick to accept that it might all be over. Why should she give up so easily? Was it so wrong that she didn't want to accept that it was over before really trying? There had to be more to be done.

'You know what? No, we're not doing this. We're not giving up.' She pulled up the ship's systems and integrities on the holo-table and beckoned everyone to gather around it. 'Between us, we've got to be able to think of a way off the ship. We have to be that smart together.'

'What're we looking for?' Volk asked.

'Anything that might get us a way off the ship,' Beatrice stated. 'As it stands, we have no chance at all. If we can get a plan that even gives us a fifty percent chance, we're taking it. Together.'

They set to work and tried. For all their might they tried to find something that would secure them a safe departure from the *Passage*. All without compromising the speed that was essential for making sure no one had the slightest chance to stop them from keeping humanity safe. They considered taking the battery power from other lifeboats, hardwiring it into another lifeboat and giving its shields extra power to survive detaching. That though would have taken more time and skill than any of them had. Had Chief Jons been alive… Maybe… She would have known just how to make that happen without thinking twice and give them more than they needed. Not even gone for a day and already Beatrice needed her friend there to help them. They quickly moved onto a new plan when Beatrice was unable to carry on thinking about her loss. Others suggested taking one of the rear lifeboats. Being at the back there was less ship to tear them up as it went by and the rest of the shielding from the forward sections of the ship would reduce the pressures exerted on them. That though risked them being spun out of control by the speed of the *Galactic Passage* going by to the point of

413

losing consciousness but there was a chance it would work. That or they would be spun until they turned into jam or caught in the engine burn and vaporised.

No matter what they tried to think of doing, nothing would give them an acceptable chance of surviving. Any chance was better than none. But she wanted to get the best odds possible.

What else was there for her to suggest so she could get her crew off the *Galactic Passage*? What other methods were there to leave the train wreck in motion behind? Then it hit her.

The SPF – their patrol ship had more than enough space for her and her remaining crew to leave with them. Being military grade, its shields were more than enough to withstand the forces being exerted on the luxury liner as well. Only problem was they were no longer docked with them. They had detached and were somewhere on the outside, probably keeping close, until the sergeant radioed for them to return and dock once more.

'Do we have any comms yet?' she asked.

'Let me check,' Dolga requested. He rushed to the comms station and his face lit up like he had just won the lottery. 'Holy shit, our system reboot after the storm has finally worked! It's not the best, but it's something.'

'Thank you,' Beatrice said. The smile on her face was uncontrollable. She opened a comm with the patrol ship. 'Helmsman Zenkovich, do you read? I say again, Zenkovich, do you read me?'

'I hear you lady,' came the pilot's response. 'What's up?'

'We need a ride,' she stated. 'We've got no way off this thing.'

'Little hard at the moment,' Ivan Zenkovich replied. 'But let me try and get through to the guys on there with you to sort something out. Either you need to be as quick as them to get to me when I re-dock or they can come pick you up before I dock. One way or another we can get you, but you need to be quick. The speeds you're going to be hitting soon mean I won't be able to stay docked with you for long. They would rip us apart as well.'

'That's understood, thank you,' Beatrice replied. She could barely contain her excitement.

'It's okay. I'll radio in when I have an update. Out.'

Prematurely or not, the crew earned the right to celebrate. This was their ticket to get off the ship safely. It was just a matter of time. They were all ready to make the move when needed, and none of them would be left behind.

Beatrice waited eagerly.

Jesa

Jesa and Professor Ainslot bagged the dead in silence, as instructed by Zenkovich, before stowing them in the freezer tucked below the floor just in front of the engine room. On the pilot's orders, they stripped the armour and weaponry off the soldiers for analysis later, to see what they had been up against. Looking at their bodies, they were not normal people – they had been highly experimented on. What looked like a thin, pale wire mesh across their entire bodies was actually scarring in a faint criss-cross pattern. Scarred blobs that looked like points of injection by hefty needles lined their limbs in symmetry. Aside from those scars, however, they looked like nearly perfect specimens of humanity. Almost Godly with their defined muscles and chiselled facial structures, like they had been created in a lab to be both beautiful and deadly.

Between them, they tried to decide what they were and why they looked that way but couldn't find an explanation good enough. If Medic Suttle were there, they were sure he would have been able to answer some of their questions for them with his medical knowledge.

The armour was equally fascinating. It was much lighter than the SPF armour, almost delicate, yet so much more advanced. Built into the armour was a reactive gel layer that solidified around any opening, creating a solid seal should there be any damage. The helmet HUD wasn't a still format, but reactive to where the eyes of the wearer looked. Each angle showing different information, perfect for making sure the wearer wasn't overloaded with too much information at any one time. Printed on the chest piece wasn't a name. It was a number. One read: 001-C-0281, the other: 001-C-0475. Clearly a unit designation, but how did that translate? She was sure that the sergeant would be able to figure it out.

When the bodies were safely stored in the fridges and their weapons and armour stored in the armoury, Jesa and Samuel gave a final goodbye to Valentina Rodriguez and Abe Udal'e before they joined Ivan Zenkovich on the flight deck. They tailed the *Galactic Passage* in close range but kept to one side. Almost as if they were stalking the liner. Ivan had his headset on, listening to chatter from within the vessel on the comms. She wondered how many Outer ships had been tailed like this by the UPN or any other Centie faction while on their day-to-day tasks.

Jesa could see the enemy frigate docked with the liner as the pilot brought them around to the other side. It was a large vessel, almost triangular in shape coning off toward the nose with enough space for at least four decks just in front of the engines going down to two decks behind the flight deck. There were no windows to the outside except for on the bridge. Panels along the hull stuck out at jagged angles giving a devilish presence. Painted along the side of the vessel was the name: *Shadow Spectre*. Clearly suggesting that the warship was never meant to be discovered or would be haunting those it pursued. What looked like point defence cannons were far and few. If it intended to defend itself, the warship must have had more weaponry stored internally that were not on display. Jesa disagreed with Ivan when he explained that it probably had more defensive features like improved shielding or engines than it did firepower. Something that advanced had to have more powerful weaponry.

'You ever seen anything like this before?' she asked Professor Ainslot.

He shook his head. 'Never. I only had to jump on and off a ship. Don't have to know anything about them or pay attention to them, I just need them to get me to my next research project.'

Ivan Zenkovich didn't reply. He was too busy with whatever was going on over the comms. He surely had seen this sort of vessel before.

'Ivan? Do you know what sort of ship that is?' she asked, tapping him gently on the shoulder.

He shook his head softly. 'Not a clue. First time I've seen it. What I can tell you about it is that it's designed to be quick and difficult to see on the radar.'

The helmsman held up his hand and silenced her from asking anything else. A commotion boomed over the headset loud enough for them to hear but not quite make out. He let out an expletive but nothing to worry about.

'What's going on in there?' she questioned when his hand was lowered.

'Same as before, they're either fighting the wolves or fighting the enemy soldiers,' he answered with a shrug. 'Last I heard we haven't lost anyone but we're doing good against the soldiers. Really good. Too good. We've pushed them back to... their... Oh? What've we got going on here?'

It was difficult to see at first what the pilot could see that Jesa couldn't. She leaned over him to get a better look at the enemy ship.

The engines started to fire up, and PDCs moved as they were brought online. The enemy frigate was coming back to life.

'Looks like they're trying to kick off,' Ivan stated, flipping several switches and keying commands into the controls. 'Don't know why they're doing that. I didn't give them permission to leave. I need you both to strap in. But not back there, kid. I need a co-pilot up here and I don't trust the lecturer to get on the stick. No offence.'

'None taken,' Professor Ainslot replied, strapping into his chair. 'Much happier back here. Thank you.'

'Why me?' Jesa questioned.

'Because, you know how to fly. I don't need to give you much of a lesson. Now move it, I need you fastened in and comfortable before shit kicks off.'

Jesa clambered into the co-pilot's chair and strapped in, pulling the restraints tight. She put on the headset Ivan passed over to her and was immediately tuned into the world outside. The team attacking the soldiers were making good grounds. Good enough to force the soldiers to abandon ship. The enemy soldiers were sealing the airlock after themselves so that the joint force couldn't follow. The docking tube retracted. Jesa watched as the frigate pushed away from the liner and the engine roared into life. It manoeuvred away from the luxury liner.

'What do you need me to do?' she asked.

'See that stick there? Take it. Ever flown something that bites?' When she didn't reply, the pilot smiled at her and pointed at the controls. 'Pull the trigger where your finger naturally wraps, and you'll fire the chin cannon. Press the left button on top and you launch missiles. Only push that one when I tell you to push it. Okay? We don't have that many and they're fucking expensive to replace. Don't want them to come out of my budget. Right button is chaff, launch it if we're targeted. They're to save us from rockets but we can't tell the difference between rockets or bullets when targeted so if we get locked push it. You'll see the lights flash around the edge of the screen when they lock on. That screen on the console is your target guidance control system. It does most of your work for you. Look at that, you've just had your crash course in gun controls.'

'So why do you need me?' Jesa replied. 'I mean, if that does most of the work for you?'

'I need to concentrate. In close quarters like this there's too much risk that I might fly into the *Passage* while keeping them in my sights for me to try and manage two jobs at once,' Ivan Zenkovich answered while taking a healthy swig from a hip flask.

'And that?'

'Helps me concentrate,' he explained, taking another mouthful. 'Now heads up, they're moving their PDCs to target us. Our shields won't hold forever against them. I need to make sure they don't hit us first when the shooting starts. Aim for the engines and when I say, pull the trigger. I'm just going to pull up behind them like so, line it up so you have a clear shot like this. Well? Fire!'

She pulled the trigger, holding it until Ivan barked the command for her to let go. Bullets peppered everything but the engines. Jesa tried again, following the instructions Zenkovich gave as close to the letter as possible. She pulled the trigger in shorter bursts this time, managing to strike the engines. They flashed and flared as the rounds slammed into them but carried on running. It was going to take more than that to stop them.

'Another salvo, fire,' Ivan ordered. 'Fire now.'

Jesa did as commanded and fired once more. Most of her shots missed as the *Shadow Spectre* evaded her shots until it turned to face them. Alarms blared as the frigate placed target locks on them for the multiple point defence cannons. Ivan took evasive manoeuvres to avoid target lock. Jesa released a burst of chaff in reaction to the alarms. Ivan Zenkovich steered the patrol ship around the *Galactic Passage*. The enemy frigate tried its best to mirror their actions but couldn't match them. It seemed their pilot wasn't up to Zen's abilities. When out of sight, Ivan sharply turned them with a line of fire pointing directly where the enemy vessel should show. Yet it didn't come into view. They continued to stare into space.

'Where are they?' Professor Ainslot asked, his breath sharp as if ready to puke.

'No idea,' Zenkovich replied. 'It should be right there. Keep your eyes... oh shit! Get ready to hurl! This is going to hurt.'

The patrol ship pushed forward at full throttle. Several target locks were being picked up, but Jesa couldn't see where they were coming from or react quick enough. All she could do was feel the weight of the world bearing down on her body as the tight rapid manoeuvre was carried out. It had been years since she felt her bones compress and muscles tense in a sharp move like that. Her hands struggled to hold onto the control stick. Being able to breathe became a challenge.

'I can't see them,' Jesa groaned as the pressures carried on piling onto her.

'It's because they're behind us!' Ivan screamed as more alarms rang out. 'I'm going to do something that's going to really hurt. But when I do, you'll know when to pull the trigger.'

As much as she didn't believe he could hurt them any more than he already was doing, Ivan Zenkovich proved he wasn't exaggerating. They were thrown into such a tight turn that Jesa thought she was going to fall straight through her seat and to the back of the ship. Maybe even through the engine and out into the void of space. Warning lights flashed and the klaxon wailed in protest. Something wasn't right. Ivan answered her pleas to know what was happening only to be told that the docking tube holding her ship in place was being strained beyond what it was meant to be put through. If it carried on any longer the tube would fail and snap. If that happened, it was a fifty-fifty chance of her ship striking the patrol ship. She wondered if when they were done, would she see her ship floating away into the distance after the docking tube breaks trailing pieces of the ships behind it.

The frigate came sharply into view. Jesa hesitated. The forces bearing down on her had been too great for a snap reaction. She needed to recover. By the time she found the strength to pull the trigger only a few rounds struck the frigate. Ivan hurtled forward and past the enemy warship, taking a few scathing strikes of return fire. They flew around the liner then took off into the distance, leading the fight away from the luxury ship and toward the black of space. The enemy ship tailed them, firing pot-shots at them hoping to strike a lucky destabilising blow on them. The fatal shot never arrived. Their ship only took a few hull shots that were predominantly deflected by the shields. Those that did strike only penetrated the outer hull plating.

Ivan pushed their bodies to the limits as he did all he could to remain out of target lock. Jesa wondered how much longer she could last before she blacked out. This was more than she had ever had to deal with before.

'Okay. When you next have a clear shot, I'll give the order. You push the left button,' Ivan Zenkovich ordered. 'Don't hesitate. Just push it.'

'The left button?' Jesa questioned, surprised that she was even asked to push it. 'Sure?'

'I'm as sure as water is wet,' Ivan said. 'You stay with me on this one. Need you to stay sharp.'

420

'Okay,' she said.

She wasn't sure. Could she do that? Since siding with the SPF, she didn't want any of that. She didn't like having a pistol in a holster strapped to her thigh, even if it was for her own protection. Jesa was never meant to handle a weapon. Hadn't really been trained to use one before. The code said it gave the smugglers too much power when they weren't supposed to have it. Offered a chance to overthrow their masters. And now she had control over missiles capable of incinerating humans to their atoms. It was all against what she had been brought up to believe.

'Good girl, now you two don't forget to keep breathing,' Ivan instructed. 'Stop breathing and neither of you are any use to me and I'll be waiting on the other side for you.'

The ship turned in a single sharp spin. It was harsh, nauseating and exhilarating all at the same time. Then the enemy frigate came back into view. Drawing closer every second. This time she didn't hesitate. She didn't forget what she had to do. When Ivan gave the order Jesa pushed the button and fired a single missile. The explosive slammed into the frigate and detonated on its shields in an explosive display of fire and light. The shielding shimmered underneath the fireball. It didn't breach the hull. The ship itself was intact. But the defensive shield protecting it was clearly weakened, if still usable at all.

The frigate still had target locks on them. They were still in the firing line. Even she knew that they needed to act first before the crew of the hostile vessel could regain control. All it would take was one well-placed shot in this standoff and they were done for.

'Fire again! Do it now!' Helmsman Zenkovich barked.

Jesa pushed the button to release a missile and pulled the trigger to pepper the vessel with PDC rounds simultaneously. The missile and heavy salvo of rounds slammed into the frigate. It's weakened shields finally wavered as they collapsed. Several shots cut through the frigate's hull. She had inflicted the pain and they were clearly hurting. Atmosphere vented into the void of space.

The *Shadow Spectre* didn't return fire. Instead, the crew powered up its engines. It sped past them before Jesa could react or be given any orders. As the helmsman turned their ship to pursue, the frigate came into view just as a wormhole opened in front of it. She didn't know what else to do except fire as much ammunition as she could at the hostile ship until it entered slip space and disappeared from the local area. They sat there gawping at the empty void. Nothing except stars in the background and somewhere out there was the liner. Only the flashing lights of a damaged docking tube and the cursing Ivan Zenkovich made disrupted the surreal view.

'They're gone,' Jesa whispered.

'I know,' Ivan growled.

'Where have they gone?' Professor Ainslot asked.

'I don't know,' Ivan replied. 'Fuck I don't know. But they got out of here.' Ivan flipped a few switches and leaned back in his chair. 'Sergeant, you there? Sergeant? Beatrice?'

'I'm here,' Beatrice replied.

'Hostile ship has left the AO,' the pilot reported. 'Returning to the ship now.'

'Understood,' the female officer said. 'Hold position around the *Galactic Passage* and wait until cleared to dock. I'm not risking anyone that's left on my ship getting off uninvited.'

'Don't you worry, no one is getting on here unless I say so,' Ivan growled.

'And me,' Jesa chimed in.

Ivan Zenkovich smiled gratefully at her support. 'We're enroute now. Keep me updated.' He cut the comms, activated the autopilot to bring them back the *Passage* and turned to Samuel. 'Right, professor, start talking.'

'What do you mean?' Professor Ainslot questioned.

'You worked with the MID. You know them better than any of us here. I want to know why they would leave when they had the stronger force,' the pilot demanded. 'When they had the resources to fight and win.'

'I don't know,' the man stuttered. 'I'm a scientist, not a soldier. I'm barely a field agent! I mean, they would go if they achieved their objective or if they were losing the fight like anyone else would. But you know the score. We don't leave anyone behind. Even I was trained to know that. Anything else, you're probably more of the expert than me.'

'So, they're gone, gone?' Jesa asked.

'I'd say so,' Professor Ainslot said. 'But what do I know?'

Jesa smiled. She was happy knowing that at least it appeared there was one less threat on the ship to hunt down the sergeant and his team. It gave them all a better chance of making it through the fight and getting off the *Galactic Passage*.

She watched as the liner came into view, while Ivan tried to get as much information as possible from the professor. With no one else to turn to the information was sketchy at best. But it was a start to understand what would be left for them if the other agents were still on the ship. The professor said something, she couldn't tell what he said, her mind wasn't anywhere near the conversation. Whatever he said had sprung Ivan Zenkovich to get back onto the radio screaming for Beatrice or the rest of his team back on-board the liner. She wondered what it could be to get him so riled up.

Jesa refocussed her attention on the conversation.

Chapter 13
16/11/2675
21:42 Earth Standard Time

Beatrice Lenoia

The Stellar Protection Force patrol ship was still some distance from the *Galactic Passage*. It had led the hostile frigate safely away from them to keep her ship out of the firing line. Beatrice watched on the holographic display in front of the command chair as the battle was underway. It appeared that the hostile ship was holding back more than it could give. She wondered why, as there was nothing to stop them. Then it disappeared, vanishing into nothing to leave the SPF patrol ship alone. After radioing in with her they fell silent to return. There, their way off the *Passage* lingered. Hundreds of miles away from them on a slow flight path. Much slower than she thought they would have moved at. The next she knew the patrol ship lurched and was accelerating at a rapid rate.

'Captain,' a voice cried from her key crew. 'The pilot's hailing us from the patrol ship again. Says it's important and can't wait.'

'Send it through,' she commanded and resumed speaking when the comms link was given to her. 'This is Beatrice.'

'Finally!' the man cried. 'I thought I wasn't going to be able to get through to you. Look. We've got a problem. By we, I mean you.'

'What's going on?' Beatrice asked.

'Turns out, that since that ship's fucked off the way it did when they could have stood their ground isn't a good thing for us. It means they've completed their mission,' the helmsman explained. 'Or they've been getting their asses handed to them. By the reports I'm listening into, it ain't that. That means they've only gone and done the job they were meant to do and are happy that we're not going to live to tell the tale.'

'Shit!' Beatrice screamed as her heart sank. All that effort, all that bloodshed, and for what? 'Fuck!'

'Oh, that's not the problem you've got,' the man added. 'You best prepare yourself for company.'

'What do you mean?'

'The agents that didn't agree with Foresc? We don't know if they're on that ship, or on your ship. If they're still on your ship their only safe way out of here now is through me and my ship. That means they will probably try to take the bridge and use you to bring me in for a ride out. We'll be back with you as soon as possible. I'm going to try to get hold of the others and tell them to get a move on. Keep your position secure and stay in touch. Be ready to make a move when we dock.'

'Understood,' she replied. 'Thanks for the heads up. Out.'

Beatrice took watched as the stellar body at the centre of the solar system grew steadily larger as they flew closer. They were hurtling through the void of space doing all they could to ensure the survival of the rest of humanity and she was sat there giving instructions and making conversation while the enemy was most likely on their way to her bridge to take control of her ship. Her hands clenched tightly into fists. What was there she could do to help but warn everyone?

She observed her bridge crew; they were as fatigued as her. Some had the remnants of coffee, energy drinks, and what she could only assume was caffeine pill packets, strewn around. Others bobbed their heads as exhaustion caught up with them and would have succumbed to the need to sleep had one or two of their peers not nudged them awake again. All shared sunken shoulders of people that had given up and knew the end was near. Hoping that soon they would be out of there.

It would all be over soon, she thought, although she knew that chances were it wasn't going to go their way.

The chatter was coming through the radio clearly. The joint force was discussing with the helmsman of the patrol ship where they would dock so they could escape. They did right to try and figure out where to go. Any of her crew that was still alive throughout the ship, if they were still alive, would also be able to regroup with them. They could get on that ship and get off the god forsaken liner.

Beatrice massaged her injured arm. It hurt. A poorly treated wound that was only getting worse with time. Hopefully, there was no long-lasting damage done to it and a bit of treatment in a hospital would put it right.

'Captain,' the guard said in her ear. He made sure that only she could hear him.

'What is it?' She whispered.

'We're going to have company. We got three hostiles, looks to me like it's those agents. They're making their way up to the bridge. Just a couple decks below us now.'

That confirmed that then. They were in trouble, and trouble was going to be with them soon. That was a good thing though because if they were on their way to them, the joint force could get out of there.

Safely. And so could everyone else. Or at least they could move a little safer.

'Can we slow them down?' she asked.

Knoxx let out a shallow sigh. 'We can do a little bit to slow them. I'll have all the blast doors shut, but they won't hold for long. Not long enough for help to get here at least. Even less time if they know what they're doing with the controls. They'll be on the bridge long before that. When they get here and through that door, there will only be so much that I can do to hold them off. I'm outnumbered.'

Beatrice hung her head momentarily then spoke slowly through clenched teeth, calculated precision behind every word. He sounded too much like he was prepared to give up. 'We all have a job on this bridge. We owe it to everyone that we hold our position for as long as we can. Regardless of if they're dead or alive. They deserve us to put up a fight. You have command of the security on this deck. Tell me what you need me to do.'

'Nothing,' he answered. 'You're to take cover and stay out of harm's way. You've already been injured. I can't risk you getting involved. We need you to continue to lead.'

'I might be your captain, but if they get on this bridge, my bridge, it won't matter. They'll kill me like they'll kill you. So, I guess I'm already involved. If I can at least help you defend the bridge, I will. I won't ask again.'

'That was asking?'

'It was. Just you wait until I'm not asking.'

Knoxx adjusted his gauntlet, pushed an unnoticeable button on the underside of it and the giant shield contained within expanded out. He flashed her a cunning smile.

'Fine, but you stay close to me or behind your command chair. That's made from the same stuff the rest of your ship is made of. Nothing that's standard issue will be able to even put a dent in it. When they get through you do your best to stay behind there for cover. Wouldn't be surprised if they were packing a few CEDs. If that's the case, they can punch their way through with only a few charges. If we're lucky and they're not packing charges, then they'll try to hack their way through the controls to get to us. It'll take a little longer but will be the same result. However, it does give me the advantage. Got a weapon? Crew, keep us up to date. We need to know what's happening or if anything changes.'

Beatrice plucked out her sidearm, and with some effort made sure it was loaded. If she had a shot of pain killers to jab into her arm, she would have pushed it in until the needle touched the bone. Anything to make loading a weapon easier. For now, adrenaline would have to ease the pain, or at the least mask it long enough to do a job. Knoxx with an automatic pistol in hand stood at the ready in front of the door to the corridor outside the bridge.

The waiting game they played in silence was torturous. Listening to the commentary of the bridge crew as they watched the progression of the enemy, she could pick up on their emotions. Her crew was scared. Understandably so. They were supposed to be getting ready to leave the ship behind, not stand their ground. It was like watching a slow-moving sand timer which only went down one grain at a time. The agents reached them soon enough and began work on the first blast door. There was no detonation on the other side, not even a mild thud. It seemed they weren't armed with explosives after all. They bypassed the security locks for the first layer of defence with ease. Beatrice flinched when the primary doors opened with a heavy clunk. They were held up a little longer at the second blast door. As she listened to the door slowly slide open, a notch at a time, Beatrice knew that it wouldn't take them much longer to open it just enough to access the final line of defence. Then they would have access onto the bridge.

She felt like a deer caught in the headlights of a monstrous vehicle, knowing the inevitable fate that approached and was powerless to do anything about. It was a sobering thought, reminding her of her own humanity. Her frail existence that, up until then, had been more than fortunate to have not been snubbed out.

'Get me a comm link with the guys still on the ship,' she instructed.

'Captain?' a man asked when the comm link was established. Ronan Moasa.

'Corporal, what's your position?'

'We're on D-Deck. Can't find those damn agents anywhere. What's going on, Captain?'

'The agents are here,' she explained. 'They'll soon be through and on the bridge. That makes it clear down there. Get your ship docked, get on it and get the hell out of here while you still can.'

'Fuck that, we're on our way to you. You're coming with us,' the soldier replied. 'That was the deal.'

'Negative. I need you to evacuate. Take this opportunity to get off safely while you have it. That's an order.'

A deep and low rumbling trembled through the blast doors. The enemy was finally through to the last set of doors and were using explosives. It turned out they had brought them, just saving them until final barrier. Smart. If it had been the other way around, they might not have succeeded.

'Sorry Captain, but we're coming to get you, then going to get our bosses,' Corporal Moasa stated. 'We don't leave anyone behind.'

'That's not happening either,' she snapped. Another explosion detonated on the other side of the doors, buckling them. 'You won't be able to get here in time. You're leaving. I can disable the ship's controls so she's flying dead ahead. No deviation, no slowdowns. Even if we lose, they will lose too. You have your chance to get out and you're taking that chance and you're leaving. Get to your ship.'

'Negative Captain, we're not leaving you,' the soldier retorted, resistance heavy in his voice.

There was another detonation. The blast doors groaned and creaked under the pressure. They were losing integrity. Soon the agents would make their way through.

'God-dammit, Corporal!' Beatrice spat as another explosion roared. 'You're getting on your ship and—'

'Captain, they're breaking through!' Knoxx cried out. 'Take cover!'

The final explosion from the other side ripped the blast doors apart. Searing heat hit her after the shockwave. Shrapnel was sent flying through the air, pinging off the guard's shield, striking terminals and cutting into her remaining crew. Their pained screams sent chills down her spine. Some were able to power through the pain to continue their work. Others succumbed to the injuries and were unable to continue.

The unmistakable crack of a gunshot boomed through the settling smoke and debris to reverberate through the bridge. Shock froze her for a moment – this was unfolding on her command deck, supposedly the safest place on the ship. Second and third shots rang through the air, slamming into the walls. It was like she was absent for a moment. When the next few rounds flew through the air, her mind went into overdrive as she accepted the reality of what was going on. Any one of those shots could be the death of them all, crew and enemy alike, as they get pulled into the void of space if it hit the glass.

'Close the heat shields!' she screamed.

Knoxx opened fire at the incoming hostiles, turning himself into a human target. The distraction gave her crew still able to work time to shut the thick metal slabs on the outside of the ship with heavy thuds, locking into place, over the glass. She could breathe a little easier knowing that her death wouldn't be any time soon because of a misplaced shot puncturing any of the viewing windows.

Beatrice turned her attention back to the oncoming assailants, helping Knoxx with the defence of the bridge. There were two attackers to the left of the opening that the guard took the liberty of targeting and one to the right that she was left with. Every time they mounted a sudden offence, she was forced into cover behind the command chair until the shots eased then she returned fire with equal ferocity. After the fourth volley, when both she and Knoxx needed to reload their weapons, the agents breached the opening and successfully entered her domain.

The enemy fired without mercy or hesitation, their targets picked out with a marksman's skill and timing. She watched for only a few seconds as her surviving crew were picked off at their posts. Some were taken out as they tried to assist in holding back the enemy, charging for the agents on instinct alone even though they had no weapons to fight with. Others were eliminated while trying to take cover.

Beatrice screamed in terror. In the commotion she couldn't hear her own cry. Only the heavy, rapid beating of her heart in her ear drum. Time seemed to slow as she watched her crew's bodies fall. Beatrice broke out from her protection. She needed to do more to keep the agents at bay, even if Knoxx tried to tell her otherwise. She squared her aim at the lone agent and squeezed her trigger repeatedly, letting off over a half dozen rounds. Several of them slammed the hostile square in the torso and seemed to not faze him. The others hit the space around the agent except for one lucky shot that went through their visor and into the forehead. The body fell back and lay motionless on the floor.

She proudly looked at her handiwork. She still had it. The killer instinct needed to take part in a fight. To more importantly be able to make it out the other side of the fight. Age apparently hadn't been that cruel to her after all.

She turned to the fight still raging between the other three present on her bridge. Knoxx was becoming overwhelmed, taking cover behind his shield. Several bullets ricocheted off it, pinging off several surfaces nearby. Then it hit her. A strange sensation went through her midsection, painful but not painful at the same time. Blood stained the front of her uniform, growing and feeding downward toward her trousers. When the pain was realised, it was intense. Almost unbearable. Her innards had been penetrated and shredded, sections turned into a purified mess after a series of deflected bullets had passed through. She fell toward her command chair, hitting her head on the way down. When she landed on the floor, her mind was fuzzy. Confused. Unfocussed. She turned her hazy gaze to see Knoxx in an almost berserk state of fury. He used the shield like an extension of his own body. Firing his pistol in quick bursts in conjunction with the defensive structure he wielded both the offensive and defensive capabilities. It was fluid. The two agents fighting against him were almost no match for his skill. Beatrice shook off the groggy weariness and returned to full sobriety in the fight in time to see Knoxx be struck a deadly clubbing blow to the face. Their eyes locked for the sharpest of seconds.

Go, he mouthed at her. His eyes darted to the helm.

Knoxx returned to the fight as if they never exchanged that moment. Screaming as he rose to his feet. Ready to fight like the warrior he was.

Beatrice used what strength she still had to lift one arm in front of the other and dragged her body along the floor as quickly as possible. Each motion was as painful as the last. Unrelenting, she crawled for the helm. When the agents realised what she was doing, they did whatever they could to get around her guard to reach her. Knoxx stayed steadfast. Fighting them valiantly. Keeping them both occupied.

'Captain, what's your situation?' Corporal Moasa questioned over the comms. 'Captain?'

She didn't respond. She couldn't. Her teeth were clenched too tightly with pain. Her hands balled into fists, grasping onto the life she could feel steadily leaving her. She just needed to hold on a little longer. Just long enough to make sure no one could change the course of history.

Knoxx cried out in a blood curdling scream of pain, barking for her to hurry before being silenced with an extended burst of sub-machine gun fire. She fought through the agony, stood up and sprinted forward the several feet to reach the helm.

'Get off the ship,' Beatrice cried over the comms as she pushed forward on the sub-light engines, increasing the thrust to maximum. 'The bridge is compromised.'

Another shot went through her shoulder. Lenoia screamed out in pain but didn't waiver. She unloaded the last of the rounds in her pistol into the station and rendered the controls useless. There was no way now that they could override the system and slow the ship down. No way to turn around and dodge the star. Not even her officer privileges would allow her to take control from the command chair after having that luxury disabled.

'Captain, we're on our way,' Corporal Moasa said. 'We'll get you out of there. Just hold on!'

'Negative,' she said weakly, falling to the floor with her back against the helm. 'I'm done. Get out.'

The soldier continued to protest. It was reassuring to say the least that he was so determined to help her. He was a good man. She regretted that there was nothing he could do for her except leave. That was more than she needed him to do.

The two remaining agents hobbled over, one crouching down in front of her holding a pistol to the side of her temple. He grinned at her with a smile through his visor that was more out of annoyance than it was out of joy. Jerome Houghton. The other was the female. Fellstrum.

'Have you done what I think you've done?' he asked her rhetorically.

She didn't say a word. She wasn't strong enough to at that point. Instead, Beatrice nodded her head slowly, with a smile of her own. A smile of victory.

The frustration flushed across his face. 'How long have we got?' When she didn't answer straight away, he nudged the muzzle of the pistol into her skull aggressively. 'How long?'

Beatrice took several deep breaths and weakly spoke, 'About an hour. Maybe an hour and half. One way. I win.'

'Fuck!' the agent screamed. 'Do you realise what you've done?'

The smile already plastered across her face only grew larger. Indeed, she knew exactly what she had done. And to know it had upset the agent this much made it all worth it. It meant that they really had won There was no way he could succeed with his mission. There was no way the agents were making it out alive. She had just saved a lot of lives throughout the UPN territories and outside the United Planetary Nations' governance. Or at least that's what she told herself, choosing to ignore the hostile frigate that had already departed.

'You know I really could kill you, right? It's not like there's anyone around that could stop me.'

'Why… Then why…'

'Why don't I just do it?' he asked, finishing her sentence for her. She nodded. 'Why do that when I can save a bullet and just let you suffer a little longer? You're either going to die when we land in that star, bleed out or, my favourite option, get eaten by one of those wolves we have on board. You're dead no matter what.'

He had a point. But the creatures were dead as well. They were all dead. What did it matter how she died in the end? Beatrice shrugged her shoulders softly then let them fall limp at her sides.

'Maybe... But you won't be long behind me.'

Jerome scoffed. 'Not any time soon. If you don't mind, I'm going to go try hitch a ride off this shipwreck.'

She watched as the agents left her bridge and the carnage behind. Left her alone. The death around her was incomprehensible. Her crew dead, murdered with barely a chance of defending themselves. Knoxx lay on his back in a pool of blood. He had been braver than anyone could have asked him to be. Had it not been for him, she would not have been able to succeed and put the ship on the collision course needed to win. They all deserved to be remembered.

When the footsteps faded away into nothing, all she could hear was the ship picking up speed. The metal structure supporting her vessel groaning under the increased forces pushing on it. The electrical discharges of damaged circuits created rain made up of sparks. It was nice in a way. A similar effect to that of listening to a waterfall with birds in the background. She could think. Though she wished that she couldn't.

Her mind was cast back over her life. Beatrice had been so proud when she was given her first command within the United Planetary Nations' Navy. It was one of the few things that were more important to her than passing the officer's academy back on Earth. Falling in love was so special to her heart. Emanuel had always been wonderful to her, taking her places she never thought of going. Together they revelled in the birth of their children. That was when she first knew she had to leave the Navy. After so many years of her life dedicated to the safety of the citizens of the UPN, she decided to leave so she could dedicate the rest of it to her family. Thanks to the move Beatrice had been able to watch her family grow. Strengthen. And she was happy going on the voyages because she would return to them.

Home. She was supposed to come home. She was supposed to hold her family close once again. But she wasn't going to. Her legacy though would live with them, and they would have to find the strength to continue without her. If they ever learnt about what happened to her on-board the *Galactic Passage*.

432

The first tear to roll down her cheek came out of nowhere. Then she wept as her life that would never happen began to unfold before her.

Duke Horren

They were almost there.

Leyton had guided the pair all the way down to the belly of the ship. There had been no encounters, but they were being watched. Every corner turned and opening clambered through was watched by prying red eyes that never came close. They only observed, keeping their distance, lurking in the shadows. Almost as if guiding them to the den, preventing them from turning down an incorrect corridor. Duke itched to turn his shotgun on them and unleash several shells per beast. He knew if he did that, their chances of catching Spike went from slim to none. The wolves would hunt them down. Spike would not be found, and all their efforts would be for nothing. Duke kept his weapon slung low to keep the temptation to pull the trigger on them prematurely.

The disorientating smell had intensified as they reached the lowest deck. The respirator built into his armour was useless. His eyes still watered at the stench. How the agent managed to cope without a helmet was beyond him. Leyton silently gestured forward to the end of the corridor – a door was wide open where the gloopy secretion that the ice wolves used to create their nest was at its thickest. The viscous substance reached out and down the hallway like a monster that was clawing out for its next victim, not realising that they were willingly walking toward it.

'You—'

Leyton silenced him almost immediately and he obeyed. It was just like hunting game in a forest. Remain quiet so that they did not alert the prey too soon. Keep the element of surprise firmly with them. They resorted to using basic hand signals for communication. Leyton confirmed that the target would be in the room ahead and that others would be there too.

When they were just a few feet away from the opening the pair could hear the chattering of the ice wolves. Their barks and huffs like glass breaking then cutting down metal permeated the air. The pair slowed their momentum down even more and waited for a moment on either side for the doorway, peering in to assess the area. Spike was there, the proud matriarch of the pack. She was at the back of the room on a wide nest of the gloopy secretion on top of what appeared to be large metal containers. A blue hue glowed from the cold storage units that originally housed the wolves beneath her. As predicted, there was a cohort of three other ice wolves in there too. Settled on their own nests. The cooing of young babies suckling was subtle. More developed youngsters played around in the murky realm. Some were half the size of a full-grown adult. It was quite cute but did nothing to deter him from what needed to be done.

Duke was suddenly very much aware of the threats that had been lingering out in the corridors following them. The sense of something behind him was no longer there. He glanced back, hoping to see something so that he knew where the others were. But he didn't. There was nothing. An empty corridor. Were the prowling wolves not allowed near the nest? Or were they waiting to catch them off guard? Maybe the pair of them had been permitted to approach the den and they were now off patrolling their territory. Either way, it was just them, four adult wolves and more pups than he could count. If he and Leyton were going to do this successfully, it had to be now. Duke held up three fingers on his left hand and waited for Leyton to see before counting down.

At the count of one his grip tightened on his shotgun. When he reached nil and was holding a fist up to the agent, they both wheeled into the storage room in unison. There was an initial pause as the wolves came to the realisation that their den had been invaded. Duke fired the first shot into the torso of the closest female as she snarled and barked at him. It took another four or five shells to put her down. A few of the larger, braver pups attempted to attack him, lunging for the pair, hurtling through the air without grace. Several were taken out mid-air or sidestepped before being put down. Leyton though was pre-occupied by an adult of his own as it charged him not long after the failed attack by the youngsters. Duke quickly reloaded and caught one of the other wolves off guard as it attempted to attack Leyton from behind, hoping to work with the other female to take out his friend. A few shots at its torso and underside downed it with ease. They forced the third female back and together they quickly despatched with the pups that were trying to protect their mothers.

'Sergeant, drop!' Leyton cried.

Duke followed the command and hit the floor, narrowly dodging the jaws of the final high-ranking female as she returned to the fight. Leyton claimed that one for himself. Leaving Duke to contend with Spike. The matriarch was on top of him before he could regain his footing. Holding the shotgun lengthways in her mouth was the only thing stopping her from biting down on his face. The gaping jaws and row upon row of teeth threatened him with every bite. The serrated tongue flicked out from under the shotgun, trying to get at his flesh. Each brush of the tongue scratched at his visor, making it harder to see with each lashing. Duke wasn't freeing himself of the predicament without help or creative thinking. He lifted a leg to awkwardly replace the grip of his right arm, and with his hand now free took control of his combat knife. Duke sliced the blade at the ice wolf's face, swinging for her neck then finally plunged it deep into her shoulder. She squealed in pain and backed away long enough for him to regain control of his shotgun. He squeezed the trigger several times, riddling her shoulders and face with shells. The amour-like flesh to her front was too thick. Nothing got deep enough to substantially weaken her.

It wasn't going to end the fight any time soon.

The wolf was bloodied and clearly hurting. She still stood her ground. The beast wasn't ready to go down. Spike glanced around and saw a cluster of her pups cowering to one side. She cried at them like any protective mother would. Ushering them to stay away or to flee. She then returned her focus on him. The matriarch charged forward, not even remotely deterred by the shells he fired at her. Spike knocked Duke back a couple feet into a mass of the sticky secretion before lunging toward him, intent on the killing blow. On instinct alone, Duke raised his weapon and squeezed out a few more shells, one striking his target square, another only a glancing shot that would cause nothing more than a graze. The final shot missed entirely. But she still came for him. He managed to prop his legs up under her throat to stop her from executing him. Her claws cut through his armour, stopping short of reaching his flesh at the gel layer under the plating. Duke brought his weapon round, pointing it straight into her mouth for the kill shot he desperately needed and pulled the trigger. The only sound was that of his heart as it sank. The trigger clicked but nothing happened. His shotgun had a jam. Its shell that was ready to finish the powerful creature unable to be fired. He instantly dropped the shotgun in panic and desperately held her back to preserve his life a little longer.

Spike edged her face forward, the spittle from each snap splashed over his visor. She was getting closer to him. His strength was failing. The rows of teeth lusted for the chance to bite him. The tongue scratched his visor. Her eyes glared deep into his soul. It wouldn't be long now.

Duke jumped a little to the shotgun blast that rang out. The matriarch jumped off him and with another shot fired she scampered out of the room. Her pups scattered and hurried after her. Whining for her to wait for them as they struggled to keep up. Spike called out for help while she fled down the corridors. Her cries fading the further she ran.

Duke hesitated, stuck in a lingering sense of being trapped. In his mind's eye he could still see her trying to kill him. Her gaping jaw striving to crunch through his helmet and rip into his skull. Leyton slapped his arm and brought his attention back to the present. He shook off the shock and reached over for his shotgun to inspect why it jammed on him. The gunk that canvassed the room had filled the barrel. He wiped out as much as he safely could until he was satisfied that it *should* fire when he needed it to.

'Are you okay?' Leyton asked, holding out a helping hand. 'Look a bit pale.'

'Fine,' he snapped. Duke recomposed himself and took the hand Leyton held out for him. As much as he didn't believe himself, he repeated his statement. 'I'm fine.'

Leyton clearly didn't believe him. His expression told that much. 'If you're sure. Come on, we need to… You feel that?'

The ship had started to surge forward. It picked up speed by the second. Subtle at first but more noticeable as he had to fight the increasing forces pushing against him to remain upright. The dampeners were either not working to their full potential or the ship was being pushed to levels that they couldn't handle.

'I do,' Duke replied. He activated an open channel comm link. 'What's going on up there? Report. Anyone out there?' Duke turned back to the agent. 'Any ideas why they're not responding?'

'None,' Leyton said then looked to the secreted padding around the cargo hold. 'Guessing all this crap has something to do with it.'

'Fuck. Let's get out of here,' Duke suggested. He glanced over to the corridor outside. 'We'll try to contact someone when we're a couple decks up.'

Duke couldn't have been keener to leave the room. Just being in the same room where the ice wolf matriarch had scared him, making his core tremble with a fear he wasn't sure how to handle. Yet he struggled to find the strength to leave, like something was holding him back. When he hesitated to leave the storage room Leyton led the way. A couple steps through the doorway and it hit him. A flashing, painful strike slammed his mind with the force of a sledgehammer controlled by a giant. All he could see when he closed his eyes was teeth. So many teeth. Each one trying to tear at his flesh. And those eyes. Those ruby red eyes that could only mean death positioned on the darkened face of the wolf.

Then it was over, but the pain resonated with him. Seared into his memory and nerve endings unlike any bullet or knife wound received before could do.

'Hey, you sure you're okay?' Leyton asked. The concern on his face turned into something more pissed off, knowing now was not the time to falter. 'If you're not then I gotta know, y'know?'

'Just a bit shaken up,' Duke admitted.

Leyton looked him square in the face. 'I ain't your babysitter or your agony aunt but listen. We got out of that. Not saying that what you just had to look at wasn't bad. But it's done. Now queen bitch is somewhere out there dying to have either one of us for payback. She's probably rounding up the rest of her pack to help her out as we speak. They're not going to be happy to see our handiwork. Or the fact we took out so many of their pups. I sure as hell ain't going to die knowing that you lost your edge. Have you lost your edge? Last time I checked; you weren't one to give up that easily.'

'No, I'm good. What's the plan then?'

'Plan is we get our troops, find out why we're speeding up then get the hell off this thing before it's too late.'

'After you then,' Duke said.

Even after they left the ice wolf den, he could smell its stench lingering on his skin, as if it permeated every pore on his flesh. It didn't matter how far away they were, or how many decks they had climbed in their pursuit of escape. The smell remained as if it had embedded himself into his cells like a virus trying to survive in a host. Haunting him.

The empty ship was eerie. Silence following them everywhere. Potentially hiding wolves around every corner. Keeping the ghosts of those that had died safe. Once full of life and now overridden with death. A sad sight.

Duke's radio crackled into life, filled with static. How much interference was there to disrupt his comms like that? 'Sergeant... read...?'

Corporal Moasa. His voice was concerned.

'I read you, what's your situation?' he replied.

'Sergeant!' Ronan exclaimed with relief. Duke had to concentrate to hear the full message from the soldier between the drops in quality from the bad reception, but at least he could get the full communication.

438

'We're going back on the patrol ship when Zen docks with the liner. The bridge is lost. Captain has fucked the controls so we're heading straight for the star at full throttle. We don't have long before we hit.'

Duke and Leyton shared a brief glance that carried the same meaning. They needed to get a move on before it was too late.

'What's your location? Same air lock?'

'Negative. We're relocating to the aft, starboard side airlock on Deck C,' Moasa explained. 'With the agent's old friends out there still, I didn't think it was smart to go back to where we were last time. It's the only way off the ship we have. I want to keep it under our control.'

'Understood and agreed,' Duke acknowledged. 'Hold your ground. We'll be with you soon.'

'Hurry, I don't know how long we've got.'

'Wilco, and Corporal, you've done well.'

'Thanks Sergeant. Out.'

That was it then. The ship was officially on a one-way trip. Everything else that had happened seemed just about pointless. Why go through all the effort to contain and defend the ship if they were going to just wind up in the middle of a star? He had lost a soldier for no reason. A member of the patrol ship's crew for nothing. So many passengers and crew had been pointlessly killed.

It was such a waste of life and it got him thinking once again. Could he really turn his back on the galaxy and leave his career when it was in such desperate need of good to be done? Even though the question was simple, it was a complicated one to answer. The universe that humanity occupied was still such a fragile place, and he now had Jesa to look after, to guide and ultimately keep on the correct side of society. What sort of a person would he be if he turned his back on everything when everything needed him the most? It took a certain type of person to forsake everyone that depended upon them. He was not that person.

'Hey, what's up?' Leyton asked. 'I know that look.'

Now was hardly the time to start to confess his feelings, but he couldn't help it. Just the one simple question being asked was like the button to release flood waters pressing against the emotional dam in his heart had been pushed with sudden and immediate force. The words were just as forceful as the rushing tide, unable to stop once they started. Set to wipe out whatever was caught in its path.

'You know how I mentioned I was supposed to retire?' Duke asked. 'How I was supposed to find somewhere to call home after this, find a shit job to keep me occupied and make a life for myself? How can I do that now? If I hadn't been here, all those people in the lifeboats on their way to the nearest safe planet would probably be dead right now. You'd probably have died by now. They only survived because of me and my team being here and responding when we did. I wouldn't have found Jesa and got her out of the mess she called life if I hadn't had a job to do.'

'And now you have no idea what to do,' Leyton added.

He nodded softly. 'That's right.'

'My advice?' Leyton offered calmly. 'Stick with what you know. You're not a lone wolf. You're no one-man army ready to take on the world. You're not even wired up for anything outside the military because you've been in it that long. You're a team player. More than that you watch over people. This life gives you what you need and what you thrive on. You retiring and taking on the rest of your life solo in a boring world will only go one of two ways: You'll either come crawling back into the military out of loneliness and lack of purpose because you've left the only thing you know, or you'll get drunk and put a bullet in your head to stop the pain from consuming any more of you than it already will have done. I think it's safe to say you're not prepared to die yet so staying where you are is the only thing that makes sense to me. Don't you think?'

Duke silently examined the reasoning. There was no flaw to it. 'I guess so.'

'Okay. Now we got that out of the way, come on. Let's get to your ship and get out of here. Then we can get you on the next job.'

Duke smiled the way he always did when he appreciated what someone was doing for him. It wasn't every day you made a friend from an enemy. Especially one that you could trust your life with. And yet it felt like they had been friends since school. The wonders of shared trauma. He knew it was all psychological, that chances were the emotions he was feeling were a way to cope with the situation at hand and that they would eventually wear off. The pleasantries of it though were worth enjoying while they had them. Maybe their connection would last after they make it off the *Passage*.

Even during his time in the covert division Special Execution of Tactics in Space, where he was pitted in some of the most dangerous situations the universe had to offer, Duke didn't build up the sort of bond he had with Agent Leyton Foresc with any of his old team. Those bonds he had were especially strong. And there he had been close to death on several occasions with his brothers and sisters. Had fought to keep his team alive. Helped them escape unspeakable torture.

He supposed though that he had never faced any ice wolves before now so that was the running contender for why he built this bond.

'I'm on your six,' Duke said, falling into step behind the agent.

Jesa

'Hold onto something!' Ivan Zenkovich cried.

Before she knew it, Jesa was being thrown around in her seat as the helmsman manoeuvred behind the flight path of the liner. The *Galactic Passage* continued to speed up on its one-way trip. She recognised the burn from the engines as the ship came into full view. The sub-lights were burning too brightly for it to be a safe speed and they were both on their way straight into the local star. As much as she wanted to turn away, Jesa knew that they needed to stay on course to save the others. Ivan polarised the glass so that the light of the stellar object ahead didn't blind them. He somehow managed to keep them close to the ship. Staying several dozen yards away at the most.

'Get on the comms,' Ivan Zenkovich ordered. 'Tell them we need them to slow down.'

'How come?' she questioned.

'Because that is something I'm not happy trying to dock with,' Ivan explained. 'If I have the choice, I want to be docking with something moving a lot slower.'

'You docked with my ship in light speed?' Jesa countered. 'What's the difference?'

'Difference was I had time to prepare, plan and get into position,' Ivan said. 'This time, I only have one shot. Add to that, their ship is falling apart, and we don't have good odds. I do it wrong, even slightly, and we're done for. No second chances. I want them to slow the fuck down.'

Jesa nodded. The comms systems were like those of her ship and easy to follow. Even if they did call her ship a piece of junk, under the armour plating they all were wired the same. She opened a comm link with the bridge and after several failed attempts she got through to Corporal Moasa.

'Corporal, I can't get the captain,' Jesa said. 'We need you to slow the liner down so we can get you off it. Can you speak to her?'

'That's not happening,' Ronan answered. 'Bridge is compromised. She's killed the controls and is probably dead by now. There's no stopping this train.'

'Shit,' she cussed. 'Where are you now?'

'Same place we agreed on. C-Deck,' the soldier said. 'Starboard side. Aft.'

'Have you heard from the sergeant?' Jesa queried.

'Not yet, we're still trying to get hold of him.'

'Okay, we're on our way,' Jesa said, grimacing at Ivan as he glared at her. 'Let me know if anything changes.'

'Will do, out.'

Ivan Zenkovich looked like he could have exploded where he sat with rage. That was not the update that he was expecting.

'Mayah, looks like we're doing this,' he snarled. 'Keep your hands off the stick and keep your eyes open. I won't be able to concentrate on anything apart from docking, so I need you to look out for anything that breaks free form the ship for me and shout out.'

At those speeds and with heat shielding being put to the test sections of the liner were crumbling away from the *Passage*. Each one a missile that would severely damage the patrol ship or destroy it and kill them in the process if it hit in the wrong place. Jesa felt out of her depth with this. She had never been in a position where she needed to spot things like that. More than that, she had to not be caught in the trance and tell Ivan about anything that was incoming. Would she be up for the job? Could her reactions call out falling debris in time or even guess correctly and call out actual debris instead of imagination?

'Hey,' Ivan said. 'You can do this. The sergeant believes in you. So, I believe in you. Okay?'

'Okay,' she whispered.

'Ready?'

'No!' Professor Ainslot shouted.

'Not really,' Jesa answered.

'Okay then, here we go!'

Ivan Zenkovich screamed as he pushed on the thrust and pulled them up alongside the liner. Debris was already falling away from the vessel ahead of where they needed to be. He brought them up the hull and past the bridge. Jesa spotted the docking port. Like the gateway to heaven, it shone under the intense light of the star. Ivan was almost there, just a few feet away. Something glistened from ahead. She called out as a piece of the hull's plating broke free and narrowly missed slamming into them. As the pilot veered to safety, he inadvertently pulled into the path of more debris. Jesa felt sick by the time Ivan had finished avoiding certain death.

The helmsman brought them in again for another attempt. He flipped a switch for the docking tube to connect, and when there should have been a heavy thud rumbling from below decks, an alarm started to blare out instead.

'Fuck!' Ivan Zenkovich blurted.

'What is it?' Jesa asked.

'The locking mechanism won't connect. We're going too damn fast for it. The safety measures are kicking in. It needs to be manually locked into place and sealed.'

'How do we do that?'

'There's a manual lever above the outer airlock door and another on the left,' Ivan explained. 'Both need to be moved into position to lock it exactly when I say. Do it too soon and we're latching onto thin air. After that, we have another manual lock above the inner airlock door that also needs to be locked into place before docking has been secured. Go. Get into position. I'll try to hold steady for you to get down there before I let you know when I'm going back in for another run.'

'I'm on it,' Jesa said.

She released the straps around her and forced herself out of her chair. Professor Ainslot unbuckled himself and joined her in the troop bay. He had a point when he told her that she might need the extra help. They stumbled as they traversed the decks and lost their footing repeatedly, finding it difficult to stay upright. When they reached the troop bay, the pair waited for the signal. Fighting the rapid changes of direction as best they could. Falling into the seats around them. A sudden jolt sent Jesa through the air, sliding along the belly of the troop bay and down the lower hatch into her ship.

Jesa slammed into the floor with a sudden thud. She gasped, coughed and fought for breath as she struggled back to her feet.

'Jesa!' Samuel screamed. 'Jesa, are you okay?'

'Fine,' she wheezed. Her body ached. Something had to be bruised.

'I'm coming to get you.'

'No, you stay up there,' Jesa insisted. 'No point two of us being down here.'

Jesa started the slow, strained rise to the transport ship. Each step up the ladders was difficult. Samuel Ainslot reached out as she came close to the top, took hold of her hand and lifted her through to the troop bay. While she regained her breath, the academic shut the door to her ship so that neither of them could fall back through.

Are you okay?' Samuel asked.

'I will be,' she replied.

'Guys, lock it!' Ivan screamed.

'I'm on it,' Professor Ainslot said.

'No,' Jesa gasped.

She clambered to her feet as the professor gawped at her in disarray.

'What?' he asked.

'I'll do it,' she insisted.

'But you're hurt!'

'I told Ivan I'll do it,' Jesa said. 'So, I'll do it.'

'But—'

'You wait here,' Jesa told the academic as she opened the inner airlock. 'If anything goes wrong pull me out and take over, yah?'

'No problem,' the professor said, perching himself on the hand holds at the side of the door. 'Be careful.'

She clambered into the airlock chamber. The ship shook violently and threw her off balance. Jesa was as ready as she would ever be. Ivan told her to get ready and when they went back into docking, she sprang into action. Jesa reached up, alarm blaring in her ears, and, under great pressure and pain, pulled the lever over to the side. First mechanism locked. Jesa turned her attention to the next one above the airlock door. Turbulence shook her around. She screamed as she tried to stabilise herself. The professor reacted in panic, fearing the worst for her, but kept back on her instructions. He would come if he needed to. Jesa tried once more and with a scream of pain pulled the lever. The second mechanism was locked into place. The red lights within the airlock turned green. Another jolt shook her off her feet, and her head hit the floor hard. In her daze, Professor Ainslot reached out and hoisted her back up. Together they locked in the third and final mechanism within the troop bay. The lights turned to green on the outer door too and to their relief the alarm stopped as well. The pair looked to each other. They had done it. Their laughter was manic, uncontrollable.

'Well done you two,' Ivan announced over the terminals. 'Now shut that door so I can get it pressurised. I'll be down soon to let our guys back in.'

Jesa followed the instructions and shut the inner airlock door. Ivan ran the process to pump atmosphere into the airlock and docking tube before he came through to the troop bay. He made a quick stop into the armoury before returning with an assault rifle in hand.

'Stay behind me,' he instructed. 'If there's anyone waiting outside that's not our guys, I'm the one that's going to end them.'

The helmsman opened the inner airlock door and waited. Confident there wasn't anything waiting on the other side Ivan unlocked the outer airlock door. He cautiously walked across the docking tube and out of Jesa's line of sight. The next time Jesa saw him, he had four companions with him. The two remaining corporals of the SPF and both agents hurried in after the helmsman. They were exhausted, bloodied and beaten. But smiling now that they were in the safety of the patrol ship. The group was lacking both of their leaders. Where was Duke? Why wasn't he there with them? What had they done to him? Jesa urgently needed to know his fate.

'Where's the sergeant?' Jesa asked, peering round the joint force hoping to see Duke come round the corner.

Ronan Moasa shook his head. 'Not here yet. They had their own thing to do but they're on their way here. Shouldn't be too far behind us.'

'I hope not,' she whispered. 'What do we do now?'

'We wait as long as we can,' Ivan Zenkovich said. 'I'll be up on the flight deck. The rest of you keep an eye out for the others. I'm not keeping us here for longer than necessary.'

'Even if it means leaving them behind?' Jesa asked.

'Especially if it means leaving them behind,' Ivan Zenkovich replied mournfully. He was already prepared to grieve. 'We can't let our emotions get the better of us. Two lives aren't worth all of ours. We can't let everyone's deaths be in vain.'

Jesa hoped that the sergeant wasn't too far away. She couldn't bear the thought of him being left behind.

'Please. Please make it.'

There was no way Jesa would be able to handle losing another father figure. It was rare to have a father to care for a child in the first place. Let alone show as much love as much as hers did. To be rewarded with a new man in her life to treat her as if she were his daughter, to speak to her with equal respect, was even rarer. Her silent prayers that he returned to her continued.

Leyton Foresc

When Leyton wheeled through the door leading them to C Deck, he found a new strength. To know that his ticket off the ship was just down the corridor was alleviating. Even the smile on Duke's face was of genuine relief. No longer forcing a fake grin. They pushed themselves to the absolute limit after fighting the ice wolves to get out from the lower decks, to climb more stairs and ladders in one go than they had dealt with before and to run kilometres of hallways with full kit. All he could think about was the chance to take the weight off his feet and lay down to rest. He didn't want to feel gravity for at least a week.

About a quarter of an hour earlier Ivan Zenkovich had made contact to updated them that he had re-docked with the liner and the rest of their teams were safely on board. They picked up the pace as soon as he told them he couldn't stay for long. The sooner they got down the hallway the better. It was just a short sprint more until they reached the patrol ship. He could almost smell the sweet smell of the airlock.

It took five shots before either of them could react. Leyton's armour took two hits, but held steady, while the other three either hit Duke or a wall. When they were able to comprehend the situation that they were in, the pair were already in cover.

'You okay over there?' Leyton gasped.

'Fine. What can you see?'

At first glance there was nothing in his visual. Then he could see the weapons. Two semi-automatics poking round the corners.

'Fuck me,' he cussed.

'That bad?' Duke asked.

'It is. The rest of my team are between us and the way out. They must have gotten wind of where the patrol ship docked. But I only count two. There's going to be a third somewhere out there. Keep your head on a swivel. They might try to get us from behind.'

'Ah shit. What do we do?'

'Get help,' Leyton instructed. 'Play them at their own game. I'll stall them.'

Duke nodded and opened a comms link with the ship. Private channel. No chance of anyone listening in from outside the SPF. He hoped they would be quick. The longer they took, the more desperate the agents would be. People in those dire situations were prepared to do anything.

'Boss, you know this can be real easy right?' Jerome called out from down the hallway. There was joy in his tone.

'For you maybe,' Leyton replied. 'For me, not so much.'

'Go on,' Jerome said. 'Why's that?'

'Well, it's easy for you because all you have to do is drop your weapons. You can't kill me, remember? You told me yourself. It's hard for me because I have a few headshots to make if you don't drop your weapons and not a lot of time to do it in if I want to live. Have to pace myself, you see? No room for error.'

'Good luck, last time I checked I'm just as good as you. I'll have you first.'

'Not quite,' Leyton corrected. 'I can score over twelve hundred on the range. Your high score was only nine hundred. Which means I have a better shot than you.'

Leyton glanced to his left. Duke remained quiet but was still speaking to his team over the comms. Leyton hoped that there weren't any other delays going on. Time was of the essence and there was none of it to spare for delays. Any hold up was the difference between making it off the ship and getting a sunburn worse than anyone in history.

When the Sergeant looked over and gave a simple nod, Leyton gripped his weapon tightly. His finger curled round the trigger, waiting for the right moment to squeeze. If the two of them were even remotely on the same wavelength, the fireworks couldn't start until the cavalry were in position to avoid a blue on blue.

He needed to continue to stall.

'Didn't you hear me?' Leyton barked. 'You can't shoot for shit! And besides. There's nothing you know that I haven't taught you. I will always be better than you. I should have known from the start that you weren't ever going to be up to standards.'

'So what? That means fuck all!' Jerome screamed, impatience and frustration getting the better of him. Just as he hoped. 'You're done! You hear me? I'm getting out of here. Not you. I'm going to win.'

'You're not going anywhere.' Leyton retorted. 'I'll make sure of that.'

'What? Like Agent Perretti? Yeah, he got taken out up on the bridge by the captain. Bet you don't care about that. Do you? Oh, and you'll be happy to know she didn't beg for her life. But I'll make you beg for yours.'

Leyton was split with his emotions. On one hand, they had one less hostile to worry about which meant he knew where his only threats were. The other, he didn't need to listen to his former friend any longer. He had no reason to. And he let his emotions get the better of him this once to vent the hot air that had been brewing for far too long.

'Will you just shut up you whiny little bitch!' Leyton snapped. 'All you ever did was question my orders, and act like you knew better when you never did. Did you? Always thinking that because it came out of your god damn mouth it was right. You can delegate like no tomorrow. You can give orders. But you could never lead by example! My God you're just like a spoilt little shit, you know that? Always have to be in the right, and when you're not you go crying to someone who will tell you that you're in the right and make it all better for you. I wish I were done with you a long time ago.'

'You know what? Fuck you! I know what's happening. I know the ship's about to go into that star. We're leaving on your ship. You can stay here. Enjoy whatever time you've got left.'

The two hostile agents started to shuffle away from them. Their footsteps gradually fading through the hallway.

'You feel better for that?' Duke asked.

Leyton shrugged. 'You know, I actually do. Not much for stalling them though, eh?'

'Might as well give them another reason to stick around if they don't want to talk,' Duke answered gleefully.

'After you,' Leyton said with a smile.

They were firing down the corridor before either of them had even zeroed their aims in on the two agents. Their opponents took cover, and a series of fire and counter-fire engagements ensued. Leyton silently begged for Jerome would poke his head a little too far out so that he could be certain that he was rid of the man permanently. Agent Tallow and Corporal Moasa charged down the corridor behind the hostile agents. Their shots forced the enemy to take cover and ultimately fall back now that they were outnumbered two to one. Their footsteps echoed between the gun shots.

'Come on you two, it's time to go,' Agent Tallow cried with a weary smile.

'Hey, no arguments from me!' Leyton replied. 'Coming, Sergeant?'

Duke took a couple steps ahead and spoke without looking back, 'Way ahead of you.'

Leyton sprinted ahead of the sergeant. He tapped on Corporal Moasa's shoulder to tell him to move as he went by. He hurtled around a couple corners and along the final stretch of corridor until he ran through the airlock, across the docking tube and into the SPF patrol ship to find everyone else except the pilot all looking at him with joy in their eyes. Ronan joined them and Duke's footsteps fell short of the docking tube. Leyton looked to the sergeant and saw him still on the *Galactic Passage.*

Duke was staring back down where they came from before turning back to face him.

'Where's Tallow?' Duke asked.

Hatty. Where was she? She was supposed to be right behind them. Right where she had been. She was right there. He had just felt her arm in his hand when he went past her. Telling her to move. It wasn't an imagination.

A scream echoed down the corridor. Agent Tallow cried out for him.

'Hatty!' Leyton cried.

His comms crackled into life in his ear. The voice he dreaded hearing spoke to him.

'Hey boss, you seriously going to go without saying bye to Hatty?' Jerome asked. She could be heard struggling in his grip swearing and doing everything she could to break free. 'It's not very nice of you considering you might not see her again.'

'What the hell are you doing?' he demanded.

'Well, I saw her trying to keep up with you all and, you know how it is, misery loves company,' Jerome explained. 'Me and Kari aren't going anywhere so we figured that we could make a party out of it. Plus, I know you. You won't leave without her.'

'Let her go!' Leyton instructed.

Jerome cackled over the comms. 'No can do. Doesn't work that way. She's sad that she can't join you by the way. Wishes you could stay for the after party. Don't worry, we'll take good care of her for you. Bye-bye now.'

The comms ceased. His heart stopped. Jerome had Hatty Tallow. She was going to die. After the ordeal he and the sergeant went through, had been too eager to get out of there. He should have taken their six and made sure she was on the ship first. That was all he needed to do. Leyton could have easily fought off Houghton. Finished him if the opportunity arose. But he didn't and now she was going to die because of him. There might have been a timer on the clock. Leyton could not have cared less. Before that ship detached from the *Galactic Passage,* he was going to rescue his agent. His friend. She didn't deserve to die. If it were her time to go, there was no way she would go alone.

He took a step forward toward the airlock. Duke was still on the other side of the docking tube. Duke reached out with his hand to the side of the airlock, pushed the controls and slammed the inner door shut before Leyton could get through. Leyton rushed to the door and beat at it as hard as he could while glaring through the porthole. Not even thinking about the controls on his side of the airlock door.

'Open the fucking door!' he screamed. 'Don't you dare take this from me!'

'Negative. I'm going to help her,' Duke replied. 'You've done more than enough already. I've lost soldiers of my own fighting to save as many people on this ship as possible. I'm going to make sure I save yours for you. Ivan Zenkovich, disengage from the airlock. We'll make our own way back to you. There are space suits at every one of these airlocks and lifeboats that we can use. I'm sure we'll figure something out. I'll see you soon.'

'No!' Leyton yelled, slamming his fists at the sealed door.

Duke reached out once more, and the outer airlock door sealed shut. The air filling the space between was vented of atmosphere. Then the docking tube started to retract as the soldier walked away from the airlock and back onto the liner while the pilot took them away. The *Galactic Passage* shrunk out of view in the porthole as they drifted further from it.

It was for nothing. The sergeant surely knew that. There was no way they could survive any of their extraction options if he succeeded. They were going to die on that ship while he lived.

'Right, take us in,' Leyton ordered. 'Get us docked with that ship. Now.'

'We can't,' Corporal Moasa replied painfully.

'We have our orders,' Corporal Arche added, standing by her peer's side sharing the same saddened expression. 'If the sergeant says he'll be out with your agent, he'll be back with her.'

Leyton shook his head in disbelief. 'How can you be so naïve? They're not getting out of there. Not now! Seen how fast that thing's going? We have to go back for them.'

Jesa stepped forward. Unlike the last time he saw her, there was no concern, apprehension or worry in her eyes. Only grit and determination. A changed person. At some point Jesa had transitioned from being a girl to a woman.

'We'll take my ship,' she announced.

'We?' he asked her. 'I'm going on my own. No one else needs to be at risk.'

'It's my ship,' she stated.

'And?'

'No one else fly's my ship,' Jesa explained. 'She's my baby. I got her, fixed her up and upgraded her. Only I fly her. I'm coming with you. Besides. I owe the sergeant one. He saved me when no one else would have cared. Can't pay him back any better than by saving his life, compre?'

Leyton nodded. 'Go prep the ship, I'll be down with you soon.'

'What do you think you're doing?' Corporal Moasa demanded.

Leyton waited until Jesa had clambered through the lower airlock and into her ship before addressing the soldier. 'I'm going to go get your sergeant and my agent off that ship. They can't use space suits. They're too close to that star now. Even if they survive pushing out of the ship, they'll be dead in seconds. They stay on that ship, they're dead. They can't even take a lifeboat! By taking the smuggler's ship, you're not being put into any danger.'

'I shouldn't let you go,' Ronan said.

'Then stop me,' Leyton goaded.

The two shared a moment where the soldier clearly wanted to stop him. Ronan had his orders that needed to be fulfilled. But he also wanted his sergeant back.

'Bring him back,' Ronan requested.

'I'll bring them all back,' Leyton said. 'Don't you worry about that.'

Chapter 14
17/11/2675
03:12 Earth Standard Time

Leyton Foresc

Docking with the liner was difficult for Jesa. She had never carried out a ship-to-ship docking procedure before, let alone a mid-flight docking routine. Add to that the fact that the liner was moving faster than it was earlier and was falling to pieces, it was just about impossible. Had it not been for Ivan Zenkovich taking remote control over the smuggler's ship for a significant proportion of the manoeuvre, they would never have made it to a docking port successfully.

While Jesa was shutting her ship down, Leyton couldn't help but admire the skeleton of the strange lizard-like organism one more time. It really was impressive. No matter how many times he looked at it, it generated a sense of awe that was almost paralysing. It was like looking up at a deity as this thing towered over him. It reminded him of the old conspiracy theories and folklore back on Earth – of lizard people dwelling underground, but in control of the humans on top. He wondered how much information Professor Ainslot had been able to gather from the skeleton for analysis. Science wasn't really his thing, but Leyton would quite readily read the report on this thing.

'You ready?' Jesa asked him, jogging down through the cargo hold toward him. 'I've taken out the ignition switch. Even if your old team somehow manage to get on-board, they can't get far without it.' she explained while patting the base of the rucksack on her back.

Leyton pointed at the bones, 'I never asked, do you know who the buyer is for this? Got to cost a whack?'

'Some Earther,' she shrugged. 'Was never told the dude's real name. They never say, compre. Got what we think is an alias to use, Ostad. Whatever stupid name that is. But whoever it is, they wanted this thing badly. They paid a fortune for it and most of the stuff on my ship.'

'You don't say.'

He really wanted to know more and find out what Ainslot knew. Never had anyone he worked with at the agency mention seeing anything remotely like this out there in the galaxy. A reptilian humanoid. More than that, the name Ostad sounded vaguely familiar.

He tried tirelessly in the fleeting moments he had to spare to remember why that name was familiar. Then it returned to him. Ostad wasn't a name. It was an acronym. The Military Intelligence Division's very own shadow division for research and development. His own superior had been in contact with gang lords to acquire the skeleton. But why? What was so important about this skeleton that it was in the same request as the ice wolves? These were questions he would get to the bottom of. One way or another he would know. But now wasn't the time to wonder.

'You good to go?' Jesa asked.

'I am,' he replied, steering his eyes away from the skeleton. He opened a comms link with the SPF patrol ship. 'Zenkovich, are you reading me?'

'Loud and clear,' the helmsman replied. 'We'll keep you updated with how long you have left. I know time keeping is going to be the last thing either of you will be focussed on. You need to be on your ship and out of there no later than at the fifteen-minute warning at a push. Any later and I can't promise you'll push off in time. That gives you at best another hour and a half give or take. Understood?'

'Understood.'

'Good luck guys,' Ivan said.

'Thanks, think we're going to need it,' Leyton muttered. 'Out.'

They disembarked from the smuggler's ship, sealed the airlock and secured it so that there wouldn't be any easy access for anyone trying to get in without invitation, then pushed through the darkened corridors of the liner. The stench of death had worked its way through the hallways and up all the decks. Jesa gipped, struggling to stomach the smell of blood that she had never encountered before to this scale. Either that or it stirred up a painful memory that made the odour and reaction all the worse. Leyton placed a reassuring arm on her shoulder.

'Where are we going?' she asked through gritted teeth. Her hand shook with the pistol wobbling in its grip. She wasn't ready for the fight regardless of how she acted earlier. Too late now. 'How do you know where Duke is going to be?'

'Couldn't tell you. Don't know how his mind works yet. But if I know Jerome half as well as I do, I can think of a couple places he could be. Either down in the lower decks where the ice wolves are nesting like a sick game or up on the bridge to watch the fireworks up close. Or maybe in the cabin quarters where there's plenty of places to hide. Doesn't matter how we do it, when we find Jerome then I guarantee we find Hatty and most likely the sergeant.'

'Which do you think it'll be?'

Leyton looked at the smuggler and shrugged. 'Same place I'd want to be. Up on the bridge.'

'Great, so let's get up there!' Jesa stated.

'Steady on,' Leyton said, holding her back. 'That's where I *think* he'd be, not guaranteed to be up there. I trained the guy. He'll know that's where I'd go so chances are he won't be anywhere near it. He'd want to keep me guessing as long as possible.'

'Where do we start, then?'

Good question. Where should they start? Like a needle in a haystack with a timer that wasn't in their favour. He let out a heavy sigh and started to see the futility in their efforts. It had been too long between the sergeant heading out on his own and them docking with the liner. He could have gone anywhere, been killed, or worse held hostage in a desperate bid by Jerome to lure Leyton out.

Jesa had taken several steps ahead into the darkness of the living quarters section and looked back at him. 'Can you hear that?'

'Not a thing,' Leyton said as he shook his head. All he could hear was the sound of the metal vibrating as the powers of gravity and thrust worked hand in hand trying to pull the ship apart.

'Come here,' she insisted, waving him over as she stepped further forward.

Leyton jogged over, held her back by her shoulder to prevent her from stepping further into any potential danger, and listened. For the first few seconds there was nothing except for the ship and their breathing. Then he heard it. The distinct repeated shots of semi-automatic weapons and the powerful blasts of a shotgun. They were near the assault. He was close to Hatty.

The pair rushed down the corridor, throwing caution to the wind to get to their friends. The shots grew louder. Then they heard the screams of argument, hostility and attempted persuasion. Almost there. And not a moment too soon.

'Slow down,' he whispered to Jesa.

Leyton took the lead and edged toward the end of the hallway to a junction and carefully peered round. Duke was there fighting the two agents. But his agent was not with either side. Where was she? Maybe Hatty was out of sight. Stowed away somewhere so she couldn't get involved. That though wasn't the most obvious option for Leyton. He wasn't so soft handed. Did that mean she was killed? Did Duke inadvertently hit her with a shotgun shell? No. The sergeant was too good a man to do that to someone he was trying to protect. He would sooner simply not take the shot. Had Jerome killed her so he could fight? That way he would have one less thing to worry about. In a hostage situation going south Leyton would have done the exact same thing once upon a time.

His blood boiled. How could he have just left her? Leyton tortured his emotions by reminding himself he should have made sure she got off that liner when they all were making their way to the patrol ship. He shook his head, trying to focus on the positive. If he couldn't see a body, it meant she could still be alive. He analysed the battlefield. There was no way of going down the corridor without being taken out. There was an old-fashioned standoff with a killing field in between. He needed to get around to the back of them if they were to win. Catch them off guard where they weren't expecting it.

'I'm going to make a distraction,' he told Jesa. 'When I do, you run down to the sergeant. Give him support to keep them occupied. I'm going round the back of them. They'll suspect something's happening when they only see you here. I won't have long. Keep chatter to the minimum and make sure you keep their attention on you guys for as long as possible. Okay?'

She nodded. Her eyes told him that she wasn't okay with it but knew if it needed to be done then she had to at least try. He could see why the sergeant took a shine to her. Her heart was in the right place.

'Okay, on the count of three you run,' he said, pulling the pin out of a flash-stun grenade he managed to swipe from the SPF patrol ship before leaving. 'Keep your head down until the flash goes. Don't look up a second before or you're done for.'

When his count reached one, he launched the grenade down the hallway. As he expected, Duke caught sight of it and took cover. He tapped on Jesa's shoulder and gave her a gentle nudge to start running. When the flash lit everything up for a second, he took his opportunity and ran across the junction. Now it was a matter of time before they figured it out that he was there.

Leyton skirted around the perimeter of the fight, taking care as he hurtled round the corners of another couple of junctions. He needed to take care to not make much noise whilst checking the open doors for potential threats that were hidden. It was a difficult process to follow when in a rush. Duke made repeated attempts to contact him over the comms, his voice hissing into Leyton's ear. He didn't respond. To do so would ruin the entire rescue operation. Leyton eventually stopped at the final corner and peered round. Agent Fellstrum was holding her ground against the sergeant and Jesa. She was a good agent. It was sad to know that she chose the wrong side. After everything that they went through, there had been no loyalty to him when it was needed most. Then Leyton reminded himself that she also took part in taking Agent Tallow before she could escape. He had to do what had to be done.

Leyton stepped out from his position unnoticed. Heart racing, he took aim at Kari. Lined up the shot for a quick, painless kill. It would be the most mercy she would receive. Agent Fellstrum had no idea he was there. One shot and she was done for.

'I'm sorry,' he whispered.

His finger wrapped around the trigger. Trembled around the metal. Then he took it away. Without realising it he talked himself out of pulling the trigger. It was just Kari Fellstrum there. Jerome was nowhere to be seen. Not even a body. To take a shot now would let Jerome know where he was.

'Where the hell are you?' Leyton asked himself.

The first strike around his face was painful. The second one was just excruciating.

Mid-daze, Leyton turned around to start defending himself against the brutal assault Jerome was delivering. The bloodlust in his former friend's eyes was terrifying even for him. He was sent spiralling into the wall and only when he dodged a punch did Leyton start to fight on an equal footing.

'Why?' Jerome demanded as they reached a standstill. 'Why did you go against our orders?'

'Because I'm not a murderer,' Leyton answered between a flurry of strikes. 'I'm a killer. A soldier. A saboteur. A spy. But I'm not a monster. I didn't join the agency to kill innocent people. I joined it to save people and keep them safe.'

'But you're supposed to follow orders!' Jerome bellowed.

Leyton broke their skirmish briefly to put his former friend in his place. 'I'm not a mindless robot! What's the point in following orders if we kill all the people that we're meant to protect in the first place? We'd be no better than the people trying to kill us every day.'

'Command has a reason,' Jerome said. 'They have a reason for everything. You always said it yourself. They play chess and what we do now they had planned months ago and have another four moves afterwards planned out too. This is just like that. Sacrifice the pawns now to check-mate the enemy king later. When the time is right. Maximum destruction.'

Leyton shook his head. 'I think this time, they had to be wrong. Can't be worth it. I refuse to accept it.'

'Well,' Jerome started, taking out his pistol. 'Right or wrong, the body count just got one higher.'

Leyton dived for cover into one of the nearby cabins as the gun shots whistled past. Two landed in the back of his shoulder. Penetrating his armour but not the gel layer underneath. They would only bruise at least. He landed on the floor next to a body that made his heart stop, his blood turn cold and the pain subside only to be replaced with heartache. Hatty Tallow. She lay there, lifeless with a single bullet wound to the skull. Execution style. The remnants of tears still glistened on her cheeks. Fear still lingered in her eyes. Jerome had killed her. Duke had let him kill her by shutting him out when he should have been there to help. She was his responsibility. Hatty Tallow shouldn't have died. She should have still been alive. Agent Tallow deserved more than an execution. She had so much going for her.

'Oh Hatty,' he sobbed.

Leyton gently placed a hand on her cheek and rubbed hit gently with his thumb. He never even realised he was crying until he took a deep breath, saw the droplets fall from his face and sniffled all the residue pouring from his nose. Leyton let out a terrible cry.

When he heard Jerome react with laughter, making comments he cared not to listen to about how she begged for her life, Leyton gripped onto his shotgun tighter than before. He stepped out of the cabin, took three pistol shots to the chest. His armour may have kept them from killing him, but the impacts ached and knocked the wind straight out of him. He marched up to Jerome and fought furiously, using his weapon as club to beat Jerome with. Leyton then placed three shells into his legs to bring the man to his knees, or at least what was left of his knees, and another shot in his right shoulder to leave him with one usable arm. The bloody grin Jerome wore was disgusting. To be so disrespectful after what he had just done was despicable. Leyton Foresc swiped him across the mouth with the butt of his shotgun.

Jerome spat out a tooth or two with a mouthful of blood and continued to look at him with that smile. He should have struck him harder to wipe the grin from his face.

'She pleaded for you to save her, you know,' he whispered. 'It almost broke my heart. Almost.'

'Why did you do it?' Leyton Foresc asked.

'Because she refused to see sense,' his former friend answered. 'Remove the weak links and potential security breaches. You know how it is. We have to keep everything contained. If we can't trust them, we end them.'

'She was your friend, as much as she was mine!' he hissed.

Jerome shook his head. 'She was a fellow agent. Then a traitor. Now she's where she belongs.'

'She's gone to a better place than you're going to,' Leyton snarled, yanking Jerome up by his collar before throwing him back down to the floor.

'No, you know that's not true. She'll be waiting for me along with everyone else,' Jerome replied, coughing up blood as he laughed at him. 'We all have blood on our hands.'

'Shut up.'

'We're all guilty. At least she's paid her debts.'

'Fuck you,' Leyton said quietly. 'This is for Hatty.' He took out his combat knife and drove it first into Jerome's neck. He slid it back out and waited a moment for Jerome to clutch at his neck with his one good arm. 'This is for the sergeant's pilot.' The knife was plunged into his ribs, puncturing a lung. 'This is for his soldier.' Leyton took the blade out and slammed it down through Houghton's collar bone. Missing his heart. 'And this. This is for me.' Leyton brought the blade out and thrust it up through Jerome's chin, through the roof of his mouth and hopefully ploughed it deep into the base of his skull to reach the brain.

Jerome gave one last gasping groan of pain before he twitched and the last of his breath escaped through his lips. Watching the body collapse to the floor was a reward far greater than anything Leyton ever had before. The satisfaction of knowing he had rights a wrong could not be summed up in words. It was just a shame that it took so much longer than it should have done.

Breathing heavily, Leyton turned to find Duke and Jesa staring at him. There was fear in their eyes, like they were looking at a monster.

'They killed her,' he said weakly. Then, pointing at Duke, 'You could have stopped this. You should have stopped it. This is your fault. You could have let me come at the start. Why didn't you?'

'That wasn't an option,' Duke said.

'Don't give me that! You could have opened the door and let me through.'

'No, I couldn't have. You know I couldn't,' Duke answered softly. 'It was always safer to risk one life than two. I wish I could tell you when they did it, but I don't know. She was probably dead before I even got here. There was nothing we could have done. I'm sorry.'

He shook his head in disbelief. There had to have been something he could have done. There was no way there couldn't have been. There was always a way. Leyton tried to process the possibility that the soldier shared none of the responsibility for her death. That Duke bore no share of the blame. No, he was to blame. But he didn't deserve to die. No more death. He would suffer though.

Before he knew what his body was doing, Leyton charged into the soldier and was throwing punches just like he had done before when they threw fists after Duke heard only what he wanted to hear. Each one was just as brutal as a kill shot should be. Duke threw punches back just as good as he took. They slugged it out until Jesa broke them up with a dangerous shot of her pistol fired overhead.

'Stop it!' she begged. 'Please! This isn't the time for this! Haven't enough people died?'

Duke stretched out his back and grunted. 'I'm sorry, but this is on us both. We should have both made sure she was on-board my ship before getting on ourselves. We'd both been through hell and back and needed off the liner after dealing with those… things. I wanted away from them more than you can believe. So, we're both to blame.'

Leyton watched as Duke looked away. His body turned rigid, and he started to shake It was like seeing a timid child in the hustle and bustle of a city for the first time where everything was terrifying. What had gone on in his mind after fighting the ice wolves? What demons now lived within him? Who was he to blame someone that was going through their own mental anguish as well?

'Sorry,' Leyton whispered. 'I just need someone to blame.'

'We've killed the ones to blame,' Duke explained.

'No, we haven't,' Leyton corrected. 'The guy in charge is still out there. I need to make him pay. Then we'll have killed them all.'

'It's a good shout,' Duke said. 'If you need help, you only have to say.'

'Thanks,' Leyton said.

'Guys, can we, you know, make our way back to my ship, yah?' Jesa asked. 'I'd feel a lot happier if you have your talk back there.'

'Zenkovich, how long we got left?' Leyton asked over the comms.

'You've got just over thirty-five minutes before your window closes,' Zen explained. 'What's happening? Have you made contact?'

'I lost my agent. We've recovered the sergeant,' he explained sombrely.

'I'm so sorry to hear that,' the pilot said. Leyton believed him. The helmsman didn't seem the type to give any false emotions. 'I'll have a drink waiting for you when you get back.'

'Thank you.' Leyton closed the comms link and turned to the others. 'We've got long enough to make our way back to the ship. Let's get going.'

A chilling sound echoed through the deck. Howling like the sound of glass breaking.

'Ice wolves,' Agent Leyton Foresc snarled, reloading his weapon immediately.

'What?' Jesa asked, moving closer to Duke for safety.

Duke. He looked at the soldier. The man was as still as a statue. Afraid and enraged at the same time. Listening intently to the howls as they faded away. Moving higher up the ship.

'Go,' Duke instructed. 'I've got something I need to finish first while they're up here.'

The sergeant took off at full speed before Leyton could explain that the soldier had no idea where they had docked. They had to go with him if they were to get him off the ship in one piece.

'Fuck me… Stay close to me kid,' Leyton instructed Jesa. 'This is going to get really rough really quickly. Okay?'

Jesa nodded. The pair hurtled on after the sergeant, using the sound of his footsteps to guide them.

Beatrice Lenoia

Beatrice was still alive, but only just. She had agonisingly pulled herself across the deck toward her command chair. Each outstretched arm grasped at the floor and took more strength than she had remaining to pull her body forward. Looking at all the death around her, knowing that she too was going to die soon, was enough to make her just roll over and accept her fate. That had never been her mentality though. Even before the military she had been brought up to take on a challenge head on, to look fear in the eye, take that fear and make it an ally to find comfort in knowing what the evil ahead really was.

She hoisted her body onto the command chair, manoeuvring uncomfortably into an upright position, and gasped for breath as the effort of crawling several feet wrecked her. She took a few moments to compose herself. The pain was nearly too much to handle but the longer she stayed still the easier it became to breathe.

With there being no gun fight to contend with, Beatrice opened the heat shields to reveal the solar system outside. The star ahead of the ship was bright. Too bright. She fumbled through the controls on the arm of her command chair wearily until the glass polarised to the point where the celestial object was dimmed and each individual nuclear explosion on its surface could be seen. Each arm of radiation and flame reaching out could be watched with clarity. All around the flaming ball in the now dimmed backdrop were spotlights of millions upon millions of other stars. Less than one percent of those stars had planets that held human colonies. And those people out there had no idea what was going on at that very moment. No idea what they had done for them. Sacrificed for them.

She smiled.

It made her think of the stories of old, how the hero always made it out of a dire situation like hers at the last possible moment to go on and live a full and happy life. Not in reality. In real life, the real hero never makes it out. Heroes only become that by making the ultimate sacrifice; those that remained knew that they were saved by the actions of the fallen. People would know something happened as the survivors were rescued and told the authorities their stories. But theirs wouldn't be the full story. Only dribs and drabs of individual events. Hers had more detail than they could offer. She had all the facts needed for something to be done. That needed to be made public. People had to know that the

UPN Military Intelligence Division had a renegade branch that was prepared to do more than it was permitted to succeed. To do so would be treason. A penalty of death hanging over those that committed it. That couldn't happen if she was already dead.

'Let's do this then,' she whispered to herself.

She flicked through the captain's commands that were still operational until she found the emergency broadcast frequency that would ensure her message would be sent everywhere, to anyone that was willing to listen. Beatrice was glad that comms had some life restored to them. It seemed like something that would happen only in the movies, but there was nothing else that she could do to pass the time to stop herself from going insane with fear and dread.

The officer opened the comms, waited a moment to try and think about what she was going to say, then started to speak from her heart instead of her mind, 'This is Captain Beatrice Lenoia of the inter-stellar luxury liner *Galactic Passage,* and this is the final message that I will be making. The purpose of this is to give the families of all that were onboard the peace of mind of knowing what has happened on this voyage and the loved ones that will not come home. What the fate of *Galactic Passage* was. I'm sending my ship into the heart of a local star to make sure an alien organism more dangerous than anything known that I never knew existed until now never makes it back to Sol as they were intended to. I don't know who will receive this message or if anyone is going to care. I just know it is important to make anyone listening aware of what has gone on and why we're not coming home.'

She paused. It felt so stupid, so silly, so childish, to be putting her thoughts and events out there like an interplanetary diary for all to hear. Her head went fuzzy for a moment, her blood loss finally taking effect. Beatrice shook her head to shake away the uneasiness and doubt. No, it wasn't immature to make the announcement. It was the right thing. Humanity had the right to know. Her family had a right to know what happened to her.

'I started this voyage with a full load of passengers, full crew and high spirits, 'she continued slowly. 'We saw so much. More wonders than anyone could have thought existed. Then we docked at Gorucia. As routine we needed to let off some passengers where that was their destination. Let on new passengers who wanted to see the galaxy. Restock our supplies. That is where routine stopped. We took on stowaways who had the right documents to be granted access. I knew something was wrong, but the level of authorisation from the UPN given to the stowaways and their cargo meant that I wasn't in any position to question it. Just give them a place to hole up and let them carry on as normal. Nothing gave any sign of something going on. How wrong we were to be complacent.'

Beatrice paused, took a shaky breath, and let a few silent tears fall down her cheeks. It was like reliving events that she never wanted to go through a second time. Seeing the ghosts of the past coming back to haunt her. But it wasn't a haunting of terror and disgust. She was tormented by the smiles, the happiness and the grasp of life all those that died once had.

'Oh God, if only I'd been more careful. Asked more questions and was less accepting. I could have saved all those people!' she screamed, before sobbing. 'It took weeks after leaving Gorucia before anything happened. We noticed an anomaly in the power system. We tried to investigate it. Every time we tried to get to it, we were stopped. Then it went wrong. We had to make an emergency jump when systems went critical. But when we dropped out, we were right in the path of a stellar storm. We couldn't recharge the drive in time and there was no way sub-light could get us around it fast enough. When it hit us, we had to reboot the entire ship's systems to regain power. I managed to get an S.O.S. out before we were hit. That was when the nightmare started. The wolves were released. When Duke and his SPF soldiers arrived, I was so relieved. It felt like I had some control over the situation again. He-

She was cut off by what sounded like cracking glass on the wind. The ice wolves. They were on the top deck. Beatrice sent out the partial transmission that she had been able to record and cut the comms. It wouldn't do anything to hide her location. She knew that much. If she could hear them now, then they will have known long ago that she was there and still alive. But it was instinct to shut off and shut down when an enemy was nearby that a soldier was powerless to fight against.

The howls and growls came closer, edging toward her. It was like the scientist said: they hunted primarily for living organisms. They had to have picked up the scent of her fresh blood and heard her voice when she was certain she was alone. Their steps casually paced over to her, taking their time. Their claws dug into the metal flooring with anticipation of her fleeing from them in a desperate bid to survive. Maybe if they knew she was in no position to run they would have killed her quickly and been done with it by now.

Her eyes shot right to see the snout of the first ice wolf poke round the side of her chair. Her gaze then immediately shifted left as another two wolves walked around that side. When the trio of beasts finished organising themselves in front of her, swirling like a flock of vultures over carrion, a fourth appeared. Bigger and bloodier than the others. This one limped and had what looked like a knife stuck deep in its shoulder. The matriarch that the scientist told them about. Trust the one that got away from Duke and Leyton to be the biggest and meanest of them all.

She stared into Spike's red eyes. Both were unblinking. Fear coursed through her veins faster than the speed of light. Even if she could have fought back, the easiest thing to do at that point was to kill herself. But with no weapon or strength, Lenoia had no choice though but to let them do with her as they pleased. She hoped the first bite was the one to end her.

'What are you waiting for then?' she asked the wolves, knowing that they couldn't respond or even understand her. Her breath was short, sharp. The monologue she made had taken so much strength out of her. 'I'm right here.'

Spike slowly stepped forward. She mounted her front legs on the arms of the command chair so that she was looking down on her. Beatrice could see the wolf sizing up her skull, calculating the chances of being able to take it in one mouthful. Spike nudged Beatrice's face, brushing its nose against Beatrice's face softly. Menacingly. The wolf must have sensed she was of no threat to it, or it wouldn't have taken so long to toy with her. To wilfully scare her like that. Funny how animals show what through the generations had been put down as human emotions or actions. This organism had such an advanced level of intelligence it had the ability to play games, have fun and ultimately do evil. It was just as if it was enjoying itself. All without human impressions.

'Just get it over with you bitch,' Beatrice gasped.

Spike complied with her demand. She opened her mouth wide, revealing all her teeth and the serrated tongue that lashed out for her. Drool and slobber dropped onto Beatrice's face. With one swift bite she had the ability to rip off at least half of Lenoia's skull. But she didn't bite.

'What the hell are you waiting for?' she questioned quietly. The anticipation was worse than going through the pain that moment.

Footsteps. Not the sound of paws on metal. Boots on metal. People were rushing down the corridor to her. The wolf didn't clamp its jaws on her. Spike pushed away to face those that were incoming.

Beatrice closed her eyes as her grip on life continued to ebb away wishing it had just ended to stop the suffering.

Duke Horren

'Get away from her!' Duke screamed at the top of his lungs before firing two shells into the ice wolf to the starboard side of the bridge. 'You two take the left flank. I've got right. Save the captain!'

'Understood,' Leyton replied.

Leyton and Jesa both swooped to the left as instructed. Neither of them had attempted to convince him to turn around while following the ice wolves up to the bridge. They simply fell into line and followed him. It was a good job, because it was a non-negotiable course of action. He had to settle his score and now that he had the matriarch in his sights, nothing was going to stop him. Not even the liner hurtling toward the star could keep him from tasting revenge.

Spike prowled away from the command chair and circled into the middle of the bridge. Her gaze never wandered away from him. When one of the subordinate males tried to charge at him, she barked and huffed until it joined the fight with the others. Even she wanted him dead enough to be unprepared to share the prey or accept assistance. That suited Duke just fine. Meant he didn't have to share his ammunition in the fight or worry about being blindsided.

Duke fell into a geosynchronous orbit with Spike. His weapon remained at the ready. After what felt like an eternity standing off against each other, the matriarch was the one to make the first move and lunged for him. He was sent flying back a few feet as the wolf clipped him. Duke collided face first with one of the workstations. His helmet took damage from the force of the attack. The HUD flickered and information was only showing half complete. Duke cast the helmet aside. No point wearing something that would not aid him anymore. The ice wolf hurtled forward again. She was only stopped as his hands held onto Spike's skull. Her teeth were inches away from his face and tongue reached out to quench its desire for flesh. There was no pain at first. Duke felt the serrated edges of its teeth and tongue run down his face as he attempted to keep the matriarch at bay. As soon as he was able to comprehend the pain, Duke let out an almighty scream.

Then the emotional defences he had built in the last few hours to keep him safe began to shut down as panic set in. His heart started to beat faster than he could comprehend, and he perspired profusely. Fear. The same fear that had him paralysed back in their den took hold of him once more. Spike's teeth were constantly on the assault, refusing to cease. Only it wasn't just her, it was every ice wolf on board, all attacking at once. All focussed entirely on him. Teeth. Teeth everywhere. So many red eyes watching. Waiting for him to die. Their howls were deafening. The pack was after them.

'No,' he pleaded. The taste of blood was coppery on his lips. 'Not like this.'

Her face was pushing closer and closer toward his own as Duke's strength began failing. He needed to get out of her grasp, and soon, before his panic attack got any worse. The knife. It still had a bit of the metal exposed. He kicked the blade still lodged in her shoulder even deeper into her flesh, forcing the wolf to retreat in pain and give him the opening he needed to end the fight at last. Duke rushed to his feet and immediately put two shells into her side, forcing her to cry out in pain. Her cries didn't go unheard by her pack. The other wolves tried to disengage from Leyton and Jesa but the two of them managed to keep the creatures occupied. When Spike realised that she wasn't going to get the help she had called out for, the matriarch went berserk, charging for Duke in a mad rush, howling wildly, knowing that this was her only chance to save not only herself but her lineage. Her pack. He fired several more shells into her, planting as many into her as possible until the matriarch was downed. Her weakened carcass slid across the floor, but she still had fight in her. Spike attempted to clamber back to her feet, pawing and scratching at anything in reach, trying to find something to push herself up with. Duke placed another few shells into the side of her skull for safe measure. The last thing he needed was to think he'd finished the job when he was far from it. She made it away from him once before. It wasn't going to happen to him again. The nightmare ended there. He needed it to end where it started. On that ship.

Duke reloaded and joined the others. Working with Leyton he put down one of the wolves that had Jesa in its sight. The remaining wolf fled once it realised that not only was it outnumbered, that its matriarch was no more. The wolf's yelps of terror echoed away into the darkness of the ship. Duke leaned over and coughed violently as he tried to catch his breath.

Are you two okay?' Duke eventually asked.

'A little beat up but not as bad as you,' Leyton replied, hinting to Duke's face.

'Mayah! What happened to you?' Jesa asked, rushing over to him.

'It's nothing serious,' Duke answered, wincing as Jesa moved his face to one side so she could inspect the wound. 'Least I don't think so.' Duke looked to the floor for a moment then glanced over to the command chair. 'Captain!'

He brushed the assistance away and led the trio over to the command chair. Beatrice sat there, slumped to her side with her eyes shut. Her skin was sickly pale. Blood stained her uniform. Duke hoped that she was dead for her sake. He couldn't imagine the pain she had to have been in until now.

Duke reached out and pat her cheek gently. 'Captain?'

'Sergeant,' she answered weakly with a forced smile, trying to hide the pain she was clearly in. Her eyes did not open. Beatrice grimaced as she took a deep breath. 'Did we win?'

'We did,' the sergeant said. 'We took out Jerome and Fellstrum. We've killed the matriarch and a few of her wolves. We're safe now.'

'That's good,' she whispered. 'At least... At least we know we can kill them.'

'Yeah,' Duke whispered. 'Yeah, we do.'

'And no one's taking any of the ones that are left away,' Leyton added. 'We've got the only way off this ship and it's just us left on board.'

Beatrice winced in pain as she smiled. 'Good. I'm glad.'

'Come on now,' Duke said, gently easing a hand behind her shoulder. 'We're getting you out of here.'

'No, no you're not,' she retorted weakly. 'I'm dead. I'll have bled out long before we get to your ship and away from here. Let alone by the time you can patch me up.'

'We have to try,' Jesa pleaded.

'Young lady. I don't think we've really had the pleasure, have we? I wasn't exactly polite when we first met,' Beatrice slowly said, taking deep, heavy gasps of air after every few words. 'I'm sure you're lovely and have your wits about you but you're young. You haven't seen what I've seen. Done what I've done. I've seen this before. Watched people try and fail to save someone this far gone. I know that there's no point in trying to save me now and I don't want you to. Look out there.' Beatrice gestured toward the forward viewing window and the star that was now filling most of the glass. 'Go on, look. Don't you think that's the most beautiful sight?' When no one answered, she gently chuckled to herself. 'I think it is. I've seen so many amazing things, but never this. Never this close. Let my last memory be a happy one. Not one reliving a nightmare. Let me go seeing this, knowing that you did everything you could to save the passengers and my crew. Please?'

Jesa had teared up. Leyton was avoiding all eye contact to keep from being subjected to his emotions. Duke, on the other hand, held his head low and couldn't tell if he was crying or if it was just blood and sweat rolling down his face. Either way she had pulled on his heartstrings, and he had to make the tough decision out of picking her up and trying to save her or allowing her to live out her last minutes her way.

'Okay,' he sighed. 'Good luck on the other side.'

Beatrice smiled weakly. 'Death will watch over me now.'

'What does that mean?' Jesa asked. 'We can't leave her like this!'

'It means she's done her bit,' Leyton answered. 'The least we can do is respect what she wants. We need to get out while we can. We have about eight minutes to get off this ship and we're thirteen minutes out. I don't like our odds but if we make a move, and don't stop, our chances are going to be better than if we stay around here.'

'We can only try. Thank you, Captain. Let's get a hustle on,' Duke instructed as he picked up his damaged helmet. 'Move it!'

Traversing the ship to the airlock where their way off was docked was far from easy. The trembling that rustled through the *Galactic Passage* had changed from just being unsteady to being almost uncontrollable as they approached the star's local gravity. It was all too much for the damaged ship to handle. Warning lights flashed aggressively throughout. Sirens wailed in pain as the ship hurtled toward its end. Electrical circuits failed, junction boxes faulted, and pipes burst all around spewing coolant and gases back into the ship to create a lethal dose of dangerous atmosphere. Fixtures and fittings started to be shaken loose. Even the gravity keeping them all on the ground had increased. Making every step taken a difficult one. Each step taking more effort to make than the last. Duke followed Leyton and Jesa, keeping as close as possible, when an explosion sent him into the wall to his side. He lost focus on the world around him as if it was all shrouded in haze. Duke pushed his way back onto his feet and before he could catch up to the others a ceiling panel struck him.

The world around him numbed. His vision blacked out, but not his consciousness. He had no idea what was up and what was down. There was no cold touch of metal or heated strike of fire. Was this what death felt like? An eternal abyss with no real answer? It wasn't as he imagined it would be. He expected more. He expected to be reunited with the ones he missed the most. To see that legendary white light to take him to his next existence.

When he eventually stirred, Duke was relieved to realise that he wasn't dead. Though he did feel like death. His mouth was dry and body weak. He was in the med bay of the patrol ship. Duke focussed his eyes in on the world around him. Medical equipment hooked up to him beeped as they administered the drugs that kept him alive. Displays hovered over him showing all his vitals. It was a while since he last had the pleasure of seeing his heart rate and blood pressure. If memory served him well, he was showing a healthy condition. To his right, Leyton sat grinning at him.

'Glad to see you back in the world of the living,' the agent said.

'Take it we made it off?' he asked. His throat hurt. 'How'd I black out? What happened?'

'I realised you need to go on a diet, that's what happened,' Leyton joked. 'You have any idea how heavy you are?'

'Give it over,' Duke snapped. 'How'd I go down?'

The agent shrugged. 'After the explosion, you just took a bad hit to the head. A ceiling panel came loose and got you bad. No chance of staying awake.'

'I was flat out then?'

'You went down like a sack of shit,' Leyton Foresc answered. 'But we made it out of there.'

They made it out of there. There were too many that didn't. Duke struggled to swallow that reality. He still wasn't sure why he made it out and others didn't.

In the silence, he needed to know how badly Spike hurt him. Duke reached up and felt his face. There was no bandaging where his face had been split by her tongue. Duke could feel something though. The ridges of healed skin that meant he had been left with scarring.

'Medic Suttle's handiwork,' Leyton explained. 'He's a damn good medic. Knows what he's doing and can fix up most people. But Dom's not exactly a miracle worker. Sorry to say but you'll never win a beauty pageant again. He's not that good just yet.'

There was a look in his eye. Even as he joked there was no humour there behind the words. Leyton was avoiding something. There was something the man wanted to say but couldn't. Jesa. Was it her? What happened to Jesa? Why wasn't she sat there with them?

'What is it?' Duke demanded.

'It isn't good,' the agent whispered.

'Tell me,' Duke said sternly.

'We picked up a hitch hiker,' Leyton told him. He was clearly thinking carefully about his wording. 'And Jesa is fond of it.'

'It? What is *it*?'

'She um… She picked up a pup,' the agent answered hesitantly. 'Looks like a runt. It broke off from the others and was on its own. She took pity on it. She said it was like how you took pity on her. She wants to try and domesticate it. Look, I'm as much against it as you are but if she can raise it for good? That would be useful for you guys. Could be a good guard dog. Well, guard wolf. And while it's still a pup, if it shows signs of being a threat to you it'll be easier to eliminate.'

His blood boiled. After everything that they had all been through. After all the death that the other wolves were responsible for. The atrocities they could have carried out if they had survived and been brought back to Sol. He would have thought that Jesa would have known better than to bring one of those things onto his ship. They were natural predators. These were not domestic dogs that had centuries of domestication hard wired into their lineage. This thing would grow up knowing its instincts were to hunt and kill, and that humans were potential prey. Eventually nature would take over any training it was put through. He needed to be rid of it now.

A sudden surge of pain split his head in two. Teeth. Rows of teeth gnawed in front of him just inches from his face. They were not there, but he could see them, the teeth as real as he was. He could even feel the heavy breathing of the wolf against his skin and smell the putrid scent of their den on its breath. Alarms started to rattle beside him as his heart rate and blood pressure went through the roof. He panicked. Duke needed to get out of his bed and do something. Anything. He needed to get away from the wolves. They were going to get him. Leyton leaned over and applied pressure to his shoulders to keep him in place, ushering for calm. The images inflicting pain upon him started to fade and eased until he was looking back at the agent once again. No more wolves. The alarms died off and fell silent.

'What the hell was that?' Leyton questioned. 'Are you okay?'

'Nothing,' Duke muttered. 'It was nothing.'

'It didn't look like nothing.'

'I… I saw the wolves again. I can't have that thing here. It needs to go.'

Leyton held his hands up and silently motioned for the sergeant to remain seated. 'I told you, I'm on your side with this. Those things have killed too many people and I regret ever being on the assignment. But she's dead set on proving that she can do for the ice wolf pup what you did for her. She had a second chance thanks to you and she's keen to make you proud. That much is clear. I say, let her try do the same back for you.'

'She can let me be rid of it,' Duke muttered.

'Give her a chance, okay?' Leyton insisted. 'She wants to try. She might be right.'

He conceded. 'Fine. But I'll have words with her.'

'That's fine. Look, I don't know what your plans are now, but there are some answers I need to get,' Leyton explained. 'And I need to go to Earth to get them.'

'What do you mean?' Duke questioned.

'I've had a look at the armour from those people who came to the ship,' Leyton said. 'I recognise the armour but can't tell you where from. Their weapons might be advanced, but I swear I've seen them somewhere before as well. I need to figure it out. Plus, we have no idea if that death squad sent after us just bailed or had the wolves with them when they left. I need to know if this nightmare ended with the *Passage* or if we're still dreaming. Also, you guys aren't going to be safe. The administrator, the guy in charge, he knows that there was an SPF patrol ship dispatched to that liner. Knows about you. He'll have all the codes and the IDs to recognise you and your ship upon arrival anywhere in the UPN zone or where we have active agents. Which means wherever you go, there's a risk that you'll be found by field agents. Until he sees a body, you're alive as far as he's concerned. We all are. On Earth, I'll be able to get the answers I need and keep him off your back. Tell him how you died so he doesn't put a mark on you.'

'Wait, what?'

'When you're on your feet, I'll be heading to Earth,' Leyton repeated. 'I can make sure you guys are safe by feeding false information and do some digging while I'm there. He won't come looking for you if you're dead. When I'm done, I can get back to you.'

'I can come with you, I did tell you that before,' Duke insisted.

'I know pal, but you guys need to stay in the outer colonies,' the agent said. 'It's safer for you out here than in the central colonies. The UPN has fewer resources out here and even if there is a bounty on your head, no Outie will want their money by doing them a favour. Take some time and figure out what you're going to do next. When you've decided what you'll do, I'll help any way I can.'

'Thanks,' Duke whispered softly. 'You shout if you need us.'

Leyton gave him a heavy pat on the arm. 'I'll be okay. And you guys will be too. I'll make sure of it. Get some rest. We'll see you in a couple days when Dom gives you the all clear.'

The agent left him to his own company.

To think that Jesa would take on one of those pups was outrageous. He didn't know much about them, if anything at all, but what he did know was that it would one day grow up like any animal would. Would it grow to be a mindless killer like the others? Duke didn't know and he didn't want to find out. It didn't belong with them. He had, however, told Leyton he'd give Jesa a chance. The honourable thing was to uphold that promise. He sighed. Duke would try to decide what he should do later.

Leyton had made a good point that Duke played around in his mind for hours. The guy in charge knew that they had been sent to the *Galactic Passage*. One of the things that would keep him from looking for them is if there was no one to look for. It would be easy since everyone perished on the liner when it went into the star. If the agent were to head back to Earth as he said he would, disinformation would go a long way to keep them safe. There would be no one else to tell him otherwise that they had survived. It was a good idea. Would it be watertight? Only Leyton could tell him. Though there would be several additional steps they would need to do to make sure it stayed that way.

After that though? What then? He did make a promise that he intended to keep. Question is, would he go it alone? Would his team want to help, or would they want to get off the ship at the nearest port to return to their lives? How their lives would look in exile was up for debate. Duke decided that these were all questions worth making note of to ask as soon as he was back on his feet. Until then, he let his eyes close and returned to his slumber while he recovered. It felt damn good to rest. Even better that he was allowed to rest in peace.

Jesa

People, understandably, had mixed feelings about the pup. The poor thing wasn't dangerous. It loved to play with them. The pup would try to nip at them as it got more excited but would stop the moment a voice was raised. No one suffered any injuries. The wolf was ugly, but the little thing was so small. It was nearly cute thanks to its ugliness. Much like one of those custom pets that were designed to be tiny. Ronan and Professor Ainslot were both more than intrigued by it. The academic wanted to study and observe the pup, advising her it was most likely going to be the runt of a litter to have been left behind like that by the adults. Ronan just thought it was funny that she had taken to it and tried to play with the wolf pup. The others though were either cautious or outright against it. Jesa didn't entertain them for that. They could think what they wanted. At the end of the day, just because it came from a pack that was intent on eating anything they could didn't mean this one would grow up to be the same. She could, she *would*, train it to be an asset to the team. The pup would grow up to help them. Only if there was really no hope would she give in and let them do whatever was necessary with it. Jesa needed to be prepared for that outcome.

They had all gathered in the briefing room in eager anticipation of the sergeant. Medic Suttle had given medical clearance for Duke, and they were waiting on him leaving the med bay. It had been two days of waiting and hoping that he would make the full recovery expected. She had avoided visiting him because of the pup. After some of the stories she had been told of his nightmares, screaming about the wolves in his sleep, she thought it best to keep away and let him recuperate. He didn't need that sort of stress, and she didn't need to see his reaction. More importantly, she didn't want to risk seeing him in case his condition was worse than they were being told.

Duke carefully walked from the med bay into the briefing room, taking each step with delicate precision. Jesa felt her heart break. How much pain was he still in to be walking like that? When he eventually came to a stop, everyone started to applaud and cheer that he was back on his feet. She on the other hand could not stop herself from crying with joy that he was okay. The scarring he was left with after fighting the matriarch suited him. It was subtle. Well blended with his skin after the recovery process, giving his face more character. She put the pup down on the holographic table and rushed over to him. Her arms wrapped around him in a tight embrace, her head tucked into his chest for comfort. It felt just like she remembered when she held her father. He too had a strong chest and arms that when wrapped around her made her feel safe in a way only a parent could do. Jesa looked up at him and smiled. Duke returned a forced smile. Having the pup in their presence clearly disappointed him. To her relief, he didn't say a thing.

Duke gestured for her to sit down and ushered the room to be calm. Jesa returned to her seat and tried to put the pup onto her lap, but instead it ran up to the edge of the holo-table and nudged into Duke's body, cooing for him to pet it much to his protest. Even in his fear of it something about the sergeant commanded its devotion in a way she couldn't have expected. What she did expect though was Professor Ainslot being all over it studying the behaviour and making notes until the sergeant told him to pay attention.

'Thank you for that,' the sergeant started. He reluctantly gave the pup a gentle pat and when satisfied it left him to return to Jesa. Duke continued, 'It's nice to be out of there. While I was on the bed, I had time to do some thinking. Jesa?'

'Yes?' Jesa replied. Her heart raced. She could feel her cheeks turn red for being singled out. Was it about her pup?

'I saved you from your former master when we arrested you,' the sergeant said. 'We took the tracker from your ship and the medic took the explosive from your arm. But that's not freedom. It only buys you time. He will not have heard about what's happened on the *Galactic Passage* or know that you were picked up by me until he realises that the buyers for all that stuff on your ship don't get their goods. When that does happen, I can promise that he will come hunting for you.'

It hurt to hear it put that way. To be reminded that, no matter how free she felt, she was still a slave to that monster. A tear rolled down her cheek. All she wanted was to be free. It wasn't living if she couldn't get through a day without looking over her shoulder.

'But he doesn't know about anything that's happened yet,' Duke followed up with. 'Which brings me to my point. I want to give Jesa her freedom. Permanently. I don't know what any of you want to do. What you're thinking of doing next. Where you want to go. What I do know is what I'm doing.' The sergeant pointed straight to her, a soft smile resting on his face. 'I want to hunt down the guy that stole Jesa from her parents after killing them. I want to bring the man who stole the innocence of her youth to justice. I want to give Jesa the peace of mind she needs to sleep at night without thinking he's out there looking for her or doing to someone else what she went through by his hand. I can do this from within the SPF but there will be that much red tape that we won't be able to do it for months. If not years. Who knows what else the guy will do in that time? From outside the SPF though? I can give her the justice she deserves with whatever methods we *have* to take to get the results. I'm prepared to do anything. I'm not asking any of you to help. I'm not even going to beg. But if you want to help, I want you on my team.'

'How do we do that? Won't people be out there looking for us?' Corporal Arche questioned.

'I'm pretty certain most sectors have stations. Won't they be able to recognise us whenever we go anywhere near a government facility?' Ronan Moasa added.

'It's true, they would be looking for us if we survived,' Duke replied. 'But we never survived the *Passage*.'

'What do you mean?' Jesa asked.

'Didn't you hear the news? We all died on the liner with its crew when it went into the star,' the sergeant explained. 'Tried our best to stop Leyton here from completing his mission after he tried to double cross us. But we weren't good enough. And it just so happened that he managed to take Jesa's ship after sabotaging ours and was the last person to make it successfully off the liner alive.'

'I see you've been thinking about what I said,' Leyton said, chuckling to himself. 'He's basically saying that if I'm the last person to make it off there... who can prove me wrong.'

'Exactly,' Duke said with a smile. 'And I've had a good thought on how to explain Jerome's information to the administrator. Just need you to verify it's a good one and make it work.'

'Go on then,' Leyton insisted. 'I'm listening.'

'There were too many double-crosses going on. Jerome got so caught up in the web of lies that he couldn't decide if you were a friend or foe and lost it. Decided the safest option was you were a threat. After that, it was only a matter of time before everything imploded and you did what had to be done to keep the lie in operation.'

Jesa looked to the agent who was now in hysterics. He looked like he had gone insane.

'You know, that's actually not too bad,' Leyton chuckled. 'Needs a bit of refinement, but I like it. I can make that work. You will all officially be dead as far as the records go by the time I'm done.'

'We can come with you,' Medic Suttle said, pointing to himself and the professor. 'We'll help.'

'No, you won't,' Leyton snapped.

'Why not?' the medic looked hurt. As if he wasn't trusted. 'We're a part of the team. More people to verify what you say.'

'Wrong. The more people that I get involved in this, the harder it will be to keep the story straight,' Leyton answered. 'They'll do everything they can to trip you up. Make you say what really happened. They get even a whiff of anything that doesn't agree to my account, and we're all done for. If it's just me, there's no one to cross check with. No one to throw a curve ball at. Feed incorrect facts to cause someone to slip up with no risk of being caught. It'll be easier if it's just me.'

'Understood,' Medic Suttle whispered.

The atmosphere in the briefing room turned thick. Jesa didn't know if she was breathing too loudly or not, or if someone needed to do something to break the silence. It was uncomfortable. The medic was going to be without his commander and the sergeant was going to be without a friend. The agent was going to risk his very life to spread the word of how they lost theirs and start the lies to keep them alive without anyone to turn to for help.

'Jesa? Do you want to do this?' Duke asked, cutting through the atmosphere, now that they had the chance to bring her the freedom she needed. When she didn't respond, the sergeant persisted, 'I can't do this without you. For all my resources, you have the most knowledge about your master our of any of us.'

Butterflies fluttered in her stomach. Nerves. Excitement. Anticipation. Fear. All wrapped up into a single emotion that she struggled to contain. The end of her lifelong terror was in sight. And her family would be able to rest in peace knowing that their daughter had her revenge for them. Avenged their deaths. That Jesa would be safe for the rest of her days thanks to the efforts of one man. There was no better reason to say yes than for her family. Her heart longed for them. She would miss them so much more when it was over, but she needed them to be able to rest. To go on to their forever resting place, happy that she would be okay.

'More than you can imagine,' she whispered eagerly. 'I want to see the bastard suffer.'

'We'll do it together,' Duke told her. She believed him. He then turned back to the others. 'I need to know, now, who's in. If you're not in, I won't hold it against you. We'll land to a nearby station. There, you can go. If you're in, be ready to be in it for the long run and to live outside the law. We will not live a life that we were trained to live by. If we get caught, there won't be any bailing out for us. No backup. Just each other. The administrator will start coming for us when we make ourselves known. Which will happen eventually. Hopefully we'll be able to take the fight when that happens.'

To Jesa's surprise, it wasn't Corporal Moasa who stepped up and spoke first. She truly expected the man bred for warfare to go first. No, it was Medic Suttle.

'I'm in,' he declared.

'Serious Doc?' Leyton asked.

'Serious,' Dom Suttle said. 'That last mission? It didn't sit with me. I don't like the fact that the guys from base were prepared to kill innocents like that. And if I can't help you, boss, I'm helping the sergeant and Jesa here. I will help make her life better. Besides, I've no doubt that the sergeant here will need fixing up at some point. I can at least keep him in the fight.'

'And I'm in,' Corporal Arche announced. She held her head up high with pride. 'We lost Abe out there. If helping you is the only way to stick it to the guy responsible for that, then you can damn well bet I'm going to help you.'

'Thank you,' Duke said. 'Ronan? You in?'

The giant of a man shrugged, 'Thought it would be obvious I'm in? It's why I didn't speak sooner. You get injured too much. If I left, I can guarantee you wouldn't last a month.'

'Thanks, I guess?' the sergeant laughed.

'I like how you guys are all jumping on this,' Ivan Zenkovich said. 'But you're missing one crucial thing. You need me.'

'Well, are you in?' Duke asked.

Ivan smiled and slapped his chest pocket that held his flask. 'As long as you keep me well stocked, I'm in.'

'I can make that happen,' Duke joked. 'So, you're in?'

Ivan Zenkovich nodded. They were all in. They all were going to help. At least, nearly all of them. The professor had yet to speak or give his opinion. Jesa turned and looked at him. He was unsure himself of what he wanted to do. That much was clear. He was fidgety. Everyone else cast their gaze upon him. The pressure was a lot for him to handle.

'Are you in?' Jesa asked him. Hopeful that his answer was yes.

'What use am I?' he replied. 'I'm just a scientist. I'm no good with a pistol. I just study alien organisms. I don't know what I can do for you.'

'Well, we have the... pup,' Duke said hesitantly. 'You'll be able to continue your studies with him. And you're easily the smartest person here. I don't know about you, but I'd like to know I've got someone smart on my team. Never know when brains are needed more than strength.'

'So? Are you in?' Jesa questioned.

She wanted him to say yes. If he did, it meant that in some way she mattered to them all.

Professor Ainslot sighed and held his hands up. 'I'm in but, I'll tell you again. I don't know how much use I'll be in the field unless I'm studying an alien lifeform.'

'Everyone has a use,' Duke said. 'We'll find yours. Thank you.'

There it was. Everyone was out to help her. The smile on her face beamed out across the holo-table to everyone around her. She had a second family. She knew she had people that she could rely on. Better still, there would be no jail cell for her. No guards, only freedom.

Second chances didn't get much sweeter than this.

Not long after everyone had decided on staying to help the sergeant and her, Leyton took Duke aside to discuss something. While Jesa was talking to everyone else in the briefing room, being told that she was going to be Ivan's co-pilot or talking about what they would do with the contraband on her ship, she was listening in on the sergeant while he spoke to Leyton. She heard words like *safehouses* and *guilds* and *contacts*. Things that sounded both dangerous and reassuring. It didn't matter where they went or what they did. What did matter was she wasn't alone. The sergeant was healthy. And alive. Her family was going to be okay.

Jesa smiled to herself. Strangely, she wouldn't have had the past several weeks go any other way.

Duke pulled her to one side. He smiled at her.

'What is it?' Jesa asked him.

'I'm keeping my word,' he answered vaguely. 'We're going to Juntah.'

'Ghavvis!' she gasped.

'Yes. I know a guy who's said he can keep us hidden for a while out there. There's a price, but we'll come to that when we're there and you've got your friend back. Don't be surprised if he doesn't take to you when you see him though. You're with Centies. He hasn't been educated like you have.'

'He'll see sense,' Jesa insisted. 'I'm just happy to see him again.'

'I thought you would be,' Duke replied. 'Then we can take care of your old boss.'

Duke left her to join the others. She walked with her pup to a porthole and gazed out to the abyss.

'I'm coming for you,' she whispered, hoping in some way Barbaros heard her. 'When I get you, you will know what it means to suffer.'

Epilogue
29/11/2675
01:42 Earth Standard Time
20:42 Local Time

Fundraiser functions. They were so predictable, so boring and unessential. Just an opportunity for philanthropists and billionaires alike to show off how much money they possessed and to throw it away carelessly without hurting their profits too much. A chance for high-ranking officials to push for their next promotion by impressing the right people or making the best connections to bring their dreams to reality. Equally they were hunting grounds for those that sought to hold leverage against a rival so that their plans faced no delay. They were places for anyone who carried influence over the lesser beings or anyone whose bank account only dreams of seeing more than five digits before the decimal. Administrator Riley Jackson of the Military Intelligence Division of the UPN would normally avoid them at all costs. This time, as the head of the division and with it being a military fundraiser, he was expected to oblige and be present, smile and shake hands. A shame. These events were nothing more than a waste of time, stealing him from real work that had purpose. He had not spent a lifetime going from that skinny kid from Yorkshire to fighting in wars and climbing the ranks of the MID, becoming the man he was today to end up being required to attend a pathetic fund raiser. This was the sort of thing spineless people in suits should attend. Not someone of importance and use like himself.

'Administrator Jackson!' cried the distinctly inebriated Senator Bromley of the Northern Territories of Luna. One of the many downsides of humanity expanding to the stars, their political titles increased in length exponentially making it nearly impossible to keep track of everyone that was of interest.

'Please, call me Riley,' the administrator replied, forcing the required pleasantries.

The senator was far from someone Riley liked to talk with. Bromley was too open about everything. Too trusting in people. He went out of his way to do what people wanted him to do, not what he should do to make things work for the better of humanity. He loved to make false promises and worse of all, he was a career politician. They were

482

nothing short of an annoyance and inconvenience in everything they did. They would quickly spring up the red tape on a project going ahead if they saw no monetary return or if enough weak-hearted, fluff ball youths who thought they knew how the world worked spoke out against the way it really worked. If only the man realised that Riley had already done his research on everyone on the guest list, the benefactors, the staff and anyone loosely associated with the event. He knew every dirty secret the guy had which, frankly, wasn't difficult at all because even though he denied all those affairs and attempted to say those indecent images on his computer were the result of a hack everyone knew they were true. He had evidence other than hush money to prove the beliefs were true. Nevertheless, the senator hadn't done anything yet. Merely came over. Administrator Jackson opted to wait until he chose the wrong set of words before revealing his hand.

'As you wish, Riley,' Bromley laughed. 'I hear you're the man to talk to about our military intelligence. All the secret spy stuff that you see in the movies. Is that so?'

'I really can't say I know what you mean,' he answered with a courteous smile. 'If I were a spy, I'd be a bad one by admitting it to you. Wouldn't I? Even if you were to drink until you forget this conversation by the morning.'

The senator laughed playfully, pushing his shoulder back a touch. Such filthy actions that politician's thought was being friendly to gain the upper hand in conversation. It was an insult. Senator Bromley had no idea who he was talking to or the power he wrought. Riley would surely find a way to make this man think twice before doing such a thing again to him.

'Now, now, we're all on the same side here,' Senator Bromley said, putting his arm around him. Administrator Jackson shrugged the arm off. 'Listen, I have to know if there is anything I need to know about the upcoming lunar elections and my position in the candidacy for Representative of Lunar? Any word on the proverbial grape vine about my chances and what people think about me? I would really like to know so I can do something about it now before the votes start coming through.'

'Easy senator. Let the man just enjoy his drink,' another man suggested. General Packton, the head of the United Planetary Nations Space Marines based in the Sol system. The large, dark-skinned man was imposing, yet somehow kept a gentle face. Packton knew it and he used it to his advantage to let people think he was weaker than he was before showing a more ruthless side. For a soldier he was quite intelligent. Respectable, but dangerous because he never stepped out of line. He ushered Senator Bromley on before turning to face Riley. 'Enjoying the evening so far?'

'Not particularly,' he replied. 'Parties aren't my thing. Too much of a risk.'

Which they were. If an operative could out skill him, or even get lucky, a party was one of the few places that they could get to him without being noticed then flee before anyone could even realise that he had hit the ground. Almost happened once. Since then, Riley always had his back close to a solid surface. No one was getting past a wall easily to get to him.

'I should imagine not, living in the shadows for a career,' Packton said.

'And for pleasure,' Riley added.

'And for pleasure,' Packton repeated with a gentle laugh. 'Listen, can we talk shop? There's something I need to discuss.'

'At an event?'

General Packton leaned in close. 'It's important. You know I respect you enough that I would normally request a meeting on this sort of subject through the correct methods, but this is urgent. I'd sleep easier having clarity if we talk it through now.'

Riley looked around. There were a lot of ears to listen in on them. Businesspeople, low ranking officials or officers eager to get an advantage to climb their career ladders and quite possibly criminals and con artists waiting for an opportunity to score the best meal ticket in their lives. Most were preoccupied with drinks, fake flatteries and dancing to the melody of the live band to even care who he was. But not everyone. Some of the suits were more bothered about what was going on around them, their eyes flickering all around looking for something potentially interesting. They probably had some idea who they were. Granted, they could just be the security but if they weren't there was too much risk. Two high profiles speaking without a smile would arouse too much attention. The pair needed to be out of sight.

In the large stately home just outside of New York City there were several rooms that could be locked from the inside. One of them was the library just a couple floors up. No more than a three-minute walk. Five if he wanted to take his time. People always avoided libraries. He could never understand why. Some of the greats in their time had works that only existed in those places. They needed to be enjoyed and not forgotten.

'Not here,' Administrator Jackson said. 'This way.'

He led General Packton down the corridors to the nearest stairwell to take them to the library, politely nodding to the security along the way. As they walked across a grand balcony, Riley couldn't help but notice the holographic images of the family that owned the property and their ancestors and statues that lined one side of the walkway and the courtyard. A grand fountain centrepiece that looked like a monument with a waterfall was adorned with well-maintained shrubs and flowers. Lavish was an understatement.

'How long did you study the layout of this place for?' General Packton questioned.

'Only needed two and a half hours. The half hour was so I could grab a bite to eat.'

Packton laughed. 'I can't tell whether you Brits are being serious or sarcastic most of the time, you know that?'

'My advice? Take it that we're always being sarcastic. Anyone that's not on the same intellectual level as us isn't worth our time of day.'

'Are you always this pleasant?' Packton asked.

'Only on special nights like tonight,' Riley answered with a smile. 'Here we are.'

He locked the door behind them in the library and took out a small metallic device, with similar dimensions to a coin, and squeezed it. Nothing obvious happened but anything electrical in that room and immediately outside was now defunct and would not work until he deactivated it. That would ensure their privacy for the duration of the conversation.

'Now that's done, how can I help you?' he asked.

'Have you had any update on these threats you keep warning us about?' Packton asked, his voice immediately turning cold as steel and straight to the point.

The threats. There was an ancient organism that, after the reports filed in from expeditions and military missions alike, Riley Jackson was certain still existed. For the last four years he had devoted time, resources and energy into searching for them. All of which cost money and he came back with only fossils and proof that they once existed. His teams continued to search for the evidence of a creature so impressive that if it existed could prove to be the end of humanity.

'Nothing new yet,' Administrator Jackson answered. 'I have agents posted all around the outer colonies keeping an eye out with more being rerouted to assist by the day as our other conflicts become more manageable by the other divisions. I also have expedition groups currently venturing into the uncharted zones trying to find outposts, bases, colonies. Anything to suggest where the threat is and when they might strike.'

'And do you even have proof that they still exist?' the office demanded, looming over him.

'Not enough for your liking,' he admitted. 'It is mainly the word and rumour of the outer colonies. They're a lot of things but they're not liars when it's their own being killed. However, I do have more evidence being brought in as we speak. I have had to go to extreme lengths to acquire the assets.'

'You better have,' Packton spat, jabbing a finger at him. 'Because right now, I have General Xun-Lee raining Hell fire down on me to find out why for this sector of the UPN military I, and the rest of the Sol division, deserve such high funding when we aren't being hit anywhere near as badly as everywhere else with terrorist groups, separatists and all the wars that are grieving the other colonies. We're not even a target for them! And all the while, he's questioning me because of our working relationship on what I know about you. If I know why you can receive blank cheques to spend however you please. Do you know what I say to him?'

He did know, of course. It was his job to know everything. But to admit it would be gloating and could easily worsen the situation. Riley needed to keep it under control to retain an ally in the war of politics. 'What do you say to him?'

'I tell him that we have an impending threat that we need to safeguard Earth against as a priority,' the officer explained. 'And every time he asks for proof, I tell him we're working on it. That he needs to have faith in the intelligence provided by the MID. It's been going on too long and holes are being burnt in the government's pockets. He's losing his patience which means I'm losing mine. When he loses his patience entirely, I lose my job and you lose your support and the major advocate of *your* funding. You've got control of so many divisions now. You're the administrator of the MID. You created and headed the Office for Intelligence and Research Development, in charge of the UPN's entire spy network, recently opened the Operations of Scientific and Technological Advancement Division and have recently acquired the rights to have your own personal military unit for your own purposes. What was that codename again? Terracotta? What the hell is that for? Security and defence? Are you sure you're just not getting greedy?'

'You'll lose more than your job if you take that tone with me again,' Riley warned, pushing himself away from the enraged man. It was one thing listening to an outburst. Tolerating an all-out attack against his success was something else. That was a personal attack that couldn't be tolerated.

'What? How dare you threaten me!'

'Oh, I dare. I dare because you won't do a thing to me. You *can't* do a thing to me. Push me, and I can make everyone believe you're a fraud. You never went through the academy and never got those impeccable grades you achieved in school or attended all those extracurricular activities to show your skill and prowess. You'll be the bastard child of some sleazy, disease-ridden whore who had an affair with a well-off official who tried to cover their tracks. If I feel creative, there might even be photographic evidence of what you get up to with the young cadets when left alone with them. Those poor boys and girls. Their parents will be livid and of course they'll deny it ever happened. Everyone denies something about someone that terrifies them. You will be a disgrace and an embarrassment when I'm done. Not even your family will want anything to do with you.'

'You wouldn't,' Packton whispered.

'I would,' he replied. 'I would and I wouldn't even think twice about it. I've made better men than you disappear for less. Just be glad that I need you. You need my help more because I cannot be as easily replaced as you can, but I still need your support to voice agreement that my work will bring the rewards I'm promising.'

'If you need me so much, what are you going to do to make sure I'm able to keep my job?' the general questioned. 'I can't help if I'm out of the office.'

'True, I can't get your help if you're out of your post. And I don't want to go through the rigor of recruiting someone else to assist me. I'm going to make sure Xun-Lee leaves you alone,' Riley explained. 'He'll be convinced that your support is vital to my research and that when we have military grade equipment to supply, he will be the first to know. His command with be the first outfitted with state-of-the-art gear and be the star of the UPN military. All you need to do is keep quiet about our arrangement and focus on voicing your support. Happy? Then I guess we're done here.'

He held out his hand politely and General Packton quickly shook it before turning around to leave him in peace. Administrator Jackson chuckled to himself. He had the best of both scenarios. He too was both strong and intimidating and he was also, without doubt, the most powerful human being within the UPN and arguably all the colonies that humanity had set up. Why? Because he was the single greatest mind that had ever come into existence. Einstein, Pythagoras, no one came close to his intelligence. Knowledge truly was the greatest weapon to exist.

His tac-pad came into life. His personal possessions worked while everything else was being disrupted – it would have been foolish if he left himself unable to communicate with anyone. A name he had not expected to appear was waiting for him to answer. Leyton. A call long overdue. It was surprising to say the least.

'Agent,' he replied cautiously. 'I hoped you were dead.'

Hoped. Expected. Both words were strongly associated in his books. It had been some time since he had his last report from the soldiers that had been despatched to the *Galactic Passage*. Their report was awfully specific. Leyton had sided with the SPF personnel to help the crew of the ship. Jerome Houghton had given reports of Leyton's change of heart to both himself and the commander of the force, 001-A-0037. The commander reported that Leyton had killed several of his soldiers by and stopped the destruction of the *Passage*. When his own team left, the remaining members of Houghton's team stayed back to finish the agent. All of which was quite accurately corroborated by the field reports from Jerome, who had been more than specific and vocal with, in his words, Leyton's treachery and betrayal. However, for all their failings they had been able to retrieve several pups and a couple adult males before having to depart the vessel amid the constant attacks form the SPF personnel and the turncoat agents. A worthy trade-off, a few soldiers for the future of humanity.

That was all good and well until he heard that final transmission from the captain of the *Galactic Passage*. A transmission that he had to work tirelessly for three days straight to silence and rescind to make sure no one else heard it. He was able to learn that the ship was no more, which nicely tied up those loose ends. That was aside from the fact that Agent Leyton Foresc had survived where his peers had not. How had he survived? If the ship went into the local star, how did he get off the liner? It should have torn him to pieces and sent him to oblivion. Who else had been able to flee from the doomed liner? Frustratingly though, the agent was not the only survivor to get off the *Passage*. Leading up to his soldiers disembarking and vacating the area, the crew of this ship had been able to save a substantial proportion of the passengers. He still had a lot to do before it was completely contained. Thankfully, Jackson had dozens of teams already out in the area hunting them down. There would be no one left to talk about the liner and the events that occurred on it. No one to ruin his plans.

'Nice to speak to you too, sir,' Leyton replied. His voice had no respect.

'Why aren't you dead?' Riley Jackson asked, going straight to the point. 'I gave Jerome orders to eliminate you after he disclosed your... sudden change of heart.'

'Because, sir, I'm here and he's not. I survived.'

'Go on, I'm intrigued. How did you survive where he didn't?'

'That's easy,' Leyton replied. 'I was the one orchestrating the deception on both sides to get into a position of control. In order to do it though, I had to double cross my own team before double crossing the SPF personnel. I was able to handle the lies that had to be told to succeed. He couldn't. So, I needed to end him before he completely ruined the mission. If it weren't for him, I'd have had a full team still and a completed mission.'

'How so?'

'I'll leave that for the debrief, sir,' Leyton said.

That was an audacious statement to make at him. If the dead agent really was to blame for everything going wrong, then he had the right to know the details. However, Leyton wanted to play it the smart way. Riley would show him what smart really was.

'Okay, how did you escape?' Administrator Jackson asked.

'I stole a smuggler vessel,' the agent explained. 'Along the way the SPF soldiers had arrested a smuggler and didn't have time to drop her off at a station before responding to the distress signal the captain of the *Passage* put out. She didn't need it anymore. I did.'

'And your original objective?' Jackson queried. It didn't matter at that point but obviously the more specimens they had the better.

'Failed. All the wolves went down with the ship. I had no means to take any with me.'

'You do realise that this isn't acceptable? They were a high priority asset. Just to have you posted out there on their home planet cost me more than a standard mission should. Then to get you back without anything to show for it. That was an additional cost in agents. I must justify this failure.'

'I understand, but there is no way even you could have prepared for what happened. That cannot be held against me. But I'm sure your guys brought something back.'

'Excuse me?' Administrator Riley replied.

'Your death squad you sent to kill us,' Leyton started, 'They left in a hurry, and I don't think it's because the SPF outgunned them. I'm certain they had pups with them.'

'That doesn't matter. You still had your orders that I intended to be followed.'

'Impossible. It couldn't be done single-handedly. Besides, I didn't come out of this empty handed.'

Leyton had something to bring back? That was something he needed to learn more about. His definition of empty handed was a wide casting net. It needed to be something extremely special to ensure that it wasn't just his job he lost.

'Explain,' Riley Jackson demanded.

'The cargo hold is full of contraband. We have weapons, armour… and something else that I have to show you.'

The agent activated the video feed on the comm link. He saw it clearly without being directed to it. The specimen he had bought that had gone off course. How did the SPF encounter that exact smuggler transporting the goods acquired? He would have to have words with the seller, Barbaros. Find out what was so difficult about his instructions that the goods were to reach Earth under any means necessary. Not by the most minimalistic methods possible that saved him costs. Compensation would be in order, one way or another.

The skeleton. He had one very much like it. Dozens of fragments. But none of the items in his possession were like this. This was taller, more imposing. It had the tail, the head crest, the stature of power. A fine specimen, and a complete one at that. The administrator had his own theories about why the skeleton Leyton was bringing back looked different. The most prevailing thought was that it was an older, purer bloodline, free of impurities. Once it was back with him, he would have his best scientists looking at it to confirm his suspicions for certain. But he needed it to arrive first – it looked like the agent had earned his safe passage.

'I haven't seen anything like this before,' Leyton stated.

'No one has,' he lied. He had to have it back. The chances, for the time being, of Leyton being honest were incredibly favourable. Anyone with a find like that and greed in mind would have sold it at the first opportunity. Only a fool, or in this case a loyalist, would be stupid enough to not realise or care for its value. 'Come back to Earth for debrief. What is your position?'

'I'm on my way to Vesti. I'll be able to resupply there before coming back.'

If he was on his way there, that meant the survivors from the liner were headed there too. Automated navigation systems in lifeboats always aimed for the nearest planet with an LSAG. That meant either they were already there, or the agent had been able to overtake them. Riley Jackson would re-route his personnel to look in that quadrant for the survivors. There would be nothing to suggest the passengers even managed to make it off. All anyone would know was that the lifeboats were launched prematurely due to system failures. That would explain to the masses how no one was able to make it off the *Passage*.

'I'll relay you the LSAG codes for the Vesti gate. Permission X-Ray One-One-One. You'll be back in a little over two weeks.'

'Thank you, sir.'

'But be warned. Your briefing will not be easy, and it will most certainly be extensive. If at any point I don't trust what you're saying to be truthful, you will be hooked up to the probe.'

Rigorous wasn't close to what his interrogation would be. Not a briefing, as he explained to the agent. There were too many answers that he needed. For all the things he was told, there was something that didn't quite sit. The agent was by everyone's account an enemy to the state, a traitor and worthy of death under treason. Yet here he was telling him it was all part of his plan, that no one was prepared to accept it. Someone was or had been lying to him and he intended to find out who.

'Understood, sir. Out,' Leyton said cautiously. He knew that it wouldn't be a simple debrief.

Riley closed the comms and took a moment. It wasn't an entire loss. He might have significant losses, but the gains from the assignments were there. They outweighed what had been lost. He had pups to start a breeding programme with. He just hoped they had different fathers to keep the gene pool as diverse as possible without newer additions to the pack being required. To fund that sort of operation would be difficult. He had the skeleton and everything else that he had bought from the black market that was to be on the same shipment on its way to him. He took some comfort in these details.

Administrator Jackson opened a new communication link with his second in command, 'Agent DuVerne. We have samples inbound. Category A priority. Ready the labs for it to arrive. I need everyone we can spare on it. I also want production of the Terracotta's increased two-fold. I want new batches of soldiers created sped up from six months to three for full development.'

'Sir,' she replied. Her eyes were weary. He had possibly woken her up. It was her own fault for needing so much sleep. Administrator Jackson failed to understand how people couldn't function on less than a few hours a day. She moved her black hair out of her face. 'Step up production? We don't have enough raw material.'

'Harvest more then. Whatever is necessary. Just gather the resources you need to make it happen. I fear we won't have long before they're needed, and we need to prepare.'

'Understood sir. I'll instruct more tubes to be set up to take on the increased production. We'll most likely have more failures during growth if we're speeding things up though.'

'What would the numbers look like?'

His second in command paused as she thought. 'I'd say we would go from a two percent failure rate to as high as an eight percent failure rate.'

'A necessary loss,' Riley answered. 'In that case make sure that we create an extra fifteen percent in the unit batches. Anything else I have already considered?'

'No sir,' DuVerne replied.

'Good. See to it that it's done. I want an initial report in two days of how everything is running. I need to see predicted figures and final totals. Out.'

He cut the link. The Terracotta programme was his brainchild. Humanity was too busy fighting itself that their military might was diminishing by the week. The UPN had the fleets but that was it. Its army was losing traction on the ground. Its air force and space forces were being shot down. He needed to provide a highly skilled military to fight any new threat the rest of humanity was too preoccupied to face in the numbers that were required. In response he grew his own military using basic human material harvested from children. The younger the better. More stem cells were available at a younger age to become whatever they needed to be. It was not a tasteful requirement and took him to levels of monstrosity that made him initially think twice about the project. The greater good of humanity took priority so he went ahead with the project. If he could speed up the production of adult soldiers, he may build a strong enough force in time for the inevitable invasion that was coming.

It was all extremely exciting, yet inspired humility. In all of humanity's arrogance, there was nothing more arrogant than to think that they were the result of a single creator. That in all the universe, with all the stars and all the planets capable of holding life for some reason humans were the only things created to have superior intelligence. Or what they perceived to be intelligence. Even with the discovery of alien species, both sentient and non-sentient, they still felt like they were the most important things in existence. This, this discovery he had of an ultimate threat, proved they weren't any creator's prized product. Humans were nothing in comparison to this thing. And it was a very real threat that, if the stories were true about, would be the end of them all. A fate he very much wanted to avoid. And he didn't care how he saved humanity. At the end of it, their survival was worth any number of sacrifices.

And speaking of aliens, he opened a new comm link with his secretary. The young Eastern European man answered straight away. Wide awake at his desk with the steam from a fresh cup of coffee flickering at the bottom of the screen. How long had he been awake for? 'Urik, what is the situation with the ambassador from the Shu'ril Sovereignty? Are we on track?'

'Ambassador Yar-Satil Besh and her Royal Guard are due to set out for Earth in three months. They'll be approximately three weeks out from their first trip to human controlled territory at planet Phall,' he advised sharply. Almost revised as if predicting the question. 'After that, they will be on track to arrive at Earth for the trade negotiations five weeks later.'

'Good,' Riley said. 'Ensure her ship is downed before she reaches Phall. Remember, the bounty is specifically for her to be captured alive. Any others kept alive is a bonus. We need to demonstrate that our Terracotta troops can carry out a successful rescue missions to put us in a better position for brokering more funding and greater secrecy to keep the program alive. Understood?'

'Understood sir,' Urik answered. 'I'll be extremely specific that the bounty is reduced depending on the severity of any injury and-or number of casualties. Will there be anything else, sir?'

493

'Nothing more,' Riley said. 'When you've finished your drink, clock out and have yourself a drink of something stronger. I'll wire you the money. We have something to celebrate today.'

'Yes sir, thank you, sir,' his secretary said.

The comm link closed.

Riley smiled and savoured another mouthful of his whisky he had brought to the room with him. Bourbon. Not quite a Scotch or Irish, but still enjoyable. The night had become one worthy of enjoying. Humanity was going to have a fighting chance now. They would soon prove yet again to be a species worthy of respect on the intergalactic platform.

He would make sure of it before his time was up.

Acknowledgements

After 4 years of work, my debut novel has come to life. This novel couldn't have been put together and brought into existence without more than just my own input. There are several people that need to be thanked for bringing this piece to life.

Editor – I would like to thank my editor for seeing the errors and inconsistencies that I couldn't after my own edits were carried out.
Cover artist – I can't thank the cover artist enough for working with me to lift my words from the page and make them into a visual for the readers to see.
Alpha Reader and Beta Readers – I also need to thank my willing volunteers for reading my novel to give their feedback and words of encouragement.

This is the first instalment of the Beyond saga. Volume 2 won't be far behind.

Where can you keep up to date?

Keep up to date on the next instalments of the Beyond Saga and all other stories I'll tell by following me on my:
Website – ddhoulden.wordpress.com
Instagram – Instagram.com/richhoulden

Printed in Great Britain
by Amazon

82495078R00285